The Ghastly Gothic Tomes

Vol. 12

The Ghastly Gothic Tomes

Vol. 12

Published by NRM Books.

ISBN: 978-1-965179-15-4

CREDITS
Cover Art by: Nathan Reese Maher

COPYRIGHT

Table of Contents

The Strange Case of Dr. Jekyll and Mr. Hyde

By Robert Lewis Stevenson

STORY OF THE DOOR

Mr. Utterson the lawyer was a man of a rugged countenance that was never lighted by a smile; cold, scanty and embarrassed in discourse; backward in sentiment; lean, long, dusty, dreary and yet somehow lovable. At friendly meetings, and when the wine was to his taste, something eminently human beaconed from his eye; something indeed which never found its way into his talk, but which spoke not only in these silent symbols of the after-dinner face, but more often and loudly in the acts of his life. He was austere with himself; drank gin when he was alone, to mortify a taste for vintages; and though he enjoyed the theatre, had not crossed the doors of one for twenty years. But he had an approved tolerance for others; sometimes wondering, almost with envy, at the high pressure of spirits involved in their misdeeds; and in any extremity inclined to help rather than to reprove. "I incline to Cain's heresy," he used to say quaintly: "I let my brother go to the devil in his own way." In this character, it was frequently his fortune to be the last reputable acquaintance and the last good influence in the lives of downgoing men. And to such as these, so long as they came about his chambers, he never marked a shade of change in his demeanour.

No doubt the feat was easy to Mr. Utterson; for he was undemonstrative at the best, and even his friendship seemed to be founded in a similar catholicity of good-nature. It is the mark of a modest man to accept his friendly circle ready-made from the hands of opportunity; and that was the lawyer's way. His friends were those of his own blood or those whom he had known the longest; his affections, like ivy, were the growth of time, they implied no aptness in the object. Hence, no doubt the bond that united him to Mr. Richard Enfield, his distant kinsman, the well-known man about town. It was a nut to crack for many, what these two could see in each other, or what subject they could find in common. It was reported by those who encountered them in their Sunday walks, that they said nothing, looked singularly dull and would hail with obvious relief the appearance of a friend. For all that, the two men put the greatest store by these excursions, counted them the chief jewel of each week, and not only set aside occasions of pleasure, but even resisted the calls of business, that they might enjoy them uninterrupted.

It chanced on one of these rambles that their way led them down a by-street in a busy quarter of London. The street was small and what is called quiet, but it drove a thriving trade on the weekdays. The inhabitants were all doing well, it seemed and all emulously hoping to do better still, and laying out the surplus of their grains in coquetry; so that the shop fronts stood along that thoroughfare with an air of invitation, like rows of smiling saleswomen. Even on Sunday, when it veiled its more florid charms and lay comparatively empty of passage, the street shone out in contrast to its dingy neighbourhood, like a fire in a forest; and with its freshly painted shutters, well-polished brasses, and general cleanliness and gaiety of note, instantly caught and pleased the eye of the passenger.

Two doors from one corner, on the left hand going east the line was broken by the entry of a court; and just at that point a certain sinister block of building thrust forward its gable on the street. It was two storeys high; showed no window, nothing but a door on the lower storey and a blind forehead of discoloured wall on the upper; and bore in every feature, the marks of prolonged and sordid negligence. The door, which was equipped with neither bell nor knocker, was blistered and distained. Tramps slouched into the recess and struck matches on the panels; children kept shop upon the steps; the schoolboy had tried his knife on the mouldings; and for close on a generation, no one had appeared to drive away these random visitors or to repair their ravages.

Mr. Enfield and the lawyer were on the other side of the by-street; but when they came abreast of the entry, the former lifted up his cane and pointed.

"Did you ever remark that door?" he asked; and when his companion had replied in the affirmative, "It is connected in my mind," added he, "with a very odd story."

"Indeed?" said Mr. Utterson, with a slight change of voice, "and what was that?"

"Well, it was this way," returned Mr. Enfield: "I was coming home from some place at the end of the world, about three o'clock of a black winter morning, and my way lay through a part of town where there was literally nothing to be seen but lamps. Street after street and all the folks asleep—street after street, all lighted up as if for a procession and all as empty as a church—till at last I got into that state of mind when a man listens and listens and begins to long for the sight of a policeman. All at once, I saw two figures: one a little man who was stumping along eastward at a good walk, and the other a girl of maybe eight or ten who was running as hard as she was able down a cross street. Well, sir, the two ran into one another naturally enough at the corner; and then came the horrible part of the thing; for the man trampled calmly over the child's body and left her screaming on the ground. It sounds nothing to hear, but it was hellish to see. It wasn't like a man; it was like some damned Juggernaut. I gave a few halloa, took to my heels, collared my gentleman, and brought him back to where there was already quite a group about the screaming child. He was perfectly cool and made no resistance, but gave me one look, so ugly that it brought out the sweat on me like running. The people who had turned out were the girl's own family; and pretty soon, the doctor, for whom she had been sent put in his appearance. Well, the child was not much the worse, more frightened, according to the sawbones; and there you might have supposed would be an end to it. But there was one curious circumstance. I had taken a loathing to my gentleman at first sight. So had the child's family, which was only natural. But the doctor's case was what struck me. He was the usual cut and dry apothecary, of no particular age and colour, with a strong Edinburgh accent and about as emotional as a bagpipe. Well, sir, he was like the rest of us; every time he looked at my prisoner, I saw that sawbones turn sick and white with the desire to kill him. I knew what was in his mind, just as he knew what was in mine; and killing being out of the question, we did the next best. We told the man we could and would make such a scandal out of this as should make his name stink from one end of London to the other. If he had any friends or any credit, we undertook that he should lose them. And all the time, as we were pitching it in red hot, we were keeping the women off him as best we could for they were as wild as harpies. I never saw a circle of such hateful faces; and there was the man in the middle, with a kind of black sneering coolness—frightened too, I could see that—but carrying it off, sir, really like Satan. 'If you choose to make capital out of this accident,' said he, 'I am naturally helpless. No gentleman but wishes to avoid a scene,' says he. 'Name your figure.' Well, we screwed him up to a hundred pounds for the child's family; he would have clearly liked to stick out; but there was something about the lot of us that meant mischief, and at last he struck. The next thing was to get the money; and where do you think he carried us but to that place with the door?—whipped out a key, went in, and presently came back with the matter of ten pounds in gold and a cheque for the balance on Coutts's, drawn payable to bearer and signed with a name that I can't mention, though it's one of the points of my story, but it was a name at least very well known and often printed. The figure was stiff; but the signature was good for more than that if it was only genuine. I took the liberty of pointing out to my gentleman that the whole business looked apocryphal, and that a man does not, in real life, walk into a cellar door at four in the morning and come out with another man's cheque for close upon a hundred pounds. But he was quite easy and sneering. 'Set your mind at rest,' says he, 'I will stay with you till the banks open and cash the cheque myself.' So we all set off, the doctor, and the child's father, and our friend and myself, and passed the rest of the night in my chambers; and next day, when we had breakfasted, went in a body to the bank. I gave in the cheque myself, and said I had every reason to believe it was a forgery. Not a bit of it. The cheque was genuine."

"Tut-tut!" said Mr. Utterson.

"I see you feel as I do," said Mr. Enfield. "Yes, it's a bad story. For my man was a fellow that nobody could have to do with, a really damnable man; and the person that drew the cheque is the very pink of the proprieties, celebrated too, and (what makes it worse) one of your fellows who do what they call good. Blackmail, I suppose; an honest man paying through the nose for some of the capers of his youth. Black Mail House is what I call the place with the door, in consequence. Though even that, you know, is far from explaining all," he added, and with the words fell into a vein of musing.

From this he was recalled by Mr. Utterson asking rather suddenly: "And you don't know if the drawer of the cheque lives there?"

"A likely place, isn't it?" returned Mr. Enfield. "But I happen to have noticed his address; he lives in some square or other."

"And you never asked about the—place with the door?" said Mr. Utterson.

"No, sir; I had a delicacy," was the reply. "I feel very strongly about putting questions; it partakes too much of the style of the day of judgment. You start a question, and it's like starting a stone. You sit quietly on the top of a hill; and away the stone goes, starting others; and presently some bland old bird (the last you would have thought of) is knocked on the head in his own back garden and the family have to change their name. No sir, I make it a rule of mine: the more it looks like Queer Street, the less I ask."

"A very good rule, too," said the lawyer.

"But I have studied the place for myself," continued Mr. Enfield. "It seems scarcely a house. There is no other door, and nobody goes in or out of that one but, once in a great while, the gentleman of my adventure. There are three windows looking on the court on the first floor; none below; the windows are always shut but they're clean. And then there is a chimney which is generally smoking; so somebody must live there. And yet it's not so sure; for the buildings are so packed together about the court, that it's hard to say where one ends and another begins."

The pair walked on again for a while in silence; and then "Enfield," said Mr. Utterson, "that's a good rule of yours."

"Yes, I think it is," returned Enfield.

"But for all that," continued the lawyer, "there's one point I want to ask. I want to ask the name of that man who walked over the child."

"Well," said Mr. Enfield, "I can't see what harm it would do. It was a man of the name of Hyde."

"Hm," said Mr. Utterson. "What sort of a man is he to see?"

"He is not easy to describe. There is something wrong with his appearance; something displeasing, something down-right detestable. I never saw a man I so disliked, and yet I scarce know why. He must be deformed somewhere; he gives a strong feeling of deformity, although I couldn't specify the point. He's an extraordinary looking man, and yet I really can name nothing out of the way. No, sir; I can make no hand of it; I can't describe him. And it's not want of memory; for I declare I can see him this moment."

Mr. Utterson again walked some way in silence and obviously under a weight of consideration. "You are sure he used a key?" he inquired at last.

"My dear sir..." began Enfield, surprised out of himself.

"Yes, I know," said Utterson; "I know it must seem strange. The fact is, if I do not ask you the name of the other party, it is because I know it already. You see, Richard, your tale has gone home. If you have been inexact in any point you had better correct it."

"I think you might have warned me," returned the other with a touch of sullenness. "But I have been pedantically exact, as you call it. The fellow had a key; and what's more, he has it still. I saw him use it not a week ago."

Mr. Utterson sighed deeply but said never a word; and the young man presently resumed. "Here is another lesson to say nothing," said he. "I am ashamed of my long tongue. Let us make a bargain never to refer to this again."

"With all my heart," said the lawyer. "I shake hands on that, Richard."

SEARCH FOR MR. HYDE

That evening Mr. Utterson came home to his bachelor house in sombre spirits and sat down to dinner without relish. It was his custom of a Sunday, when this meal was over, to sit close by the fire, a volume of some dry divinity on his reading desk, until the clock of the neighbouring church rang out the hour of twelve, when he would go soberly and gratefully to bed. On this night however, as soon as the cloth was taken away, he took up a candle and went into his business room. There he opened his safe, took from the most private part of it a document endorsed on the envelope as Dr. Jekyll's Will and sat down with a clouded brow to study its contents. The will was holograph, for Mr. Utterson though he took charge of it now that it was made, had refused to lend the least assistance in the making of it; it provided not only that, in case of the decease of Henry Jekyll, M.D., D.C.L., L.L.D., F.R.S., etc., all his possessions were to pass into the hands of his "friend and benefactor Edward Hyde," but that in case of Dr. Jekyll's "disappearance or unexplained absence for any period exceeding three calendar months," the said Edward Hyde should step into the said Henry Jekyll's shoes without further delay and free from any burthen or obligation beyond the payment of a few small sums to the members of the doctor's household. This document had long been the lawyer's eyesore. It offended him both as a lawyer and as a lover of the sane and customary sides of life, to whom the fanciful was the immodest. And hitherto it was his ignorance of Mr. Hyde that had swelled his indignation; now, by a sudden turn, it was his knowledge. It was already bad enough when the name was but a name of which he could learn no more. It was worse when it began to be clothed upon with detestable attributes; and out of the shifting, insubstantial mists that had so long baffled his eye, there leaped up the sudden, definite presentment of a fiend.

"I thought it was madness," he said, as he replaced the obnoxious paper in the safe, "and now I begin to fear it is disgrace."

With that he blew out his candle, put on a greatcoat, and set forth in the direction of Cavendish Square, that citadel of medicine, where his friend, the great Dr. Lanyon, had his house and received his crowding patients. "If anyone knows, it will be

Lanyon," he had thought.

The solemn butler knew and welcomed him; he was subjected to no stage of delay, but ushered direct from the door to the dining-room where Dr. Lanyon sat alone over his wine. This was a hearty, healthy, dapper, red-faced gentleman, with a shock of hair prematurely white, and a boisterous and decided manner. At sight of Mr. Utterson, he sprang up from his chair and welcomed him with both hands. The geniality, as was the way of the man, was somewhat theatrical to the eye; but it reposed on genuine feeling. For these two were old friends, old mates both at school and college, both thorough respectors of themselves and of each other, and what does not always follow, men who thoroughly enjoyed each other's company.

After a little rambling talk, the lawyer led up to the subject which so disagreeably preoccupied his mind.

"I suppose, Lanyon," said he, "you and I must be the two oldest friends that Henry Jekyll has?"

"I wish the friends were younger," chuckled Dr. Lanyon. "But I suppose we are. And what of that? I see little of him now."

"Indeed?" said Utterson. "I thought you had a bond of common interest."

"We had," was the reply. "But it is more than ten years since Henry Jekyll became too fanciful for me. He began to go wrong, wrong in mind; and though of course I continue to take an interest in him for old sake's sake, as they say, I see and I have seen devilish little of the man. Such unscientific balderdash," added the doctor, flushing suddenly purple, "would have estranged Damon and Pythias."

This little spirit of temper was somewhat of a relief to Mr. Utterson. "They have only differed on some point of science," he thought; and being a man of no scientific passions (except in the matter of conveyancing), he even added: "It is nothing worse than that!" He gave his friend a few seconds to recover his composure, and then approached the question he had come to put. "Did you ever come across a protégé of his—one Hyde?" he asked.

"Hyde?" repeated Lanyon. "No. Never heard of him. Since

my time."

That was the amount of information that the lawyer carried back with him to the great, dark bed on which he tossed to and fro, until the small hours of the morning began to grow large. It was a night of little ease to his toiling mind, toiling in mere darkness and besieged by questions.

Six o'clock struck on the bells of the church that was so conveniently near to Mr. Utterson's dwelling, and still he was digging at the problem. Hitherto it had touched him on the intellectual side alone; but now his imagination also was engaged, or rather enslaved; and as he lay and tossed in the gross darkness of the night and the curtained room, Mr. Enfield's tale went by before his mind in a scroll of lighted pictures. He would be aware of the great field of lamps of a nocturnal city; then of the figure of a man walking swiftly; then of a child running from the doctor's; and then these met, and that human Juggernaut trod the child down and passed on regardless of her screams. Or else he would see a room in a rich house, where his friend lay asleep, dreaming and smiling at his dreams; and then the door of that room would be opened, the curtains of the bed plucked apart, the sleeper recalled, and lo! there would stand by his side a figure to whom power was given, and even at that dead hour, he must rise and do its bidding. The figure in these two phases haunted the lawyer all night; and if at any time he dozed over, it was but to see it glide more stealthily through sleeping houses, or move the more swiftly and still the more swiftly, even to dizziness, through wider labyrinths of lamplighted city, and at every street corner crush a child and leave her screaming. And still the figure had no face by which he might know it; even in his dreams, it had no face, or one that baffled him and melted before his eyes; and thus it was that there sprang up and grew apace in the lawyer's mind a singularly strong, almost an inordinate, curiosity to behold the features of the real Mr. Hyde. If he could but once set eyes on him, he thought the mystery would lighten and perhaps roll altogether away, as was the habit of mysterious things when well examined. He might see a reason for his friend's strange preference or bondage (call it which you please) and even for the startling clause of the will. At least it would be a face worth seeing: the face of a man who was without bowels of mercy: a face which had but to show itself to raise up, in the mind of the unimpressionable Enfield, a spirit of enduring hatred.

From that time forward, Mr. Utterson began to haunt the door in the by-street of shops. In the morning before office hours, at noon when business was plenty and time scarce, at night under the face of the fogged city moon, by all lights and at all hours of solitude or concourse, the lawyer was to be found on his chosen post.

"If he be Mr. Hyde," he had thought, "I shall be Mr. Seek."

And at last his patience was rewarded. It was a fine dry night; frost in the air; the streets as clean as a ballroom floor; the lamps, unshaken by any wind, drawing a regular pattern of light and shadow. By ten o'clock, when the shops were closed, the by-street was very solitary and, in spite of the low growl of London from all round, very silent. Small sounds carried far; domestic sounds out of the houses were clearly audible on either side of the roadway; and the rumour of the approach of any passenger preceded him by a long time. Mr. Utterson had been some minutes at his post, when he was aware of an odd light footstep drawing near. In the course of his nightly patrols, he had long grown accustomed to the quaint effect with which the footfalls of a single person, while he is still a great way off, suddenly spring out distinct from the vast hum and clatter of the city. Yet his attention had never before been so sharply and decisively arrested; and it was with a strong, superstitious prevision of success that he withdrew into the entry of the court.

The steps drew swiftly nearer, and swelled out suddenly louder as they turned the end of the street. The lawyer, looking forth from the entry, could soon see what manner of man he had to deal with. He was small and very plainly dressed and the look of him, even at that distance, went somehow strongly against the watcher's inclination. But he made straight for the door, crossing the roadway to save time; and as he came, he drew a key from his pocket like one approaching home.

Mr. Utterson stepped out and touched him on the shoulder as he passed. "Mr. Hyde, I think?"

Mr. Hyde shrank back with a hissing intake of the breath. But his fear was only momentary; and though he did not look the lawyer in the face, he answered coolly enough: "That is my name. What do you want?"

"I see you are going in," returned the lawyer. "I am an old friend of Dr. Jekyll's—Mr. Utterson of Gaunt Street—you must have heard of my name; and meeting you so conveniently, I thought you might admit me."

"You will not find Dr. Jekyll; he is from home," replied Mr. Hyde, blowing in the key. And then suddenly, but still without looking up, "How did you know me?" he asked.

"On your side," said Mr. Utterson "will you do me a favour?"

"With pleasure," replied the other. "What shall it be?"

"Will you let me see your face?" asked the lawyer.

Mr. Hyde appeared to hesitate, and then, as if upon some sudden reflection, fronted about with an air of defiance; and the pair stared at each other pretty fixedly for a few seconds. "Now I shall know you again," said Mr. Utterson. "It may be useful."

"Yes," returned Mr. Hyde, "It is as well we have met; and à propos, you should have my address." And he gave a number of a street in Soho.

"Good God!" thought Mr. Utterson, "can he, too, have been thinking of the will?" But he kept his feelings to himself and only grunted in acknowledgment of the address.

"And now," said the other, "how did you know me?"

"By description," was the reply.

"Whose description?"

"We have common friends," said Mr. Utterson.

"Common friends," echoed Mr. Hyde, a little hoarsely. "Who are they?"

"Jekyll, for instance," said the lawyer.

"He never told you," cried Mr. Hyde, with a flush of anger. "I did not think you would have lied."

"Come," said Mr. Utterson, "that is not fitting language."

The other snarled aloud into a savage laugh; and the next

moment, with extraordinary quickness, he had unlocked the door and disappeared into the house.

The lawyer stood awhile when Mr. Hyde had left him, the picture of disquietude. Then he began slowly to mount the street, pausing every step or two and putting his hand to his brow like a man in mental perplexity. The problem he was thus debating as he walked, was one of a class that is rarely solved. Mr. Hyde was pale and dwarfish, he gave an impression of deformity without any nameable malformation, he had a displeasing smile, he had borne himself to the lawyer with a sort of murderous mixture of timidity and boldness, and he spoke with a husky, whispering and somewhat broken voice; all these were points against him, but not all of these together could explain the hitherto unknown disgust, loathing and fear with which Mr. Utterson regarded him. "There must be something else," said the perplexed gentleman. "There is something more, if I could find a name for it. God bless me, the man seems hardly human! Something troglodytic, shall we say? or can it be the old story of Dr. Fell? or is it the mere radiance of a foul soul that thus transpires through, and transfigures, its clay continent? The last, I think; for, O my poor old Harry Jekyll, if ever I read Satan's signature upon a face, it is on that of your new friend."

Round the corner from the by-street, there was a square of ancient, handsome houses, now for the most part decayed from their high estate and let in flats and chambers to all sorts and conditions of men; map-engravers, architects, shady lawyers and the agents of obscure enterprises. One house, however, second from the corner, was still occupied entire; and at the door of this, which wore a great air of wealth and comfort, though it was now plunged in darkness except for the fanlight, Mr. Utterson stopped and knocked. A well-dressed, elderly servant opened the door.

"Is Dr. Jekyll at home, Poole?" asked the lawyer.

"I will see, Mr. Utterson," said Poole, admitting the visitor, as he spoke, into a large, low-roofed, comfortable hall paved with flags, warmed (after the fashion of a country house) by a bright, open fire, and furnished with costly cabinets of oak. "Will you wait here by the fire, sir? or shall I give you a light in the dining-room?"

"Here, thank you," said the lawyer, and he drew near and leaned on the tall fender. This hall, in which he was now left alone, was a pet fancy of his friend the doctor's; and Utterson himself was wont to speak of it as the pleasantest room in London. But tonight there was a shudder in his blood; the face of Hyde sat heavy on his memory; he felt (what was rare with him) a nausea and distaste of life; and in the gloom of his spirits, he seemed to read a menace in the flickering of the firelight on the polished cabinets and the uneasy starting of the shadow on the roof. He was ashamed of his relief, when Poole presently returned to announce that Dr. Jekyll was gone out.

"I saw Mr. Hyde go in by the old dissecting room, Poole," he said. "Is that right, when Dr. Jekyll is from home?"

"Quite right, Mr. Utterson, sir," replied the servant. "Mr. Hyde has a key."

"Your master seems to repose a great deal of trust in that young man, Poole," resumed the other musingly.

"Yes, sir, he does indeed," said Poole. "We have all orders to obey him."

"I do not think I ever met Mr. Hyde?" asked Utterson.

"O, dear no, sir. He never dines here," replied the butler. "Indeed we see very little of him on this side of the house; he mostly comes and goes by the laboratory."

"Well, good-night, Poole."

"Good-night, Mr. Utterson."

And the lawyer set out homeward with a very heavy heart. "Poor Harry Jekyll," he thought, "my mind misgives me he is in deep waters! He was wild when he was young; a long while ago to be sure; but in the law of God, there is no statute of limitations. Ay, it must be that; the ghost of some old sin, the cancer of some concealed disgrace: punishment coming, pede claudo, years after memory has forgotten and self-love condoned the fault." And the lawyer, scared by the thought, brooded awhile on his own past, groping in all the corners of memory, least by chance some Jack-in-the-Box of an old iniquity should leap to light there. His past was fairly blameless; few men could read the rolls of their life with less apprehension; yet he was humbled to the dust by the many ill things he had done, and raised up again into a sober and fearful gratitude by the many he had come so near to doing yet avoided. And then by a return on his former subject, he conceived a spark of hope. "This Master Hyde, if he were studied," thought he, "must have secrets of his own; black secrets, by the look of him; secrets compared to which poor Jekyll's worst would be like sunshine. Things cannot continue as they are. It turns me cold to think of this creature stealing like a thief to Harry's bedside; poor Harry, what a wakening! And the danger of it; for if this Hyde suspects the existence of the will, he may grow impatient to inherit. Ay, I must put my shoulders to the wheel—if Jekyll will but let me," he added, "if Jekyll will only let me." For once more he saw before his mind's eye, as clear as transparency, the strange clauses of the will.

DR. JEKYLL WAS QUITE AT EASE

A fortnight later, by excellent good fortune, the doctor gave one of his pleasant dinners to some five or six old cronies, all intelligent, reputable men and all judges of good wine; and Mr. Utterson so contrived that he remained behind after the others had departed. This was no new arrangement, but a thing that had befallen many scores of times. Where Utterson was liked, he was liked well. Hosts loved to detain the dry lawyer, when the light-hearted and loose-tongued had already their foot on the threshold; they liked to sit a while in his unobtrusive company, practising for solitude, sobering their minds in the man's rich silence after the expense and strain of gaiety. To this rule, Dr. Jekyll was no exception; and as he now sat on the opposite side of the fire—a large, well-made, smooth-faced man of fifty, with something of a slyish cast perhaps, but every mark of capacity and kindness—you could see by his looks that he cherished for Mr. Utterson a sincere and warm affection.

"I have been wanting to speak to you, Jekyll," began the latter. "You know that will of yours?"

A close observer might have gathered that the topic was distasteful; but the doctor carried it off gaily. "My poor Utterson," said he, "you are unfortunate in such a client. I never saw a man so distressed as you were by my will; unless it were that hide-bound pedant, Lanyon, at what he called my scientific heresies. O, I know he's a good fellow—you needn't frown—an excellent fellow, and I always mean to see more of him; but a hide-bound pedant for all that; an ignorant, blatant pedant. I was never more disappointed in any man than Lanyon."

"You know I never approved of it," pursued Utterson, ruthlessly disregarding the fresh topic.

"My will? Yes, certainly, I know that," said the doctor, a trifle sharply. "You have told me so."

"Well, I tell you so again," continued the lawyer. "I have been learning something of young Hyde."

The large handsome face of Dr. Jekyll grew pale to the very lips, and there came a blackness about his eyes. "I do not care to hear more," said he. "This is a matter I thought we had agreed to drop."

"What I heard was abominable," said Utterson.

"It can make no change. You do not understand my position," returned the doctor, with a certain incoherency of manner. "I am painfully situated, Utterson; my position is a very strange—a very strange one. It is one of those affairs that cannot be mended by talking."

"Jekyll," said Utterson, "you know me: I am a man to be trusted. Make a clean breast of this in confidence; and I make no doubt I can get you out of it."

"My good Utterson," said the doctor, "this is very good of you, this is downright good of you, and I cannot find words to thank you in. I believe you fully; I would trust you before any man alive, ay, before myself, if I could make the choice; but indeed it isn't what you fancy; it is not as bad as that; and just to put your good heart at rest, I will tell you one thing: the moment I choose, I can be rid of Mr. Hyde. I give you my hand upon that; and I thank you again and again; and I will just add one little word, Utterson, that I'm sure you'll take in good part: this is a private matter, and I beg of you to let it sleep."

Utterson reflected a little, looking in the fire.

"I have no doubt you are perfectly right," he said at last, getting to his feet.

"Well, but since we have touched upon this business, and for the last time I hope," continued the doctor, "there is one point I should like you to understand. I have really a very great interest in poor Hyde. I know you have seen him; he told me so; and I fear he was rude. But I do sincerely take a great, a very great interest in that young man; and if I am taken away, Utterson, I wish you to promise me that you will bear with him and get his rights for him. I think you would, if you knew all; and it would be a weight off my mind if you would promise."

"I can't pretend that I shall ever like him," said the lawyer.

"I don't ask that," pleaded Jekyll, laying his hand upon the other's arm; "I only ask for justice; I only ask you to help him for my sake, when I am no longer here."

Utterson heaved an irrepressible sigh. "Well," said he, "I promise."

THE CAREW MURDER CASE

Nearly a year later, in the month of October, 18—, London was startled by a crime of singular ferocity and rendered all the more notable by the high position of the victim. The details were few and startling. A maid servant living alone in a house not far from the river, had gone upstairs to bed about eleven. Although a fog rolled over the city in the small hours, the early part of the night was cloudless, and the lane, which the maid's window overlooked, was brilliantly lit by the full moon. It seems she was romantically given, for she sat down upon her box, which stood immediately under the window, and fell into a dream of musing. Never (she used to say, with streaming tears, when she narrated that experience), never had she felt more at peace with all men or thought more kindly of the world. And as she so sat she became aware of an aged beautiful gentleman with white hair, drawing near along the lane; and advancing to meet him, another and very small gentleman, to whom at first she paid less attention. When they had come within speech (which was just under the maid's eyes) the older man bowed and accosted the other with a very pretty manner of politeness. It did not seem as if the subject of his address were of great importance; indeed, from his pointing, it sometimes appeared as if he were only inquiring his way; but the moon shone on his face as he spoke, and the girl was pleased to watch it, it seemed to breathe such an innocent and old-world kindness of disposition, yet with something high too, as of a well-founded self-content. Presently her eye wandered to the other, and she was surprised to recognise in him a certain Mr. Hyde, who had once visited her master and for whom she had conceived a dislike. He had in his hand a heavy cane, with which he was trifling; but he answered never a word, and seemed to listen with an ill-contained impatience. And then all of a sudden he broke out in a great flame of anger, stamping with his foot, brandishing the cane, and carrying on (as the maid described it) like a madman. The old gentleman took a step back, with the air of one very much surprised and a trifle hurt; and at that Mr. Hyde broke out of all bounds and clubbed him to the earth. And next moment, with ape-like fury, he was trampling his victim under foot and hailing down a storm of blows, under which the bones were audibly shattered and the body jumped upon the roadway. At the horror of these sights and sounds, the maid fainted.

It was two o'clock when she came to herself and called for the police. The murderer was gone long ago; but there lay his victim in the middle of the lane, incredibly mangled. The stick with which the deed had been done, although it was of some rare and very tough and heavy wood, had broken in the middle under the stress of this insensate cruelty; and one splintered half had rolled in the neighbouring gutter—the other, without doubt, had been carried away by the murderer. A purse and gold watch were found upon the victim: but no cards or papers, except a sealed and stamped envelope, which he had been probably carrying to the post, and which bore the name and address of Mr. Utterson.

This was brought to the lawyer the next morning, before he was out of bed; and he had no sooner seen it and been told the circumstances, than he shot out a solemn lip. "I shall say nothing till I have seen the body," said he; "this may be very serious. Have the kindness to wait while I dress." And with the same grave countenance he hurried through his breakfast and drove to the police station, whither the body had been carried. As soon as he came into the cell, he nodded.

"Yes," said he, "I recognise him. I am sorry to say that this is Sir Danvers Carew."

"Good God, sir," exclaimed the officer, "is it possible?" And the next moment his eye lighted up with professional ambition. "This will make a deal of noise," he said. "And perhaps you can help us to the man." And he briefly narrated what the maid had seen, and showed the broken stick.

Mr. Utterson had already quailed at the name of Hyde; but when the stick was laid before him, he could doubt no longer; broken and battered as it was, he recognised it for one that he had himself presented many years before to Henry Jekyll.

"Is this Mr. Hyde a person of small stature?" he inquired.

"Particularly small and particularly wicked-looking, is what the maid calls him," said the officer.

Mr. Utterson reflected; and then, raising his head, "If you will come with me in my cab," he said, "I think I can take you to his house."

It was by this time about nine in the morning, and the first fog of the season. A great chocolate-coloured pall lowered over heaven, but the wind was continually charging and routing these embattled vapours; so that as the cab crawled from street to street, Mr. Utterson beheld a marvelous number of degrees and hues of twilight; for here it would be dark like the back-end of evening; and there would be a glow of a rich, lurid brown, like the light of some strange conflagration; and here, for a moment, the fog would be quite broken up, and a haggard shaft of daylight would glance in between the swirling wreaths. The dismal quarter of Soho seen under these changing glimpses, with its muddy ways, and slatternly passengers, and its lamps, which had never been extinguished or had been kindled afresh to combat this mournful reinvasion of darkness, seemed, in the lawyer's eyes, like a district of some city in a nightmare. The thoughts of his mind, besides, were of the gloomiest dye; and when he glanced at the companion of his drive, he was conscious of some touch of that terror of the law and the law's officers, which may at times assail the most honest.

As the cab drew up before the address indicated, the fog lifted a little and showed him a dingy street, a gin palace, a low French eating house, a shop for the retail of penny numbers and twopenny salads, many ragged children huddled in the doorways, and many women of many different nationalities passing out, key in hand, to have a morning glass; and the next moment the fog settled down again upon that part, as brown as umber, and cut him off from his blackguardly surroundings. This was the home of Henry Jekyll's favourite; of a man who was heir to a quarter of a million sterling.

An ivory-faced and silvery-haired old woman opened the door. She had an evil face, smoothed by hypocrisy: but her manners were excellent. Yes, she said, this was Mr. Hyde's, but he was not at home; he had been in that night very late, but he had gone away again in less than an hour; there was nothing strange in that; his habits were very irregular, and he was often absent; for instance, it was nearly two months since she had seen him till yesterday.

"Very well, then, we wish to see his rooms," said the lawyer; and when the woman began to declare it was impossible, "I had better tell you who this person is," he added. "This is Inspector

Newcomen of Scotland Yard."

A flash of odious joy appeared upon the woman's face. "Ah!" said she, "he is in trouble! What has he done?"

Mr. Utterson and the inspector exchanged glances. "He don't seem a very popular character," observed the latter. "And now, my good woman, just let me and this gentleman have a look about us."

In the whole extent of the house, which but for the old woman remained otherwise empty, Mr. Hyde had only used a couple of rooms; but these were furnished with luxury and good taste. A closet was filled with wine; the plate was of silver, the napery elegant; a good picture hung upon the walls, a gift (as Utterson supposed) from Henry Jekyll, who was much of a connoisseur; and the carpets were of many plies and agreeable in colour. At this moment, however, the rooms bore every mark of having been recently and hurriedly ransacked; clothes lay about the floor, with their pockets inside out; lock-fast drawers stood open; and on the hearth there lay a pile of grey ashes, as though many papers had been burned. From these embers the inspector disinterred the butt end of a green cheque book, which had resisted the action of the fire; the other half of the stick was found behind the door; and as this clinched his suspicions, the officer declared himself delighted. A visit to the bank, where several thousand pounds were found to be lying to the murderer's credit, completed his gratification.

"You may depend upon it, sir," he told Mr. Utterson: "I have him in my hand. He must have lost his head, or he never would have left the stick or, above all, burned the cheque book. Why, money's life to the man. We have nothing to do but wait for him at the bank, and get out the handbills."

This last, however, was not so easy of accomplishment; for Mr. Hyde had numbered few familiars—even the master of the servant maid had only seen him twice; his family could nowhere be traced; he had never been photographed; and the few who could describe him differed widely, as common observers will. Only on one point were they agreed; and that was the haunting sense of unexpressed deformity with which the fugitive impressed his beholders.

INCIDENT OF THE LETTER

It was late in the afternoon, when Mr. Utterson found his way to Dr. Jekyll's door, where he was at once admitted by Poole, and carried down by the kitchen offices and across a yard which had once been a garden, to the building which was indifferently known as the laboratory or dissecting rooms. The doctor had bought the house from the heirs of a celebrated surgeon; and his own tastes being rather chemical than anatomical, had changed the destination of the block at the bottom of the garden. It was the first time that the lawyer had been received in that part of his friend's quarters; and he eyed the dingy, windowless structure with curiosity, and gazed round with a distasteful sense of strangeness as he crossed the theatre, once crowded with eager students and now lying gaunt and silent, the tables laden with chemical apparatus, the floor strewn with crates and littered with packing straw, and the light falling dimly through the foggy cupola. At the further end, a flight of stairs mounted to a door covered with red baize; and through this, Mr. Utterson was at last received into the doctor's cabinet. It was a large room fitted round with glass presses, furnished, among other things, with a cheval-glass and a business table, and looking out upon the court by three dusty windows barred with iron. The fire burned in the grate; a lamp was set lighted on the chimney shelf, for even in the houses the fog began to lie thickly; and there, close up to the warmth, sat Dr. Jekyll, looking deathly sick. He did not rise to meet his visitor, but held out a cold hand and bade him welcome in a changed voice.

"And now," said Mr. Utterson, as soon as Poole had left them, "you have heard the news?"

The doctor shuddered. "They were crying it in the square," he said. "I heard them in my dining-room."

"One word," said the lawyer. "Carew was my client, but so are you, and I want to know what I am doing. You have not been mad enough to hide this fellow?"

"Utterson, I swear to God," cried the doctor, "I swear to God I will never set eyes on him again. I bind my honour to you that I am done with him in this world. It is all at an end. And indeed he does not want my help; you do not know him as I do; he is safe, he is quite safe; mark my words, he will never more be heard of."

The lawyer listened gloomily; he did not like his friend's feverish manner. "You seem pretty sure of him," said he; "and for your sake, I hope you may be right. If it came to a trial, your name might appear."

"I am quite sure of him," replied Jekyll; "I have grounds for certainty that I cannot share with any one. But there is one thing on which you may advise me. I have—I have received a letter; and I am at a loss whether I should show it to the police. I should like to leave it in your hands, Utterson; you would judge wisely, I am sure; I have so great a trust in you."

"You fear, I suppose, that it might lead to his detection?" asked the lawyer.

"No," said the other. "I cannot say that I care what becomes of Hyde; I am quite done with him. I was thinking of my own character, which this hateful business has rather exposed."

Utterson ruminated awhile; he was surprised at his friend's selfishness, and yet relieved by it. "Well," said he, at last, "let me see the letter."

The letter was written in an odd, upright hand and signed "Edward Hyde": and it signified, briefly enough, that the writer's benefactor, Dr. Jekyll, whom he had long so unworthily repaid for a thousand generosities, need labour under no alarm for his safety, as he had means of escape on which he placed a sure dependence. The lawyer liked this letter well enough; it put a better colour on the intimacy than he had looked for; and he blamed himself for some of his past suspicions.

"Have you the envelope?" he asked.

"I burned it," replied Jekyll, "before I thought what I was about. But it bore no postmark. The note was handed in."

"Shall I keep this and sleep upon it?" asked Utterson.

"I wish you to judge for me entirely," was the reply. "I have lost confidence in myself."

"Well, I shall consider," returned the lawyer. "And now one word more: it was Hyde who dictated the terms in your will about that disappearance?"

The doctor seemed seized with a qualm of faintness; he shut his mouth tight and nodded.

"I knew it," said Utterson. "He meant to murder you. You had a fine escape."

"I have had what is far more to the purpose," returned the doctor solemnly: "I have had a lesson—O God, Utterson, what a lesson I have had!" And he covered his face for a moment with his hands.

On his way out, the lawyer stopped and had a word or two with Poole. "By the bye," said he, "there was a letter handed in to-day: what was the messenger like?" But Poole was positive nothing had come except by post; "and only circulars by that," he added.

This news sent off the visitor with his fears renewed. Plainly the letter had come by the laboratory door; possibly, indeed, it had been written in the cabinet; and if that were so, it must be differently judged, and handled with the more caution. The newsboys, as he went, were crying themselves hoarse along the footways: "Special edition. Shocking murder of an M.P." That was the funeral oration of one friend and client; and he could not help a certain apprehension lest the good name of another should be sucked down in the eddy of the scandal. It was, at least, a ticklish decision that he had to make; and self-reliant as he was by habit, he began to cherish a longing for advice. It was not to be had directly; but perhaps, he thought, it might be fished for.

Presently after, he sat on one side of his own hearth, with Mr. Guest, his head clerk, upon the other, and midway between, at a nicely calculated distance from the fire, a bottle of a particular old wine that had long dwelt unsunned in the foundations of his house. The fog still slept on the wing above the drowned city, where the lamps glimmered like carbuncles; and through the muffle and smother of these fallen clouds, the procession of the town's life was still rolling in through the great arteries with a sound as of a mighty wind. But the room was gay with firelight. In the bottle the acids were long ago resolved; the imperial dye had softened with time, as the colour grows richer in stained windows; and the glow of hot autumn afternoons on hillside vineyards, was ready to be set free and to disperse the fogs of London. Insensibly the lawyer melted. There was no man from whom he kept fewer secrets than Mr. Guest; and he was not always sure that he kept as many as he meant. Guest had often been on business to the doctor's; he knew Poole; he could scarce have failed to hear of Mr. Hyde's familiarity about the house; he might draw conclusions: was it not as well, then, that he should see a letter which put that mystery to right? and above all since Guest, being a great student and critic of handwriting, would consider the step natural and obliging? The clerk, besides, was a man of counsel; he could scarce read so strange a document without dropping a remark; and by that remark Mr. Utterson might shape his future course.

"This is a sad business about Sir Danvers," he said.

"Yes, sir, indeed. It has elicited a great deal of public feeling," returned Guest. "The man, of course, was mad."

"I should like to hear your views on that," replied Utterson. "I have a document here in his handwriting; it is between ourselves, for I scarce know what to do about it; it is an ugly business at the best. But there it is; quite in your way: a murderer's autograph."

Guest's eyes brightened, and he sat down at once and studied it with passion. "No sir," he said: "not mad; but it is an odd hand."

"And by all accounts a very odd writer," added the lawyer.

Just then the servant entered with a note.

"Is that from Dr. Jekyll, sir?" inquired the clerk. "I thought I knew the writing. Anything private, Mr. Utterson?"

"Only an invitation to dinner. Why? Do you want to see it?"

"One moment. I thank you, sir;" and the clerk laid the two sheets of paper alongside and sedulously compared their contents. "Thank you, sir," he said at last, returning both; "it's a very interesting autograph."

There was a pause, during which Mr. Utterson struggled with himself. "Why did you compare them, Guest?" he inquired suddenly.

"Well, sir," returned the clerk, "there's a rather singular resemblance; the two hands are in many points identical: only differently sloped."

"Rather quaint," said Utterson.

"It is, as you say, rather quaint," returned Guest.

"I wouldn't speak of this note, you know," said the master.

"No, sir," said the clerk. "I understand."

But no sooner was Mr. Utterson alone that night, than he locked the note into his safe, where it reposed from that time forward. "What!" he thought. "Henry Jekyll forge for a murderer!" And his blood ran cold in his veins.

INCIDENT OF DR. LANYON

Time ran on; thousands of pounds were offered in reward, for the death of Sir Danvers was resented as a public injury; but Mr. Hyde had disappeared out of the ken of the police as though he had never existed. Much of his past was unearthed, indeed, and all disreputable: tales came out of the man's cruelty, at once so callous and violent; of his vile life, of his strange associates, of the hatred that seemed to have surrounded his career; but of his present whereabouts, not a whisper. From the time he had left the house in Soho on the morning of the murder, he was simply blotted out; and gradually, as time drew on, Mr. Utterson began to recover from the hotness of his alarm, and to grow more at quiet with himself. The death of Sir Danvers was, to his way of thinking, more than paid for by the disappearance of Mr. Hyde. Now that that evil influence had been withdrawn, a new life began for Dr. Jekyll. He came out of his seclusion, renewed relations with his friends, became once more their familiar guest and entertainer; and whilst he had always been known for charities, he was now no less distinguished for religion. He was busy, he was much in the open air, he did good; his face seemed to open and brighten, as if with an inward consciousness of service; and for more than two months, the doctor was at peace.

On the 8th of January Utterson had dined at the doctor's with a small party; Lanyon had been there; and the face of the host had looked from one to the other as in the old days when the trio were inseparable friends. On the 12th, and again on the 14th, the door was shut against the lawyer. "The doctor was confined to the house," Poole said, "and saw no one." On the 15th, he tried again, and was again refused; and having now been used for the last two months to see his friend almost daily, he found this return of solitude to weigh upon his spirits. The fifth night he had in Guest to dine with him; and the sixth he betook himself to Dr. Lanyon's.

There at least he was not denied admittance; but when he came in, he was shocked at the change which had taken place in the doctor's appearance. He had his death-warrant written legibly upon his face. The rosy man had grown pale; his flesh had fallen away; he was visibly balder and older; and yet it was not so much these tokens of a swift physical decay that arrested the lawyer's notice, as a look in the eye and quality of manner that seemed to testify to some deep-seated terror of the mind. It was unlikely that the doctor should fear death; and yet that was what Utterson was tempted to suspect. "Yes," he thought; "he is a doctor, he must know his own state and that his days are counted; and the knowledge is more than he can bear." And yet when Utterson remarked on his ill looks, it was with an air of great firmness that Lanyon declared himself a doomed man.

"I have had a shock," he said, "and I shall never recover. It is a question of weeks. Well, life has been pleasant; I liked it; yes, sir, I used to like it. I sometimes think if we knew all, we should be more glad to get away."

"Jekyll is ill, too," observed Utterson. "Have you seen him?"

But Lanyon's face changed, and he held up a trembling hand. "I wish to see or hear no more of Dr. Jekyll," he said in a loud, unsteady voice. "I am quite done with that person; and I beg that you will spare me any allusion to one whom I regard as dead."

"Tut, tut!" said Mr. Utterson; and then after a considerable pause, "Can't I do anything?" he inquired. "We are three very old friends, Lanyon; we shall not live to make others."

"Nothing can be done," returned Lanyon; "ask himself."

"He will not see me," said the lawyer.

"I am not surprised at that," was the reply. "Some day, Utterson, after I am dead, you may perhaps come to learn the right and wrong of this. I cannot tell you. And in the meantime, if you can sit and talk with me of other things, for God's sake, stay and do so; but if you cannot keep clear of this accursed topic, then in God's name, go, for I cannot bear it."

As soon as he got home, Utterson sat down and wrote to Jekyll, complaining of his exclusion from the house, and asking the cause of this unhappy break with Lanyon; and the next day brought him a long answer, often very pathetically worded, and sometimes darkly mysterious in drift. The quarrel with Lanyon was incurable. "I do not blame our old friend," Jekyll wrote, "but I share his view that we must never meet. I mean from henceforth to lead a life of extreme seclusion; you must not be surprised, nor must you doubt my friendship, if my door is often shut even to you. You must suffer me to go my own dark way. I have brought on myself a punishment and a danger that I cannot name. If I am the chief of sinners, I am the chief of sufferers also. I could not think that this earth contained a place for sufferings and terrors so unmanning; and you can do but one thing, Utterson, to lighten this destiny, and that is to respect my silence." Utterson was amazed; the dark influence of Hyde had been withdrawn, the doctor had returned to his old tasks and amities; a week ago, the prospect had smiled with every promise of a cheerful and an honoured age; and now in a moment, friendship, and peace of mind, and the whole tenor of his life were wrecked. So great and unprepared a change pointed to madness; but in view of Lanyon's manner and words, there must lie for it some deeper ground.

A week afterwards Dr. Lanyon took to his bed, and in something less than a fortnight he was dead. The night after the funeral, at which he had been sadly affected, Utterson locked the door of his business room, and sitting there by the light of a melancholy candle, drew out and set before him an envelope addressed by the hand and sealed with the seal of his dead friend. "PRIVATE: for the hands of G. J. Utterson ALONE, and in case of his predecease to be destroyed unread," so it was emphatically superscribed; and the lawyer dreaded to behold the contents. "I have buried one friend to-day," he thought: "what if this should cost me another?" And then he condemned the fear as a disloyalty, and broke the seal. Within there was another enclosure, likewise sealed, and marked upon the cover as "not to be opened till the death or disappearance of Dr. Henry Jekyll." Utterson could not trust his eyes. Yes, it was disappearance; here again, as in the mad will which he had long ago restored to its author, here again were the idea of a disappearance and the name of Henry Jekyll bracketted. But in the will, that idea had sprung from the sinister suggestion of the man Hyde; it was set there with a purpose all too plain and horrible. Written by the hand of Lanyon, what should it mean? A great curiosity came on the trustee, to disregard the prohibition and dive at once to the bottom of these mysteries; but professional honour and faith to his dead friend were stringent obligations; and the packet slept in the inmost corner of his private safe.

It is one thing to mortify curiosity, another to conquer it; and it may be doubted if, from that day forth, Utterson desired the society of his surviving friend with the same eagerness. He thought of him kindly; but his thoughts were disquieted and fearful. He went to call indeed; but he was perhaps relieved to be denied admittance; perhaps, in his heart, he preferred to speak with Poole upon the doorstep and surrounded by the air and sounds of the open city, rather than to be admitted into that house of voluntary bondage, and to sit and speak with its inscrutable recluse. Poole had, indeed, no very pleasant news to communicate. The doctor, it appeared, now more than ever confined himself to the cabinet over the laboratory, where he would sometimes even sleep; he was out of spirits, he had grown very silent, he did not read; it seemed as if he had something on his mind. Utterson became so used to the unvarying character of these reports, that he fell off little by little in the frequency of his visits.

INCIDENT AT THE WINDOW

It chanced on Sunday, when Mr. Utterson was on his usual walk with Mr. Enfield, that their way lay once again through the by-street; and that when they came in front of the door, both stopped to gaze on it.

"Well," said Enfield, "that story's at an end at least. We shall never see more of Mr. Hyde."

"I hope not," said Utterson. "Did I ever tell you that I once saw him, and shared your feeling of repulsion?"

"It was impossible to do the one without the other," returned Enfield. "And by the way, what an ass you must have thought me, not to know that this was a back way to Dr. Jekyll's! It was partly your own fault that I found it out, even when I did."

"So you found it out, did you?" said Utterson. "But if that be so, we may step into the court and take a look at the windows. To tell you the truth, I am uneasy about poor Jekyll; and even outside, I feel as if the presence of a friend might do him good."

The court was very cool and a little damp, and full of premature twilight, although the sky, high up overhead, was still bright with sunset. The middle one of the three windows was half-way open; and sitting close beside it, taking the air with an infinite sadness of mien, like some disconsolate prisoner, Utterson saw Dr. Jekyll.

"What! Jekyll!" he cried. "I trust you are better."

"I am very low, Utterson," replied the doctor drearily, "very low. It will not last long, thank God."

"You stay too much indoors," said the lawyer. "You should be out, whipping up the circulation like Mr. Enfield and me. (This is my cousin—Mr. Enfield—Dr. Jekyll.) Come now; get your hat and take a quick turn with us."

"You are very good," sighed the other. "I should like to very much; but no, no, no, it is quite impossible; I dare not. But indeed, Utterson, I am very glad to see you; this is really a great pleasure; I would ask you and Mr. Enfield up, but the place is really not fit."

"Why, then," said the lawyer, good-naturedly, "the best thing we can do is to stay down here and speak with you from where we are."

"That is just what I was about to venture to propose," returned the doctor with a smile. But the words were hardly uttered, before the smile was struck out of his face and succeeded by an expression of such abject terror and despair, as froze the very blood of the two gentlemen below. They saw it but for a glimpse for the window was instantly thrust down; but that glimpse had been sufficient, and they turned and left the court without a word. In silence, too, they traversed the by-street; and it was not until they had come into a neighbouring thoroughfare, where even upon a Sunday there were still some stirrings of life, that Mr. Utterson at last turned and looked at his companion. They were both pale; and there was an answering horror in their eyes.

"God forgive us, God forgive us," said Mr. Utterson.

But Mr. Enfield only nodded his head very seriously, and walked on once more in silence.

THE LAST NIGHT

Mr. Utterson was sitting by his fireside one evening after dinner, when he was surprised to receive a visit from Poole.

"Bless me, Poole, what brings you here?" he cried; and then taking a second look at him, "What ails you?" he added; "is the doctor ill?"

"Mr. Utterson," said the man, "there is something wrong."

"Take a seat, and here is a glass of wine for you," said the lawyer. "Now, take your time, and tell me plainly what you want."

"You know the doctor's ways, sir," replied Poole, "and how he shuts himself up. Well, he's shut up again in the cabinet; and I don't like it, sir—I wish I may die if I like it. Mr. Utterson, sir, I'm afraid."

"Now, my good man," said the lawyer, "be explicit. What are you afraid of?"

"I've been afraid for about a week," returned Poole, doggedly disregarding the question, "and I can bear it no more."

The man's appearance amply bore out his words; his manner was altered for the worse; and except for the moment when he had first announced his terror, he had not once looked the lawyer in the face. Even now, he sat with the glass of wine untasted on his knee, and his eyes directed to a corner of the floor. "I can bear it no more," he repeated.

"Come," said the lawyer, "I see you have some good reason, Poole; I see there is something seriously amiss. Try to tell me what it is."

"I think there's been foul play," said Poole, hoarsely.

"Foul play!" cried the lawyer, a good deal frightened and rather inclined to be irritated in consequence. "What foul play! What does the man mean?"

"I daren't say, sir," was the answer; "but will you come along with me and see for yourself?"

Mr. Utterson's only answer was to rise and get his hat and

greatcoat; but he observed with wonder the greatness of the relief that appeared upon the butler's face, and perhaps with no less, that the wine was still untasted when he set it down to follow.

It was a wild, cold, seasonable night of March, with a pale moon, lying on her back as though the wind had tilted her, and flying wrack of the most diaphanous and lawny texture. The wind made talking difficult, and flecked the blood into the face. It seemed to have swept the streets unusually bare of passengers, besides; for Mr. Utterson thought he had never seen that part of London so deserted. He could have wished it otherwise; never in his life had he been conscious of so sharp a wish to see and touch his fellow-creatures; for struggle as he might, there was borne in upon his mind a crushing anticipation of calamity. The square, when they got there, was full of wind and dust, and the thin trees in the garden were lashing themselves along the railing. Poole, who had kept all the way a pace or two ahead, now pulled up in the middle of the pavement, and in spite of the biting weather, took off his hat and mopped his brow with a red pocket-handkerchief. But for all the hurry of his coming, these were not the dews of exertion that he wiped away, but the moisture of some strangling anguish; for his face was white and his voice, when he spoke, harsh and broken.

"Well, sir," he said, "here we are, and God grant there be nothing wrong."

"Amen, Poole," said the lawyer.

Thereupon the servant knocked in a very guarded manner; the door was opened on the chain; and a voice asked from within, "Is that you, Poole?"

"It's all right," said Poole. "Open the door."

The hall, when they entered it, was brightly lighted up; the fire was built high; and about the hearth the whole of the servants, men and women, stood huddled together like a flock of sheep. At the sight of Mr. Utterson, the housemaid broke into hysterical whimpering; and the cook, crying out "Bless God! it's Mr. Utterson," ran forward as if to take him in her arms.

"What, what? Are you all here?" said the lawyer peevishly.

"Very irregular, very unseemly; your master would be far from pleased."

"They're all afraid," said Poole.

Blank silence followed, no one protesting; only the maid lifted her voice and now wept loudly.

"Hold your tongue!" Poole said to her, with a ferocity of accent that testified to his own jangled nerves; and indeed, when the girl had so suddenly raised the note of her lamentation, they had all started and turned towards the inner door with faces of dreadful expectation. "And now," continued the butler, addressing the knife-boy, "reach me a candle, and we'll get this through hands at once." And then he begged Mr. Utterson to follow him, and led the way to the back garden.

"Now, sir," said he, "you come as gently as you can. I want you to hear, and I don't want you to be heard. And see here, sir, if by any chance he was to ask you in, don't go."

Mr. Utterson's nerves, at this unlooked-for termination, gave a jerk that nearly threw him from his balance; but he recollected his courage and followed the butler into the laboratory building through the surgical theatre, with its lumber of crates and bottles, to the foot of the stair. Here Poole motioned him to stand on one side and listen; while he himself, setting down the candle and making a great and obvious call on his resolution, mounted the steps and knocked with a somewhat uncertain hand on the red baize of the cabinet door.

"Mr. Utterson, sir, asking to see you," he called; and even as he did so, once more violently signed to the lawyer to give ear.

A voice answered from within: "Tell him I cannot see anyone," it said complainingly.

"Thank you, sir," said Poole, with a note of something like triumph in his voice; and taking up his candle, he led Mr. Utterson back across the yard and into the great kitchen, where the fire was out and the beetles were leaping on the floor.

"Sir," he said, looking Mr. Utterson in the eyes, "Was that my master's voice?"

"It seems much changed," replied the lawyer, very pale, but giving look for look.

"Changed? Well, yes, I think so," said the butler. "Have I been twenty years in this man's house, to be deceived about his voice? No, sir; master's made away with; he was made away with eight days ago, when we heard him cry out upon the name of God; and who's in there instead of him, and why it stays there, is a thing that cries to Heaven, Mr. Utterson!"

"This is a very strange tale, Poole; this is rather a wild tale my man," said Mr. Utterson, biting his finger. "Suppose it were as you suppose, supposing Dr. Jekyll to have been—well, murdered, what could induce the murderer to stay? That won't hold water; it doesn't commend itself to reason."

"Well, Mr. Utterson, you are a hard man to satisfy, but I'll do it yet," said Poole. "All this last week (you must know) him, or it, whatever it is that lives in that cabinet, has been crying night and day for some sort of medicine and cannot get it to his mind. It was sometimes his way—the master's, that is—to write his orders on a sheet of paper and throw it on the stair. We've had nothing else this week back; nothing but papers, and a closed door, and the very meals left there to be smuggled in when nobody was looking. Well, sir, every day, ay, and twice and thrice in the same day, there have been orders and complaints, and I have been sent flying to all the wholesale chemists in town. Every time I brought the stuff back, there would be another paper telling me to return it, because it was not pure, and another order to a different firm. This drug is wanted bitter bad, sir, whatever for."

"Have you any of these papers?" asked Mr. Utterson.

Poole felt in his pocket and handed out a crumpled note, which the lawyer, bending nearer to the candle, carefully examined. Its contents ran thus: "Dr. Jekyll presents his compliments to Messrs. Maw. He assures them that their last sample is impure and quite useless for his present purpose. In the year 18—, Dr. J. purchased a somewhat large quantity from Messrs. M. He now begs them to search with most sedulous care, and should any of the same quality be left, forward it to him at once. Expense is no consideration. The importance of this to Dr. J. can hardly be exaggerated." So far the letter had run composedly enough, but here with a sudden splutter of the pen, the writer's emotion had broken loose. "For God's sake," he added, "find me some of the old."

"This is a strange note," said Mr. Utterson; and then sharply, "How do you come to have it open?"

"The man at Maw's was main angry, sir, and he threw it back to me like so much dirt," returned Poole.

"This is unquestionably the doctor's hand, do you know?" resumed the lawyer.

"I thought it looked like it," said the servant rather sulkily; and then, with another voice, "But what matters hand of write?" he said. "I've seen him!"

"Seen him?" repeated Mr. Utterson. "Well?"

"That's it!" said Poole. "It was this way. I came suddenly into the theatre from the garden. It seems he had slipped out to look for this drug or whatever it is; for the cabinet door was open, and there he was at the far end of the room digging among the crates. He looked up when I came in, gave a kind of cry, and whipped upstairs into the cabinet. It was but for one minute that I saw him, but the hair stood upon my head like quills. Sir, if that was my master, why had he a mask upon his face? If it was my master, why did he cry out like a rat, and run from me? I have served him long enough. And then..." The man paused and passed his hand over his face.

"These are all very strange circumstances," said Mr. Utterson, "but I think I begin to see daylight. Your master, Poole, is plainly seized with one of those maladies that both torture and deform the sufferer; hence, for aught I know, the alteration of his voice; hence the mask and the avoidance of his friends; hence his eagerness to find this drug, by means of which the poor soul retains some hope of ultimate recovery—God grant that he be not deceived! There is my explanation; it is sad enough, Poole, ay, and appalling to consider; but it is plain and natural, hangs well together, and delivers us from all exorbitant alarms."

"Sir," said the butler, turning to a sort of mottled pallor, "that thing was not my master, and there's the truth. My master"—here he looked round him and began to whisper—"is a tall, fine build of a man, and this was more of a dwarf." Utterson attempted to protest. "O, sir," cried Poole, "do you think I do not know my master after twenty years? Do you think I do not know where his head comes to in the cabinet door, where I saw him every morning of my life? No, sir, that thing in the mask was never Dr. Jekyll—God knows what it was, but it was never Dr. Jekyll; and it is the belief of my heart that there was murder done."

"Poole," replied the lawyer, "if you say that, it will become my duty to make certain. Much as I desire to spare your master's feelings, much as I am puzzled by this note which seems to prove him to be still alive, I shall consider it my duty to break in that door."

"Ah, Mr. Utterson, that's talking!" cried the butler.

"And now comes the second question," resumed Utterson: "Who is going to do it?"

"Why, you and me, sir," was the undaunted reply.

"That's very well said," returned the lawyer; "and whatever comes of it, I shall make it my business to see you are no loser."

"There is an axe in the theatre," continued Poole; "and you might take the kitchen poker for yourself."

The lawyer took that rude but weighty instrument into his hand, and balanced it. "Do you know, Poole," he said, looking up, "that you and I are about to place ourselves in a position of some peril?"

"You may say so, sir, indeed," returned the butler.

"It is well, then that we should be frank," said the other. "We both think more than we have said; let us make a clean breast. This masked figure that you saw, did you recognise it?"

"Well, sir, it went so quick, and the creature was so doubled up, that I could hardly swear to that," was the answer. "But if you mean, was it Mr. Hyde?—why, yes, I think it was! You see, it was much of the same bigness; and it had the same quick, light way with it; and then who else could have got in by the laboratory door? You have not forgot, sir, that at the time of the murder he had still the key with him? But that's not all. I don't know, Mr. Utterson, if you ever met this Mr. Hyde?"

"Yes," said the lawyer, "I once spoke with him."

"Then you must know as well as the rest of us that there was something queer about that gentleman—something that gave a man a turn—I don't know rightly how to say it, sir, beyond this: that you felt in your marrow kind of cold and thin."

"I own I felt something of what you describe," said Mr. Utterson.

"Quite so, sir," returned Poole. "Well, when that masked thing like a monkey jumped from among the chemicals and whipped into the cabinet, it went down my spine like ice. O, I know it's not evidence, Mr. Utterson; I'm book-learned enough for that; but a man has his feelings, and I give you my bible-word it was Mr. Hyde!"

"Ay, ay," said the lawyer. "My fears incline to the same point. Evil, I fear, founded—evil was sure to come—of that connection. Ay truly, I believe you; I believe poor Harry is killed; and I believe his murderer (for what purpose, God alone can tell) is still lurking in his victim's room. Well, let our name be vengeance. Call Bradshaw."

The footman came at the summons, very white and nervous.

"Pull yourself together, Bradshaw," said the lawyer. "This suspense, I know, is telling upon all of you; but it is now our intention to make an end of it. Poole, here, and I are going to force our way into the cabinet. If all is well, my shoulders are broad enough to bear the blame. Meanwhile, lest anything should really be amiss, or any malefactor seek to escape by the back, you and the boy must go round the corner with a pair of good sticks and take your post at the laboratory door. We give you ten minutes to get to your stations."

As Bradshaw left, the lawyer looked at his watch. "And now, Poole, let us get to ours," he said; and taking the poker under his arm, led the way into the yard. The scud had banked over the moon, and it was now quite dark. The wind, which only broke in puffs and draughts into that deep well of building, tossed the light of the candle to and fro about their steps, until they came into the shelter of the theatre, where they sat down silently to wait. London hummed solemnly all around; but nearer at hand, the stillness was only broken by the sounds of a footfall moving to and fro along the cabinet floor.

"So it will walk all day, sir," whispered Poole; "ay, and the better part of the night. Only when a new sample comes from the chemist, there's a bit of a break. Ah, it's an ill conscience that's such an enemy to rest! Ah, sir, there's blood foully shed in every step of it! But hark again, a little closer—put your heart in your ears, Mr. Utterson, and tell me, is that the doctor's foot?"

The steps fell lightly and oddly, with a certain swing, for all they went so slowly; it was different indeed from the heavy creaking tread of Henry Jekyll. Utterson sighed. "Is there never anything else?" he asked.

Poole nodded. "Once," he said. "Once I heard it weeping!"

"Weeping? how that?" said the lawyer, conscious of a sudden chill of horror.

"Weeping like a woman or a lost soul," said the butler. "I came away with that upon my heart, that I could have wept too."

But now the ten minutes drew to an end. Poole disinterred the axe from under a stack of packing straw; the candle was set upon the nearest table to light them to the attack; and they drew near with bated breath to where that patient foot was still going up and down, up and down, in the quiet of the night.

"Jekyll," cried Utterson, with a loud voice, "I demand to see you." He paused a moment, but there came no reply. "I give you fair warning, our suspicions are aroused, and I must and shall see you," he resumed; "if not by fair means, then by foul—if not of your consent, then by brute force!"

"Utterson," said the voice, "for God's sake, have mercy!"

"Ah, that's not Jekyll's voice—it's Hyde's!" cried Utterson. "Down with the door, Poole!"

Poole swung the axe over his shoulder; the blow shook the building, and the red baize door leaped against the lock and hinges. A dismal screech, as of mere animal terror, rang from the cabinet. Up went the axe again, and again the panels crashed and the frame bounded; four times the blow fell; but the wood was tough and the fittings were of excellent workmanship; and it was not until the fifth, that the lock burst and the wreck of the door fell inwards on the carpet.

The besiegers, appalled by their own riot and the stillness

that had succeeded, stood back a little and peered in. There lay the cabinet before their eyes in the quiet lamplight, a good fire glowing and chattering on the hearth, the kettle singing its thin strain, a drawer or two open, papers neatly set forth on the business table, and nearer the fire, the things laid out for tea; the quietest room, you would have said, and, but for the glazed presses full of chemicals, the most commonplace that night in London.

Right in the middle there lay the body of a man sorely contorted and still twitching. They drew near on tiptoe, turned it on its back and beheld the face of Edward Hyde. He was dressed in clothes far too large for him, clothes of the doctor's bigness; the cords of his face still moved with a semblance of life, but life was quite gone; and by the crushed phial in the hand and the strong smell of kernels that hung upon the air, Utterson knew that he was looking on the body of a self-destroyer.

"We have come too late," he said sternly, "whether to save or punish. Hyde is gone to his account; and it only remains for us to find the body of your master."

The far greater proportion of the building was occupied by the theatre, which filled almost the whole ground storey and was lighted from above, and by the cabinet, which formed an upper storey at one end and looked upon the court. A corridor joined the theatre to the door on the by-street; and with this the cabinet communicated separately by a second flight of stairs. There were besides a few dark closets and a spacious cellar. All these they now thoroughly examined. Each closet needed but a glance, for all were empty, and all, by the dust that fell from their doors, had stood long unopened. The cellar, indeed, was filled with crazy lumber, mostly dating from the times of the surgeon who was Jekyll's predecessor; but even as they opened the door they were advertised of the uselessness of further search, by the fall of a perfect mat of cobweb which had for years sealed up the entrance. Nowhere was there any trace of Henry Jekyll, dead or alive.

Poole stamped on the flags of the corridor. "He must be buried here," he said, hearkening to the sound.

"Or he may have fled," said Utterson, and he turned to

examine the door in the by-street. It was locked; and lying near by on the flags, they found the key, already stained with rust.

"This does not look like use," observed the lawyer.

"Use!" echoed Poole. "Do you not see, sir, it is broken? much as if a man had stamped on it."

"Ay," continued Utterson, "and the fractures, too, are rusty." The two men looked at each other with a scare. "This is beyond me, Poole," said the lawyer. "Let us go back to the cabinet."

They mounted the stair in silence, and still with an occasional awestruck glance at the dead body, proceeded more thoroughly to examine the contents of the cabinet. At one table, there were traces of chemical work, various measured heaps of some white salt being laid on glass saucers, as though for an experiment in which the unhappy man had been prevented.

"That is the same drug that I was always bringing him," said Poole; and even as he spoke, the kettle with a startling noise boiled over.

This brought them to the fireside, where the easy-chair was drawn cosily up, and the tea things stood ready to the sitter's elbow, the very sugar in the cup. There were several books on a shelf; one lay beside the tea things open, and Utterson was amazed to find it a copy of a pious work, for which Jekyll had several times expressed a great esteem, annotated, in his own hand with startling blasphemies.

Next, in the course of their review of the chamber, the searchers came to the cheval-glass, into whose depths they looked with an involuntary horror. But it was so turned as to show them nothing but the rosy glow playing on the roof, the fire sparkling in a hundred repetitions along the glazed front of the presses, and their own pale and fearful countenances stooping to look in.

"This glass has seen some strange things, sir," whispered Poole.

"And surely none stranger than itself," echoed the lawyer in the same tones. "For what did Jekyll"—he caught himself up at the word with a start, and then conquering the weakness—"what could Jekyll want with it?" he said.

"You may say that!" said Poole.

Next they turned to the business table. On the desk, among the neat array of papers, a large envelope was uppermost, and bore, in the doctor's hand, the name of Mr. Utterson. The lawyer unsealed it, and several enclosures fell to the floor. The first was a will, drawn in the same eccentric terms as the one which he had returned six months before, to serve as a testament in case of death and as a deed of gift in case of disappearance; but in place of the name of Edward Hyde, the lawyer, with indescribable amazement read the name of Gabriel John Utterson. He looked at Poole, and then back at the paper, and last of all at the dead malefactor stretched upon the carpet.

"My head goes round," he said. "He has been all these days in possession; he had no cause to like me; he must have raged to see himself displaced; and he has not destroyed this document."

He caught up the next paper; it was a brief note in the doctor's hand and dated at the top. "O Poole!" the lawyer cried, "he was alive and here this day. He cannot have been disposed of in so short a space; he must be still alive, he must have fled! And then, why fled? and how? and in that case, can we venture to declare this suicide? O, we must be careful. I foresee that we may yet involve your master in some dire catastrophe."

"Why don't you read it, sir?" asked Poole.

"Because I fear," replied the lawyer solemnly. "God grant I have no cause for it!" And with that he brought the paper to his eyes and read as follows:

"My dear Utterson,—When this shall fall into your hands, I shall have disappeared, under what circumstances I have not the penetration to foresee, but my instinct and all the circumstances of my nameless situation tell me that the end is sure and must be early. Go then, and first read the narrative which Lanyon warned me he was to place in your hands; and if you care to hear more, turn to the confession of

"Your unworthy and unhappy friend,

"HENRY JEKYLL."

"There was a third enclosure?" asked Utterson.

"Here, sir," said Poole, and gave into his hands a

considerable packet sealed in several places.

The lawyer put it in his pocket. "I would say nothing of this paper. If your master has fled or is dead, we may at least save his credit. It is now ten; I must go home and read these documents in quiet; but I shall be back before midnight, when we shall send for the police."

They went out, locking the door of the theatre behind them; and Utterson, once more leaving the servants gathered about the fire in the hall, trudged back to his office to read the two narratives in which this mystery was now to be explained.

DR. LANYON'S NARRATIVE

On the ninth of January, now four days ago, I received by the evening delivery a registered envelope, addressed in the hand of my colleague and old school companion, Henry Jekyll. I was a good deal surprised by this; for we were by no means in the habit of correspondence; I had seen the man, dined with him, indeed, the night before; and I could imagine nothing in our intercourse that should justify formality of registration. The contents increased my wonder; for this is how the letter ran:

"10th December, 18—.

"Dear Lanyon,—You are one of my oldest friends; and although we may have differed at times on scientific questions, I cannot remember, at least on my side, any break in our affection. There was never a day when, if you had said to me, 'Jekyll, my life, my honour, my reason, depend upon you,' I would not have sacrificed my left hand to help you. Lanyon, my life, my honour, my reason, are all at your mercy; if you fail me to-night, I am lost. You might suppose, after this preface, that I am going to ask you for something dishonourable to grant. Judge for yourself.

"I want you to postpone all other engagements for to-night—ay, even if you were summoned to the bedside of an emperor; to take a cab, unless your carriage should be actually at the door; and with this letter in your hand for consultation, to drive straight to my house. Poole, my butler, has his orders; you will find him waiting your arrival with a locksmith. The door of my cabinet is then to be forced; and you are to go in alone; to open the glazed press (letter E) on the left hand, breaking the lock if it be shut; and to draw out, with all its contents as they stand, the fourth drawer from the top or (which is the same thing) the third from the bottom. In my extreme distress of mind, I have a morbid fear of misdirecting you; but even if I am in error, you may know the right drawer by its contents: some powders, a phial and a paper book. This drawer I beg of you to carry back with you to Cavendish Square exactly as it stands.

"That is the first part of the service: now for the second. You should be back, if you set out at once on the receipt of this, long before midnight; but I will leave you that amount of margin, not only in the fear of one of those obstacles that can neither be prevented nor foreseen, but because an hour when your servants are in bed is to be preferred for what will then remain to do. At midnight, then, I have to ask you to be alone in your consulting room, to admit with your own hand into the house a man who will present himself in my name, and to place in his hands the drawer that you will have brought with you from my cabinet. Then you will have played your part and earned my gratitude completely. Five minutes afterwards, if you insist upon an explanation, you will have understood that these arrangements are of capital importance; and that by the neglect of one of them, fantastic as they must appear, you might have charged your conscience with my death or the shipwreck of my reason.

"Confident as I am that you will not trifle with this appeal, my heart sinks and my hand trembles at the bare thought of such a possibility. Think of me at this hour, in a strange place, labouring under a blackness of distress that no fancy can exaggerate, and yet well aware that, if you will but punctually serve me, my troubles will roll away like a story that is told. Serve me, my dear Lanyon and save

"Your friend,

"H.J.

"P.S.—I had already sealed this up when a fresh terror struck upon my soul. It is possible that the post-office may fail me, and this letter not come into your hands until to-morrow morning. In that case, dear Lanyon, do my errand when it shall be most convenient for you in the course of the day; and once more expect my messenger at midnight. It may then already be too late; and if that night passes without event, you will know that you have seen the last of Henry Jekyll."

Upon the reading of this letter, I made sure my colleague was insane; but till that was proved beyond the possibility of doubt, I felt bound to do as he requested. The less I understood of this farrago, the less I was in a position to judge of its importance; and an appeal so worded could not be set aside without a grave responsibility. I rose accordingly from table, got into a hansom, and drove straight to Jekyll's house. The butler was awaiting my arrival; he had received by the same post as mine a registered letter of instruction, and had sent at once for a locksmith and a carpenter. The tradesmen came while we were yet speaking; and we moved in a body to old Dr. Denman's surgical theatre, from which (as you are doubtless aware) Jekyll's private cabinet is most conveniently entered. The door was very strong, the lock excellent; the carpenter avowed he would have great trouble and have to do much damage, if force were to be used; and the locksmith was near despair. But this last was a handy fellow, and after two hour's work, the door stood open. The press marked E was unlocked; and I took out the drawer, had it filled up with straw and tied in a sheet, and returned with it to Cavendish Square.

Here I proceeded to examine its contents. The powders were neatly enough made up, but not with the nicety of the dispensing chemist; so that it was plain they were of Jekyll's private manufacture; and when I opened one of the wrappers I found what seemed to me a simple crystalline salt of a white colour. The phial, to which I next turned my attention, might have been about half full of a blood-red liquor, which was highly pungent to the sense of smell and seemed to me to contain phosphorus and some volatile ether. At the other ingredients I could make no guess. The book was an ordinary version book and contained little but a series of dates. These covered a period of many years, but I observed that the entries ceased nearly a year ago and quite abruptly. Here and there a brief remark was appended to a date, usually no more than a single word: "double" occurring perhaps six times in a total of several hundred entries; and once very early in the list and followed by several marks of exclamation, "total failure!!!" All this, though it whetted my curiosity, told me little that was definite. Here were a phial of some salt, and the record of a series of experiments that had led (like too many of Jekyll's investigations) to no end of practical usefulness. How could the presence of these articles in my house affect either the honour, the sanity, or the life of my flighty colleague? If his messenger could go to one place, why could he not go to another? And even granting some impediment, why was this gentleman to be received by me in secret? The more I reflected the more convinced I grew that I was dealing with a case of cerebral disease; and though I dismissed my servants to bed, I loaded an old revolver, that I might be found in some posture of self-defence.

Twelve o'clock had scarce rung out over London, ere the knocker sounded very gently on the door. I went myself at the summons, and found a small man crouching against the pillars of the portico.

"Are you come from Dr. Jekyll?" I asked.

He told me "yes" by a constrained gesture; and when I had bidden him enter, he did not obey me without a searching backward glance into the darkness of the square. There was a policeman not far off, advancing with his bull's eye open; and at the sight, I thought my visitor started and made greater haste.

These particulars struck me, I confess, disagreeably; and as I followed him into the bright light of the consulting room, I kept my hand ready on my weapon. Here, at last, I had a chance of clearly seeing him. I had never set eyes on him before, so much was certain. He was small, as I have said; I was struck besides with the shocking expression of his face, with his remarkable combination of great muscular activity and great apparent debility of constitution, and—last but not least—with the odd, subjective disturbance caused by his neighbourhood. This bore some resemblance to incipient rigour, and was accompanied by a marked sinking of the pulse. At the time, I set it down to some idiosyncratic, personal distaste, and merely wondered at the acuteness of the symptoms; but I have since had reason to believe the cause to lie much deeper in the nature of man, and to turn on some nobler hinge than the principle of hatred.

This person (who had thus, from the first moment of his entrance, struck in me what I can only describe as a disgustful curiosity) was dressed in a fashion that would have made an ordinary person laughable; his clothes, that is to say, although they were of rich and sober fabric, were enormously too large for him in every measurement—the trousers hanging on his legs and rolled up to keep them from the ground, the waist of the coat below his haunches, and the collar sprawling wide upon his shoulders. Strange to relate, this ludicrous accoutrement was far from moving me to laughter. Rather, as there was something abnormal and misbegotten in the very essence of the creature that now faced me—something seizing, surprising and revolting—this fresh disparity seemed but to fit in with and to reinforce it; so that to my interest in the man's nature and character, there was added a curiosity as to his origin, his life, his fortune and status in the world.

These observations, though they have taken so great a space to be set down in, were yet the work of a few seconds. My visitor was, indeed, on fire with sombre excitement.

"Have you got it?" he cried. "Have you got it?" And so lively was his impatience that he even laid his hand upon my arm and sought to shake me.

I put him back, conscious at his touch of a certain icy pang along my blood. "Come, sir," said I. "You forget that I have not yet the pleasure of your acquaintance. Be seated, if you please." And I showed him an example, and sat down myself in my customary seat and with as fair an imitation of my ordinary manner to a patient, as the lateness of the hour, the nature of my preoccupations, and the horror I had of my visitor, would suffer me to muster.

"I beg your pardon, Dr. Lanyon," he replied civilly enough. "What you say is very well founded; and my impatience has shown its heels to my politeness. I come here at the instance of your colleague, Dr. Henry Jekyll, on a piece of business of some moment; and I understood..." He paused and put his hand to his throat, and I could see, in spite of his collected manner, that he was wrestling against the approaches of the hysteria—"I understood, a drawer..."

But here I took pity on my visitor's suspense, and some perhaps on my own growing curiosity.

"There it is, sir," said I, pointing to the drawer, where it lay on the floor behind a table and still covered with the sheet.

He sprang to it, and then paused, and laid his hand upon his heart; I could hear his teeth grate with the convulsive action of his jaws; and his face was so ghastly to see that I grew alarmed both for his life and reason.

"Compose yourself," said I.

He turned a dreadful smile to me, and as if with the decision of despair, plucked away the sheet. At sight of the contents, he uttered one loud sob of such immense relief that I sat petrified. And the next moment, in a voice that was already fairly well under control, "Have you a graduated glass?" he asked.

I rose from my place with something of an effort and gave him what he asked.

He thanked me with a smiling nod, measured out a few minims of the red tincture and added one of the powders. The mixture, which was at first of a reddish hue, began, in proportion as the crystals melted, to brighten in colour, to effervesce audibly, and to throw off small fumes of vapour. Suddenly and at the same moment, the ebullition ceased and the compound changed to a dark purple, which faded again more slowly to a watery green. My visitor, who had watched these metamorphoses with a keen eye, smiled, set down the glass upon the table, and then turned and looked upon me with an air of scrutiny.

"And now," said he, "to settle what remains. Will you be wise? will you be guided? will you suffer me to take this glass in my hand and to go forth from your house without further parley? or has the greed of curiosity too much command of you? Think before you answer, for it shall be done as you decide. As you decide, you shall be left as you were before, and neither richer nor wiser, unless the sense of service rendered to a man in mortal distress may be counted as a kind of riches of the soul. Or, if you shall so prefer to choose, a new province of knowledge and new avenues to fame and power shall be laid open to you, here, in this room, upon the instant; and your sight shall be blasted by a prodigy to stagger the unbelief of Satan."

"Sir," said I, affecting a coolness that I was far from truly possessing, "you speak enigmas, and you will perhaps not wonder that I hear you with no very strong impression of belief. But I have gone too far in the way of inexplicable services to pause before I see the end."

"It is well," replied my visitor. "Lanyon, you remember your vows: what follows is under the seal of our profession. And now, you who have so long been bound to the most narrow and material views, you who have denied the virtue of transcendental medicine, you who have derided your superiors—behold!"

He put the glass to his lips and drank at one gulp. A cry followed; he reeled, staggered, clutched at the table and held on, staring with injected eyes, gasping with open mouth; and as I looked there came, I thought, a change—he seemed to swell—his face became suddenly black and the features seemed to melt and alter—and the next moment, I had sprung to my feet and leaped back against the wall, my arms raised to shield me from that prodigy, my mind submerged in terror.

"O God!" I screamed, and "O God!" again and again; for there before my eyes—pale and shaken, and half fainting, and groping before him with his hands, like a man restored from death—there stood Henry Jekyll!

What he told me in the next hour, I cannot bring my mind to set on paper. I saw what I saw, I heard what I heard, and my soul sickened at it; and yet now when that sight has faded from my eyes, I ask myself if I believe it, and I cannot answer. My life is shaken to its roots; sleep has left me; the deadliest terror sits by me at all hours of the day and night; and I feel that my days are numbered, and that I must die; and yet I shall die incredulous. As for the moral turpitude that man unveiled to me, even with tears of penitence, I cannot, even in memory, dwell on it without a start of horror. I will say but one thing, Utterson, and that (if you can bring your mind to credit it) will be more than enough. The creature who crept into my house that night was, on Jekyll's own confession, known by the name of Hyde and hunted for in every corner of the land as the murderer of Carew.

HASTIE LANYON.

HENRY JEKYLL'S FULL STATEMENT OF THE CASE

I was born in the year 18— to a large fortune, endowed besides with excellent parts, inclined by nature to industry, fond of the respect of the wise and good among my fellowmen, and thus, as might have been supposed, with every guarantee of an honourable and distinguished future. And indeed the worst of my faults was a certain impatient gaiety of disposition, such as has made the happiness of many, but such as I found it hard to reconcile with my imperious desire to carry my head high, and wear a more than commonly grave countenance before the public. Hence it came about that I concealed my pleasures; and that when I reached years of reflection, and began to look round me and take stock of my progress and position in the world, I stood already committed to a profound duplicity of life. Many a man would have even blazoned such irregularities as I was guilty of; but from the high views that I had set before me, I regarded and hid them with an almost morbid sense of shame. It was thus rather the exacting nature of my aspirations than any particular degradation in my faults, that made me what I was, and, with even a deeper trench than in the majority of men, severed in me those provinces of good and ill which divide and compound man's dual nature. In this case, I was driven to reflect deeply and inveterately on that hard law of life, which lies at the root of religion and is one of the most plentiful springs of distress. Though so profound a double-dealer, I was in no sense a hypocrite; both sides of me were in dead earnest; I was no more myself when I laid aside restraint and plunged in shame, than when I laboured, in the eye of day, at the furtherance of knowledge or the relief of sorrow and suffering. And it chanced that the direction of my scientific studies, which led wholly towards the mystic and the transcendental, reacted and shed a strong light on this consciousness of the perennial war among my members. With every day, and from both sides of my intelligence, the moral and the intellectual, I thus drew steadily nearer to that truth, by whose partial discovery I have been doomed to such a dreadful shipwreck: that man is not truly one, but truly two. I say two, because the state of my own knowledge does not pass beyond that point. Others will follow, others will outstrip me on the same lines; and I hazard the guess that man will be ultimately known for a mere polity of multifarious, incongruous and independent denizens. I, for my part, from the nature of my life, advanced infallibly in one direction and in one direction only. It was on the moral side, and in my own person, that I learned to recognise the thorough and primitive duality of man; I saw that, of the two natures that contended in the field of my consciousness, even if I could rightly be said to be either, it was only because I was radically both; and from an early date, even before the course of my scientific discoveries had begun to suggest the most naked possibility of such a miracle, I had learned to dwell with pleasure, as a beloved daydream, on the thought of the separation of these elements. If each, I told myself, could be housed in separate identities, life would be relieved of all that was unbearable; the unjust might go his way, delivered from the aspirations and remorse of his more upright twin; and the just could walk steadfastly and securely on his upward path, doing the good things in which he found his pleasure, and no longer exposed to disgrace and penitence by the hands of this extraneous evil. It was the curse of mankind that these incongruous faggots were thus bound together—that in the agonised womb of consciousness, these polar twins should be continuously struggling. How, then were they dissociated?

I was so far in my reflections when, as I have said, a side light began to shine upon the subject from the laboratory table. I began to perceive more deeply than it has ever yet been stated, the trembling immateriality, the mistlike transience, of this seemingly so solid body in which we walk attired. Certain agents I found to have the power to shake and pluck back that fleshly vestment, even as a wind might toss the curtains of a pavilion. For two good reasons, I will not enter deeply into this scientific branch of my confession. First, because I have been made to learn that the doom and burthen of our life is bound for ever on man's shoulders, and when the attempt is made to cast it off, it but returns upon us with more unfamiliar and more awful pressure. Second, because, as my narrative will make, alas! too evident, my discoveries were incomplete. Enough then, that I not only recognised my natural body from the mere aura and effulgence of certain of the powers that made up my spirit, but managed to compound a drug by which these powers should be dethroned from their supremacy, and a second form and countenance substituted, none the less natural to me because they were the expression, and bore the stamp of lower elements in my soul.

I hesitated long before I put this theory to the test of practice. I knew well that I risked death; for any drug that so potently controlled and shook the very fortress of identity, might, by the least scruple of an overdose or at the least inopportunity in the moment of exhibition, utterly blot out that immaterial tabernacle which I looked to it to change. But the temptation of a discovery so singular and profound at last overcame the suggestions of alarm. I had long since prepared my tincture; I purchased at once, from a firm of wholesale chemists, a large quantity of a particular salt which I knew, from my experiments, to be the last ingredient required; and late one accursed night, I compounded the elements, watched them boil and smoke together in the glass, and when the ebullition had subsided, with a strong glow of courage, drank off the potion.

The most racking pangs succeeded: a grinding in the bones, deadly nausea, and a horror of the spirit that cannot be exceeded at the hour of birth or death. Then these agonies began swiftly to subside, and I came to myself as if out of a great sickness. There was something strange in my sensations, something indescribably new and, from its very novelty, incredibly sweet. I felt younger, lighter, happier in body; within I was conscious of a heady recklessness, a current of disordered sensual images running like a millrace in my fancy, a solution of the bonds of obligation, an unknown but not an innocent freedom of the soul. I knew myself, at the first breath of this new life, to be more wicked, tenfold more wicked, sold a slave to my original evil; and the thought, in that moment, braced and delighted me like wine. I stretched out my hands, exulting in the freshness of these sensations; and in the act, I was suddenly aware that I had lost in stature.

There was no mirror, at that date, in my room; that which stands beside me as I write, was brought there later on and for the very purpose of these transformations. The night however, was far gone into the morning—the morning, black as it was, was nearly ripe for the conception of the day—the inmates of my house were locked in the most rigorous hours of slumber;

and I determined, flushed as I was with hope and triumph, to venture in my new shape as far as to my bedroom. I crossed the yard, wherein the constellations looked down upon me, I could have thought, with wonder, the first creature of that sort that their unsleeping vigilance had yet disclosed to them; I stole through the corridors, a stranger in my own house; and coming to my room, I saw for the first time the appearance of Edward Hyde.

I must here speak by theory alone, saying not that which I know, but that which I suppose to be most probable. The evil side of my nature, to which I had now transferred the stamping efficacy, was less robust and less developed than the good which I had just deposed. Again, in the course of my life, which had been, after all, nine tenths a life of effort, virtue and control, it had been much less exercised and much less exhausted. And hence, as I think, it came about that Edward Hyde was so much smaller, slighter and younger than Henry Jekyll. Even as good shone upon the countenance of the one, evil was written broadly and plainly on the face of the other. Evil besides (which I must still believe to be the lethal side of man) had left on that body an imprint of deformity and decay. And yet when I looked upon that ugly idol in the glass, I was conscious of no repugnance, rather of a leap of welcome. This, too, was myself. It seemed natural and human. In my eyes it bore a livelier image of the spirit, it seemed more express and single, than the imperfect and divided countenance I had been hitherto accustomed to call mine. And in so far I was doubtless right. I have observed that when I wore the semblance of Edward Hyde, none could come near to me at first without a visible misgiving of the flesh. This, as I take it, was because all human beings, as we meet them, are commingled out of good and evil: and Edward Hyde, alone in the ranks of mankind, was pure evil.

I lingered but a moment at the mirror: the second and conclusive experiment had yet to be attempted; it yet remained to be seen if I had lost my identity beyond redemption and must flee before daylight from a house that was no longer mine; and hurrying back to my cabinet, I once more prepared and drank the cup, once more suffered the pangs of dissolution, and came to myself once more with the character, the stature and the face of Henry Jekyll.

That night I had come to the fatal cross-roads. Had I approached my discovery in a more noble spirit, had I risked the experiment while under the empire of generous or pious aspirations, all must have been otherwise, and from these agonies of death and birth, I had come forth an angel instead of a fiend. The drug had no discriminating action; it was neither diabolical nor divine; it but shook the doors of the prisonhouse of my disposition; and like the captives of Philippi, that which stood within ran forth. At that time my virtue slumbered; my evil, kept awake by ambition, was alert and swift to seize the occasion; and the thing that was projected was Edward Hyde. Hence, although I had now two characters as well as two appearances, one was wholly evil, and the other was still the old Henry Jekyll, that incongruous compound of whose reformation and improvement I had already learned to despair. The movement was thus wholly toward the worse.

Even at that time, I had not conquered my aversions to the dryness of a life of study. I would still be merrily disposed at times; and as my pleasures were (to say the least) undignified, and I was not only well known and highly considered, but growing towards the elderly man, this incoherency of my life was daily growing more unwelcome. It was on this side that my new power tempted me until I fell in slavery. I had but to drink the cup, to doff at once the body of the noted professor, and to assume, like a thick cloak, that of Edward Hyde. I smiled at the notion; it seemed to me at the time to be humourous; and I made my preparations with the most studious care. I took and furnished that house in Soho, to which Hyde was tracked by the police; and engaged as a housekeeper a creature whom I knew well to be silent and unscrupulous. On the other side, I announced to my servants that a Mr. Hyde (whom I described) was to have full liberty and power about my house in the square; and to parry mishaps, I even called and made myself a familiar object, in my second character. I next drew up that will to which you so much objected; so that if anything befell me in the person of Dr. Jekyll, I could enter on that of Edward Hyde without pecuniary loss. And thus fortified, as I supposed, on every side, I began to profit by the strange immunities of my position.

Men have before hired bravos to transact their crimes, while their own person and reputation sat under shelter. I was the first that ever did so for his pleasures. I was the first that could plod in the public eye with a load of genial respectability, and in a moment, like a schoolboy, strip off these lendings and spring headlong into the sea of liberty. But for me, in my impenetrable mantle, the safety was complete. Think of it—I did not even exist! Let me but escape into my laboratory door, give me but a second or two to mix and swallow the draught that I had always standing ready; and whatever he had done, Edward Hyde would pass away like the stain of breath upon a mirror; and there in his stead, quietly at home, trimming the midnight lamp in his study, a man who could afford to laugh at suspicion, would be Henry Jekyll.

The pleasures which I made haste to seek in my disguise were, as I have said, undignified; I would scarce use a harder term. But in the hands of Edward Hyde, they soon began to turn toward the monstrous. When I would come back from these excursions, I was often plunged into a kind of wonder at my vicarious depravity. This familiar that I called out of my own soul, and sent forth alone to do his good pleasure, was a being inherently malign and villainous; his every act and thought centered on self; drinking pleasure with bestial avidity from any degree of torture to another; relentless like a man of stone. Henry Jekyll stood at times aghast before the acts of Edward Hyde; but the situation was apart from ordinary laws, and insidiously relaxed the grasp of conscience. It was Hyde, after all, and Hyde alone, that was guilty. Jekyll was no worse; he woke again to his good qualities seemingly unimpaired; he would even make haste, where it was possible, to undo the evil done by Hyde. And thus his conscience slumbered.

Into the details of the infamy at which I thus connived (for even now I can scarce grant that I committed it) I have no design of entering; I mean but to point out the warnings and the successive steps with which my chastisement approached. I met with one accident which, as it brought on no consequence, I shall no more than mention. An act of cruelty to a child aroused against me the anger of a passer-by, whom I recognised the other day in the person of your kinsman; the doctor and the child's family joined him; there were moments when I feared for my life; and at last, in order to pacify their too just resentment, Edward Hyde had to bring them to the door, and pay them in a cheque drawn in the name of Henry Jekyll. But this danger was easily eliminated from the future, by opening an account at another bank in the name of Edward Hyde himself; and when, by sloping my own hand backward, I had supplied my double with a signature, I thought I sat beyond the reach of fate.

Some two months before the murder of Sir Danvers, I had been out for one of my adventures, had returned at a late hour, and woke the next day in bed with somewhat odd sensations. It was in vain I looked about me; in vain I saw the decent furniture and tall proportions of my room in the square; in vain that I recognised the pattern of the bed curtains and the design of the mahogany frame; something still kept insisting that I was not where I was, that I had not wakened where I seemed to be, but in the little room in Soho where I was accustomed to sleep in the body of Edward Hyde. I smiled to myself, and in my psychological way, began lazily to inquire into the elements of this illusion, occasionally, even as I did so, dropping back into a comfortable morning doze. I was still so engaged when, in one of my more wakeful moments, my eyes fell upon my hand. Now the hand of Henry Jekyll (as you have often remarked) was professional in shape and size; it was large, firm, white and comely. But the hand which I now saw, clearly enough, in the yellow light of a mid-London morning, lying half shut on the bedclothes, was lean, corded, knuckly, of a dusky pallor and thickly shaded with a swart growth of hair. It was the hand of Edward Hyde.

I must have stared upon it for near half a minute, sunk as I was in the mere stupidity of wonder, before terror woke up in my breast as sudden and startling as the crash of cymbals; and bounding from my bed I rushed to the mirror. At the sight that met my eyes, my blood was changed into something exquisitely thin and icy. Yes, I had gone to bed Henry Jekyll, I had awakened Edward Hyde. How was this to be explained? I asked myself; and then, with another bound of terror—how was it to be remedied? It was well on in the morning; the servants were up; all my drugs were in the cabinet—a long journey down two pairs of stairs, through the back passage, across the open court and through the anatomical theatre, from where I was then standing horror-struck. It might indeed be possible to cover my face; but of what use was that, when I was unable to conceal the alteration in my stature? And then with an overpowering sweetness of relief, it came back upon my mind that the servants were already used to the coming and going of my second self. I had soon dressed, as well as I was able, in clothes of my own size: had soon passed through the house, where Bradshaw stared and drew back at seeing Mr. Hyde at such an hour and in such a strange array; and ten minutes later, Dr. Jekyll had returned to his own shape and was sitting down, with a darkened brow, to make a feint of breakfasting.

Small indeed was my appetite. This inexplicable incident, this reversal of my previous experience, seemed, like the Babylonian finger on the wall, to be spelling out the letters of my judgment; and I began to reflect more seriously than ever before on the issues and possibilities of my double existence. That part of me which I had the power of projecting, had lately been much exercised and nourished; it had seemed to me of late as though the body of Edward Hyde had grown in stature, as though (when I wore that form) I were conscious of a more generous tide of blood; and I began to spy a danger that, if this were much prolonged, the balance of my nature might be permanently overthrown, the power of voluntary change be forfeited, and the character of Edward Hyde become irrevocably mine. The power of the drug had not been always equally displayed. Once, very early in my career, it had totally failed me; since then I had been obliged on more than one occasion to double, and once, with infinite risk of death, to treble the amount; and these rare uncertainties had cast hitherto the sole shadow on my contentment. Now, however, and in the light of that morning's accident, I was led to remark that whereas, in the beginning, the difficulty had been to throw off the body of Jekyll, it had of late gradually but decidedly transferred itself to the other side. All things therefore seemed to point to this; that I was slowly losing hold of my original and better self, and becoming slowly incorporated with my second and worse.

Between these two, I now felt I had to choose. My two natures had memory in common, but all other faculties were most unequally shared between them. Jekyll (who was composite) now with the most sensitive apprehensions, now with a greedy gusto, projected and shared in the pleasures and adventures of Hyde; but Hyde was indifferent to Jekyll, or but remembered him as the mountain bandit remembers the cavern in which he conceals himself from pursuit. Jekyll had more than a father's interest; Hyde had more than a son's indifference. To cast in my lot with Jekyll, was to die to those appetites which I had long secretly indulged and had of late begun to pamper. To cast it in with Hyde, was to die to a thousand interests and aspirations, and to become, at a blow and forever, despised and friendless. The bargain might appear unequal; but there was still another consideration in the scales; for while Jekyll would suffer smartingly in the fires of abstinence, Hyde would be not even conscious of all that he had lost. Strange as my circumstances were, the terms of this debate are as old and commonplace as man; much the same inducements and alarms cast the die for any tempted and trembling sinner; and it fell out with me, as it falls with so vast a majority of my fellows, that I chose the better part and was found wanting in the strength to keep to it.

Yes, I preferred the elderly and discontented doctor, surrounded by friends and cherishing honest hopes; and bade a resolute farewell to the liberty, the comparative youth, the light step, leaping impulses and secret pleasures, that I had enjoyed in the disguise of Hyde. I made this choice perhaps with some unconscious reservation, for I neither gave up the house in Soho, nor destroyed the clothes of Edward Hyde, which still lay ready in my cabinet. For two months, however, I was true to my determination; for two months, I led a life of such severity as I had never before attained to, and enjoyed the compensations of an approving conscience. But time began at last to obliterate the freshness of my alarm; the praises of conscience began to grow into a thing of course; I began to be tortured with throes and longings, as of Hyde struggling after freedom; and at last, in an hour of moral weakness, I once again compounded and swallowed the transforming draught.

I do not suppose that, when a drunkard reasons with himself upon his vice, he is once out of five hundred times affected by the dangers that he runs through his brutish, physical insensibility; neither had I, long as I had considered my position, made enough allowance for the complete moral insensibility and insensate readiness to evil, which were the leading characters of Edward Hyde. Yet it was by these that I was punished. My devil had been long caged, he came out roaring. I was conscious, even when I took the draught, of a more unbridled, a more furious propensity to ill. It must have been this, I suppose, that stirred in my soul that tempest of impatience with which I listened to the civilities of my unhappy victim; I declare, at least, before God, no man morally sane could have been guilty of that crime upon so pitiful a provocation; and that I struck in no more reasonable spirit than that in which a sick child may break a plaything. But I had voluntarily stripped myself of all those balancing instincts by which even the worst of us continues to walk with some degree of steadiness among temptations; and in my case, to be tempted, however slightly, was to fall.

Instantly the spirit of hell awoke in me and raged. With a transport of glee, I mauled the unresisting body, tasting delight from every blow; and it was not till weariness had begun to succeed, that I was suddenly, in the top fit of my delirium, struck through the heart by a cold thrill of terror. A mist dispersed; I saw my life to be forfeit; and fled from the scene of these excesses, at once glorying and trembling, my lust of evil gratified and stimulated, my love of life screwed to the topmost peg. I ran to the house in Soho, and (to make assurance doubly sure) destroyed my papers; thence I set out through the lamplit streets, in the same divided ecstasy of mind, gloating on my crime, light-headedly devising others in the future, and yet still hastening and still hearkening in my wake for the steps of the avenger. Hyde had a song upon his lips as he compounded the draught, and as he drank it, pledged the dead man. The pangs of transformation had not done tearing him, before Henry Jekyll, with streaming tears of gratitude and remorse, had fallen upon his knees and lifted his clasped hands to God. The veil of self-indulgence was rent from head to foot. I saw my life as a whole: I followed it up from the days of childhood, when I had walked with my father's hand, and through the self-denying toils of my professional life, to arrive again and again, with the same sense of unreality, at the damned horrors of the evening. I could have screamed aloud; I sought with tears and prayers to smother down the crowd of hideous images and sounds with which my memory swarmed against me; and still, between the petitions, the ugly face of my iniquity stared into my soul. As the acuteness of this remorse began to die away, it was succeeded by a sense of joy. The problem of my conduct was solved. Hyde was thenceforth impossible; whether I would or not, I was now confined to the better part of my existence; and

O, how I rejoiced to think of it! with what willing humility I embraced anew the restrictions of natural life! with what sincere renunciation I locked the door by which I had so often gone and come, and ground the key under my heel!

The next day, came the news that the murder had not been overlooked, that the guilt of Hyde was patent to the world, and that the victim was a man high in public estimation. It was not only a crime, it had been a tragic folly. I think I was glad to know it; I think I was glad to have my better impulses thus buttressed and guarded by the terrors of the scaffold. Jekyll was now my city of refuge; let but Hyde peep out an instant, and the hands of all men would be raised to take and slay him.

I resolved in my future conduct to redeem the past; and I can say with honesty that my resolve was fruitful of some good. You know yourself how earnestly, in the last months of the last year, I laboured to relieve suffering; you know that much was done for others, and that the days passed quietly, almost happily for myself. Nor can I truly say that I wearied of this beneficent and innocent life; I think instead that I daily enjoyed it more completely; but I was still cursed with my duality of purpose; and as the first edge of my penitence wore off, the lower side of me, so long indulged, so recently chained down, began to growl for licence. Not that I dreamed of resuscitating Hyde; the bare idea of that would startle me to frenzy: no, it was in my own person that I was once more tempted to trifle with my conscience; and it was as an ordinary secret sinner that I at last fell before the assaults of temptation.

There comes an end to all things; the most capacious measure is filled at last; and this brief condescension to my evil finally destroyed the balance of my soul. And yet I was not alarmed; the fall seemed natural, like a return to the old days before I had made my discovery. It was a fine, clear, January day, wet under foot where the frost had melted, but cloudless overhead; and the Regent's Park was full of winter chirrupings and sweet with spring odours. I sat in the sun on a bench; the animal within me licking the chops of memory; the spiritual side a little drowsed, promising subsequent penitence, but not yet moved to begin. After all, I reflected, I was like my neighbours; and then I smiled, comparing myself with other men, comparing my active good-will with the lazy cruelty of their neglect. And at the very moment of that vainglorious thought, a qualm came over me, a horrid nausea and the most deadly shuddering. These passed away, and left me faint; and then as in its turn faintness subsided, I began to be aware of a change in the temper of my thoughts, a greater boldness, a contempt of danger, a solution of the bonds of obligation. I looked down; my clothes hung formlessly on my shrunken limbs; the hand that lay on my knee was corded and hairy. I was once more Edward Hyde. A moment before I had been safe of all men's respect, wealthy, beloved—the cloth laying for me in the dining-room at home; and now I was the common quarry of mankind, hunted, houseless, a known murderer, thrall to the gallows.

My reason wavered, but it did not fail me utterly. I have more than once observed that in my second character, my faculties seemed sharpened to a point and my spirits more tensely elastic; thus it came about that, where Jekyll perhaps might have succumbed, Hyde rose to the importance of the moment. My drugs were in one of the presses of my cabinet; how was I to reach them? That was the problem that (crushing my temples in my hands) I set myself to solve. The laboratory door I had closed. If I sought to enter by the house, my own servants would consign me to the gallows. I saw I must employ another hand, and thought of Lanyon. How was he to be reached? how persuaded? Supposing that I escaped capture in the streets, how was I to make my way into his presence? and how should I, an unknown and displeasing visitor, prevail on the famous physician to rifle the study of his colleague, Dr. Jekyll? Then I remembered that of my original character, one part remained to me: I could write my own hand; and once I had conceived that kindling spark, the way that I must follow became lighted up from end to end.

Thereupon, I arranged my clothes as best I could, and summoning a passing hansom, drove to an hotel in Portland Street, the name of which I chanced to remember. At my appearance (which was indeed comical enough, however tragic a fate these garments covered) the driver could not conceal his mirth. I gnashed my teeth upon him with a gust of devilish fury; and the smile withered from his face—happily for him—yet more happily for myself, for in another instant I had certainly dragged him from his perch. At the inn, as I entered, I looked about me with so black a countenance as made the attendants tremble; not a look did they exchange in my presence; but obsequiously took my orders, led me to a private room, and brought me wherewithal to write. Hyde in danger of his life was a creature new to me; shaken with inordinate anger, strung to the pitch of murder, lusting to inflict pain. Yet the creature was astute; mastered his fury with a great effort of the will; composed his two important letters, one to Lanyon and one to Poole; and that he might receive actual evidence of their being posted, sent them out with directions that they should be registered. Thenceforward, he sat all day over the fire in the private room, gnawing his nails; there he dined, sitting alone with his fears, the waiter visibly quailing before his eye; and thence, when the night was fully come, he set forth in the corner of a closed cab, and was driven to and fro about the streets of the city. He, I say—I cannot say, I. That child of Hell had nothing human; nothing lived in him but fear and hatred. And when at last, thinking the driver had begun to grow suspicious, he discharged the cab and ventured on foot, attired in his misfitting clothes, an object marked out for observation, into the midst of the nocturnal passengers, these two base passions raged within him like a tempest. He walked fast, hunted by his fears, chattering to himself, skulking through the less frequented thoroughfares, counting the minutes that still divided him from midnight. Once a woman spoke to him, offering, I think, a box of lights. He smote her in the face, and she fled.

When I came to myself at Lanyon's, the horror of my old friend perhaps affected me somewhat: I do not know; it was at least but a drop in the sea to the abhorrence with which I looked back upon these hours. A change had come over me. It was no longer the fear of the gallows, it was the horror of being Hyde that racked me. I received Lanyon's condemnation partly in a dream; it was partly in a dream that I came home to my own house and got into bed. I slept after the prostration of the day, with a stringent and profound slumber which not even the nightmares that wrung me could avail to break. I awoke in the morning shaken, weakened, but refreshed. I still hated and feared the thought of the brute that slept within me, and I had not of course forgotten the appalling dangers of the day before; but I was once more at home, in my own house and close to my drugs; and gratitude for my escape shone so strong in my soul that it almost rivalled the brightness of hope.

I was stepping leisurely across the court after breakfast, drinking the chill of the air with pleasure, when I was seized again with those indescribable sensations that heralded the change; and I had but the time to gain the shelter of my cabinet, before I was once again raging and freezing with the passions of Hyde. It took on this occasion a double dose to recall me to myself; and alas! six hours after, as I sat looking sadly in the fire, the pangs returned, and the drug had to be re-administered. In short, from that day forth it seemed only by a great effort as of gymnastics, and only under the immediate stimulation of the drug, that I was able to wear the countenance of Jekyll. At all hours of the day and night, I would be taken with the premonitory shudder; above all, if I slept, or even dozed for a moment in my chair, it was always as Hyde that I awakened. Under the strain of this continually impending doom and by the sleeplessness to which I now condemned myself, ay, even beyond what I had thought possible to man, I became, in my own person, a creature eaten up and emptied by fever, languidly weak both in body and mind, and solely occupied by one thought: the horror of my other self. But when I slept, or when the virtue of the medicine wore off, I would leap almost without transition (for the pangs of transformation grew daily less marked) into the possession of a fancy brimming with images of terror, a soul boiling with causeless hatreds, and a body that seemed not strong enough to contain the raging energies of life. The powers of Hyde seemed to have grown with the sickliness of Jekyll. And certainly the hate that now divided them was equal on each side. With Jekyll, it was a thing of vital instinct. He had now seen the full deformity of that creature that shared with him some of the phenomena of consciousness, and was co-heir with him to death: and beyond these links of community, which in themselves made the most poignant part of his distress, he thought of Hyde, for all his energy of life, as of something not only hellish but inorganic. This was the shocking thing; that the slime of the pit seemed to utter cries and voices; that the amorphous dust gesticulated and sinned; that what was dead, and had no shape, should usurp the offices of life. And this again, that that insurgent horror was knit to him closer than a wife, closer than an eye; lay caged in his flesh, where he heard it mutter and felt it struggle to be born; and at every hour of weakness, and in the confidence of slumber, prevailed against him, and deposed him out of life. The hatred of Hyde for Jekyll was of a different order. His terror of the gallows drove him continually to commit temporary suicide, and return to his subordinate station of a part instead of a person; but he loathed the necessity, he loathed the despondency into which Jekyll was now fallen, and he resented the dislike with which he was himself regarded. Hence the ape-like tricks that he would play me, scrawling in my own hand blasphemies on the pages of my books, burning the letters and destroying the portrait of my father; and indeed, had it not been for his fear of death, he would long ago have ruined himself in order to involve me in the ruin. But his love of life is wonderful; I go further: I, who sicken and freeze at the mere thought of him, when I recall the abjection and passion of this attachment, and when I know how he fears my power to cut him off by suicide, I find it in my heart to pity him.

It is useless, and the time awfully fails me, to prolong this description; no one has ever suffered such torments, let that suffice; and yet even to these, habit brought—no, not alleviation—but a certain callousness of soul, a certain acquiescence of despair; and my punishment might have gone on for years, but for the last calamity which has now fallen, and which has finally severed me from my own face and nature. My provision of the salt, which had never been renewed since the date of the first experiment, began to run low. I sent out for a fresh supply and mixed the draught; the ebullition followed, and the first change of colour, not the second; I drank it and it was without efficiency. You will learn from Poole how I have had London ransacked; it was in vain; and I am now persuaded that my first supply was impure, and that it was that unknown impurity which lent efficacy to the draught.

About a week has passed, and I am now finishing this statement under the influence of the last of the old powders. This, then, is the last time, short of a miracle, that Henry Jekyll can think his own thoughts or see his own face (now how sadly altered!) in the glass. Nor must I delay too long to bring my writing to an end; for if my narrative has hitherto escaped destruction, it has been by a combination of great prudence and great good luck. Should the throes of change take me in the act of writing it, Hyde will tear it in pieces; but if some time shall have elapsed after I have laid it by, his wonderful selfishness and circumscription to the moment will probably save it once again from the action of his ape-like spite. And indeed the doom that is closing on us both has already changed and crushed him. Half an hour from now, when I shall again and forever reindue that hated personality, I know how I shall sit shuddering and weeping in my chair, or continue, with the most strained and fearstruck ecstasy of listening, to pace up and down this room (my last earthly refuge) and give ear to every sound of menace. Will Hyde die upon the scaffold? or will he find courage to release himself at the last moment? God knows; I am careless; this is my true hour of death, and what is to follow concerns another than myself. Here then, as I lay down the pen and proceed to seal up my confession, I bring the life of that unhappy Henry Jekyll to an end.

The Great God Pan

By Arthur Machen

I

THE EXPERIMENT

"I am glad you came, Clarke; very glad indeed. I was not sure you could spare the time."

"I was able to make arrangements for a few days; things are not very lively just now. But have you no misgivings, Raymond? Is it absolutely safe?"

The two men were slowly pacing the terrace in front of Dr. Raymond's house. The sun still hung above the western mountain-line, but it shone with a dull red glow that cast no shadows, and all the air was quiet; a sweet breath came from the great wood on the hillside above, and with it, at intervals, the soft murmuring call of the wild doves. Below, in the long lovely valley, the river wound in and out between the lonely hills, and, as the sun hovered and vanished into the west, a faint mist, pure white, began to rise from the hills. Dr. Raymond turned sharply to his friend.

"Safe? Of course it is. In itself the operation is a perfectly simple one; any surgeon could do it."

"And there is no danger at any other stage?"

"None; absolutely no physical danger whatsoever, I give you my word. You are always timid, Clarke, always; but you know my history. I have devoted myself to transcendental medicine for the last twenty years. I have heard myself called quack and charlatan and impostor, but all the while I knew I was on the right path. Five years ago I reached the goal, and since then every day has been a preparation for what we shall do tonight."

"I should like to believe it is all true." Clarke knit his brows, and looked doubtfully at Dr. Raymond. "Are you perfectly sure, Raymond, that your theory is not a phantasmagoria—a splendid vision, certainly, but a mere vision after all?"

Dr. Raymond stopped in his walk and turned sharply. He was

a middle-aged man, gaunt and thin, of a pale yellow complexion, but as he answered Clarke and faced him, there was a flush on his cheek.

"Look about you, Clarke. You see the mountain, and hill following after hill, as wave on wave, you see the woods and orchard, the fields of ripe corn, and the meadows reaching to the reed-beds by the river. You see me standing here beside you, and hear my voice; but I tell you that all these things—yes, from that star that has just shone out in the sky to the solid ground beneath our feet—I say that all these are but dreams and shadows; the shadows that hide the real world from our eyes. There is a real world, but it is beyond this glamour and this vision, beyond these 'chases in Arras, dreams in a career,' beyond them all as beyond a veil. I do not know whether any human being has ever lifted that veil; but I do know, Clarke, that you and I shall see it lifted this very night from before another's eyes. You may think this all strange nonsense; it may be strange, but it is true, and the ancients knew what lifting the veil means. They called it seeing the god Pan."

Clarke shivered; the white mist gathering over the river was chilly.

"It is wonderful indeed," he said. "We are standing on the brink of a strange world, Raymond, if what you say is true. I suppose the knife is absolutely necessary?"

"Yes; a slight lesion in the grey matter, that is all; a trifling rearrangement of certain cells, a microscopical alteration that would escape the attention of ninety-nine brain specialists out of a hundred. I don't want to bother you with 'shop,' Clarke; I might give you a mass of technical detail which would sound very imposing, and would leave you as enlightened as you are now. But I suppose you have read, casually, in out-of-the-way corners of your paper, that immense strides have been made recently in the physiology of the brain. I saw a paragraph the other day about Digby's theory, and Browne Faber's discoveries. Theories and discoveries! Where they are standing now, I stood fifteen years ago, and I need not tell you that I have not been standing still for the last fifteen years. It will be enough if I say that five years ago I made the discovery that I alluded to when I said that ten years ago I reached the goal. After years of labour, after years of toiling and groping in the dark, after days and nights of disappointments and sometimes of despair, in which I used now and then to tremble and grow cold with the thought that perhaps there were others seeking for what I sought, at last, after so long, a pang of sudden joy thrilled my soul, and I knew the long journey was at an end. By what seemed then and still seems a chance, the suggestion of a moment's idle thought followed up upon familiar lines and paths that I had tracked a hundred times already, the great truth burst upon me, and I saw, mapped out in lines of sight, a whole world, a sphere unknown; continents and islands, and great oceans in which no ship has sailed (to my belief) since a Man first lifted up his eyes and beheld the sun, and the stars of heaven, and the quiet earth beneath. You will think this all high-flown language, Clarke, but it is hard to be literal. And yet; I do not know whether what I am hinting at cannot be set forth in plain and lonely terms. For instance, this world of ours is pretty well girded now with the telegraph wires and cables; thought, with something less than the speed of thought, flashes from sunrise to sunset, from north to south, across the floods and the desert places. Suppose that an electrician of today were suddenly to perceive that he and his friends have merely been playing with pebbles and mistaking them for the foundations of the world; suppose that such a man saw uttermost space lie open before the current, and words of men flash forth to the sun and beyond the sun into the systems beyond, and the voice of articulate-speaking men echo in the waste void that bounds our thought. As analogies go, that is a pretty good analogy of what I have done; you can understand now a little of what I felt as I stood here one evening; it was a summer evening, and the valley looked much as it does now; I stood here, and saw before me the unutterable, the unthinkable gulf that yawns profound between two worlds, the world of matter and the world of spirit; I saw the great empty deep stretch dim before me, and in that instant a bridge of light leapt from the earth to the unknown shore, and the abyss was spanned. You may look in Browne Faber's book, if you like, and you will find that to the present day men of science are unable to account for the presence, or to specify the functions of a certain group of nerve-cells in the brain. That group is, as it were, land to let, a mere waste place for fanciful theories. I am not in the position of Browne Faber and the specialists, I am perfectly instructed as to the possible functions of those nerve-centers in the scheme of things. With a touch I can bring them into play, with a touch, I say, I can set free the current, with a touch I can complete the communication between this world of sense and—we shall be able to finish the sentence later on. Yes, the knife is necessary; but think what that knife will effect. It will level utterly the solid wall of sense, and probably, for the first time since man was made, a spirit will gaze on a spirit-world. Clarke, Mary will see the god Pan!"

"But you remember what you wrote to me? I thought it would be requisite that she—"

He whispered the rest into the doctor's ear.

"Not at all, not at all. That is nonsense. I assure you. Indeed, it is better as it is; I am quite certain of that."

"Consider the matter well, Raymond. It's a great responsibility. Something might go wrong; you would be a miserable man for the rest of your days."

"No, I think not, even if the worst happened. As you know, I rescued Mary from the gutter, and from almost certain starvation, when she was a child; I think her life is mine, to use as I see fit. Come, it's getting late; we had better go in."

Dr. Raymond led the way into the house, through the hall, and down a long dark passage. He took a key from his pocket and opened a heavy door, and motioned Clarke into his laboratory. It had once been a billiard-room, and was lighted by a glass dome in the centre of the ceiling, whence there still shone a sad grey light on the figure of the doctor as he lit a lamp with a heavy shade and placed it on a table in the middle of the room.

Clarke looked about him. Scarcely a foot of wall remained bare; there were shelves all around laden with bottles and phials of all shapes and colours, and at one end stood a little Chippendale book-case. Raymond pointed to this.

"You see that parchment Oswald Crollius? He was one of the first to show me the way, though I don't think he ever found it himself. That is a strange saying of his: 'In every grain of wheat there lies hidden the soul of a star.'"

There was not much furniture in the laboratory. The table in the centre, a stone slab with a drain in one corner, the two armchairs on which Raymond and Clarke were sitting; that was all, except an odd-looking chair at the furthest end of the room. Clarke looked at it, and raised his eyebrows.

"Yes, that is the chair," said Raymond. "We may as well place it in position." He got up and wheeled the chair to the light, and began raising and lowering it, letting down the seat, setting the back at various angles, and adjusting the foot-rest. It looked comfortable enough, and Clarke passed his hand over the soft green velvet, as the doctor manipulated the levers.

"Now, Clarke, make yourself quite comfortable. I have a couple hours' work before me; I was obliged to leave certain matters to the last."

Raymond went to the stone slab, and Clarke watched him

drearily as he bent over a row of phials and lit the flame under the crucible. The doctor had a small hand-lamp, shaded as the larger one, on a ledge above his apparatus, and Clarke, who sat in the shadows, looked down at the great shadowy room, wondering at the bizarre effects of brilliant light and undefined darkness contrasting with one another. Soon he became conscious of an odd odour, at first the merest suggestion of odour, in the room, and as it grew more decided he felt surprised that he was not reminded of the chemist's shop or the surgery. Clarke found himself idly endeavouring to analyse the sensation, and half conscious, he began to think of a day, fifteen years ago, that he had spent roaming through the woods and meadows near his own home. It was a burning day at the beginning of August, the heat had dimmed the outlines of all things and all distances with a faint mist, and people who observed the thermometer spoke of an abnormal register, of a temperature that was almost tropical. Strangely that wonderful hot day of the fifties rose up again in Clarke's imagination; the sense of dazzling all-pervading sunlight seemed to blot out the shadows and the lights of the laboratory, and he felt again the heated air beating in gusts about his face, saw the shimmer rising from the turf, and heard the myriad murmur of the summer.

"I hope the smell doesn't annoy you, Clarke; there's nothing unwholesome about it. It may make you a bit sleepy, that's all."

Clarke heard the words quite distinctly, and knew that Raymond was speaking to him, but for the life of him he could not rouse himself from his lethargy. He could only think of the lonely walk he had taken fifteen years ago; it was his last look at the fields and woods he had known since he was a child, and now it all stood out in brilliant light, as a picture, before him. Above all there came to his nostrils the scent of summer, the smell of flowers mingled, and the odour of the woods, of cool shaded places, deep in the green depths, drawn forth by the sun's heat; and the scent of the good earth, lying as it were with arms stretched forth, and smiling lips, overpowered all. His fancies made him wander, as he had wandered long ago, from the fields into the wood, tracking a little path between the shining undergrowth of beech-trees; and the trickle of water dropping from the limestone rock sounded as a clear melody in the dream. Thoughts began to go astray and to mingle with other thoughts; the beech alley was transformed to a path between ilex-trees, and here and there a vine climbed from bough to bough, and sent up waving tendrils and drooped with purple grapes, and the sparse grey-green leaves of a wild olive-tree stood out against the dark shadows of the ilex. Clarke, in the deep folds of dream, was conscious that the path from his father's house had led him into an undiscovered country, and he was wondering at the strangeness of it all, when suddenly, in place of the hum and murmur of the summer, an infinite silence seemed to fall on all things, and the wood was hushed, and for a moment in time he stood face to face there with a presence, that was neither man nor beast, neither the living nor the dead, but all things mingled, the form of all things but devoid of all form. And in that moment, the sacrament of body and soul was dissolved, and a voice seemed to cry "Let us go hence," and then the darkness of darkness beyond the stars, the darkness of everlasting.

When Clarke woke up with a start he saw Raymond pouring a few drops of some oily fluid into a green phial, which he stoppered tightly.

"You have been dozing," he said; "the journey must have tired you out. It is done now. I am going to fetch Mary; I shall be back in ten minutes."

Clarke lay back in his chair and wondered. It seemed as if he had but passed from one dream into another. He half expected to see the walls of the laboratory melt and disappear, and to awake in London, shuddering at his own sleeping fancies. But at last the door opened, and the doctor returned, and behind him came a girl of about seventeen, dressed all in white. She was so beautiful that Clarke did not wonder at what the doctor had written to him. She was blushing now over face and neck and arms, but Raymond seemed unmoved.

"Mary," he said, "the time has come. You are quite free. Are you willing to trust yourself to me entirely?"

"Yes, dear."

"Do you hear that, Clarke? You are my witness. Here is the chair, Mary. It is quite easy. Just sit in it and lean back. Are you ready?"

"Yes, dear, quite ready. Give me a kiss before you begin."

The doctor stooped and kissed her mouth, kindly enough. "Now shut your eyes," he said. The girl closed her eyelids, as if she were tired, and longed for sleep, and Raymond placed the green phial to her nostrils. Her face grew white, whiter than her dress; she struggled faintly, and then with the feeling of submission strong within her, crossed her arms upon her breast as a little child about to say her prayers. The bright light of the lamp fell full upon her, and Clarke watched changes fleeting over her face as the changes of the hills when the summer clouds float across the sun. And then she lay all white and still, and the doctor turned up one of her eyelids. She was quite unconscious. Raymond pressed hard on one of the levers and the chair instantly sank back. Clarke saw him cutting away a circle, like a tonsure, from her hair, and the lamp was moved nearer. Raymond took a small glittering instrument from a little case, and Clarke turned away shudderingly. When he looked again the doctor was binding up the wound he had made.

"She will awake in five minutes." Raymond was still perfectly cool. "There is nothing more to be done; we can only wait."

The minutes passed slowly; they could hear a slow, heavy, ticking. There was an old clock in the passage. Clarke felt sick and faint; his knees shook beneath him, he could hardly stand.

Suddenly, as they watched, they heard a long-drawn sigh, and suddenly did the colour that had vanished return to the girl's cheeks, and suddenly her eyes opened. Clarke quailed before them. They shone with an awful light, looking far away, and a great wonder fell upon her face, and her hands stretched out as if to touch what was invisible; but in an instant the wonder faded, and gave place to the most awful terror. The muscles of her face were hideously convulsed, she shook from head to foot; the soul seemed struggling and shuddering within the house of flesh. It was a horrible sight, and Clarke rushed forward, as she fell shrieking to the floor.

Three days later Raymond took Clarke to Mary's bedside. She was lying wide-awake, rolling her head from side to side, and grinning vacantly.

"Yes," said the doctor, still quite cool, "it is a great pity; she is a hopeless idiot. However, it could not be helped; and, after all, she has seen the Great God Pan."

II

MR. CLARKE'S MEMOIRS

Mr. Clarke, the gentleman chosen by Dr. Raymond to witness the strange experiment of the god Pan, was a person in whose character caution and curiosity were oddly mingled; in his sober moments he thought of the unusual and eccentric with undisguised aversion, and yet, deep in his heart, there was a wide-eyed inquisitiveness with respect to all the more recondite and esoteric elements in the nature of men. The latter tendency had prevailed when he accepted Raymond's invitation, for though his considered judgment had always repudiated the doctor's theories as the wildest nonsense, yet he secretly hugged a belief in fantasy, and would have rejoiced to see that belief confirmed. The horrors that he witnessed in the dreary laboratory were to a certain extent salutary; he was conscious of being involved in an affair not altogether reputable, and for many years afterwards he clung bravely to the commonplace, and rejected all occasions of occult investigation. Indeed, on some homeopathic principle, he for some time attended the seances of distinguished mediums, hoping that the clumsy tricks of these gentlemen would make him altogether disgusted with mysticism of every kind, but the remedy, though caustic, was not efficacious. Clarke knew that he still pined for the unseen, and little by little, the old passion began to reassert itself, as the face of Mary, shuddering and convulsed with an unknown terror, faded slowly from his memory. Occupied all day in pursuits both serious and lucrative, the temptation to relax in the evening was too great, especially in the winter months, when the fire cast a warm glow over his snug bachelor apartment, and a bottle of some choice claret stood ready by his elbow. His dinner digested, he would make a brief pretence of reading the evening paper, but the mere catalogue of news soon palled upon him, and Clarke would find himself casting glances of warm desire in the direction of an old Japanese bureau, which stood at a pleasant distance from the hearth. Like a boy before a jam-closet, for a few minutes he would hover indecisive, but lust always prevailed, and Clarke ended by drawing up his chair, lighting a candle, and sitting down before the bureau. Its pigeon-holes and drawers teemed with documents on the most morbid subjects, and in the well reposed a large manuscript volume, in which he had painfully entered the gems of his collection. Clarke had a fine contempt for published literature; the most ghostly story ceased to interest him if it happened to be printed; his sole pleasure was in the reading, compiling, and rearranging what he called his "Memoirs to prove the Existence of the Devil," and engaged in this pursuit the evening seemed to fly and the night appeared too short.

On one particular evening, an ugly December night, black with fog, and raw with frost, Clarke hurried over his dinner, and scarcely deigned to observe his customary ritual of taking up the paper and laying it down again. He paced two or three times up and down the room, and opened the bureau, stood still a moment, and sat down. He leant back, absorbed in one of those dreams to which he was subject, and at length drew out his book, and opened it at the last entry. There were three or four pages densely covered with Clarke's round, set penmanship, and at the beginning he had written in a somewhat larger hand:

Singular Narrative told me by my Friend, Dr. Phillips. He assures me that all the facts related therein are strictly and wholly True, but refuses to give either the Surnames of the Persons Concerned, or the Place where these Extraordinary Events occurred.

Mr. Clarke began to read over the account for the tenth time, glancing now and then at the pencil notes he had made when it was told him by his friend. It was one of his humours to pride himself on a certain literary ability; he thought well of his style, and took pains in arranging the circumstances in dramatic order. He read the following story:—

The persons concerned in this statement are Helen V., who, if she is still alive, must now be a woman of twenty-three, Rachel M., since deceased, who was a year younger than the above, and Trevor W., an imbecile, aged eighteen. These persons were at the period of the story inhabitants of a village on the borders of Wales, a place of some importance in the time of the Roman occupation, but now a scattered hamlet, of not more than five hundred souls. It is situated on rising ground, about six miles from the sea, and is sheltered by a large and picturesque forest.

Some eleven years ago, Helen V. came to the village under rather peculiar circumstances. It is understood that she, being an orphan, was adopted in her infancy by a distant relative, who brought her up in his own house until she was twelve years old. Thinking, however, that it would be better for the child to have playmates of her own age, he advertised in several local papers for a good home in a comfortable farmhouse for a girl of twelve, and this advertisement was answered by Mr. R., a well-to-do farmer in the above-mentioned village. His references proving satisfactory, the gentleman sent his adopted daughter to Mr. R., with a letter, in which he stipulated that the girl should have a room to herself, and stated that her guardians need be at no trouble in the matter of education, as she was already sufficiently educated for the position in life which she would occupy. In fact, Mr. R. was given to understand that the girl be allowed to find her own occupations and to spend her time almost as she liked. Mr. R. duly met her at the nearest station, a town seven miles away from his house, and seems to have remarked nothing extraordinary about the child except that she was reticent as to her former life and her adopted father. She was, however, of a very different type from the inhabitants of the village; her skin was a pale, clear olive, and her features were strongly marked, and of a somewhat foreign character. She appears to have settled down easily enough into farmhouse life, and became a favourite with the children, who sometimes went with her on her rambles in the forest, for this was her amusement. Mr. R. states that he has known her to go out by herself directly after their early breakfast, and not return till after dusk, and that, feeling uneasy at a young girl being out alone for so many hours, he communicated with her adopted father, who replied in a brief note that Helen must do as she chose. In the winter, when the forest paths are impassable, she spent most of her time in her bedroom, where she slept alone, according to the instructions of her relative. It was on one of these expeditions to the forest that the first of the singular incidents with which this girl is connected occurred, the date being about a year after her arrival at the village. The preceding winter had been remarkably severe, the snow drifting to a great depth, and the frost continuing for an unexampled period, and the summer following was as noteworthy for its extreme heat. On one of the very hottest days in this summer, Helen V. left the farmhouse for one of her long rambles in the forest, taking with her, as usual, some bread and meat for lunch. She was seen by some men in the fields making for the old Roman Road, a green causeway which traverses the highest part of the wood, and they were astonished to observe that the girl had taken off her hat, though the heat of the sun was already tropical. As it happened, a labourer, Joseph W. by name, was working in the forest near the Roman Road, and at twelve o'clock his little son, Trevor, brought the man his dinner of bread and cheese. After the meal, the boy, who was about seven years old at the time, left his father at work, and, as he said, went to look for flowers in the wood, and the man, who could hear him shouting with delight at his discoveries, felt no uneasiness. Suddenly, however, he was horrified at hearing the most dreadful screams, evidently the result of great terror, proceeding from the direction in which his son had gone, and he hastily threw down his tools and ran to see what had happened. Tracing his path by the sound, he met the little boy, who was running headlong, and was evidently terribly frightened, and on questioning him the man elicited that after picking a posy of flowers he felt tired, and lay down on the grass and fell asleep. He was suddenly awakened, as he stated, by a peculiar noise, a sort of singing he called it, and on peeping through the branches he saw Helen V. playing on the grass with a "strange naked man," who he seemed unable to describe more fully. He said he felt dreadfully frightened and ran away crying for his father. Joseph W. proceeded in the direction indicated by his son, and found Helen V. sitting on the grass in the middle of a glade or open space left by charcoal burners. He angrily charged her with frightening his little boy, but she entirely denied the accusation and laughed at the child's story of a "strange man," to which he himself did not attach much credence. Joseph W. came to the conclusion that the boy had woke up with a sudden fright, as children sometimes do, but Trevor persisted in his story, and continued in such evident distress that at last his father took him home, hoping that his mother would be able to soothe him. For many weeks, however, the boy gave his parents much anxiety; he became nervous and strange in his manner, refusing to leave the cottage by himself, and constantly alarming the household by waking in the night with cries of "The man in the wood! father! father!"

In course of time, however, the impression seemed to have worn off, and about three months later he accompanied his father to the home of a gentleman in the neighborhood, for whom Joseph W. occasionally did work. The man was shown into the study, and the little boy was left sitting in the hall, and a few minutes later, while the gentleman was giving W. his instructions, they were both horrified by a piercing shriek and the sound of a fall, and rushing out they found the child lying senseless on the floor, his face contorted with terror. The doctor was immediately summoned, and after some examination he pronounced the child to be suffering form a kind of fit, apparently produced by a sudden shock. The boy was taken to one of the bedrooms, and after some time recovered consciousness, but only to pass into a condition described by the medical man as one of violent hysteria. The doctor exhibited a strong sedative, and in the course of two hours pronounced him fit to walk home, but in passing through the hall the paroxysms of fright returned and with additional violence. The father perceived that the child was pointing at some object, and heard the old cry, "The man in the wood," and looking in the direction indicated saw a stone head of grotesque appearance, which had been built into the wall above one of the doors. It seems the owner of the house had recently made alterations in his premises, and on digging the foundations for some offices, the men had found a curious head, evidently of the Roman period, which had been placed in the manner described. The head is pronounced by the most experienced archaeologists of the district to be that of a faun or satyr.[*]

[* Dr. Phillips tells me that he has seen the head in question, and assures me that he has never received such a vivid presentment of intense evil.]

From whatever cause arising, this second shock seemed too severe for the boy Trevor, and at the present date he suffers from a weakness of intellect, which gives but little promise of amending. The matter caused a good deal of sensation at the time, and the girl Helen was closely questioned by Mr. R., but to no purpose, she steadfastly denying that she had frightened or in any way molested Trevor.

The second event with which this girl's name is connected took place about six years ago, and is of a still more extraordinary character.

At the beginning of the summer of 1882, Helen contracted a friendship of a peculiarly intimate character with Rachel M., the daughter of a prosperous farmer in the neighbourhood. This girl, who was a year younger than Helen, was considered by most people to be the prettier of the two, though Helen's features had to a great extent softened as she became older. The two girls, who were together on every available opportunity, presented a singular contrast, the one with her clear, olive skin and almost Italian appearance, and the other of the proverbial red and white of our rural districts. It must be stated that the payments made to Mr. R. for the maintenance of Helen were known in the village for their excessive liberality, and the impression was general that she would one day inherit a large sum of money from her relative. The parents of Rachel were therefore not averse from their daughter's friendship with the girl, and even encouraged the intimacy, though they now bitterly regret having done so. Helen still retained her extraordinary fondness for the forest, and on several occasions Rachel accompanied her, the two friends setting out early in the morning, and remaining in the wood until dusk. Once or twice after these excursions Mrs. M. thought her daughter's manner rather peculiar; she seemed languid and dreamy, and as it has been expressed, "different from herself," but these peculiarities seem to have been thought too trifling for remark. One evening, however, after Rachel had come home, her mother heard a noise which sounded like suppressed weeping in the girl's room, and on going in found her lying, half undressed, upon the bed, evidently in the greatest distress. As soon as she saw her mother, she exclaimed, "Ah, mother, mother, why did you let me go to the forest with Helen?" Mrs. M. was astonished at so strange a question, and proceeded to make inquiries. Rachel told her a wild story. She said—

Clarke closed the book with a snap, and turned his chair towards the fire. When his friend sat one evening in that very chair, and told his story, Clarke had interrupted him at a point a little subsequent to this, had cut short his words in a paroxysm of horror. "My God!" he had exclaimed, "think, think what you are saying. It is too incredible, too monstrous; such things can never be in this quiet world, where men and women live and die, and struggle, and conquer, or maybe fail, and fall down under sorrow, and grieve and suffer strange fortunes for many a year; but not this, Phillips, not such things as this. There must be some explanation, some way out of the terror. Why, man, if such a case were possible, our earth would be a nightmare."

But Phillips had told his story to the end, concluding:

"Her flight remains a mystery to this day; she vanished in broad sunlight; they saw her walking in a meadow, and a few moments later she was not there."

Clarke tried to conceive the thing again, as he sat by the fire, and again his mind shuddered and shrank back, appalled before the sight of such awful, unspeakable elements enthroned as it were, and triumphant in human flesh. Before him stretched the long dim vista of the green causeway in the forest, as his friend had described it; he saw the swaying leaves and the quivering shadows on the grass, he saw the sunlight and the flowers, and far away, far in the long distance, the two figures moved toward him. One was Rachel, but the other?

Clarke had tried his best to disbelieve it all, but at the end of the account, as he had written it in his book, he had placed the inscription:

Et Diabolus incarnatus est. Et homo factus est.

III

THE CITY OF RESURRECTIONS

"Herbert! Good God! Is it possible?"

"Yes, my name's Herbert. I think I know your face, too, but I don't remember your name. My memory is very queer."

"Don't you recollect Villiers of Wadham?"

"So it is, so it is. I beg your pardon, Villiers, I didn't think I was begging of an old college friend. Good-night."

"My dear fellow, this haste is unnecessary. My rooms are close by, but we won't go there just yet. Suppose we walk up Shaftesbury Avenue a little way? But how in heaven's name have you come to this pass, Herbert?"

"It's a long story, Villiers, and a strange one too, but you can hear it if you like."

"Come on, then. Take my arm, you don't seem very strong."

The ill-assorted pair moved slowly up Rupert Street; the one in dirty, evil-looking rags, and the other attired in the regulation uniform of a man about town, trim, glossy, and eminently well-to-do. Villiers had emerged from his restaurant after an excellent dinner of many courses, assisted by an ingratiating little flask of Chianti, and, in that frame of mind which was with him almost chronic, had delayed a moment by the door, peering round in the dimly-lighted street in search of those mysterious incidents and persons with which the streets of London teem in every quarter and every hour. Villiers prided himself as a practised explorer of such obscure mazes and byways of London life, and in this unprofitable pursuit he displayed an assiduity which was worthy of more serious employment. Thus he stood by the lamp-post surveying the passers-by with undisguised curiosity, and with that gravity known only to the systematic diner, had just enunciated in his mind the formula: "London has been called the city of encounters; it is more than that, it is the city of Resurrections," when these reflections were suddenly interrupted by a piteous whine at his elbow, and a deplorable appeal for alms. He looked around in some irritation, and with a sudden shock found himself confronted with the embodied proof of his somewhat stilted fancies. There, close beside him, his face altered and disfigured by poverty and disgrace, his body barely covered by greasy ill-fitting rags, stood his old friend Charles Herbert, who had matriculated on the same day as himself, with whom he had been merry and wise for twelve revolving terms. Different occupations and varying interests had interrupted the friendship, and it was six years since Villiers had seen Herbert; and now he looked upon this wreck of a man with grief and dismay, mingled with a certain inquisitiveness as to what dreary chain of circumstances had dragged him down to such a doleful pass. Villiers felt together with compassion all the relish of the amateur in mysteries, and congratulated himself on his leisurely speculations outside the restaurant.

They walked on in silence for some time, and more than one passer-by stared in astonishment at the unaccustomed spectacle of a well-dressed man with an unmistakable beggar hanging on to his arm, and, observing this, Villiers led the way to an obscure street in Soho. Here he repeated his question.

"How on earth has it happened, Herbert? I always understood you would succeed to an excellent position in Dorsetshire. Did your father disinherit you? Surely not?"

"No, Villiers; I came into all the property at my poor father's death; he died a year after I left Oxford. He was a very good father to me, and I mourned his death sincerely enough. But you know what young men are; a few months later I came up to town and went a good deal into society. Of course I had excellent introductions, and I managed to enjoy myself very much in a harmless sort of way. I played a little, certainly, but never for heavy stakes, and the few bets I made on races brought me in money—only a few pounds, you know, but enough to pay for cigars and such petty pleasures. It was in my second season that the tide turned. Of course you have heard of my marriage?"

"No, I never heard anything about it."

"Yes, I married, Villiers. I met a girl, a girl of the most wonderful and most strange beauty, at the house of some people whom I knew. I cannot tell you her age; I never knew it, but, so far as I can guess, I should think she must have been about nineteen when I made her acquaintance. My friends had come to know her at Florence; she told them she was an orphan, the child of an English father and an Italian mother, and she charmed them as she charmed me. The first time I saw her was at an evening party. I was standing by the door talking to a friend, when suddenly above the hum and babble of conversation I heard a voice which seemed to thrill to my heart. She was singing an Italian song. I was introduced to her that evening, and in three months I married Helen. Villiers, that woman, if I can call her woman, corrupted my soul. The night of the wedding I found myself sitting in her bedroom in the hotel, listening to her talk. She was sitting up in bed, and I listened to her as she spoke in her beautiful voice, spoke of things which even now I would not dare whisper in the blackest night, though I stood in the midst of a wilderness. You, Villiers, you may think you know life, and London, and what goes on day and night in this dreadful city; for all I can say you may have heard the talk of the vilest, but I tell you you can have no conception of what I know, not in your most fantastic, hideous dreams can you have imaged forth the faintest shadow of what I have heard—and seen. Yes, seen. I have seen the incredible, such horrors that even I myself sometimes stop in the middle of the street and ask whether it is possible for a man to behold such things and live. In a year, Villiers, I was a ruined man, in body and soul—in body and soul."

"But your property, Herbert? You had land in Dorset."

"I sold it all; the fields and woods, the dear old house—everything."

"And the money?"

"She took it all from me."

"And then left you?"

"Yes; she disappeared one night. I don't know where she went, but I am sure if I saw her again it would kill me. The rest of my story is of no interest; sordid misery, that is all. You may think, Villiers, that I have exaggerated and talked for effect; but I have not told you half. I could tell you certain things which would convince you, but you would never know a happy day again. You would pass the rest of your life, as I pass mine, a haunted man, a man who has seen hell."

Villiers took the unfortunate man to his rooms, and gave him a meal. Herbert could eat little, and scarcely touched the glass of wine set before him. He sat moody and silent by the fire, and seemed relieved when Villiers sent him away with a small present of money.

"By the way, Herbert," said Villiers, as they parted at the door, "what was your wife's name? You said Helen, I think? Helen what?"

"The name she passed under when I met her was Helen Vaughan, but what her real name was I can't say. I don't think she had a name. No, no, not in that sense. Only human beings have names, Villiers; I can't say anymore. Good-bye; yes, I will not fail to call if I see any way in which you can help me. Good-night."

The man went out into the bitter night, and Villiers returned to his fireside. There was something about Herbert which shocked him inexpressibly; not his poor rags nor the marks which poverty had set upon his face, but rather an indefinite terror which hung about him like a mist. He had acknowledged that he himself was not devoid of blame; the woman, he had avowed, had corrupted him body and soul, and Villiers felt that this man, once his friend, had been an actor in scenes evil beyond the power of words. His story needed no confirmation: he himself was the embodied proof of it. Villiers mused curiously over the story he had heard, and wondered whether he had heard both the first and the last of it. "No," he thought, "certainly not the last, probably only the beginning. A case like this is like a nest of Chinese boxes; you open one after the other and find a quainter workmanship in every box. Most likely poor Herbert is merely one of the outside boxes; there are stranger ones to follow."

Villiers could not take his mind away from Herbert and his story, which seemed to grow wilder as the night wore on. The fire seemed to burn low, and the chilly air of the morning crept into the room; Villiers got up with a glance over his shoulder, and, shivering slightly, went to bed.

A few days later he saw at his club a gentleman of his acquaintance, named Austin, who was famous for his intimate knowledge of London life, both in its tenebrous and luminous phases. Villiers, still full of his encounter in Soho and its consequences, thought Austin might possibly be able to shed some light on Herbert's history, and so after some casual talk he suddenly put the question:

"Do you happen to know anything of a man named Herbert—Charles Herbert?"

Austin turned round sharply and stared at Villiers with some astonishment.

"Charles Herbert? Weren't you in town three years ago? No; then you have not heard of the Paul Street case? It caused a good deal of sensation at the time."

"What was the case?"

"Well, a gentleman, a man of very good position, was found

dead, stark dead, in the area of a certain house in Paul Street, off Tottenham Court Road. Of course the police did not make the discovery; if you happen to be sitting up all night and have a light in your window, the constable will ring the bell, but if you happen to be lying dead in somebody's area, you will be left alone. In this instance, as in many others, the alarm was raised by some kind of vagabond; I don't mean a common tramp, or a public-house loafer, but a gentleman, whose business or pleasure, or both, made him a spectator of the London streets at five o'clock in the morning. This individual was, as he said, 'going home,' it did not appear whence or whither, and had occasion to pass through Paul Street between four and five a.m. Something or other caught his eye at Number 20; he said, absurdly enough, that the house had the most unpleasant physiognomy he had ever observed, but, at any rate, he glanced down the area and was a good deal astonished to see a man lying on the stones, his limbs all huddled together, and his face turned up. Our gentleman thought his face looked peculiarly ghastly, and so set off at a run in search of the nearest policeman. The constable was at first inclined to treat the matter lightly, suspecting common drunkenness; however, he came, and after looking at the man's face, changed his tone, quickly enough. The early bird, who had picked up this fine worm, was sent off for a doctor, and the policeman rang and knocked at the door till a slatternly servant girl came down looking more than half asleep. The constable pointed out the contents of the area to the maid, who screamed loudly enough to wake up the street, but she knew nothing of the man; had never seen him at the house, and so forth. Meanwhile, the original discoverer had come back with a medical man, and the next thing was to get into the area. The gate was open, so the whole quartet stumped down the steps. The doctor hardly needed a moment's examination; he said the poor fellow had been dead for several hours, and it was then the case began to get interesting. The dead man had not been robbed, and in one of his pockets were papers identifying him as—well, as a man of good family and means, a favourite in society, and nobody's enemy, as far as could be known. I don't give his name, Villiers, because it has nothing to do with the story, and because it's no good raking up these affairs about the dead when there are no relations living. The next curious point was that the medical men couldn't agree as to how he met his death. There were some slight bruises on his shoulders, but they were so slight that it looked as if he had been pushed roughly out of the kitchen door, and not thrown over the railings from the street or even dragged down the steps. But there were positively no other marks of violence about him, certainly none that would account for his death; and when they came to the autopsy there wasn't a trace of poison of any kind. Of course the police wanted to know all about the people at Number 20, and here again, so I have heard from private sources, one or two other very curious points came out. It appears that the occupants of the house were a Mr. and Mrs. Charles Herbert; he was said to be a landed proprietor, though it struck most people that Paul Street was not exactly the place to look for country gentry. As for Mrs. Herbert, nobody seemed to know who or what she was, and, between ourselves, I fancy the divers after her history found themselves in rather strange waters. Of course they both denied knowing anything about the deceased, and in default of any evidence against them they were discharged. But some very odd things came out about them. Though it was between five and six in the morning when the dead man was removed, a large crowd had collected, and several of the neighbours ran to see what was going on. They were pretty free with their comments, by all accounts, and from these it appeared that Number 20 was in very bad odour in Paul Street. The detectives tried to trace down these rumours to some solid foundation of fact, but could not get hold of anything. People shook their heads and raised their eyebrows and thought the Herberts rather 'queer,' 'would rather not be seen going into their house,' and so on, but there was nothing tangible. The authorities were morally certain the man met his death in some way or another in the house and was thrown out by the kitchen door, but they couldn't prove it, and the absence of any indications of violence or poisoning left them helpless. An odd case, wasn't it? But curiously enough, there's something more that I haven't told you. I happened to know one of the doctors who was consulted as to the cause of death, and some time after the inquest I met him, and asked him about it. 'Do you really mean to tell me,' I said, 'that you were baffled by the case, that you actually don't know what the man died of?' 'Pardon me,' he replied, 'I know perfectly well what caused death. Blank died of fright, of sheer, awful terror; I never saw features so hideously contorted in the entire course of my practice, and I have seen the faces of a whole host of dead.' The doctor was usually a cool customer enough, and a certain vehemence in his manner struck me, but I couldn't get anything more out of him. I suppose the Treasury didn't see their way to prosecuting the Herberts for frightening a man to death; at any rate, nothing was done, and the case dropped out of men's minds. Do you happen to know anything of Herbert?"

"Well," replied Villiers, "he was an old college friend of mine."

"You don't say so? Have you ever seen his wife?"

"No, I haven't. I have lost sight of Herbert for many years."

"It's queer, isn't it, parting with a man at the college gate or at Paddington, seeing nothing of him for years, and then finding him pop up his head in such an odd place. But I should like to have seen Mrs. Herbert; people said extraordinary things about her."

"What sort of things?"

"Well, I hardly know how to tell you. Everyone who saw her at the police court said she was at once the most beautiful woman and the most repulsive they had ever set eyes on. I have spoken to a man who saw her, and I assure you he positively shuddered as he tried to describe the woman, but he couldn't tell why. She seems to have been a sort of enigma; and I expect if that one dead man could have told tales, he would have told some uncommonly queer ones. And there you are again in another puzzle; what could a respectable country gentleman like Mr. Blank (we'll call him that if you don't mind) want in such a very queer house as Number 20? It's altogether a very odd case, isn't it?"

"It is indeed, Austin; an extraordinary case. I didn't think, when I asked you about my old friend, I should strike on such strange metal. Well, I must be off; good-day."

Villiers went away, thinking of his own conceit of the Chinese boxes; here was quaint workmanship indeed.

IV

THE DISCOVERY IN PAUL STREET

A few months after Villiers' meeting with Herbert, Mr. Clarke was sitting, as usual, by his after-dinner hearth, resolutely guarding his fancies from wandering in the direction of the bureau. For more than a week he had succeeded in keeping away from the "Memoirs," and he cherished hopes of a complete self-reformation; but, in spite of his endeavours, he could not hush the wonder and the strange curiosity that the last case he had written down had excited within him. He had put the case, or rather the outline of it, conjecturally to a scientific friend, who shook his head, and thought Clarke getting queer, and on this particular evening Clarke was making an effort to rationalize the story, when a sudden knock at the door roused him from his meditations.

"Mr. Villiers to see you sir."

"Dear me, Villiers, it is very kind of you to look me up; I have not seen you for many months; I should think nearly a year. Come in, come in. And how are you, Villiers? Want any advice about investments?"

"No, thanks, I fancy everything I have in that way is pretty safe. No, Clarke, I have really come to consult you about a rather curious matter that has been brought under my notice of late. I am afraid you will think it all rather absurd when I tell my tale. I sometimes think so myself, and that's just why I made up my mind to come to you, as I know you're a practical man."

Mr. Villiers was ignorant of the "Memoirs to prove the Existence of the Devil."

"Well, Villiers, I shall be happy to give you my advice, to the best of my ability. What is the nature of the case?"

"It's an extraordinary thing altogether. You know my ways; I always keep my eyes open in the streets, and in my time I have chanced upon some queer customers, and queer cases too, but this, I think, beats all. I was coming out of a restaurant one nasty winter night about three months ago; I had had a capital dinner and a good bottle of Chianti, and I stood for a moment on the pavement, thinking what a mystery there is about London streets and the companies that pass along them. A bottle of red wine encourages these fancies, Clarke, and I dare say I should have thought a page of small type, but I was cut short by a beggar who had come behind me, and was making the usual appeals. Of course I looked round, and this beggar turned out to be what was left of an old friend of mine, a man named Herbert. I asked him how he had come to such a wretched pass, and he told me. We walked up and down one of those long and dark Soho streets, and there I listened to his story. He said he had married a beautiful girl, some years younger than himself, and, as he put it, she had corrupted him body and soul. He wouldn't go into details; he said he dare not, that what he had seen and heard haunted him by night and day, and when I looked in his face I knew he was speaking the truth. There was something about the man that made me shiver. I don't know why, but it was there. I gave him a little money and sent him away, and I assure you that when he was gone I gasped for breath. His presence seemed to chill one's blood."

"Isn't this all just a little fanciful, Villiers? I suppose the poor fellow had made an imprudent marriage, and, in plain English, gone to the bad."

"Well, listen to this." Villiers told Clarke the story he had heard from Austin.

"You see," he concluded, "there can be but little doubt that this Mr. Blank, whoever he was, died of sheer terror; he saw something so awful, so terrible, that it cut short his life. And what he saw, he most certainly saw in that house, which, somehow or other, had got a bad name in the neighbourhood. I had the curiosity to go and look at the place for myself. It's a saddening kind of street; the houses are old enough to be mean and dreary, but not old enough to be quaint. As far as I could see most of them are let in lodgings, furnished and unfurnished, and almost every door has three bells to it. Here and there the ground floors have been made into shops of the commonest kind; it's a dismal street in every way. I found Number 20 was to let, and I went to the agent's and got the key. Of course I should have heard nothing of the Herberts in that quarter, but I asked the man, fair and square, how long they had left the house and whether there had been other tenants in the meanwhile. He looked at me queerly for a minute, and told me the Herberts had left immediately after the unpleasantness, as he called it, and since then the house had been empty."

Mr. Villiers paused for a moment.

"I have always been rather fond of going over empty houses; there's a sort of fascination about the desolate empty rooms, with the nails sticking in the walls, and the dust thick upon the window-sills. But I didn't enjoy going over Number 20, Paul Street. I had hardly put my foot inside the passage when I noticed a queer, heavy feeling about the air of the house. Of course all empty houses are stuffy, and so forth, but this was something quite different; I can't describe it to you, but it seemed to stop the breath. I went into the front room and the back room, and the kitchens downstairs; they were all dirty and dusty enough, as you would expect, but there was something strange about them all. I couldn't define it to you, I only know I felt queer. It was one of the rooms on the first floor, though, that was the worst. It was a largish room, and once on a time the paper must have been cheerful enough, but when I saw it, paint, paper, and everything were most doleful. But the room was full of horror; I felt my teeth grinding as I put my hand on the door, and when I went in, I thought I should have fallen fainting to the floor. However, I pulled myself together, and stood against the end wall, wondering what on earth there could be about the room to make my limbs tremble, and my heart beat as if I were at the hour of death. In one corner there was a pile of newspapers littered on the floor, and I began looking at them; they were papers of three or four years ago, some of them half torn, and some crumpled as if they had been used for packing. I turned the whole pile over, and amongst them I found a curious drawing; I will show it to you presently. But I couldn't stay in the room; I felt it was overpowering me. I was thankful to come out, safe and sound, into the open air. People stared at me as I walked along the street, and one man said I was drunk. I was staggering about from one side of the pavement to the other, and it was as much as I could do to take the key back to the agent and get home. I was in bed for a week, suffering from what my doctor called nervous shock and exhaustion. One of those days I was reading the evening paper, and happened to notice a paragraph headed: 'Starved to Death.' It was the usual style of thing; a model lodging-house in Marylebone, a door locked for several days, and a dead man in his chair when they broke in. 'The deceased,' said the paragraph, 'was known as Charles Herbert, and is believed to have been once a prosperous country gentleman. His name was familiar to the public three years ago in connection with the mysterious death in Paul Street, Tottenham Court Road, the deceased being the tenant of the house Number 20, in the area of which a gentleman of good position was found dead under circumstances not devoid of suspicion.' A tragic ending, wasn't it? But after all, if what he told me were true, which I am sure it was, the man's life was all a tragedy, and a tragedy of a stranger sort than they put on the boards."

"And that is the story, is it?" said Clarke musingly.

"Yes, that is the story."

"Well, really, Villiers, I scarcely know what to say about it. There are, no doubt, circumstances in the case which seem peculiar, the finding of the dead man in the area of Herbert's house, for instance, and the extraordinary opinion of the physician as to the cause of death; but, after all, it is conceivable that the facts may be explained in a straightforward manner. As to your own sensations, when you went to see the house, I would suggest that they were due to a vivid imagination; you must have been brooding, in a semi-conscious way, over what you had heard. I don't exactly see what more can be said or done in the matter; you evidently think there is a mystery of some kind, but Herbert is dead; where then do you propose to look?"

"I propose to look for the woman; the woman whom he married. She is the mystery."

The two men sat silent by the fireside; Clarke secretly congratulating himself on having successfully kept up the character of advocate of the commonplace, and Villiers wrapped in his gloomy fancies.

"I think I will have a cigarette," he said at last, and put his hand in his pocket to feel for the cigarette-case.

"Ah!" he said, starting slightly, "I forgot I had something to show you. You remember my saying that I had found a rather curious sketch amongst the pile of old newspapers at the house in Paul Street? Here it is."

Villiers drew out a small thin parcel from his pocket. It was covered with brown paper, and secured with string, and the knots were troublesome. In spite of himself Clarke felt inquisitive; he bent forward on his chair as Villiers painfully undid the string, and unfolded the outer covering. Inside was a second wrapping of tissue, and Villiers took it off and handed the small piece of paper to Clarke without a word.

There was dead silence in the room for five minutes or more; the two men sat so still that they could hear the ticking of the tall old-fashioned clock that stood outside in the hall, and in the mind of one of them the slow monotony of sound woke up a far, far memory. He was looking intently at the small pen-and-ink sketch of the woman's head; it had evidently been drawn with great care, and by a true artist, for the woman's soul looked out of the eyes, and the lips were parted with a strange smile. Clarke gazed still at the face; it brought to his memory one summer evening, long ago; he saw again the long lovely valley, the river winding between the hills, the meadows and the cornfields, the dull red sun, and the cold white mist rising from the water. He heard a voice speaking to him across the waves of many years, and saying "Clarke, Mary will see the god

Pan!" and then he was standing in the grim room beside the doctor, listening to the heavy ticking of the clock, waiting and watching, watching the figure lying on the green chair beneath the lamplight. Mary rose up, and he looked into her eyes, and his heart grew cold within him.

"Who is this woman?" he said at last. His voice was dry and hoarse.

"That is the woman who Herbert married."

Clarke looked again at the sketch; it was not Mary after all. There certainly was Mary's face, but there was something else, something he had not seen on Mary's features when the white-clad girl entered the laboratory with the doctor, nor at her terrible awakening, nor when she lay grinning on the bed. Whatever it was, the glance that came from those eyes, the smile on the full lips, or the expression of the whole face, Clarke shuddered before it at his inmost soul, and thought, unconsciously, of Dr. Phillip's words, "the most vivid presentment of evil I have ever seen." He turned the paper over mechanically in his hand and glanced at the back.

"Good God! Clarke, what is the matter? You are as white as death."

Villiers had started wildly from his chair, as Clarke fell back with a groan, and let the paper drop from his hands.

"I don't feel very well, Villiers, I am subject to these attacks. Pour me out a little wine; thanks, that will do. I shall feel better in a few minutes."

Villiers picked up the fallen sketch and turned it over as Clarke had done.

"You saw that?" he said. "That's how I identified it as being a portrait of Herbert's wife, or I should say his widow. How do you feel now?"

"Better, thanks, it was only a passing faintness. I don't think I quite catch your meaning. What did you say enabled you to identify the picture?"

"This word—'Helen'—was written on the back. Didn't I tell you her name was Helen? Yes; Helen Vaughan."

Clarke groaned; there could be no shadow of doubt.

"Now, don't you agree with me," said Villiers, "that in the story I have told you to-night, and in the part this woman plays in it, there are some very strange points?"

"Yes, Villiers," Clarke muttered, "it is a strange story indeed; a strange story indeed. You must give me time to think it over; I may be able to help you or I may not. Must you be going now? Well, good-night, Villiers, good-night. Come and see me in the course of a week."

V

THE LETTER OF ADVICE

"Do you know, Austin," said Villiers, as the two friends were pacing sedately along Piccadilly one pleasant morning in May, "do you know I am convinced that what you told me about Paul Street and the Herberts is a mere episode in an extraordinary history? I may as well confess to you that when I asked you about Herbert a few months ago I had just seen him."

"You had seen him? Where?"

"He begged of me in the street one night. He was in the most pitiable plight, but I recognized the man, and I got him to tell me his history, or at least the outline of it. In brief, it amounted to this—he had been ruined by his wife."

"In what manner?"

"He would not tell me; he would only say that she had destroyed him, body and soul. The man is dead now."

"And what has become of his wife?"

"Ah, that's what I should like to know, and I mean to find her sooner or later. I know a man named Clarke, a dry fellow, in fact a man of business, but shrewd enough. You understand my meaning; not shrewd in the mere business sense of the word, but a man who really knows something about men and life. Well, I laid the case before him, and he was evidently impressed. He said it needed consideration, and asked me to come again in the course of a week. A few days later I received this extraordinary letter."

Austin took the envelope, drew out the letter, and read it curiously. It ran as follows:—

"MY DEAR VILLIERS,—I have thought over the matter on which you consulted me the other night, and my advice to you is this. Throw the portrait into the fire, blot out the story from your mind. Never give it another thought, Villiers, or you will be sorry. You will think, no doubt, that I am in possession of some secret information, and to a certain extent that is the case. But I only know a little; I am like a traveller who has peered over an abyss, and has drawn back in terror. What I know is strange enough and horrible enough, but beyond my knowledge there are depths and horrors more frightful still, more incredible than any tale told of winter nights about the fire. I have resolved, and nothing shall shake that resolve, to explore no whit farther, and if you value your happiness you will make the same determination.

"Come and see me by all means; but we will talk on more cheerful topics than this."

Austin folded the letter methodically, and returned it to Villiers.

"It is certainly an extraordinary letter," he said, "what does he mean by the portrait?"

"Ah! I forgot to tell you I have been to Paul Street and have made a discovery."

Villiers told his story as he had told it to Clarke, and Austin listened in silence. He seemed puzzled.

"How very curious that you should experience such an unpleasant sensation in that room!" he said at length. "I hardly gather that it was a mere matter of the imagination; a feeling of repulsion, in short."

"No, it was more physical than mental. It was as if I were inhaling at every breath some deadly fume, which seemed to penetrate to every nerve and bone and sinew of my body. I felt racked from head to foot, my eyes began to grow dim; it was like the entrance of death."

"Yes, yes, very strange certainly. You see, your friend confesses that there is some very black story connected with this woman. Did you notice any particular emotion in him when you were telling your tale?"

"Yes, I did. He became very faint, but he assured me that it was a mere passing attack to which he was subject."

"Did you believe him?"

"I did at the time, but I don't now. He heard what I had to say with a good deal of indifference, till I showed him the portrait. It was then that he was seized with the attack of which I spoke. He looked ghastly, I assure you."

"Then he must have seen the woman before. But there might be another explanation; it might have been the name, and not the face, which was familiar to him. What do you think?"

"I couldn't say. To the best of my belief it was after turning the portrait in his hands that he nearly dropped from the chair. The name, you know, was written on the back."

"Quite so. After all, it is impossible to come to any resolution in a case like this. I hate melodrama, and nothing strikes me as more commonplace and tedious than the ordinary ghost story of commerce; but really, Villiers, it looks as if there were something very queer at the bottom of all this."

The two men had, without noticing it, turned up Ashley Street, leading northward from Piccadilly. It was a long street, and rather a gloomy one, but here and there a brighter taste had illuminated the dark houses with flowers, and gay curtains, and a cheerful paint on the doors. Villiers glanced up as Austin stopped speaking, and looked at one of these houses; geraniums, red and white, drooped from every sill, and daffodil-coloured curtains were draped back from each window.

"It looks cheerful, doesn't it?" he said.

"Yes, and the inside is still more cheery. One of the pleasantest houses of the season, so I have heard. I haven't been there myself, but I've met several men who have, and they tell me it's uncommonly jovial."

"Whose house is it?"

"A Mrs. Beaumont's."

"And who is she?"

"I couldn't tell you. I have heard she comes from South America, but after all, who she is is of little consequence. She is a very wealthy woman, there's no doubt of that, and some of the best people have taken her up. I hear she has some wonderful claret, really marvellous wine, which must have cost a fabulous sum. Lord Argentine was telling me about it; he was there last Sunday evening. He assures me he has never tasted such a wine, and Argentine, as you know, is an expert. By the way, that reminds me, she must be an oddish sort of woman, this Mrs. Beaumont. Argentine asked her how old the wine was, and what do you think she said? 'About a thousand years, I believe.' Lord Argentine thought she was chaffing him, you know, but when he laughed she said she was speaking quite seriously and offered to show him the jar. Of course, he couldn't say anything more after that; but it seems rather antiquated for a beverage, doesn't it? Why, here we are at my rooms. Come in, won't you?"

"Thanks, I think I will. I haven't seen the curiosity-shop for a while."

It was a room furnished richly, yet oddly, where every jar and bookcase and table, and every rug and jar and ornament seemed to be a thing apart, preserving each its own individuality.

"Anything fresh lately?" said Villiers after a while.

"No; I think not; you saw those queer jugs, didn't you? I thought so. I don't think I have come across anything for the last few weeks."

Austin glanced around the room from cupboard to cupboard, from shelf to shelf, in search of some new oddity. His eyes fell at last on an odd chest, pleasantly and quaintly carved, which stood in a dark corner of the room.

"Ah," he said, "I was forgetting, I have got something to show you." Austin unlocked the chest, drew out a thick quarto volume, laid it on the table, and resumed the cigar he had put down.

"Did you know Arthur Meyrick the painter, Villiers?"

"A little; I met him two or three times at the house of a friend of mine. What has become of him? I haven't heard his name mentioned for some time."

"He's dead."

"You don't say so! Quite young, wasn't he?"

"Yes; only thirty when he died."

"What did he die of?"

"I don't know. He was an intimate friend of mine, and a thoroughly good fellow. He used to come here and talk to me for hours, and he was one of the best talkers I have met. He could even talk about painting, and that's more than can be said of most painters. About eighteen months ago he was feeling rather overworked, and partly at my suggestion he went off on a sort of roving expedition, with no very definite end or aim about it. I believe New York was to be his first port, but I never heard from him. Three months ago I got this book, with a very civil letter from an English doctor practising at Buenos Ayres, stating that he had attended the late Mr. Meyrick during his illness, and that the deceased had expressed an earnest wish that the enclosed packet should be sent to me after his death. That was all."

"And haven't you written for further particulars?"

"I have been thinking of doing so. You would advise me to write to the doctor?"

"Certainly. And what about the book?"

"It was sealed up when I got it. I don't think the doctor had seen it."

"It is something very rare? Meyrick was a collector, perhaps?"

"No, I think not, hardly a collector. Now, what do you think of these Ainu jugs?"

"They are peculiar, but I like them. But aren't you going to show me poor Meyrick's legacy?"

"Yes, yes, to be sure. The fact is, it's rather a peculiar sort of thing, and I haven't shown it to any one. I wouldn't say anything about it if I were you. There it is."

Villiers took the book, and opened it at haphazard.

"It isn't a printed volume, then?" he said.

"No. It is a collection of drawings in black and white by my poor friend Meyrick."

Villiers turned to the first page, it was blank; the second bore a brief inscription, which he read:

Silet per diem universus, nec sine horrore secretus est; lucet nocturnis ignibus, chorus Ægipanum undique personatur: audiuntur et cantus tibiarum, et tinnitus cymbalorum per oram maritimam.

On the third page was a design which made Villiers start and look up at Austin; he was gazing abstractedly out of the window. Villiers turned page after page, absorbed, in spite of himself, in the frightful Walpurgis Night of evil, strange monstrous evil, that the dead artist had set forth in hard black and white. The figures of Fauns and Satyrs and Ægipans danced before his eyes, the darkness of the thicket, the dance on the mountain-top, the scenes by lonely shores, in green vineyards, by rocks and desert places, passed before him: a world before which the human soul seemed to shrink back and shudder. Villiers whirled over the remaining pages; he had seen enough, but the picture on the last leaf caught his eye, as he almost closed the book.

"Austin!"

"Well, what is it?"

"Do you know who that is?"

It was a woman's face, alone on the white page.

"Know who it is? No, of course not."

"I do."

"Who is it?"

"It is Mrs. Herbert."

"Are you sure?"

"I am perfectly sure of it. Poor Meyrick! He is one more chapter in her history."

"But what do you think of the designs?"

"They are frightful. Lock the book up again, Austin. If I were you I would burn it; it must be a terrible companion even though it be in a chest."

"Yes, they are singular drawings. But I wonder what connection there could be between Meyrick and Mrs. Herbert, or what link between her and these designs?"

"Ah, who can say? It is possible that the matter may end here, and we shall never know, but in my own opinion this Helen Vaughan, or Mrs. Herbert, is only the beginning. She will come back to London, Austin; depend on it, she will come back, and we shall hear more about her then. I doubt it will be very pleasant news."

VI

THE SUICIDES

Lord Argentine was a great favourite in London Society. At twenty he had been a poor man, decked with the surname of an illustrious family, but forced to earn a livelihood as best he could, and the most speculative of money-lenders would not have entrusted him with fifty pounds on the chance of his ever changing his name for a title, and his poverty for a great fortune. His father had been near enough to the fountain of good things to secure one of the family livings, but the son, even if he had taken orders, would scarcely have obtained so much as this, and moreover felt no vocation for the ecclesiastical estate. Thus he fronted the world with no better armour than the bachelor's gown and the wits of a younger son's grandson, with which equipment he contrived in some way to make a very tolerable fight of it. At twenty-five Mr. Charles Aubernon saw himself still a man of struggles and of warfare with the world, but out of the seven who stood before him and the high places of his family three only remained. These three, however, were "good lives," but yet not proof against the Zulu assegais and typhoid fever, and so one morning Aubernon woke up and found himself Lord Argentine, a man of thirty who had faced the difficulties of existence, and had conquered. The situation amused him immensely, and he resolved that riches should be as pleasant to him as poverty had always been. Argentine, after some little consideration, came to the conclusion that dining, regarded as a fine art, was perhaps the most amusing pursuit open to fallen humanity, and thus his dinners became famous in London, and an invitation to his table a thing covetously desired. After ten years of lordship and dinners Argentine still declined to be jaded, still persisted in enjoying life, and by a kind of infection had become recognized as the cause of joy in others, in short, as the best of company. His sudden and tragical death therefore caused a wide and deep sensation. People could scarcely believe it, even though the newspaper was before their eyes, and the cry of "Mysterious Death of a Nobleman" came ringing up from the street. But there stood the brief paragraph: "Lord Argentine was found dead this morning by his valet under distressing circumstances. It is stated that there can be no doubt that his lordship committed suicide, though no motive can be assigned for the act. The deceased nobleman was widely known in society, and much liked for his genial manner and sumptuous hospitality. He is succeeded by," etc., etc.

By slow degrees the details came to light, but the case still remained a mystery. The chief witness at the inquest was the deceased's valet, who said that the night before his death Lord

Argentine had dined with a lady of good position, whose name was suppressed in the newspaper reports. At about eleven o'clock Lord Argentine had returned, and informed his man that he should not require his services till the next morning. A little later the valet had occasion to cross the hall and was somewhat astonished to see his master quietly letting himself out at the front door. He had taken off his evening clothes, and was dressed in a Norfolk coat and knickerbockers, and wore a low brown hat. The valet had no reason to suppose that Lord Argentine had seen him, and though his master rarely kept late hours, thought little of the occurrence till the next morning, when he knocked at the bedroom door at a quarter to nine as usual. He received no answer, and, after knocking two or three times, entered the room, and saw Lord Argentine's body leaning forward at an angle from the bottom of the bed. He found that his master had tied a cord securely to one of the short bed-posts, and, after making a running noose and slipping it round his neck, the unfortunate man must have resolutely fallen forward, to die by slow strangulation. He was dressed in the light suit in which the valet had seen him go out, and the doctor who was summoned pronounced that life had been extinct for more than four hours. All papers, letters, and so forth seemed in perfect order, and nothing was discovered which pointed in the most remote way to any scandal either great or small. Here the evidence ended; nothing more could be discovered. Several persons had been present at the dinner-party at which Lord Argentine had assisted, and to all these he seemed in his usual genial spirits. The valet, indeed, said he thought his master appeared a little excited when he came home, but confessed that the alteration in his manner was very slight, hardly noticeable, indeed. It seemed hopeless to seek for any clue, and the suggestion that Lord Argentine had been suddenly attacked by acute suicidal mania was generally accepted.

It was otherwise, however, when within three weeks, three more gentlemen, one of them a nobleman, and the two others men of good position and ample means, perished miserably in the almost precisely the same manner. Lord Swanleigh was found one morning in his dressing-room, hanging from a peg affixed to the wall, and Mr. Collier-Stuart and Mr. Herries had chosen to die as Lord Argentine. There was no explanation in either case; a few bald facts; a living man in the evening, and a body with a black swollen face in the morning. The police had been forced to confess themselves powerless to arrest or to explain the sordid murders of Whitechapel; but before the horrible suicides of Piccadilly and Mayfair they were dumbfoundered, for not even the mere ferocity which did duty as an explanation of the crimes of the East End, could be of service in the West. Each of these men who had resolved to die a tortured shameful death was rich, prosperous, and to all appearances in love with the world, and not the acutest research should ferret out any shadow of a lurking motive in either case. There was a horror in the air, and men looked at one another's faces when they met, each wondering whether the other was to be the victim of the fifth nameless tragedy. Journalists sought in vain for their scrapbooks for materials whereof to concoct reminiscent articles; and the morning paper was unfolded in many a house with a feeling of awe; no man knew when or where the next blow would light.

A short while after the last of these terrible events, Austin came to see Mr. Villiers. He was curious to know whether Villiers had succeeded in discovering any fresh traces of Mrs. Herbert, either through Clarke or by other sources, and he asked the question soon after he had sat down.

"No," said Villiers, "I wrote to Clarke, but he remains obdurate, and I have tried other channels, but without any result. I can't find out what became of Helen Vaughan after she left Paul Street, but I think she must have gone abroad. But to tell the truth, Austin, I haven't paid much attention to the matter for the last few weeks; I knew poor Herries intimately, and his terrible death has been a great shock to me, a great shock."

"I can well believe it," answered Austin gravely, "you know Argentine was a friend of mine. If I remember rightly, we were speaking of him that day you came to my rooms."

"Yes; it was in connection with that house in Ashley Street, Mrs. Beaumont's house. You said something about Argentine's dining there."

"Quite so. Of course you know it was there Argentine dined the night before—before his death."

"No, I had not heard that."

"Oh, yes; the name was kept out of the papers to spare Mrs. Beaumont. Argentine was a great favourite of hers, and it is said she was in a terrible state for sometime after."

A curious look came over Villiers' face; he seemed undecided whether to speak or not. Austin began again.

"I never experienced such a feeling of horror as when I read the account of Argentine's death. I didn't understand it at the time, and I don't now. I knew him well, and it completely passes my understanding for what possible cause he—or any of the others for the matter of that—could have resolved in cold blood to die in such an awful manner. You know how men babble away each other's characters in London, you may be sure any buried scandal or hidden skeleton would have been brought to light in such a case as this; but nothing of the sort has taken place. As for the theory of mania, that is very well, of course, for the coroner's jury, but everybody knows that it's all nonsense. Suicidal mania is not small-pox."

Austin relapsed into gloomy silence. Villiers sat silent, also, watching his friend. The expression of indecision still fleeted across his face; he seemed as if weighing his thoughts in the balance, and the considerations he was resolving left him still silent. Austin tried to shake off the remembrance of tragedies as hopeless and perplexed as the labyrinth of Daedalus, and began to talk in an indifferent voice of the more pleasant incidents and adventures of the season.

"That Mrs. Beaumont," he said, "of whom we were speaking, is a great success; she has taken London almost by storm. I met her the other night at Fulham's; she is really a remarkable woman."

"You have met Mrs. Beaumont?"

"Yes; she had quite a court around her. She would be called very handsome, I suppose, and yet there is something about her face which I didn't like. The features are exquisite, but the expression is strange. And all the time I was looking at her, and afterwards, when I was going home, I had a curious feeling that very expression was in some way or another familiar to me."

"You must have seen her in the Row."

"No, I am sure I never set eyes on the woman before; it is that which makes it puzzling. And to the best of my belief I have never seen anyone like her; what I felt was a kind of dim far-off memory, vague but persistent. The only sensation I can compare it to, is that odd feeling one sometimes has in a dream, when fantastic cities and wondrous lands and phantom personages appear familiar and accustomed."

Villiers nodded and glanced aimlessly round the room, possibly in search of something on which to turn the conversation. His eyes fell on an old chest somewhat like that in which the artist's strange legacy lay hid beneath a Gothic scutcheon.

"Have you written to the doctor about poor Meyrick?" he asked.

"Yes; I wrote asking for full particulars as to his illness and death. I don't expect to have an answer for another three weeks or a month. I thought I might as well inquire whether Meyrick knew an Englishwoman named Herbert, and if so, whether the doctor could give me any information about her. But it's very possible that Meyrick fell in with her at New York, or Mexico, or San Francisco; I have no idea as to the extent or direction of his travels."

"Yes, and it's very possible that the woman may have more than one name."

"Exactly. I wish I had thought of asking you to lend me the portrait of her which you possess. I might have enclosed it in my letter to Dr. Matthews."

"So you might; that never occurred to me. We might send it now. Hark! what are those boys calling?"

While the two men had been talking together a confused noise of shouting had been gradually growing louder. The noise rose from the eastward and swelled down Piccadilly, drawing nearer and nearer, a very torrent of sound; surging up streets usually quiet, and making every window a frame for a face, curious or excited. The cries and voices came echoing up the silent street where Villiers lived, growing more distinct as they advanced, and, as Villiers spoke, an answer rang up from the pavement:

"The West End Horrors; Another Awful Suicide; Full Details!"

Austin rushed down the stairs and bought a paper and read out the paragraph to Villiers as the uproar in the street rose and fell. The window was open and the air seemed full of noise and terror.

"Another gentleman has fallen a victim to the terrible epidemic of suicide which for the last month has prevailed in the West End. Mr. Sidney Crashaw, of Stoke House, Fulham, and King's Pomeroy, Devon, was found, after a prolonged search, hanging dead from the branch of a tree in his garden at one o'clock today. The deceased gentleman dined last night at the Carlton Club and seemed in his usual health and spirits. He left the club at about ten o'clock, and was seen walking leisurely up St. James's Street a little later. Subsequent to this his movements cannot be traced. On the discovery of the body medical aid was at once summoned, but life had evidently been long extinct. So far as is known, Mr. Crashaw had no trouble or anxiety of any kind. This painful suicide, it will be remembered, is the fifth of the kind in the last month. The authorities at Scotland Yard are unable to suggest any explanation of these terrible occurrences."

Austin put down the paper in mute horror.

"I shall leave London to-morrow," he said, "it is a city of nightmares. How awful this is, Villiers!"

Mr. Villiers was sitting by the window quietly looking out into the street. He had listened to the newspaper report attentively, and the hint of indecision was no longer on his face.

"Wait a moment, Austin," he replied, "I have made up my mind to mention a little matter that occurred last night. It stated, I think, that Crashaw was last seen alive in St. James's Street shortly after ten?"

"Yes, I think so. I will look again. Yes, you are quite right."

"Quite so. Well, I am in a position to contradict that statement at all events. Crashaw was seen after that; considerably later indeed."

"How do you know?"

"Because I happened to see Crashaw myself at about two o'clock this morning."

"You saw Crashaw? You, Villiers?"

"Yes, I saw him quite distinctly; indeed, there were but a few feet between us."

"Where, in Heaven's name, did you see him?"

"Not far from here. I saw him in Ashley Street. He was just leaving a house."

"Did you notice what house it was?"

"Yes. It was Mrs. Beaumont's."

"Villiers! Think what you are saying; there must be some mistake. How could Crashaw be in Mrs. Beaumont's house at two o'clock in the morning? Surely, surely, you must have been dreaming, Villiers; you were always rather fanciful."

"No; I was wide awake enough. Even if I had been dreaming as you say, what I saw would have roused me effectually."

"What you saw? What did you see? Was there anything strange about Crashaw? But I can't believe it; it is impossible."

"Well, if you like I will tell you what I saw, or if you please, what I think I saw, and you can judge for yourself."

"Very good, Villiers."

The noise and clamour of the street had died away, though now and then the sound of shouting still came from the distance, and the dull, leaden silence seemed like the quiet after an earthquake or a storm. Villiers turned from the window and began speaking.

"I was at a house near Regent's Park last night, and when I came away the fancy took me to walk home instead of taking a hansom. It was a clear pleasant night enough, and after a few minutes I had the streets pretty much to myself. It's a curious thing, Austin, to be alone in London at night, the gas-lamps stretching away in perspective, and the dead silence, and then perhaps the rush and clatter of a hansom on the stones, and the fire starting up under the horse's hoofs. I walked along pretty briskly, for I was feeling a little tired of being out in the night, and as the clocks were striking two I turned down Ashley Street, which, you know, is on my way. It was quieter than ever there, and the lamps were fewer; altogether, it looked as dark and gloomy as a forest in winter. I had done about half the length of the street when I heard a door closed very softly, and naturally I looked up to see who was abroad like myself at such an hour. As it happens, there is a street lamp close to the house in question, and I saw a man standing on the step. He had just shut the door and his face was towards me, and I recognized Crashaw directly. I never knew him to speak to, but I had often seen him, and I am positive that I was not mistaken in my man. I looked into his face for a moment, and then—I will confess the truth—I set off at a good run, and kept it up till I was within my own door."

"Why?"

"Why? Because it made my blood run cold to see that man's face. I could never have supposed that such an infernal medley of passions could have glared out of any human eyes; I almost fainted as I looked. I knew I had looked into the eyes of a lost soul, Austin, the man's outward form remained, but all hell was within it. Furious lust, and hate that was like fire, and the loss of all hope and horror that seemed to shriek aloud to the night, though his teeth were shut; and the utter blackness of despair. I am sure that he did not see me; he saw nothing that you or I can see, but what he saw I hope we never shall. I do not know when he died; I suppose in an hour, or perhaps two, but when I passed down Ashley Street and heard the closing door, that man no longer belonged to this world; it was a devil's face I looked upon."

There was an interval of silence in the room when Villiers ceased speaking. The light was failing, and all the tumult of an hour ago was quite hushed. Austin had bent his head at the close of the story, and his hand covered his eyes.

"What can it mean?" he said at length.

"Who knows, Austin, who knows? It's a black business, but I think we had better keep it to ourselves, for the present at any rate. I will see if I cannot learn anything about that house through private channels of information, and if I do light upon anything I will let you know."

VII

THE ENCOUNTER IN SOHO

Three weeks later Austin received a note from Villiers, asking him to call either that afternoon or the next. He chose the nearer date, and found Villiers sitting as usual by the window, apparently lost in meditation on the drowsy traffic of the street. There was a bamboo table by his side, a fantastic thing, enriched with gilding and queer painted scenes, and on it lay a little pile of papers arranged and docketed as neatly as anything in Mr. Clarke's office.

"Well, Villiers, have you made any discoveries in the last three weeks?"

"I think so; I have here one or two memoranda which struck me as singular, and there is a statement to which I shall call your attention."

"And these documents relate to Mrs. Beaumont? It was really Crashaw whom you saw that night standing on the doorstep of the house in Ashley Street?"

"As to that matter my belief remains unchanged, but neither my inquiries nor their results have any special relation to Crashaw. But my investigations have had a strange issue. I have found out who Mrs. Beaumont is!"

"Who is she? In what way do you mean?"

"I mean that you and I know her better under another name."

"What name is that?"

"Herbert."

"Herbert!" Austin repeated the word, dazed with astonishment.

"Yes, Mrs. Herbert of Paul Street, Helen Vaughan of earlier adventures unknown to me. You had reason to recognize the expression of her face; when you go home look at the face in Meyrick's book of horrors, and you will know the sources of your recollection."

"And you have proof of this?"

"Yes, the best of proof; I have seen Mrs. Beaumont, or shall we say Mrs. Herbert?"

"Where did you see her?"

"Hardly in a place where you would expect to see a lady who lives in Ashley Street, Piccadilly. I saw her entering a house in one of the meanest and most disreputable streets in Soho. In fact, I had made an appointment, though not with her, and she was precise to both time and place."

"All this seems very wonderful, but I cannot call it incredible. You must remember, Villiers, that I have seen this woman, in the ordinary adventure of London society, talking and laughing, and sipping her coffee in a commonplace drawing-room with commonplace people. But you know what you are saying."

"I do; I have not allowed myself to be led by surmises or fancies. It was with no thought of finding Helen Vaughan that I searched for Mrs. Beaumont in the dark waters of the life of London, but such has been the issue."

"You must have been in strange places, Villiers."

"Yes, I have been in very strange places. It would have been useless, you know, to go to Ashley Street, and ask Mrs. Beaumont to give me a short sketch of her previous history. No; assuming, as I had to assume, that her record was not of the cleanest, it would be pretty certain that at some previous time she must have moved in circles not quite so refined as her present ones. If you see mud at the top of a stream, you may be sure that it was once at the bottom. I went to the bottom. I have always been fond of diving into Queer Street for my amusement, and I found my knowledge of that locality and its inhabitants very useful. It is, perhaps, needless to say that my friends had never heard the name of Beaumont, and as I had never seen the lady, and was quite unable to describe her, I had to set to work in an indirect way. The people there know me; I have been able to do some of them a service now and again, so they made no difficulty about giving their information; they were aware I had no communication direct or indirect with Scotland Yard. I had to cast out a good many lines, though, before I got what I wanted, and when I landed the fish I did not for a moment suppose it was my fish. But I listened to what I was told out of a constitutional liking for useless information, and I found myself in possession of a very curious story, though, as I imagined, not the story I was looking for. It was to this effect. Some five or six years ago, a woman named Raymond suddenly made her appearance in the neighbourhood to which I am referring. She was described to me as being quite young, probably not more than seventeen or eighteen, very handsome, and looking as if she came from the country. I should be wrong in saying that she found her level in going to this particular quarter, or associating with these people, for from what I was told, I should think the worst den in London far too good for her. The person from whom I got my information, as you may suppose, no great Puritan, shuddered and grew sick in telling me of the nameless infamies which were laid to her charge. After living there for a year, or perhaps a little more, she disappeared as suddenly as she came, and they saw nothing of her till about the time of the Paul Street case. At first she came to her old haunts only occasionally, then more frequently, and finally took up her abode there as before, and remained for six or eight months. It's of no use my going into details as to the life that woman led; if you want particulars you can look at Meyrick's legacy. Those designs were not drawn from his imagination. She again disappeared, and the people of the place saw nothing of her till a few months ago. My informant told me that she had taken some rooms in a house which he pointed out, and these rooms she was in the habit of visiting two or three times a week and always at ten in the morning. I was led to expect that one of these visits would be paid on a certain day about a week ago, and I accordingly managed to be on the look-out in company with my cicerone at a quarter to ten, and the hour and the lady came with equal punctuality. My friend and I were standing under an archway, a little way back from the street, but she saw us, and gave me a glance that I shall be long in forgetting. That look was quite enough for me; I knew Miss Raymond to be Mrs. Herbert; as for Mrs. Beaumont she had quite gone out of my head. She went into the house, and I watched it till four o'clock, when she came out, and then I followed her. It was a long chase, and I had to be very careful to keep a long way in the background, and yet not lose sight of the woman. She took me down to the Strand, and then to Westminster, and then up St. James's Street, and along Piccadilly. I felt queerish when I saw her turn up Ashley Street; the thought that Mrs. Herbert was Mrs. Beaumont came into my mind, but it seemed too impossible to be true. I waited at the corner, keeping my eye on her all the time, and I took particular care to note the house at which she stopped. It was the house with the gay curtains, the home of flowers, the house out of which Crashaw came the night he hanged himself in his garden. I was just going away with my discovery, when I saw an empty carriage come round and draw up in front of the house, and I came to the conclusion that Mrs. Herbert was going out for a drive, and I was right. There, as it happened, I met a man I know, and we stood talking together a little distance from the carriage-way, to which I had my back. We had not been there for ten minutes when my friend took off his hat, and I glanced round and saw the lady I had been following all day. 'Who is that?' I said, and his answer was 'Mrs. Beaumont; lives in

Ashley Street.' Of course there could be no doubt after that. I don't know whether she saw me, but I don't think she did. I went home at once, and, on consideration, I thought that I had a sufficiently good case with which to go to Clarke."

"Why to Clarke?"

"Because I am sure that Clarke is in possession of facts about this woman, facts of which I know nothing."

"Well, what then?"

Mr. Villiers leaned back in his chair and looked reflectively at Austin for a moment before he answered:

"My idea was that Clarke and I should call on Mrs. Beaumont."

"You would never go into such a house as that? No, no, Villiers, you cannot do it. Besides, consider; what result..."

"I will tell you soon. But I was going to say that my information does not end here; it has been completed in an extraordinary manner.

"Look at this neat little packet of manuscript; it is paginated, you see, and I have indulged in the civil coquetry of a ribbon of red tape. It has almost a legal air, hasn't it? Run your eye over it, Austin. It is an account of the entertainment Mrs. Beaumont provided for her choicer guests. The man who wrote this escaped with his life, but I do not think he will live many years. The doctors tell him he must have sustained some severe shock to the nerves."

Austin took the manuscript, but never read it. Opening the neat pages at haphazard his eye was caught by a word and a phrase that followed it; and, sick at heart, with white lips and a cold sweat pouring like water from his temples, he flung the paper down.

"Take it away, Villiers, never speak of this again. Are you made of stone, man? Why, the dread and horror of death itself, the thoughts of the man who stands in the keen morning air on the black platform, bound, the bell tolling in his ears, and waits for the harsh rattle of the bolt, are as nothing compared to this. I will not read it; I should never sleep again."

"Very good. I can fancy what you saw. Yes; it is horrible enough; but after all, it is an old story, an old mystery played in our day, and in dim London streets instead of amidst the vineyards and the olive gardens. We know what happened to those who chanced to meet the Great God Pan, and those who are wise know that all symbols are symbols of something, not of nothing. It was, indeed, an exquisite symbol beneath which men long ago veiled their knowledge of the most awful, most secret forces which lie at the heart of all things; forces before which the souls of men must wither and die and blacken, as their bodies blacken under the electric current. Such forces cannot be named, cannot be spoken, cannot be imagined except under a veil and a symbol, a symbol to the most of us appearing a quaint, poetic fancy, to some a foolish tale. But you and I, at all events, have known something of the terror that may dwell in the secret place of life, manifested under human flesh; that which is without form taking to itself a form. Oh, Austin, how can it be? How is it that the very sunlight does not turn to blackness before this thing, the hard earth melt and boil beneath such a burden?"

Villiers was pacing up and down the room, and the beads of sweat stood out on his forehead. Austin sat silent for a while, but Villiers saw him make a sign upon his breast.

"I say again, Villiers, you will surely never enter such a house as that? You would never pass out alive."

"Yes, Austin, I shall go out alive—I, and Clarke with me."

"What do you mean? You cannot, you would not dare..."

"Wait a moment. The air was very pleasant and fresh this morning; there was a breeze blowing, even through this dull street, and I thought I would take a walk. Piccadilly stretched before me a clear, bright vista, and the sun flashed on the carriages and on the quivering leaves in the park. It was a joyous morning, and men and women looked at the sky and smiled as they went about their work or their pleasure, and the wind blew as blithely as upon the meadows and the scented gorse. But somehow or other I got out of the bustle and the gaiety, and found myself walking slowly along a quiet, dull street, where there seemed to be no sunshine and no air, and where the few foot-passengers loitered as they walked, and hung indecisively about corners and archways. I walked along, hardly knowing where I was going or what I did there, but feeling impelled, as one sometimes is, to explore still further, with a vague idea of reaching some unknown goal. Thus I forged up the street, noting the small traffic of the milk-shop, and wondering at the incongruous medley of penny pipes, black tobacco, sweets, newspapers, and comic songs which here and there jostled one another in the short compass of a single window. I think it was a cold shudder that suddenly passed through me that first told me that I had found what I wanted. I looked up from the pavement and stopped before a dusty shop, above which the lettering had faded, where the red bricks of two hundred years ago had grimed to black; where the windows had gathered to themselves the dust of winters innumerable. I saw what I required; but I think it was five minutes before I had steadied myself and could walk in and ask for it in a cool voice and with a calm face. I think there must even then have been a tremor in my words, for the old man who came out of the back parlour, and fumbled slowly amongst his goods, looked oddly at me as he tied the parcel. I paid what he asked, and stood leaning by the counter, with a strange reluctance to take up my goods and go. I asked about the business, and learnt that trade was bad and the profits cut down sadly; but then the street was not what it was before traffic had been diverted, but that was done forty years ago, 'just before my father died,' he said. I got away at last, and walked along sharply; it was a dismal street indeed, and I was glad to return to the bustle and the noise. Would you like to see my purchase?"

Austin said nothing, but nodded his head slightly; he still looked white and sick. Villiers pulled out a drawer in the bamboo table, and showed Austin a long coil of cord, hard and new; and at one end was a running noose.

"It is the best hempen cord," said Villiers, "just as it used to be made for the old trade, the man told me. Not an inch of jute from end to end."

Austin set his teeth hard, and stared at Villiers, growing whiter as he looked.

"You would not do it," he murmured at last. "You would not have blood on your hands. My God!" he exclaimed, with sudden vehemence, "you cannot mean this, Villiers, that you will make yourself a hangman?"

"No. I shall offer a choice, and leave Helen Vaughan alone with this cord in a locked room for fifteen minutes. If when we go in it is not done, I shall call the nearest policeman. That is all."

"I must go now. I cannot stay here any longer; I cannot bear this. Good-night."

"Good-night, Austin."

The door shut, but in a moment it was open again, and Austin stood, white and ghastly, in the entrance.

"I was forgetting," he said, "that I too have something to tell. I have received a letter from Dr. Harding of Buenos Ayres. He says that he attended Meyrick for three weeks before his death."

"And does he say what carried him off in the prime of life? It was not fever?"

"No, it was not fever. According to the doctor, it was an utter collapse of the whole system, probably caused by some severe shock. But he states that the patient would tell him nothing, and that he was consequently at some disadvantage in treating the case."

"Is there anything more?"

"Yes. Dr. Harding ends his letter by saying: 'I think this is all the information I can give you about your poor friend. He had not been long in Buenos Ayres, and knew scarcely any one, with the exception of a person who did not bear the best of characters, and has since left—a Mrs. Vaughan.'"

VIII
THE FRAGMENTS

[Amongst the papers of the well-known physician, Dr. Robert Matheson, of Ashley Street, Piccadilly, who died suddenly, of apoplectic seizure, at the beginning of 1892, a leaf of manuscript paper was found, covered with pencil jottings. These notes were in Latin, much abbreviated, and had evidently been made in great haste. The MS. was only deciphered with difficulty, and some words have up to the present time evaded all the efforts of the expert employed. The date, "XXV Jul. 1888," is written on the right-hand corner of the MS. The following is a translation of Dr. Matheson's manuscript.]

"Whether science would benefit by these brief notes if they could be published, I do not know, but rather doubt. But certainly I shall never take the responsibility of publishing or divulging one word of what is here written, not only on account of my oath given freely to those two persons who were present, but also because the details are too abominable. It is probably that, upon mature consideration, and after weighting the good and evil, I shall one day destroy this paper, or at least leave it under seal to my friend D., trusting in his discretion, to use it or to burn it, as he may think fit.

"As was befitting, I did all that my knowledge suggested to make sure that I was suffering under no delusion. At first astounded, I could hardly think, but in a minute's time I was sure that my pulse was steady and regular, and that I was in my real and true senses. I then fixed my eyes quietly on what was before me.

"Though horror and revolting nausea rose up within me, and an odour of corruption choked my breath, I remained firm. I was then privileged or accursed, I dare not say which, to see that which was on the bed, lying there black like ink, transformed before my eyes. The skin, and the flesh, and the muscles, and the bones, and the firm structure of the human body that I had thought to be unchangeable, and permanent as adamant, began to melt and dissolve.

"I know that the body may be separated into its elements by external agencies, but I should have refused to believe what I saw. For here there was some internal force, of which I knew nothing, that caused dissolution and change.

"Here too was all the work by which man had been made repeated before my eyes. I saw the form waver from sex to sex, dividing itself from itself, and then again reunited. Then I saw the body descend to the beasts whence it ascended, and that which was on the heights go down to the depths, even to the abyss of all being. The principle of life, which makes organism, always remained, while the outward form changed.

"The light within the room had turned to blackness, not the darkness of night, in which objects are seen dimly, for I could see clearly and without difficulty. But it was the negation of light; objects were presented to my eyes, if I may say so, without any medium, in such a manner that if there had been a prism in the room I should have seen no colours represented in it.

"I watched, and at last I saw nothing but a substance as jelly. Then the ladder was ascended again... [here the MS. is illegible] ...for one instance I saw a Form, shaped in dimness before me, which I will not farther describe. But the symbol of this form may be seen in ancient sculptures, and in paintings which survived beneath the lava, too foul to be spoken of... as a horrible and unspeakable shape, neither man nor beast, was changed into human form, there came finally death.

"I who saw all this, not without great horror and loathing of soul, here write my name, declaring all that I have set on this paper to be true.

"ROBERT MATHESON, Med. Dr."

...Such, Raymond, is the story of what I know and what I have seen. The burden of it was too heavy for me to bear alone, and yet I could tell it to none but you. Villiers, who was with me at the last, knows nothing of that awful secret of the wood, of how what we both saw die, lay upon the smooth, sweet turf amidst the summer flowers, half in sun and half in shadow, and holding the girl Rachel's hand, called and summoned those companions, and shaped in solid form, upon the earth we tread upon, the horror which we can but hint at, which we can only name under a figure. I would not tell Villiers of this, nor of that resemblance, which struck me as with a blow upon my heart, when I saw the portrait, which filled the cup of terror at the end. What this can mean I dare not guess. I know that what I saw perish was not Mary, and yet in the last agony Mary's eyes looked into mine. Whether there can be any one who can show the last link in this chain of awful mystery, I do not know, but if there be any one who can do this, you, Raymond, are the man. And if you know the secret, it rests with you to tell it or not, as you please.

I am writing this letter to you immediately on my getting back to town. I have been in the country for the last few days;

perhaps you may be able to guess in which part. While the horror and wonder of London was at its height—for "Mrs. Beaumont," as I have told you, was well known in society—I wrote to my friend Dr. Phillips, giving some brief outline, or rather hint, of what happened, and asking him to tell me the name of the village where the events he had related to me occurred. He gave me the name, as he said with the less hesitation, because Rachel's father and mother were dead, and the rest of the family had gone to a relative in the State of Washington six months before. The parents, he said, had undoubtedly died of grief and horror caused by the terrible death of their daughter, and by what had gone before that death. On the evening of the day which I received Phillips' letter I was at Caermaen, and standing beneath the mouldering Roman walls, white with the winters of seventeen hundred years, I looked over the meadow where once had stood the older temple of the "God of the Deeps," and saw a house gleaming in the sunlight. It was the house where Helen had lived. I stayed at Caermaen for several days. The people of the place, I found, knew little and had guessed less. Those whom I spoke to on the matter seemed surprised that an antiquarian (as I professed myself to be) should trouble about a village tragedy, of which they gave a very commonplace version, and, as you may imagine, I told nothing of what I knew. Most of my time was spent in the great wood that rises just above the village and climbs the hillside, and goes down to the river in the valley; such another long lovely valley, Raymond, as that on which we looked one summer night, walking to and fro before your house. For many an hour I strayed through the maze of the forest, turning now to right and now to left, pacing slowly down long alleys of undergrowth, shadowy and chill, even under the midday sun, and halting beneath great oaks; lying on the short turf of a clearing where the faint sweet scent of wild roses came to me on the wind and mixed with the heavy perfume of the elder, whose mingled odour is like the odour of the room of the dead, a vapour of incense and corruption. I stood at the edges of the wood, gazing at all the pomp and procession of the foxgloves towering amidst the bracken and shining red in the broad sunshine, and beyond them into deep thickets of close undergrowth where springs boil up from the rock and nourish the water-weeds, dank and evil. But in all my wanderings I avoided one part of the wood; it was not till yesterday that I climbed to the summit of the hill, and stood upon the ancient Roman road that threads the highest ridge of the wood. Here they had walked, Helen and Rachel, along this quiet causeway, upon the pavement of green turf, shut in on either side by high banks of red earth, and tall hedges of shining beech, and here I followed in their steps, looking out, now and again, through partings in the boughs, and seeing on one side the sweep of the wood stretching far to right and left, and sinking into the broad level, and beyond, the yellow sea, and the land over the sea. On the other side was the valley and the river and hill following hill as wave on wave, and wood and meadow, and cornfield, and white houses gleaming, and a great wall of mountain, and far blue peaks in the north. And so at last I came to the place. The track went up a gentle slope, and widened out into an open space with a wall of thick undergrowth around it, and then, narrowing again, passed on into the distance and the faint blue mist of summer heat. And into this pleasant summer glade Rachel passed a girl, and left it, who shall say what? I did not stay long there.

In a small town near Caermaen there is a museum, containing for the most part Roman remains which have been found in the neighbourhood at various times. On the day after my arrival in Caermaen I walked over to the town in question, and took the opportunity of inspecting the museum. After I had seen most of the sculptured stones, the coffins, rings, coins, and fragments of tessellated pavement which the place contains, I was shown a small square pillar of white stone, which had been recently discovered in the wood of which I have been speaking, and, as I found on inquiry, in that open space where the Roman road broadens out. On one side of the pillar was an inscription, of which I took a note. Some of the letters have been defaced, but I do not think there can be any doubt as to those which I supply. The inscription is as follows:

DEVOMNODENTi

FLAvIVSSENILISPOSSVit

PROPTERNVPtias

quaSVIDITSVBVMBra

"To the great god Nodens (the god of the Great Deep or Abyss) Flavius Senilis has erected this pillar on account of the marriage which he saw beneath the shade."

The custodian of the museum informed me that local antiquaries were much puzzled, not by the inscription, or by any difficulty in translating it, but as to the circumstance or rite to which allusion is made.

...And now, my dear Clarke, as to what you tell me about Helen Vaughan, whom you say you saw die under circumstances of the utmost and almost incredible horror. I was interested in your account, but a good deal, nay all, of what you told me I knew already. I can understand the strange likeness you remarked in both the portrait and in the actual face; you have seen Helen's mother. You remember that still summer night so many years ago, when I talked to you of the world beyond the shadows, and of the god Pan. You remember Mary. She was the mother of Helen Vaughan, who was born nine months after that night.

Mary never recovered her reason. She lay, as you saw her, all the while upon her bed, and a few days after the child was born she died. I fancy that just at the last she knew me; I was standing by the bed, and the old look came into her eyes for a second, and then she shuddered and groaned and died. It was an ill work I did that night when you were present; I broke open the door of the house of life, without knowing or caring what might pass forth or enter in. I recollect your telling me at the time, sharply enough, and rightly too, in one sense, that I had ruined the reason of a human being by a foolish experiment, based on an absurd theory. You did well to blame me, but my theory was not all absurdity. What I said Mary would see she saw, but I forgot that no human eyes can look on such a sight with impunity. And I forgot, as I have just said, that when the house of life is thus thrown open, there may enter in that for which we have no name, and human flesh may become the veil of a horror one dare not express. I played with energies which I did not understand, you have seen the ending of it. Helen Vaughan did well to bind the cord about her neck and die, though the death was horrible. The blackened face, the hideous form upon the bed, changing and melting before your eyes from woman to man, from man to beast, and from beast to worse than beast, all the strange horror that you witness, surprises me but little. What you say the doctor whom you sent for saw and shuddered at I noticed long ago; I knew what I had done the moment the child was born, and when it was scarcely five years old I surprised it, not once or twice but several times with a playmate, you may guess of what kind. It was for me a constant, an incarnate horror, and after a few years I felt I could bear it no more, and I sent Helen Vaughan away. You know now what frightened the boy in the wood. The rest of the strange story, and all else that you tell me, as discovered by your friend, I have contrived to learn from time to time, almost to the last chapter. And now Helen is with her companions...

THE END.

The Picture of Dorian Grey

By Oscar Wilde

CHAPTER I

The studio was filled with the rich odor of roses, and when the light summer wind stirred amidst the trees of the garden there came through the open door the heavy scent of the lilac, or the more delicate perfume of the pink-flowering thorn.

From the corner of the divan of Persian saddle-bags on which he was lying, smoking, as usual, innumerable cigarettes, Lord Henry Wotton could just catch the gleam of the honey-sweet and honey-colored blossoms of the laburnum, whose tremulous branches seemed hardly able to bear the burden of a beauty so flame-like as theirs; and now and then the fantastic shadows of birds in flight flitted across the long tussore-silk curtains that were stretched in front of the huge window, producing a kind of momentary Japanese effect, and making him think of those pallid jade-faced painters who, in an art that is necessarily immobile, seek to convey the sense of swiftness and motion. The sullen murmur of the bees shouldering their way through the long unmown grass, or circling with monotonous insistence round the black-crocketed spires of the early June hollyhocks, seemed to make the stillness more oppressive, and the dim roar of London was like the bourdon note of a distant organ.

In the centre of the room, clamped to an upright easel, stood the full-length portrait of a young man of extraordinary personal beauty, and in front of it, some little distance away, was sitting the artist himself, Basil Hallward, whose sudden disappearance some years ago caused, at the time, such public excitement, and gave rise to so many strange conjectures.

As he looked at the gracious and comely form he had so skilfully mirrored in his art, a smile of pleasure passed across his face, and seemed about to linger there. But he suddenly started up, and, closing his eyes, placed his fingers upon the lids, as though he sought to imprison within his brain some curious dream from which he feared he might awake.

"It is your best work, Basil, the best thing you have ever done," said Lord Henry, languidly. "You must certainly send it next year to the Grosvenor. The Academy is too large and too vulgar. The Grosvenor is the only place."

"I don't think I will send it anywhere," he answered, tossing his head back in that odd way that used to make his friends laugh at him at Oxford. "No: I won't send it anywhere."

Lord Henry elevated his eyebrows, and looked at him in amazement through the thin blue wreaths of smoke that curled up in such fanciful whorls from his heavy opium-tainted cigarette. "Not send it anywhere? My dear fellow, why? Have you any reason? What odd chaps you painters are! You do anything in the world to gain a reputation. As soon as you have one, you seem to want to throw it away. It is silly of you, for there is only one thing in the world worse than being talked about, and that is not being talked about. A portrait like this would set you far above all the young men in England, and make the old men quite jealous, if old men are ever capable of any emotion."

"I know you will laugh at me," he replied, "but I really can't exhibit it. I have put too much of myself into it."

Lord Henry stretched his long legs out on the divan and shook with laughter.

"Yes, I knew you would laugh; but it is quite true, all the same."

"Too much of yourself in it! Upon my word, Basil, I didn't know you were so vain; and I really can't see any resemblance between you, with your rugged strong face and your coal-black hair, and this young Adonis, who looks as if he was made of ivory and rose-leaves. Why, my dear Basil, he is a Narcissus, and you--well, of course you have an intellectual expression, and all that. But beauty, real beauty, ends where an intellectual expression begins. Intellect is in itself an exaggeration, and destroys the harmony of any face. The moment one sits down to think, one becomes all nose, or all forehead, or something horrid. Look at the successful men in any of the learned professions. How perfectly hideous they are! Except, of course, in the Church. But then in the Church they don't think. A bishop keeps on saying at the age of eighty what he was told to say when he was a boy of eighteen, and consequently he always looks absolutely delightful. Your mysterious young friend, whose name you have never told me, but whose picture really fascinates me, never thinks. I feel quite sure of that. He is a brainless, beautiful thing, who should be always here in winter when we have no flowers to look at, and always here in summer when we want something to chill our intelligence. Don't flatter yourself, Basil: you are not in the least like him."

"You don't understand me, Harry. Of course I am not like him. I know that perfectly well. Indeed, I should be sorry to look like him. You shrug your shoulders? I am telling you the truth. There is a fatality about all physical and intellectual distinction, the sort of fatality that seems to dog through history the faltering steps of kings. It is better not to be different from one's fellows. The ugly and the stupid have the best of it in this world. They can sit quietly and gape at the play. If they know nothing of victory, they are at least spared the knowledge of defeat. They live as we all should live, undisturbed, indifferent, and without disquiet. They neither bring ruin upon others nor ever receive it from alien hands. Your rank and wealth, Harry; my brains, such as they are,--my fame, whatever it may be worth; Dorian Gray's good looks,--we will all suffer for what the gods have given us, suffer terribly."

"Dorian Gray? is that his name?" said Lord Henry, walking across the studio towards Basil Hallward.

"Yes; that is his name. I didn't intend to tell it to you."

"But why not?"

"Oh, I can't explain. When I like people immensely I never tell their names to any one. It seems like surrendering a part of them. You know how I love secrecy. It is the only thing that can make modern life wonderful or mysterious to us. The commonest thing is delightful if one only hides it. When I leave town I never tell my people where I am going. If I did, I would lose all my pleasure. It is a silly habit, I dare say, but somehow it seems to bring a great deal of romance into one's life. I suppose you think me awfully foolish about it?"

"Not at all," answered Lord Henry, laying his hand upon his shoulder; "not at all, my dear Basil. You seem to forget that I am married, and the one charm of marriage is that it makes a life of deception necessary for both parties. I never know where my wife is, and my wife never knows what I am doing. When we meet,--we do meet occasionally, when we dine out together, or go down to the duke's,--we tell each other the most absurd stories with the most serious faces. My wife is very good at it,--much better, in fact, than I am. She never gets confused over her dates, and I always do. But when she does find me out, she makes no row at all. I sometimes wish she would; but she merely laughs at me."

"I hate the way you talk about your married life, Harry," said Basil Hallward, shaking his hand off, and strolling towards the door that led into the garden. "I believe that you are really a very good husband, but that you are thoroughly ashamed of your own virtues. You are an extraordinary fellow. You never say a moral thing, and you never do a wrong thing. Your cynicism is simply a pose."

"Being natural is simply a pose, and the most irritating pose I know," cried Lord Henry, laughing; and the two young men went out into the garden together, and for a time they did not speak.

After a long pause Lord Henry pulled out his watch. "I am afraid I must be going, Basil," he murmured, "and before I go I insist on your answering a question I put to you some time ago."

"What is that?" asked Basil Hallward, keeping his eyes fixed on the ground.

"You know quite well."

"I do not, Harry."

"Well, I will tell you what it is."

"Please don't."

"I must. I want you to explain to me why you won't exhibit Dorian Gray's picture. I want the real reason."

"I told you the real reason."

"No, you did not. You said it was because there was too much of yourself in it. Now, that is childish."

"Harry," said Basil Hallward, looking him straight in the face, "every portrait that is painted with feeling is a portrait of the artist, not of the sitter. The sitter is merely the accident, the occasion. It is not he who is revealed by the painter; it is rather the painter who, on the colored canvas, reveals himself. The reason I will not exhibit this picture is that I am afraid that I have shown with it the secret of my own soul."

Lord Harry laughed. "And what is that?" he asked.

"I will tell you," said Hallward; and an expression of perplexity came over his face.

"I am all expectation, Basil," murmured his companion, looking at him.

"Oh, there is really very little to tell, Harry," answered the young painter; "and I am afraid you will hardly understand it. Perhaps you will hardly believe it."

Lord Henry smiled, and, leaning down, plucked a pink-petalled daisy from the grass, and examined it. "I am quite sure I shall understand it," he replied, gazing intently at the little golden white-feathered disk, "and I can believe anything, provided that it is incredible."

The wind shook some blossoms from the trees, and the heavy lilac blooms, with their clustering stars, moved to and fro in the languid air. A grasshopper began to chirrup in the grass, and a long thin dragon-fly floated by on its brown gauze wings. Lord Henry felt as if he could hear Basil Hallward's heart beating, and he wondered what was coming.

"Well, this is incredible," repeated Hallward, rather bitterly,--"incredible to me at times. I don't know what it means. The story is simply this. Two months ago I went to a crush at Lady Brandon's. You know we poor painters have to show ourselves in society from time to time, just to remind the public that we are not savages. With an evening coat and a white tie, as you told me once, anybody, even a stock-broker, can gain a reputation for being civilized. Well, after I had been in the room about ten minutes, talking to huge overdressed dowagers and tedious Academicians, I suddenly became conscious that some one was looking at me. I turned half-way round, and saw Dorian Gray for the first time. When our eyes met, I felt that I was growing pale. A curious instinct of terror came over me. I knew that I had come face to face with some one whose mere personality was so fascinating that, if I allowed it to do so, it would absorb my whole nature, my whole soul, my very art itself. I did not want any external influence in my life. You know yourself, Harry, how independent I am by nature. My father destined me for the army. I insisted on going to Oxford. Then he made me enter my name at the Middle Temple. Before I had eaten half a dozen dinners I gave up the Bar, and announced my intention of becoming a painter. I have always been my own master; had at least always been so, till I met Dorian Gray. Then--But I don't know how to explain it to you. Something seemed to tell me that I was on the verge of a terrible crisis in my life. I had a strange feeling that Fate had in store for me exquisite joys and exquisite sorrows. I knew that if I spoke to Dorian I would become absolutely devoted to him, and that I ought not to speak to him. I grew afraid, and turned to quit the room. It was not conscience that made me do so: it was cowardice. I take no credit to myself for trying to escape."

"Conscience and cowardice are really the same things, Basil. Conscience is the trade-name of the firm. That is all."

"I don't believe that, Harry. However, whatever was my motive,--and it may have been pride, for I used to be very proud,--I certainly struggled to the door. There, of course, I stumbled against Lady Brandon. 'You are not going to run away so soon, Mr. Hallward?' she screamed out. You know her shrill horrid voice?"

"Yes; she is a peacock in everything but beauty," said Lord Henry, pulling the daisy to bits with his long, nervous fingers.

"I could not get rid of her. She brought me up to Royalties, and people with Stars and Garters, and elderly ladies with gigantic tiaras and hooked noses. She spoke of me as her dearest friend. I had only met her once before, but she took it into her head to lionize me. I believe some picture of mine had made a great success at the time, at least had been chattered about in the penny newspapers, which is the nineteenth-century standard of immortality. Suddenly I found myself face to face with the young man whose personality had so strangely stirred me. We were quite close, almost touching. Our eyes met again. It was mad of me, but I asked Lady Brandon to introduce me to him. Perhaps it was not so mad, after all. It was simply inevitable. We would have spoken to each other without any introduction. I am sure of that. Dorian told me so afterwards. He, too, felt that we were destined to know each other."

"And how did Lady Brandon describe this wonderful young man? I know she goes in for giving a rapid précis of all her guests. I remember her bringing me up to a most truculent and red-faced old gentleman covered all over with orders and ribbons, and hissing into my ear, in a tragic whisper which must have been perfectly audible to everybody in the room, something like 'Sir Humpty Dumpty--you know--Afghan frontier--Russian intrigues: very successful man--wife killed by an elephant--quite inconsolable--wants to marry a beautiful American widow--everybody does nowadays--hates Mr. Gladstone--but very much interested in beetles: ask him what he thinks of Schouvaloff.' I simply fled. I like to find out people for myself. But poor Lady Brandon treats her guests exactly as an auctioneer treats his goods. She either explains them entirely away, or tells one everything about them except what one wants to know. But what did she say about Mr. Dorian Gray?"

"Oh, she murmured, 'Charming boy--poor dear mother and I quite inseparable--engaged to be married to the same man--I mean married on the same day--how very silly of me! Quite forget what he does--afraid he--doesn't do anything--oh, yes, plays the piano--or is it the violin, dear Mr. Gray?' We could neither of us help laughing, and we became friends at once."

"Laughter is not a bad beginning for a friendship, and it is the best ending for one," said Lord Henry, plucking another daisy.

Hallward buried his face in his hands. "You don't understand what friendship is, Harry," he murmured,--"or what enmity is, for that matter. You like every one; that is to say, you are indifferent to every one."

"How horribly unjust of you!" cried Lord Henry, tilting his hat back, and looking up at the little clouds that were drifting across the hollowed turquoise of the summer sky, like ravelled skeins of glossy white silk. "Yes; horribly unjust of you. I make a great difference between people. I choose my friends for their good looks, my acquaintances for their characters, and my enemies for their brains. A man can't be too careful in the choice of his enemies. I have not got one who is a fool. They are all men of some intellectual power, and consequently they all appreciate me. Is that very vain of me? I think it is rather vain."

"I should think it was, Harry. But according to your category I must be merely an acquaintance."

"My dear old Basil, you are much more than an acquaintance."

"And much less than a friend. A sort of brother, I suppose?"

"Oh, brothers! I don't care for brothers. My elder brother won't die, and my younger brothers seem never to do anything else."

"Harry!"

"My dear fellow, I am not quite serious. But I can't help detesting my relations. I suppose it comes from the fact that we can't stand other people having the same faults as ourselves. I quite sympathize with the rage of the English democracy against what they call the vices of the upper classes. They feel that drunkenness, stupidity, and immorality should be their own special property, and that if any one of us makes an ass of himself he is poaching on their preserves. When poor Southwark got into the Divorce Court, their indignation was quite magnificent. And yet I don't suppose that ten per cent of the lower orders live correctly."

"I don't agree with a single word that you have said, and, what is more, Harry, I don't believe you do either."

Lord Henry stroked his pointed brown beard, and tapped the toe of his patent-leather boot with a tasselled malacca cane. "How English you are, Basil! If one puts forward an idea to a real Englishman,--always a rash thing to do,--he never dreams of considering whether the idea is right or wrong. The only thing he considers of any importance is whether one believes it one's self. Now, the value of an idea has nothing whatsoever to do with the sincerity of the man who expresses it. Indeed, the probabilities are that the more insincere the man is, the more purely intellectual will the idea be, as in that case it will not be colored by either his wants, his desires, or his prejudices. However, I don't propose to discuss politics, sociology, or metaphysics with you. I like persons better than principles. Tell me more about Dorian Gray. How often do you see him?"

"Every day. I couldn't be happy if I didn't see him every day. Of course sometimes it is only for a few minutes. But a few minutes with somebody one worships mean a great deal."

"But you don't really worship him?"

"I do."

"How extraordinary! I thought you would never care for anything but your painting,--your art, I should say. Art sounds better, doesn't it?"

"He is all my art to me now. I sometimes think, Harry, that there are only two eras of any importance in the history of the world. The first is the appearance of a new medium for art, and the second is the appearance of a new personality for art also. What the invention of oil-painting was to the Venetians, the face of Antinoüs was to late Greek sculpture, and the face of Dorian Gray will some day be to me. It is not merely that I paint from him, draw from him, model from him. Of course I have done all that. He has stood as Paris in dainty armor, and as Adonis with huntsman's cloak and polished boar-spear. Crowned with heavy lotus-blossoms, he has sat on the prow of Adrian's barge, looking into the green, turbid Nile. He has leaned over the still pool of some Greek woodland, and seen in the water's silent silver the wonder of his own beauty. But he is much more to me than that. I won't tell you that I am dissatisfied with what I have done of him, or that his beauty is such that art cannot express it. There is nothing that art cannot express, and I know that the work I have done since I met Dorian Gray is good work, is the best work of my life. But in some curious way--I wonder will you understand me?--his personality has suggested to me an entirely new manner in art, an entirely new mode of style. I see things differently, I think of them differently. I can now re-create life in a way that was hidden from me before. 'A dream of form in days of thought,'--who is it who says that? I forget; but it is what Dorian Gray has been to me. The merely visible presence of this lad,--for he seems to me little more than a lad, though he is really over twenty,--his merely visible presence,--ah! I wonder can you realize all that that means? Unconsciously he defines for me the lines of a fresh school, a school that is to have in itself all the passion of the romantic spirit, all the perfection of the spirit that is Greek. The harmony of soul and body,--how much that is! We in our madness have separated the two, and have invented a realism that is bestial, an ideality that is void. Harry! Harry! if you only knew what Dorian Gray is to me! You remember that landscape of mine, for which Agnew offered me such a huge price, but which I would not part with? It is one of the best things I have ever done. And why is it so? Because, while I was painting it, Dorian Gray sat beside me."

"Basil, this is quite wonderful! I must see Dorian Gray." Hallward got up from the seat, and walked up and down the garden. After some time he came back. "You don't understand, Harry," he said. "Dorian Gray is merely to me a motive in art. He is never more present in my work than when no image of him is there. He is simply a suggestion, as I have said, of a new manner. I see him in the curves of certain lines, in the loveliness and the subtleties of certain colors. That is all."

"Then why won't you exhibit his portrait?"

"Because I have put into it all the extraordinary romance of which, of course, I have never dared to speak to him. He knows nothing about it. He will never know anything about it. But the world might guess it; and I will not bare my soul to their shallow, prying eyes. My heart shall never be put under their microscope. There is too much of myself in the thing, Harry,--too much of myself!"

"Poets are not so scrupulous as you are. They know how useful passion is for publication. Nowadays a broken heart will run to many editions."

"I hate them for it. An artist should create beautiful things, but should put nothing of his own life into them. We live in an age when men treat art as if it were meant to be a form of autobiography. We have lost the abstract sense of beauty. If I live, I will show the world what it is; and for that reason the world shall never see my portrait of Dorian Gray."

"I think you are wrong, Basil, but I won't argue with you. It is only the intellectually lost who ever argue. Tell me, is Dorian Gray very fond of you?"

Hallward considered for a few moments. "He likes me," he answered, after a pause; "I know he likes me. Of course I flatter him dreadfully. I find a strange pleasure in saying things to him that I know I shall be sorry for having said. I give myself away. As a rule, he is charming to me, and we walk home together from the club arm in arm, or sit in the studio and talk of a thousand things. Now and then, however, he is horribly thoughtless, and seems to take a real delight in giving me pain. Then I feel, Harry, that I have given away my whole soul to some one who treats it as if it were a flower to put in his coat, a bit of decoration to charm his vanity, an ornament for a summer's day."

"Days in summer, Basil, are apt to linger. Perhaps you will tire sooner than he will. It is a sad thing to think of, but there is no doubt that Genius lasts longer than Beauty. That accounts for the fact that we all take such pains to over-educate ourselves. In the wild struggle for existence, we want to have something that endures, and so we fill our minds with rubbish and facts, in the silly hope of keeping our place. The thoroughly well informed man,--that is the modern ideal. And the mind of the thoroughly well informed man is a dreadful thing. It is like a bric-à-brac shop, all monsters and dust, and everything priced above its proper value. I think you will tire first, all the same. Some day you will look at Gray, and he will seem to you to be a little out of drawing, or you won't like his tone of color, or something. You will bitterly reproach him in your own heart, and seriously think that he has behaved very badly to you. The next time he calls, you will be perfectly cold and indifferent. It will be a great pity, for it will alter you. The worst of having a romance is that it leaves one so unromantic."

"Harry, don't talk like that. As long as I live, the personality of Dorian Gray will dominate me. You can't feel what I feel. You change too often."

"Ah, my dear Basil, that is exactly why I can feel it. Those who are faithful know only the pleasures of love: it is the faithless who know love's tragedies." And Lord Henry struck a light on a dainty silver case, and began to smoke a cigarette with a self-conscious and self-satisfied air, as if he had summed up life in a phrase. There was a rustle of chirruping sparrows in the ivy, and the blue cloud-shadows chased themselves across the grass like swallows. How pleasant it was in the garden! And how delightful other people's emotions were!--much more delightful than their ideas, it seemed to him. One's own soul, and the passions of one's friends,--those were the fascinating things in life. He thought with pleasure of the tedious luncheon that he had missed by staying so long with Basil Hallward. Had he gone to his aunt's, he would have been sure to meet Lord Goodbody there, and the whole conversation would have been about the housing of the poor, and the necessity for model lodging-houses. It was charming to have escaped all that! As he thought of his aunt, an idea seemed to strike him. He turned to Hallward, and said, "My dear fellow, I have just remembered."

"Remembered what, Harry?"

"Where I heard the name of Dorian Gray."

"Where was it?" asked Hallward, with a slight frown.

"Don't look so angry, Basil. It was at my aunt's, Lady Agatha's. She told me she had discovered a wonderful young man, who was going to help her in the East End, and that his name was Dorian Gray. I am bound to state that she never told me he was good-looking. Women have no appreciation of good looks. At least, good women have not. She said that he was very earnest, and had a beautiful nature. I at once pictured to myself a creature with spectacles and lank hair, horridly freckled, and tramping about on huge feet. I wish I had known it was your friend."

"I am very glad you didn't, Harry."

"Why?"

"I don't want you to meet him."

"Mr. Dorian Gray is in the studio, sir," said the butler, coming into the garden.

"You must introduce me now," cried Lord Henry, laughing.

Basil Hallward turned to the servant, who stood blinking in the sunlight. "Ask Mr. Gray to wait, Parker: I will be in in a few moments." The man bowed, and went up the walk.

Then he looked at Lord Henry. "Dorian Gray is my dearest friend," he said. "He has a simple and a beautiful nature. Your aunt was quite right in what she said of him. Don't spoil him for me. Don't try to influence him. Your influence would be bad. The world is wide, and has many marvellous people in it. Don't take away from me the one person that makes life absolutely lovely to me, and that gives to my art whatever wonder or charm it possesses. Mind, Harry, I trust you." He spoke very slowly, and the words seemed wrung out of him almost against his will.

"What nonsense you talk!" said Lord Henry, smiling, and, taking Hallward by the arm, he almost led him into the house.

CHAPTER II

As they entered they saw Dorian Gray. He was seated at the piano, with his back to them, turning over the pages of a volume of Schumann's "Forest Scenes." "You must lend me these, Basil," he cried. "I want to learn them. They are perfectly charming."

"That entirely depends on how you sit to-day, Dorian."

"Oh, I am tired of sitting, and I don't want a life-sized portrait of myself," answered the lad, swinging round on the music-stool, in a wilful, petulant manner. When he caught sight of Lord Henry, a faint blush colored his cheeks for a moment, and he started up. "I beg your pardon, Basil, but I didn't know you had any one with you."

"This is Lord Henry Wotton, Dorian, an old Oxford friend of mine. I have just been telling him what a capital sitter you were, and now you have spoiled everything."

"You have not spoiled my pleasure in meeting you, Mr. Gray," said Lord Henry, stepping forward and shaking him by the hand. "My aunt has often spoken to me about you. You are one of her favorites, and, I am afraid, one of her victims also."

"I am in Lady Agatha's black books at present," answered Dorian, with a funny look of penitence. "I promised to go to her club in Whitechapel with her last Tuesday, and I really forgot all about it. We were to have played a duet together,--three duets, I believe. I don't know what she will say to me. I am far too frightened to call."

"Oh, I will make your peace with my aunt. She is quite devoted to you. And I don't think it really matters about your not being there. The audience probably thought it was a duet. When Aunt Agatha sits down to the piano she makes quite enough noise for two people."

"That is very horrid to her, and not very nice to me," answered Dorian, laughing.

Lord Henry looked at him. Yes, he was certainly wonderfully handsome, with his finely-curved scarlet lips, his frank blue eyes, his crisp gold hair. There was something in his face that made one trust him at once. All the candor of youth was there, as well as all youth's passionate purity. One felt that he had kept himself unspotted from the world. No wonder Basil Hallward worshipped him. He was made to be worshipped.

"You are too charming to go in for philanthropy, Mr. Gray,--far too charming." And Lord Henry flung himself down on the divan, and opened his cigarette-case.

Hallward had been busy mixing his colors and getting his brushes ready. He was looking worried, and when he heard Lord Henry's last remark he glanced at him, hesitated for a moment, and then said, "Harry, I want to finish this picture to-day. Would you think it awfully rude of me if I asked you to go away?"

Lord Henry smiled, and looked at Dorian Gray. "Am I to go, Mr. Gray?" he asked.

"Oh, please don't, Lord Henry. I see that Basil is in one of his sulky moods; and I can't bear him when he sulks. Besides, I want you to tell me why I should not go in for philanthropy."

"I don't know that I shall tell you that, Mr. Gray. But I certainly will not run away, now that you have asked me to stop. You don't really mind, Basil, do you? You have often told me that you liked your sitters to have some one to chat to."

Hallward bit his lip. "If Dorian wishes it, of course you must stay. Dorian's whims are laws to everybody, except himself."

Lord Henry took up his hat and gloves. "You are very pressing, Basil, but I am afraid I must go. I have promised to meet a man at the Orleans.--Good-by, Mr. Gray. Come and see me some afternoon in Curzon Street. I am nearly always at home at five o'clock. Write to me when you are coming. I should be sorry to miss you."

"Basil," cried Dorian Gray, "if Lord Henry goes I shall go too. You never open your lips while you are painting, and it is horribly dull standing on a platform and trying to look pleasant. Ask him to stay. I insist upon it."

"Stay, Harry, to oblige Dorian, and to oblige me," said Hallward, gazing intently at his picture. "It is quite true, I never talk when I am working, and never listen either, and it must be dreadfully tedious for my unfortunate sitters. I beg you to stay."

"But what about my man at the Orleans?"

Hallward laughed. "I don't think there will be any difficulty about that. Sit down again, Harry.--And now, Dorian, get up on the platform, and don't move about too much, or pay any attention to what Lord Henry says. He has a very bad influence over all his friends, with the exception of myself."

Dorian stepped up on the dais, with the air of a young Greek martyr, and made a little moue of discontent to Lord Henry, to whom he had rather taken a fancy. He was so unlike Hallward. They made a delightful contrast. And he had such a beautiful voice. After a few moments he said to him, "Have you really a very bad influence, Lord Henry? As bad as Basil says?"

"There is no such thing as a good influence, Mr. Gray. All influence is immoral,--immoral from the scientific point of view."

"Why?"

"Because to influence a person is to give him one's own soul. He does not think his natural thoughts, or burn with his natural passions. His virtues are not real to him. His sins, if there are such things as sins, are borrowed. He becomes an echo of some one else's music, an actor of a part that has not been written for him. The aim of life is self-development. To realize one's nature perfectly,--that is what each of us is here for. People are afraid of themselves, nowadays. They have forgotten the highest of all duties, the duty that one owes to one's self. Of course they are charitable. They feed the hungry, and clothe the beggar. But their own souls starve, and are naked. Courage has gone out of our race. Perhaps we never really had it. The terror of society, which is the basis of morals, the terror of God, which is the secret of religion,--these are the two things that govern us. And yet--"

"Just turn your head a little more to the right, Dorian, like a good boy," said Hallward, deep in his work, and conscious only that a look had come into the lad's face that he had never seen there before.

"And yet," continued Lord Henry, in his low, musical voice, and with that graceful wave of the hand that was always so characteristic of him, and that he had even in his Eton days, "I believe that if one man were to live his life out fully and completely, were to give form to every feeling, expression to every thought, reality to every dream,--I believe that the world would gain such a fresh impulse of joy that we would forget all the maladies of mediaevalism, and return to the Hellenic ideal,--to something finer, richer, than the Hellenic ideal, it may be. But the bravest man among us is afraid of himself. The mutilation of the savage has its tragic survival in the self-denial that mars our lives. We are punished for our refusals. Every impulse that we strive to strangle broods in the mind, and poisons us. The body sins once, and has done with its sin, for action is a mode of purification. Nothing remains then but the recollection of a pleasure, or the luxury of a regret. The only way to get rid of a temptation is to yield to it. Resist it, and your soul grows sick with longing for the things it has forbidden to itself, with desire for what its monstrous laws have made monstrous and unlawful. It has been said that the great events of the world take place in the brain. It is in the brain, and the brain only, that the great sins of the world take place also. You, Mr. Gray, you yourself, with your rose-red youth and your rose-white boyhood, you have had passions that have made you afraid, thoughts that have filled you with terror, day-dreams and sleeping dreams whose mere memory might stain your cheek with shame--"

"Stop!" murmured Dorian Gray, "stop! you bewilder me. I don't know what to say. There is some answer to you, but I cannot find it. Don't speak. Let me think, or, rather, let me try not to think."

For nearly ten minutes he stood there motionless, with parted lips, and eyes strangely bright. He was dimly conscious that entirely fresh impulses were at work within him, and they seemed to him to have come really from himself. The few words that Basil's friend had said to him--words spoken by chance, no doubt, and with wilful paradox in them--had yet touched some secret chord, that had never been touched before, but that he felt was now vibrating and throbbing to curious pulses.

Music had stirred him like that. Music had troubled him many times. But music was not articulate. It was not a new world, but rather a new chaos, that it created in us. Words! Mere words! How terrible they were! How clear, and vivid, and cruel! One could not escape from them. And yet what a subtle magic there was in them! They seemed to be able to give a plastic form to formless things, and to have a music of their own as sweet as that of viol or of lute. Mere words! Was there anything so real as words?

Yes; there had been things in his boyhood that he had not understood. He understood them now. Life suddenly became fiery-colored to him. It seemed to him that he had been walking in fire. Why had he not known it?

Lord Henry watched him, with his sad smile. He knew the precise psychological moment when to say nothing. He felt intensely interested. He was amazed at the sudden impression that his words had produced, and, remembering a book that he had read when he was sixteen, which had revealed to him much that he had not known before, he wondered whether Dorian Gray was passing through the same experience. He had merely shot an arrow into the air. Had it hit the mark? How fascinating the lad was!

Hallward painted away with that marvellous bold touch of his, that had the true refinement and perfect delicacy that come only from strength. He was unconscious of the silence.

"Basil, I am tired of standing," cried Dorian Gray, suddenly. "I must go out and sit in the garden. The air is stifling here."

"My dear fellow, I am so sorry. When I am painting, I can't think of anything else. But you never sat better. You were perfectly still. And I have caught the effect I wanted,--the half-parted lips, and the bright look in the eyes. I don't know what Harry has been saying to you, but he has certainly made you have the most wonderful expression. I suppose he has been paying you compliments. You mustn't believe a word that he says."

"He has certainly not been paying me compliments. Perhaps that is the reason I don't think I believe anything he has told me."

"You know you believe it all," said Lord Henry, looking at him with his dreamy, heavy-lidded eyes. "I will go out to the garden with you. It is horridly hot in the studio.--Basil, let us have something iced to drink, something with strawberries in it."

"Certainly, Harry. Just touch the bell, and when Parker comes I will tell him what you want. I have got to work up this background, so I will join you later on. Don't keep Dorian too long. I have never been in better form for painting than I am to-day. This is going to be my masterpiece. It is my masterpiece as it stands."

Lord Henry went out to the garden, and found Dorian Gray burying his face in the great cool lilac-blossoms, feverishly drinking in their perfume as if it had been wine. He came close to him, and put his hand upon his shoulder. "You are quite right to do that," he murmured. "Nothing can cure the soul but the senses, just as nothing can cure the senses but the soul."

The lad started and drew back. He was bareheaded, and the leaves had tossed his rebellious curls and tangled all their gilded threads. There was a look of fear in his eyes, such as people have when they are suddenly awakened. His finely-chiselled nostrils quivered, and some hidden nerve shook the scarlet of his lips and left them trembling.

"Yes," continued Lord Henry, "that is one of the great secrets of life,--to cure the soul by means of the senses, and the senses by means of the soul. You are a wonderful creature. You know more than you think you know, just as you know less than you want to know."

Dorian Gray frowned and turned his head away. He could not help liking the tall, graceful young man who was standing by him. His romantic olive-colored face and worn expression interested him. There was something in his low, languid voice that was absolutely fascinating. His cool, white, flower-like hands, even, had a curious charm. They moved, as he spoke, like music, and seemed to have a language of their own. But he felt afraid of him, and ashamed of being afraid. Why had it been left for a stranger to reveal him to himself? He had known Basil Hallward for months, but the friendship between then had never altered him. Suddenly there had come some one across his life who seemed to have disclosed to him life's mystery. And, yet, what was there to be afraid of? He was not a school-boy, or a girl. It was absurd to be frightened.

"Let us go and sit in the shade," said Lord Henry. "Parker has brought out the drinks, and if you stay any longer in this glare you will be quite spoiled, and Basil will never paint you again. You really must not let yourself become sunburnt. It would be very unbecoming to you."

"What does it matter?" cried Dorian, laughing, as he sat down on the seat at the end of the garden.

"It should matter everything to you, Mr. Gray."

"Why?"

"Because you have now the most marvellous youth, and youth is the one thing worth having."

"I don't feel that, Lord Henry."

"No, you don't feel it now. Some day, when you are old and wrinkled and ugly, when thought has seared your forehead with its lines, and passion branded your lips with its hideous fires, you will feel it, you will feel it terribly. Now, wherever you go, you charm the world. Will it always be so?

"You have a wonderfully beautiful face, Mr. Gray. Don't frown. You have. And Beauty is a form of Genius,--is higher, indeed, than Genius, as it needs no explanation. It is one of the great facts of the world, like sunlight, or spring-time, or the reflection in dark waters of that silver shell we call the moon. It cannot be questioned. It has its divine right of sovereignty. It makes princes of those who have it. You smile? Ah! when you have lost it you won't smile.

"People say sometimes that Beauty is only superficial. That may be so. But at least it is not so superficial as Thought. To me, Beauty is the wonder of wonders. It is only shallow people who do not judge by appearances. The true mystery of the world is the visible, not the invisible.

"Yes, Mr. Gray, the gods have been good to you. But what the gods give they quickly take away. You have only a few years in which really to live. When your youth goes, your beauty will go with it, and then you will suddenly discover that there are no triumphs left for you, or have to content yourself with those mean triumphs that the memory of your past will make more bitter than defeats. Every month as it wanes brings you nearer to something dreadful. Time is jealous of you, and wars against your lilies and your roses. You will become sallow, and hollow-cheeked, and dull-eyed. You will suffer horribly.

"Realize your youth while you have it. Don't squander the gold of your days, listening to the tedious, trying to improve the hopeless failure, or giving away your life to the ignorant, the common, and the vulgar, which are the aims, the false ideals, of our age. Live! Live the wonderful life that is in you! Let nothing be lost upon you. Be always searching for new sensations. Be afraid of nothing.

"A new hedonism,--that is what our century wants. You might be its visible symbol. With your personality there is nothing you could not do. The world belongs to you for a season.

"The moment I met you I saw that you were quite unconscious of what you really are, what you really might be. There was so much about you that charmed me that I felt I must tell you something about yourself. I thought how tragic it would be if you were wasted. For there is such a little time that your youth will last,--such a little time.

"The common hill-flowers wither, but they blossom again. The laburnum will be as golden next June as it is now. In a month there will be purple stars on the clematis, and year after year the green night of its leaves will have its purple stars. But we never get back our youth. The pulse of joy that beats in us at twenty, becomes sluggish. Our limbs fail, our senses rot. We degenerate into hideous puppets, haunted by the memory of the passions of which we were too much afraid, and the exquisite temptations that we did not dare to yield to. Youth! Youth! There is absolutely nothing in the world but youth!"

Dorian Gray listened, open-eyed and wondering. The spray of lilac fell from his hand upon the gravel. A furry bee came and buzzed round it for a moment. Then it began to scramble all over the fretted purple of the tiny blossoms. He watched it with that strange interest in trivial things that we try to develop when things of high import make us afraid, or when we are stirred by some new emotion, for which we cannot find expression, or when some thought that terrifies us lays sudden siege to the brain and calls on us to yield. After a time it flew away. He saw it creeping into the stained trumpet of a Tyrian convolvulus. The flower seemed to quiver, and then swayed gently to and fro.

Suddenly Hallward appeared at the door of the studio, and made frantic signs for them to come in. They turned to each other, and smiled.

"I am waiting," cried Hallward. "Do come in. The light is quite perfect, and you can bring your drinks."

They rose up, and sauntered down the walk together. Two green-and-white butterflies fluttered past them, and in the pear-tree at the end of the garden a thrush began to sing.

"You are glad you have met me, Mr. Gray," said Lord Henry, looking at him.

"Yes, I am glad now. I wonder shall I always be glad?"

"Always! That is a dreadful word. It makes me shudder when I hear it. Women are so fond of using it. They spoil every romance by trying to make it last forever. It is a meaningless word, too. The only difference between a caprice and a life-long passion is that the caprice lasts a little longer."

As they entered the studio, Dorian Gray put his hand upon Lord Henry's arm. "In that case, let our friendship be a caprice," he murmured, flushing at his own boldness, then stepped upon the platform and resumed his pose.

Lord Henry flung himself into a large wicker arm-chair, and watched him. The sweep and dash of the brush on the canvas made the only sound that broke the stillness, except when Hallward stepped back now and then to look at his work from a distance. In the slanting beams that streamed through the open door-way the dust danced and was golden. The heavy scent of the roses seemed to brood over everything.

After about a quarter of an hour, Hallward stopped painting, looked for a long time at Dorian Gray, and then for a long time at the picture, biting the end of one of his huge brushes, and smiling. "It is quite finished," he cried, at last, and stooping down he wrote his name in thin vermilion letters on the left-hand corner of the canvas.

Lord Henry came over and examined the picture. It was certainly a wonderful work of art, and a wonderful likeness as well.

"My dear fellow, I congratulate you most warmly," he said.--"Mr. Gray, come and look at yourself."

The lad started, as if awakened from some dream. "Is it really finished?" he murmured, stepping down from the platform.

"Quite finished," said Hallward. "And you have sat splendidly to-day. I am awfully obliged to you."

"That is entirely due to me," broke in Lord Henry. "Isn't it, Mr. Gray?"

Dorian made no answer, but passed listlessly in front of his picture and turned towards it. When he saw it he drew back, and his cheeks flushed for a moment with pleasure. A look of joy came into his eyes, as if he had recognized himself for the first time. He stood there motionless, and in wonder, dimly conscious that Hallward was speaking to him, but not catching the meaning of his words. The sense of his own beauty came on him like a revelation. He had never felt it before. Basil Hallward's compliments had seemed to him to be merely the charming exaggerations of friendship. He had listened to them, laughed at them, forgotten them. They had not influenced his nature. Then had come Lord Henry, with his strange panegyric on youth, his terrible warning of its brevity. That had stirred him at the time, and now, as he stood gazing at the shadow of his own loveliness, the full reality of the description flashed across him. Yes, there would be a day when his face would be wrinkled and wizen, his eyes dim and colorless, the grace of his figure broken and deformed. The scarlet would pass away from his lips, and the gold steal from his hair. The life that was to make his soul would mar his body. He would become ignoble, hideous, and uncouth.

As he thought of it, a sharp pang of pain struck like a knife across him, and made each delicate fibre of his nature quiver. His eyes deepened into amethyst, and a mist of tears came across them. He felt as if a hand of ice had been laid upon his heart.

"Don't you like it?" cried Hallward at last, stung a little by the lad's silence, and not understanding what it meant.

"Of course he likes it," said Lord Henry. "Who wouldn't like it? It is one of the greatest things in modern art. I will give you anything you like to ask for it. I must have it."

"It is not my property, Harry."

"Whose property is it?"

"Dorian's, of course."

"He is a very lucky fellow."

"How sad it is!" murmured Dorian Gray, with his eyes still fixed upon his own portrait. "How sad it is! I shall grow old, and horrid, and dreadful. But this picture will remain always young. It will never be older than this particular day of June. . . . If it was only the other way! If it was I who were to be always young, and the picture that were to grow old! For this--for this--I would give everything! Yes, there is nothing in the whole world I would not give!"

"You would hardly care for that arrangement, Basil," cried Lord Henry, laughing. "It would be rather hard lines on you."

"I should object very strongly, Harry."

Dorian Gray turned and looked at him. "I believe you would, Basil. You like your art better than your friends. I am no more to you than a green bronze figure. Hardly as much, I dare say."

Hallward stared in amazement. It was so unlike Dorian to speak like that. What had happened? He seemed almost angry. His face was flushed and his cheeks burning.

"Yes," he continued, "I am less to you than your ivory Hermes or your silver Faun. You will like them always. How long will you like me? Till I have my first wrinkle, I suppose. I know, now, that when one loses one's good looks, whatever they may be, one loses everything. Your picture has taught me that. Lord Henry is perfectly right. Youth is the only thing worth having. When I find that I am growing old, I will kill myself."

Hallward turned pale, and caught his hand. "Dorian! Dorian!" he cried, "don't talk like that. I have never had such a friend as you, and I shall never have such another. You are not jealous of material things, are you?"

"I am jealous of everything whose beauty does not die. I am jealous of the portrait you have painted of me. Why should it keep what I must lose? Every moment that passes takes something from me, and gives something to it. Oh, if it was only the other way! If the picture could change, and I could be always what I am now! Why did you paint it? It will mock me some day,--mock me horribly!" The hot tears welled into his eyes; he tore his hand away, and, flinging himself on the divan, he buried his face in the cushions, as if he was praying.

"This is your doing, Harry," said Hallward, bitterly.

"My doing?"

"Yes, yours, and you know it."

Lord Henry shrugged his shoulders. "It is the real Dorian Gray,--that is all," he answered.

"It is not."

"If it is not, what have I to do with it?"

"You should have gone away when I asked you."

"I stayed when you asked me."

"Harry, I can't quarrel with my two best friends at once, but between you both you have made me hate the finest piece of work I have ever done, and I will destroy it. What is it but canvas and color? I will not let it come across our three lives and mar them."

Dorian Gray lifted his golden head from the pillow, and looked at him with pallid face and tear-stained eyes, as he walked over to the deal painting-table that was set beneath the large curtained window. What was he doing there? His fingers were straying about among the litter of tin tubes and dry brushes, seeking for something. Yes, it was the long palette-knife, with its thin blade of lithe steel. He had found it at last. He was going to rip up the canvas.

With a stifled sob he leaped from the couch, and, rushing over to Hallward, tore the knife out of his hand, and flung it to the end of the studio. "Don't, Basil, don't!" he cried. "It would be murder!"

"I am glad you appreciate my work at last, Dorian," said Hallward, coldly, when he had recovered from his surprise. "I never thought you would."

"Appreciate it? I am in love with it, Basil. It is part of myself, I feel that."

"Well, as soon as you are dry, you shall be varnished, and framed, and sent home. Then you can do what you like with yourself." And he walked across the room and rang the bell for tea. "You will have tea, of course, Dorian? And so will you, Harry? Tea is the only simple pleasure left to us."

"I don't like simple pleasures," said Lord Henry. "And I don't like scenes, except on the stage. What absurd fellows you are, both of you! I wonder who it was defined man as a rational animal. It was the most premature definition ever given. Man is many things, but he is not rational. I am glad he is not, after all: though I wish you chaps would not squabble over the picture. You had much better let me have it, Basil. This silly boy doesn't really want it, and I do."

"If you let any one have it but me, Basil, I will never forgive you!" cried Dorian Gray. "And I don't allow people to call me a silly boy."

"You know the picture is yours, Dorian. I gave it to you before it existed."

"And you know you have been a little silly, Mr. Gray, and that you don't really mind being called a boy."

"I should have minded very much this morning, Lord Henry."

"Ah! this morning! You have lived since then."

There came a knock to the door, and the butler entered with the tea-tray and set it down upon a small Japanese table. There was a rattle of cups and saucers and the hissing of a fluted Georgian urn. Two globe-shaped china dishes were brought in by a page. Dorian Gray went over and poured the tea out. The two men sauntered languidly to the table, and examined what was under the covers.

"Let us go to the theatre to-night," said Lord Henry. "There is sure to be something on, somewhere. I have promised to dine at White's, but it is only with an old friend, so I can send him a wire and say that I am ill, or that I am prevented from coming in consequence of a subsequent engagement. I think that would be a rather nice excuse: it would have the surprise of candor."

"It is such a bore putting on one's dress-clothes," muttered Hallward. "And, when one has them on, they are so horrid."

"Yes," answered Lord Henry, dreamily, "the costume of our day is detestable. It is so sombre, so depressing. Sin is the only color-element left in modern life."

"You really must not say things like that before Dorian, Harry."

"Before which Dorian? The one who is pouring out tea for us, or the one in the picture?"

"Before either."

"I should like to come to the theatre with you, Lord Henry," said the lad.

"Then you shall come; and you will come too, Basil, won't you?"

"I can't, really. I would sooner not. I have a lot of work to do."

"Well, then, you and I will go alone, Mr. Gray."

"I should like that awfully."

Basil Hallward bit his lip and walked over, cup in hand, to the picture. "I will stay with the real Dorian," he said, sadly.

"Is it the real Dorian?" cried the original of the portrait, running across to him. "Am I really like that?"

"Yes; you are just like that."

"How wonderful, Basil!"

"At least you are like it in appearance. But it will never alter," said Hallward. "That is something."

"What a fuss people make about fidelity!" murmured Lord

Henry.

"And, after all, it is purely a question for physiology. It has nothing to do with our own will. It is either an unfortunate accident, or an unpleasant result of temperament. Young men want to be faithful, and are not; old men want to be faithless, and cannot: that is all one can say."

"Don't go to the theatre to-night, Dorian," said Hallward. "Stop and dine with me."

"I can't, really."

"Why?"

"Because I have promised Lord Henry to go with him."

"He won't like you better for keeping your promises. He always breaks his own. I beg you not to go."

Dorian Gray laughed and shook his head.

"I entreat you."

The lad hesitated, and looked over at Lord Henry, who was watching them from the tea-table with an amused smile.

"I must go, Basil," he answered.

"Very well," said Hallward; and he walked over and laid his cup down on the tray. "It is rather late, and, as you have to dress, you had better lose no time. Good-by, Harry; good-by, Dorian. Come and see me soon. Come to-morrow."

"Certainly."

"You won't forget?"

"No, of course not."

"And . . . Harry!"

"Yes, Basil?"

"Remember what I asked you, when in the garden this morning."

"I have forgotten it."

"I trust you."

"I wish I could trust myself," said Lord Henry, laughing.--"Come, Mr. Gray, my hansom is outside, and I can drop you at your own place.--Good-by, Basil. It has been a most interesting afternoon."

As the door closed behind them, Hallward flung himself down on a sofa, and a look of pain came into his face.

CHAPTER III

One afternoon, a month later, Dorian Gray was reclining in a luxurious arm-chair, in the little library of Lord Henry's house in Curzon Street. It was, in its way, a very charming room, with its high panelled wainscoting of olive-stained oak, its cream-colored frieze and ceiling of raised plaster-work, and its brick-dust felt carpet strewn with long-fringed silk Persian rugs. On a tiny satinwood table stood a statuette by Clodion, and beside it lay a copy of "Les Cent Nouvelles," bound for Margaret of Valois by Clovis Eve, and powdered with the gilt daisies that the queen had selected for her device. Some large blue china jars, filled with parrot-tulips, were ranged on the mantel-shelf, and through the small leaded panes of the window streamed the apricot-colored light of a summer's day in London.

Lord Henry had not come in yet. He was always late on principle, his principle being that punctuality is the thief of time. So the lad was looking rather sulky, as with listless fingers he turned over the pages of an elaborately-illustrated edition of "Manon Lescaut" that he had found in one of the bookcases. The formal monotonous ticking of the Louis Quatorze clock annoyed him. Once or twice he thought of going away.

At last he heard a light step outside, and the door opened. "How late you are, Harry!" he murmured.

"I am afraid it is not Harry, Mr. Gray," said a woman's voice.

He glanced quickly round, and rose to his feet. "I beg your pardon. I thought--"

"You thought it was my husband. It is only his wife. You must let me introduce myself. I know you quite well by your photographs. I think my husband has got twenty-seven of them."

"Not twenty-seven, Lady Henry?"

"Well, twenty-six, then. And I saw you with him the other night at the Opera." She laughed nervously, as she spoke, and watched him with her vague forget-me-not eyes. She was a curious woman, whose dresses always looked as if they had been designed in a rage and put on in a tempest. She was always in love with somebody, and, as her passion was never returned, she had kept all her illusions. She tried to look picturesque, but only succeeded in being untidy. Her name was Victoria, and she had a perfect mania for going to church.

"That was at 'Lohengrin,' Lady Henry, I think?"

"Yes; it was at dear 'Lohengrin.' I like Wagner's music better than any other music. It is so loud that one can talk the whole time, without people hearing what one says. That is a great advantage: don't you think so, Mr. Gray?"

The same nervous staccato laugh broke from her thin lips, and her fingers began to play with a long paper-knife.

Dorian smiled, and shook his head: "I am afraid I don't think so, Lady Henry. I never talk during music,--at least during good music. If one hears bad music, it is one's duty to drown it by conversation."

"Ah! that is one of Harry's views, isn't it, Mr. Gray? But you must not think I don't like good music. I adore it, but I am afraid of it. It makes me too romantic. I have simply worshipped pianists,--two at a time, sometimes. I don't know what it is about them. Perhaps it is that they are foreigners. They all are, aren't they? Even those that are born in England become foreigners after a time, don't they? It is so clever of them, and such a compliment to art. Makes it quite cosmopolitan, doesn't it? You have never been to any of my parties, have you, Mr. Gray? You must come. I can't afford orchids, but I spare no expense in foreigners. They make one's rooms look so picturesque. But here is Harry!--Harry, I came in to look for you, to ask you something,--I forget what it was,--and I found Mr. Gray here. We have had such a pleasant chat about music. We have quite the same views. No; I think our views are quite different. But he has been most pleasant. I am so glad I've seen him."

"I am charmed, my love, quite charmed," said Lord Henry, elevating his dark crescent-shaped eyebrows and looking at them both with an amused smile.--"So sorry I am late, Dorian. I went to look after a piece of old brocade in Wardour Street, and had to bargain for hours for it. Nowadays people know the price of everything, and the value of nothing."

"I am afraid I must be going," exclaimed Lady Henry, after an awkward silence, with her silly sudden laugh. "I have promised to drive with the duchess.--Good-by, Mr. Gray.--Good-by, Harry. You are dining out, I suppose? So am I. Perhaps I shall see you at Lady Thornbury's."

"I dare say, my dear," said Lord Henry, shutting the door behind her, as she flitted out of the room, looking like a bird-of-paradise that had been out in the rain, and leaving a faint odor of patchouli behind her. Then he shook hands with Dorian

Gray, lit a cigarette, and flung himself down on the sofa.

"Never marry a woman with straw-colored hair, Dorian," he said, after a few puffs.

"Why, Harry?"

"Because they are so sentimental."

"But I like sentimental people."

"Never marry at all, Dorian. Men marry because they are tired; women, because they are curious: both are disappointed."

"I don't think I am likely to marry, Harry. I am too much in love. That is one of your aphorisms. I am putting it into practice, as I do everything you say."

"Whom are you in love with?" said Lord Henry, looking at him with a curious smile.

"With an actress," said Dorian Gray, blushing.

Lord Henry shrugged his shoulders. "That is a rather common-place début," he murmured.

"You would not say so if you saw her, Harry."

"Who is she?"

"Her name is Sibyl Vane."

"Never heard of her."

"No one has. People will some day, however. She is a genius."

"My dear boy, no woman is a genius: women are a decorative sex. They never have anything to say, but they say it charmingly. They represent the triumph of matter over mind, just as we men represent the triumph of mind over morals. There are only two kinds of women, the plain and the colored. The plain women are very useful. If you want to gain a reputation for respectability, you have merely to take them down to supper. The other women are very charming. They commit one mistake, however. They paint in order to try to look young. Our grandmothers painted in order to try to talk brilliantly. Rouge and esprit used to go together. That has all gone out now. As long as a woman can look ten years younger than her own daughter, she is perfectly satisfied. As for conversation, there are only five women in London worth talking to, and two of these can't be admitted into decent society. However, tell me about your genius. How long have you known her?"

"About three weeks. Not so much. About two weeks and two days."

"How did you come across her?"

"I will tell you, Harry; but you mustn't be unsympathetic about it. After all, it never would have happened if I had not met you. You filled me with a wild desire to know everything about life. For days after I met you, something seemed to throb in my veins. As I lounged in the Park, or strolled down Piccadilly, I used to look at every one who passed me, and wonder with a mad curiosity what sort of lives they led. Some of them fascinated me. Others filled me with terror. There was an exquisite poison in the air. I had a passion for sensations.

"One evening about seven o'clock I determined to go out in search of some adventure. I felt that this gray, monstrous London of ours, with its myriads of people, its splendid sinners, and its sordid sins, as you once said, must have something in store for me. I fancied a thousand things.

"The mere danger gave me a sense of delight. I remembered what you had said to me on that wonderful night when we first dined together, about the search for beauty being the poisonous secret of life. I don't know what I expected, but I went out, and wandered eastward, soon losing my way in a labyrinth of grimy streets and black, grassless squares. About half-past eight I passed by a little third-rate theatre, with great flaring gas-jets and gaudy play-bills. A hideous Jew, in the most amazing waistcoat I ever beheld in my life, was standing at the entrance, smoking a vile cigar. He had greasy ringlets, and an enormous diamond blazed in the centre of a soiled shirt. "Ave a box, my lord?' he said, when he saw me, and he took off his hat with an act of gorgeous servility. There was something about him, Harry, that amused me. He was such a monster. You will laugh at me, I know, but I really went in and paid a whole guinea for the stage-box. To the present day I can't make out why I did so; and yet if I hadn't!--my dear Harry, if I hadn't, I would have missed the greatest romance of my life. I see you are laughing. It is horrid of you!"

"I am not laughing, Dorian; at least I am not laughing at you. But you should not say the greatest romance of your life. You should say the first romance of your life. You will always be loved, and you will always be in love with love. There are exquisite things in store for you. This is merely the beginning."

"Do you think my nature so shallow?" cried Dorian Gray, angrily.

"No; I think your nature so deep."

"How do you mean?"

"My dear boy, people who only love once in their lives are really shallow people. What they call their loyalty, and their fidelity, I call either the lethargy of custom or the lack of imagination. Faithlessness is to the emotional life what consistency is to the intellectual life,--simply a confession of failure. But I don't want to interrupt you. Go on with your story."

"Well, I found myself seated in a horrid little private box, with a vulgar drop-scene staring me in the face. I looked out behind the curtain, and surveyed the house. It was a tawdry affair, all Cupids and cornucopias, like a third-rate wedding-cake. The gallery and pit were fairly full, but the two rows of dingy stalls were quite empty, and there was hardly a person in what I suppose they called the dress-circle. Women went about with oranges and ginger-beer, and there was a terrible consumption of nuts going on."

"It must have been just like the palmy days of the British Drama."

"Just like, I should fancy, and very horrid. I began to wonder what on earth I should do, when I caught sight of the play-bill. What do you think the play was, Harry?"

"I should think 'The Idiot Boy, or Dumb but Innocent.' Our fathers used to like that sort of piece, I believe. The longer I live, Dorian, the more keenly I feel that whatever was good enough for our fathers is not good enough for us. In art, as in politics, les grand pères ont toujours tort."

"This play was good enough for us, Harry. It was 'Romeo and Juliet.' I must admit I was rather annoyed at the idea of seeing Shakespeare done in such a wretched hole of a place. Still, I felt interested, in a sort of way. At any rate, I determined to wait for the first act. There was a dreadful orchestra, presided over by a young Jew who sat at a cracked piano, that nearly drove me away, but at last the drop-scene was drawn up, and the play began. Romeo was a stout elderly gentleman, with corked eyebrows, a husky tragedy voice, and a figure like a beer-barrel. Mercutio was almost as bad. He was played by the low-comedian, who had introduced gags of his own and was on most familiar terms with the pit. They were as grotesque as the scenery, and that looked as if it had come out of a pantomime of fifty years ago. But Juliet! Harry, imagine a girl, hardly seventeen years of age, with a little flower-like face, a small Greek head with plaited coils of dark-brown hair, eyes that were violet wells of passion, lips that were like the petals of a rose. She was the loveliest thing I had ever seen in my life. You said to me once that pathos left you unmoved, but that beauty, mere beauty, could fill your eyes with tears. I tell you, Harry, I could hardly see this girl for the mist of tears that came across me. And her voice,--I never heard such a voice. It was very low at first, with deep mellow notes, that seemed to fall singly upon one's ear. Then it became a little louder, and sounded like a flute or a distant hautbois. In the garden-scene it had all the tremulous ecstasy that one hears just before dawn when nightingales are singing. There were moments, later on, when it had the wild passion of violins. You know how a voice can stir one. Your voice and the voice of Sibyl Vane are two things that I shall never forget. When I close my eyes, I hear them, and each of them says something different. I don't know which to follow. Why should I not love her? Harry, I do love her. She is everything to me in life. Night after night I go to see her play. One evening she is Rosalind, and the next evening she is Imogen. I have seen her die in the gloom of an Italian tomb, sucking the poison from her lover's lips. I have watched her wandering through the forest of Arden, disguised as a pretty boy in hose and doublet and dainty cap. She has been mad, and has come into the presence of a guilty king, and given him rue to wear, and bitter herbs to taste of. She has been innocent, and the black hands of jealousy have crushed her reed-like throat. I have seen her in every age and in every costume. Ordinary women never appeal to one's imagination. They are limited to their century. No glamour ever transfigures them. One knows their minds as easily as one knows their bonnets. One can always find them. There is no mystery in one of them. They ride in the Park in the morning, and chatter at tea-parties in the afternoon. They have their stereotyped smile, and their fashionable manner. They are quite obvious. But an actress! How different an actress is! Why didn't you tell me that the only thing worth loving is an actress?"

"Because I have loved so many of them, Dorian."

"Oh, yes, horrid people with dyed hair and painted faces."

"Don't run down dyed hair and painted faces. There is an extraordinary charm in them, sometimes."

"I wish now I had not told you about Sibyl Vane."

"You could not have helped telling me, Dorian. All through your life you will tell me everything you do."

"Yes, Harry, I believe that is true. I cannot help telling you things. You have a curious influence over me. If I ever did a crime, I would come and confide it to you. You would understand me."

"People like you--the wilful sunbeams of life--don't commit crimes, Dorian. But I am much obliged for the compliment, all the same. And now tell me,--reach me the matches, like a good boy: thanks,--tell me, what are your relations with Sibyl Vane?"

Dorian Gray leaped to his feet, with flushed cheeks and burning eyes. "Harry, Sibyl Vane is sacred!"

"It is only the sacred things that are worth touching, Dorian," said Lord Henry, with a strange touch of pathos in his voice. "But why should you be annoyed? I suppose she will be yours some day. When one is in love, one always begins by deceiving one's self, and one always ends by deceiving others. That is what the world calls romance. You know her, at any rate, I suppose?"

"Of course I know her. On the first night I was at the theatre, the horrid old Jew came round to the box after the performance was over, and offered to bring me behind the scenes and introduce me to her. I was furious with him, and told him that Juliet had been dead for hundreds of years, and that her body was lying in a marble tomb in Verona. I think, from his blank look of amazement, that he thought I had taken too much champagne, or something."

"I am not surprised."

"I was not surprised either. Then he asked me if I wrote for any of the newspapers. I told him I never even read them. He seemed terribly disappointed at that, and confided to me that all the dramatic critics were in a conspiracy against him, and that they were all to be bought."

"I believe he was quite right there. But, on the other hand, most of them are not at all expensive."

"Well, he seemed to think they were beyond his means. By this time the lights were being put out in the theatre, and I had to go. He wanted me to try some cigars which he strongly recommended. I declined. The next night, of course, I arrived at the theatre again. When he saw me he made me a low bow, and assured me that I was a patron of art. He was a most offensive brute, though he had an extraordinary passion for Shakespeare. He told me once, with an air of pride, that his three bankruptcies were entirely due to the poet, whom he insisted on calling 'The Bard.' He seemed to think it a distinction."

"It was a distinction, my dear Dorian,--a great distinction. But when did you first speak to Miss Sibyl Vane?"

"The third night. She had been playing Rosalind. I could not help going round. I had thrown her some flowers, and she had looked at me; at least I fancied that she had. The old Jew was persistent. He seemed determined to bring me behind, so I consented. It was curious my not wanting to know her, wasn't it?"

"No; I don't think so."

"My dear Harry, why?"

"I will tell you some other time. Now I want to know about the girl."

"Sibyl? Oh, she was so shy, and so gentle. There is something of a child about her. Her eyes opened wide in exquisite wonder when I told her what I thought of her performance, and she seemed quite unconscious of her power. I think we were both rather nervous. The old Jew stood grinning at the door-way of the dusty greenroom, making elaborate speeches about us both, while we stood looking at each other like children. He would insist on calling me 'My Lord,' so I had to assure Sibyl that I was not anything of the kind. She said quite simply to me, 'You look more like a prince.'"

"Upon my word, Dorian, Miss Sibyl knows how to pay compliments."

"You don't understand her, Harry. She regarded me merely as a person in a play. She knows nothing of life. She lives with her mother, a faded tired woman who played Lady Capulet in a sort of magenta dressing-wrapper on the first night, and who looks as if she had seen better days."

"I know that look. It always depresses me."

"The Jew wanted to tell me her history, but I said it did not interest me."

"You were quite right. There is always something infinitely mean about other people's tragedies."

"Sibyl is the only thing I care about. What is it to me where she came from? From her little head to her little feet, she is absolutely and entirely divine. I go to see her act every night of my life, and every night she is more marvellous."

"That is the reason, I suppose, that you will never dine with me now. I thought you must have some curious romance on hand. You have; but it is not quite what I expected."

"My dear Harry, we either lunch or sup together every day, and I have been to the Opera with you several times."

"You always come dreadfully late."

"Well, I can't help going to see Sibyl play, even if it is only for an act. I get hungry for her presence; and when I think of the wonderful soul that is hidden away in that little ivory body, I am filled with awe."

"You can dine with me to-night, Dorian, can't you?"

He shook his head. "To-night she is Imogen," he answered, "and tomorrow night she will be Juliet."

"When is she Sibyl Vane?"

"Never."

"I congratulate you."

"How horrid you are! She is all the great heroines of the world in one. She is more than an individual. You laugh, but I tell you she has genius. I love her, and I must make her love me. You, who know all the secrets of life, tell me how to charm Sibyl Vane to love me! I want to make Romeo jealous. I want the dead lovers of the world to hear our laughter, and grow sad. I want a breath of our passion to stir their dust into consciousness, to wake their ashes into pain. My God, Harry, how I worship her!" He was walking up and down the room as he spoke. Hectic spots of red burned on his cheeks. He was terribly excited.

Lord Henry watched him with a subtle sense of pleasure. How different he was now from the shy, frightened boy he had met in Basil Hallward's studio! His nature had developed like a flower, had borne blossoms of scarlet flame. Out of its secret hiding-place had crept his Soul, and Desire had come to meet it on the way.

"And what do you propose to do?" said Lord Henry, at last.

"I want you and Basil to come with me some night and see her act. I have not the slightest fear of the result. You won't be able to refuse to recognize her genius. Then we must get her out of the Jew's hands. She is bound to him for three years--at least for two years and eight months--from the present time. I will have to pay him something, of course. When all that is settled, I will take a West-End theatre and bring her out properly. She will make the world as mad as she has made me."

"Impossible, my dear boy!"

"Yes, she will. She has not merely art, consummate art-instinct, in her, but she has personality also; and you have often told me that it is personalities, not principles, that move the age."

"Well, what night shall we go?"

"Let me see. To-day is Tuesday. Let us fix to-morrow. She plays Juliet to-morrow."

"All right. The Bristol at eight o'clock; and I will get Basil."

"Not eight, Harry, please. Half-past six. We must be there before the curtain rises. You must see her in the first act, where she meets Romeo."

"Half-past six! What an hour! It will be like having a meat-tea. However, just as you wish. Shall you see Basil between this and then? Or shall I write to him?"

"Dear Basil! I have not laid eyes on him for a week. It is rather horrid of me, as he has sent me my portrait in the most wonderful frame, designed by himself, and, though I am a little jealous of it for being a whole month younger than I am, I must admit that I delight in it. Perhaps you had better write to him. I don't want to see him alone. He says things that annoy me."

Lord Henry smiled. "He gives you good advice, I suppose. People are very fond of giving away what they need most themselves."

"You don't mean to say that Basil has got any passion or any romance in him?"

"I don't know whether he has any passion, but he certainly has romance," said Lord Henry, with an amused look in his eyes. "Has he never let you know that?"

"Never. I must ask him about it. I am rather surprised to hear it. He is the best of fellows, but he seems to me to be just a bit of a Philistine. Since I have known you, Harry, I have discovered that."

"Basil, my dear boy, puts everything that is charming in him into his work. The consequence is that he has nothing left for life but his prejudices, his principles, and his common sense. The only artists I have ever known who are personally delightful are bad artists. Good artists give everything to their art, and consequently are perfectly uninteresting in themselves. A great poet, a really great poet, is the most unpoetical of all creatures. But inferior poets are absolutely fascinating. The worse their rhymes are, the more picturesque they look. The mere fact of having published a book of second-rate sonnets makes a man quite irresistible. He lives the poetry that he cannot write. The others write the poetry that they dare not realize."

"I wonder is that really so, Harry?" said Dorian Gray, putting some perfume on his handkerchief out of a large gold-topped bottle that stood on the table. "It must be, if you say so. And now I must be off. Imogen is waiting for me. Don't forget about to-morrow. Good-by."

As he left the room, Lord Henry's heavy eyelids drooped, and he began to think. Certainly few people had ever interested him so much as Dorian Gray, and yet the lad's mad adoration of some one else caused him not the slightest pang of annoyance or jealousy. He was pleased by it. It made him a more interesting study. He had been always enthralled by the methods of science, but the ordinary subject-matter of science had seemed to him trivial and of no import. And so he had begun by vivisecting himself, as he had ended by vivisecting others. Human life,--that appeared to him the one thing worth investigating. There was nothing else of any value, compared to it. It was true that as one watched life in its curious crucible of pain and pleasure, one could not wear over one's face a mask of glass, or keep the sulphurous fumes from troubling the brain and making the imagination turbid with monstrous fancies and misshapen dreams. There were poisons so subtle that to know their properties one had to sicken of them. There were maladies so strange that one had to pass through them if one sought to understand their nature. And, yet, what a great reward one received! How wonderful the whole world became to one! To note the curious hard logic of passion, and the emotional colored life of the intellect,--to observe where they met, and where they separated, at what point they became one, and at what point they were at discord,--there was a delight in that! What matter what the cost was? One could never pay too high a price for any sensation.

He was conscious--and the thought brought a gleam of pleasure into his brown agate eyes--that it was through certain words of his, musical words said with musical utterance, that Dorian Gray's soul had turned to this white girl and bowed in worship before her. To a large extent, the lad was his own creation. He had made him premature. That was something. Ordinary people waited till life disclosed to them its secrets, but to the few, to the elect, the mysteries of life were revealed before the veil was drawn away. Sometimes this was the effect of art, and chiefly of the art of literature, which dealt immediately with the passions and the intellect. But now and then a complex personality took the place and assumed the office of art, was indeed, in its way, a real work of art, Life having its elaborate masterpieces, just as poetry has, or sculpture, or painting.

Yes, the lad was premature. He was gathering his harvest while it was yet spring. The pulse and passion of youth were in him, but he was becoming self-conscious. It was delightful to watch him. With his beautiful face, and his beautiful soul, he was a thing to wonder at. It was no matter how it all ended, or was destined to end. He was like one of those gracious figures in a pageant or a play, whose joys seem to be remote from one, but whose sorrows stir one's sense of beauty, and whose wounds are like red roses.

Soul and body, body and soul--how mysterious they were! There was animalism in the soul, and the body had its moments of spirituality. The senses could refine, and the intellect could degrade. Who could say where the fleshly impulse ceased, or the psychical impulse began? How shallow were the arbitrary definitions of ordinary psychologists! And yet how difficult to decide between the claims of the various schools! Was the soul a shadow seated in the house of sin? Or was the body really in the soul, as Giordano Bruno thought? The separation of spirit from matter was a mystery, and the union of spirit with matter was a mystery also.

He began to wonder whether we should ever make psychology so absolute a science that each little spring of life would be revealed to us. As it was, we always misunderstood ourselves, and rarely understood others. Experience was of no ethical value. It was merely the name we gave to our mistakes. Men had, as a rule, regarded it as a mode of warning, had claimed for it a certain moral efficacy in the formation of character, had praised it as something that taught us what to follow and showed us what to avoid. But there was no motive power in experience. It was as little of an active cause as conscience itself. All that it really demonstrated was that our future would be the same as our past, and that the sin we had done once, and with loathing, we would do many times, and with joy.

It was clear to him that the experimental method was the only method by which one could arrive at any scientific analysis of the passions; and certainly Dorian Gray was a subject made to his hand, and seemed to promise rich and fruitful results. His sudden mad love for Sibyl Vane was a psychological phenomenon of no small interest. There was no doubt that curiosity had much to do with it, curiosity and the desire for new experiences; yet it was not a simple but rather a very complex passion. What there was in it of the purely sensuous instinct of boyhood had been transformed by the workings of the imagination, changed into something that seemed to the boy himself to be remote from sense, and was for that very reason all the more dangerous. It was the passions about whose origin we deceived ourselves that tyrannized most strongly over us. Our weakest motives were those of whose nature we were conscious. It often happened that when we thought we were experimenting on others we were really experimenting on ourselves.

While Lord Henry sat dreaming on these things, a knock came to the door, and his valet entered, and reminded him it was time to dress for dinner. He got up and looked out into the street. The sunset had smitten into scarlet gold the upper windows of the houses opposite. The panes glowed like plates of heated metal. The sky above was like a faded rose. He thought of Dorian Gray's young fiery-colored life, and wondered how it was all going to end.

When he arrived home, about half-past twelve o'clock, he saw a telegram lying on the hall-table. He opened it and found it was from Dorian. It was to tell him that he was engaged to be married to Sibyl Vane.

CHAPTER IV

"I suppose you have heard the news, Basil?" said Lord Henry on the following evening, as Hallward was shown into a little private room at the Bristol where dinner had been laid for three.

"No, Harry," answered Hallward, giving his hat and coat to the bowing waiter. "What is it? Nothing about politics, I hope? They don't interest me. There is hardly a single person in the House of Commons worth painting; though many of them would be the better for a little whitewashing."

"Dorian Gray is engaged to be married," said Lord Henry, watching him as he spoke.

Hallward turned perfectly pale, and a curious look flashed for a moment into his eyes, and then passed away, leaving them dull. "Dorian engaged to be married!" he cried. "Impossible!"

"It is perfectly true."

"To whom?"

"To some little actress or other."

"I can't believe it. Dorian is far too sensible."

"Dorian is far too wise not to do foolish things now and then, my dear Basil."

"Marriage is hardly a thing that one can do now and then, Harry," said Hallward, smiling.

"Except in America. But I didn't say he was married. I said he was engaged to be married. There is a great difference. I have a distinct remembrance of being married, but I have no recollection at all of being engaged. I am inclined to think that I never was engaged."

"But think of Dorian's birth, and position, and wealth. It would be absurd for him to marry so much beneath him."

"If you want him to marry this girl, tell him that, Basil. He is sure to do it then. Whenever a man does a thoroughly stupid thing, it is always from the noblest motives."

"I hope the girl is good, Harry. I don't want to see Dorian tied to some vile creature, who might degrade his nature and ruin his intellect."

"Oh, she is more than good--she is beautiful," murmured Lord Henry, sipping a glass of vermouth and orange-bitters. "Dorian says she is beautiful; and he is not often wrong about things of that kind. Your portrait of him has quickened his appreciation of the personal appearance of other people. It has had that excellent effect, among others. We are to see her to-night, if that boy doesn't forget his appointment."

"But do you approve of it, Harry?" asked Hallward, walking up and down the room, and biting his lip. "You can't approve of it, really. It is some silly infatuation."

"I never approve, or disapprove, of anything now. It is an absurd attitude to take towards life. We are not sent into the world to air our moral prejudices. I never take any notice of what common people say, and I never interfere with what charming people do. If a personality fascinates me, whatever the personality chooses to do is absolutely delightful to me. Dorian Gray falls in love with a beautiful girl who acts Shakespeare, and proposes to marry her. Why not? If he wedded Messalina he would be none the less interesting. You know I am not a champion of marriage. The real drawback to marriage is that it makes one unselfish. And unselfish people are colorless. They lack individuality. Still, there are certain temperaments that marriage makes more complex. They retain their egotism, and add to it many other egos. They are forced to have more than one life. They become more highly organized. Besides, every experience is of value, and, whatever one may say against marriage, it is certainly an experience. I hope that Dorian Gray will make this girl his wife, passionately adore her for six months, and then suddenly become fascinated by some one else. He would be a wonderful study."

"You don't mean all that, Harry; you know you don't. If Dorian Gray's life were spoiled, no one would be sorrier than yourself. You are much better than you pretend to be."

Lord Henry laughed. "The reason we all like to think so well of others is that we are all afraid for ourselves. The basis of optimism is sheer terror. We think that we are generous because we credit our neighbor with those virtues that are likely to benefit ourselves. We praise the banker that we may overdraw our account, and find good qualities in the highwayman in the hope that he may spare our pockets. I mean everything that I have said. I have the greatest contempt for optimism. And as for a spoiled life, no life is spoiled but one whose growth is arrested. If you want to mar a nature, you have merely to reform it. But here is Dorian himself. He will tell you more than

I can."

"My dear Harry, my dear Basil, you must both congratulate me!" said the boy, throwing off his evening cape with its satin-lined wings, and shaking each of his friends by the hand in turn. "I have never been so happy. Of course it is sudden: all really delightful things are. And yet it seems to me to be the one thing I have been looking for all my life." He was flushed with excitement and pleasure, and looked extraordinarily handsome.

"I hope you will always be very happy, Dorian," said Hallward, "but I don't quite forgive you for not having let me know of your engagement. You let Harry know."

"And I don't forgive you for being late for dinner," broke in Lord Henry, putting his hand on the lad's shoulder, and smiling as he spoke. "Come, let us sit down and try what the new chef here is like, and then you will tell us how it all came about."

"There is really not much to tell," cried Dorian, as they took their seats at the small round table. "What happened was simply this. After I left you yesterday evening, Harry, I had some dinner at that curious little Italian restaurant in Rupert Street, you introduced me to, and went down afterwards to the theatre. Sibyl was playing Rosalind. Of course the scenery was dreadful, and the Orlando absurd. But Sibyl! You should have seen her! When she came on in her boy's dress she was perfectly wonderful. She wore a moss-colored velvet jerkin with cinnamon sleeves, slim brown cross-gartered hose, a dainty little green cap with a hawk's feather caught in a jewel, and a hooded cloak lined with dull red. She had never seemed to me more exquisite. She had all the delicate grace of that Tanagra figurine that you have in your studio, Basil. Her hair clustered round her face like dark leaves round a pale rose. As for her acting--well, you will see her to-night. She is simply a born artist. I sat in the dingy box absolutely enthralled. I forgot that I was in London and in the nineteenth century. I was away with my love in a forest that no man had ever seen. After the performance was over I went behind, and spoke to her. As we were sitting together, suddenly there came a look into her eyes that I had never seen there before. My lips moved towards hers. We kissed each other. I can't describe to you what I felt at that moment. It seemed to me that all my life had been narrowed to one perfect point of rose-colored joy. She trembled all over, and shook like a white narcissus. Then she flung herself on her knees and kissed my hands. I feel that I should not tell you all this, but I can't help it. Of course our engagement is a dead secret. She has not even told her own mother. I don't know what my guardians will say. Lord Radley is sure to be furious. I don't care. I shall be of age in less than a year, and then I can do what

I like. I have been right, Basil, haven't I, to take my love out of poetry, and to find my wife in Shakespeare's plays? Lips that Shakespeare taught to speak have whispered their secret in my ear. I have had the arms of Rosalind around me, and kissed Juliet on the mouth."

"Yes, Dorian, I suppose you were right," said Hallward, slowly.

"Have you seen her to-day?" asked Lord Henry.

Dorian Gray shook his head. "I left her in the forest of Arden, I shall find her in an orchard in Verona."

Lord Henry sipped his champagne in a meditative manner. "At what particular point did you mention the word marriage, Dorian? and what did she say in answer? Perhaps you forgot all about it."

"My dear Harry, I did not treat it as a business transaction, and I did not make any formal proposal. I told her that I loved her, and she said she was not worthy to be my wife. Not worthy! Why, the whole world is nothing to me compared to her."

"Women are wonderfully practical," murmured Lord Henry, --"much more practical than we are. In situations of that kind we often forget to say anything about marriage, and they always remind us."

Hallward laid his hand upon his arm. "Don't, Harry. You have annoyed Dorian. He is not like other men. He would never bring misery upon any one. His nature is too fine for that."

Lord Henry looked across the table. "Dorian is never annoyed with me," he answered. "I asked the question for the best reason possible, for the only reason, indeed, that excuses one for asking any question,--simple curiosity. I have a theory that it is always the women who propose to us, and not we who propose to the women, except, of course, in middle-class life. But then the middle classes are not modern."

Dorian Gray laughed, and tossed his head. "You are quite incorrigible, Harry; but I don't mind. It is impossible to be angry with you. When you see Sibyl Vane you will feel that the man who could wrong her would be a beast without a heart. I cannot understand how any one can wish to shame what he loves. I love Sibyl Vane. I wish to place her on a pedestal of gold, and to see the world worship the woman who is mine. What is marriage? An irrevocable vow. And it is an irrevocable vow that I want to take. Her trust makes me faithful, her belief makes me good. When I am with her, I regret all that you have taught me. I become different from what you have known me to be. I am changed, and the mere touch of Sibyl Vane's hand makes me forget you and all your wrong, fascinating, poisonous, delightful theories."

"You will always like me, Dorian," said Lord Henry. "Will you have some coffee, you fellows?--Waiter, bring coffee, and fine-champagne, and some cigarettes. No: don't mind the cigarettes; I have some.--Basil, I can't allow you to smoke cigars. You must have a cigarette. A cigarette is the perfect type of a perfect pleasure. It is exquisite, and it leaves one unsatisfied. What more can you want?--Yes, Dorian, you will always be fond of me. I represent to you all the sins you have never had the courage to commit."

"What nonsense you talk, Harry!" cried Dorian Gray, lighting his cigarette from a fire-breathing silver dragon that the waiter had placed on the table. "Let us go down to the theatre. When you see Sibyl you will have a new ideal of life. She will represent something to you that you have never known."

"I have known everything," said Lord Henry, with a sad look in his eyes, "but I am always ready for a new emotion. I am afraid that there is no such thing, for me at any rate. Still, your wonderful girl may thrill me. I love acting. It is so much more real than life. Let us go. Dorian, you will come with me.--I am so sorry, Basil, but there is only room for two in the brougham. You must follow us in a hansom."

They got up and put on their coats, sipping their coffee standing. Hallward was silent and preoccupied. There was a gloom over him. He could not bear this marriage, and yet it seemed to him to be better than many other things that might have happened. After a few moments, they all passed downstairs. He drove off by himself, as had been arranged, and watched the flashing lights of the little brougham in front of him. A strange sense of loss came over him. He felt that Dorian Gray would never again be to him all that he had been in the past. His eyes darkened, and the crowded flaring streets became blurred to him. When the cab drew up at the doors of the theatre, it seemed to him that he had grown years older.

CHAPTER V

For some reason or other, the house was crowded that night, and the fat Jew manager who met them at the door was beaming from ear to ear with an oily, tremulous smile. He escorted them to their box with a sort of pompous humility, waving his fat jewelled hands, and talking at the top of his voice. Dorian Gray loathed him more than ever. He felt as if he had come to look for Miranda and had been met by Caliban. Lord Henry, upon the other hand, rather liked him. At least he declared he did, and insisted on shaking him by the hand, and assured him that he was proud to meet a man who had discovered a real genius and gone bankrupt over Shakespeare. Hallward amused himself with watching the faces in the pit. The heat was terribly oppressive, and the huge sunlight flamed like a monstrous dahlia with petals of fire. The youths in the gallery had taken off their coats and waistcoats and hung them over the side. They talked to each other across the theatre, and shared their oranges with the tawdry painted girls who sat by them. Some women were laughing in the pit; their voices were horribly shrill and discordant. The sound of the popping of corks came from the bar.

"What a place to find one's divinity in!" said Lord Henry.

"Yes!" answered Dorian Gray. "It was here I found her, and she is divine beyond all living things. When she acts you will forget everything. These common people here, with their coarse faces and brutal gestures, become quite different when she is on the stage. They sit silently and watch her. They weep and laugh as she wills them to do. She makes them as responsive as a violin. She spiritualizes them, and one feels that they are of the same flesh and blood as one's self."

"Oh, I hope not!" murmured Lord Henry, who was scanning the occupants of the gallery through his opera-glass.

"Don't pay any attention to him, Dorian," said Hallward. "I understand what you mean, and I believe in this girl. Any one you love must be marvellous, and any girl that has the effect you describe must be fine and noble. To spiritualize one's age,--that is something worth doing. If this girl can give a soul to those who have lived without one, if she can create the sense of beauty in people whose lives have been sordid and ugly, if she can strip them of their selfishness and lend them tears for sorrows that are not their own, she is worthy of all your adoration, worthy of the adoration of the world. This marriage is quite right. I did not think so at first, but I admit it now. God made Sibyl Vane for you. Without her you would have been incomplete."

"Thanks, Basil," answered Dorian Gray, pressing his hand. "I knew that you would understand me. Harry is so cynical, he terrifies me. But here is the orchestra. It is quite dreadful, but it only lasts for about five minutes. Then the curtain rises, and you will see the girl to whom I am going to give all my life, to whom I have given everything that is good in me."

A quarter of an hour afterwards, amidst an extraordinary turmoil of applause, Sibyl Vane stepped on to the stage. Yes, she was certainly lovely to look at,--one of the loveliest creatures, Lord Henry thought, that he had ever seen. There was something of the fawn in her shy grace and startled eyes. A faint blush, like the shadow of a rose in a mirror of silver, came to her cheeks as she glanced at the crowded, enthusiastic house. She stepped back a few paces, and her lips seemed to tremble. Basil Hallward leaped to his feet and began to applaud. Dorian Gray sat motionless, gazing on her, like a man in a dream. Lord Henry peered through his opera-glass, murmuring, "Charming! charming!"

The scene was the hall of Capulet's house, and Romeo in his pilgrim's dress had entered with Mercutio and his friends. The band, such as it was, struck up a few bars of music, and the dance began. Through the crowd of ungainly, shabbily-dressed actors, Sibyl Vane moved like a creature from a finer world. Her body swayed, as she danced, as a plant sways in the water. The curves of her throat were like the curves of a white lily. Her hands seemed to be made of cool ivory.

Yet she was curiously listless. She showed no sign of joy when her eyes rested on Romeo. The few lines she had to speak, --

Good pilgrim, you do wrong your hand too much,

Which mannerly devotion shows in this;

For saints have hands that pilgrims' hands do touch,

And palm to palm is holy palmers' kiss,--

with the brief dialogue that follows, were spoken in a thoroughly artificial manner. The voice was exquisite, but from the point of view of tone it was absolutely false. It was wrong in color. It took away all the life from the verse. It made the passion unreal.

Dorian Gray grew pale as he watched her. Neither of his friends dared to say anything to him. She seemed to them to be absolutely incompetent. They were horribly disappointed.

Yet they felt that the true test of any Juliet is the balcony scene of the second act. They waited for that. If she failed there, there was nothing in her.

She looked charming as she came out in the moonlight. That could not be denied. But the staginess of her acting was unbearable, and grew worse as she went on. Her gestures became absurdly artificial. She over-emphasized everything that she had to say. The beautiful passage,--

Thou knowest the mask of night is on my face,

Else would a maiden blush bepaint my cheek

For that which thou hast heard me speak to-night,--was declaimed with the painful precision of a school-girl who has been taught to recite by some second-rate professor of elocution. When she leaned over the balcony and came to those wonderful lines,--

Although I joy in thee,

I have no joy of this contract to-night:

It is too rash, too unadvised, too sudden;

Too like the lightning, which doth cease to be

Ere one can say, "It lightens." Sweet, good-night!

This bud of love by summer's ripening breath

May prove a beauteous flower when next we meet,--

she spoke the words as if they conveyed no meaning to her. It was not nervousness. Indeed, so far from being nervous, she seemed absolutely self-contained. It was simply bad art. She was a complete failure.

Even the common uneducated audience of the pit and gallery lost their interest in the play. They got restless, and began to talk loudly and to whistle. The Jew manager, who was standing at the back of the dress-circle, stamped and swore with rage. The only person unmoved was the girl herself.

When the second act was over there came a storm of hisses, and Lord Henry got up from his chair and put on his coat. "She is quite beautiful, Dorian," he said, "but she can't act. Let us go."

"I am going to see the play through," answered the lad, in a hard, bitter voice. "I am awfully sorry that I have made you waste an evening, Harry. I apologize to both of you."

"My dear Dorian, I should think Miss Vane was ill," interrupted Hallward. "We will come some other night."

"I wish she was ill," he rejoined. "But she seems to me to be simply callous and cold. She has entirely altered. Last night she was a great artist. To-night she is merely a commonplace, mediocre actress."

"Don't talk like that about any one you love, Dorian. Love is a more wonderful thing than art."

"They are both simply forms of imitation," murmured Lord Henry. "But do let us go. Dorian, you must not stay here any longer. It is not good for one's morals to see bad acting. Besides, I don't suppose you will want your wife to act. So what does it matter if she plays Juliet like a wooden doll? She is very lovely, and if she knows as little about life as she does about acting, she will be a delightful experience. There are only two kinds of people who are really fascinating,--people who know absolutely everything, and people who know absolutely nothing. Good heavens, my dear boy, don't look so tragic! The secret of remaining young is never to have an emotion that is unbecoming. Come to the club with Basil and myself. We will smoke cigarettes and drink to the beauty of Sibyl Vane. She is beautiful. What more can you want?"

"Please go away, Harry," cried the lad. "I really want to be alone.--Basil, you don't mind my asking you to go? Ah! can't you see that my heart is breaking?" The hot tears came to his eyes. His lips trembled, and, rushing to the back of the box, he leaned up against the wall, hiding his face in his hands.

"Let us go, Basil," said Lord Henry, with a strange tenderness in his voice; and the two young men passed out together.

A few moments afterwards the footlights flared up, and the curtain rose on the third act. Dorian Gray went back to his seat. He looked pale, and proud, and indifferent. The play dragged on, and seemed interminable. Half of the audience went out, tramping in heavy boots, and laughing. The whole thing was a fiasco. The last act was played to almost empty benches.

As soon as it was over, Dorian Gray rushed behind the scenes into the greenroom. The girl was standing alone there, with a look of triumph on her face. Her eyes were lit with an exquisite fire. There was a radiance about her. Her parted lips were smiling over some secret of their own.

When he entered, she looked at him, and an expression of infinite joy came over her. "How badly I acted to-night, Dorian!" she cried.

"Horribly!" he answered, gazing at her in amazement,--"horribly! It was dreadful. Are you ill? You have no idea what it was. You have no idea what I suffered."

The girl smiled. "Dorian," she answered, lingering over his name with long-drawn music in her voice, as though it were sweeter than honey to the red petals of her lips,--"Dorian, you should have understood. But you understand now, don't you?"

"Understand what?" he asked, angrily.

"Why I was so bad to-night. Why I shall always be bad. Why I shall never act well again."

He shrugged his shoulders. "You are ill, I suppose. When you are ill you shouldn't act. You make yourself ridiculous. My friends were bored. I was bored."

She seemed not to listen to him. She was transfigured with joy. An ecstasy of happiness dominated her.

"Dorian, Dorian," she cried, "before I knew you, acting was the one reality of my life. It was only in the theatre that I lived. I thought that it was all true. I was Rosalind one night, and Portia the other. The joy of Beatrice was my joy, and the sorrows of Cordelia were mine also. I believed in everything. The common people who acted with me seemed to me to be godlike. The painted scenes were my world. I knew nothing but shadows, and I thought them real. You came,--oh, my beautiful love!--and you freed my soul from prison. You taught me what reality really is. To-night, for the first time in my life, I saw through the hollowness, the sham, the silliness, of the empty pageant in which I had always played. To-night, for the first time, I became conscious that the Romeo was hideous, and old, and painted, that the moonlight in the orchard was false, that the scenery was vulgar, and that the words I had to speak were unreal, were not my words, not what I wanted to say. You had brought me something higher, something of which all art is but a reflection. You have made me understand what love really is. My love! my love! I am sick of shadows. You are more to me than all art can ever be. What have I to do with the puppets of a play? When I came on to-night, I could not understand how it was that everything had gone from me. Suddenly it dawned on my soul what it all meant. The knowledge was exquisite to me. I heard them hissing, and I smiled. What should they know of love? Take me away, Dorian--take me away with you, where we can be quite alone. I hate the stage. I might mimic a passion that I do not feel, but I cannot mimic one that burns me like fire. Oh, Dorian, Dorian, you understand now what it all means? Even if I could do it, it would be profanation for me to play at being in love. You have made me see that."

He flung himself down on the sofa, and turned away his face. "You have killed my love," he muttered.

She looked at him in wonder, and laughed. He made no answer. She came across to him, and stroked his hair with her little fingers. She knelt down and pressed his hands to her lips. He drew them away, and a shudder ran through him.

Then he leaped up, and went to the door. "Yes," he cried, "you have killed my love. You used to stir my imagination. Now you don't even stir my curiosity. You simply produce no effect. I loved you because you were wonderful, because you had genius and intellect, because you realized the dreams of great poets and gave shape and substance to the shadows of art. You have thrown it all away. You are shallow and stupid. My God! how mad I was to love you! What a fool I have been! You are nothing to me now. I will never see you again. I will never think of you. I will never mention your name. You don't know what you were to me, once. Why, once . . . . Oh, I can't bear to think of it! I wish I had never laid eyes upon you! You have spoiled the romance of my life. How little you can know of love, if you say it mars your art! What are you without your art? Nothing. I would have made you famous, splendid, magnificent. The world would have worshipped you, and you would have belonged to me. What are you now? A third-rate actress with a pretty face."

The girl grew white, and trembled. She clinched her hands together, and her voice seemed to catch in her throat. "You are not serious, Dorian?" she murmured. "You are acting."

"Acting! I leave that to you. You do it so well," he answered, bitterly.

She rose from her knees, and, with a piteous expression of

pain in her face, came across the room to him. She put her hand upon his arm, and looked into his eyes. He thrust her back. "Don't touch me!" he cried.

A low moan broke from her, and she flung herself at his feet, and lay there like a trampled flower. "Dorian, Dorian, don't leave me!" she whispered. "I am so sorry I didn't act well. I was thinking of you all the time. But I will try,--indeed, I will try. It came so suddenly across me, my love for you. I think I should never have known it if you had not kissed me,--if we had not kissed each other. Kiss me again, my love. Don't go away from me. I couldn't bear it. Can't you forgive me for to-night? I will work so hard, and try to improve. Don't be cruel to me because I love you better than anything in the world. After all, it is only once that I have not pleased you. But you are quite right, Dorian. I should have shown myself more of an artist. It was foolish of me; and yet I couldn't help it. Oh, don't leave me, don't leave me." A fit of passionate sobbing choked her. She crouched on the floor like a wounded thing, and Dorian Gray, with his beautiful eyes, looked down at her, and his chiselled lips curled in exquisite disdain. There is always something ridiculous about the passions of people whom one has ceased to love. Sibyl Vane seemed to him to be absurdly melodramatic. Her tears and sobs annoyed him.

"I am going," he said at last, in his calm, clear voice. "I don't wish to be unkind, but I can't see you again. You have disappointed me."

She wept silently, and made no answer, but crept nearer to him. Her little hands stretched blindly out, and appeared to be seeking for him. He turned on his heel, and left the room. In a few moments he was out of the theatre.

Where he went to, he hardly knew. He remembered wandering through dimly-lit streets with gaunt black-shadowed archways and evil-looking houses. Women with hoarse voices and harsh laughter had called after him. Drunkards had reeled by cursing, and chattering to themselves like monstrous apes. He had seen grotesque children huddled upon door-steps, and had heard shrieks and oaths from gloomy courts.

When the dawn was just breaking he found himself at Covent Garden. Huge carts filled with nodding lilies rumbled slowly down the polished empty street. The air was heavy with the perfume of the flowers, and their beauty seemed to bring him an anodyne for his pain. He followed into the market, and watched the men unloading their wagons. A white-smocked carter offered him some cherries. He thanked him, wondered why he refused to accept any money for them, and began to eat them listlessly. They had been plucked at midnight, and the coldness of the moon had entered into them. A long line of boys carrying crates of striped tulips, and of yellow and red roses, defiled in front of him, threading their way through the huge jade-green piles of vegetables. Under the portico, with its gray sun-bleached pillars, loitered a troop of draggled bareheaded girls, waiting for the auction to be over. After some time he hailed a hansom and drove home. The sky was pure opal now, and the roofs of the houses glistened like silver against it. As he was passing through the library towards the door of his bedroom, his eye fell upon the portrait Basil Hallward had painted of him. He started back in surprise, and then went over to it and examined it. In the dim arrested light that struggled through the cream-colored silk blinds, the face seemed to him to be a little changed. The expression looked different. One would have said that there was a touch of cruelty in the mouth. It was certainly curious.

He turned round, and, walking to the window, drew the blinds up. The bright dawn flooded the room, and swept the fantastic shadows into dusky corners, where they lay shuddering. But the strange expression that he had noticed in the face of the portrait seemed to linger there, to be more intensified even. The quivering, ardent sunlight showed him the lines of cruelty round the mouth as clearly as if he had been looking into a mirror after he had done some dreadful thing.

He winced, and, taking up from the table an oval glass framed in ivory Cupids, that Lord Henry had given him, he glanced hurriedly into it. No line like that warped his red lips. What did it mean?

He rubbed his eyes, and came close to the picture, and examined it again. There were no signs of any change when he looked into the actual painting, and yet there was no doubt that the whole expression had altered. It was not a mere fancy of his own. The thing was horribly apparent.

He threw himself into a chair, and began to think. Suddenly there flashed across his mind what he had said in Basil Hallward's studio the day the picture had been finished. Yes, he remembered it perfectly. He had uttered a mad wish that he himself might remain young, and the portrait grow old; that his own beauty might be untarnished, and the face on the canvas bear the burden of his passions and his sins; that the painted image might be seared with the lines of suffering and thought, and that he might keep all the delicate bloom and loveliness of his then just conscious boyhood. Surely his prayer had not been answered? Such things were impossible. It seemed monstrous even to think of them. And, yet, there was the picture before him, with the touch of cruelty in the mouth.

Cruelty! Had he been cruel? It was the girl's fault, not his. He had dreamed of her as a great artist, had given his love to her because he had thought her great. Then she had disappointed him. She had been shallow and unworthy. And, yet, a feeling of infinite regret came over him, as he thought of her lying at his feet sobbing like a little child. He remembered with what callousness he had watched her. Why had he been made like that? Why had such a soul been given to him? But he had suffered also. During the three terrible hours that the play had lasted, he had lived centuries of pain, aeon upon aeon of torture. His life was well worth hers. She had marred him for a moment, if he had wounded her for an age. Besides, women were better suited to bear sorrow than men. They lived on their emotions. They only thought of their emotions. When they took lovers, it was merely to have some one with whom they could have scenes. Lord Henry had told him that, and Lord Henry knew what women were. Why should he trouble about Sibyl Vane? She was nothing to him now.

But the picture? What was he to say of that? It held the secret of his life, and told his story. It had taught him to love his own beauty. Would it teach him to loathe his own soul? Would he ever look at it again?

No; it was merely an illusion wrought on the troubled senses. The horrible night that he had passed had left phantoms behind it. Suddenly there had fallen upon his brain that tiny scarlet speck that makes men mad. The picture had not changed. It was folly to think so.

Yet it was watching him, with its beautiful marred face and its cruel smile. Its bright hair gleamed in the early sunlight. Its blue eyes met his own. A sense of infinite pity, not for himself, but for the painted image of himself, came over him. It had altered already, and would alter more. Its gold would wither into gray. Its red and white roses would die. For every sin that he committed, a stain would fleck and wreck its fairness. But he would not sin. The picture, changed or unchanged, would be to him the visible emblem of conscience. He would resist temptation. He would not see Lord Henry any more,--would not, at any rate, listen to those subtle poisonous theories that in Basil Hallward's garden had first stirred within him the passion for impossible things. He would go back to Sibyl Vane, make her amends, marry her, try to love her again. Yes, it was his duty to do so. She must have suffered more than he had. Poor child! He had been selfish and cruel to her. The fascination that she had exercised over him would return. They would be happy together. His life with her would be beautiful and pure.

He got up from his chair, and drew a large screen right in front of the portrait, shuddering as he glanced at it. "How horrible!" he murmured to himself, and he walked across to the window and opened it. When he stepped out on the grass, he drew a deep breath. The fresh morning air seemed to drive away all his sombre passions. He thought only of Sibyl Vane. A faint echo of his love came back to him. He repeated her name over and over again. The birds that were singing in the dew-drenched garden seemed to be telling the flowers about her.

CHAPTER VI

It was long past noon when he awoke. His valet had crept several times into the room on tiptoe to see if he was stirring, and had wondered what made his young master sleep so late. Finally his bell sounded, and Victor came in softly with a cup of tea, and a pile of letters, on a small tray of old Sèvres china, and drew back the olive-satin curtains, with their shimmering blue lining, that hung in front of the three tall windows.

"Monsieur has well slept this morning," he said, smiling.

"What o'clock is it, Victor?" asked Dorian Gray, sleepily.

"One hour and a quarter, monsieur."

How late it was! He sat up, and, having sipped some tea, turned over his letters. One of them was from Lord Henry, and had been brought by hand that morning. He hesitated for a moment, and then put it aside. The others he opened listlessly. They contained the usual collection of cards, invitations to dinner, tickets for private views, programmes of charity concerts, and the like, that are showered on fashionable young men every morning during the season. There was a rather heavy bill, for a chased silver Louis-Quinze toilet-set, that he had not yet had the courage to send on to his guardians, who were extremely old-fashioned people and did not realize that we live in an age when only unnecessary things are absolutely necessary to us; and there were several very courteously worded communications from Jermyn Street money-lenders offering to advance any sum of money at a moment's notice and at the most reasonable rates of interest.

After about ten minutes he got up, and, throwing on an elaborate dressing-gown, passed into the onyx-paved bath-room. The cool water refreshed him after his long sleep. He seemed to have forgotten all that he had gone through. A dim sense of having taken part in some strange tragedy came to him once or twice, but there was the unreality of a dream about it.

As soon as he was dressed, he went into the library and sat down to a light French breakfast, that had been laid out for him on a small round table close to an open window. It was an exquisite day. The warm air seemed laden with spices. A bee flew in, and buzzed round the blue-dragon bowl, filled with sulphur-yellow roses, that stood in front of him. He felt perfectly happy.

Suddenly his eye fell on the screen that he had placed in

front of the portrait, and he started.

"Too cold for Monsieur?" asked his valet, putting an omelette on the table. "I shut the window?"

Dorian shook his head. "I am not cold," he murmured.

Was it all true? Had the portrait really changed? Or had it been simply his own imagination that had made him see a look of evil where there had been a look of joy? Surely a painted canvas could not alter? The thing was absurd. It would serve as a tale to tell Basil some day. It would make him smile.

And, yet, how vivid was his recollection of the whole thing! First in the dim twilight, and then in the bright dawn, he had seen the touch of cruelty in the warped lips. He almost dreaded his valet leaving the room. He knew that when he was alone he would have to examine the portrait. He was afraid of certainty. When the coffee and cigarettes had been brought and the man turned to go, he felt a mad desire to tell him to remain. As the door closed behind him he called him back. The man stood waiting for his orders. Dorian looked at him for a moment. "I am not at home to any one, Victor," he said, with a sigh. The man bowed and retired.

He rose from the table, lit a cigarette, and flung himself down on a luxuriously-cushioned couch that stood facing the screen. The screen was an old one of gilt Spanish leather, stamped and wrought with a rather florid Louis-Quatorze pattern. He scanned it curiously, wondering if it had ever before concealed the secret of a man's life.

Should he move it aside, after all? Why not let it stay there? What was the use of knowing? If the thing was true, it was terrible. If it was not true, why trouble about it? But what if, by some fate or deadlier chance, other eyes than his spied behind, and saw the horrible change? What should he do if Basil Hallward came and asked to look at his own picture? He would be sure to do that. No; the thing had to be examined, and at once. Anything would be better than this dreadful state of doubt.

He got up, and locked both doors. At least he would be alone when he looked upon the mask of his shame. Then he drew the screen aside, and saw himself face to face. It was perfectly true. The portrait had altered.

As he often remembered afterwards, and always with no small wonder, he found himself at first gazing at the portrait with a feeling of almost scientific interest. That such a change should have taken place was incredible to him. And yet it was a fact. Was there some subtle affinity between the chemical atoms, that shaped themselves into form and color on the canvas, and the soul that was within him? Could it be that what that soul thought, they realized?--that what it dreamed, they made true? Or was there some other, more terrible reason? He shuddered, and felt afraid, and, going back to the couch, lay there, gazing at the picture in sickened horror.

One thing, however, he felt that it had done for him. It had made him conscious how unjust, how cruel, he had been to Sibyl Vane. It was not too late to make reparation for that. She could still be his wife. His unreal and selfish love would yield to some higher influence, would be transformed into some nobler passion, and the portrait that Basil Hallward had painted of him would be a guide to him through life, would be to him what holiness was to some, and conscience to others, and the fear of God to us all. There were opiates for remorse, drugs that could lull the moral sense to sleep. But here was a visible symbol of the degradation of sin. Here was an ever-present sign of the ruin men brought upon their souls.

Three o'clock struck, and four, and half-past four, but he did not stir. He was trying to gather up the scarlet threads of life, and to weave them into a pattern; to find his way through the sanguine labyrinth of passion through which he was wandering. He did not know what to do, or what to think. Finally, he went over to the table and wrote a passionate letter to the girl he had loved, imploring her forgiveness, and accusing himself of madness. He covered page after page with wild words of sorrow, and wilder words of pain. There is a luxury in self-reproach. When we blame ourselves we feel that no one else has a right to blame us. It is the confession, not the priest, that gives us absolution. When Dorian Gray had finished the letter, he felt that he had been forgiven.

Suddenly there came a knock to the door, and he heard Lord Henry's voice outside. "My dear Dorian, I must see you. Let me in at once. I can't bear your shutting yourself up like this."

He made no answer at first, but remained quite still. The knocking still continued, and grew louder. Yes, it was better to let Lord Henry in, and to explain to him the new life he was going to lead, to quarrel with him if it became necessary to quarrel, to part if parting was inevitable. He jumped up, drew the screen hastily across the picture, and unlocked the door.

"I am so sorry for it all, my dear boy," said Lord Henry, coming in. "But you must not think about it too much."

"Do you mean about Sibyl Vane?" asked Dorian.

"Yes, of course," answered Lord Henry, sinking into a chair, and slowly pulling his gloves off. "It is dreadful, from one point of view, but it was not your fault. Tell me, did you go behind and see her after the play was over?"

"Yes."

"I felt sure you had. Did you make a scene with her?"

"I was brutal, Harry,--perfectly brutal. But it is all right now. I am not sorry for anything that has happened. It has taught me to know myself better."

"Ah, Dorian, I am so glad you take it in that way! I was afraid I would find you plunged in remorse, and tearing your nice hair."

"I have got through all that," said Dorian, shaking his head, and smiling. "I am perfectly happy now. I know what conscience is, to begin with. It is not what you told me it was. It is the divinest thing in us. Don't sneer at it, Harry, any more,--at least not before me. I want to be good. I can't bear the idea of my soul being hideous."

"A very charming artistic basis for ethics, Dorian! I congratulate you on it. But how are you going to begin?"

"By marrying Sibyl Vane."

"Marrying Sibyl Vane!" cried Lord Henry, standing up, and looking at him in perplexed amazement. "But, my dear Dorian--"

"Yes, Harry, I know what you are going to say. Something dreadful about marriage. Don't say it. Don't ever say things of that kind to me again. Two days ago I asked Sibyl to marry me. I am not going to break my word to her. She is to be my wife."

"Your wife! Dorian! . . . Didn't you get my letter? I wrote to you this morning, and sent the note down, by my own man."

"Your letter? Oh, yes, I remember. I have not read it yet, Harry. I was afraid there might be something in it that I wouldn't like."

Lord Henry walked across the room, and, sitting down by Dorian Gray, took both his hands in his, and held them tightly.

"Dorian," he said, "my letter--don't be frightened--was to tell you that Sibyl Vane is dead."

A cry of pain rose from the lad's lips, and he leaped to his feet, tearing his hands away from Lord Henry's grasp. "Dead! Sibyl dead! It is not true! It is a horrible lie!"

"It is quite true, Dorian," said Lord Henry, gravely. "It is in all the morning papers. I wrote down to you to ask you not to see any one till I came. There will have to be an inquest, of course, and you must not be mixed up in it. Things like that make a man fashionable in Paris. But in London people are so prejudiced. Here, one should never make one's début with a scandal. One should reserve that to give an interest to one's old age. I don't suppose they know your name at the theatre. If they don't, it is all right. Did any one see you going round to her room? That is an important point."

Dorian did not answer for a few moments. He was dazed with horror. Finally he murmured, in a stifled voice, "Harry, did you say an inquest? What did you mean by that? Did Sibyl--? Oh, Harry, I can't bear it! But be quick. Tell me everything at once."

"I have no doubt it was not an accident, Dorian, though it must be put in that way to the public. As she was leaving the theatre with her mother, about half-past twelve or so, she said she had forgotten something up-stairs. They waited some time for her, but she did not come down again. They ultimately found her lying dead on the floor of her dressing-room. She had swallowed something by mistake, some dreadful thing they use at theatres. I don't know what it was, but it had either prussic acid or white lead in it. I should fancy it was prussic acid, as she seems to have died instantaneously. It is very tragic, of course, but you must not get yourself mixed up in it. I see by the Standard that she was seventeen. I should have thought she was almost younger than that. She looked such a child, and seemed to know so little about acting. Dorian, you mustn't let this thing get on your nerves. You must come and dine with me, and afterwards we will look in at the Opera. It is a Patti night, and everybody will be there. You can come to my sister's box. She has got some smart women with her."

"So I have murdered Sibyl Vane," said Dorian Gray, half to himself,--"murdered her as certainly as if I had cut her little throat with a knife. And the roses are not less lovely for all that. The birds sing just as happily in my garden. And to-night I am to dine with you, and then go on to the Opera, and sup somewhere, I suppose, afterwards. How extraordinarily dramatic life is! If I had read all this in a book, Harry, I think I would have wept over it. Somehow, now that it has happened actually, and to me, it seems far too wonderful for tears. Here is the first passionate love-letter I have ever written in my life. Strange, that my first passionate love-letter should have been addressed to a dead girl. Can they feel, I wonder, those white silent people we call the dead? Sibyl! Can she feel, or know, or listen? Oh, Harry, how I loved her once! It seems years ago to me now. She was everything to me. Then came that dreadful night--was it really only last night?--when she played so badly, and my heart almost broke. She explained it all to me. It was terribly pathetic. But I was not moved a bit. I thought her shallow. Then something happened that made me afraid. I can't tell you what it was, but it was awful. I said I would go back to her. I felt I had done wrong. And now she is dead. My God! my God! Harry, what shall I do? You don't know the danger I am in, and there is nothing to keep me straight. She would have done that for me. She had no right to kill herself. It was selfish of her."

"My dear Dorian, the only way a woman can ever reform a man is by boring him so completely that he loses all possible interest in life. If you had married this girl you would have been wretched. Of course you would have treated her kindly. One can always be kind to people about whom one cares nothing. But she would have soon found out that you were absolutely indifferent to her. And when a woman finds that out about her husband, she either becomes dreadfully dowdy, or wears very smart bonnets that some other woman's husband has to pay for. I say nothing about the social mistake, but I assure you that in any case the whole thing would have been an absolute failure."

"I suppose it would," muttered the lad, walking up and down the room, and looking horribly pale. "But I thought it was my duty. It is not my fault that this terrible tragedy has prevented my doing what was right. I remember your saying once that there is a fatality about good resolutions,--that they are always made too late. Mine certainly were."

"Good resolutions are simply a useless attempt to interfere with scientific laws. Their origin is pure vanity. Their result is absolutely nil. They give us, now and then, some of those luxurious sterile emotions that have a certain charm for us. That is all that can be said for them."

"Harry," cried Dorian Gray, coming over and sitting down beside him, "why is it that I cannot feel this tragedy as much as I want to? I don't think I am heartless. Do you?"

"You have done too many foolish things in your life to be entitled to give yourself that name, Dorian," answered Lord

Henry, with his sweet, melancholy smile.

The lad frowned. "I don't like that explanation, Harry," he rejoined, "but I am glad you don't think I am heartless. I am nothing of the kind. I know I am not. And yet I must admit that this thing that has happened does not affect me as it should. It seems to me to be simply like a wonderful ending to a wonderful play. It has all the terrible beauty of a great tragedy, a tragedy in which I took part, but by which I have not been wounded."

"It is an interesting question," said Lord Henry, who found an exquisite pleasure in playing on the lad's unconscious egotism,--"an extremely interesting question. I fancy that the explanation is this. It often happens that the real tragedies of life occur in such an inartistic manner that they hurt us by their crude violence, their absolute incoherence, their absurd want of meaning, their entire lack of style. They affect us just as vulgarity affects us. They give us an impression of sheer brute force, and we revolt against that. Sometimes, however, a tragedy that has artistic elements of beauty crosses our lives. If these elements of beauty are real, the whole thing simply appeals to our sense of dramatic effect. Suddenly we find that we are no longer the actors, but the spectators of the play. Or rather we are both. We watch ourselves, and the mere wonder of the spectacle enthralls us. In the present case, what is it that has really happened? Some one has killed herself for love of you. I wish I had ever had such an experience. It would have made me in love with love for the rest of my life. The people who have adored me--there have not been very many, but there have been some--have always insisted on living on, long after I had ceased to care for them, or they to care for me. They have become stout and tedious, and when I meet them they go in at once for reminiscences. That awful memory of woman! What a fearful thing it is! And what an utter intellectual stagnation it reveals! One should absorb the color of life, but one should never remember its details. Details are always vulgar.

"Of course, now and then things linger. I once wore nothing but violets all through one season, as mourning for a romance that would not die. Ultimately, however, it did die. I forget what killed it. I think it was her proposing to sacrifice the whole world for me. That is always a dreadful moment. It fills one with the terror of eternity. Well,--would you believe it?--a week ago, at Lady Hampshire's, I found myself seated at dinner next the lady in question, and she insisted on going over the whole thing again, and digging up the past, and raking up the future. I had buried my romance in a bed of poppies. She dragged it out again, and assured me that I had spoiled her life. I am bound to state that she ate an enormous dinner, so I did not feel any anxiety. But what a lack of taste she showed! The one charm of the past is that it is the past. But women never know when the curtain has fallen. They always want a sixth act, and as soon as the interest of the play is entirely over they propose to continue it. If they were allowed to have their way, every comedy would have a tragic ending, and every tragedy would culminate in a farce. They are charmingly artificial, but they have no sense of art. You are more fortunate than I am. I assure you, Dorian, that not one of the women I have known would have done for me what Sibyl Vane did for you. Ordinary women always console themselves. Some of them do it by going in for sentimental colors. Never trust a woman who wears mauve, whatever her age may be, or a woman over thirty-five who is fond of pink ribbons. It always means that they have a history. Others find a great consolation in suddenly discovering the good qualities of their husbands. They flaunt their conjugal felicity in one's face, as if it was the most fascinating of sins. Religion consoles some. Its mysteries have all the charm of a flirtation, a woman once told me; and I can quite understand it. Besides, nothing makes one so vain as being told that one is a sinner. There is really no end to the consolations that women find in modern life. Indeed, I have not mentioned the most important one of all."

"What is that, Harry?" said Dorian Gray, listlessly.

"Oh, the obvious one. Taking some one else's admirer when one loses one's own. In good society that always whitewashes a woman. But really, Dorian, how different Sibyl Vane must have been from all the women one meets! There is something to me quite beautiful about her death. I am glad I am living in a century when such wonders happen. They make one believe in the reality of the things that shallow, fashionable people play with, such as romance, passion, and love."

"I was terribly cruel to her. You forget that."

"I believe that women appreciate cruelty more than anything else. They have wonderfully primitive instincts. We have emancipated them, but they remain slaves looking for their masters, all the same. They love being dominated. I am sure you were splendid. I have never seen you angry, but I can fancy how delightful you looked. And, after all, you said something to me the day before yesterday that seemed to me at the time to be merely fanciful, but that I see now was absolutely true, and it explains everything."

"What was that, Harry?"

"You said to me that Sibyl Vane represented to you all the heroines of romance--that she was Desdemona one night, and

Ophelia the other; that if she died as Juliet, she came to life as Imogen."

"She will never come to life again now," murmured the lad, burying his face in his hands.

"No, she will never come to life. She has played her last part. But you must think of that lonely death in the tawdry dressing-room simply as a strange lurid fragment from some Jacobean tragedy, as a wonderful scene from Webster, or Ford, or Cyril Tourneur. The girl never really lived, and so she has never really died. To you at least she was always a dream, a phantom that flitted through Shakespeare's plays and left them lovelier for its presence, a reed through which Shakespeare's music sounded richer and more full of joy. The moment she touched actual life, she marred it, and it marred her, and so she passed away. Mourn for Ophelia, if you like. Put ashes on your head because Cordelia was strangled. Cry out against Heaven because the daughter of Brabantio died. But don't waste your tears over Sibyl Vane. She was less real than they are."

There was a silence. The evening darkened in the room. Noiselessly, and with silver feet, the shadows crept in from the garden. The colors faded wearily out of things.

After some time Dorian Gray looked up. "You have explained me to myself, Harry," he murmured, with something of a sigh of relief. "I felt all that you have said, but somehow I was afraid of it, and I could not express it to myself. How well you know me! But we will not talk again of what has happened. It has been a marvellous experience. That is all. I wonder if life has still in store for me anything as marvellous."

"Life has everything in store for you, Dorian. There is nothing that you, with your extraordinary good looks, will not be able to do."

"But suppose, Harry, I became haggard, and gray, and wrinkled? What then?"

"Ah, then," said Lord Henry, rising to go,--"then, my dear Dorian, you would have to fight for your victories. As it is, they are brought to you. No, you must keep your good looks. We live in an age that reads too much to be wise, and that thinks too much to be beautiful. We cannot spare you. And now you had better dress, and drive down to the club. We are rather late, as it is."

"I think I shall join you at the Opera, Harry. I feel too tired to eat anything. What is the number of your sister's box?"

"Twenty-seven, I believe. It is on the grand tier. You will see her name on the door. But I am sorry you won't come and dine."

"I don't feel up to it," said Dorian, wearily. "But I am awfully obliged to you for all that you have said to me. You are certainly my best friend. No one has ever understood me as you have."

"We are only at the beginning of our friendship, Dorian," answered Lord Henry, shaking him by the hand. "Good-by. I shall see you before nine-thirty, I hope. Remember, Patti is singing."

As he closed the door behind him, Dorian Gray touched the bell, and in a few minutes Victor appeared with the lamps and drew the blinds down. He waited impatiently for him to go. The man seemed to take an interminable time about everything.

As soon as he had left, he rushed to the screen, and drew it back. No; there was no further change in the picture. It had received the news of Sibyl Vane's death before he had known of it himself. It was conscious of the events of life as they occurred. The vicious cruelty that marred the fine lines of the mouth had, no doubt, appeared at the very moment that the girl had drunk the poison, whatever it was. Or was it indifferent to results? Did it merely take cognizance of what passed within the soul? he wondered, and hoped that some day he would see the change taking place before his very eyes, shuddering as he hoped it.

Poor Sibyl! what a romance it had all been! She had often mimicked death on the stage, and at last Death himself had touched her, and brought her with him. How had she played that dreadful scene? Had she cursed him, as she died? No; she had died for love of him, and love would always be a sacrament to him now. She had atoned for everything, by the sacrifice she had made of her life. He would not think any more of what she had made him go through, that horrible night at the theatre. When he thought of her, it would be as a wonderful tragic figure to show Love had been a great reality. A wonderful tragic figure? Tears came to his eyes as he remembered her child-like look and winsome fanciful ways and shy tremulous grace. He wiped them away hastily, and looked again at the picture.

He felt that the time had really come for making his choice. Or had his choice already been made? Yes, life had decided that for him,--life, and his own infinite curiosity about life. Eternal youth, infinite passion, pleasures subtle and secret, wild joys and wilder sins,--he was to have all these things. The portrait was to bear the burden of his shame: that was all.

A feeling of pain came over him as he thought of the desecration that was in store for the fair face on the canvas. Once, in boyish mockery of Narcissus, he had kissed, or feigned to kiss, those painted lips that now smiled so cruelly at him. Morning after morning he had sat before the portrait wondering at its beauty, almost enamoured of it, as it seemed to him at times. Was it to alter now with every mood to which he yielded? Was it to become a hideous and loathsome thing, to be hidden away in a locked room, to be shut out from the sunlight that had so often touched to brighter gold the waving wonder of the hair? The pity of it! the pity of it!

For a moment he thought of praying that the horrible sympathy that existed between him and the picture might cease. It had changed in answer to a prayer; perhaps in answer to a prayer it might remain unchanged. And, yet, who, that knew anything about Life, would surrender the chance of remaining always young, however fantastic that chance might be, or with what fateful consequences it might be fraught? Besides, was it really under his control? Had it indeed been prayer that had produced the substitution? Might there not be some curious scientific reason for it all? If thought could exercise its influence upon a living organism, might not thought exercise an influence upon dead and inorganic things? Nay, without thought or conscious desire, might not things external to ourselves vibrate in unison with our moods and passions, atom calling to atom, in secret love or strange affinity? But the reason was of no importance. He would never again tempt by a prayer any terrible power. If the picture was to alter, it was to alter. That was all. Why inquire too closely into it?

For there would be a real pleasure in watching it. He would be able to follow his mind into its secret places. This portrait would be to him the most magical of mirrors. As it had revealed to him his own body, so it would reveal to him his own soul. And when winter came upon it, he would still be standing where spring trembles on the verge of summer. When the blood crept from its face, and left behind a pallid mask of chalk with leaden eyes, he would keep the glamour of boyhood. Not one blossom of his loveliness would ever fade. Not one pulse of his life would ever weaken. Like the gods of the Greeks, he would be strong, and fleet, and joyous. What did it matter what happened to the colored image on the canvas? He would be safe. That was everything.

He drew the screen back into its former place in front of the picture, smiling as he did so, and passed into his bedroom, where his valet was already waiting for him. An hour later he was at the Opera, and Lord Henry was leaning over his chair.

CHAPTER VII

As he was sitting at breakfast next morning, Basil Hallward was shown into the room.

"I am so glad I have found you, Dorian," he said, gravely. "I called last night, and they told me you were at the Opera. Of course I knew that was impossible. But I wish you had left word where you had really gone to. I passed a dreadful evening, half afraid that one tragedy might be followed by another. I think you might have telegraphed for me when you heard of it first. I read of it quite by chance in a late edition of the Globe, that I picked up at the club. I came here at once, and was miserable at not finding you. I can't tell you how heart-broken I am about the whole thing. I know what you must suffer. But where were you? Did you go down and see the girl's mother? For a moment I thought of following you there. They gave the address in the paper. Somewhere in the Euston Road, isn't it? But I was afraid of intruding upon a sorrow that I could not lighten. Poor woman! What a state she must be in! And her only child, too! What did she say about it all?"

"My dear Basil, how do I know?" murmured Dorian, sipping some pale-yellow wine from a delicate gold-beaded bubble of Venetian glass, and looking dreadfully bored. "I was at the Opera. You should have come on there. I met Lady Gwendolen, Harry's sister, for the first time. We were in her box. She is perfectly charming; and Patti sang divinely. Don't talk about horrid subjects. If one doesn't talk about a thing, it has never happened. It is simply expression, as Harry says, that gives reality to things. Tell me about yourself and what you are painting."

"You went to the Opera?" said Hallward, speaking very slowly, and with a strained touch of pain in his voice. "You went to the Opera while Sibyl Vane was lying dead in some sordid lodging? You can talk to me of other women being charming, and of Patti singing divinely, before the girl you loved has even the quiet of a grave to sleep in? Why, man, there are horrors in store for that little white body of hers!"

"Stop, Basil! I won't hear it!" cried Dorian, leaping to his feet. "You must not tell me about things. What is done is done. What is past is past."

"You call yesterday the past?"

"What has the actual lapse of time got to do with it? It is only shallow people who require years to get rid of an emotion. A man who is master of himself can end a sorrow as easily as he can invent a pleasure. I don't want to be at the mercy of my emotions. I want to use them, to enjoy them, and to dominate them."

"Dorian, this is horrible! Something has changed you completely. You look exactly the same wonderful boy who used to come down to my studio, day after day, to sit for his picture. But you were simple, natural, and affectionate then. You were the most unspoiled creature in the whole world. Now, I don't know what has come over you. You talk as if you had no heart, no pity in you. It is all Harry's influence. I see that."

The lad flushed up, and, going to the window, looked out on the green, flickering garden for a few moments. "I owe a great deal to Harry, Basil," he said, at last,--"more than I owe to you. You only taught me to be vain."

"Well, I am punished for that, Dorian,--or shall be some day."

"I don't know what you mean, Basil," he exclaimed, turning round. "I don't know what you want. What do you want?"

"I want the Dorian Gray I used to know."

"Basil," said the lad, going over to him, and putting his hand on his shoulder, "you have come too late. Yesterday when I heard that Sibyl Vane had killed herself--"

"Killed herself! Good heavens! is there no doubt about that?" cried Hallward, looking up at him with an expression of horror.

"My dear Basil! Surely you don't think it was a vulgar accident? Of course she killed herself It is one of the great romantic tragedies of the age. As a rule, people who act lead the most commonplace lives. They are good husbands, or faithful wives, or something tedious. You know what I mean,--middle-class virtue, and all that kind of thing. How different Sibyl was! She lived her finest tragedy. She was always a heroine. The last night she played--the night you saw her--she acted badly because she had known the reality of love. When she knew its unreality, she died, as Juliet might have died. She passed again into the sphere of art. There is something of the martyr about her. Her death has all the pathetic uselessness of martyrdom, all its wasted beauty. But, as I was saying, you must not think I have not suffered. If you had come in yesterday at a particular moment,--about half-past five, perhaps, or a quarter to six,--you would have found me in tears. Even Harry, who was here, who brought me the news, in fact, had no idea what I was going through. I suffered immensely, then it passed away. I cannot repeat an emotion. No one can, except sentimentalists. And you are awfully unjust, Basil. You come down here to console me. That is charming of you. You find me consoled, and you are furious. How like a sympathetic person! You remind me of a story Harry told me about a certain philanthropist who spent twenty years of his life in trying to get some grievance redressed, or some unjust law altered,--I forget exactly what it was. Finally he succeeded, and nothing could exceed his disappointment. He had absolutely nothing to do, almost died of ennui, and became a confirmed misanthrope. And besides, my dear old Basil, if you really want to console me, teach me rather to forget what has happened, or to see it from a proper artistic point of view. Was it not Gautier who used to write about la consolation des arts? I remember picking up a little vellum-covered book in your studio one day and chancing on that delightful phrase. Well, I am not like that young man you told me of when we were down at Marlowe together, the young man who used to say that yellow satin could console one for all the miseries of life. I love beautiful things that one can touch and handle. Old brocades, green bronzes, lacquer-work, carved ivories, exquisite surroundings, luxury, pomp,--there is much to be got from all these. But the artistic temperament that they create, or at any rate reveal, is still more to me. To become the spectator of one's own life, as Harry says, is to escape the suffering of life. I know you are surprised at my talking to you like this. You have not realized how I have developed. I was a school-boy when you knew me. I am a man now. I have new passions, new thoughts, new ideas. I am different, but you must not like me less. I am changed, but you must always be my friend. Of course I am very fond of Harry. But I know that you are better than he is. You are not stronger,--you are too much afraid of life,--but you are better. And how happy we used to be together! Don't leave me, Basil, and don't quarrel with me. I am what I am. There is nothing more to be said."

Hallward felt strangely moved. Rugged and straightforward as he was, there was something in his nature that was purely feminine in its tenderness. The lad was infinitely dear to him, and his personality had been the great turning-point in his art. He could not bear the idea of reproaching him any more. After all, his indifference was probably merely a mood that would pass away. There was so much in him that was good, so much in him that was noble.

"Well, Dorian," he said, at length, with a sad smile, "I won't speak to you again about this horrible thing, after to-day. I only trust your name won't be mentioned in connection with it. The inquest is to take place this afternoon. Have they summoned you?"

Dorian shook his head, and a look of annoyance passed over his face at the mention of the word "inquest." There was something so crude and vulgar about everything of the kind. "They don't know my name," he answered.

"But surely she did?"

"Only my Christian name, and that I am quite sure she never mentioned to any one. She told me once that they were all rather curious to learn who I was, and that she invariably told them my name was Prince Charming. It was pretty of her. You must do me a drawing of her, Basil. I should like to have something more of her than the memory of a few kisses and some broken pathetic words."

"I will try and do something, Dorian, if it would please you. But you must come and sit to me yourself again. I can't get on without you."

"I will never sit to you again, Basil. It is impossible!" he exclaimed, starting back.

Hallward stared at him, "My dear boy, what nonsense!" he cried. "Do you mean to say you don't like what I did of you? Where is it? Why have you pulled the screen in front of it? Let me look at it. It is the best thing I have ever painted. Do take that screen away, Dorian. It is simply horrid of your servant hiding my work like that. I felt the room looked different as I came in."

"My servant has nothing to do with it, Basil. You don't imagine I let him arrange my room for me? He settles my flowers for me sometimes,--that is all. No; I did it myself. The light was too strong on the portrait."

"Too strong! Impossible, my dear fellow! It is an admirable place for it. Let me see it." And Hallward walked towards the corner of the room.

A cry of terror broke from Dorian Gray's lips, and he rushed between Hallward and the screen. "Basil," he said, looking very pale, "you must not look at it. I don't wish you to."

"Not look at my own work! you are not serious. Why shouldn't I look at it?" exclaimed Hallward, laughing.

"If you try to look at it, Basil, on my word of honor I will never speak to you again as long as I live. I am quite serious. I don't offer any explanation, and you are not to ask for any. But, remember, if you touch this screen, everything is over between us."

Hallward was thunderstruck. He looked at Dorian Gray in absolute amazement. He had never seen him like this before. The lad was absolutely pallid with rage. His hands were clinched, and the pupils of his eyes were like disks of blue fire. He was trembling all over.

"Dorian!"

"Don't speak!"

"But what is the matter? Of course I won't look at it if you don't want me to," he said, rather coldly, turning on his heel, and going over towards the window. "But, really, it seems rather absurd that I shouldn't see my own work, especially as I am going to exhibit it in Paris in the autumn. I shall probably have to give it another coat of varnish before that, so I must see it some day, and why not to-day?"

"To exhibit it! You want to exhibit it?" exclaimed Dorian Gray, a strange sense of terror creeping over him. Was the world going to be shown his secret? Were people to gape at the mystery of his life? That was impossible. Something--he did not know what--had to be done at once.

"Yes: I don't suppose you will object to that. Georges Petit is going to collect all my best pictures for a special exhibition in the Rue de Sèze, which will open the first week in October. The portrait will only be away a month. I should think you could easily spare it for that time. In fact, you are sure to be out of town. And if you hide it always behind a screen, you can't care much about it."

Dorian Gray passed his hand over his forehead. There were beads of perspiration there. He felt that he was on the brink of a horrible danger. "You told me a month ago that you would never exhibit it," he said. "Why have you changed your mind? You people who go in for being consistent have just as many moods as others. The only difference is that your moods are rather meaningless. You can't have forgotten that you assured me most solemnly that nothing in the world would induce you to send it to any exhibition. You told Harry exactly the same thing." He stopped suddenly, and a gleam of light came into his eyes. He remembered that Lord Henry had said to him once, half seriously and half in jest, "If you want to have an interesting quarter of an hour, get Basil to tell you why he won't exhibit your picture. He told me why he wouldn't, and it was a revelation to me." Yes, perhaps Basil, too, had his secret. He would ask him and try.

"Basil," he said, coming over quite close, and looking him straight in the face, "we have each of us a secret. Let me know yours, and I will tell you mine. What was your reason for refusing to exhibit my picture?"

Hallward shuddered in spite of himself. "Dorian, if I told you, you might like me less than you do, and you would certainly laugh at me. I could not bear your doing either of those two things. If you wish me never to look at your picture again, I am content. I have always you to look at. If you wish the best work I have ever done to be hidden from the world, I am satisfied. Your friendship is dearer to me than any fame or reputation."

"No, Basil, you must tell me," murmured Dorian Gray. "I think I have a right to know." His feeling of terror had passed away, and curiosity had taken its place. He was determined to find out Basil Hallward's mystery.

"Let us sit down, Dorian," said Hallward, looking pale and pained. "Let us sit down. I will sit in the shadow, and you shall sit in the sunlight. Our lives are like that. Just answer me one question. Have you noticed in the picture something that you did not like?--something that probably at first did not strike you, but that revealed itself to you suddenly?"

"Basil!" cried the lad, clutching the arms of his chair with trembling hands, and gazing at him with wild, startled eyes.

"I see you did. Don't speak. Wait till you hear what I have to say. It is quite true that I have worshipped you with far more romance of feeling than a man usually gives to a friend. Somehow, I had never loved a woman. I suppose I never had time. Perhaps, as Harry says, a really 'grande passion' is the privilege of those who have nothing to do, and that is the use of the idle classes in a country. Well, from the moment I met you, your personality had the most extraordinary influence over me. I quite admit that I adored you madly, extravagantly, absurdly. I was jealous of every one to whom you spoke. I wanted to have you all to myself. I was only happy when I was with you. When I was away from you, you were still present in my art. It was all wrong and foolish. It is all wrong and foolish still. Of course I never let you know anything about this. It would have been impossible. You would not have understood it; I did not understand it myself. One day I determined to paint a wonderful portrait of you. It was to have been my masterpiece.

It is my masterpiece. But, as I worked at it, every flake and film of color seemed to me to reveal my secret. I grew afraid that the world would know of my idolatry. I felt, Dorian, that I had told too much. Then it was that I resolved never to allow the picture to be exhibited. You were a little annoyed; but then you did not realize all that it meant to me. Harry, to whom I talked about it, laughed at me. But I did not mind that. When the picture was finished, and I sat alone with it, I felt that I was right. Well, after a few days the portrait left my studio, and as soon as I had got rid of the intolerable fascination of its presence it seemed to me that I had been foolish in imagining that I had said anything in it, more than that you were extremely good-looking and that I could paint. Even now I cannot help feeling that it is a mistake to think that the passion one feels in creation is ever really shown in the work one creates. Art is more abstract than we fancy. Form and color tell us of form and color,--that is all. It often seems to me that art conceals the artist far more completely than it ever reveals him. And so when I got this offer from Paris I determined to make your portrait the principal thing in my exhibition. It never occurred to me that you would refuse. I see now that you were right. The picture must not be shown. You must not be angry with me, Dorian, for what I have told you. As I said to Harry, once, you are made to be worshipped."

Dorian Gray drew a long breath. The color came back to his cheeks, and a smile played about his lips. The peril was over. He was safe for the time. Yet he could not help feeling infinite pity for the young man who had just made this strange confession to him. He wondered if he would ever be so dominated by the personality of a friend. Lord Harry had the charm of being very dangerous. But that was all. He was too clever and too cynical to be really fond of. Would there ever be some one who would fill him with a strange idolatry? Was that one of the things that life had in store?

"It is extraordinary to me, Dorian," said Hallward, "that you should have seen this in the picture. Did you really see it?"

"Of course I did."

"Well, you don't mind my looking at it now?"

Dorian shook his head. "You must not ask me that, Basil. I could not possibly let you stand in front of that picture."

"You will some day, surely?"

"Never."

"Well, perhaps you are right. And now good-by, Dorian. You have been the one person in my life of whom I have been really fond. I don't suppose I shall often see you again. You don't know what it cost me to tell you all that I have told you."

"My dear Basil," cried Dorian, "what have you told me? Simply that you felt that you liked me too much. That is not even a compliment."

"It was not intended as a compliment. It was a confession."

"A very disappointing one."

"Why, what did you expect, Dorian? You didn't see anything else in the picture, did you? There was nothing else to see?"

"No: there was nothing else to see. Why do you ask? But you mustn't talk about not meeting me again, or anything of that kind. You and I are friends, Basil, and we must always remain so."

"You have got Harry," said Hallward, sadly.

"Oh, Harry!" cried the lad, with a ripple of laughter. "Harry spends his days in saying what is incredible, and his evenings in doing what is improbable. Just the sort of life I would like to lead. But still I don't think I would go to Harry if I was in trouble. I would sooner go to you, Basil."

"But you won't sit to me again?"

"Impossible!"

"You spoil my life as an artist by refusing, Dorian. No man comes across two ideal things. Few come across one."

"I can't explain it to you, Basil, but I must never sit to you again. I will come and have tea with you. That will be just as pleasant."

"Pleasanter for you, I am afraid," murmured Hallward, regretfully. "And now good-by. I am sorry you won't let me look at the picture once again. But that can't be helped. I quite understand what you feel about it."

As he left the room, Dorian Gray smiled to himself. Poor Basil! how little he knew of the true reason! And how strange it was that, instead of having been forced to reveal his own secret, he had succeeded, almost by chance, in wresting a secret from his friend! How much that strange confession explained to him! Basil's absurd fits of jealousy, his wild devotion, his extravagant panegyrics, his curious reticences,--he understood them all now, and he felt sorry. There was something tragic in a friendship so colored by romance.

He sighed, and touched the bell. The portrait must be hidden away at all costs. He could not run such a risk of discovery again. It had been mad of him to have the thing remain, even for an hour, in a room to which any of his friends had access.

CHAPTER VIII

When his servant entered, he looked at him steadfastly, and wondered if he had thought of peering behind the screen. The man was quite impassive, and waited for his orders. Dorian lit a cigarette, and walked over to the glass and glanced into it. He could see the reflection of Victor's face perfectly. It was like a placid mask of servility. There was nothing to be afraid of, there. Yet he thought it best to be on his guard.

Speaking very slowly, he told him to tell the housekeeper that he wanted to see her, and then to go to the frame-maker's and ask him to send two of his men round at once. It seemed to him that as the man left the room he peered in the direction of the screen. Or was that only his fancy?

After a few moments, Mrs. Leaf, a dear old lady in a black silk dress, with a photograph of the late Mr. Leaf framed in a large gold brooch at her neck, and old-fashioned thread mittens on her wrinkled hands, bustled into the room.

"Well, Master Dorian," she said, "what can I do for you? I beg your pardon, sir,"--here came a courtesy,--"I shouldn't call you Master Dorian any more. But, Lord bless you, sir, I have known you since you were a baby, and many's the trick you've played on poor old Leaf. Not that you were not always a good boy, sir; but boys will be boys, Master Dorian, and jam is a temptation to the young, isn't it, sir?"

He laughed. "You must always call me Master Dorian, Leaf. I will be very angry with you if you don't. And I assure you I am quite as fond of jam now as I used to be. Only when I am asked out to tea I am never offered any. I want you to give me the key of the room at the top of the house."

"The old school-room, Master Dorian? Why, it's full of dust. I must get it arranged and put straight before you go into it. It's not fit for you to see, Master Dorian. It is not, indeed."

"I don't want it put straight, Leaf. I only want the key."

"Well, Master Dorian, you'll be covered with cobwebs if you goes into it. Why, it hasn't been opened for nearly five years,--not since his lordship died."

He winced at the mention of his dead uncle's name. He had hateful memories of him. "That does not matter, Leaf," he replied. "All I want is the key."

"And here is the key, Master Dorian," said the old lady, after going over the contents of her bunch with tremulously uncertain hands. "Here is the key. I'll have it off the ring in a moment. But you don't think of living up there, Master Dorian, and you so comfortable here?"

"No, Leaf, I don't. I merely want to see the place, and perhaps store something in it,--that is all. Thank you, Leaf. I hope your rheumatism is better; and mind you send me up jam for breakfast."

Mrs. Leaf shook her head. "Them foreigners doesn't understand jam, Master Dorian. They calls it 'compot.' But I'll bring it to you myself some morning, if you lets me."

"That will be very kind of you, Leaf," he answered, looking at the key; and, having made him an elaborate courtesy, the old lady left the room, her face wreathed in smiles. She had a strong objection to the French valet. It was a poor thing, she felt, for any one to be born a foreigner.

As the door closed, Dorian put the key in his pocket, and looked round the room. His eye fell on a large purple satin coverlet heavily embroidered with gold, a splendid piece of late seventeenth-century Venetian work that his uncle had found in a convent near Bologna. Yes, that would serve to wrap the dreadful thing in. It had perhaps served often as a pall for the dead. Now it was to hide something that had a corruption of its own, worse than the corruption of death itself,--something that would breed horrors and yet would never die. What the worm was to the corpse, his sins would be to the painted image on the canvas. They would mar its beauty, and eat away its grace. They would defile it, and make it shameful. And yet the thing would still live on. It would be always alive.

He shuddered, and for a moment he regretted that he had not told Basil the true reason why he had wished to hide the picture away. Basil would have helped him to resist Lord Henry's influence, and the still more poisonous influences that came from his own temperament. The love that he bore him--for it was really love--had something noble and intellectual in it. It was not that mere physical admiration of beauty that is born of the senses, and that dies when the senses tire. It was such love as Michael Angelo had known, and Montaigne, and Winckelmann, and Shakespeare himself. Yes, Basil could have saved him. But it was too late now. The past could always be annihilated. Regret, denial, or forgetfulness could do that. But the future was inevitable. There were passions in him that would find their terrible outlet, dreams that would make the shadow of their evil real.

He took up from the couch the great purple-and-gold texture that covered it, and, holding it in his hands, passed behind the screen. Was the face on the canvas viler than before? It seemed to him that it was unchanged; and yet his loathing of it was intensified. Gold hair, blue eyes, and rose-red lips,--they all were there. It was simply the expression that had altered. That was horrible in its cruelty. Compared to what he saw in it of censure or rebuke, how shallow Basil's reproaches about Sibyl Vane had been!--how shallow, and of what little account! His own soul was looking out at him from the canvas and calling him to judgment. A look of pain came across him, and he flung the rich pall over the picture. As he did so, a knock came to the door. He passed out as his servant entered.

"The persons are here, monsieur."

He felt that the man must be got rid of at once. He must not be allowed to know where the picture was being taken to. There was something sly about him, and he had thoughtful, treacherous eyes. Sitting down at the writing-table, he scribbled a note to Lord Henry, asking him to send him round something to read, and reminding him that they were to meet at eight-fifteen that evening.

"Wait for an answer," he said, handing it to him, "and show the men in here."

In two or three minutes there was another knock, and Mr. Ashton himself, the celebrated frame-maker of South Audley Street, came in with a somewhat rough-looking young assistant. Mr. Ashton was a florid, red-whiskered little man, whose admiration for art was considerably tempered by the inveterate impecuniosity of most of the artists who dealt with him. As a rule, he never left his shop. He waited for people to come to him. But he always made an exception in favor of Dorian Gray. There was something about Dorian that charmed everybody. It was a pleasure even to see him.

"What can I do for you, Mr. Gray?" he said, rubbing his fat freckled hands. "I thought I would do myself the honor of coming round in person. I have just got a beauty of a frame, sir. Picked it up at a sale. Old Florentine. Came from Fonthill, I believe. Admirably suited for a religious picture, Mr. Gray."

"I am so sorry you have given yourself the trouble of coming round, Mr. Ashton. I will certainly drop in and look at the frame,--though I don't go in much for religious art,--but to-day I only want a picture carried to the top of the house for me. It is rather heavy, so I thought I would ask you to lend me a couple of your men."

"No trouble at all, Mr. Gray. I am delighted to be of any service to you. Which is the work of art, sir?"

"This," replied Dorian, moving the screen back. "Can you move it, covering and all, just as it is? I don't want it to get scratched going up-stairs."

"There will be no difficulty, sir," said the genial frame-maker, beginning, with the aid of his assistant, to unhook the picture from the long brass chains by which it was suspended. "And, now, where shall we carry it to, Mr. Gray?"

"I will show you the way, Mr. Ashton, if you will kindly follow me. Or perhaps you had better go in front. I am afraid it is right at the top of the house. We will go up by the front staircase, as it is wider."

He held the door open for them, and they passed out into the hall and began the ascent. The elaborate character of the frame had made the picture extremely bulky, and now and then, in spite of the obsequious protests of Mr. Ashton, who had a true tradesman's dislike of seeing a gentleman doing anything useful, Dorian put his hand to it so as to help them.

"Something of a load to carry, sir," gasped the little man, when they reached the top landing. And he wiped his shiny forehead.

"A terrible load to carry," murmured Dorian, as he unlocked the door that opened into the room that was to keep for him the curious secret of his life and hide his soul from the eyes of men.

He had not entered the place for more than four years,--not, indeed, since he had used it first as a play-room when he was a child and then as a study when he grew somewhat older. It was a large, well-proportioned room, which had been specially built by the last Lord Sherard for the use of the little nephew whom, being himself childless, and perhaps for other reasons, he had always hated and desired to keep at a distance. It did not appear to Dorian to have much changed. There was the huge Italian cassone, with its fantastically-painted panels and its tarnished gilt mouldings, in which he had so often hidden himself as a boy. There was the satinwood bookcase filled with his dog-eared school-books. On the wall behind it was hanging the same ragged Flemish tapestry where a faded king and queen were playing chess in a garden, while a company of hawkers rode by, carrying hooded birds on their gauntleted wrists. How well he recalled it all! Every moment of his lonely childhood came back to him, as he looked round. He remembered the stainless purity of his boyish life, and it seemed horrible to him that it was here that the fatal portrait was to be hidden away. How little he had thought, in those dead days, of all that was in store for him!

But there was no other place in the house so secure from prying eyes as this. He had the key, and no one else could enter it. Beneath its purple pall, the face painted on the canvas could grow bestial, sodden, and unclean. What did it matter? No one could see it. He himself would not see it. Why should he watch the hideous corruption of his soul? He kept his youth,--that was enough. And, besides, might not his nature grow finer, after all? There was no reason that the future should be so full of shame. Some love might come across his life, and purify him, and shield him from those sins that seemed to be already stirring in spirit and in flesh,--those curious unpictured sins whose very mystery lent them their subtlety and their charm. Perhaps, some day, the cruel look would have passed away from the scarlet sensitive mouth, and he might show to the world Basil Hallward's masterpiece.

No; that was impossible. The thing upon the canvas was growing old, hour by hour, and week by week. Even if it escaped the hideousness of sin, the hideousness of age was in store for it. The cheeks would become hollow or flaccid. Yellow crow's-feet would creep round the fading eyes and make them horrible. The hair would lose its brightness, the mouth would gape or droop, would be foolish or gross, as the mouths of old men are. There would be the wrinkled throat, the cold blue-veined hands, the twisted body, that he remembered in the uncle who had been so stern to him in his boyhood. The picture had to be concealed. There was no help for it.

"Bring it in, Mr. Ashton, please," he said, wearily, turning round. "I am sorry I kept you so long. I was thinking of something else."

"Always glad to have a rest, Mr. Gray," answered the frame-maker, who was still gasping for breath. "Where shall we put it, sir?"

"Oh, anywhere, Here, this will do. I don't want to have it hung up. Just lean it against the wall. Thanks."

"Might one look at the work of art, sir?"

Dorian started. "It would not interest you, Mr. Ashton," he said, keeping his eye on the man. He felt ready to leap upon him and fling him to the ground if he dared to lift the gorgeous hanging that concealed the secret of his life. "I won't trouble you any more now. I am much obliged for your kindness in coming round."

"Not at all, not at all, Mr. Gray. Ever ready to do anything for you, sir." And Mr. Ashton tramped down-stairs, followed by the assistant, who glanced back at Dorian with a look of shy wonder in his rough, uncomely face. He had never seen any one so marvellous.

When the sound of their footsteps had died away, Dorian locked the door, and put the key in his pocket. He felt safe now. No one would ever look on the horrible thing. No eye but his would ever see his shame.

On reaching the library he found that it was just after five o'clock, and that the tea had been already brought up. On a little table of dark perfumed wood thickly incrusted with nacre, a present from his guardian's wife, Lady Radley, who had spent the preceding winter in Cairo, was lying a note from Lord Henry, and beside it was a book bound in yellow paper, the cover slightly torn and the edges soiled. A copy of the third edition of the St. James's Gazette had been placed on the tea-tray. It was evident that Victor had returned. He wondered if he had met the men in the hall as they were leaving the house and had wormed out of them what they had been doing. He would be sure to miss the picture,--had no doubt missed it already, while he had been laying the tea-things. The screen had not been replaced, and the blank space on the wall was visible. Perhaps some night he might find him creeping up-stairs and trying to force the door of the room. It was a horrible thing to have a spy in one's house. He had heard of rich men who had been blackmailed all their lives by some servant who had read a letter, or overheard a conversation, or picked up a card with an address, or found beneath a pillow a withered flower or a bit of crumpled lace.

He sighed, and, having poured himself out some tea, opened Lord Henry's note. It was simply to say that he sent him round the evening paper, and a book that might interest him, and that he would be at the club at eight-fifteen. He opened the St. James's languidly, and looked through it. A red pencil-mark on the fifth page caught his eye. He read the following paragraph:

"INQUEST ON AN ACTRESS.--An inquest was held this morning at the Bell Tavern, Hoxton Road, by Mr. Danby, the District Coroner, on the body of Sibyl Vane, a young actress recently engaged at the Royal Theatre, Holborn. A verdict of death by misadventure was returned. Considerable sympathy was expressed for the mother of the deceased, who was greatly affected during the giving of her own evidence, and that of Dr. Birrell, who had made the post-mortem examination of the deceased."

He frowned slightly, and, tearing the paper in two, went across the room and flung the pieces into a gilt basket. How ugly it all was! And how horribly real ugliness made things! He felt a little annoyed with Lord Henry for having sent him the account. And it was certainly stupid of him to have marked it with red pencil. Victor might have read it. The man knew more than enough English for that.

Perhaps he had read it, and had begun to suspect something. And, yet, what did it matter? What had Dorian Gray to do with Sibyl Vane's death? There was nothing to fear. Dorian Gray had not killed her.

His eye fell on the yellow book that Lord Henry had sent him. What was it, he wondered. He went towards the little pearl-colored octagonal stand, that had always looked to him like the work of some strange Egyptian bees who wrought in silver, and took the volume up. He flung himself into an arm-chair, and began to turn over the leaves. After a few minutes, he became absorbed. It was the strangest book he had ever read. It seemed to him that in exquisite raiment, and to the delicate sound of flutes, the sins of the world were passing in dumb show before him. Things that he had dimly dreamed of were suddenly made real to him. Things of which he had never dreamed were gradually revealed.

It was a novel without a plot, and with only one character, being, indeed, simply a psychological study of a certain young Parisian, who spent his life trying to realize in the nineteenth century all the passions and modes of thought that belonged to every century except his own, and to sum up, as it were, in himself the various moods through which the world-spirit had ever passed, loving for their mere artificiality those renunciations that men have unwisely called virtue, as much as those natural rebellions that wise men still call sin. The style in which it was written was that curious jewelled style, vivid and obscure at once, full of argot and of archaisms, of technical expressions and of elaborate paraphrases, that characterizes the work of some of the finest artists of the French school of Décadents. There were in it metaphors as monstrous as orchids, and as evil in color. The life of the senses was described in the terms of mystical philosophy. One hardly knew at times whether one was reading the spiritual ecstasies of some mediaeval saint or the morbid confessions of a modern sinner. It was a poisonous book. The heavy odor of incense seemed to cling about its pages and to trouble the brain. The mere cadence of the sentences, the subtle monotony of their music, so full as it was of complex refrains and movements elaborately repeated, produced in the mind of the lad, as he passed from chapter to chapter, a form of revery, a malady of dreaming, that made him unconscious of the falling day and the creeping shadows.

Cloudless, and pierced by one solitary star, a copper-green sky gleamed through the windows. He read on by its wan light till he could read no more. Then, after his valet had reminded him several times of the lateness of the hour, he got up, and, going into the next room, placed the book on the little Florentine table that always stood at his bedside, and began to dress for dinner.

It was almost nine o'clock before he reached the club, where he found Lord Henry sitting alone, in the morning-room, looking very bored.

"I am so sorry, Harry," he cried, "but really it is entirely your fault. That book you sent me so fascinated me that I forgot what the time was."

"I thought you would like it," replied his host, rising from his chair.

"I didn't say I liked it, Harry. I said it fascinated me. There is a great difference."

"Ah, if you have discovered that, you have discovered a great deal," murmured Lord Henry, with his curious smile. "Come, let us go in to dinner. It is dreadfully late, and I am afraid the champagne will be too much iced."

CHAPTER IX

For years, Dorian Gray could not free himself from the memory of this book. Or perhaps it would be more accurate to say that he never sought to free himself from it. He procured from Paris no less than five large-paper copies of the first edition, and had them bound in different colors, so that they might suit his various moods and the changing fancies of a nature over which he seemed, at times, to have almost entirely lost control. The hero, the wonderful young Parisian, in whom the romantic temperament and the scientific temperament were so strangely blended, became to him a kind of prefiguring type of himself. And, indeed, the whole book seemed to him to contain the story of his own life, written before he had lived it.

In one point he was more fortunate than the book's fantastic hero. He never knew--never, indeed, had any cause to know--that somewhat grotesque dread of mirrors, and polished metal surfaces, and still water, which came upon the young Parisian so early in his life, and was occasioned by the sudden decay of a beauty that had once, apparently, been so remarkable. It was with an almost cruel joy--and perhaps in nearly every joy, as certainly in every pleasure, cruelty has its place--that he used to read the latter part of the book, with its really tragic, if somewhat over-emphasized, account of the sorrow and despair of one who had himself lost what in others, and in the world, he had most valued.

He, at any rate, had no cause to fear that. The boyish beauty that had so fascinated Basil Hallward, and many others besides him, seemed never to leave him. Even those who had heard the most evil things against him (and from time to time strange rumors about his mode of life crept through London and became the chatter of the clubs) could not believe anything to his dishonor when they saw him. He had always the look of one who had kept himself unspotted from the world. Men who talked grossly became silent when Dorian Gray entered the room. There was something in the purity of his face that rebuked them. His mere presence seemed to recall to them the innocence that they had tarnished. They wondered how one so charming and graceful as he was could have escaped the stain of an age that was at once sordid and sensuous.

He himself, on returning home from one of those mysterious and prolonged absences that gave rise to such strange conjecture among those who were his friends, or thought that they were so, would creep up-stairs to the locked room, open the door with the key that never left him, and stand, with a mirror, in front of the portrait that Basil Hallward had painted of him, looking now at the evil and aging face on the canvas, and now at the fair young face that laughed back at him from the polished glass. The very sharpness of the contrast used to quicken his sense of pleasure. He grew more and more enamoured of his own beauty, more and more interested in the corruption of his own soul. He would examine with minute care, and often with a monstrous and terrible delight, the hideous lines that seared the wrinkling forehead or crawled around the heavy sensual mouth, wondering sometimes which were the more horrible, the signs of sin or the signs of age. He would place his white hands beside the coarse bloated hands of the picture, and smile. He mocked the misshapen body and the failing limbs.

There were moments, indeed, at night, when, lying sleepless in his own delicately-scented chamber, or in the sordid room of the little ill-famed tavern near the Docks, which, under an assumed name, and in disguise, it was his habit to frequent, he would think of the ruin he had brought upon his soul, with a pity that was all the more poignant because it was purely selfish. But moments such as these were rare. That curiosity about life that, many years before, Lord Henry had first stirred in him, as they sat together in the garden of their friend, seemed to increase with gratification. The more he knew, the more he desired to know. He had mad hungers that grew more ravenous as he fed them.

Yet he was not really reckless, at any rate in his relations to society. Once or twice every month during the winter, and on each Wednesday evening while the season lasted, he would throw open to the world his beautiful house and have the most celebrated musicians of the day to charm his guests with the wonders of their art. His little dinners, in the settling of which Lord Henry always assisted him, were noted as much for the careful selection and placing of those invited, as for the exquisite taste shown in the decoration of the table, with its subtle symphonic arrangements of exotic flowers, and embroidered cloths, and antique plate of gold and silver. Indeed, there were many, especially among the very young men, who saw, or fancied that they saw, in Dorian Gray the true realization of a type of which they had often dreamed in Eton or Oxford days, a type that was to combine something of the real culture of the scholar with all the grace and distinction and perfect manner of a citizen of the world. To them he seemed to belong to those whom Dante describes as having sought to "make themselves perfect by the worship of beauty." Like Gautier, he was one for whom "the visible world existed."

And, certainly, to him life itself was the first, the greatest, of the arts, and for it all the other arts seemed to be but a preparation. Fashion, by which what is really fantastic becomes for a moment universal, and Dandyism, which, in its own way, is an attempt to assert the absolute modernity of beauty, had, of course, their fascination for him. His mode of dressing, and the particular styles that he affected from time to time, had their marked influence on the young exquisites of the Mayfair balls and Pall Mall club windows, who copied him in everything that he did, and tried to reproduce the accidental charm of his graceful, though to him only half-serious, fopperies.

For, while he was but too ready to accept the position that was almost immediately offered to him on his coming of age, and found, indeed, a subtle pleasure in the thought that he might really become to the London of his own day what to imperial Neronian Rome the author of the "Satyricon" had once been, yet in his inmost heart he desired to be something more than a mere arbiter elegantiarum, to be consulted on the wearing of a jewel, or the knotting of a necktie, or the conduct of a cane. He sought to elaborate some new scheme of life that would have its reasoned philosophy and its ordered principles and find in the spiritualizing of the senses its highest realization.

The worship of the senses has often, and with much justice, been decried, men feeling a natural instinct of terror about passions and sensations that seem stronger than ourselves, and that we are conscious of sharing with the less highly organized forms of existence. But it appeared to Dorian Gray that the true nature of the senses had never been understood, and that they had remained savage and animal merely because the world had sought to starve them into submission or to kill them by pain, instead of aiming at making them elements of a new spirituality, of which a fine instinct for beauty was to be the dominant characteristic. As he looked back upon man moving through History, he was haunted by a feeling of loss. So much had been surrendered! and to such little purpose! There had been mad wilful rejections, monstrous forms of self-torture and self-denial, whose origin was fear, and whose result was a degradation infinitely more terrible than that fancied degradation from which, in their ignorance, they had sought to escape, Nature in her wonderful irony driving the anchorite out to herd with the wild animals of the desert and giving to the hermit the beasts of the field as his companions.

Yes, there was to be, as Lord Henry had prophesied, a new hedonism that was to re-create life, and to save it from that harsh, uncomely puritanism that is having, in our own day, its curious revival. It was to have its service of the intellect, certainly; yet it was never to accept any theory or system that would involve the sacrifice of any mode of passionate experience. Its aim, indeed, was to be experience itself, and not the fruits of experience, sweet or bitter as they might be. Of the asceticism that deadens the senses, as of the vulgar profligacy that dulls them, it was to know nothing. But it was to teach man to concentrate himself upon the moments of a life that is itself but a moment.

There are few of us who have not sometimes wakened before dawn, either after one of those dreamless nights that make one almost enamoured of death, or one of those nights of horror and misshapen joy, when through the chambers of the brain sweep phantoms more terrible than reality itself, and instinct with that vivid life that lurks in all grotesques, and that lends to Gothic art its enduring vitality, this art being, one might fancy, especially the art of those whose minds have been troubled with the malady of revery. Gradually white fingers creep through the curtains, and they appear to tremble. Black fantastic shadows crawl into the corners of the room, and crouch there. Outside, there is the stirring of birds among the leaves, or the sound of men going forth to their work, or the sigh and sob of the wind coming down from the hills, and wandering round the silent house, as though it feared to wake the sleepers. Veil after veil of thin dusky gauze is lifted, and by degrees the forms and colors of things are restored to them, and we watch the dawn remaking the world in its antique pattern. The wan mirrors get back their mimic life. The flameless tapers stand where we have left them, and beside them lies the half-read book that we had been studying, or the wired flower that we had worn at the ball, or the letter that we had been afraid to read, or that we had read too often. Nothing seems to us changed. Out of the unreal shadows of the night comes back the real life that we had known. We have to resume it where we had left off, and there steals over us a terrible sense of the necessity for the continuance of energy in the same wearisome round of stereotyped habits, or a wild longing, it may be, that our eyelids might open some morning upon a world that had been re-fashioned anew for our pleasure in the darkness, a world in which things would have fresh shapes and colors, and be changed, or have other secrets, a world in which the past would have little or no place, or survive, at any rate, in no conscious form of obligation or regret, the remembrance even of joy having its bitterness, and the memories of pleasure their pain.

It was the creation of such worlds as these that seemed to Dorian Gray to be the true object, or among the true objects, of life; and in his search for sensations that would be at once new and delightful, and possess that element of strangeness that is so essential to romance, he would often adopt certain modes of thought that he knew to be really alien to his nature, abandon himself to their subtle influences, and then, having, as it were, caught their color and satisfied his intellectual curiosity, leave them with that curious indifference that is not incompatible with a real ardor of temperament, and that indeed, according to certain modern psychologists, is often a condition of it.

It was rumored of him once that he was about to join the Roman Catholic communion; and certainly the Roman ritual had always a great attraction for him. The daily sacrifice, more awful really than all the sacrifices of the antique world, stirred him as much by its superb rejection of the evidence of the senses as by the primitive simplicity of its elements and the eternal pathos of the human tragedy that it sought to symbolize. He loved to kneel down on the cold marble pavement, and with the priest, in his stiff flowered cope, slowly and with white hands moving aside the veil of the tabernacle, and raising aloft the jewelled lantern-shaped monstrance with that pallid wafer that at times, one would fain think, is indeed the "panis caelestis," the bread of angels, or, robed in the garments of the Passion of Christ, breaking the Host into the chalice, and smiting his breast for his sins. The fuming censers, that the grave boys, in their lace and scarlet, tossed into the air like great gilt flowers, had their subtle fascination for him. As he passed out, he used to look with wonder at the black confessionals, and long to sit in the dim shadow of one of them and listen to men and women whispering through the tarnished grating the true story of their lives.

But he never fell into the error of arresting his intellectual development by any formal acceptance of creed or system, or of mistaking, for a house in which to live, an inn that is but suitable for the sojourn of a night, or for a few hours of a night in which there are no stars and the moon is in travail. Mysticism, with its marvellous power of making common things strange to us, and the subtle antinomianism that always seems to accompany it, moved him for a season; and for a season he inclined to the materialistic doctrines of the Darwinismus movement in Germany, and found a curious pleasure in tracing the thoughts and passions of men to some pearly cell in the brain, or some white nerve in the body, delighting in the conception of the absolute dependence of the spirit on certain physical conditions, morbid or healthy, normal or diseased. Yet, as has been said of him before, no theory of life seemed to him to be of any importance compared with life itself. He felt keenly conscious of how barren all intellectual speculation is when separated from action and experiment. He knew that the senses, no less than the soul, have their mysteries to reveal.

And so he would now study perfumes, and the secrets of

their manufacture, distilling heavily-scented oils, and burning odorous gums from the East. He saw that there was no mood of the mind that had not its counterpart in the sensuous life, and set himself to discover their true relations, wondering what there was in frankincense that made one mystical, and in ambergris that stirred one's passions, and in violets that woke the memory of dead romances, and in musk that troubled the brain, and in champak that stained the imagination; and seeking often to elaborate a real psychology of perfumes, and to estimate the several influences of sweet-smelling roots, and scented pollen-laden flowers, of aromatic balms, and of dark and fragrant woods, of spikenard that sickens, of hovenia that makes men mad, and of aloes that are said to be able to expel melancholy from the soul.

At another time he devoted himself entirely to music, and in a long latticed room, with a vermilion-and-gold ceiling and walls of olive-green lacquer, he used to give curious concerts in which mad gypsies tore wild music from little zithers, or grave yellow-shawled Tunisians plucked at the strained strings of monstrous lutes, while grinning negroes beat monotonously upon copper drums, or turbaned Indians, crouching upon scarlet mats, blew through long pipes of reed or brass, and charmed, or feigned to charm, great hooded snakes and horrible horned adders. The harsh intervals and shrill discords of barbaric music stirred him at times when Schubert's grace, and Chopin's beautiful sorrows, and the mighty harmonies of Beethoven himself, fell unheeded on his ear. He collected together from all parts of the world the strangest instruments that could be found, either in the tombs of dead nations or among the few savage tribes that have survived contact with Western civilizations, and loved to touch and try them. He had the mysterious juruparis of the Rio Negro Indians, that women are not allowed to look at, and that even youths may not see till they have been subjected to fasting and scourging, and the earthen jars of the Peruvians that have the shrill cries of birds, and flutes of human bones such as Alfonso de Ovalle heard in Chili, and the sonorous green stones that are found near Cuzco and give forth a note of singular sweetness. He had painted gourds filled with pebbles that rattled when they were shaken; the long clarin of the Mexicans, into which the performer does not blow, but through which he inhales the air; the harsh turé of the Amazon tribes, that is sounded by the sentinels who sit all day long in trees, and that can be heard, it is said, at a distance of three leagues; the teponaztli, that has two vibrating tongues of wood, and is beaten with sticks that are smeared with an elastic gum obtained from the milky juice of plants; the yotl-bells of the Aztecs, that are hung in clusters like grapes; and a huge cylindrical drum, covered with the skins of great serpents, like the one that Bernal Diaz saw when he went with Cortes into the Mexican temple, and of whose doleful sound he has left us so vivid a description. The fantastic character of these instruments fascinated him, and he felt a curious delight in the thought that Art, like Nature, has her monsters, things of bestial shape and with hideous voices. Yet, after some time, he wearied of them, and would sit in his box at the Opera, either alone or with Lord Henry, listening in rapt pleasure to "Tannhäuser," and seeing in that great work of art a presentation of the tragedy of his own soul.

On another occasion he took up the study of jewels, and appeared at a costume ball as Anne de Joyeuse, Admiral of France, in a dress covered with five hundred and sixty pearls. He would often spend a whole day settling and resettling in their cases the various stones that he had collected, such as the olive-green chrysoberyl that turns red by lamplight, the cymophane with its wire-like line of silver, the pistachio-colored peridot, rose-pink and wine-yellow topazes, carbuncles of fiery scarlet with tremulous four-rayed stars, flame-red cinnamon-stones, orange and violet spinels, and amethysts with their alternate layers of ruby and sapphire. He loved the red gold of the sunstone, and the moonstone's pearly whiteness, and the broken rainbow of the milky opal. He procured from Amsterdam three emeralds of extraordinary size and richness of color, and had a turquoise de la vieille roche that was the envy of all the connoisseurs.

He discovered wonderful stories, also, about jewels. In Alphonso's "Clericalis Disciplina" a serpent was mentioned with eyes of real jacinth, and in the romantic history of Alexander he was said to have found snakes in the vale of Jordan "with collars of real emeralds growing on their backs." There was a gem in the brain of the dragon, Philostratus told us, and "by the exhibition of golden letters and a scarlet robe" the monster could be thrown into a magical sleep, and slain. According to the great alchemist Pierre de Boniface, the diamond rendered a man invisible, and the agate of India made him eloquent. The cornelian appeased anger, and the hyacinth provoked sleep, and the amethyst drove away the fumes of wine. The garnet cast out demons, and the hydropicus deprived the moon of her color. The selenite waxed and waned with the moon, and the meloceus, that discovers thieves, could be affected only by the blood of kids. Leonardus Camillus had seen a white stone taken from the brain of a newly-killed toad, that was a certain antidote against poison. The bezoar, that was found in the heart of the Arabian deer, was a charm that could cure the plague. In the nests of Arabian birds was the aspilates, that, according to Democritus, kept the wearer from any danger by fire.

The King of Ceilan rode through his city with a large ruby in his hand, as the ceremony of his coronation. The gates of the palace of John the Priest were "made of sardius, with the horn of the horned snake inwrought, so that no man might bring poison within." Over the gable were "two golden apples, in which were two carbuncles," so that the gold might shine by day, and the carbuncles by night. In Lodge's strange romance "A Margarite of America" it was stated that in the chamber of Margarite were seen "all the chaste ladies of the world, inchased out of silver, looking through fair mirrours of chrysolites, carbuncles, sapphires, and greene emeraults." Marco Polo had watched the inhabitants of Zipangu place a rose-colored pearl in the mouth of the dead. A sea-monster had been enamoured of the pearl that the diver brought to King Perozes, and had slain the thief, and mourned for seven moons over his loss. When the Huns lured the king into the great pit, he flung it away,--Procopius tells the story,--nor was it ever found again, though the Emperor Anastasius offered five hundred-weight of gold pieces for it. The King of Malabar had shown a Venetian a rosary of one hundred and four pearls, one for every god that he worshipped.

When the Duke de Valentinois, son of Alexander VI., visited Louis XII. of France, his horse was loaded with gold leaves, according to Brantôme, and his cap had double rows of rubies that threw out a great light. Charles of England had ridden in stirrups hung with three hundred and twenty-one diamonds. Richard II. had a coat, valued at thirty thousand marks, which was covered with balas rubies. Hall described Henry VIII., on his way to the Tower previous to his coronation, as wearing "a jacket of raised gold, the placard embroidered with diamonds and other rich stones, and a great bauderike about his neck of large balasses." The favorites of James I. wore ear-rings of emeralds set in gold filigrane. Edward II. gave to Piers Gaveston a suit of red-gold armor studded with jacinths, and a collar of gold roses set with turquoise-stones, and a skull-cap parsemé with pearls. Henry II. wore jewelled gloves reaching to the elbow, and had a hawk-glove set with twelve rubies and fifty-two great pearls. The ducal hat of Charles the Rash, the last Duke of Burgundy of his race, was studded with sapphires and hung with pear-shaped pearls.

How exquisite life had once been! How gorgeous in its pomp and decoration! Even to read of the luxury of the dead was wonderful.

Then he turned his attention to embroideries, and to the tapestries that performed the office of frescos in the chill rooms of the Northern nations of Europe. As he investigated the subject,--and he always had an extraordinary faculty of becoming absolutely absorbed for the moment in whatever he took up,--he was almost saddened by the reflection of the ruin that time brought on beautiful and wonderful things. He, at any rate, had escaped that. Summer followed summer, and the yellow jonquils bloomed and died many times, and nights of horror repeated the story of their shame, but he was unchanged. No winter marred his face or stained his flower-like bloom. How different it was with material things! Where had they gone to? Where was the great crocus-colored robe, on which the gods fought against the giants, that had been worked for Athena? Where the huge velarium that Nero had stretched across the Colosseum at Rome, on which were represented the starry sky, and Apollo driving a chariot drawn by white gilt-reined steeds? He longed to see the curious table-napkins wrought for Elagabalus, on which were displayed all the dainties and viands that could be wanted for a feast; the mortuary cloth of King Chilperic, with its three hundred golden bees; the fantastic robes that excited the indignation of the Bishop of Pontus, and were figured with "lions, panthers, bears, dogs, forests, rocks, hunters,--all, in fact, that a painter can copy from nature;" and the coat that Charles of Orleans once wore, on the sleeves of which were embroidered the verses of a song beginning "Madame, je suis tout joyeux," the musical accompaniment of the words being wrought in gold thread, and each note, a square shape in those days, formed with four pearls. He read of the room that was prepared at the palace at Rheims for the use of Queen Joan of Burgundy, and was decorated with "thirteen hundred and twenty-one parrots, made in broidery, and blazoned with the king's arms, and five hundred and sixty-one butterflies, whose wings were similarly ornamented with the arms of the queen, the whole worked in gold." Catherine de Médicis had a mourning-bed made for her of black velvet powdered with crescents and suns. Its curtains were of damask, with leafy wreaths and garlands, figured upon a gold and silver ground, and fringed along the edges with broideries of pearls, and it stood in a room hung with rows of the queen's devices in cut black velvet upon cloth of silver. Louis XIV. had gold-embroidered caryatides fifteen feet high in his apartment. The state bed of Sobieski, King of Poland, was made of Smyrna gold brocade embroidered in turquoises with verses from the Koran. Its supports were of silver gilt, beautifully chased, and profusely set with enamelled and jewelled medallions. It had been taken from the Turkish camp before Vienna, and the standard of Mohammed had stood under it.

And so, for a whole year, he sought to accumulate the most exquisite specimens that he could find of textile and embroidered work, getting the dainty Delhi muslins, finely wrought, with gold-threat palmates, and stitched over with iridescent beetles' wings; the Dacca gauzes, that from their transparency are known in the East as "woven air," and "running water," and "evening dew;" strange figured cloths from Java; elaborate yellow Chinese hangings; books bound in tawny satins or fair blue silks and wrought with fleurs de lys, birds, and images; veils of lacis worked in Hungary point; Sicilian brocades, and stiff Spanish velvets; Georgian work with its gilt coins, and Japanese Foukousas with their green-toned golds and their marvellously-plumaged birds.

He had a special passion, also, for ecclesiastical vestments, as indeed he had for everything connected with the service of the Church. In the long cedar chests that lined the west gallery of his house he had stored away many rare and beautiful specimens of what is really the raiment of the Bride of Christ, who must wear purple and jewels and fine linen that she may hide the pallid macerated body that is worn by the suffering that she seeks for, and wounded by self-inflicted pain. He had a gorgeous cope of crimson silk and gold-thread damask, figured with a repeating pattern of golden pomegranates set in six-petalled formal blossoms, beyond which on either side was the pine-apple device wrought in seed-pearls. The orphreys were divided into panels representing scenes from the life of the Virgin, and the coronation of the Virgin was figured in colored silks upon the hood. This was Italian work of the fifteenth century. Another cope was of green velvet, embroidered with heart-shaped groups of acanthus-leaves, from which spread long-stemmed white blossoms, the details of which were picked out with silver thread and colored crystals. The morse bore a seraph's head in gold-thread raised work. The orphreys were woven in a diaper of red and gold silk, and were starred with medallions of many saints and martyrs, among whom was St. Sebastian. He had chasubles, also, of amber-colored silk, and blue silk and gold brocade, and yellow silk damask and cloth of gold, figured with representations of the Passion and Crucifixion of Christ, and embroidered with lions and peacocks and other emblems; dalmatics of white satin and pink silk damask, decorated with tulips and dolphins and fleurs de lys; altar frontals of crimson velvet and blue linen; and many corporals, chalice-veils, and sudaria. In the mystic offices to which these things were put there was something that quickened his imagination.

For these things, and everything that he collected in his lovely house, were to be to him means of forgetfulness, modes by which he could escape, for a season, from the fear that seemed to him at times to be almost too great to be borne. Upon the walls of the lonely locked room where he had spent so much of his boyhood, he had hung with his own hands the terrible portrait whose changing features showed him the real degradation of his life, and had draped the purple-and-gold pall in front of it as a curtain. For weeks he would not go there, would forget the hideous painted thing, and get back his light heart, his wonderful joyousness, his passionate pleasure in mere existence. Then, suddenly, some night he would creep out of the house, go down to dreadful places near Blue Gate Fields, and stay there, day after day, until he was driven away. On his return he would sit in front of the picture, sometimes loathing it and himself, but filled, at other times, with that pride of rebellion that is half the fascination of sin, and smiling, with secret pleasure, at the misshapen shadow that had to bear the burden that should have been his own.

After a few years he could not endure to be long out of England, and gave up the villa that he had shared at Trouville with Lord Henry, as well as the little white walled-in house at Algiers where he had more than once spent his winter. He hated to be separated from the picture that was such a part of his life, and he was also afraid that during his absence some one might gain access to the room, in spite of the elaborate bolts and bars that he had caused to be placed upon the door.

He was quite conscious that this would tell them nothing. It was true that the portrait still preserved, under all the foulness and ugliness of the face, its marked likeness to himself; but what could they learn from that? He would laugh at any one who tried to taunt him. He had not painted it. What was it to him how vile and full of shame it looked? Even if he told them, would they believe it?

Yet he was afraid. Sometimes when he was down at his great house in Nottinghamshire, entertaining the fashionable young men of his own rank who were his chief companions, and astounding the county by the wanton luxury and gorgeous splendor of his mode of life, he would suddenly leave his guests and rush back to town to see that the door had not been tampered with and that the picture was still there. What if it should be stolen? The mere thought made him cold with horror. Surely the world would know his secret then. Perhaps the world already suspected it.

For, while he fascinated many, there were not a few who distrusted him. He was blackballed at a West End club of which his birth and social position fully entitled him to become a member, and on one occasion, when he was brought by a friend into the smoking-room of the Carlton, the Duke of Berwick and another gentleman got up in a marked manner and went out. Curious stories became current about him after he had passed his twenty-fifth year. It was said that he had been seen brawling with foreign sailors in a low den in the distant parts of Whitechapel, and that he consorted with thieves and coiners and knew the mysteries of their trade. His extraordinary absences became notorious, and, when he used to reappear again in society, men would whisper to each other in corners, or pass him with a sneer, or look at him with cold searching eyes, as if they were determined to discover his secret.

Of such insolences and attempted slights he, of course, took no notice, and in the opinion of most people his frank debonair manner, his charming boyish smile, and the infinite grace of that wonderful youth that seemed never to leave him, were in themselves a sufficient answer to the calumnies (for so they called them) that were circulated about him. It was remarked, however, that those who had been most intimate with him appeared, after a time, to shun him. Of all his friends, or so-called friends, Lord Henry Wotton was the only one who remained loyal to him. Women who had wildly adored him, and for his sake had braved all social censure and set convention at defiance, were seen to grow pallid with shame or horror if Dorian Gray entered the room.

Yet these whispered scandals only lent him, in the eyes of many, his strange and dangerous charm. His great wealth was a certain element of security. Society, civilized society at least, is never very ready to believe anything to the detriment of those who are both rich and charming. It feels instinctively that manners are of more importance than morals, and the highest respectability is of less value in its opinion than the possession of a good chef. And, after all, it is a very poor consolation to be told that the man who has given one a bad dinner, or poor wine, is irreproachable in his private life. Even the cardinal virtues cannot atone for cold entrées, as Lord Henry remarked once, in a discussion on the subject; and there is possibly a good deal to be said for his view. For the canons of good society are, or should be, the same as the canons of art. Form is absolutely essential to it. It should have the dignity of a ceremony, as well as its unreality, and should combine the insincere character of a romantic play with the wit and beauty that make such plays charming. Is insincerity such a terrible thing? I think not. It is merely a method by which we can multiply our personalities.

Such, at any rate, was Dorian Gray's opinion. He used to wonder at the shallow psychology of those who conceive the Ego in man as a thing simple, permanent, reliable, and of one essence. To him, man was a being with myriad lives and myriad sensations, a complex multiform creature that bore within itself strange legacies of thought and passion, and whose very flesh was tainted with the monstrous maladies of the dead. He loved to stroll through the gaunt cold picture-gallery of his country-house and look at the various portraits of those whose blood flowed in his veins. Here was Philip Herbert, described by Francis Osborne, in his "Memoires on the Reigns of Queen

Elizabeth and King James," as one who was "caressed by the court for his handsome face, which kept him not long company." Was it young Herbert's life that he sometimes led? Had some strange poisonous germ crept from body to body till it had reached his own? Was it some dim sense of that ruined grace that had made him so suddenly, and almost without cause, give utterance, in Basil Hallward's studio, to that mad prayer that had so changed his life? Here, in gold-embroidered red doublet, jewelled surcoat, and gilt-edged ruff and wrist-bands, stood Sir Anthony Sherard, with his silver-and-black armor piled at his feet. What had this man's legacy been? Had the lover of Giovanna of Naples bequeathed him some inheritance of sin and shame? Were his own actions merely the dreams that the dead man had not dared to realize? Here, from the fading canvas, smiled Lady Elizabeth Devereux, in her gauze hood, pearl stomacher, and pink slashed sleeves. A flower was in her right hand, and her left clasped an enamelled collar of white and damask roses. On a table by her side lay a mandolin and an apple. There were large green rosettes upon her little pointed shoes. He knew her life, and the strange stories that were told about her lovers. Had he something of her temperament in him? Those oval heavy-lidded eyes seemed to look curiously at him. What of George Willoughby, with his powdered hair and fantastic patches? How evil he looked! The face was saturnine and swarthy, and the sensual lips seemed to be twisted with disdain. Delicate lace ruffles fell over the lean yellow hands that were so overladen with rings. He had been a macaroni of the eighteenth century, and the friend, in his youth, of Lord Ferrars. What of the second Lord Sherard, the companion of the Prince Regent in his wildest days, and one of the witnesses at the secret marriage with Mrs. Fitzherbert? How proud and handsome he was, with his chestnut curls and insolent pose! What passions had he bequeathed? The world had looked upon him as infamous. He had led the orgies at Carlton House. The star of the Garter glittered upon his breast. Beside him hung the portrait of his wife, a pallid, thin-lipped woman in black. Her blood, also, stirred within him. How curious it all seemed!

Yet one had ancestors in literature, as well as in one's own race, nearer perhaps in type and temperament, many of them, and certainly with an influence of which one was more absolutely conscious. There were times when it seemed to Dorian Gray that the whole of history was merely the record of his own life, not as he had lived it in act and circumstance, but as his imagination had created it for him, as it had been in his brain and in his passions. He felt that he had known them all, those strange terrible figures that had passed across the stage of the world and made sin so marvellous and evil so full of wonder. It seemed to him that in some mysterious way their lives had been his own.

The hero of the dangerous novel that had so influenced his life had himself had this curious fancy. In a chapter of the book he tells how, crowned with laurel, lest lightning might strike him, he had sat, as Tiberius, in a garden at Capri, reading the shameful books of Elephantis, while dwarfs and peacocks strutted round him and the flute-player mocked the swinger of the censer; and, as Caligula, had caroused with the green-shirted jockeys in their stables, and supped in an ivory manger with a jewel-frontleted horse; and, as Domitian, had wandered through a corridor lined with marble mirrors, looking round with haggard eyes for the reflection of the dagger that was to end his days, and sick with that ennui, that taedium vitae, that comes on those to whom life denies nothing; and had peered through a clear emerald at the red shambles of the Circus, and then, in a litter of pearl and purple drawn by silver-shod mules, been carried through the Street of Pomegranates to a House of Gold, and heard men cry on Nero Caesar as he passed by; and, as Elagabalus, had painted his face with colors, and plied the distaff among the women, and brought the Moon from Carthage, and given her in mystic marriage to the Sun.

Over and over again Dorian used to read this fantastic chapter, and the chapter immediately following, in which the hero describes the curious tapestries that he had had woven for him from Gustave Moreau's designs, and on which were pictured the awful and beautiful forms of those whom Vice and Blood and Weariness had made monstrous or mad: Filippo, Duke of Milan, who slew his wife, and painted her lips with a scarlet poison; Pietro Barbi, the Venetian, known as Paul the Second, who sought in his vanity to assume the title of Formosus, and whose tiara, valued at two hundred thousand florins, was bought at the price of a terrible sin; Gian Maria Visconti, who used hounds to chase living men, and whose murdered body was covered with roses by a harlot who had loved him; the Borgia on his white horse, with Fratricide riding beside him, and his mantle stained with the blood of Perotto; Pietro Riario, the young Cardinal Archbishop of Florence, child and minion of Sixtus IV., whose beauty was equalled only by his debauchery, and who received Leonora of Aragon in a pavilion of white and crimson silk, filled with nymphs and centaurs, and gilded a boy that he might serve her at the feast as Ganymede or Hylas; Ezzelin, whose melancholy could be cured only by the spectacle of death, and who had a passion for red blood, as other men have for red wine,--the son of the Fiend, as was reported, and one who had cheated his father at dice when gambling with him for his own soul; Giambattista Cibo, who in mockery took the name of Innocent, and into whose torpid veins the blood of three lads was infused by a Jewish doctor;

Sigismondo Malatesta, the lover of Isotta, and the lord of Rimini, whose effigy was burned at Rome as the enemy of God and man, who strangled Polyssena with a napkin, and gave poison to Ginevra d'Este in a cup of emerald, and in honor of a shameful passion built a pagan church for Christian worship; Charles VI., who had so wildly adored his brother's wife that a leper had warned him of the insanity that was coming on him, and who could only be soothed by Saracen cards painted with the images of Love and Death and Madness; and, in his trimmed jerkin and jewelled cap and acanthus-like curls, Grifonetto Baglioni, who slew Astorre with his bride, and Simonetto with his page, and whose comeliness was such that, as he lay dying in the yellow piazza of Perugia, those who had hated him could not choose but weep, and Atalanta, who had cursed him, blessed him.

There was a horrible fascination in them all. He saw them at night, and they troubled his imagination in the day. The Renaissance knew of strange manners of poisoning,--poisoning by a helmet and a lighted torch, by an embroidered glove and a jewelled fan, by a gilded pomander and by an amber chain. Dorian Gray had been poisoned by a book. There were moments when he looked on evil simply as a mode through which he could realize his conception of the beautiful.

CHAPTER X

It was on the 7th of November, the eve of his own thirty-second birthday, as he often remembered afterwards.

He was walking home about eleven o'clock from Lord Henry's, where he had been dining, and was wrapped in heavy furs, as the night was cold and foggy. At the corner of Grosvenor Square and South Audley Street a man passed him in the mist, walking very fast, and with the collar of his gray ulster turned up. He had a bag in his hand. He recognized him. It was Basil Hallward. A strange sense of fear, for which he could not account, came over him. He made no sign of recognition, and went on slowly, in the direction of his own house.

But Hallward had seen him. Dorian heard him first stopping, and then hurrying after him. In a few moments his hand was on his arm.

"Dorian! What an extraordinary piece of luck! I have been waiting for you ever since nine o'clock in your library. Finally I took pity on your tired servant, and told him to go to bed, as he let me out. I am off to Paris by the midnight train, and I wanted particularly to see you before I left. I thought it was you, or rather your fur coat, as you passed me. But I wasn't quite sure. Didn't you recognize me?"

"In this fog, my dear Basil? Why, I can't even recognize Grosvenor Square. I believe my house is somewhere about here, but I don't feel at all certain about it. I am sorry you are going away, as I have not seen you for ages. But I suppose you will be back soon?"

"No: I am going to be out of England for six months. I intend to take a studio in Paris, and shut myself up till I have finished a great picture I have in my head. However, it wasn't about myself I wanted to talk. Here we are at your door. Let me come in for a moment. I have something to say to you."

"I shall be charmed. But won't you miss your train?" said Dorian Gray, languidly, as he passed up the steps and opened the door with his latch-key.

The lamp-light struggled out through the fog, and Hallward looked at his watch. "I have heaps of time," he answered. "The train doesn't go till twelve-fifteen, and it is only just eleven. In fact, I was on my way to the club to look for you, when I met you. You see, I shan't have any delay about luggage, as I have sent on my heavy things. All I have with me is in this bag, and I can easily get to Victoria in twenty minutes."

Dorian looked at him and smiled. "What a way for a fashionable painter to travel! A Gladstone bag, and an ulster! Come in, or the fog will get into the house. And mind you don't talk about anything serious. Nothing is serious nowadays. At least nothing should be."

Hallward shook his head, as he entered, and followed Dorian into the library. There was a bright wood fire blazing in the large open hearth. The lamps were lit, and an open Dutch silver spirit-case stood, with some siphons of soda-water and large cut-glass tumblers, on a little table.

"You see your servant made me quite at home, Dorian. He gave me everything I wanted, including your best cigarettes. He is a most hospitable creature. I like him much better than the Frenchman you used to have. What has become of the Frenchman, by the bye?"

Dorian shrugged his shoulders. "I believe he married Lady Ashton's maid, and has established her in Paris as an English dressmaker. Anglomanie is very fashionable over there now, I hear. It seems silly of the French, doesn't it? But--do you know?--he was not at all a bad servant. I never liked him, but I had nothing to complain about. One often imagines things that are quite absurd. He was really very devoted to me, and seemed quite sorry when he went away. Have another brandy-and-soda? Or would you like hock-and-seltzer? I always take hock-and-seltzer myself. There is sure to be some in the next room."

"Thanks, I won't have anything more," said Hallward, taking his cap and coat off, and throwing them on the bag that he had placed in the corner. "And now, my dear fellow, I want to speak to you seriously. Don't frown like that. You make it so much more difficult for me."

"What is it all about?" cried Dorian, in his petulant way, flinging himself down on the sofa. "I hope it is not about myself. I am tired of myself to-night. I should like to be somebody else."

"It is about yourself," answered Hallward, in his grave, deep voice, "and I must say it to you. I shall only keep you half an hour."

Dorian sighed, and lit a cigarette. "Half an hour!" he murmured.

"It is not much to ask of you, Dorian, and it is entirely for your own sake that I am speaking. I think it right that you should know that the most dreadful things are being said about you in London,--things that I could hardly repeat to you."

"I don't wish to know anything about them. I love scandals about other people, but scandals about myself don't interest me. They have not got the charm of novelty."

"They must interest you, Dorian. Every gentleman is interested in his good name. You don't want people to talk of you as something vile and degraded. Of course you have your position, and your wealth, and all that kind of thing. But position and wealth are not everything. Mind you, I don't believe these rumors at all. At least, I can't believe them when I see you. Sin is a thing that writes itself across a man's face. It cannot be concealed. People talk of secret vices. There are no such things as secret vices. If a wretched man has a vice, it shows itself in the lines of his mouth, the droop of his eyelids, the moulding of his hands even. Somebody--I won't mention his name, but you know him--came to me last year to have his portrait done. I had never seen him before, and had never heard anything about him at the time, though I have heard a good deal since. He offered an extravagant price. I refused him. There was something in the shape of his fingers that I hated. I know now that I was quite right in what I fancied about him. His life is dreadful. But you, Dorian, with your pure, bright, innocent face, and your marvellous untroubled youth,--I can't believe anything against you. And yet I see you very seldom, and you never come down to the studio now, and when I am away from you, and I hear all these hideous things that people are whispering about you, I don't know what to say. Why is it, Dorian, that a man like the Duke of Berwick leaves the room of a club when you enter it? Why is it that so many gentlemen in London will neither go to your house nor invite you to theirs? You used to be a friend of Lord Cawdor. I met him at dinner last week. Your name happened to come up in conversation, in connection with the miniatures you have lent to the exhibition at the Dudley. Cawdor curled his lip, and said that you might have the most artistic tastes, but that you were a man whom no pure-minded girl should be allowed to know, and whom no chaste woman should sit in the same room with. I reminded him that I was a friend of yours, and asked him what he meant. He told me. He told me right out before everybody. It was horrible! Why is your friendship so fateful to young men? There was that wretched boy in the Guards who committed suicide. You were his great friend. There was Sir Henry Ashton, who had to leave England, with a tarnished name. You and he were inseparable. What about Adrian Singleton, and his dreadful end? What about Lord Kent's only son, and his career? I met his father yesterday in St. James Street. He seemed broken with shame and sorrow. What about the young Duke of Perth? What sort of life has he got now? What gentleman would associate with him? Dorian, Dorian, your reputation is infamous. I know you and Harry are great friends. I say nothing about that now, but surely you need not have made his sister's name a by-word. When you met Lady Gwendolen, not a breath of scandal had ever touched her. Is there a single decent woman in London now who would drive with her in the Park? Why, even her children are not allowed to live with her. Then there are other stories,--stories that you have been seen creeping at dawn out of dreadful houses and slinking in disguise into the foulest dens in London. Are they true? Can they be true? When I first heard them, I laughed. I hear them now, and they make me shudder. What about your country-house, and the life that is led there? Dorian, you don't know what is said about you. I won't tell you that I don't want to preach to you. I remember Harry saying once that every man who turned himself into an amateur curate for the moment always said that, and then broke his word. I do want to preach to you. I want you to lead such a life as will make the world respect you. I want you to have a clean name and a fair record. I want you to get rid of the dreadful people you associate with. Don't shrug your shoulders like that. Don't be so indifferent. You have a wonderful influence. Let it be for good, not for evil. They say that you corrupt every one whom you become intimate with, and that it is quite sufficient for you to enter a house, for shame of some kind to follow after you. I don't know whether it is so or not. How should I know? But it is said of you. I am told things that it seems impossible to doubt. Lord Gloucester was one of my greatest friends at Oxford. He showed me a letter that his wife had written to him when she was dying alone in her villa at Mentone. Your name was implicated in the most terrible confession I ever read. I told him that it was absurd,--that I knew you thoroughly, and that you were incapable of anything of the kind. Know you? I wonder do I know you? Before I could answer that, I should have to see your soul."

"To see my soul!" muttered Dorian Gray, starting up from the sofa and turning almost white from fear.

"Yes," answered Hallward, gravely, and with infinite sorrow in his voice,--"to see your soul. But only God can do that."

A bitter laugh of mockery broke from the lips of the younger man. "You shall see it yourself, to-night!" he cried, seizing a lamp from the table. "Come: it is your own handiwork. Why shouldn't you look at it? You can tell the world all about it afterwards, if you choose. Nobody would believe you. If they did believe you, they'd like me all the better for it. I know the age better than you do, though you will prate about it so tediously. Come, I tell you. You have chattered enough about corruption. Now you shall look on it face to face."

There was the madness of pride in every word he uttered. He stamped his foot upon the ground in his boyish insolent manner. He felt a terrible joy at the thought that some one else was to share his secret, and that the man who had painted the portrait that was the origin of all his shame was to be burdened for the rest of his life with the hideous memory of what he had done.

"Yes," he continued, coming closer to him, and looking steadfastly into his stern eyes, "I will show you my soul. You shall see the thing that you fancy only God can see."

Hallward started back. "This is blasphemy, Dorian!" he cried. "You must not say things like that. They are horrible, and they don't mean anything."

"You think so?" He laughed again.

"I know so. As for what I said to you to-night, I said it for your good. You know I have been always devoted to you."

"Don't touch me. Finish what you have to say."

A twisted flash of pain shot across Hallward's face. He paused for a moment, and a wild feeling of pity came over him. After all, what right had he to pry into the life of Dorian Gray? If he had done a tithe of what was rumored about him, how much he must have suffered! Then he straightened himself up, and walked over to the fireplace, and stood there, looking at the burning logs with their frost-like ashes and their throbbing cores of flame.

"I am waiting, Basil," said the young man, in a hard, clear voice.

He turned round. "What I have to say is this," he cried. "You must give me some answer to these horrible charges that are made against you. If you tell me that they are absolutely untrue from beginning to end, I will believe you. Deny them, Dorian, deny them! Can't you see what I am going through? My God! don't tell me that you are infamous!"

Dorian Gray smiled. There was a curl of contempt in his lips. "Come up-stairs, Basil," he said, quietly. "I keep a diary of my life from day to day, and it never leaves the room in which it is written. I will show it to you if you come with me."

"I will come with you, Dorian, if you wish it. I see I have missed my train. That makes no matter. I can go to-morrow. But don't ask me to read anything to-night. All I want is a plain answer to my question."

"That will be given to you up-stairs. I could not give it here. You won't have to read long. Don't keep me waiting."

CHAPTER XI

He passed out of the room, and began the ascent, Basil Hallward following close behind. They walked softly, as men instinctively do at night. The lamp cast fantastic shadows on the wall and staircase. A rising wind made some of the windows rattle.

When they reached the top landing, Dorian set the lamp down on the floor, and taking out the key turned it in the lock. "You insist on knowing, Basil?" he asked, in a low voice.

"Yes."

"I am delighted," he murmured, smiling. Then he added, somewhat bitterly, "You are the one man in the world who is entitled to know everything about me. You have had more to do with my life than you think." And, taking up the lamp, he opened the door and went in. A cold current of air passed them, and the light shot up for a moment in a flame of murky orange. He shuddered. "Shut the door behind you," he said, as he placed the lamp on the table.

Hallward glanced round him, with a puzzled expression. The room looked as if it had not been lived in for years. A faded Flemish tapestry, a curtained picture, an old Italian cassone, and an almost empty bookcase,--that was all that it seemed to contain, besides a chair and a table. As Dorian Gray was lighting a half-burned candle that was standing on the mantel-shelf, he saw that the whole place was covered with dust, and that the carpet was in holes. A mouse ran scuffling behind the wainscoting. There was a damp odor of mildew.

"So you think that it is only God who sees the soul, Basil? Draw that curtain back, and you will see mine."

The voice that spoke was cold and cruel. "You are mad, Dorian, or playing a part," muttered Hallward, frowning.

"You won't? Then I must do it myself," said the young man; and he tore the curtain from its rod, and flung it on the ground.

An exclamation of horror broke from Hallward's lips as he saw in the dim light the hideous thing on the canvas leering at him. There was something in its expression that filled him with disgust and loathing. Good heavens! it was Dorian Gray's own face that he was looking at! The horror, whatever it was, had not yet entirely marred that marvellous beauty. There was still some gold in the thinning hair and some scarlet on the sensual lips. The sodden eyes had kept something of the loveliness of their blue, the noble curves had not yet passed entirely away from chiselled nostrils and from plastic throat. Yes, it was Dorian himself. But who had done it? He seemed to recognize his own brush-work, and the frame was his own design. The idea was monstrous, yet he felt afraid. He seized the lighted candle, and held it to the picture. In the left-hand corner was his own name, traced in long letters of bright vermilion.

It was some foul parody, some infamous, ignoble satire. He had never done that. Still, it was his own picture. He knew it, and he felt as if his blood had changed from fire to sluggish ice in a moment. His own picture! What did it mean? Why had it altered? He turned, and looked at Dorian Gray with the eyes of a sick man. His mouth twitched, and his parched tongue seemed unable to articulate. He passed his hand across his forehead. It was dank with clammy sweat.

The young man was leaning against the mantel-shelf, watching him with that strange expression that is on the faces of those who are absorbed in a play when a great artist is acting. There was neither real sorrow in it nor real joy. There was simply the passion of the spectator, with perhaps a flicker of triumph in the eyes. He had taken the flower out of his coat, and was smelling it, or pretending to do so.

"What does this mean?" cried Hallward, at last. His own voice sounded shrill and curious in his ears.

"Years ago, when I was a boy," said Dorian Gray, "you met me, devoted yourself to me, flattered me, and taught me to be vain of my good looks. One day you introduced me to a friend of yours, who explained to me the wonder of youth, and you finished a portrait of me that revealed to me the wonder of beauty. In a mad moment, that I don't know, even now, whether I regret or not, I made a wish. Perhaps you would call it a prayer . . . ."

"I remember it! Oh, how well I remember it! No! the thing is impossible. The room is damp. The mildew has got into the canvas. The paints I used had some wretched mineral poison in them. I tell you the thing is impossible."

"Ah, what is impossible?" murmured the young man, going over to the window, and leaning his forehead against the cold, mist-stained glass.

"You told me you had destroyed it."

"I was wrong. It has destroyed me."

"I don't believe it is my picture."

"Can't you see your romance in it?" said Dorian, bitterly.

"My romance, as you call it . . ."

"As you called it."

"There was nothing evil in it, nothing shameful. This is the face of a satyr."

"It is the face of my soul."

"God! what a thing I must have worshipped! This has the eyes of a devil."

"Each of us has Heaven and Hell in him, Basil," cried Dorian, with a wild gesture of despair.

Hallward turned again to the portrait, and gazed at it. "My God! if it is true," he exclaimed, "and this is what you have done with your life, why, you must be worse even than those who talk against you fancy you to be!" He held the light up again to the canvas, and examined it. The surface seemed to be quite undisturbed, and as he had left it. It was from within, apparently, that the foulness and horror had come. Through some strange quickening of inner life the leprosies of sin were slowly eating the thing away. The rotting of a corpse in a watery grave was not so fearful.

His hand shook, and the candle fell from its socket on the floor, and lay there sputtering. He placed his foot on it and put it out. Then he flung himself into the rickety chair that was standing by the table and buried his face in his hands.

"Good God, Dorian, what a lesson! what an awful lesson!" There was no answer, but he could hear the young man sobbing at the window.

"Pray, Dorian, pray," he murmured. "What is it that one was taught to say in one's boyhood? 'Lead us not into temptation. Forgive us our sins. Wash away our iniquities.' Let us say that together. The prayer of your pride has been answered. The prayer of your repentance will be answered also. I worshipped you too much. I am punished for it. You worshipped yourself too much. We are both punished."

Dorian Gray turned slowly around, and looked at him with tear-dimmed eyes. "It is too late, Basil," he murmured.

"It is never too late, Dorian. Let us kneel down and try if we can remember a prayer. Isn't there a verse somewhere, 'Though your sins be as scarlet, yet I will make them as white as snow'?"

"Those words mean nothing to me now."

"Hush! don't say that. You have done enough evil in your life. My God! don't you see that accursed thing leering at us?"

Dorian Gray glanced at the picture, and suddenly an uncontrollable feeling of hatred for Basil Hallward came over him. The mad passions of a hunted animal stirred within him, and he loathed the man who was seated at the table, more than he had ever loathed anything in his whole life. He glanced wildly around. Something glimmered on the top of the painted chest that faced him. His eye fell on it. He knew what it was. It was a knife that he had brought up, some days before, to cut a piece of cord, and had forgotten to take away with him. He moved slowly towards it, passing Hallward as he did so. As soon as he got behind him, he seized it, and turned round. Hallward moved in his chair as if he was going to rise. He rushed at him, and dug the knife into the great vein that is behind the ear, crushing the man's head down on the table, and stabbing again and again.

There was a stifled groan, and the horrible sound of some one choking with blood. The outstretched arms shot up convulsively three times, waving grotesque stiff-fingered hands in the air. He stabbed him once more, but the man did not move. Something began to trickle on the floor. He waited for a moment, still pressing the head down. Then he threw the knife on the table, and listened.

He could hear nothing, but the drip, drip on the threadbare carpet. He opened the door, and went out on the landing. The house was quite quiet. No one was stirring.

He took out the key, and returned to the room, locking himself in as he did so.

The thing was still seated in the chair, straining over the table with bowed head, and humped back, and long fantastic arms. Had it not been for the red jagged tear in the neck, and the clotted black pool that slowly widened on the table, one would have said that the man was simply asleep.

How quickly it had all been done! He felt strangely calm, and, walking over to the window, opened it, and stepped out on the balcony. The wind had blown the fog away, and the sky was like a monstrous peacock's tail, starred with myriads of golden eyes. He looked down, and saw the policeman going his rounds and flashing a bull's-eye lantern on the doors of the silent houses. The crimson spot of a prowling hansom gleamed at the corner, and then vanished. A woman in a ragged shawl was creeping round by the railings, staggering as she went. Now and then she stopped, and peered back. Once, she began to sing in a hoarse voice. The policeman strolled over and said something to her. She stumbled away, laughing. A bitter blast swept across the Square. The gas-lamps flickered, and became blue, and the leafless trees shook their black iron branches as if in pain. He shivered, and went back, closing the window behind him.

He passed to the door, turned the key, and opened it. He did not even glance at the murdered man. He felt that the secret of the whole thing was not to realize the situation. The friend who had painted the fatal portrait, the portrait to which all his misery had been due, had gone out of his life. That was enough.

Then he remembered the lamp. It was a rather curious one of Moorish workmanship, made of dull silver inlaid with arabesques of burnished steel. Perhaps it might be missed by his servant, and questions would be asked. He turned back, and took it from the table. How still the man was! How horribly white the long hands looked! He was like a dreadful wax image.

He locked the door behind him, and crept quietly downstairs. The wood-work creaked, and seemed to cry out as if in pain. He stopped several times, and waited. No: everything was still. It was merely the sound of his own footsteps.

When he reached the library, he saw the bag and coat in the corner. They must be hidden away somewhere. He unlocked a secret press that was in the wainscoting, and put them into it. He could easily burn them afterwards. Then he pulled out his watch. It was twenty minutes to two.

He sat down, and began to think. Every year--every month, almost--men were strangled in England for what he had done. There had been a madness of murder in the air. Some red star had come too close to the earth.

Evidence? What evidence was there against him? Basil Hallward had left the house at eleven. No one had seen him come in again. Most of the servants were at Selby Royal. His valet had gone to bed.

Paris! Yes. It was to Paris that Basil had gone, by the midnight train, as he had intended. With his curious reserved habits, it would be months before any suspicions would be aroused. Months? Everything could be destroyed long before then.

A sudden thought struck him. He put on his fur coat and hat, and went out into the hall. There he paused, hearing the slow heavy tread of the policeman outside on the pavement, and seeing the flash of the lantern reflected in the window. He waited, holding his breath.

After a few moments he opened the front door, and slipped out, shutting it very gently behind him. Then he began ringing the bell. In about ten minutes his valet appeared, half dressed, and looking very drowsy.

"I am sorry to have had to wake you up, Francis," he said, stepping in; "but I had forgotten my latch-key. What time is it?"

"Five minutes past two, sir," answered the man, looking at the clock and yawning.

"Five minutes past two? How horribly late! You must wake me at nine to-morrow. I have some work to do."

"All right, sir."

"Did any one call this evening?"

"Mr. Hallward, sir. He stayed here till eleven, and then he went away to catch his train."

"Oh! I am sorry I didn't see him. Did he leave any message?"

"No, sir, except that he would write to you."

"That will do, Francis. Don't forget to call me at nine tomorrow."

"No, sir."

The man shambled down the passage in his slippers.

Dorian Gray threw his hat and coat upon the yellow marble table, and passed into the library. He walked up and down the room for a quarter of an hour, biting his lip, and thinking. Then he took the Blue Book down from one of the shelves, and began to turn over the leaves. "Alan Campbell, 152, Hertford Street, Mayfair." Yes; that was the man he wanted.

CHAPTER XII

At nine o'clock the next morning his servant came in with a cup of chocolate on a tray, and opened the shutters. Dorian was sleeping quite peacefully, lying on his right side, with one hand underneath his cheek. He looked like a boy who had been tired out with play, or study.

The man had to touch him twice on the shoulder before he woke, and as he opened his eyes a faint smile passed across his lips, as though he had been having some delightful dream. Yet he had not dreamed at all. His night had been untroubled by any images of pleasure or of pain. But youth smiles without any reason. It is one of its chiefest charms.

He turned round, and, leaning on his elbow, began to drink his chocolate. The mellow November sun was streaming into the room. The sky was bright blue, and there was a genial warmth in the air. It was almost like a morning in May.

Gradually the events of the preceding night crept with silent blood-stained feet into his brain, and reconstructed themselves there with terrible distinctness. He winced at the memory of all that he had suffered, and for a moment the same curious feeling of loathing for Basil Hallward, that had made him kill him as he sat in the chair, came back to him, and he grew cold with passion. The dead man was still sitting there, too, and in the sunlight now. How horrible that was! Such hideous things were for the darkness, not for the day.

He felt that if he brooded on what he had gone through he would sicken or grow mad. There were sins whose fascination was more in the memory than in the doing of them, strange triumphs that gratified the pride more than the passions, and gave to the intellect a quickened sense of joy, greater than any joy they brought, or could ever bring, to the senses. But this was not one of them. It was a thing to be driven out of the mind, to be drugged with poppies, to be strangled lest it might strangle one itself.

He passed his hand across his forehead, and then got up hastily, and dressed himself with even more than his usual attention, giving a good deal of care to the selection of his necktie and scarf-pin, and changing his rings more than once.

He spent a long time over breakfast, tasting the various dishes, talking to his valet about some new liveries that he was thinking of getting made for the servants at Selby, and going through his correspondence. Over some of the letters he smiled.

Three of them bored him. One he read several times over, and then tore up with a slight look of annoyance in his face. "That awful thing, a woman's memory!" as Lord Henry had once said.

When he had drunk his coffee, he sat down at the table, and wrote two letters. One he put in his pocket, the other he handed to the valet.

"Take this round to 152, Hertford Street, Francis, and if Mr. Campbell is out of town, get his address."

As soon as he was alone, he lit a cigarette, and began sketching upon a piece of paper, drawing flowers, and bits of architecture, first, and then faces. Suddenly he remarked that every face that he drew seemed to have an extraordinary likeness to Basil Hallward. He frowned, and, getting up, went over to the bookcase and took out a volume at hazard. He was determined that he would not think about what had happened, till it became absolutely necessary to do so.

When he had stretched himself on the sofa, he looked at the title-page of the book. It was Gautier's "Emaux et Camées," Charpentier's Japanese-paper edition, with the Jacquemart etching. The binding was of citron-green leather with a design of gilt trellis-work and dotted pomegranates. It had been given to him by Adrian Singleton. As he turned over the pages his eye fell on the poem about the hand of Lacenaire, the cold yellow hand "du supplice encore mal lavée," with its downy red hairs and its "doigts de faune." He glanced at his own white taper fingers, and passed on, till he came to those lovely verses upon Venice:

Sur une gamme chromatique,

  Le sein de perles ruisselant,

La Vénus de l'Adriatique

  Sort de l'eau son corps rose et blanc.

Les dômes, sur l'azur des ondes

  Suivant la phrase au pur contour,

S'enflent comme des gorges rondes

  Que soulève un soupir d'amour.

L'esquif aborde et me dépose,

Jetant son amarre au pilier,

Devant une façade rose,

Sur le marbre d'un escalier.

How exquisite they were! As one read them, one seemed to be floating down the green water-ways of the pink and pearl city, lying in a black gondola with silver prow and trailing curtains. The mere lines looked to him like those straight lines of turquoise-blue that follow one as one pushes out to the Lido. The sudden flashes of color reminded him of the gleam of the opal-and-iris-throated birds that flutter round the tall honey-combed Campanile, or stalk, with such stately grace, through the dim arcades. Leaning back with half-closed eyes, he kept saying over and over to himself,--

Devant une façade rose,

Sur le marbre d'un escalier.

The whole of Venice was in those two lines. He remembered the autumn that he had passed there, and a wonderful love that had stirred him to delightful fantastic follies. There was romance in every place. But Venice, like Oxford, had kept the background for romance, and background was everything, or almost everything. Basil had been with him part of the time, and had gone wild over Tintoret. Poor Basil! what a horrible way for a man to die!

He sighed, and took up the book again, and tried to forget. He read of the swallows that fly in and out of the little café at Smyrna where the Hadjis sit counting their amber beads and the turbaned merchants smoke their long tasselled pipes and talk gravely to each other; of the Obelisk in the Place de la Concorde that weeps tears of granite in its lonely sunless exile, and longs to be back by the hot lotus-covered Nile, where there are Sphinxes, and rose-red ibises, and white vultures with gilded claws, and crocodiles, with small beryl eyes, that crawl over the green steaming mud; and of that curious statue that Gautier compares to a contralto voice, the "monstre charmant" that couches in the porphyry-room of the Louvre. But after a time the book fell from his hand. He grew nervous, and a horrible fit of terror came over him. What if Alan Campbell should be out of England? Days would elapse before he could come back. Perhaps he might refuse to come. What could he do then? Every moment was of vital importance.

They had been great friends once, five years before,--almost inseparable, indeed. Then the intimacy had come suddenly to an end. When they met in society now, it was only Dorian Gray who smiled: Alan Campbell never did.

He was an extremely clever young man, though he had no real appreciation of the visible arts, and whatever little sense of the beauty of poetry he possessed he had gained entirely from Dorian. His dominant intellectual passion was for science. At Cambridge he had spent a great deal of his time working in the Laboratory, and had taken a good class in the Natural Science tripos of his year. Indeed, he was still devoted to the study of chemistry, and had a laboratory of his own, in which he used to shut himself up all day long, greatly to the annoyance of his mother, who had set her heart on his standing for Parliament and had a vague idea that a chemist was a person who made up prescriptions. He was an excellent musician, however, as well, and played both the violin and the piano better than most amateurs. In fact, it was music that had first brought him and Dorian Gray together,--music and that indefinable attraction that Dorian seemed to be able to exercise whenever he wished, and indeed exercised often without being conscious of it. They had met at Lady Berkshire's the night that Rubinstein played there, and after that used to be always seen together at the Opera, and wherever good music was going on. For eighteen months their intimacy lasted. Campbell was always either at Selby Royal or in Grosvenor Square. To him, as to many others, Dorian Gray was the type of everything that is wonderful and fascinating in life. Whether or not a quarrel had taken place between them no one ever knew. But suddenly people remarked that they scarcely spoke when they met, and that Campbell seemed always to go away early from any party at which Dorian Gray was present. He had changed, too,--was strangely melancholy at times, appeared almost to dislike hearing music of any passionate character, and would never himself play, giving as his excuse, when he was called upon, that he was so absorbed in science that he had no time left in which to practise. And this was certainly true. Every day he seemed to become more interested in biology, and his name appeared once or twice in some of the scientific reviews, in connection with certain curious experiments.

This was the man that Dorian Gray was waiting for, pacing up and down the room, glancing every moment at the clock, and becoming horribly agitated as the minutes went by. At last the door opened, and his servant entered.

"Mr. Alan Campbell, sir."

A sigh of relief broke from his parched lips, and the color came back to his cheeks.

"Ask him to come in at once, Francis."

The man bowed, and retired. In a few moments Alan Campbell walked in, looking very stern and rather pale, his pallor being intensified by his coal-black hair and dark eyebrows.

"Alan! this is kind of you. I thank you for coming."

"I had intended never to enter your house again, Gray. But you said it was a matter of life and death." His voice was hard and cold. He spoke with slow deliberation. There was a look of contempt in the steady searching gaze that he turned on Dorian. He kept his hands in the pockets of his Astrakhan coat, and appeared not to have noticed the gesture with which he had been greeted.

"It is a matter of life and death, Alan, and to more than one person. Sit down."

Campbell took a chair by the table, and Dorian sat opposite to him. The two men's eyes met. In Dorian's there was infinite pity. He knew that what he was going to do was dreadful.

After a strained moment of silence, he leaned across and said, very quietly, but watching the effect of each word upon the face of the man he had sent for, "Alan, in a locked room at the top of this house, a room to which nobody but myself has access, a dead man is seated at a table. He has been dead ten hours now. Don't stir, and don't look at me like that. Who the man is, why he died, how he died, are matters that do not concern you. What you have to do is this--"

"Stop, Gray. I don't want to know anything further. Whether what you have told me is true or not true, doesn't concern me. I entirely decline to be mixed up in your life. Keep your horrible secrets to yourself. They don't interest me any more."

"Alan, they will have to interest you. This one will have to interest you. I am awfully sorry for you, Alan. But I can't help myself. You are the one man who is able to save me. I am forced to bring you into the matter. I have no option. Alan, you are a scientist. You know about chemistry, and things of that kind. You have made experiments. What you have got to do is to destroy the thing that is up-stairs,--to destroy it so that not a vestige will be left of it. Nobody saw this person come into the house. Indeed, at the present moment he is supposed to be in Paris. He will not be missed for months. When he is missed, there must be no trace of him found here. You, Alan, you must change him, and everything that belongs to him, into a handful of ashes that I may scatter in the air."

"You are mad, Dorian."

"Ah! I was waiting for you to call me Dorian."

"You are mad, I tell you,--mad to imagine that I would raise a finger to help you, mad to make this monstrous confession. I will have nothing to do with this matter, whatever it is. Do you think I am going to peril my reputation for you? What is it to me what devil's work you are up to?"

"It was a suicide, Alan."

"I am glad of that. But who drove him to it? You, I should fancy."

"Do you still refuse to do this, for me?"

"Of course I refuse. I will have absolutely nothing to do with it. I don't care what shame comes on you. You deserve it all. I should not be sorry to see you disgraced, publicly disgraced. How dare you ask me, of all men in the world, to mix myself up in this horror? I should have thought you knew more about people's characters. Your friend Lord Henry Wotton can't have taught you much about psychology, whatever else he has taught you. Nothing will induce me to stir a step to help you. You have come to the wrong man. Go to some of your friends. Don't come to me."

"Alan, it was murder. I killed him. You don't know what he had made me suffer. Whatever my life is, he had more to do with the making or the marring of it than poor Harry has had. He may not have intended it, the result was the same."

"Murder! Good God, Dorian, is that what you have come to? I shall not inform upon you. It is not my business. Besides, you are certain to be arrested, without my stirring in the matter. Nobody ever commits a murder without doing something stupid. But I will have nothing to do with it."

"All I ask of you is to perform a certain scientific experiment. You go to hospitals and dead-houses, and the horrors that you do there don't affect you. If in some hideous dissecting-room or fetid laboratory you found this man lying on a leaden table with red gutters scooped out in it, you would simply look upon him as an admirable subject. You would not turn a hair. You would not believe that you were doing anything wrong. On the contrary, you would probably feel that you were benefiting the human race, or increasing the sum of knowledge in the world, or gratifying intellectual curiosity, or something of that kind. What I want you to do is simply what you have often done before. Indeed, to destroy a body must be less horrible than what you are accustomed to work at. And, remember, it is the only piece of evidence against me. If it is discovered, I am lost; and it is sure to be discovered unless you help me."

"I have no desire to help you. You forget that. I am simply indifferent to the whole thing. It has nothing to do with me."

"Alan, I entreat you. Think of the position I am in. Just before you came I almost fainted with terror. No! don't think of that. Look at the matter purely from the scientific point of view. You don't inquire where the dead things on which you experiment come from. Don't inquire now. I have told you too much as it is. But I beg of you to do this. We were friends once, Alan."

"Don't speak about those days, Dorian: they are dead."

"The dead linger sometimes. The man up-stairs will not go away. He is sitting at the table with bowed head and outstretched arms. Alan! Alan! if you don't come to my assistance I am ruined. Why, they will hang me, Alan! Don't you understand? They will hang me for what I have done."

"There is no good in prolonging this scene. I refuse absolutely to do anything in the matter. It is insane of you to ask me."

"You refuse absolutely?"

"Yes."

The same look of pity came into Dorian's eyes, then he stretched out his hand, took a piece of paper, and wrote something on it. He read it over twice, folded it carefully, and pushed it across the table. Having done this, he got up, and went over to the window.

Campbell looked at him in surprise, and then took up the paper, and opened it. As he read it, his face became ghastly pale, and he fell back in his chair. A horrible sense of sickness came over him. He felt as if his heart was beating itself to death in some empty hollow.

After two or three minutes of terrible silence, Dorian turned round, and came and stood behind him, putting his hand upon his shoulder.

"I am so sorry, Alan," he murmured, "but you leave me no alternative. I have a letter written already. Here it is. You see the address. If you don't help me, I must send it. You know what the result will be. But you are going to help me. It is impossible for you to refuse now. I tried to spare you. You will do me the justice to admit that. You were stern, harsh, offensive. You treated me as no man has ever dared to treat me,--no living man, at any rate. I bore it all. Now it is for me to dictate terms."

Campbell buried his face in his hands, and a shudder passed through him.

"Yes, it is my turn to dictate terms, Alan. You know what they are. The thing is quite simple. Come, don't work yourself into this fever. The thing has to be done. Face it, and do it."

A groan broke from Campbell's lips, and he shivered all over. The ticking of the clock on the mantel-piece seemed to him to be dividing time into separate atoms of agony, each of which was too terrible to be borne. He felt as if an iron ring was being slowly tightened round his forehead, and as if the disgrace with which he was threatened had already come upon him. The hand upon his shoulder weighed like a hand of lead. It was intolerable. It seemed to crush him.

"Come, Alan, you must decide at once."

He hesitated a moment. "Is there a fire in the room up-stairs?" he murmured.

"Yes, there is a gas-fire with asbestos."

"I will have to go home and get some things from the laboratory."

"No, Alan, you need not leave the house. Write on a sheet of note-paper what you want, and my servant will take a cab and bring the things back to you."

Campbell wrote a few lines, blotted them, and addressed an envelope to his assistant. Dorian took the note up and read it carefully. Then he rang the bell, and gave it to his valet, with orders to return as soon as possible, and to bring the things with him.

When the hall door shut, Campbell started, and, having got up from the chair, went over to the chimney-piece. He was shivering with a sort of ague. For nearly twenty minutes, neither of the men spoke. A fly buzzed noisily about the room, and the ticking of the clock was like the beat of a hammer.

As the chime struck one, Campbell turned around, and, looking at Dorian Gray, saw that his eyes were filled with tears. There was something in the purity and refinement of that sad face that seemed to enrage him. "You are infamous, absolutely infamous!" he muttered.

"Hush, Alan: you have saved my life," said Dorian.

"Your life? Good heavens! what a life that is! You have gone from corruption to corruption, and now you have culminated in crime. In doing what I am going to do, what you force me to do, it is not of your life that I am thinking."

"Ah, Alan," murmured Dorian, with a sigh, "I wish you had a thousandth part of the pity for me that I have for you." He turned away, as he spoke, and stood looking out at the garden. Campbell made no answer.

After about ten minutes a knock came to the door, and the servant entered, carrying a mahogany chest of chemicals, with a small electric battery set on top of it. He placed it on the table, and went out again, returning with a long coil of steel and platinum wire and two rather curiously-shaped iron clamps.

"Shall I leave the things here, sir?" he asked Campbell.

"Yes," said Dorian. "And I am afraid, Francis, that I have another errand for you. What is the name of the man at Richmond who supplies Selby with orchids?"

"Harden, sir."

"Yes,--Harden. You must go down to Richmond at once, see Harden personally, and tell him to send twice as many orchids as I ordered, and to have as few white ones as possible. In fact, I don't want any white ones. It is a lovely day, Francis, and Richmond is a very pretty place, otherwise I wouldn't bother you about it."

"No trouble, sir. At what time shall I be back?"

Dorian looked at Campbell. "How long will your experiment take, Alan?" he said, in a calm, indifferent voice. The presence of a third person in the room seemed to give him extraordinary courage.

Campbell frowned, and bit his lip. "It will take about five hours," he answered.

"It will be time enough, then, if you are back at half-past seven, Francis. Or stay: just leave my things out for dressing. You can have the evening to yourself. I am not dining at home, so I shall not want you."

"Thank you, sir," said the man, leaving the room.

"Now, Alan, there is not a moment to be lost. How heavy this chest is! I'll take it for you. You bring the other things." He spoke rapidly, and in an authoritative manner. Campbell felt dominated by him. They left the room together.

When they reached the top landing, Dorian took out the key and turned it in the lock. Then he stopped, and a troubled look came into his eyes. He shuddered. "I don't think I can go in, Alan," he murmured.

"It is nothing to me. I don't require you," said Campbell, coldly.

Dorian half opened the door. As he did so, he saw the face of the portrait grinning in the sunlight. On the floor in front of it the torn curtain was lying. He remembered that the night before, for the first time in his life, he had forgotten to hide it, when he crept out of the room.

But what was that loathsome red dew that gleamed, wet and glistening, on one of the hands, as though the canvas had sweated blood? How horrible it was!--more horrible, it seemed to him for the moment, than the silent thing that he knew was stretched across the table, the thing whose grotesque misshapen shadow on the spotted carpet showed him that it had not stirred, but was still there, as he had left it.

He opened the door a little wider, and walked quickly in, with half-closed eyes and averted head, determined that he would not look even once upon the dead man. Then, stooping down, and taking up the gold-and-purple hanging, he flung it over the picture.

He stopped, feeling afraid to turn round, and his eyes fixed themselves on the intricacies of the pattern before him. He heard Campbell bringing in the heavy chest, and the irons, and the other things that he had required for his dreadful work. He began to wonder if he and Basil Hallward had ever met, and, if so, what they had thought of each other.

"Leave me now," said Campbell.

He turned and hurried out, just conscious that the dead man had been thrust back into the chair and was sitting up in it, with Campbell gazing into the glistening yellow face. As he was going downstairs he heard the key being turned in the lock.

It was long after seven o'clock when Campbell came back into the library. He was pale, but absolutely calm. "I have done what you asked me to do," he muttered. "And now, good-by. Let us never see each other again."

"You have saved me from ruin, Alan. I cannot forget that," said Dorian, simply.

As soon as Campbell had left, he went up-stairs. There was a horrible smell of chemicals in the room. But the thing that had been sitting at the table was gone.

CHAPTER XIII

"There is no good telling me you are going to be good, Dorian," cried Lord Henry, dipping his white fingers into a red copper bowl filled with rose-water. "You are quite perfect. Pray don't change."

Dorian shook his head. "No, Harry, I have done too many dreadful things in my life. I am not going to do any more. I began my good actions yesterday."

"Where were you yesterday?"

"In the country, Harry. I was staying at a little inn by myself."

"My dear boy," said Lord Henry smiling, "anybody can be good in the country. There are no temptations there. That is the reason why people who live out of town are so uncivilized. There are only two ways, as you know, of becoming civilized. One is by being cultured, the other is by being corrupt. Country-people have no opportunity of being either, so they stagnate."

"Culture and corruption," murmured Dorian. "I have known something of both. It seems to me curious now that they should ever be found together. For I have a new ideal, Harry. I am going to alter. I think I have altered."

"You have not told me yet what your good action was. Or did you say you had done more than one?"

"I can tell you, Harry. It is not a story I could tell to any one else. I spared somebody. It sounds vain, but you understand what I mean. She was quite beautiful, and wonderfully like Sibyl Vane. I think it was that which first attracted me to her. You remember Sibyl, don't you? How long ago that seems! Well, Hetty was not one of our own class, of course. She was simply a girl in a village. But I really loved her. I am quite sure that I loved her. All during this wonderful May that we have been having, I used to run down and see her two or three times a week. Yesterday she met me in a little orchard. The apple-blossoms kept tumbling down on her hair, and she was laughing. We were to have gone away together this morning at dawn. Suddenly I determined to leave her as flower-like as I had found her."

"I should think the novelty of the emotion must have given you a thrill of real pleasure, Dorian," interrupted Lord Henry. "But I can finish your idyl for you. You gave her good advice, and broke her heart. That was the beginning of your reformation."

"Harry, you are horrible! You mustn't say these dreadful things. Hetty's heart is not broken. Of course she cried, and all that. But there is no disgrace upon her. She can live, like Perdita, in her garden."

"And weep over a faithless Florizel," said Lord Henry, laughing. "My dear Dorian, you have the most curious boyish moods. Do you think this girl will ever be really contented now with any one of her own rank? I suppose she will be married some day to a rough carter or a grinning ploughman. Well, having met you, and loved you, will teach her to despise her husband, and she will be wretched. From a moral point of view I really don't think much of your great renunciation. Even as a beginning, it is poor. Besides, how do you know that Hetty isn't floating at the present moment in some mill-pond, with water-lilies round her, like Ophelia?"

"I can't bear this, Harry! You mock at everything, and then suggest the most serious tragedies. I am sorry I told you now. I don't care what you say to me, I know I was right in acting as I did. Poor Hetty! As I rode past the farm this morning, I saw her white face at the window, like a spray of jasmine. Don't let me talk about it any more, and don't try to persuade me that the first good action I have done for years, the first little bit of self-sacrifice I have ever known, is really a sort of sin. I want to be better. I am going to be better. Tell me something about yourself. What is going on in town? I have not been to the club for days."

"The people are still discussing poor Basil's disappearance."

"I should have thought they had got tired of that by this time," said Dorian, pouring himself out some wine, and frowning slightly.

"My dear boy, they have only been talking about it for six weeks, and the public are really not equal to the mental strain of having more than one topic every three months. They have been very fortunate lately, however. They have had my own divorce-case, and Alan Campbell's suicide. Now they have got the mysterious disappearance of an artist. Scotland Yard still insists that the man in the gray ulster who left Victoria by the midnight train on the 7th of November was poor Basil, and the French police declare that Basil never arrived in Paris at all. I suppose in about a fortnight we will be told that he has been seen in San Francisco. It is an odd thing, but every one who disappears is said to be seen at San Francisco. It must be a delightful city, and possess all the attractions of the next world."

"What do you think has happened to Basil?" asked Dorian, holding up his Burgundy against the light, and wondering how it was that he could discuss the matter so calmly.

"I have not the slightest idea. If Basil chooses to hide himself, it is no business of mine. If he is dead, I don't want to think about him. Death is the only thing that ever terrifies me. I hate it. One can survive everything nowadays except that. Death and vulgarity are the only two facts in the nineteenth century that one cannot explain away. Let us have our coffee in the music-room, Dorian. You must play Chopin to me. The man with whom my wife ran away played Chopin exquisitely. Poor Victoria! I was very fond of her. The house is rather lonely without her."

Dorian said nothing, but rose from the table, and, passing into the next room, sat down to the piano and let his fingers stray across the keys. After the coffee had been brought in, he stopped, and, looking over at Lord Henry, said, "Harry, did it ever occur to you that Basil was murdered?"

Lord Henry yawned. "Basil had no enemies, and always wore a Waterbury watch. Why should he be murdered? He was not clever enough to have enemies. Of course he had a wonderful genius for painting. But a man can paint like Velasquez and yet be as dull as possible. Basil was really rather dull. He only interested me once, and that was when he told me, years ago, that he had a wild adoration for you."

"I was very fond of Basil," said Dorian, with a sad look in his eyes. "But don't people say that he was murdered?"

"Oh, some of the papers do. It does not seem to be probable. I know there are dreadful places in Paris, but Basil was not the sort of man to have gone to them. He had no curiosity. It was his chief defect. Play me a nocturne, Dorian, and, as you play, tell me, in a low voice, how you have kept your youth. You must have some secret. I am only ten years older than you are, and I am wrinkled, and bald, and yellow. You are really wonderful, Dorian. You have never looked more charming than you do to-night. You remind me of the day I saw you first. You were rather cheeky, very shy, and absolutely extraordinary. You have changed, of course, but not in appearance. I wish you would tell me your secret. To get back my youth I would do anything in the world, except take exercise, get up early, or be respectable. Youth! There is nothing like it. It's absurd to talk of the ignorance of youth. The only people whose opinions I listen to now with any respect are people much younger than myself. They seem in front of me. Life has revealed to them her last wonder. As for the aged, I always contradict the aged. I do it on principle. If you ask them their opinion on something that happened yesterday, they solemnly give you the opinions current in 1820, when people wore high stocks and knew absolutely nothing. How lovely that thing you are playing is! I wonder did Chopin write it at Majorca, with the sea weeping round the villa, and the salt spray dashing against the panes? It is marvelously romantic. What a blessing it is that there is one art left to us that is not imitative! Don't stop. I want music to-night. It seems to me that you are the young Apollo, and that I am Marsyas listening to you. I have sorrows, Dorian, of my own, that even you know nothing of. The tragedy of old age is not that one is old, but that one is young. I am amazed sometimes at my own sincerity. Ah, Dorian, how happy you are! What an exquisite life you have had! You have drunk deeply of everything. You have crushed the grapes against your palate. Nothing has been hidden from you. But it has all been to you no more than the sound of music. It has not marred you. You are still the same.

"I wonder what the rest of your life will be. Don't spoil it by renunciations. At present you are a perfect type. Don't make yourself incomplete. You are quite flawless now. You need not shake your head: you know you are. Besides, Dorian, don't deceive yourself. Life is not governed by will or intention. Life is a question of nerves, and fibres, and slowly-built-up cells in which thought hides itself and passion has its dreams. You may fancy yourself safe, and think yourself strong. But a chance tone of color in a room or a morning sky, a particular perfume that you had once loved and that brings strange memories with it, a line from a forgotten poem that you had come across again, a cadence from a piece of music that you had ceased to play,--I tell you, Dorian, that it is on things like these that our lives depend. Browning writes about that somewhere; but our own senses will imagine them for us. There are moments when the odor of heliotrope passes suddenly across me, and I have to live the strangest year of my life over again.

"I wish I could change places with you, Dorian. The world has cried out against us both, but it has always worshipped you. It always will worship you. You are the type of what the age is searching for, and what it is afraid it has found. I am so glad that you have never done anything, never carved a statue, or painted a picture, or produced anything outside of yourself! Life has been your art. You have set yourself to music. Your days have been your sonnets."

Dorian rose up from the piano, and passed his hand through his hair. "Yes, life has been exquisite," he murmured, "but I am not going to have the same life, Harry. And you must not say these extravagant things to me. You don't know everything about me. I think that if you did, even you would turn from me. You laugh. Don't laugh."

"Why have you stopped playing, Dorian? Go back and play the nocturne over again. Look at that great honey-colored moon that hangs in the dusky air. She is waiting for you to charm her, and if you play she will come closer to the earth. You won't? Let us go to the club, then. It has been a charming evening, and we must end it charmingly. There is some one at the club who wants immensely to know you,--young Lord Poole, Bournmouth's eldest son. He has already copied your neckties, and has begged me to introduce him to you. He is quite delightful, and rather reminds me of you."

"I hope not," said Dorian, with a touch of pathos in his voice. "But I am tired to-night, Harry. I won't go to the club. It is nearly eleven, and I want to go to bed early."

"Do stay. You have never played so well as to-night. There was something in your touch that was wonderful. It had more expression than I had ever heard from it before."

"It is because I am going to be good," he answered, smiling. "I am a little changed already."

"Don't change, Dorian; at any rate, don't change to me. We must always be friends."

"Yet you poisoned me with a book once. I should not forgive that. Harry, promise me that you will never lend that book to any one. It does harm."

"My dear boy, you are really beginning to moralize. You will soon be going about warning people against all the sins of which you have grown tired. You are much too delightful to do that. Besides, it is no use. You and I are what we are, and will be what we will be. Come round tomorrow. I am going to ride at eleven, and we might go together. The Park is quite lovely now. I don't think there have been such lilacs since the year I met you."

"Very well. I will be here at eleven," said Dorian. "Good-night, Harry." As he reached the door he hesitated for a moment, as if he had something more to say. Then he sighed and went out.

It was a lovely night, so warm that he threw his coat over his arm, and did not even put his silk scarf round his throat. As he strolled home, smoking his cigarette, two young men in evening dress passed him. He heard one of them whisper to the other, "That is Dorian Gray." He remembered how pleased he used to be when he was pointed out, or stared at, or talked about. He was tired of hearing his own name now. Half the charm of the little village where he had been so often lately was that no one knew who he was. He had told the girl whom he had made love him that he was poor, and she had believed him. He had told her once that he was wicked, and she had laughed at him, and told him that wicked people were always very old and very ugly. What a laugh she had!--just like a thrush singing. And how pretty she had been in her cotton dresses and her large hats! She knew nothing, but she had everything that he had lost.

When he reached home, he found his servant waiting up for him. He sent him to bed, and threw himself down on the sofa in the library, and began to think over some of the things that Lord Henry had said to him.

Was it really true that one could never change? He felt a wild longing for the unstained purity of his boyhood,--his rose-white boyhood, as Lord Henry had once called it. He knew that he had tarnished himself, filled his mind with corruption, and given horror to his fancy; that he had been an evil influence to others, and had experienced a terrible joy in being so; and that of the lives that had crossed his own it had been the fairest and the most full of promise that he had brought to shame. But was it all irretrievable? Was there no hope for him?

It was better not to think of the past. Nothing could alter that. It was of himself, and of his own future, that he had to think. Alan Campbell had shot himself one night in his laboratory, but had not revealed the secret that he had been forced to know. The excitement, such as it was, over Basil Hallward's disappearance would soon pass away. It was already waning. He was perfectly safe there. Nor, indeed, was it the death of Basil Hallward that weighed most upon his mind. It was the living death of his own soul that troubled him. Basil had painted the portrait that had marred his life. He could not forgive him that. It was the portrait that had done everything. Basil had said things to him that were unbearable, and that he had yet borne with patience. The murder had been simply the madness of a moment. As for Alan Campbell, his suicide had been his own act. He had chosen to do it. It was nothing to him.

A new life! That was what he wanted. That was what he was waiting for. Surely he had begun it already. He had spared one innocent thing, at any rate. He would never again tempt innocence. He would be good.

As he thought of Hetty Merton, he began to wonder if the portrait in the locked room had changed. Surely it was not still so horrible as it had been? Perhaps if his life became pure, he would be able to expel every sign of evil passion from the face. Perhaps the signs of evil had already gone away. He would go and look.

He took the lamp from the table and crept up-stairs. As he unlocked the door, a smile of joy flitted across his young face and lingered for a moment about his lips. Yes, he would be good, and the hideous thing that he had hidden away would no longer be a terror to him. He felt as if the load had been lifted from him already.

He went in quietly, locking the door behind him, as was his custom, and dragged the purple hanging from the portrait. A cry of pain and indignation broke from him. He could see no change, unless that in the eyes there was a look of cunning, and in the mouth the curved wrinkle of the hypocrite. The thing was still loathsome,--more loathsome, if possible, than before,--and the scarlet dew that spotted the hand seemed brighter, and more like blood newly spilt.

Had it been merely vanity that had made him do his one good deed? Or the desire of a new sensation, as Lord Henry had hinted, with his mocking laugh? Or that passion to act a part that sometimes makes us do things finer than we are ourselves? Or, perhaps, all these?

Why was the red stain larger than it had been? It seemed to have crept like a horrible disease over the wrinkled fingers. There was blood on the painted feet, as though the thing had dripped,--blood even on the hand that had not held the knife.

Confess? Did it mean that he was to confess? To give himself up, and be put to death? He laughed. He felt that the idea was monstrous. Besides, who would believe him, even if he did confess? There was no trace of the murdered man anywhere. Everything belonging to him had been destroyed. He himself had burned what had been below-stairs. The world would simply say he was mad. They would shut him up if he persisted in his story.

Yet it was his duty to confess, to suffer public shame, and to make public atonement. There was a God who called upon men to tell their sins to earth as well as to heaven. Nothing that he could do would cleanse him till he had told his own sin. His sin? He shrugged his shoulders. The death of Basil Hallward seemed very little to him. He was thinking of Hetty Merton.

It was an unjust mirror, this mirror of his soul that he was looking at. Vanity? Curiosity? Hypocrisy? Had there been nothing more in his renunciation than that? There had been something more. At least he thought so. But who could tell?

And this murder,--was it to dog him all his life? Was he never to get rid of the past? Was he really to confess? No. There was only one bit of evidence left against him. The picture itself,--that was evidence.

He would destroy it. Why had he kept it so long? It had given him pleasure once to watch it changing and growing old. Of late he had felt no such pleasure. It had kept him awake at night. When he had been away, he had been filled with terror lest other eyes should look upon it. It had brought melancholy across his passions. Its mere memory had marred many moments of joy. It had been like conscience to him. Yes, it had been conscience. He would destroy it.

He looked round, and saw the knife that had stabbed Basil Hallward. He had cleaned it many times, till there was no stain left upon it. It was bright, and glistened. As it had killed the painter, so it would kill the painter's work, and all that that meant. It would kill the past, and when that was dead he would be free. He seized it, and stabbed the canvas with it, ripping the thing right up from top to bottom.

There was a cry heard, and a crash. The cry was so horrible in its agony that the frightened servants woke, and crept out of their rooms. Two gentlemen, who were passing in the Square below, stopped, and looked up at the great house. They walked on till they met a policeman, and brought him back. The man rang the bell several times, but there was no answer. The house was all dark, except for a light in one of the top windows. After a time, he went away, and stood in the portico of the next house and watched.

"Whose house is that, constable?" asked the elder of the two gentlemen.

"Mr. Dorian Gray's, sir," answered the policeman.

They looked at each other, as they walked away, and sneered. One of them was Sir Henry Ashton's uncle.

Inside, in the servants' part of the house, the half-clad domestics were talking in low whispers to each other. Old Mrs. Leaf was crying, and wringing her hands. Francis was as pale as death.

After about a quarter of an hour, he got the coachman and one of the footmen and crept up-stairs. They knocked, but there was no reply. They called out. Everything was still. Finally, after vainly trying to force the door, they got on the roof, and dropped down on to the balcony. The windows yielded easily: the bolts were old.

When they entered, they found hanging upon the wall a splendid portrait of their master as they had last seen him, in all the wonder of his exquisite youth and beauty. Lying on the floor was a dead man, in evening dress, with a knife in his heart. He was withered, wrinkled, and loathsome of visage. It was not till they had examined the rings that they recognized who it was.

Lot No. 249

By Arthur Conan Doyle

Of the dealings of Edward Bellingham with William Monkhouse Lee, and of the cause of the great terror of Abercrombie Smith, it may be that no absolute and final judgment will ever be delivered. It is true that we have the full and clear narrative of Smith himself, and such corroboration as he could look for from Thomas Styles the servant, from the Reverend Plumptree Peterson, Fellow of Old's, and from such other people as chanced to gain some passing glance at this or that incident in a singular chain of events. Yet, in the main, the story must rest upon Smith alone, and the most will think that it is more likely that one brain, however outwardly sane, has some subtle warp in its texture, some strange flaw in its workings, than that the path of Nature has been overstepped in open day in so famed a centre of learning and light as the University of Oxford. Yet when we think how narrow and how devious this path of Nature is, how dimly we can trace it, for all our lamps of science, and how from the darkness which girds it round great and terrible possibilities loom ever shadowly upwards, it is a bold and confident man who will put a limit to the strange by-paths into which the human spirit may wander.

In a certain wing of what we will call Old College in Oxford there is a corner turret of an exceeding great age. The heavy arch which spans the open door has bent downwards in the centre under the weight of its years, and the grey, lichen-blotched blocks of stone are, bound and knitted together with withes and strands of ivy, as though the old mother had set herself to brace them up against wind and weather. From the door a stone stair curves upward spirally, passing two landings, and terminating in a third one, its steps all shapeless and hollowed by the tread of so many generations of the seekers after knowledge. Life has flowed like water down this winding stair, and, waterlike, has left these smooth-worn grooves behind it. From the long-gowned, pedantic scholars of Plantagenet days down to the young bloods of a later age, how full and strong had been that tide of young English life. And what was left now of all those hopes, those strivings, those fiery energies, save here and there in some old-world churchyard a few scratches upon a stone, and perchance a handful of dust in a mouldering coffin?

Yet here were the silent stair and the grey old wall, with bend and saltire and many another heraldic device still to be read upon its surface, like grotesque shadows thrown back from the days that had passed.

In the month of May, in the year 1884, three young men occupied the sets of rooms which opened on to the separate landings of the old stair. Each set consisted simply of a sitting-room and of a bedroom, while the two corresponding rooms upon the ground-floor were used, the one as a coal-cellar, and the other as the living-room of the servant, or gyp, Thomas Styles, whose duty it was to wait upon the three men above him. To right and to left was a line of lecture-rooms and of offices, so that the dwellers in the old turret enjoyed a certain seclusion, which made the chambers popular among the more studious undergraduates. Such were the three who occupied them now—Abercrombie Smith above, Edward Bellingham beneath him, and William Monkhouse Lee upon the lowest storey.

It was ten o'clock on a bright spring night, and Abercrombie Smith lay back in his arm-chair, his feet upon the fender, and his briar-root pipe between his lips. In a similar chair, and equally at his ease, there lounged on the other side of the fireplace his old school friend Jephro Hastie. Both men were in flannels, for they had spent their evening upon the river, but apart from their dress no one could look at their hard-cut, alert faces without seeing that they were open-air men—men whose minds and tastes turned naturally to all that was manly and robust. Hastie, indeed, was stroke of his college boat, and Smith was an even better oar, but a coming examination had already cast its shadow over him and held him to his work, save for the few hours a week which health demanded. A litter of medical books upon the table, with scattered bones, models and anatomical plates, pointed to the extent as well as the nature of his studies, while a couple of single-sticks and a set of boxing-gloves above the mantelpiece hinted at the means by which, with Hastie's help, he might take his exercise in its most compressed and least distant form. They knew each other very well—so well that they could sit now in that soothing silence which is the very highest development of companionship.

"Have some whisky," said Abercrombie Smith at last between two cloudbursts. "Scotch in the jug and Irish in the bottle."

"No, thanks. I'm in for the sculls. I don't liquor when I'm training. How about you?"

"I'm reading hard. I think it best to leave it alone."

Hastie nodded, and they relapsed into a contented silence.

"By-the-way, Smith," asked Hastie, presently, "have you made the acquaintance of either of the fellows on your stair yet?"

"Just a nod when we pass. Nothing more."

"Hum! I should be inclined to let it stand at that. I know something of them both. Not much, but as much as I want. I don't think I should take them to my bosom if I were you. Not that there's much amiss with Monkhouse Lee."

"Meaning the thin one?"

"Precisely. He is a gentlemanly little fellow. I don't think there is any vice in him. But then you can't know him without knowing Bellingham."

"Meaning the fat one?"

"Yes, the fat one. And he's a man whom I, for one, would rather not know."

Abercrombie Smith raised his eyebrows and glanced across at his companion.

"What's up, then?" he asked. "Drink? Cards? Cad? You used not to be censorious."

"Ah! you evidently don't know the man, or you wouldn't ask. There's something damnable about him—something reptilian. My gorge always rises at him. I should put him down as a man with secret vices—an evil liver. He's no fool, though. They say that he is one of the best men in his line that they have ever had in the college."

"Medicine or classics?"

"Eastern languages. He's a demon at them. Chillingworth met him somewhere above the second cataract last long, and he told me that he just prattled to the Arabs as if he had been born and nursed and weaned among them. He talked Coptic to the Copts, and Hebrew to the Jews, and Arabic to the Bedouins, and they were all ready to kiss the hem of his frock-coat. There are some old hermit Johnnies up in those parts who sit on rocks and scowl and spit at the casual stranger. Well, when they saw this chap Bellingham, before he had said five words they just lay down on their bellies and wriggled. Chillingworth said that he never saw anything like it. Bellingham seemed to take it as his right, too, and strutted about among them and talked down to them like a Dutch uncle. Pretty good for an undergrad. of Old's, wasn't it?"

"Why do you say you can't know Lee without knowing Bellingham?"

"Because Bellingham is engaged to his sister Eveline. Such a bright little girl, Smith! I know the whole family well. It's disgusting to see that brute with her. A toad and a dove, that's what they always remind me of."

Abercrombie Smith grinned and knocked his ashes out against the side of the grate.

"You show every card in your hand, old chap," said he. "What a prejudiced, green-eyed, evil-thinking old man it is! You have really nothing against the fellow except that."

"Well, I've known her ever since she was as long as that cherry-wood pipe, and I don't like to see her taking risks. And it is a risk. He looks beastly. And he has a beastly temper, a venomous temper. You remember his row with Long Norton?"

"No; you always forget that I am a freshman."

"Ah, it was last winter. Of course. Well, you know the towpath along by the river. There were several fellows going along it, Bellingham in front, when they came on an old market-woman coming the other way. It had been raining—you know what those fields are like when it has rained—and the path ran between the river and a great puddle that was nearly as broad. Well, what does this swine do but keep the path, and push the old girl into the mud, where she and her marketings came to terrible grief. It was a blackguard thing to do, and Long Norton, who is as gentle a fellow as ever stepped, told him what he thought of it. One word led to another, and it ended in Norton laying his stick across the fellow's shoulders. There was the deuce of a fuss about it, and it's a treat to see the way in which Bellingham looks at Norton when they meet now. By Jove, Smith, it's nearly eleven o'clock!"

"No hurry. Light your pipe again."

"Not I. I'm supposed to be in training. Here I've been sitting gossiping when I ought to have been safely tucked up. I'll borrow your skull, if you can share it. Williams has had mine for a month. I'll take the little bones of your ear, too, if you are sure you won't need them. Thanks very much. Never mind a bag, I can carry them very well under my arm. Good-night, my son, and take my tip as to your neighbour."

When Hastie, bearing his anatomical plunder, had clattered off down the winding stair, Abercrombie Smith hurled his pipe into the wastepaper basket, and drawing his chair nearer to the lamp, plunged into a formidable green-covered volume, adorned with great colored maps of that strange internal kingdom of which we are the hapless and helpless monarchs. Though a freshman at Oxford, the student was not so in medicine, for he had worked for four years at Glasgow and at Berlin, and this coming examination would place him finally as a member of his profession. With his firm mouth, broad forehead, and clear-cut, somewhat hard-featured face, he was a man who, if he had no brilliant talent, was yet so dogged, so patient, and so strong that he might in the end overtop a more showy genius. A man who can hold his own among Scotchmen and North Germans is not a man to be easily set back. Smith had left a name at Glasgow and at Berlin, and he was bent now upon doing as much at Oxford, if hard work and devotion could accomplish it.

He had sat reading for about an hour, and the hands of the noisy carriage clock upon the side table were rapidly closing together upon the twelve, when a sudden sound fell upon the student's ear—a sharp, rather shrill sound, like the hissing intake of a man's breath who gasps under some strong emotion. Smith laid down his book and slanted his ear to listen. There was no one on either side or above him, so that the interruption came certainly from the neighbour beneath—the same neighbour of whom Hastie had given so unsavoury an account. Smith knew him only as a flabby, pale-faced man of silent and studious habits, a man, whose lamp threw a golden bar from the old turret even after he had extinguished his own. This community in lateness had formed a certain silent bond between them. It was soothing to Smith when the hours stole on towards dawning to feel that there was another so close who set as small a value upon his sleep as he did. Even now, as his thoughts turned towards him, Smith's feelings were kindly. Hastie was a good fellow, but he was rough, strong-fibred, with no imagination or sympathy. He could not tolerate departures from what he looked upon as the model type of manliness. If a man could not be measured by a public-school standard, then he was beyond the pale with Hastie. Like so many who are themselves robust, he was apt to confuse the constitution with the character, to ascribe to want of principle what was really a want of circulation. Smith, with his stronger mind, knew his friend's habit, and made allowance for it now as his thoughts turned towards the man beneath him.

There was no return of the singular sound, and Smith was about to turn to his work once more, when suddenly there broke out in the silence of the night a hoarse cry, a positive scream—the call of a man who is moved and shaken beyond all control. Smith sprang out of his chair and dropped his book. He was a man of fairly firm fibre, but there was something in this sudden, uncontrollable shriek of horror which chilled his blood and pringled in his skin. Coming in such a place and at such an hour, it brought a thousand fantastic possibilities into his head. Should he rush down, or was it better to wait? He had all the national hatred of making a scene, and he knew so little of his neighbour that he would not lightly intrude upon his affairs. For a moment he stood in doubt and even as he balanced the matter there was a quick rattle of footsteps upon the stairs, and young Monkhouse Lee, half dressed and as white as ashes, burst into his room.

"Come down!" he gasped. "Bellingham's ill."

Abercrombie Smith followed him closely down stairs into the sitting-room which was beneath his own, and intent as he was upon the matter in hand, he could not but take an amazed glance around him as he crossed the threshold. It was such a chamber as he had never seen before—a museum rather than a study. Walls and ceiling were thickly covered with a thousand strange relics from Egypt and the East. Tall, angular figures bearing burdens or weapons stalked in an uncouth frieze round the apartments. Above were bull-headed, stork-headed, cat-headed, owl-headed statues, with viper-crowned, almond-eyed monarchs, and strange, beetle-like deities cut out of the blue Egyptian lapis lazuli. Horus and Isis and Osiris peeped down from every niche and shelf, while across the ceiling a true son of Old Nile, a great, hanging-jawed crocodile, was slung in a double noose.

In the centre of this singular chamber was a large, square table, littered with papers, bottles, and the dried leaves of some graceful, palm-like plant. These varied objects had all been heaped together in order to make room for a mummy case, which had been conveyed from the wall, as was evident from the gap there, and laid across the front of the table. The mummy itself, a horrid, black, withered thing, like a charred head on a gnarled bush, was lying half out of the case, with its clawlike hand and bony forearm resting upon the table. Propped up against the sarcophagus was an old yellow scroll of papyrus, and in front of it, in a wooden armchair, sat the owner of the room, his head thrown back, his widely-opened eyes directed in a horrified stare to the crocodile above him, and his blue, thick lips puffing loudly with every expiration.

"My God! he's dying!" cried Monkhouse Lee distractedly.

He was a slim, handsome young fellow, olive-skinned and dark-eyed, of a Spanish rather than of an English type, with a Celtic intensity of manner which contrasted with the Saxon phlegm of Abercombie Smith.

"Only a faint, I think," said the medical student. "Just give me a hand with him. You take his feet. Now on to the sofa. Can you kick all those little wooden devils off? What a litter it is! Now he will be all right if we undo his collar and give him some water. What has he been up to at all?"

"I don't know. I heard him cry out. I ran up. I know him pretty well, you know. It is very good of you to come down."

"His heart is going like a pair of castanets," said Smith, laying his hand on the breast of the unconscious man. "He seems to me to be frightened all to pieces. Chuck the water over him! What a face he has got on him!"

It was indeed a strange and most repellent face, for colour and outline were equally unnatural. It was white, not with the ordinary pallor of fear but with an absolutely bloodless white, like the under side of a sole. He was very fat, but gave the impression of having at some time been considerably fatter, for his skin hung loosely in creases and folds, and was shot with a meshwork of wrinkles. Short, stubbly brown hair bristled up from his scalp, with a pair of thick, wrinkled ears protruding on either side. His light grey eyes were still open, the pupils dilated and the balls projecting in a fixed and horrid stare. It seemed to Smith as he looked down upon him that he had never seen nature's danger signals flying so plainly upon a man's countenance, and his thoughts turned more seriously to the warning which Hastie had given him an hour before.

"What the deuce can have frightened him so?" he asked.

"It's the mummy."

"The mummy? How, then?"

"I don't know. It's beastly and morbid. I wish he would drop it. It's the second fright he has given me. It was the same last winter. I found him just like this, with that horrid thing in front of him."

"What does he want with the mummy, then?"

"Oh, he's a crank, you know. It's his hobby. He knows more about these things than any man in England. But I wish he wouldn't! Ah, he's beginning to come to."

A faint tinge of colour had begun to steal back into Bellingham's ghastly cheeks, and his eyelids shivered like a sail after a calm. He clasped and unclasped his hands, drew a long, thin breath between his teeth, and suddenly jerking up his head, threw a glance of recognition around him. As his eyes fell upon the mummy, he sprang off the sofa, seized the roll of papyrus, thrust it into a drawer, turned the key, and then staggered back on to the sofa.

"What's up?" he asked. "What do you chaps want?"

"You've been shrieking out and making no end of a fuss," said Monkhouse Lee. "If our neighbour here from above hadn't come down, I'm sure I don't know what I should have done with you."

"Ah, it's Abercrombie Smith," said Bellingham, glancing up at him. "How very good of you to come in! What a fool I am! Oh, my God, what a fool I am!"

He sunk his head on to his hands, and burst into peal after peal of hysterical laughter.

"Look here! Drop it!" cried Smith, shaking him roughly by the shoulder.

"Your nerves are all in a jangle. You must drop these little midnight games with mummies, or you'll be going off your chump. You're all on wires now."

"I wonder," said Bellingham, "whether you would be as cool as I am if you had seen— —"

"What then?"

"Oh, nothing. I meant that I wonder if you could sit up at night with a mummy without trying your nerves. I have no doubt that you are quite right. I dare say that I have been taking it out of myself too much lately. But I am all right now. Please don't go, though. Just wait for a few minutes until I am quite myself."

"The room is very close," remarked Lee, throwing open the window and letting in the cool night air.

"It's balsamic resin," said Bellingham. He lifted up one of the dried palmate leaves from the table and frizzled it over the chimney of the lamp. It broke away into heavy smoke wreaths, and a pungent, biting odour filled the chamber. "It's the sacred plant—the plant of the priests," he remarked. "Do you know anything of Eastern languages, Smith?"

"Nothing at all. Not a word."

The answer seemed to lift a weight from the Egyptologist's mind.

"By-the-way," he continued, "how long was it from the time that you ran down, until I came to my senses?"

"Not long. Some four or five minutes."

"I thought it could not be very long," said he, drawing a long breath. "But what a strange thing unconsciousness is! There is no measurement to it. I could not tell from my own sensations if it were seconds or weeks. Now that gentleman on the table was packed up in the days of the eleventh dynasty, some forty centuries ago, and yet if he could find his tongue he would tell us that this lapse of time has been but a closing of the eyes and a reopening of them. He is a singularly fine mummy, Smith."

Smith stepped over to the table and looked down with a professional eye at the black and twisted form in front of him. The features, though horribly discoloured, were perfect, and two little nut-like eyes still lurked in the depths of the black, hollow sockets. The blotched skin was drawn tightly from bone to bone, and a tangled wrap of black coarse hair fell over the ears. Two thin teeth, like those of a rat, overlay the shrivelled lower lip. In its crouching position, with bent joints and craned head, there was a suggestion of energy about the horrid thing which made Smith's gorge rise. The gaunt ribs, with their parchment-like covering, were exposed, and the sunken, leaden-hued abdomen, with the long slit where the embalmer had left his mark; but the lower limbs were wrapt round with coarse yellow bandages. A number of little clove-like pieces of myrrh and of cassia were sprinkled over the body, and lay scattered on the inside of the case.

"I don't know his name," said Bellingham, passing his hand over the shrivelled head. "You see the outer sarcophagus with the inscriptions is missing. Lot 249 is all the title he has now. You see it printed on his case. That was his number in the auction at which I picked him up."

"He has been a very pretty sort of fellow in his day," remarked Abercrombie Smith.

"He has been a giant. His mummy is six feet seven in length, and that would be a giant over there, for they were never a very robust race. Feel these great knotted bones, too. He would be a nasty fellow to tackle."

"Perhaps these very hands helped to build the stones into the pyramids," suggested Monkhouse Lee, looking down with disgust in his eyes at the crooked, unclean talons.

"No fear. This fellow has been pickled in natron, and looked after in the most approved style. They did not serve hodsmen in that fashion. Salt or bitumen was enough for them. It has been calculated that this sort of thing cost about seven hundred and thirty pounds in our money. Our friend was a noble at the least. What do you make of that small inscription near his feet, Smith?"

"I told you that I know no Eastern tongue."

"Ah, so you did. It is the name of the embalmer, I take it. A very conscientious worker he must have been. I wonder how many modern works will survive four thousand years?"

He kept on speaking lightly and rapidly, but it was evident to Abercrombie Smith that he was still palpitating with fear. His hands shook, his lower lip trembled, and look where he would, his eye always came sliding round to his gruesome companion. Through all his fear, however, there was a suspicion of triumph in his tone and manner. His eye shone, and his footstep, as he paced the room, was brisk and jaunty. He gave the impression of a man who has gone through an ordeal, the marks of which he still bears upon him, but which has helped him to his end.

"You're not going yet?" he cried, as Smith rose from the sofa.

At the prospect of solitude, his fears seemed to crowd back upon him, and he stretched out a hand to detain him.

"Yes, I must go. I have my work to do. You are all right now. I think that with your nervous system you should take up some less morbid study."

"Oh, I am not nervous as a rule; and I have unwrapped mummies before."

"You fainted last time," observed Monkhouse Lee.

"Ah, yes, so I did. Well, I must have a nerve tonic or a course of electricity. You are not going, Lee?"

"I'll do whatever you wish, Ned."

"Then I'll come down with you and have a shake-down on your sofa. Good-night, Smith. I am so sorry to have disturbed you with my foolishness."

They shook hands, and as the medical student stumbled up the spiral and irregular stair he heard a key turn in a door, and the steps of his two new acquaintances as they descended to the lower floor.

In this strange way began the acquaintance between Edward Bellingham and Abercrombie Smith, an acquaintance which the latter, at least, had no desire to push further. Bellingham, however, appeared to have taken a fancy to his rough-spoken neighbour, and made his advances in such a way that he could hardly be repulsed without absolute brutality. Twice he called to thank Smith for his assistance, and many times afterwards he looked in with books, papers, and such other civilities as two bachelor neighbours can offer each other. He was, as Smith soon found, a man of wide reading, with catholic tastes and an extraordinary memory. His manner, too, was so pleasing and suave that one came, after a time, to overlook his repellent appearance. For a jaded and wearied man he was no unpleasant companion, and Smith found himself, after a time, looking forward to his visits, and even returning them.

Clever as he undoubtedly was, however, the medical student seemed to detect a dash of insanity in the man. He broke out at times into a high, inflated style of talk which was in contrast with the simplicity of his life.

"It is a wonderful thing," he cried, "to feel that one can command powers of good and of evil—a ministering angel or a demon of vengeance." And again, of Monkhouse Lee, he said, —"Lee is a good fellow, an honest fellow, but he is without strength or ambition. He would not make a fit partner for a man with a great enterprise. He would not make a fit partner for me."

At such hints and innuendoes stolid Smith, puffing solemnly at his pipe, would simply raise his eyebrows and shake his head, with little interjections of medical wisdom as to earlier hours and fresher air.

One habit Bellingham had developed of late which Smith knew to be a frequent herald of a weakening mind. He appeared to be forever talking to himself. At late hours of the night, when there could be no visitor with him, Smith could still hear his voice beneath him in a low, muffled monologue, sunk almost to a whisper, and yet very audible in the silence. This solitary babbling annoyed and distracted the student, so that he spoke more than once to his neighbour about it. Bellingham, however, flushed up at the charge, and denied curtly that he had uttered a sound; indeed, he showed more annoyance over the matter than the occasion seemed to demand.

Had Abercrombie Smith had any doubt as to his own ears he had not to go far to find corroboration. Tom Styles, the little wrinkled man-servant who had attended to the wants of the lodgers in the turret for a longer time than any man's memory could carry him, was sorely put to it over the same matter.

"If you please, sir," said he, as he tidied down the top chamber one morning, "do you think Mr. Bellingham is all right, sir?"

"All right, Styles?"

"Yes sir. Right in his head, sir."

"Why should he not be, then?"

"Well, I don't know, sir. His habits has changed of late. He's not the same man he used to be, though I make free to say that he was never quite one of my gentlemen, like Mr. Hastie or yourself, sir. He's took to talkin' to himself something awful. I wonder it don't disturb you. I don't know what to make of him, sir."

"I don't know what business it is of yours, Styles."

"Well, I takes an interest, Mr. Smith. It may be forward of me, but I can't help it. I feel sometimes as if I was mother and father to my young gentlemen. It all falls on me when things go wrong and the relations come. But Mr. Bellingham, sir. I want to know what it is that walks about his room sometimes when he's out and when the door's locked on the outside."

"Eh! you're talking nonsense, Styles."

"Maybe so, sir; but I heard it more'n once with my own ears."

"Rubbish, Styles."

"Very good, sir. You'll ring the bell if you want me."

Abercrombie Smith gave little heed to the gossip of the old man-servant, but a small incident occurred a few days later which left an unpleasant effect upon his mind, and brought the words of Styles forcibly to his memory.

Bellingham had come up to see him late one night, and was entertaining him with an interesting account of the rock tombs of Beni Hassan in Upper Egypt, when Smith, whose hearing was remarkably acute, distinctly heard the sound of a door opening on the landing below.

"There's some fellow gone in or out of your room," he remarked.

Bellingham sprang up and stood helpless for a moment, with the expression of a man who is half incredulous and half afraid.

"I surely locked it. I am almost positive that I locked it," he stammered. "No one could have opened it."

"Why, I hear someone coming up the steps now," said Smith.

Bellingham rushed out through the door, slammed it loudly behind him, and hurried down the stairs. About half-way down Smith heard him stop, and thought he caught the sound of whispering. A moment later the door beneath him shut, a key creaked in a lock, and Bellingham, with beads of moisture upon his pale face, ascended the stairs once more, and re-entered the room.

"It's all right," he said, throwing himself down in a chair. "It was that fool of a dog. He had pushed the door open. I don't know how I came to forget to lock it."

"I didn't know you kept a dog," said Smith, looking very thoughtfully at the disturbed face of his companion.

"Yes, I haven't had him long. I must get rid of him. He's a great nuisance."

"He must be, if you find it so hard to shut him up. I should have thought that shutting the door would have been enough, without locking it."

"I want to prevent old Styles from letting him out. He's of some value, you know, and it would be awkward to lose him."

"I am a bit of a dog-fancier myself," said Smith, still gazing hard at his companion from the corner of his eyes. "Perhaps you'll let me have a look at it."

"Certainly. But I am afraid it cannot be to-night; I have an appointment. Is that clock right? Then I am a quarter of an hour late already. You'll excuse me, I am sure."

He picked up his cap and hurried from the room. In spite of his appointment, Smith heard him re-enter his own chamber and lock his door upon the inside.

This interview left a disagreeable impression upon the medical student's mind. Bellingham had lied to him, and lied so clumsily that it looked as if he had desperate reasons for concealing the truth. Smith knew that his neighbour had no dog. He knew, also, that the step which he had heard upon the stairs was not the step of an animal. But if it were not, then what could it be? There was old Styles's statement about the something which used to pace the room at times when the owner was absent. Could it be a woman? Smith rather inclined to the view. If so, it would mean disgrace and expulsion to Bellingham if it were discovered by the authorities, so that his anxiety and falsehoods might be accounted for. And yet it was inconceivable that an undergraduate could keep a woman in his rooms without being instantly detected. Be the explanation what it might, there was something ugly about it, and Smith determined, as he turned to his books, to discourage all further attempts at intimacy on the part of his soft-spoken and ill-favoured neighbour.

But his work was destined to interruption that night. He had hardly caught tip the broken threads when a firm, heavy footfall came three steps at a time from below, and Hastie, in blazer and flannels, burst into the room.

"Still at it!" said he, plumping down into his wonted arm-chair. "What a chap you are to stew! I believe an earthquake might come and knock Oxford into a cocked hat, and you would sit perfectly placid with your books among the rains. However, I won't bore you long. Three whiffs of baccy, and I am off."

"What's the news, then?" asked Smith, cramming a plug of bird's-eye into his briar with his forefinger.

"Nothing very much. Wilson made 70 for the freshmen against the eleven. They say that they will play him instead of Buddicomb, for Buddicomb is clean off colour. He used to be able to bowl a little, but it's nothing but half-vollies and long hops now."

"Medium right," suggested Smith, with the intense gravity which comes upon a 'varsity man when he speaks of athletics.

"Inclining to fast, with a work from leg. Comes with the arm about three inches or so. He used to be nasty on a wet wicket. Oh, by-the-way, have you heard about Long Norton?"

"What's that?"

"He's been attacked."

"Attacked?"

"Yes, just as he was turning out of the High Street, and within a hundred yards of the gate of Old's."

"But who——"

"Ah, that's the rub! If you said 'what,' you would be more grammatical. Norton swears that it was not human, and, indeed, from the scratches on his throat, I should be inclined to agree with him."

"What, then? Have we come down to spooks?"

Abercrombie Smith puffed his scientific contempt.

"Well, no; I don't think that is quite the idea, either. I am inclined to think that if any showman has lost a great ape lately, and the brute is in these parts, a jury would find a true bill against it. Norton passes that way every night, you know, about the same hour. There's a tree that hangs low over the path—the big elm from Rainy's garden. Norton thinks the thing dropped on him out of the tree. Anyhow, he was nearly strangled by two arms, which, he says, were as strong and as thin as steel bands. He saw nothing; only those beastly arms that tightened and tightened on him. He yelled his head nearly off, and a couple of chaps came running, and the thing went over the wall like a cat. He never got a fair sight of it the whole time. It gave Norton a shake up, I can tell you. I tell him it has been as good as a change at the sea-side for him."

"A garrotter, most likely," said Smith.

"Very possibly. Norton says not; but we don't mind what he says. The garrotter had long nails, and was pretty smart at swinging himself over walls. By-the-way, your beautiful neighbour would be pleased if he heard about it. He had a grudge against Norton, and he's not a man, from what I know of him, to forget his little debts. But hallo, old chap, what have you got in your noddle?"

"Nothing," Smith answered curtly.

He had started in his chair, and the look had flashed over his face which comes upon a man who is struck suddenly by some unpleasant idea.

"You looked as if something I had said had taken you on the raw. By-the-way, you have made the acquaintance of Master B. since I looked in last, have you not? Young Monkhouse Lee told me something to that effect."

"Yes; I know him slightly. He has been up here once or twice."

"Well, you're big enough and ugly enough to take care of yourself. He's not what I should call exactly a healthy sort of Johnny, though, no doubt, he's very clever, and all that. But you'll soon find out for yourself. Lee is all right; he's a very decent little fellow. Well, so long, old chap! I row Mullins for the Vice-Chancellor's pot on Wednesday week, so mind you come down, in case I don't see you before."

Bovine Smith laid down his pipe and turned stolidly to his

books once more. But with all the will in the world, he found it very hard to keep his mind upon his work. It would slip away to brood upon the man beneath him, and upon the little mystery which hung round his chambers. Then his thoughts turned to this singular attack of which Hastie had spoken, and to the grudge which Bellingham was said to owe the object of it. The two ideas would persist in rising together in his mind, as though there were some close and intimate connection between them. And yet the suspicion was so dim and vague that it could not be put down in words.

"Confound the chap!" cried Smith, as he shied his book on pathology across the room. "He has spoiled my night's reading, and that's reason enough, if there were no other, why I should steer clear of him in the future."

For ten days the medical student confined himself so closely to his studies that he neither saw nor heard anything of either of the men beneath him. At the hours when Bellingham had been accustomed to visit him, he took care to sport his oak, and though he more than once heard a knocking at his outer door, he resolutely refused to answer it. One afternoon, however, he was descending the stairs when, just as he was passing it, Bellingham's door flew open, and young Monkhouse Lee came out with his eyes sparkling and a dark flush of anger upon his olive cheeks. Close at his heels followed Bellingham, his fat, unhealthy face all quivering with malignant passion.

"You fool!" he hissed. "You'll be sorry."

"Very likely," cried the other. "Mind what I say. It's off! I won't hear of it!"

"You've promised, anyhow."

"Oh, I'll keep that! I won't speak. But I'd rather little Eva was in her grave. Once for all, it's off. She'll do what I say. We don't want to see you again."

So much Smith could not avoid hearing, but he hurried on, for he had no wish to be involved in their dispute. There had been a serious breach between them, that was clear enough, and Lee was going to cause the engagement with his sister to be broken off. Smith thought of Hastie's comparison of the toad and the dove, and was glad to think that the matter was at an end. Bellingham's face when he was in a passion was not pleasant to look upon. He was not a man to whom an innocent girl could be trusted for life. As he walked, Smith wondered languidly what could have caused the quarrel, and what the promise might be which Bellingham had been so anxious that Monkhouse Lee should keep.

It was the day of the sculling match between Hastie and Mullins, and a stream of men were making their way down to the banks of the Isis. A May sun was shining brightly, and the yellow path was barred with the black shadows of the tall elm-trees. On either side the grey colleges lay back from the road, the hoary old mothers of minds looking out from their high, mullioned windows at the tide of young life which swept so merrily past them. Black-clad tutors, prim officials, pale reading men, brown-faced, straw-hatted young athletes in white sweaters or many-coloured blazers, all were hurrying towards the blue winding river which curves through the Oxford meadows.

Abercrombie Smith, with the intuition of an old oarsman, chose his position at the point where he knew that the struggle, if there were a struggle, would come. Far off he heard the hum which announced the start, the gathering roar of the approach, the thunder of running feet, and the shouts of the men in the boats beneath him. A spray of half-clad, deep-breathing runners shot past him, and craning over their shoulders, he saw Hastie pulling a steady thirty-six, while his opponent, with a jerky forty, was a good boat's length behind him. Smith gave a cheer for his friend, and pulling out his watch, was starting off again for his chambers, when he felt a touch upon his shoulder, and found that young Monkhouse Lee was beside him.

"I saw you there," he said, in a timid, deprecating way. "I wanted to speak to you, if you could spare me a half-hour. This cottage is mine. I share it with Harrington of King's. Come in and have a cup of tea."

"I must be back presently," said Smith. "I am hard on the grind at present. But I'll come in for a few minutes with pleasure. I wouldn't have come out only Hastie is a friend of mine."

"So he is of mine. Hasn't he a beautiful style? Mullins wasn't in it. But come into the cottage. It's a little den of a place, but it is pleasant to work in during the summer months."

It was a small, square, white building, with green doors and shutters, and a rustic trellis-work porch, standing back some fifty yards from the river's bank. Inside, the main room was roughly fitted up as a study—deal table, unpainted shelves with books, and a few cheap oleographs upon the wall. A kettle sang upon a spirit-stove, and there were tea things upon a tray on the table.

"Try that chair and have a cigarette," said Lee. "Let me pour you out a cup of tea. It's so good of you to come in, for I know that your time is a good deal taken up. I wanted to say to you that, if I were you, I should change my rooms at once."

"Eh?"

Smith sat staring with a lighted match in one hand and his unlit cigarette in the other.

"Yes; it must seem very extraordinary, and the worst of it is that I cannot give my reasons, for I am under a solemn promise—a very solemn promise. But I may go so far as to say that I don't think Bellingham is a very safe man to live near. I intend to camp out here as much as I can for a time."

"Not safe! What do you mean?"

"Ah, that's what I mustn't say. But do take my advice, and move your rooms. We had a grand row to-day. You must have heard us, for you came down the stairs."

"I saw that you had fallen out."

"He's a horrible chap, Smith. That is the only word for him. I have had doubts about him ever since that night when he fainted—you remember, when you came down. I taxed him to-day, and he told me things that made my hair rise, and wanted me to stand in with him. I'm not strait-laced, but I am a clergyman's son, you know, and I think there are some things which are quite beyond the pale. I only thank God that I found him out before it was too late, for he was to have married into my family."

"This is all very fine, Lee," said Abercrombie Smith curtly. "But either you are saying a great deal too much or a great deal too little."

"I give you a warning."

"If there is real reason for warning, no promise can bind you. If I see a rascal about to blow a place up with dynamite no pledge will stand in my way of preventing him."

"Ah, but I cannot prevent him, and I can do nothing but warn you."

"Without saying what you warn me against."

"Against Bellingham."

"But that is childish. Why should I fear him, or any man?"

"I can't tell you. I can only entreat you to change your rooms. You are in danger where you are. I don't even say that Bellingham would wish to injure you. But it might happen, for he is a dangerous neighbour just now."

"Perhaps I know more than you think," said Smith, looking keenly at the young man's boyish, earnest face. "Suppose I tell you that some one else shares Bellingham's rooms."

Monkhouse Lee sprang from his chair in uncontrollable excitement.

"You know, then?" he gasped.

"A woman."

Lee dropped back again with a groan.

"My lips are sealed," he said. "I must not speak."

"Well, anyhow," said Smith, rising, "it is not likely that I should allow myself to be frightened out of rooms which suit me very nicely. It would be a little too feeble for me to move out all my goods and chattels because you say that Bellingham might in some unexplained way do me an injury. I think that I'll just take my chance, and stay where I am, and as I see that it's nearly five o'clock, I must ask you to excuse me."

He bade the young student adieu in a few curt words, and made his way homeward through the sweet spring evening feeling half-ruffled, half-amused, as any other strong, unimaginative man might who has been menaced by a vague and shadowy danger.

There was one little indulgence which Abercrombie Smith always allowed himself, however closely his work might press upon him. Twice a week, on the Tuesday and the Friday, it was his invariable custom to walk over to Farlingford, the residence of Dr. Plumptree Peterson, situated about a mile and a half out of Oxford. Peterson had been a close friend of Smith's elder brother Francis, and as he was a bachelor, fairly well-to-do, with a good cellar and a better library, his house was a pleasant goal for a man who was in need of a brisk walk. Twice a week, then, the medical student would swing out there along the dark country roads, and spend a pleasant hour in Peterson's comfortable study, discussing, over a glass of old port, the gossip of the 'varsity or the latest developments of medicine or of surgery.

On the day which followed his interview with Monkhouse Lee, Smith shut up his books at a quarter past eight, the hour when he usually started for his friend's house. As he was leaving his room, however, his eyes chanced to fall upon one of the books which Bellingham had lent him, and his conscience pricked him for not having returned it. However repellent the man might be, he should not be treated with discourtesy. Taking the book, he walked downstairs and knocked at his neighbour's door. There was no answer; but on turning the handle he found that it was unlocked. Pleased at the thought of avoiding an interview, he stepped inside, and placed the book with his card upon the table.

The lamp was turned half down, but Smith could see the details of the room plainly enough. It was all much as he had seen it before—the frieze, the animal-headed gods, the banging crocodile, and the table littered over with papers and dried leaves. The mummy case stood upright against the wall, but the mummy itself was missing. There was no sign of any second occupant of the room, and he felt as he withdrew that he had probably done Bellingham an injustice. Had he a guilty secret to preserve, he would hardly leave his door open so that all the world might enter.

The spiral stair was as black as pitch, and Smith was slowly making his way down its irregular steps, when he was suddenly conscious that something had passed him in the darkness. There was a faint sound, a whiff of air, a light brushing past his elbow, but so slight that he could scarcely be certain of it. He stopped and listened, but the wind was rustling among the ivy outside, and he could hear nothing else.

"Is that you, Styles?" he shouted.

There was no answer, and all was still behind him. It must have been a sudden gust of air, for there were crannies and cracks in the old turret. And yet he could almost have sworn that he heard a footfall by his very side. He had emerged into the quadrangle, still turning the matter over in his head, when a man came running swiftly across the smooth-cropped lawn.

"Is that you, Smith?"

"Hullo, Hastie!"

"For God's sake come at once! Young Lee is drowned! Here's Harrington of King's with the news. The doctor is out. You'll do, but come along at once. There may be life in him."

"Have you brandy?"

"No."

"I'll bring some. There's a flask on my table."

Smith bounded up the stairs, taking three at a time, seized the flask, and was rushing down with it, when, as he passed Bellingham's room, his eyes fell upon something which left him gasping and staring upon the landing.

The door, which he had closed behind him, was now open, and right in front of him, with the lamp-light shining upon it, was the mummy case. Three minutes ago it had been empty. He could swear to that. Now it framed the lank body of its horrible occupant, who stood, grim and stark, with his black shrivelled face towards the door. The form was lifeless and inert, but it seemed to Smith as he gazed that there still lingered a lurid spark of vitality, some faint sign of consciousness in the little eyes which lurked in the depths of the hollow sockets. So astounded and shaken was he that he had forgotten his errand, and was still staring at the lean, sunken figure when the voice of his friend below recalled him to himself.

"Come on, Smith!" he shouted. "It's life and death, you know. Hurry up! Now, then," he added, as the medical student reappeared, "let us do a sprint. It is well under a mile, and we should do it in five minutes. A human life is better worth running for than a pot."

Neck and neck they dashed through the darkness, and did not pull up until, panting and spent, they had reached the little cottage by the river. Young Lee, limp and dripping like a broken water-plant, was stretched upon the sofa, the green scum of the river upon his black hair, and a fringe of white foam upon his leaden-hued lips. Beside him knelt his fellow-student Harrington, endeavouring to chafe some warmth back into his rigid limbs.

"I think there's life in him," said Smith, with his hand to the lad's side. "Put your watch glass to his lips. Yes, there's dimming on it. You take one arm, Hastie. Now work it as I do, and we'll soon pull him round."

For ten minutes they worked in silence, inflating and depressing the chest of the unconscious man. At the end of that time a shiver ran through his body, his lips trembled, and he opened his eyes. The three students burst out into an irrepressible cheer.

"Wake up, old chap. You've frightened us quite enough."

"Have some brandy. Take a sip from the flask."

"He's all right now," said his companion Harrington. "Heavens, what a fright I got! I was reading here, and he had gone for a stroll as far as the river, when I heard a scream and a splash. Out I ran, and by the time that I could find him and fish him out, all life seemed to have gone. Then Simpson couldn't get a doctor, for he has a game-leg, and I had to run, and I don't know what I'd have done without you fellows. That's right, old chap. Sit up."

Monkhouse Lee had raised himself on his hands, and looked wildly about him.

"What's up?" he asked. "I've been in the water. Ah, yes; I remember."

A look of fear came into his eyes, and he sank his face into his hands.

"How did you fall in?"

"I didn't fall in."

"How, then?"

"I was thrown in. I was standing by the bank, and something from behind picked me up like a feather and hurled me in. I heard nothing, and I saw nothing. But I know what it was, for all that."

"And so do I," whispered Smith.

Lee looked up with a quick glance of surprise. "You've learned, then!" he said. "You remember the advice I gave you?"

"Yes, and I begin to think that I shall take it."

"I don't know what the deuce you fellows are talking about," said Hastie, "but I think, if I were you, Harrington, I should get Lee to bed at once. It will be time enough to discuss the why and the wherefore when he is a little stronger. I think, Smith, you and I can leave him alone now. I am walking back to college; if you are coming in that direction, we can have a chat."

But it was little chat that they had upon their homeward path. Smith's mind was too full of the incidents of the evening, the absence of the mummy from his neighbour's rooms, the step that passed him on the stair, the reappearance—the extraordinary, inexplicable reappearance of the grisly thing—and then this attack upon Lee, corresponding so closely to the previous outrage upon another man against whom Bellingham bore a grudge. All this settled in his thoughts, together with the many little incidents which had previously turned him against his neighbour, and the singular circumstances under which he was first called in to him. What had been a dim suspicion, a vague, fantastic conjecture, had suddenly taken form, and stood out in his mind as a grim fact, a thing not to be denied. And yet, how monstrous it was! how unheard of! how entirely beyond all bounds of human experience. An impartial judge, or even the friend who walked by his side, would simply tell him that his eyes had deceived him, that the mummy had been there all the time, that young Lee had tumbled into the river as any other man tumbles into a river, and that a blue pill was the best thing for a disordered liver. He felt that he would have said as much if the positions had been reversed. And yet he could swear that Bellingham was a murderer at heart, and that he wielded a weapon such as no man had ever used in all the grim history of crime.

Hastie had branched off to his rooms with a few crisp and emphatic comments upon his friend's unsociability, and Abercrombie Smith crossed the quadrangle to his corner turret with a strong feeling of repulsion for his chambers and their associations. He would take Lee's advice, and move his quarters as soon as possible, for how could a man study when his ear was ever straining for every murmur or footstep in the room below? He observed, as he crossed over the lawn, that the light was still shining in Bellingham's window, and as he passed up the staircase the door opened, and the man himself looked out at him. With his fat, evil face he was like some bloated spider fresh from the weaving of his poisonous web.

"Good-evening," said he. "Won't you come in?"

"No," cried Smith, fiercely.

"No? You are busy as ever? I wanted to ask you about Lee. I was sorry to hear that there was a rumour that something was amiss with him."

His features were grave, but there was the gleam of a hidden laugh in his eyes as he spoke. Smith saw it, and he could have knocked him down for it.

"You'll be sorrier still to hear that Monkhouse Lee is doing very well, and is out of all danger," he answered. "Your hellish tricks have not come off this time. Oh, you needn't try to brazen it out. I know all about it."

Bellingham took a step back from the angry student, and half-closed the door as if to protect himself.

"You are mad," he said. "What do you mean? Do you assert that I had anything to do with Lee's accident?"

"Yes," thundered Smith. "You and that bag of bones behind you; you worked it between you. I tell you what it is, Master B., they have given up burning folk like you, but we still keep a hangman, and, by George! if any man in this college meets his death while you are here, I'll have you up, and if you don't swing for it, it won't be my fault. You'll find that your filthy Egyptian tricks won't answer in England."

"You're a raving lunatic," said Bellingham.

"All right. You just remember what I say, for you'll find that I'll be better than my word."

The door slammed, and Smith went fuming up to his chamber, where he locked the door upon the inside, and spent half the night in smoking his old briar and brooding over the strange events of the evening.

Next morning Abercrombie Smith heard nothing of his neighbour, but Harrington called upon him in the afternoon to say that Lee was almost himself again. All day Smith stuck fast to his work, but in the evening he determined to pay the visit to his friend Dr. Peterson upon which he had started upon the night before. A good walk and a friendly chat would be welcome to his jangled nerves.

Bellingham's door was shut as he passed, but glancing back when he was some distance from the turret, he saw his neighbour's head at the window outlined against the lamp-light, his face pressed apparently against the glass as he gazed out into the darkness. It was a blessing to be away from all contact with him, but if for a few hours, and Smith stepped out briskly, and breathed the soft spring air into his lungs. The half-moon lay in the west between two Gothic pinnacles, and threw upon the silvered street a dark tracery from the stone-work above. There was a brisk breeze, and light, fleecy clouds drifted swiftly across the sky. Old's was on the very border of the town, and in five minutes Smith found himself beyond the houses and between the hedges of a May-scented Oxfordshire lane.

It was a lonely and little frequented road which led to his friend's house. Early as it was, Smith did not meet a single soul upon his way. He walked briskly along until he came to the avenue gate, which opened into the long gravel drive leading up to Farlingford. In front of him he could see the cosy red light of the windows glimmering through the foliage. He stood with his hand upon the iron latch of the swinging gate, and he glanced back at the road along which he had come. Something was coming swiftly down it.

It moved in the shadow of the hedge, silently and furtively, a dark, crouching figure, dimly visible against the black background. Even as he gazed back at it, it had lessened its distance by twenty paces, and was fast closing upon him. Out of the darkness he had a glimpse of a scraggy neck, and of two eyes that will ever haunt him in his dreams. He turned, and with a cry of terror he ran for his life up the avenue. There were the red lights, the signals of safety, almost within a stone's throw of him. He was a famous runner, but never had he run as he ran that night.

The heavy gate had swung into place behind him, but he heard it dash open again before his pursuer. As he rushed madly and wildly through the night, he could hear a swift, dry patter behind him, and could see, as he threw back a glance, that this horror was bounding like a tiger at his heels, with blazing eyes and one stringy arm outthrown. Thank God, the door was ajar. He could see the thin bar of light which shot from the lamp in the hall. Nearer yet sounded the clatter from behind. He heard a hoarse gurgling at his very shoulder. With a shriek he flung himself against the door, slammed and bolted it behind him, and sank half-fainting on to the hall chair.

"My goodness, Smith, what's the matter?" asked Peterson, appearing at the door of his study.

"Give me some brandy!"

Peterson disappeared, and came rushing out again with a glass and a decanter.

"You need it," he said, as his visitor drank off what he poured out for him. "Why, man, you are as white as a cheese."

Smith laid down his glass, rose up, and took a deep breath.

"I am my own man again now," said he. "I was never so unmanned before. But, with your leave, Peterson, I will sleep here to-night, for I don't think I could face that road again except by daylight. It's weak, I know, but I can't help it."

Peterson looked at his visitor with a very questioning eye.

"Of course you shall sleep here if you wish. I'll tell Mrs. Burney to make up the spare bed. Where are you off to now?"

"Come up with me to the window that overlooks the door. I want you to see what I have seen."

They went up to the window of the upper hall whence they could look down upon the approach to the house. The drive and the fields on either side lay quiet and still, bathed in the peaceful moonlight.

"Well, really, Smith," remarked Peterson, "it is well that I know you to be an abstemious man. What in the world can have frightened you?"

"I'll tell you presently. But where can it have gone? Ah, now look, look! See the curve of the road just beyond your gate."

"Yes, I see; you needn't pinch my arm off. I saw someone pass. I should say a man, rather thin, apparently, and tall, very tall. But what of him? And what of yourself? You are still shaking like an aspen leaf."

"I have been within hand-grip of the devil, that's all. But come down to your study, and I shall tell you the whole story."

He did so. Under the cheery lamplight, with a glass of wine on the table beside him, and the portly form and florid face of his friend in front, he narrated, in their order, all the events, great and small, which had formed so singular a chain, from the night on which he had found Bellingham fainting in front of the mummy case until his horrid experience of an hour ago.

"There now," he said as he concluded, "that's the whole black business. It is monstrous and incredible, but it is true."

Dr. Plumptree Peterson sat for some time in silence with a very puzzled expression upon his face.

"I never heard of such a thing in my life, never!" he said at last. "You have told me the facts. Now tell me your inferences."

"You can draw your own."

"But I should like to hear yours. You have thought over the matter, and I have not."

"Well, it must be a little vague in detail, but the main points seem to me to be clear enough. This fellow Bellingham, in his Eastern studies, has got hold of some infernal secret by which a mummy—or possibly only this particular mummy—can be temporarily brought to life. He was trying this disgusting business on the night when he fainted. No doubt the sight of the creature moving had shaken his nerve, even though he had expected it. You remember that almost the first words he said were to call out upon himself as a fool. Well, he got more hardened afterwards, and carried the matter through without fainting. The vitality which he could put into it was evidently only a passing thing, for I have seen it continually in its case as dead as this table. He has some elaborate process, I fancy, by which he brings the thing to pass. Having done it, he naturally bethought him that he might use the creature as an agent. It has intelligence and it has strength. For some purpose he took Lee into his confidence; but Lee, like a decent Christian, would have nothing to do with such a business. Then they had a row, and Lee vowed that he would tell his sister of Bellingham's true character. Bellingham's game was to prevent him, and he nearly managed it, by setting this creature of his on his track. He had already tried its powers upon another man—Norton—towards whom he had a grudge. It is the merest chance that he has not two murders upon his soul. Then, when I taxed him with the matter, he had the strongest reasons for wishing to get me out of the way before I could convey my knowledge to anyone else. He got his chance when I went out, for he knew my habits, and where I was bound for. I have had a narrow shave, Peterson, and it is mere luck you didn't find me on your doorstep in the morning. I'm not a nervous man as a rule, and I never thought to have the fear of death put upon me as it was to-night."

"My dear boy, you take the matter too seriously," said his companion. "Your nerves are out of order with your work, and you make too much of it. How could such a thing as this stride about the streets of Oxford, even at night, without being seen?"

"It has been seen. There is quite a scare in the town about an escaped ape, as they imagine the creature to be. It is the talk of the place."

"Well, it's a striking chain of events. And yet, my dear fellow, you must allow that each incident in itself is capable of a more natural explanation."

"What! even my adventure of to-night?"

"Certainly. You come out with your nerves all unstrung, and your head full of this theory of yours. Some gaunt, half-famished tramp steals after you, and seeing you run, is emboldened to pursue you. Your fears and imagination do the rest."

"It won't do, Peterson; it won't do."

"And again, in the instance of your finding the mummy case empty, and then a few moments later with an occupant, you know that it was lamplight, that the lamp was half turned down, and that you had no special reason to look hard at the case. It is quite possible that you may have overlooked the creature in the first instance."

"No, no; it is out of the question."

"And then Lee may have fallen into the river, and Norton been garrotted. It is certainly a formidable indictment that you have against Bellingham; but if you were to place it before a police magistrate, he would simply laugh in your face."

"I know he would. That is why I mean to take the matter into my own hands."

"Eh?"

"Yes; I feel that a public duty rests upon me, and, besides, I must do it for my own safety, unless I choose to allow myself to be hunted by this beast out of the college, and that would be a little too feeble. I have quite made up my mind what I shall do. And first of all, may I use your paper and pens for an hour?"

"Most certainly. You will find all that you want upon that side table."

Abercrombie Smith sat down before a sheet of foolscap, and for an hour, and then for a second hour his pen travelled swiftly over it. Page after page was finished and tossed aside while his friend leaned back in his arm-chair, looking across at him with patient curiosity. At last, with an exclamation of satisfaction, Smith sprang to his feet, gathered his papers up into order, and laid the last one upon Peterson's desk.

"Kindly sign this as a witness," he said.

"A witness? Of what?"

"Of my signature, and of the date. The date is the most important. Why, Peterson, my life might hang upon it."

"My dear Smith, you are talking wildly. Let me beg you to go to bed."

"On the contrary, I never spoke so deliberately in my life. And I will promise to go to bed the moment you have signed it."

"But what is it?"

"It is a statement of all that I have been telling you to-night. I wish you to witness it."

"Certainly," said Peterson, signing his name under that of his companion. "There you are! But what is the idea?"

"You will kindly retain it, and produce it in case I am arrested."

"Arrested? For what?"

"For murder. It is quite on the cards. I wish to be ready for every event. There is only one course open to me, and I am determined to take it."

"For Heaven's sake, don't do anything rash!"

"Believe me, it would be far more rash to adopt any other course. I hope that we won't need to bother you, but it will ease my mind to know that you have this statement of my motives. And now I am ready to take your advice and to go to roost, for I want to be at my best in the morning."

Abercrombie Smith was not an entirely pleasant man to have as an enemy. Slow and easytempered, he was formidable when driven to action. He brought to every purpose in life the same deliberate resoluteness which had distinguished him as a scientific student. He had laid his studies aside for a day, but he intended that the day should not be wasted. Not a word did he say to his host as to his plans, but by nine o'clock he was well on his way to Oxford.

In the High Street he stopped at Clifford's, the gun-maker's, and bought a heavy revolver, with a box of central-fire cartridges. Six of them he slipped into the chambers, and half-cocking the weapon, placed it in the pocket of his coat. He then made his way to Hastie's rooms, where the big oarsman was lounging over his breakfast, with the Sporting Times propped up against the coffeepot.

"Hullo! What's up?" he asked. "Have some coffee?"

"No, thank you. I want you to come with me, Hastie, and do what I ask you."

"Certainly, my boy."

"And bring a heavy stick with you."

"Hullo!" Hastie stared. "Here's a hunting-crop that would fell an ox."

"One other thing. You have a box of amputating knives. Give me the longest of them."

"There you are. You seem to be fairly on the war trail. Anything else?"

"No; that will do." Smith placed the knife inside his coat, and led the way to the quadrangle. "We are neither of us chickens, Hastie," said he. "I think I can do this job alone, but I take you as a precaution. I am going to have a little talk with Bellingham. If I have only him to deal with, I won't, of course, need you. If I shout, however, up you come, and lam out with your whip as hard as you can lick. Do you understand?"

"All right. I'll come if I hear you bellow."

"Stay here, then. It may be a little time, but don't budge until I come down."

"I'm a fixture."

Smith ascended the stairs, opened Bellingham's door and stepped in. Bellingham was seated behind his table, writing. Beside him, among his litter of strange possessions, towered the mummy case, with its sale number 249 still stuck upon its front, and its hideous occupant stiff and stark within it. Smith looked very deliberately round him, closed the door, locked it, took the key from the inside, and then stepping across to the fireplace, struck a match and set the fire alight. Bellingham sat staring, with amazement and rage upon his bloated face.

"Well, really now, you make yourself at home," he gasped.

Smith sat himself deliberately down, placing his watch upon the table, drew out his pistol, cocked it, and laid it in his lap. Then he took the long amputating knife from his bosom, and threw it down in front of Bellingham.

"Now, then," said he, "just get to work and cut up that mummy."

"Oh, is that it?" said Bellingham with a sneer.

"Yes, that is it. They tell me that the law can't touch you. But I have a law that will set matters straight. If in five minutes you have not set to work, I swear by the God who made me that I will put a bullet through your brain!"

"You would murder me?"

Bellingham had half risen, and his face was the colour of putty.

"Yes."

"And for what?"

"To stop your mischief. One minute has gone."

"But what have I done?"

"I know and you know."

"This is mere bullying."

"Two minutes are gone."

"But you must give reasons. You are a madman—a dangerous madman. Why should I destroy my own property? It is a valuable mummy."

"You must cut it up, and you must burn it."

"I will do no such thing."

"Four minutes are gone."

Smith took up the pistol and he looked towards Bellingham with an inexorable face. As the second-hand stole round, he raised his hand, and the finger twitched upon the trigger.

"There! there! I'll do it!" screamed Bellingham.

In frantic haste he caught up the knife and hacked at the figure of the mummy, ever glancing round to see the eye and the weapon of his terrible visitor bent upon him. The creature crackled and snapped under every stab of the keen blade. A thick yellow dust rose up from it. Spices and dried essences rained down upon the floor. Suddenly, with a rending crack, its backbone snapped asunder, and it fell, a brown heap of sprawling limbs, upon the floor.

"Now into the fire!" said Smith.

The flames leaped and roared as the dried and tinderlike debris was piled upon it. The little room was like the stoke-hole of a steamer and the sweat ran down the faces of the two men; but still the one stooped and worked, while the other sat watching him with a set face. A thick, fat smoke oozed out from the fire, and a heavy smell of burned rosin and singed hair filled the air. In a quarter of an hour a few charred and brittle sticks were all that was left of Lot No. 249.

"Perhaps that will satisfy you," snarled Bellingham, with hate and fear in his little grey eyes as he glanced back at his tormenter.

"No; I must make a clean sweep of all your materials. We must have no more devil's tricks. In with all these leaves! They may have something to do with it."

"And what now?" asked Bellingham, when the leaves also had been added to the blaze.

"Now the roll of papyrus which you had on the table that night. It is in that drawer, I think."

"No, no," shouted Bellingham. "Don't burn that! Why, man, you don't know what you do. It is unique; it contains wisdom which is nowhere else to be found."

"Out with it!"

"But look here, Smith, you can't really mean it. I'll share the knowledge with you. I'll teach you all that is in it. Or, stay, let me only copy it before you burn it!"

Smith stepped forward and turned the key in the drawer. Taking out the yellow, curled roll of paper, he threw it into the fire, and pressed it down with his heel. Bellingham screamed, and grabbed at it; but Smith pushed him back, and stood over it until it was reduced to a formless grey ash.

"Now, Master B.," said he, "I think I have pretty well drawn your teeth. You'll hear from me again, if you return to your old tricks. And now good-morning, for I must go back to my studies."

And such is the narrative of Abercrombie Smith as to the singular events which occurred in Old College, Oxford, in the spring of '84. As Bellingham left the university immediately afterwards, and was last heard of in the Soudan, there is no one who can contradict his statement. But the wisdom of men is small, and the ways of nature are strange, and who shall put a bound to the dark things which may be found by those who seek for them?

The Yellow Wallpaper

By Charlotte Perkins Gilman

It is very seldom that mere ordinary people like John and myself secure ancestral halls for the summer.

A colonial mansion, a hereditary estate, I would say a haunted house, and reach the height of romantic felicity—but that would be asking too much of fate!

Still I will proudly declare that there is something queer about it.

Else, why should it be let so cheaply? And why have stood so long untenanted?

John laughs at me, of course, but one expects that in marriage.

John is practical in the extreme. He has no patience with faith, an intense horror of superstition, and he scoffs openly at any talk of things not to be felt and seen and put down in figures.

John is a physician, and perhaps—(I would not say it to a living soul, of course, but this is dead paper and a great relief to my mind)—perhaps that is one reason I do not get well faster.

You see, he does not believe I am sick!

And what can one do?

If a physician of high standing, and one's own husband, assures friends and relatives that there is really nothing the matter with one but temporary nervous depression—a slight hysterical tendency—what is one to do?

My brother is also a physician, and also of high standing, and he says the same thing.

So I take phosphates or phosphites—whichever it is, and tonics, and journeys, and air, and exercise, and am absolutely forbidden to "work" until I am well again.

Personally, I disagree with their ideas.

Personally, I believe that congenial work, with excitement and change, would do me good.

But what is one to do?

I did write for a while in spite of them; but it does exhaust me a good deal—having to be so sly about it, or else meet with heavy opposition.

I sometimes fancy that in my condition if I had less opposition and more society and stimulus—but John says the very worst thing I can do is to think about my condition, and I confess it always makes me feel bad.

So I will let it alone and talk about the house.

The most beautiful place! It is quite alone, standing well back from the road, quite three miles from the village. It makes me think of English places that you read about, for there are hedges and walls and gates that lock, and lots of separate little houses for the gardeners and people.

There is a delicious garden! I never saw such a garden—large and shady, full of box-bordered paths, and lined with long grape-covered arbors with seats under them.

There were greenhouses, too, but they are all broken now.

There was some legal trouble, I believe, something about the heirs and co-heirs; anyhow, the place has been empty for years.

That spoils my ghostliness, I am afraid; but I don't care—there is something strange about the house—I can feel it.

I even said so to John one moonlight evening, but he said what I felt was a draught, and shut the window.

I get unreasonably angry with John sometimes. I'm sure I never used to be so sensitive. I think it is due to this nervous condition.

But John says if I feel so I shall neglect proper self-control; so I take pains to control myself,—before him, at least,—and that makes me very tired.

I don't like our room a bit. I wanted one downstairs that

opened on the piazza and had roses all over the window, and such pretty old-fashioned chintz hangings! but John would not hear of it.

He said there was only one window and not room for two beds, and no near room for him if he took another.

He is very careful and loving, and hardly lets me stir without special direction.

I have a schedule prescription for each hour in the day; he takes all care from me, and so I feel basely ungrateful not to value it more.

He said we came here solely on my account, that I was to have perfect rest and all the air I could get. "Your exercise depends on your strength, my dear," said he, "and your food somewhat on your appetite; but air you can absorb all the time." So we took the nursery, at the top of the house.

It is a big, airy room, the whole floor nearly, with windows that look all ways, and air and sunshine galore. It was nursery first and then playground and gymnasium, I should judge; for the windows are barred for little children, and there are rings and things in the walls.

The paint and paper look as if a boys' school had used it. It is stripped off—the paper—in great patches all around the head of my bed, about as far as I can reach, and in a great place on the other side of the room low down. I never saw a worse paper in my life.

One of those sprawling flamboyant patterns committing every artistic sin.

It is dull enough to confuse the eye in following, pronounced enough to constantly irritate, and provoke study, and when you follow the lame, uncertain curves for a little distance they suddenly commit suicide—plunge off at outrageous angles, destroy themselves in unheard-of contradictions.

The color is repellant, almost revolting; a smouldering, unclean yellow, strangely faded by the slow-turning sunlight.

It is a dull yet lurid orange in some places, a sickly sulphur tint in others.

No wonder the children hated it! I should hate it myself if I had to live in this room long.

There comes John, and I must put this away,—he hates to have me write a word.

We have been here two weeks, and I haven't felt like writing before, since that first day.

I am sitting by the window now, up in this atrocious nursery, and there is nothing to hinder my writing as much as I please, save lack of strength.

John is away all day, and even some nights when his cases are serious.

I am glad my case is not serious!

But these nervous troubles are dreadfully depressing.

John does not know how much I really suffer. He knows there is no reason to suffer, and that satisfies him.

Of course it is only nervousness. It does weigh on me so not to do my duty in any way!

I meant to be such a help to John, such a real rest and comfort, and here I am a comparative burden already!

Nobody would believe what an effort it is to do what little I am able—to dress and entertain, and order things.

It is fortunate Mary is so good with the baby. Such a dear baby!

And yet I cannot be with him, it makes me so nervous.

I suppose John never was nervous in his life. He laughs at me so about this wallpaper!

At first he meant to repaper the room, but afterwards he said that I was letting it get the better of me, and that nothing was worse for a nervous patient than to give way to such fancies.

He said that after the wallpaper was changed it would be the heavy bedstead, and then the barred windows, and then that gate at the head of the stairs, and so on.

"You know the place is doing you good," he said, "and

really, dear, I don't care to renovate the house just for a three months' rental."

"Then do let us go downstairs," I said, "there are such pretty rooms there."

Then he took me in his arms and called me a blessed little goose, and said he would go down cellar if I wished, and have it whitewashed into the bargain.

But he is right enough about the beds and windows and things.

It is as airy and comfortable a room as any one need wish, and, of course, I would not be so silly as to make him uncomfortable just for a whim.

I'm really getting quite fond of the big room, all but that horrid paper.

Out of one window I can see the garden, those mysterious deep-shaded arbors, the riotous old-fashioned flowers, and bushes and gnarly trees.

Out of another I get a lovely view of the bay and a little private wharf belonging to the estate. There is a beautiful shaded lane that runs down there from the house. I always fancy I see people walking in these numerous paths and arbors, but John has cautioned me not to give way to fancy in the least. He says that with my imaginative power and habit of story-making a nervous weakness like mine is sure to lead to all manner of excited fancies, and that I ought to use my will and good sense to check the tendency. So I try.

I think sometimes that if I were only well enough to write a little it would relieve the press of ideas and rest me.

But I find I get pretty tired when I try.

It is so discouraging not to have any advice and companionship about my work. When I get really well John says we will ask Cousin Henry and Julia down for a long visit; but he says he would as soon put fire-works in my pillow-case as to let me have those stimulating people about now.

I wish I could get well faster.

But I must not think about that. This paper looks to me as if it knew what a vicious influence it had!

There is a recurrent spot where the pattern lolls like a broken neck and two bulbous eyes stare at you upside-down.

I get positively angry with the impertinence of it and the everlastingness. Up and down and sideways they crawl, and those absurd, unblinking eyes are everywhere. There is one place where two breadths didn't match, and the eyes go all up and down the line, one a little higher than the other.

I never saw so much expression in an inanimate thing before, and we all know how much expression they have! I used to lie awake as a child and get more entertainment and terror out of blank walls and plain furniture than most children could find in a toy-store.

I remember what a kindly wink the knobs of our big old bureau used to have, and there was one chair that always seemed like a strong friend.

I used to feel that if any of the other things looked too fierce I could always hop into that chair and be safe.

The furniture in this room is no worse than inharmonious, however, for we had to bring it all from downstairs. I suppose when this was used as a playroom they had to take the nursery things out, and no wonder! I never saw such ravages as the children have made here.

The wallpaper, as I said before, is torn off in spots, and it sticketh closer than a brother—they must have had perseverance as well as hatred.

Then the floor is scratched and gouged and splintered, the plaster itself is dug out here and there, and this great heavy bed, which is all we found in the room, looks as if it had been through the wars.

But I don't mind it a bit—only the paper.

There comes John's sister. Such a dear girl as she is, and so careful of me! I must not let her find me writing.

She is a perfect, and enthusiastic housekeeper, and hopes for no better profession. I verily believe she thinks it is the writing which made me sick!

But I can write when she is out, and see her a long way off from these windows.

There is one that commands the road, a lovely, shaded, winding road, and one that just looks off over the country. A lovely country, too, full of great elms and velvet meadows.

This wallpaper has a kind of sub-pattern in a different shade, a particularly irritating one, for you can only see it in certain lights, and not clearly then.

But in the places where it isn't faded, and where the sun is just so, I can see a strange, provoking, formless sort of figure, that seems to sulk about behind that silly and conspicuous front design.

There's sister on the stairs!

Well, the Fourth of July is over! The people are gone and I am tired out. John thought it might do me good to see a little company, so we just had mother and Nellie and the children down for a week.

Of course I didn't do a thing. Jennie sees to everything now.

But it tired me all the same.

John says if I don't pick up faster he shall send me to Weir Mitchell in the fall.

But I don't want to go there at all. I had a friend who was in his hands once, and she says he is just like John and my brother, only more so!

Besides, it is such an undertaking to go so far.

I don't feel as if it was worth while to turn my hand over for anything, and I'm getting dreadfully fretful and querulous.

I cry at nothing, and cry most of the time.

Of course I don't when John is here, or anybody else, but when I am alone.

And I am alone a good deal just now. John is kept in town very often by serious cases, and Jennie is good and lets me alone when I want her to.

So I walk a little in the garden or down that lovely lane, sit on the porch under the roses, and lie down up here a good deal.

I'm getting really fond of the room in spite of the wallpaper. Perhaps because of the wallpaper.

It dwells in my mind so!

I lie here on this great immovable bed—it is nailed down, I believe—and follow that pattern about by the hour. It is as good as gymnastics, I assure you. I start, we'll say, at the bottom, down in the corner over there where it has not been touched, and I determine for the thousandth time that I will follow that pointless pattern to some sort of a conclusion.

I know a little of the principle of design, and I know this thing was not arranged on any laws of radiation, or alternation, or repetition, or symmetry, or anything else that I ever heard of.

It is repeated, of course, by the breadths, but not otherwise.

Looked at in one way each breadth stands alone, the bloated curves and flourishes—a kind of "debased Romanesque" with delirium tremens—go waddling up and down in isolated columns of fatuity.

But, on the other hand, they connect diagonally, and the sprawling outlines run off in great slanting waves of optic horror, like a lot of wallowing seaweeds in full chase.

The whole thing goes horizontally, too, at least it seems so, and I exhaust myself in trying to distinguish the order of its going in that direction.

They have used a horizontal breadth for a frieze, and that adds wonderfully to the confusion.

There is one end of the room where it is almost intact, and there, when the cross-lights fade and the low sun shines directly upon it, I can almost fancy radiation after all,—the interminable grotesques seem to form around a common centre and rush off in headlong plunges of equal distraction.

It makes me tired to follow it. I will take a nap, I guess.

I don't know why I should write this.

I don't want to.

I don't feel able.

And I know John would think it absurd. But I must say what I feel and think in some way—it is such a relief!

But the effort is getting to be greater than the relief.

Half the time now I am awfully lazy, and lie down ever so much.

John says I musn't lose my strength, and has me take cod-liver oil and lots of tonics and things, to say nothing of ale and wine and rare meat.

Dear John! He loves me very dearly, and hates to have me sick. I tried to have a real earnest reasonable talk with him the other day, and tell him how I wish he would let me go and make a visit to Cousin Henry and Julia.

But he said I wasn't able to go, nor able to stand it after I got there; and I did not make out a very good case for myself, for I was crying before I had finished.

It is getting to be a great effort for me to think straight. Just this nervous weakness, I suppose.

And dear John gathered me up in his arms, and just carried me upstairs and laid me on the bed, and sat by me and read to me till it tired my head.

He said I was his darling and his comfort and all he had, and that I must take care of myself for his sake, and keep well.

He says no one but myself can help me out of it, that I must use my will and self-control and not let any silly fancies run away with me.

There's one comfort, the baby is well and happy, and does not have to occupy this nursery with the horrid wallpaper.

If we had not used it that blessed child would have! What a fortunate escape! Why, I wouldn't have a child of mine, an impressionable little thing, live in such a room for worlds.

I never thought of it before, but it is lucky that John kept me here after all. I can stand it so much easier than a baby, you see.

Of course I never mention it to them any more,—I am too

wise,—but I keep watch of it all the same.

There are things in that paper that nobody knows but me, or ever will.

Behind that outside pattern the dim shapes get clearer every day.

It is always the same shape, only very numerous.

And it is like a woman stooping down and creeping about behind that pattern. I don't like it a bit. I wonder—I begin to think—I wish John would take me away from here!

It is so hard to talk with John about my case, because he is so wise, and because he loves me so.

But I tried it last night.

It was moonlight. The moon shines in all around, just as the sun does.

I hate to see it sometimes, it creeps so slowly, and always comes in by one window or another.

John was asleep and I hated to waken him, so I kept still and watched the moonlight on that undulating wallpaper till I felt creepy.

The faint figure behind seemed to shake the pattern, just as if she wanted to get out.

I got up softly and went to feel and see if the paper did move, and when I came back John was awake.

"What is it, little girl?" he said. "Don't go walking about like that—you'll get cold."

I thought it was a good time to talk, so I told him that I really was not gaining here, and that I wished he would take me away.

"Why darling!" said he, "our lease will be up in three weeks, and I can't see how to leave before.

"The repairs are not done at home, and I cannot possibly leave town just now. Of course if you were in any danger I could and would, but you really are better, dear, whether you can see it or not. I am a doctor, dear, and I know. You are gaining flesh and color, your appetite is better. I feel really much easier about you."

"I don't weigh a bit more," said I, "nor as much; and my appetite may be better in the evening, when you are here, but it is worse in the morning when you are away."

"Bless her little heart!" said he with a big hug; "she shall be as sick as she pleases! But now let's improve the shining hours by going to sleep, and talk about it in the morning!"

"And you won't go away?" I asked gloomily.

"Why, how can I, dear? It is only three weeks more and then we will take a nice little trip of a few days while Jennie is getting the house ready. Really, dear, you are better!"

"Better in body perhaps"—I began, and stopped short, for he sat up straight and looked at me with such a stern, reproachful look that I could not say another word.

"My darling," said he, "I beg of you, for my sake and for our child's sake, as well as for your own, that you will never for one instant let that idea enter your mind! There is nothing so dangerous, so fascinating, to a temperament like yours. It is a false and foolish fancy. Can you not trust me as a physician when I tell you so?"

So of course I said no more on that score, and we went to sleep before long. He thought I was asleep first, but I wasn't,—I lay there for hours trying to decide whether that front pattern and the back pattern really did move together or separately.

On a pattern like this, by daylight, there is a lack of sequence, a defiance of law, that is a constant irritant to a normal mind.

The color is hideous enough, and unreliable enough, and infuriating enough, but the pattern is torturing.

You think you have mastered it, but just as you get well under way in following, it turns a back somersault and there you are. It slaps you in the face, knocks you down, and tramples upon you. It is like a bad dream.

The outside pattern is a florid arabesque, reminding one of a fungus. If you can imagine a toadstool in joints, an interminable string of toadstools, budding and sprouting in endless convolutions,—why, that is something like it.

That is, sometimes!

There is one marked peculiarity about this paper, a thing nobody seems to notice but myself, and that is that it changes as the light changes.

When the sun shoots in through the east window—I always watch for that first long, straight ray—it changes so quickly that I never can quite believe it.

That is why I watch it always.

By moonlight—the moon shines in all night when there is a moon—I wouldn't know it was the same paper.

At night in any kind of light, in twilight, candlelight, lamplight, and worst of all by moonlight, it becomes bars! The outside pattern I mean, and the woman behind it is as plain as can be.

I didn't realize for a long time what the thing was that showed behind,—that dim sub-pattern,—but now I am quite sure it is a woman.

By daylight she is subdued, quiet. I fancy it is the pattern that keeps her so still. It is so puzzling. It keeps me quiet by the hour.

I lie down ever so much now. John says it is good for me, and to sleep all I can.

Indeed, he started the habit by making me lie down for an hour after each meal.

It is a very bad habit, I am convinced, for, you see, I don't sleep.

And that cultivates deceit, for I don't tell them I'm awake,—oh, no!

The fact is, I am getting a little afraid of John.

He seems very queer sometimes, and even Jennie has an inexplicable look.

It strikes me occasionally, just as a scientific hypothesis, that perhaps it is the paper!

I have watched John when he did not know I was looking, and come into the room suddenly on the most innocent excuses, and I've caught him several times looking at the paper! And Jennie too. I caught Jennie with her hand on it once.

She didn't know I was in the room, and when I asked her in a quiet, a very quiet voice, with the most restrained manner possible, what she was doing with the paper she turned around as if she had been caught stealing, and looked quite angry—asked me why I should frighten her so!

Then she said that the paper stained everything it touched, that she had found yellow smooches on all my clothes and John's, and she wished we would be more careful!

Did not that sound innocent? But I know she was studying that pattern, and I am determined that nobody shall find it out but myself!

Life is very much more exciting now than it used to be. You see I have something more to expect, to look forward to, to watch. I really do eat better, and am more quiet than I was.

John is so pleased to see me improve! He laughed a little the other day, and said I seemed to be flourishing in spite of my wallpaper.

I turned it off with a laugh. I had no intention of telling him it was because of the wallpaper—he would make fun of me. He might even want to take me away.

I don't want to leave now until I have found it out. There is a week more, and I think that will be enough.

I'm feeling ever so much better! I don't sleep much at night, for it is so interesting to watch developments; but I sleep a good deal in the daytime.

In the daytime it is tiresome and perplexing.

There are always new shoots on the fungus, and new shades of yellow all over it. I cannot keep count of them, though I have tried conscientiously.

It is the strangest yellow, that wallpaper! It makes me think of all the yellow things I ever saw—not beautiful ones like buttercups, but old foul, bad yellow things.

But there is something else about that paper—the smell! I noticed it the moment we came into the room, but with so much air and sun it was not bad. Now we have had a week of fog and rain, and whether the windows are open or not, the smell is here.

It creeps all over the house.

I find it hovering in the dining-room, skulking in the parlor, hiding in the hall, lying in wait for me on the stairs.

It gets into my hair.

Even when I go to ride, if I turn my head suddenly and surprise it—there is that smell!

Such a peculiar odor, too! I have spent hours in trying to analyze it, to find what it smelled like.

It is not bad—at first, and very gentle, but quite the subtlest, most enduring odor I ever met.

In this damp weather it is awful. I wake up in the night and find it hanging over me.

It used to disturb me at first. I thought seriously of burning the house—to reach the smell.

But now I am used to it. The only thing I can think of that it is like is the color of the paper! A yellow smell.

There is a very funny mark on this wall, low down, near the mopboard. A streak that runs round the room. It goes behind every piece of furniture, except the bed, a long, straight, even smooch, as if it had been rubbed over and over.

I wonder how it was done and who did it, and what they did it for. Round and round and round—round and round and round—it makes me dizzy!

I really have discovered something at last.

Through watching so much at night, when it changes so, I have finally found out.

The front pattern does move—and no wonder! The woman behind shakes it!

Sometimes I think there are a great many women behind, and sometimes only one, and she crawls around fast, and her crawling shakes it all over.

Then in the very bright spots she keeps still, and in the very shady spots she just takes hold of the bars and shakes them hard.

And she is all the time trying to climb through. But nobody could climb through that pattern—it strangles so; I think that is why it has so many heads.

They get through, and then the pattern strangles them off and turns them upside-down, and makes their eyes white!

If those heads were covered or taken off it would not be half so bad.

I think that woman gets out in the daytime!

And I'll tell you why—privately—I've seen her!

I can see her out of every one of my windows!

It is the same woman, I know, for she is always creeping, and most women do not creep by daylight.

I see her on that long shaded lane, creeping up and down. I see her in those dark grape arbors, creeping all around the garden.

I see her on that long road under the trees, creeping along, and when a carriage comes she hides under the blackberry vines.

I don't blame her a bit. It must be very humiliating to be caught creeping by daylight!

I always lock the door when I creep by daylight. I can't do it at night, for I know John would suspect something at once.

And John is so queer now, that I don't want to irritate him. I wish he would take another room! Besides, I don't want anybody to get that woman out at night but myself.

I often wonder if I could see her out of all the windows at once.

But, turn as fast as I can, I can only see out of one at one time.

And though I always see her she may be able to creep faster than I can turn!

I have watched her sometimes away off in the open country, creeping as fast as a cloud shadow in a high wind.

If only that top pattern could be gotten off from the under one! I mean to try it, little by little.

I have found out another funny thing, but I shan't tell it this time! It does not do to trust people too much.

There are only two more days to get this paper off, and I believe John is beginning to notice. I don't like the look in his eyes.

And I heard him ask Jennie a lot of professional questions about me. She had a very good report to give.

She said I slept a good deal in the daytime.

John knows I don't sleep very well at night, for all I'm so quiet!

He asked me all sorts of questions, too, and pretended to be very loving and kind.

As if I couldn't see through him!

Still, I don't wonder he acts so, sleeping under this paper for three months.

It only interests me, but I feel sure John and Jennie are secretly affected by it.

Hurrah! This is the last day, but it is enough. John is to stay in town over night, and won't be out until this evening.

Jennie wanted to sleep with me—the sly thing! but I told her I should undoubtedly rest better for a night all alone.

That was clever, for really I wasn't alone a bit! As soon as it was moonlight, and that poor thing began to crawl and shake the pattern, I got up and ran to help her.

I pulled and she shook, I shook and she pulled, and before morning we had peeled off yards of that paper.

A strip about as high as my head and half around the room.

And then when the sun came and that awful pattern began to laugh at me I declared I would finish it to-day!

We go away to-morrow, and they are moving all my furniture down again to leave things as they were before.

Jennie looked at the wall in amazement, but I told her merrily that I did it out of pure spite at the vicious thing.

She laughed and said she wouldn't mind doing it herself, but I must not get tired.

How she betrayed herself that time!

But I am here, and no person touches this paper but me—not alive!

She tried to get me out of the room—it was too patent! But I said it was so quiet and empty and clean now that I believed I would lie down again and sleep all I could; and not to wake me even for dinner—I would call when I woke.

So now she is gone, and the servants are gone, and the things are gone, and there is nothing left but that great bedstead nailed down, with the canvas mattress we found on it.

We shall sleep downstairs to-night, and take the boat home to-morrow.

I quite enjoy the room, now it is bare again.

How those children did tear about here!

This bedstead is fairly gnawed!

But I must get to work.

I have locked the door and thrown the key down into the front path.

I don't want to go out, and I don't want to have anybody come in, till John comes.

I want to astonish him.

I've got a rope up here that even Jennie did not find. If that woman does get out, and tries to get away, I can tie her!

But I forgot I could not reach far without anything to stand on!

This bed will not move!

I tried to lift and push it until I was lame, and then I got so angry I bit off a little piece at one corner—but it hurt my teeth.

Then I peeled off all the paper I could reach standing on the floor. It sticks horribly and the pattern just enjoys it! All those strangled heads and bulbous eyes and waddling fungus growths just shriek with derision!

I am getting angry enough to do something desperate. To jump out of the window would be admirable exercise, but the bars are too strong even to try.

Besides I wouldn't do it. Of course not. I know well enough that a step like that is improper and might be misconstrued.

I don't like to look out of the windows even—there are so many of those creeping women, and they creep so fast.

I wonder if they all come out of that wallpaper as I did?

But I am securely fastened now by my well-hidden rope—you don't get me out in the road there!

I suppose I shall have to get back behind the pattern when it comes night, and that is hard!

It is so pleasant to be out in this great room and creep around as I please!

I don't want to go outside. I won't, even if Jennie asks me to.

For outside you have to creep on the ground, and everything is green instead of yellow.

But here I can creep smoothly on the floor, and my shoulder

just fits in that long smooch around the wall, so I cannot lose my way.

Why, there's John at the door!

It is no use, young man, you can't open it!

How he does call and pound!

Now he's crying for an axe.

It would be a shame to break down that beautiful door!

"John dear!" said I in the gentlest voice, "the key is down by the front steps, under a plantain leaf!"

That silenced him for a few moments.

Then he said—very quietly indeed, "Open the door, my darling!"

"I can't," said I. "The key is down by the front door under a plantain leaf!"

And then I said it again, several times, very gently and slowly, and said it so often that he had to go and see, and he got it, of course, and came in. He stopped short by the door.

"What is the matter?" he cried. "For God's sake, what are you doing!"

I kept on creeping just the same, but I looked at him over my shoulder.

"I've got out at last," said I, "in spite of you and Jane! And I've pulled off most of the paper, so you can't put me back!"

Now why should that man have fainted? But he did, and right across my path by the wall, so that I had to creep over him every time!

The Beetle: A Mystery

By Richard Marsh

BOOK I.

The House with the Open Window

The Surprising Narration of Robert Holt

CHAPTER I.

OUTSIDE

'No room!—Full up!'

He banged the door in my face.

That was the final blow.

To have tramped about all day looking for work; to have begged even for a job which would give me money enough to buy a little food; and to have tramped and to have begged in vain,—that was bad. But, sick at heart, depressed in mind and in body, exhausted by hunger and fatigue, to have been compelled to pocket any little pride I might have left, and solicit, as the penniless, homeless tramp which indeed I was, a night's lodging in the casual ward,—and to solicit it in vain!—that was worse. Much worse. About as bad as bad could be.

I stared, stupidly, at the door which had just been banged in my face. I could scarcely believe that the thing was possible. I had hardly expected to figure as a tramp; but, supposing it conceivable that I could become a tramp, that I should be refused admission to that abode of all ignominy, the tramp's ward, was to have attained a depth of misery of which never even in nightmares I had dreamed.

As I stood wondering what I should do, a man slouched towards me out of the shadow of the wall.

'Won't 'e let yer in?'

'He says it's full.'

'Says it's full, does 'e? That's the lay at Fulham,—they always says it's full. They wants to keep the number down.'

I looked at the man askance. His head hung forward; his hands were in his trouser pockets; his clothes were rags; his tone was husky.

'Do you mean that they say it's full when it isn't,—that they won't let me in although there's room?'

'That's it,—bloke's a-kiddin' yer.'

'But, if there's room, aren't they bound to let me in?'

'Course they are,—and, blimey, if I was you I'd make 'em. Blimey I would!'

He broke into a volley of execrations.

'But what am I to do?'

'Why, give 'em another rouser—let 'em know as you won't be kidded!'

I hesitated; then, acting on his suggestion, for the second time I rang the bell. The door was flung wide open, and the grizzled pauper, who had previously responded to my summons, stood in the open doorway. Had he been the Chairman of the Board of Guardians himself he could not have addressed me with greater scorn.

'What, here again! What's your little game? Think I've nothing better to do than to wait upon the likes of you?'

'I want to be admitted.'

'Then you won't be admitted!'

'I want to see someone in authority.'

'Ain't yer seein' someone in authority?'

'I want to see someone besides you,—I want to see the master.'

'Then you won't see the master!'

He moved the door swiftly to; but, prepared for such a manoeuvre, I thrust my foot sufficiently inside to prevent his shutting it. I continued to address him.

'Are you sure that the ward is full?'

'Full two hours ago!'

'But what am I to do?'

'I don't know what you're to do!'

'Which is the next nearest workhouse?'

'Kensington.'

Suddenly opening the door, as he answered me, putting out his arm he thrust me backwards. Before I could recover the door was closed. The man in rags had continued a grim spectator of the scene. Now he spoke.

'Nice bloke, ain't he?'

'He's only one of the paupers,—has he any right to act as one of the officials?'

'I tell yer some of them paupers is wuss than the orficers,—a long sight wuss! They thinks they owns the 'ouses, blimey they do. Oh it's a— —fine world, this is!'

He paused. I hesitated. For some time there had been a suspicion of rain in the air. Now it was commencing to fall in a fine but soaking drizzle. It only needed that to fill my cup to overflowing. My companion was regarding me with a sort of sullen curiosity.

'Ain't you got no money?'

'Not a farthing.'

'Done much of this sort of thing?'

'It's the first time I've been to a casual ward,—and it doesn't seem as if I'm going to get in now.'

'I thought you looked as if you was a bit fresh.—What are yer goin' to do?'

'How far is it to Kensington?'

'Work'us?—about three mile;—but, if I was you, I'd try St George's.'

'Where's that?'

'In the Fulham Road. Kensington's only a small place, they do you well there, and it's always full as soon as the door's opened;—you'd 'ave more chawnce at St George's.'

He was silent. I turned his words over in my mind, feeling as little disposed to try the one place as the other. Presently he began again.

'I've travelled from Reading this——day, I 'ave,—tramped every——foot!—and all the way as I come along, I'll 'ave a shakedown at 'Ammersmith, I says,—and now I'm as fur off from it as ever! This is a——fine country, this is,—I wish every——soul in it was swept into the——sea, blimey I do! But I ain't goin' to go no further,—I'll 'ave a bed in 'Ammersmith or I'll know the reason why.'

'How are you going to manage it,—have you got any money?'

'Got any money?—My crikey!—I look as though I 'ad,—I sound as though I 'ad too! I ain't 'ad no brads, 'cept now and then a brown, this larst six months.'

'How are you going to get a bed then?'

''Ow am I going to?—why, like this way.' He picked up two stones, one in either hand. The one in his left he flung at the glass which was over the door of the casual ward. It crashed through it, and through the lamp beyond. 'That's 'ow I'm goin' to get a bed.'

The door was hastily opened. The grizzled pauper reappeared. He shouted, as he peered at us in the darkness,

'Who done that?'

'I done it, guvnor,—and, if you like, you can see me do the other. It might do your eyesight good.'

Before the grizzled pauper could interfere, he had hurled the stone in his right hand through another pane. I felt that it was time for me to go. He was earning a night's rest at a price which, even in my extremity, I was not disposed to pay.

When I left two or three other persons had appeared upon the scene, and the man in rags was addressing them with a degree of frankness, which, in that direction, left little to be desired. I slunk away unnoticed. But had not gone far before I had almost decided that I might as well have thrown in my fortune with the bolder wretch, and smashed a window too. Indeed, more than once my feet faltered, as I all but returned to do the feat which I had left undone.

A more miserable night for an out-of-door excursion I could hardly have chosen. The rain was like a mist, and was not only drenching me to the skin, but it was rendering it difficult to see more than a little distance in any direction. The neighbourhood was badly lighted. It was one in which I was a stranger. I had come to Hammersmith as a last resource. It had seemed to me that I had tried to find some occupation which would enable me to keep body and soul together in every other part of London, and that now only Hammersmith was left. And, at Hammersmith, even the workhouse would have none of me!

Retreating from the inhospitable portal of the casual ward, I had taken the first turning to the left,—and, at the moment, had been glad to take it. In the darkness and the rain, the locality which I was entering appeared unfinished. I seemed to be leaving civilisation behind me. The path was unpaved; the road rough and uneven, as if it had never been properly made. Houses were few and far between. Those which I did encounter, seemed, in the imperfect light, amid the general desolation, to be cottages which were crumbling to decay.

Exactly where I was I could not tell. I had a faint notion that, if I only kept on long enough, I should strike some part of Walham Green. How long I should have to keep on I could only guess. Not a creature seemed to be about of whom I could make inquiries. It was as if I was in a land of desolation.

I suppose it was between eleven o'clock and midnight. I had not given up my quest for work till all the shops were closed,—and in Hammersmith, that night, at any rate, they were not early closers. Then I had lounged about dispiritedly, wondering what was the next thing I could do. It was only because I feared that if I attempted to spend the night in the open air, without food, when the morning came I should be broken up, and fit for nothing, that I sought a night's free board and lodging. It was really hunger which drove me to the workhouse door. That was Wednesday. Since the Sunday night preceding nothing had passed my lips save water from the public fountains,—with the exception of a crust of bread which a man had given me whom I had found crouching at the root of a tree in Holland Park. For three days I had been fasting,—practically all the time upon my feet. It seemed to me that if I had to go hungry till the morning I should collapse—there would be an end. Yet, in that strange and inhospitable place, where was I to get food at that time of night, and how?

I do not know how far I went. Every yard I covered, my feet dragged more. I was dead beat, inside and out. I had neither strength nor courage left. And within there was that frightful craving, which was as though it shrieked aloud. I leant against some palings, dazed and giddy. If only death had come upon me quickly, painlessly, how true a friend I should have thought it! It was the agony of dying inch by inch which was so hard to bear.

It was some minutes before I could collect myself sufficiently to withdraw from the support of the railings, and to start afresh. I stumbled blindly over the uneven road. Once, like a drunken man, I lurched forward, and fell upon my knees. Such was my backboneless state that for some seconds I remained where I was, half disposed to let things slide, accept the good the gods had sent me, and make a night of it just there. A long night, I fancy, it would have been, stretching from time unto eternity.

Having regained my feet, I had gone perhaps another couple of hundred yards along the road—Heaven knows that it seemed to me just then a couple of miles!—when there came over me again that overpowering giddiness which, I take it, was born of my agony of hunger. I staggered, helplessly, against a low wall which, just there, was at the side of the path. Without it I should have fallen in a heap. The attack appeared to last for hours; I suppose it was only seconds; and, when I came to myself, it was as though I had been aroused from a swoon of sleep,—aroused, to an extremity of pain. I exclaimed aloud,

'For a loaf of bread what wouldn't I do!'

I looked about me, in a kind of frenzy. As I did so I for the first time became conscious that behind me was a house. It was not a large one. It was one of those so-called villas which are springing up in multitudes all round London, and which are let at rentals of from twenty-five to forty pounds a year. It was detached. So far as I could see, in the imperfect light, there was not another building within twenty or thirty yards of either side of it. It was in two storeys. There were three windows in the upper storey. Behind each the blinds were closely drawn. The hall door was on my right. It was approached by a little wooden gate.

The house itself was so close to the public road that by leaning over the wall I could have touched either of the windows on the lower floor. There were two of them. One of them was a bow window. The bow window was open. The bottom centre sash was raised about six inches.

CHAPTER II.

INSIDE

I realised, and, so to speak, mentally photographed all the little details of the house in front of which I was standing with what almost amounted to a gleam of preternatural perception. An instant before, the world swam before my eyes. I saw nothing. Now I saw everything, with a clearness which, as it were, was shocking.

Above all, I saw the open window. I stared at it, conscious, as I did so, of a curious catching of the breath. It was so near to me; so very near. I had but to stretch out my hand to thrust it through the aperture. Once inside, my hand would at least be dry. How it rained out there! My scanty clothing was soaked; I was wet to the skin! I was shivering. And, each second, it seemed to rain still faster. My teeth were chattering. The damp was liquefying the very marrow in my bones.

And, inside that open window, it was, it must be, so warm, so dry!

There was not a soul in sight. Not a human being anywhere near. I listened; there was not a sound. I alone was at the mercy of the sodden night. Of all God's creatures the only one unsheltered from the fountains of Heaven which He had opened. There was not one to see what I might do; not one to care. I need fear no spy.

Perhaps the house was empty; nay, probably. It was my plain duty to knock at the door, rouse the inmates, and call attention to their oversight,—the open window. The least they could do would be to reward me for my pains. But, suppose the place was empty, what would be the use of knocking? It would be to make a useless clatter. Possibly to disturb the neighbourhood, for nothing. And, even if the people were at home, I might go unrewarded. I had learned, in a hard school, the world's ingratitude. To have caused the window to be closed—the inviting window, the tempting window, the convenient window!—and then to be no better for it after all, but still to be penniless, hopeless, hungry, out in the cold and the rain—better anything than that. In such a situation, too late, I should say to myself that mine had been the conduct of a fool. And I should say it justly too. To be sure.

Leaning over the low wall I found that I could very easily put my hand inside the room. How warm it was in there! I could feel the difference of temperature in my fingertips. Very quietly I stepped right over the wall. There was just room to stand in comfort between the window and the wall. The ground felt to the foot as if it were cemented. Stooping down, I peered through the opening. I could see nothing. It was black as pitch inside. The blind was drawn right up; it seemed incredible that anyone could be at home, and have gone to bed, leaving the blind up, and the window open. I placed my ear to the crevice. How still it was! Beyond doubt, the place was empty.

I decided to push the window up another inch or two, so as to enable me to reconnoitre. If anyone caught me in the act, then there would be an opportunity to describe the circumstances, and to explain how I was just on the point of giving the alarm. Only, I must go carefully. In such damp weather it was probable that the sash would creak.

Not a bit of it. It moved as readily and as noiselessly as if it had been oiled. This silence of the sash so emboldened me that I raised it more than I intended. In fact, as far as it would go. Not by a sound did it betray me. Bending over the sill I put my head and half my body into the room. But I was no forwarder. I could see nothing. Not a thing. For all I could tell the room might be unfurnished. Indeed, the likelihood of such an explanation began to occur to me. I might have chanced upon an empty house. In the darkness there was nothing to suggest the contrary. What was I to do?

Well, if the house was empty, in such a plight as mine I might be said to have a moral, if not a legal, right, to its bare shelter. Who, with a heart in his bosom, would deny it me? Hardly the most punctilious landlord. Raising myself by means of the sill I slipped my legs into the room.

The moment I did so I became conscious that, at any rate, the room was not entirely unfurnished. The floor was carpeted. I have had my feet on some good carpets in my time; I know what carpets are; but never did I stand upon a softer one than that. It reminded me, somehow, even then, of the turf in Richmond Park,—it caressed my instep, and sprang beneath my tread. To my poor, travel-worn feet, it was luxury after the puddly, uneven road. Should I, now I had ascertained that the room was, at least, partially furnished, beat a retreat? Or should I push my researches further? It would have been rapture to have thrown off my clothes, and to have sunk down, on the carpet, then and there, to sleep. But,—I was so hungry, so famine-goaded; what would I not have given to have lighted on something good to eat!

I moved a step or two forward, gingerly, reaching out with my hands, lest I struck, unawares, against some unseen thing. When I had taken three or four such steps, without encountering an obstacle, or, indeed, anything at all, I began, all at once, to wish I had not seen the house; that I had passed it by; that I had not come through the window; that I were safely out of it again. I became, on a sudden, aware, that something was with me in the room. There was nothing, ostensible, to lead me to such a conviction; it may be that my faculties were unnaturally keen; but, all at once, I knew that there was something there. What was more, I had a horrible persuasion that, though unseeing, I was seen; that my every movement was being watched.

What it was that was with me I could not tell; I could not even guess. It was as though something in my mental organisation had been stricken by a sudden paralysis. It may seem childish to use such language; but I was overwrought, played out; physically speaking, at my last counter; and, in an instant, without the slightest warning, I was conscious of a very curious sensation, the like of which I had never felt before, and the like of which I pray that I never may feel again,—a sensation of panic fear. I remained rooted to the spot on which I stood, not daring to move, fearing to draw my breath. I felt that the presence with me in the room was something strange, something evil.

I do not know how long I stood there, spell-bound, but certainly for some considerable space of time. By degrees, as nothing moved, nothing was seen, nothing was heard, and nothing happened, I made an effort to better play the man. I knew that, at the moment, I played the cur. And endeavoured to ask myself of what it was I was afraid. I was shivering at my own imaginings. What could be in the room, to have suffered me to open the window and to enter unopposed? Whatever it was, was surely to the full as great a coward as I was, or why permit, unchecked, my burglarious entry. Since I had been allowed to enter, the probability was that I should be at liberty to retreat,—and I was sensible of a much keener desire to retreat than I had ever had to enter.

I had to put the greatest amount of pressure upon myself before I could summon up sufficient courage to enable me to even turn my head upon my shoulders,—and the moment I did so I turned it back again. What constrained me, to save my soul I could not have said,—but I was constrained. My heart was palpitating in my bosom; I could hear it beat. I was trembling so that I could scarcely stand. I was overwhelmed by a fresh flood of terror. I stared in front of me with eyes in which, had it been light, would have been seen the frenzy of unreasoning fear. My ears were strained so that I listened with an acuteness of tension which was painful.

Something moved. Slightly, with so slight a sound, that it would scarcely have been audible to other ears save mine. But I heard. I was looking in the direction from which the movement came, and, as I looked, I saw in front of me two specks of light. They had not been there a moment before, that I would swear. They were there now. They were eyes,—I told myself they were eyes. I had heard how cats' eyes gleam in the dark, though I had never seen them, and I said to myself that these were cats' eyes; that the thing in front of me was nothing but a cat. But I knew I lied. I knew that these were eyes, and I knew they were not cats' eyes, but what eyes they were I did not know,—nor dared to think.

They moved,—towards me. The creature to which the eyes belonged was coming closer. So intense was my desire to fly that I would much rather have died than stood there still; yet I could not control a limb; my limbs were as if they were not mine. The eyes came on,—noiselessly. At first they were between two and three feet from the ground; but, on a sudden, there was a squelching sound, as if some yielding body had been squashed upon the floor. The eyes vanished,—to reappear, a moment afterwards, at what I judged to be a distance of some six inches from the floor. And they again came on.

So it seemed that the creature, whatever it was to which the eyes belonged, was, after all, but small. Why I did not obey the frantic longing which I had to flee from it, I cannot tell; I only know, I could not. I take it that the stress and privations which I had lately undergone, and which I was, even then, still undergoing, had much to do with my conduct at that moment, and with the part I played in all that followed. Ordinarily I believe that I have as high a spirit as the average man, and as solid a resolution; but when one has been dragged through the Valley of Humiliation, and plunged, again and again, into the Waters of Bitterness and Privation, a man can be constrained to a course of action of which, in his happier moments, he would have deemed himself incapable. I know this of my own knowledge.

Slowly the eyes came on, with a strange slowness, and as they came they moved from side to side as if their owner walked unevenly. Nothing could have exceeded the horror with which I awaited their approach,—except my incapacity to escape them.

Not for an instant did my glance pass from them,—I could not have shut my eyes for all the gold the world contains!—so that as they came closer I had to look right down to what seemed to be almost the level of my feet. And, at last, they reached my feet. They never paused. On a sudden I felt something on my boot, and, with a sense of shrinking, horror, nausea, rendering me momentarily more helpless, I realised that the creature was beginning to ascend my legs, to climb my body. Even then what it was I could not tell,—it mounted me, apparently, with as much ease as if I had been horizontal instead of perpendicular. It was as though it were some gigantic spider,—a spider of the nightmares; a monstrous conception of some dreadful vision. It pressed lightly against my clothing with what might, for all the world, have been spider's legs. There was an amazing host of them,—I felt the pressure of each separate one. They embraced me softly, stickily, as if the creature glued and unglued them, each time it moved.

Higher and higher! It had gained my loins. It was moving towards the pit of my stomach. The helplessness with which I suffered its invasion was not the least part of my agony,—it was that helplessness which we know in dreadful dreams. I understood, quite well, that if I did but give myself a hearty shake, the creature would fall off; but I had not a muscle at my command.

As the creature mounted its eyes began to play the part of two small lamps; they positively emitted rays of light. By their rays I began to perceive faint outlines of its body. It seemed larger than I had supposed. Either the body itself was slightly phosphorescent, or it was of a peculiar yellow hue. It gleamed in the darkness. What it was there was still nothing to positively show, but the impression grew upon me that it was some member of the spider family, some monstrous member, of the like of which I had never heard or read. It was heavy, so heavy indeed, that I wondered how, with so slight a pressure, it managed to retain its hold,—that it did so by the aid of some adhesive substance at the end of its legs I was sure,—I could feel it stick. Its weight increased as it ascended,—and it smelt! I had been for some time aware that it emitted an unpleasant, foetid odour; as it neared my face it became so intense as to be unbearable.

It was at my chest. I became more and more conscious of an uncomfortable wobbling motion, as if each time it breathed its body heaved. Its forelegs touched the bare skin about the base of my neck; they stuck to it,—shall I ever forget the feeling? I have it often in my dreams. While it hung on with those in front it seemed to draw its other legs up after it. It crawled up my neck, with hideous slowness, a quarter of an inch at a time, its weight compelling me to brace the muscles of my back. It reached my chin, it touched my lips,—and I stood still and bore it all, while it enveloped my face with its huge, slimy, evil-smelling body, and embraced me with its myriad legs. The horror of it made me mad. I shook myself like one stricken by the shaking ague. I shook the creature off. It squashed upon the floor. Shrieking like some lost spirit, turning, I dashed towards the window. As I went, my foot, catching in some obstacle, I fell headlong to the floor.

Picking myself up as quickly as I could I resumed my flight,—rain or no rain, oh to get out of that room! I already had my hand upon the sill, in another instant I should have been over it,—then, despite my hunger, my fatigues, let anyone have stopped me if they could!—when someone behind me struck a light.

CHAPTER III.

THE MAN IN THE BED

The illumination which instantly followed was unexpected. It startled me, causing a moment's check, from which I was just recovering when a voice said,

'Keep still!'

There was a quality in the voice which I cannot describe. Not only an accent of command, but a something malicious, a something saturnine. It was a little guttural, though whether it was a man speaking I could not have positively said; but I had no doubt it was a foreigner. It was the most disagreeable voice I had ever heard, and it had on me the most disagreeable effect; for when it said, 'Keep still!' I kept still. It was as though there was nothing else for me to do.

'Turn round!'

I turned round, mechanically, like an automaton. Such passivity was worse than undignified, it was galling; I knew that well. I resented it with secret rage. But in that room, in that presence, I was invertebrate.

When I turned I found myself confronting someone who was lying in bed. At the head of the bed was a shelf. On the shelf was a small lamp which gave the most brilliant light I had ever seen. It caught me full in the eyes, having on me such a blinding effect that for some seconds I could see nothing. Throughout the whole of that strange interview I cannot affirm that I saw clearly; the dazzling glare caused dancing specks to obscure my vision. Yet, after an interval of time, I did see something; and what I did see I had rather have left unseen.

I saw someone in front of me lying in a bed. I could not at once decide if it was a man or a woman. Indeed at first I doubted if it was anything human. But, afterwards, I knew it to be a man,—for this reason, if for no other, that it was impossible such a creature could be feminine. The bedclothes were drawn up to his shoulders; only his head was visible. He lay on his left side, his head resting on his left hand; motionless, eyeing me as if he sought to read my inmost soul. And, in very truth, I believe he read it. His age I could not guess; such a look of age I had never imagined. Had he asserted that he had been living through the ages, I should have been forced to admit that, at least, he looked it. And yet I felt that it was quite within the range of possibility that he was no older than myself,—there was a vitality in his eyes which was startling. It might have been that he had been afflicted by some terrible disease, and it was that which had made him so supernaturally ugly.

There was not a hair upon his face or head, but, to make up for it, the skin, which was a saffron yellow, was an amazing mass of wrinkles. The cranium, and, indeed, the whole skull, was so small as to be disagreeably suggestive of something animal. The nose, on the other hand, was abnormally large; so extravagant were its dimensions, and so peculiar its shape, it resembled the beak of some bird of prey. A characteristic of the face—and an uncomfortable one!—was that, practically, it stopped short at the mouth. The mouth, with its blubber lips, came immediately underneath the nose, and chin, to all intents and purposes, there was none. This deformity—for the absence of chin amounted to that—it was which gave to the face the appearance of something not human,—that, and the eyes. For so marked a feature of the man were his eyes, that, ere long, it seemed to me that he was nothing but eyes.

His eyes ran, literally, across the whole of the upper portion of his face,—remember, the face was unwontedly small, and the columna of the nose was razor-edged. They were long, and they looked out of narrow windows, and they seemed to be lighted by some internal radiance, for they shone out like lamps in a lighthouse tower. Escape them I could not, while, as I endeavoured to meet them, it was as if I shrivelled into nothingness. Never before had I realised what was meant by the power of the eye. They held me enchained, helpless, spell-bound. I felt that they could do with me as they would; and they did. Their gaze was unfaltering, having the bird-like trick of never blinking; this man could have glared at me for hours and never moved an eyelid.

It was he who broke the silence. I was speechless.

'Shut the window.' I did as he bade me. 'Pull down the blind.' I obeyed. 'Turn round again.' I was still obedient. 'What is your name?'

Then I spoke,—to answer him. There was this odd thing about the words I uttered, that they came from me, not in response to my will power, but in response to his. It was not I who willed that I should speak; it was he. What he willed that I should say, I said. Just that, and nothing more. For the time I was no longer a man; my manhood was merged in his. I was, in the extremest sense, an example of passive obedience.

'Robert Holt.'

'What are you?'

'A clerk.'

'You look as if you were a clerk.' There was a flame of scorn in his voice which scorched me even then. 'What sort of a clerk are you?'

'I am out of a situation.'

'You look as if you were out of a situation.' Again the scorn. 'Are you the sort of clerk who is always out of a situation? You are a thief.'

'I am not a thief.'

'Do clerks come through the window?' I was still,—he putting no constraint on me to speak. 'Why did you come through the window?'

'Because it was open.'

'So!—Do you always come through a window which is open?'

'No.'

'Then why through this?'

'Because I was wet—and cold—and hungry—and tired.'

The words came from me as if he had dragged them one by one,—which, in fact, he did.

'Have you no home?'

'No.'

'Money?'

'No.'

'Friends?'

'No.'

'Then what sort of a clerk are you?'

I did not answer him,—I did not know what it was he wished me to say. I was the victim of bad luck, nothing else,—I swear it. Misfortune had followed hard upon misfortune. The firm by whom I had been employed for years suspended payment. I obtained a situation with one of their creditors, at a lower salary. They reduced their staff, which entailed my going. After an interval I obtained a temporary engagement; the occasion which required my services passed, and I with it. After another, and a longer interval, I again found temporary employment, the pay for which was but a pittance. When that was over I could find nothing. That was nine months ago, and since then I had not earned a penny. It is so easy to grow shabby, when you are on the everlasting tramp, and are living on your stock of clothes. I had trudged all over London in search of work,—work of any kind would have been welcome, so long as it would have enabled me to keep body and soul together. And I had trudged in vain. Now I had been refused admittance as a casual,—how easy is the descent! But I did not tell the man lying on the bed all this. He did not wish to hear,—had he wished he would have made me tell him.

It may be that he read my story, unspoken though it was,—it is conceivable. His eyes had powers of penetration which were peculiarly their own,—that I know.

'Undress!'

When he spoke again that was what he said, in those guttural tones of his in which there was a reminiscence of some foreign land. I obeyed, letting my sodden, shabby clothes fall anyhow upon the floor. A look came on his face, as I stood naked in front of him, which, if it was meant for a smile, was a satyr's smile, and which filled me with a sensation of shuddering repulsion.

'What a white skin you have,—how white! What would I not give for a skin as white as that,—ah yes!' He paused, devouring me with his glances; then continued. 'Go to the cupboard; you will find a cloak; put it on.'

I went to a cupboard which was in a corner of the room, his eyes following me as I moved. It was full of clothing,—garments which might have formed the stock-in-trade of a costumier whose speciality was providing costumes for masquerades. A long dark cloak hung on a peg. My hand moved towards it, apparently of its own volition. I put it on, its ample folds falling to my feet.

'In the other cupboard you will find meat, and bread, and wine. Eat and drink.'

On the opposite side of the room, near the head of his bed, there was a second cupboard. In this, upon a shelf, I found what looked like pressed beef, several round cakes of what tasted like rye bread, and some thin, sour wine, in a straw-covered flask. But I was in no mood to criticise; I crammed myself, I believe, like some famished wolf, he watching me, in silence, all the time. When I had done, which was when I had eaten and drunk as much as I could hold, there returned to his face that satyr's grin.

'I would that I could eat and drink like that,—ah yes!—Put back what is left.' I put it back,—which seemed an unnecessary exertion, there was so little to put. 'Look me in the face.'

I looked him in the face,—and immediately became conscious, as I did so, that something was going from me,—the capacity, as it were, to be myself. His eyes grew larger and larger, till they seemed to fill all space—till I became lost in their immensity. He moved his hand, doing something to me, I know not what, as it passed through the air—cutting the solid ground from underneath my feet, so that I fell headlong to the ground. Where I fell, there I lay, like a log.

And the light went out.

CHAPTER IV.

A LONELY VIGIL

I knew that the light went out. For not the least singular, nor, indeed, the least distressing part of my condition was the fact that, to the best of my knowledge and belief, I never once lost consciousness during the long hours which followed. I was aware of the extinction of the lamp, and of the black darkness which ensued. I heard a rustling sound, as if the man in the bed was settling himself between the sheets. Then all was still. And throughout that interminable night I remained, my brain awake, my body dead, waiting, watching, for the day. What had happened to me I could not guess. That I probably wore some of the external evidences of death my instinct told me,—I knew I did. Paradoxical though it may sound, I felt as a man might feel who had actually died,—as, in moments of speculation, in the days gone by, I had imagined it as quite possible that he would feel. It is very far from certain that feeling necessarily expires with what we call life. I continually asked myself if I could be dead,—the inquiry pressed itself on me with awful iteration. Does the body die, and the brain—the I, the ego—still live on? God only knows. But, then! the agony of the thought.

The hours passed. By slow degrees, the silence was eclipsed. Sounds of traffic, of hurrying footsteps,—life!—were ushers of the morn. Outside the window sparrows twittered,—a cat mewed, a dog barked—there was the clatter of a milk can. Shafts of light stole past the blind, increasing in intensity. It still rained, now and again it pattered against the pane. The wind must have shifted, because, for the first time, there came, on a sudden, the clang of a distant clock striking the hour,—seven. Then, with the interval of a lifetime between each chiming, eight,—nine,—ten.

So far, in the room itself there had not been a sound. When the clock had struck ten, as it seemed to me, years ago, there came a rustling noise, from the direction of the bed. Feet stepped upon the floor,—moving towards where I was lying. It was, of course, now broad day, and I, presently, perceived that a figure, clad in some queer coloured garment, was standing at my side, looking down at me. It stooped, then knelt. My only covering was unceremoniously thrown from off me, so that I lay there in my nakedness. Fingers prodded me then and there, as if I had been some beast ready for the butcher's stall. A face looked into mine, and, in front of me, were those dreadful eyes. Then, whether I was dead or living, I said to myself that this could be nothing human,—nothing fashioned in God's image could wear such a shape as that. Fingers were pressed into my cheeks, they were thrust into my mouth, they touched my staring eyes, shut my eyelids, then opened them again, and—horror of horrors!—the blubber lips were pressed to mine—the soul of something evil entered into me in the guise of a kiss.

Then this travesty of manhood reascended to his feet, and said, whether speaking to me or to himself I could not tell,

'Dead!—dead!—as good as dead!—and better! We'll have him buried.'

He moved away from me. I heard a door open and shut, and knew that he was gone.

And he continued gone throughout the day. I had no actual knowledge of his issuing out into the street, but he must have done so, because the house appeared deserted. What had become of the dreadful creature of the night before I could not guess. My first fear was that he had left it behind him in the room with me,—it might be, as a sort of watchdog. But, as the minutes and the hours passed, and there was still no sign or sound of anything living, I concluded that, if the thing was there, it was, possibly, as helpless as myself, and that during its owner's absence, at any rate, I had nothing to fear from its too pressing attentions.

That, with the exception of myself, the house held nothing human, I had strong presumptive proof more than once in the course of the day. Several times, both in the morning and the afternoon, people without endeavoured to attract the attention of whoever was within. Vehicles—probably tradesmen's carts—drew up in front, their stopping being followed by more or less assiduous assaults upon the knocker and the bell. But in every case their appeals remained unheeded. Whatever it was they wanted, they had to go unsatisfied away. Lying there, torpid, with nothing to do but listen, I was, possibly, struck by very little, but it did occur to me that one among the callers was more persistent than the rest.

The distant clock had just struck noon when I heard the gate open, and someone approached the front door. Since nothing but silence followed, I supposed that the occupant of the place had returned, and had chosen to do so as silently as he had gone. Presently, however, there came from the doorstep a slight but peculiar call, as if a rat was squeaking. It was repeated three times, and then there was the sound of footsteps quietly retreating, and the gate re-closing. Between one and two the caller came again; there was a repetition of the same signal,—that it was a signal I did not doubt; followed by the same retreat. About three the mysterious visitant returned. The signal was repeated, and, when there was no response, fingers tapped softly against the panels of the front door. When there was still no answer, footsteps stole softly round the side of the house, and there came the signal from the rear,—and then, again, tapping of fingers against what was, apparently, the back door. No notice being taken of these various proceedings, the footsteps returned the way they went, and, as before, the gate was closed.

Shortly after darkness had fallen this assiduous caller returned, to make a fourth and more resolute attempt to call attention to his presence. From the peculiar character of his manoeuvres it seemed that he suspected that whoever was within had particular reasons for ignoring him without. He went through the familiar pantomime of the three squeaky calls both at the front door and the back,—followed by the tapping of the fingers on the panels. This time, however, he also tried the window panes,—I could hear, quite distinctly, the clear, yet distinct, noise of what seemed like knuckles rapping against the windows behind. Disappointed there, he renewed his efforts at the front. The curiously quiet footsteps came round the house, to pause before the window of the room in which I lay,—and then something singular occurred.

While I waited for the tapping, there came, instead, the sound of someone or something, scrambling on to the window-sill,—as if some creature, unable to reach the window from the ground, was endeavouring to gain the vantage of the sill. Some ungainly creature, unskilled in surmounting such an obstacle as a perpendicular brick wall. There was the noise of what seemed to be the scratching of claws, as if it experienced considerable difficulty in obtaining a hold on the unyielding surface. What kind of creature it was I could not think,—I was astonished to find that it was a creature at all. I had taken it for granted that the persevering visitor was either a woman or a man. If, however, as now seemed likely, it was some sort of animal, the fact explained the squeaking sounds,—though what, except a rat, did squeak like that was more than I could say—and the absence of any knocking or ringing.

Whatever it was, it had gained the summit of its desires,—the window-sill. It panted as if its efforts at climbing had made it short of breath. Then began the tapping. In the light of my new discovery, I perceived, clearly enough, that the tapping was hardly that which was likely to be the product of human fingers,—it was sharp and definite, rather resembling the striking of the point of a nail against the glass. It was not loud, but in time—it continued with much persistency—it became plainly vicious. It was accompanied by what I can only describe as the most extraordinary noises. There were squeaks, growing angrier and shriller as the minutes passed; what seemed like gaspings for breath; and a peculiar buzzing sound like, yet unlike, the purring of a cat.

The creature's resentment at its want of success in attracting attention was unmistakable. The tapping became like the clattering of hailstones; it kept up a continuous noise with its cries and pantings; there was the sound as of some large body being rubbed against the glass, as if it were extending itself against the window, and endeavouring, by force of pressure, to gain an entrance through the pane. So violent did its contortions become that I momentarily anticipated the yielding of the glass, and the excited assailant coming crashing through. Considerably to my relief the window proved more impregnable than seemed at one time likely. The stolid resistance proved, in the end, to be too much either for its endurance or its patience. Just as I was looking for some fresh manifestation of fury, it seemed rather to tumble than to spring off the sill; then came, once more, the same sound of quietly retreating footsteps; and what, under the circumstances, seemed odder still, the same closing of the gate.

During the two or three hours which immediately ensued nothing happened at all out of the way,—and then took place the most surprising incident of all. The clock had struck ten some time before. Since before the striking of the hour nothing and no one had passed along what was evidently the little frequented road in front of that uncanny house. On a sudden two sounds broke the stillness without,—of someone running, and of cries. Judging from his hurrying steps someone seemed to be flying for his life,—to the accompaniment of curious cries. It was only when the runner reached the front of the house that, in the cries, I recognised the squeaks of the persistent caller. I imagined that he had returned, as before, alone, to renew his attacks upon the window,—until it was made plain, as it quickly was, that, with him, was some sort of a companion. Immediately there arose, from without, the noise of battle. Two creatures, whose cries were, to me, of so unusual a character, that I found it impossible to even guess at their identity, seemed to be waging war to the knife upon the doorstep. After a minute or two of furious contention, victory seemed to rest with one of the combatants, for the other fled, squeaking as with pain. While I listened, with strained attention, for the next episode in this queer drama, expecting that now would come another assault upon the window, to my unbounded surprise I heard a key thrust in the keyhole, the lock turned, and the front door thrown open with a furious bang. It was closed as loudly as it was opened. Then the door of the room in which I was, was dashed open, with the same display of excitement, and of clamour, footsteps came hurrying in, the door was slammed to with a force which shook the house to its foundations, there was a rustling as of bed-clothes, the brilliant illumination of the night before, and a voice, which I had only too good reason to remember said,

'Stand up.'

I stood up, automatically, at the word of command, facing towards the bed.

There, between the sheets, with his head resting on his hand, in the attitude in which I had seen him last, was the being I had made acquaintance with under circumstances which I was never likely to forget,—the same, yet not the same.

CHAPTER V.

AN INSTRUCTION TO COMMIT BURGLARY

That the man in the bed was the one whom, to my cost, I had suffered myself to stumble on the night before, there could, of course, not be the faintest doubt. And yet, directly I saw him, I recognised that some astonishing alteration had taken place in his appearance. To begin with, he seemed younger,—the decrepitude of age had given place to something very like the fire of youth. His features had undergone some subtle change. His nose, for instance, was not by any means so grotesque; its beak-like quality was less conspicuous. The most part of his wrinkles had disappeared, as if by magic. And, though his skin was still as yellow as saffron, his contours had rounded,—he had even come into possession of a modest allowance of chin. But the most astounding novelty was that about the face there was something which was essentially feminine; so feminine, indeed, that I wondered if I could by any possibility have blundered, and mistaken a woman for a man; some ghoulish example of her sex, who had so yielded to her depraved instincts as to have become nothing but a ghastly reminiscence of womanhood.

The effect of the changes which had come about in his appearance—for, after all, I told myself that it was impossible that I could have been such a simpleton as to have been mistaken on such a question as gender—was heightened by the self-evident fact that, very recently, he had been engaged in some pitched battle; some hand to hand, and, probably, discreditable encounter, from which he had borne away uncomfortable proofs of his opponent's prowess. His antagonist could hardly have been a chivalrous fighter, for his countenance was marked by a dozen different scratches which seemed to suggest that the weapons used had been someone's finger-nails. It was, perhaps, because the heat of the battle was still in his veins that he was in such a state of excitement. He seemed to be almost overwhelmed by the strength of his own feelings. His eyes seemed literally to flame with fire. The muscles of his face were working as if they were wholly beyond his own control. When he spoke his accent was markedly foreign; the words rushed from his lips in an inarticulate torrent; he kept repeating the same thing over and over again in a fashion which was not a little suggestive of insanity.

'So you're not dead!—you're not dead:—you're alive!—you're

alive! Well,—how does it feel to be dead? I ask you!—Is it not good to be dead? To keep dead is better,—it is the best of all! To have made an end of all things, to cease to strive and to cease to weep, to cease to want and to cease to have, to cease to annoy and to cease to long, to no more care,—no!—not for anything, to put from you the curse of life,—forever!—is that not the best? Oh yes!—I tell you!—do I not know? But for you such knowledge is not yet. For you there is the return to life, the coming out of death,—you shall live on!—for me!—Live on!'

He made a movement with his hand, and, directly he did so, it happened as on the previous evening, that a metamorphosis took place in the very abysses of my being. I woke from my torpor, as he put it, I came out of death, and was alive again. I was far, yet, from being my own man; I realised that he exercised on me a degree of mesmeric force which I had never dreamed that one creature could exercise on another; but, at least, I was no longer in doubt as to whether I was or was not dead. I knew I was alive.

He lay, watching me, as if he was reading the thoughts which occupied my brain,—and, for all I know, he was.

'Robert Holt, you are a thief.'

'I am not.'

My own voice, as I heard it, startled me,—it was so long since it had sounded in my ears.

'You are a thief! Only thieves come through windows,—did you not come through the window?' I was still,—what would my contradiction have availed me? 'But it is well that you came through the window,—well you are a thief,—well for me! for me! It is you that I am wanting,—at the happy moment you have dropped yourself into my hands,—in the nick of time. For you are my slave,—at my beck and call,—my familiar spirit, to do with as I will,—you know this,—eh?'

I did know it, and the knowledge of my impotence was terrible. I felt that if I could only get away from him; only release myself from the bonds with which he had bound me about; only remove myself from the horrible glamour of his near neighbourhood; only get one or two square meals and have an opportunity of recovering from the enervating stress of mental and bodily fatigue;—I felt that then I might be something like his match, and that, a second time, he would endeavour in vain to bring me within the compass of his magic.

But, as it was, I was conscious that I was helpless, and the consciousness was agony. He persisted in reiterating his former falsehood.

'I say you are a thief!—a thief, Robert Holt, a thief! You came through a window for your own pleasure, now you will go through a window for mine,—not this window, but another.' Where the jest lay I did not perceive; but it tickled him, for a grating sound came from his throat which was meant for laughter. 'This time it is as a thief that you will go,—oh yes, be sure.'

He paused, as it seemed, to transfix me with his gaze. His unblinking eyes never for an instant quitted my face. With what a frightful fascination they constrained me,—and how I loathed them!

When he spoke again there was a new intonation in his speech,—something bitter, cruel, unrelenting.

'Do you know Paul Lessingham?'

He pronounced the name as if he hated it,—and yet as if he loved to have it on his tongue.

'What Paul Lessingham?'

'There is only one Paul Lessingham! The Paul Lessingham,—the great Paul Lessingham!'

He shrieked, rather than said this, with an outburst of rage so frenzied that I thought, for the moment, that he was going to spring on me and rend me. I shook all over. I do not doubt that, as I replied, my voice was sufficiently tremulous.

'All the world knows Paul Lessingham,—the politician,—the statesman.'

As he glared at me his eyes dilated. I still stood in expectation of a physical assault. But, for the present, he contented himself with words.

'To-night you are going through his window like a thief!'

I had no inkling of his meaning,—and, apparently, judging from his next words, I looked something of the bewilderment I felt.

'You do not understand?—no!—it is simple!—what could be simpler? I say that to-night—to-night!—you are going through his window like a thief. You came through my window,—why not through the window of Paul Lessingham, the politician—the statesman.'

He repeated my words as if in mockery. I am—I make it my boast!—of that great multitude which regards Paul Lessingham as the greatest living force in practical politics; and which looks to him, with confidence, to carry through that great work of constitutional and social reform which he has set himself to do. I daresay that my tone, in speaking of him, savoured of laudation,—which, plainly, the man in the bed resented. What he meant by his wild words about my going through Paul Lessingham's window like a thief, I still had not the faintest notion. They sounded like the ravings of a madman.

As I continued silent, and he yet stared, there came into his tone another note,—a note of tenderness,—a note of which I had not deemed him capable.

'He is good to look at, Paul Lessingham,—is he not good to look at?'

I was aware that, physically, Mr Lessingham was a fine specimen of manhood, but I was not prepared for the assertion of the fact in such a quarter,—nor for the manner in which the temporary master of my fate continued to harp and enlarge upon the theme.

'He is straight,—straight as the mast of a ship,—he is tall,—his skin is white; he is strong—do I not know that he is strong—how strong!—oh yes! Is there a better thing than to be his wife? his well-beloved? the light of his eyes? Is there for a woman a happier chance? Oh no, not one! His wife!—Paul Lessingham!'

As, with soft cadences, he gave vent to these unlooked-for sentiments, the fashion of his countenance was changed. A look of longing came into his face—of savage, frantic longing—which, unalluring though it was, for the moment transfigured him. But the mood was transient.

'To be his wife,—oh yes!—the wife of his scorn! the despised and rejected!'

The return to the venom of his former bitterness was rapid,—I could not but feel that this was the natural man. Though why a creature such as he was should go out of his way to apostrophise, in such a manner, a publicist of Mr Lessingham's eminence, surpassed my comprehension. Yet he stuck to his subject like a leech,—as if it had been one in which he had an engrossing personal interest.

'He is a devil,—hard as the granite rock,—cold as the snows of Ararat. In him there is none of life's warm blood,—he is accursed! He is false,—ay, false as the fables of those who lie for love of lies,—he is all treachery. Her whom he has taken to his bosom he would put away from him as if she had never been,—he would steal from her like a thief in the night,—he would forget she ever was! But the avenger follows after, lurking in the shadows, hiding among the rocks, waiting, watching, till his time shall come. And it shall come!—the day of the avenger!—ay, the day!'

Raising himself to a sitting posture, he threw his arms above his head, and shrieked with a demoniac fury. Presently he became a trifle calmer. Reverting to his recumbent position, resting his head upon his hand, he eyed me steadily; then asked me a question which struck me as being, under the circumstances, more than a little singular.

'You know his house,—the house of the great Paul Lessingham,—the politician,—the statesman?'

'I do not.'

'You lie!—you do!'

The words came from him with a sort of snarl,—as if he would have lashed me across the face with them.

'I do not. Men in my position are not acquainted with the residences of men in his. I may, at some time, have seen his address in print; but, if so, I have forgotten it.'

He looked at me intently, for some moments, as if to learn if I spoke the truth; and apparently, at last, was satisfied that I did.

'You do not know it?—Well!—I will show it you,—I will show the house of the great Paul Lessingham.'

What he meant I did not know; but I was soon to learn,—an astounding revelation it proved to be. There was about his manner something hardly human; something which, for want of a better phrase, I would call vulpine. In his tone there was a mixture of mockery and bitterness, as if he wished his words to have the effect of corrosive sublimate, and to sear me as he uttered them.

'Listen with all your ears. Give me your whole attention. Hearken to my bidding, so that you may do as I bid you. Not that I fear your obedience,—oh no!'

He paused,—as if to enable me to fully realise the picture of my helplessness conjured up by his jibes.

'You came through my window, like a thief. You will go through my window, like a fool. You will go to the house of the great Paul Lessingham. You say you do not know it? Well, I will show it you. I will be your guide. Unseen, in the darkness and the night, I will stalk beside you, and will lead you to where I would have you go.—You will go just as you are, with bare feet, and head uncovered, and with but a single garment to hide your nakedness. You will be cold, your feet will be cut and bleeding,—but what better does a thief deserve? If any see you, at the least they will take you for a madman; there will be trouble. But have no fear; bear a bold heart. None shall see you while I stalk at your side. I will cover you with the cloak of invisibility,—so that you may come in safety to the house of the great Paul Lessingham.'

He paused again. What he said, wild and wanton though it was, was beginning to fill me with a sense of the most extreme discomfort. His sentences, in some strange, indescribable way, seemed, as they came from his lips, to warp my limbs; to enwrap themselves about me; to confine me, tighter and tighter, within, as it were, swaddling clothes; to make me more and more helpless. I was already conscious that whatever mad freak he chose to set me on, I should have no option but to carry it through.

'When you come to the house, you will stand, and look, and seek for a window convenient for entry. It may be that you will find one open, as you did mine; if not, you will open one. How,—that is your affair, not mine. You will practise the arts of a thief to steal into his house.'

The monstrosity of his suggestion fought against the spell which he again was casting upon me, and forced me into speech,—endowed me with the power to show that there still was in me something of a man; though every second the strands of my manhood, as it seemed, were slipping faster through the fingers which were strained to clutch them.

'I will not.'

He was silent. He looked at me. The pupils of his eyes dilated, —until they seemed all pupil.

'You will.—Do you hear?—I say you will.'

'I am not a thief, I am an honest man,—why should I do this thing?'

'Because I bid you.'

'Have mercy!'

'On whom—on you, or on Paul Lessingham?—Who, at any time, has shown mercy unto me, that I should show mercy unto any?'

He stopped, and then again went on,—reiterating his former incredible suggestion with an emphasis which seemed to eat its way into my brain.

'You will practise the arts of a thief to steal into his house; and, being in, will listen. If all be still, you will make your way to the room he calls his study.'

'How shall I find it? I know nothing of his house.'

The question was wrung from me; I felt that the sweat was standing in great drops upon my brow.

'I will show it you.'

'Shall you go with me?'

'Ay,—I shall go with you. All the time I shall be with you. You will not see me, but I shall be there. Be not afraid.'

His claim to supernatural powers, for what he said amounted to nothing less, was, on the face of it, preposterous, but, then, I was in no condition to even hint at its absurdity. He continued.

'When you have gained the study, you will go to a certain drawer, which is in a certain bureau, in a corner of the room—I see it now; when you are there you shall see it too—and you will open it.'

'Should it be locked?'

'You still will open it.'

'But how shall I open it if it is locked?'

'By those arts in which a thief is skilled. I say to you again that that is your affair, not mine.'

I made no attempt to answer him. Even supposing that he forced me, by the wicked, and unconscionable exercise of what, I presumed, were the hypnotic powers with which nature had to such a dangerous degree endowed him, to carry the adventure to a certain stage, since he could hardly, at an instant's notice, endow me with the knack of picking locks, should the drawer he alluded to be locked—which might Providence permit!—nothing serious might issue from it after all. He read my thoughts.

'You will open it,—though it be doubly and trebly locked, I say that you will open it.—In it you will find—' he hesitated, as if to reflect—'some letters; it may be two or three,—I know not just how many,—they are bound about by a silken ribbon. You will take them out of the drawer, and, having taken them, you will make the best of your way out of the house, and bear them back to me.'

'And should anyone come upon me while engaged in these nefarious proceedings,—for instance, should I encounter Mr Lessingham himself, what then?'

'Paul Lessingham?—You need have no fear if you encounter him.'

'I need have no fear!—If he finds me, in his own house, at dead of night, committing burglary!'

'You need have no fear of him.'

'On your account, or on my own?—At least he will have me haled to gaol.'

'I say you need have no fear of him. I say what I mean.'

'How, then, shall I escape his righteous vengeance? He is not the man to suffer a midnight robber to escape him scatheless,—shall I have to kill him?'

'You will not touch him with a finger,—nor will he touch you.'

'By what spell shall I prevent him?'

'By the spell of two words.'

'What words are they?'

'Should Paul Lessingham chance to come upon you, and find you in his house, a thief, and should seek to stay you from whatever it is you may be at, you will not flinch nor flee from him, but you will stand still, and you will say—'

Something in the crescendo accents of his voice, something weird and ominous, caused my heart to press against my ribs, so that when he stopped, in my eagerness I cried out,

'What?'

'THE BEETLE!'

As the words came from him in a kind of screech, the lamp went out, and the place was all in darkness, and I knew, so that the knowledge filled me with a sense of loathing, that with me, in the room, was the evil presence of the night before. Two bright specks gleamed in front of me; something flopped from off the bed on to the ground; the thing was coming towards me across the floor. It came slowly on, and on, and on. I stood still, speechless in the sickness of my horror. Until, on my bare feet, it touched me with slimy feelers, and my terror lest it should creep up my naked body lent me voice, and I fell shrieking like a soul in agony.

It may be that my shrieking drove it from me. At least, it went. I knew it went. And all was still. Until, on a sudden, the lamp flamed out again, and there, lying, as before, in bed, glaring at me with his baleful eyes, was the being whom, in my folly, or in my wisdom,—whichever it was!—I was beginning to credit with the possession of unhallowed, unlawful powers.

'You will say that to him; those two words; they only; no more. And you will see what you will see. But Paul Lessingham is a man of resolution. Should he still persist in interference, or seek to hinder you, you will say those two words again. You need do no more. Twice will suffice, I promise you.—Now go.—Draw up the blind; open the window; climb through it. Hasten to do what I have bidden you. I wait here for your return,—and all the way I shall be with you.'

CHAPTER VI.

A SINGULAR FELONY

I went to the window; I drew up the blind, unlatching the sash, I threw it open; and clad, or, rather, unclad as I was, I clambered through it into the open air. I was not only incapable of resistance, I was incapable of distinctly formulating the desire to offer resistance. Some compelling influence moved me hither and hither, with completest disregard of whether I would or would not.

And yet, when I found myself without, I was conscious of a sense of exultation at having escaped from the miasmic atmosphere of that room of unholy memories. And a faint hope began to dawn within my bosom that, as I increased the distance between myself and it, I might shake off something of the nightmare helplessness which numbed and tortured me. I lingered for a moment by the window; then stepped over the short dividing wall into the street; and then again I lingered.

My condition was one of dual personality,—while, physically, I was bound, mentally, to a considerable extent, I was free. But this measure of freedom on my mental side made my plight no better. For, among other things, I realised what a ridiculous figure I must be cutting, barefooted and bareheaded, abroad, at such an hour of the night, in such a boisterous breeze,—for I quickly discovered that the wind amounted to something like a gale. Apart from all other considerations, the notion of parading the streets in such a condition filled me with profound disgust. And I do believe that if my tyrannical oppressor had only permitted me to attire myself in my own garments, I should have started with a comparatively light heart on the felonious mission on which he apparently was sending me. I believe, too, that the consciousness of the incongruity of my attire increased my sense of helplessness, and that, had I been dressed as Englishmen are wont to be, who take their walks abroad, he would not have found in me, on that occasion, the facile instrument which, in fact, he did.

There was a moment, in which the gravelled pathway first made itself known to my naked feet, and the cutting wind to my naked flesh, when I think it possible that, had I gritted my teeth, and strained my every nerve, I might have shaken myself free from the bonds which shackled me, and bade defiance to the ancient sinner who, for all I knew, was peeping at me through the window. But so depressed was I by the knowledge of the ridiculous appearance I presented that, before I could take advantage of it the moment passed,—not to return again that night.

I did catch, as it were, at its fringe, as it was flying past me, making a hurried movement to one side,—the first I had made, of my own initiative, for hours. But it was too late. My tormentor,—as if, though unseen, he saw—tightened his grip, I was whirled round, and sped hastily onwards in a direction in which I certainly had no desire of travelling.

All the way I never met a soul. I have since wondered whether in that respect my experience was not a normal one; whether it might not have happened to any. If so, there are streets in London, long lines of streets, which, at a certain period of the night, in a certain sort of weather—probably the weather had something to do with it—are clean deserted; in which there is neither foot-passenger nor vehicle,—not even a policeman. The greater part of the route along which I was driven—I know no juster word—was one with which I had some sort of acquaintance. It led, at first, through what, I take it, was some part of Walham Green; then along the Lillie Road, through Brompton, across the Fulham Road, through the network of streets leading to Sloane Street, across Sloane Street into Lowndes Square. Who goes that way goes some distance, and goes through some important thoroughfares; yet not a creature did I see, nor, I imagine, was there a creature who saw me. As I crossed Sloane Street, I fancied that I heard the distant rumbling of a vehicle along the Knightsbridge Road, but that was the only sound I heard.

It is painful even to recollect the plight in which I was when I was stopped,—for stopped I was, as shortly and as sharply, as the beast of burden, with a bridle in its mouth, whose driver puts a period to his career. I was wet,—intermittent gusts of rain were borne on the scurrying wind; in spite of the pace at which I had been brought, I was chilled to the bone; and—worst of all! —my mud-stained feet, all cut and bleeding, were so painful—for, unfortunately, I was still susceptible enough to pain—that it was agony to have them come into contact with the cold and the slime of the hard, unyielding pavement.

I had been stopped on the opposite side of the square,—that nearest to the hospital; in front of a house which struck me as being somewhat smaller than the rest. It was a house with a portico; about the pillars of this portico was trelliswork, and on the trelliswork was trained some climbing plant. As I stood, shivering, wondering what would happen next, some strange impulse mastered me, and, immediately, to my own unbounded amazement, I found myself scrambling up the trellis towards the verandah above. I am no gymnast, either by nature or by education; I doubt whether, previously, I had ever attempted to climb anything more difficult than a step ladder. The result was, that, though the impulse might be given me, the skill could not, and I had only ascended a yard or so when, losing my footing, I came slithering down upon my back. Bruised and shaken though I was, I was not allowed to inquire into my injuries. In a moment I was on my feet again, and again I was impelled to climb,—only, however, again to come to grief. This time the demon, or whatever it was, that had entered into me, seeming to appreciate the impossibility of getting me to the top of that verandah, directed me to try another way. I mounted the steps leading to the front door, got on to the low parapet which was at one side, thence on to the sill of the adjacent window,—had I slipped then I should have fallen a sheer descent of at least twenty feet to the bottom of the deep area down below. But the sill was broad, and—if it is proper to use such language in connection with a transaction of the sort in which I was engaged—fortune favoured me. I did not fall. In my clenched fist I had a stone. With this I struck the pane of glass, as with a hammer. Through the hole which resulted, I could just insert my hand, and reach the latch within. In another minute the sash was raised, and I was in the house,—I had committed burglary.

As I look back and reflect upon the audacity of the whole proceeding, even now I tremble. Hapless slave of another's will although in very truth I was, I cannot repeat too often that I realised to the full just what it was that I was being compelled to do—a fact which was very far from rendering my situation less distressful!—and every detail of my involuntary actions was projected upon my brain in a series of pictures, whose clear-cut outlines, so long as memory endures, will never fade. Certainly no professional burglar, nor, indeed, any creature in his senses, would have ventured to emulate my surprising rashness. The process of smashing the pane of glass—it was plate glass—was anything but a noiseless one. There was, first, the blow itself, then the shivering of the glass, then the clattering of fragments into the area beneath. One would have thought that the whole thing would have made din enough to have roused the Seven Sleepers. But, here, again the weather was on my side. About that time the wind was howling wildly,—it came shrieking across the square. It is possible that the tumult which it made deadened all other sounds.

Anyhow, as I stood within the room which I had violated, listening for signs of someone being on the alert, I could hear nothing. Within the house there seemed to be the silence of the grave. I drew down the window, and made for the door.

It proved by no means easy to find. The windows were obscured by heavy curtains, so that the room inside was dark as pitch. It appeared to be unusually full of furniture,—an appearance due, perhaps, to my being a stranger in the midst of such Cimmerian blackness. I had to feel my way, very gingerly indeed, among the various impedimenta. As it was I seemed to come into contact with most of the obstacles there were to come into contact with, stumbling more than once over footstools, and over what seemed to be dwarf chairs. It was a miracle that my movements still continued to be unheard,—but I believe that the explanation was, that the house was well built; that the servants were the only persons in it at the time; that their bedrooms were on the top floor; that they were fast asleep; and that they were little likely to be disturbed by anything that might occur in the room which I had entered.

Reaching the door at last, I opened it,—listening for any promise of being interrupted—and—to adapt a hackneyed phrase—directed by the power which shaped my end, I went across the hall and up the stairs. I passed up the first landing, and, on the second, moved to a door upon the right. I turned the handle, it yielded, the door opened, I entered, closing it behind me. I went to the wall just inside the door, found a handle, jerked it, and switched on the electric light,—doing, I make no doubt, all these things, from a spectator's point of view, so naturally, that a judge and jury would have been with difficulty persuaded that they were not the product of my own volition.

In the brilliant glow of the electric light I took a leisurely survey of the contents of the room. It was, as the man in the bed had said it would be, a study,—a fine, spacious apartment, evidently intended rather for work than for show. There were three separate writing-tables, one very large and two smaller ones, all covered with an orderly array of manuscripts and papers. A typewriter stood at the side of one. On the floor, under and about them, were piles of books, portfolios, and official-looking documents. Every available foot of wall space on three sides of the room was lined with shelves, full as they could hold with books. On the fourth side, facing the door, was a large lock-up oak bookcase, and, in the farther corner, a quaint old bureau. So soon as I saw this bureau I went for it, straight as an arrow from a bow,—indeed, it would be no abuse of metaphor to say that I was propelled towards it like an arrow from a bow.

It had drawers below, glass doors above, and between the drawers and the doors was a flap to let down. It was to this flap my attention was directed. I put out my hand to open it; it was locked at the top. I pulled at it with both hands; it refused to budge.

So this was the lock I was, if necessary, to practise the arts of a thief to open. I was no picklock; I had flattered myself that nothing, and no one, could make me such a thing. Yet now that I found myself confronted by that unyielding flap, I found that pressure, irresistible pressure, was being put upon me to gain, by any and every means, access to its interior. I had no option but to yield. I looked about me in search of some convenient tool with which to ply the felon's trade. I found it close beside me. Leaning against the wall, within a yard of where I stood, were examples of various kinds of weapons,—among them, spear-heads. Taking one of these spear-heads, with much difficulty I forced the point between the flap and the bureau. Using the leverage thus obtained, I attempted to prise it open. The flap held fast; the spear-head snapped in two. I tried another, with the same result; a third, to fail again. There were no more. The most convenient thing remaining was a queer, heavy-headed, sharp-edged hatchet. This I took, brought the sharp edge down with all my force upon the refractory flap. The hatchet went through,—before I had done with it, it was open with a vengeance.

But I was destined on the occasion of my first—and, I trust, last—experience of the burglar's calling, to carry the part completely through. I had gained access to the flap itself only to find that at the back were several small drawers, on one of which my observation was brought to bear in a fashion which it was quite impossible to disregard. As a matter of course it was locked, and, once more, I had to search for something which would serve as a rough-and-ready substitute for the missing key.

There was nothing at all suitable among the weapons,—I could hardly for such a purpose use the hatchet; the drawer in question was such a little one that to have done so would have been to shiver it to splinters. On the mantelshelf, in an open leather case, were a pair of revolvers. Statesmen, nowadays, sometimes stand in actual peril of their lives. It is possible that Mr Lessingham, conscious of continually threatened danger, carried them about with him as a necessary protection. They were serviceable weapons, large, and somewhat weighty,—of the type with which, I believe, upon occasion the police are armed. Not only were all the barrels loaded, but, in the case itself there was a supply of cartridges more than sufficient to charge them all again.

I was handling the weapons, wondering—if, in my condition, the word was applicable—what use I could make of them to enable me to gain admission to that drawer, when there came, on a sudden, from the street without, the sound of approaching wheels. There was a whirring within my brain, as if someone was endeavouring to explain to me to what service to apply the revolvers, and I, perforce, strained every nerve to grasp the meaning of my invisible mentor. While I did so, the wheels drew rapidly nearer, and, just as I was expecting them to go whirling by, stopped,—in front of the house. My heart leapt in my bosom. In a convulsion of frantic terror, again, during the passage of one frenzied moment, I all but burst the bonds that held me, and fled, haphazard, from the imminent peril. But the bonds were stronger than I,—it was as if I had been rooted to the ground.

A key was inserted in the keyhole of the front door, the lock was turned, the door thrown open, firm footsteps entered the house. If I could I would not have stood upon the order of my going, but gone at once, anywhere, anyhow; but, at that moment, my comings and goings were not matters in which I was consulted. Panic fear raging within, outwardly I was calm as possible, and stood, turning the revolvers over and over, asking myself what it could be that I was intended to do with them. All at once it came to me in an illuminating flash,—I was to fire at the lock of the drawer, and blow it open.

A madder scheme it would have been impossible to hit upon. The servants had slept through a good deal, but they would hardly sleep through the discharge of a revolver in a room below them,—not to speak of the person who had just entered the premises, and whose footsteps were already audible as he came up the stairs. I struggled to make a dumb protest against the insensate folly which was hurrying me to infallible destruction, without success. For me there was only obedience. With a revolver in either hand I marched towards the bureau as unconcernedly as if I would not have given my life to have escaped the dénouement which I needed but a slight modicum of common sense to be aware was close at hand. I placed the muzzle of one of the revolvers against the keyhole of the drawer to which my unseen guide had previously directed me, and pulled the trigger. The lock was shattered, the contents of the drawer were at my mercy. I snatched up a bundle of letters, about which a pink ribbon was wrapped. Startled by a noise behind me, immediately following the report of the pistol, I glanced over my shoulder.

The room door was open, and Mr Lessingham was standing with the handle in his hand.

CHAPTER VII.

THE GREAT PAUL LESSINGHAM

He was in evening dress. He carried a small portfolio in his left hand. If the discovery of my presence startled him, as it could scarcely have failed to do, he allowed no sign of surprise to escape him. Paul Lessingham's impenetrability is proverbial. Whether on platforms addressing excited crowds, or in the midst of heated discussion in the House of Commons, all the world knows that his coolness remains unruffled. It is generally understood that he owes his success in the political arena in no slight measure to the adroitness which is born of his invulnerable presence of mind. He gave me a taste of its quality then. Standing in the attitude which has been familiarised to us by caricaturists, his feet apart, his broad shoulders well set back, his handsome head a little advanced, his keen blue eyes having in them something suggestive of a bird of prey considering just when, where, and how to pounce, he regarded me for some seconds in perfect silence,—whether outwardly I flinched I cannot say; inwardly I know I did. When he spoke, it was without moving from where he stood, and in the calm, airy tones in which he might have addressed an acquaintance who had just dropped in.

'May I ask, sir, to what I am indebted for the pleasure of your company?'

He paused, as if waiting for my answer. When none came, he put his question in another form.

'Pray, sir, who are you, and on whose invitation do I find you here?'

As I still stood speechless, motionless, meeting his glance without a twitching of an eyebrow, nor a tremor of the hand, I imagine that he began to consider me with an even closer intentness than before. And that the—to say the least of it—peculiarity of my appearance, caused him to suspect that he was face to face with an adventure of a peculiar kind. Whether he took me for a lunatic I cannot certainly say; but, from his manner, I think it possible he did. He began to move towards me from across the room, addressing me with the utmost suavity and courtesy.

'Be so good as to give me the revolver, and the papers you are holding in your hand.'

As he came on, something entered into me, and forced itself from between my lips, so that I said, in a low, hissing voice, which I vow was never mine,

'THE BEETLE!'

Whether it was, or was not, owing, in some degree, to a trick of my imagination, I cannot determine, but, as the words were spoken, it seemed to me that the lights went low, so that the place was all in darkness, and I again was filled with the nauseous consciousness of the presence of something evil in the room. But if, in that matter, my abnormally strained imagination played me a trick, there could be no doubt whatever as to the effect which the words had on Mr Lessingham. When the mist of the blackness—real or supposititious—had passed from before my eyes, I found that he had retreated to the extremest limits of the room, and was crouching, his back against the bookshelves, clutching at them, in the attitude of a man who has received a staggering blow, from which, as yet, he has had no opportunity of recovering. A most extraordinary change had taken place in the expression of his face; in his countenance amazement, fear, and horror seemed struggling for the mastery. I was filled with a most discomforting qualm, as I gazed at the frightened figure in front of me, and realised that it was that of the great Paul Lessingham, the god of my political idolatry.

'Who are you?—In God's name, who are you?'

His very voice seemed changed; his frenzied, choking accents would hardly have been recognised by either friend or foe.

'Who are you?—Do you hear me ask, who are you? In the name of God, I bid you say!'

As he perceived that I was still, he began to show a species of excitement which it was unpleasant to witness, especially as he continued to crouch against the bookshelf, as if he was afraid to stand up straight. So far from exhibiting the impassivity for which he was renowned, all the muscles in his face and all the limbs in his body seemed to be in motion at once; he was like a man afflicted with the shivering ague,—his very fingers were twitching aimlessly, as they were stretched out on either side of him, as if seeking for support from the shelves against which he leaned.

'Where have you come from? what do you want? who sent you here? what concern have you with me? is it necessary that you should come and play these childish tricks with me? why? why?'

The questions came from him with astonishing rapidity. When he saw that I continued silent, they came still faster, mingled with what sounded to me like a stream of inchoate abuse.

'Why do you stand there in that extraordinary garment,—it's worse than nakedness, yes, worse than nakedness! For that alone I could have you punished, and I will!—and try to play the fool? Do you think I am a boy to be bamboozled by every bogey a blunderer may try to conjure up? If so, you're wrong, as whoever sent you might have had sense enough to let you know. If you tell me who you are, and who sent you here, and what it is you want, I will be merciful; if not, the police shall be sent for, and the law shall take its course,—to the bitter end!—I warn you.—Do you hear? You fool! tell me who you are?'

The last words came from him in what was very like a burst of childish fury. He himself seemed conscious, the moment after, that his passion was sadly lacking in dignity, and to be ashamed of it. He drew himself straight up. With a pocket-handkerchief which he took from an inner pocket of his coat, he wiped his lips. Then, clutching it tightly in his hand, he eyed me with a fixedness which, under any other circumstances, I should have found unbearable.

'Well, sir, is your continued silence part of the business of the rôle you have set yourself to play?'

His tone was firmer, and his bearing more in keeping with his character.

'If it be so, I presume that I, at least have liberty to speak. When I find a gentleman, even one gifted with your eloquence of silence, playing the part of burglar, I think you will grant that a few words on my part cannot justly be considered to be out of place.'

Again he paused. I could not but feel that he was employing the vehicle of somewhat cumbrous sarcasm to gain time, and to give himself the opportunity of recovering, if the thing was possible, his pristine courage. That, for some cause wholly hidden from me, the mysterious utterance had shaken his nature to its deepest foundations, was made plainer by his endeavour to treat the whole business with a sort of cynical levity.

'To commence with, may I ask if you have come through London, or through any portion of it, in that costume,—or, rather, in that want of costume? It would seem out of place in a Cairene street,—would it not?—even in the Rue de Rabagas,—was it not the Rue de Rabagas?'

He asked the question with an emphasis the meaning of which was wholly lost on me. What he referred to either then, or in what immediately followed, I, of course, knew no more than the man in the moon,—though I should probably have found great difficulty in convincing him of my ignorance.

'I take it that you are a reminiscence of the Rue de Rabagas,—that, of course;—is it not of course? The little house with the blue-grey venetians, and the piano with the F sharp missing? Is there still the piano? with the tinny treble,—indeed, the whole atmosphere, was it not tinny?—You agree with me?—I have not forgotten. I am not even afraid to remember,—you perceive it?'

A new idea seemed to strike him,—born, perhaps, of my continued silence.

'You look English,—is it possible that you are not English? What are you then—French? We shall see!'

He addressed me in a tongue which I recognised as French, but with which I was not sufficiently acquainted to understand. Although, I flatter myself that,—as the present narrative should show—I have not made an ill-use of the opportunities which I have had to improve my, originally, modest education, I regret that I have never had so much as a ghost of a chance to acquire an even rudimentary knowledge of any language except my own. Recognising, I suppose, from my looks, that he was addressing me in a tongue to which I was a stranger, after a time he stopped, added something with a smile, and then began to talk to me in a lingo to which, in a manner of speaking, I was even stranger, for this time I had not the faintest notion what it was,—it might have been gibberish for all that I could tell. Quickly perceiving that he had succeeded no better than before, he returned to English.

'You do not know French?—nor the patois of the Rue de Rabagas? Very good,—then what is it that you do know? Are you under a vow of silence, or are you dumb,—except upon occasion? Your face is English,—what can be seen of it, and I will take it, therefore, that English spoken words convey some meaning to your brain. So listen, sir, to what I have to say,—do me the favour to listen carefully.'

He was becoming more and more his former self. In his clear, modulated tones there was a ring of something like a threat,—a something which went very far beyond his words.

'You know something of a period which I choose to have forgotten,—that is plain; you come from a person who, probably, knows still more. Go back to that person and say that what I have forgotten I have forgotten; nothing will be gained by anyone by an endeavour to induce me to remember,—be very sure upon that point, say that nothing will be gained by anyone. That time was one of mirage, of delusion, of disease. I was in a condition, mentally and bodily, in which pranks could have been played upon me by any trickster. Such pranks were played. I know that now quite well. I do not pretend to be proficient in the modus operandi of the hankey-pankey man, but I know that he has a method, all the same,—one susceptible, too, of facile explanation. Go back to your friend, and tell him that I am not again likely to be made the butt of his old method,—nor of his new one either.—You hear me, sir?'

I remained motionless and silent,—an attitude which, plainly, he resented.

'Are you deaf and dumb? You certainly are not dumb, for you spoke to me just now. Be advised by me, and do not compel me to resort to measures which will be the cause to you of serious discomfort.—You hear me, sir?'

Still, from me, not a sign of comprehension,—to his increased annoyance.

'So be it. Keep your own counsel, if you choose. Yours will be the bitterness, not mine. You may play the lunatic, and play it excellently well, but that you do understand what is said to you is clear.—Come to business, sir. Give me that revolver, and the packet of letters which you have stolen from my desk.'

He had been speaking with the air of one who desired to convince himself as much as me,—and about his last words there was almost a flavour of braggadocio. I remained unheeding.

'Are you going to do as I require, or are you insane enough to refuse?—in which case I shall summon assistance, and there will quickly be an end of it. Pray do not imagine that you can trick me into supposing that you do not grasp the situation. I know better.—Once more, are you going to give me that revolver and those letters?'

Yet no reply. His anger was growing momentarily greater,—and his agitation too. On my first introduction to Paul Lessingham I was not destined to discover in him any one of those qualities of which the world held him to be the undisputed possessor. He showed himself to be as unlike the statesman I had conceived, and esteemed, as he easily could have done.

'Do you think I stand in awe of you?—you!—of such a thing as you! Do as I tell you, or I myself will make you,—and, at the same time, teach you a much-needed lesson.'

He raised his voice. In his bearing there was a would-be defiance. He might not have been aware of it, but the repetitions of the threats were, in themselves, confessions of weakness. He came a step or two forward,—then, stopping short, began to tremble. The perspiration broke out upon his brow; he made spasmodic little dabs at it with his crumpled-up handkerchief. His eyes wandered hither and thither, as if searching for something which they feared to see yet were constrained to seek. He began to talk to himself, out loud, in odd disconnected sentences,—apparently ignoring me entirely.

'What was that?—It was nothing.—It was my imagination.—My nerves are out of order.—I have been working too hard.—I am not well.—What's that?'

This last inquiry came from him in a half-stifled shriek,—as the door opened to admit the head and body of an elderly man in a state of considerable undress. He had the tousled appearance of one who had been unexpectedly roused out of slumber, and unwillingly dragged from bed. Mr Lessingham stared at him as if he had been a ghost, while he stared back at Mr Lessingham as if he found a difficulty in crediting the evidence of his own eyes. It was he who broke the silence,—stutteringly.

'I am sure I beg your pardon, sir, but one of the maids thought that she heard the sound of a shot, and we came down to see if there was anything the matter,—I had no idea, sir, that you were here.' His eyes travelled from Mr Lessingham towards me,—suddenly increasing, when they saw me, to about twice their previous size. 'God save us!—who is that?'

The man's self-evident cowardice possibly impressed Mr Lessingham with the conviction that he himself was not cutting the most dignified of figures. At any rate, he made a notable effort to, once more, assume a bearing of greater determination.

'You are quite right, Matthews, quite right. I am obliged by your watchfulness. At present you may leave the room—I propose to deal with this fellow myself,—only remain with the other men upon the landing, so that, if I call, you may come to my assistance.'

Matthews did as he was told, he left the room,—with, I fancy, more rapidity than he had entered it. Mr Lessingham returned to me, his manner distinctly more determined, as if he found his resolution reinforced by the near neighbourhood of his retainers.

'Now, my man, you see how the case stands, at a word from me you will be overpowered and doomed to undergo a long period of imprisonment. Yet I am still willing to listen to the dictates of mercy. Put down that revolver, give me those letters, —you will not find me disposed to treat you hardly.'

For all the attention I paid him, I might have been a graven image. He misunderstood, or pretended to misunderstand, the cause of my silence.

'Come, I see that you suppose my intentions to be harsher than they really are,—do not let us have a scandal, and a scene, —be sensible!—give me those letters!'

Again he moved in my direction; again, after he had taken a step or two, to stumble and stop, and look about him with frightened eyes; again to begin to mumble to himself aloud.

'It's a conjurer's trick!—Of course!—Nothing more.—What else could it be?—I'm not to be fooled.—I'm older than I was. I've been overdoing it,—that's all.'

Suddenly he broke into cries.

'Matthews! Matthews!—Help! help!'

Matthews entered the room, followed by three other men, younger than himself. Evidently all had slipped into the first articles of clothing they could lay their hands upon, and each carried a stick, or some similar rudimentary weapon.

Their master spurred them on.

'Strike the revolver out of his hand, Matthews!—knock him down!—take the letters from him!—don't be afraid!—I'm not afraid!'

In proof of it, he rushed at me, as it seemed half blindly. As he did so I was constrained to shout out, in tones which I should not have recognised as mine,

'THE BEETLE!'

And that moment the room was all in darkness, and there were screams as of someone in an agony of terror or of pain. I felt that something had come into the room, I knew not whence nor how,—something of horror. And the next action of which I was conscious was, that under cover of the darkness, I was flying from the room, propelled by I knew not what.

CHAPTER VIII.

THE MAN IN THE STREET

Whether anyone pursued I cannot say. I have some dim recollection, as I came out of the room, of women being huddled against the wall upon the landing, and of their screaming as I went past. But whether any effort was made to arrest my progress I cannot tell. My own impression is that not the slightest attempt to impede my headlong flight was made by anyone.

In what direction I was going I did not know. I was like a man flying through the phantasmagoric happenings of a dream, knowing neither how nor whither. I tore along what I suppose was a broad passage, through a door at the end into what, I fancy, was a drawing-room. Across this room I dashed, helter-skelter, bringing down, in the gloom, unseen articles of furniture, with myself sometimes on top, and sometimes under them. In a trice, each time I fell, I was on my feet again,—until I went crashing against a window which was concealed by curtains. It would not have been strange had I crashed through it,—but I was spared that. Thrusting aside the curtains, I fumbled for the fastening of the window. It was a tall French casement, extending, so far as I could judge, from floor to ceiling. When I had it open I stepped through it on to the verandah without,—to find that I was on the top of the portico which I had vainly essayed to ascend from below.

I tried the road down which I had tried up,—proceeding with a breakneck recklessness of which now I shudder to think. It was, probably, some thirty feet above the pavement, yet I rushed at the descent with as much disregard for the safety of life and limb as if it had been only three. Over the edge of the parapet I went, obtaining, with my naked feet, a precarious foothold on the latticework,—then down I commenced to scramble. I never did get a proper hold, and when I had descended, perhaps, rather more than half the distance—scraping, as it seemed to me, every scrap of skin off my body in the process—I lost what little hold I had. Down to the bottom I went tumbling, rolling right across the pavement into the muddy road. It was a miracle I was not seriously injured,—but in that sense, certainly, that night the miracles were on my side. Hardly was I down, than I was up again,—mud and all.

Just as I was getting on to my feet I felt a firm hand grip me by the shoulder. Turning I found myself confronted by a tall, slenderly built man, with a long, drooping moustache, and an overcoat buttoned up to the chin, who held me with a grasp of steel. He looked at me,—and I looked back at him.

'After the ball,—eh?'

Even then I was struck by something pleasant in his voice, and some quality as of sunshine in his handsome face.

Seeing that I said nothing he went on,—with a curious, half mocking smile.

'Is that the way to come slithering down the Apostle's pillar? —Is it simple burglary, or simpler murder?—Tell me the glad tidings that you've killed St Paul, and I'll let you go.'

Whether he was mad or not I cannot say,—there was some excuse for thinking so. He did not look mad, though his words and actions alike were strange.

'Although you have confined yourself to gentle felony, shall I not shower blessings on the head of him who has been robbing Paul?—Away with you!'

He removed his grip, giving me a gentle push as he did so,—and I was away. I neither stayed nor paused.

I knew little of records, but if anyone has made a better record than I did that night between Lowndes Square and Walham Green I should like to know just what it was,—I should, too, like to have seen it done.

In an incredibly short space of time I was once more in front of the house with the open window,—the packet of letters—which were like to have cost me so dear!—gripped tightly in my hand.

CHAPTER IX.

THE CONTENTS OF THE PACKET

I pulled up sharply,—as if a brake had been suddenly, and even mercilessly, applied to bring me to a standstill. In front of the window I stood shivering. A shower had recently commenced,—the falling rain was being blown before the breeze. I was in a terrible sweat,—yet tremulous as with cold; covered with mud; bruised, and cut, and bleeding,—as piteous an object as you would care to see. Every limb in my body ached; every muscle was exhausted; mentally and physically I was done; had I not been held up, willy nilly, by the spell which was upon me, I should have sunk down, then and there, in a hopeless, helpless, hapless heap.

But my tormentor was not yet at an end with me.

As I stood there, like some broken and beaten hack, waiting for the word of command, it came. It was as if some strong magnetic current had been switched on to me through the window to draw me into the room. Over the low wall I went, over the sill,—once more I stood in that chamber of my humiliation and my shame. And once again I was conscious of that awful sense of the presence of an evil thing. How much of it was fact, and how much of it was the product of imagination I cannot say; but, looking back, it seems to me that it was as if I had been taken out of the corporeal body to be plunged into the inner chambers of all nameless sin. There was the sound of something flopping from off the bed on to the ground, and I knew that the thing was coming at me across the floor. My stomach quaked, my heart melted within me,—the very anguish of my terror gave me strength to scream,—and scream! Sometimes, even now, I seem to hear those screams of mine ringing through the night, and I bury my face in the pillow, and it is as though I was passing through the very Valley of the Shadow.

The thing went back,—I could hear it slipping and sliding across the floor. There was silence. And, presently, the lamp was lit, and the room was all in brightness. There, on the bed, in the familiar attitude between the sheets, his head resting on his hand, his eyes blazing like living coals, was the dreadful cause of all my agonies. He looked at me with his unpitying, unblinking glance.

'So!—Through the window again!—like a thief!—Is it always through that door that you come into a house?'

He paused,—as if to give me time to digest his gibe.

'You saw Paul Lessingham,—well?—the great Paul Lessingham!—Was he, then, so great?'

His rasping voice, with its queer foreign twang, reminded me, in some uncomfortable way, of a rusty saw,—the things he said, and the manner in which he said them, were alike intended to add to my discomfort. It was solely because the feat was barely possible that he only partially succeeded.

'Like a thief you went into his house,—did I not tell you that you would? Like a thief he found you,—were you not ashamed? Since, like a thief he found you, how comes it that you have escaped,—by what robber's artifice have you saved yourself from gaol?'

His manner changed,—so that, all at once, he seemed to snarl at me.

'Is he great?—well!—is he great,—Paul Lessingham? You are small, but he is smaller,—your great Paul Lessingham!—Was there ever a man so less than nothing?'

With the recollection fresh upon me of Mr Lessingham as I had so lately seen him I could not but feel that there might be a modicum of truth in what, with such an intensity of bitterness, the speaker suggested. The picture which, in my mental gallery, I had hung in the place of honour, seemed, to say the least, to have become a trifle smudged.

As usual, the man in the bed seemed to experience not the slightest difficulty in deciphering what was passing through my mind.

'That is so,—you and he, you are a pair,—the great Paul Lessingham is as great a thief as you,—and greater!—for, at least, than you he has more courage.'

For some moments he was still; then exclaimed, with sudden fierceness,

'Give me what you have stolen!'

I moved towards the bed—most unwillingly—and held out to him the packet of letters which I had abstracted from the little drawer. Perceiving my disinclination to his near neighbourhood, he set himself to play with it. Ignoring my outstretched hand, he stared me straight in the face.

'What ails you? Are you not well? Is it not sweet to stand close at my side? You, with your white skin, if I were a woman, would you not take me for a wife?'

There was something about the manner in which this was said which was so essentially feminine that once more I wondered if I could possibly be mistaken in the creature's sex. I would have given much to have been able to strike him across the face,—or, better, to have taken him by the neck, and thrown him through the window, and rolled him in the mud.

He condescended to notice what I was holding out to him.

'So!—that is what you have stolen!—That is what you have taken from the drawer in the bureau—the drawer which was locked—and which you used the arts in which a thief is skilled to enter. Give it to me,—thief!'

He snatched the packet from me, scratching the back of my hand as he did so, as if his nails had been talons. He turned the packet over and over, glaring at it as he did so,—it was strange what a relief it was to have his glance removed from off my face.

'You kept it in your inner drawer, Paul Lessingham, where none but you could see it,—did you? You hid it as one hides treasure. There should be something here worth having, worth seeing, worth knowing,—yes, worth knowing!—since you found it worth your while to hide it up so closely.'

As I have said, the packet was bound about by a string of pink ribbon,—a fact on which he presently began to comment.

'With what a pretty string you have encircled it,—and how neatly it is tied! Surely only a woman's hand could tie a knot like that,—who would have guessed yours were such agile fingers?—So! An endorsement on the cover! What's this?—let's see what's written!—"The letters of my dear love, Marjorie Lindon."'

As he read these words, which, as he said, were endorsed upon the outer sheet of paper which served as a cover for the letters which were enclosed within, his face became transfigured. Never did I suppose that rage could have so possessed a human countenance. His jaw dropped open so that his yellow fangs gleamed through his parted lips,—he held his breath so long that each moment I looked to see him fall down in a fit; the veins stood out all over his face and head like seams of blood. I know not how long he continued speechless. When his breath returned, it was with chokings and gaspings, in the midst of which he hissed out his words, as if their mere passage through his throat brought him near to strangulation.

'The letters of his dear love!—of his dear love!—his!—Paul Lessingham's!—So!—It is as I guessed,—as I knew,—as I saw!—Marjorie Lindon!—Sweet Marjorie!—His dear love!—Paul Lessingham's dear love!—She with the lily face, the corn-hued hair!—What is it his dear love has found in her fond heart to write Paul Lessingham?'

Sitting up in bed he tore the packet open. It contained, perhaps, eight or nine letters,—some mere notes, some long epistles. But, short or long, he devoured them with equal appetite, each one over and over again, till I thought he never would have done re-reading them. They were on thick white paper, of a peculiar shade of whiteness, with untrimmed edges. On each sheet a crest and an address were stamped in gold, and all the sheets were of the same shape and size. I told myself that if anywhere, at any time, I saw writing paper like that again, I should not fail to know it. The caligraphy was, like the paper, unusual, bold, decided, and, I should have guessed, produced by a J pen.

All the time that he was reading he kept emitting sounds, more resembling yelps and snarls than anything more human, —like some savage beast nursing its pent-up rage. When he had made an end of reading,—for the season,—he let his passion have full vent.

'So!—That is what his dear love has found it in her heart to write Paul Lessingham!—Paul Lessingham!'

Pen cannot describe the concentrated frenzy of hatred with which the speaker dwelt upon the name,—it was demoniac.

'It is enough!—it is the end!—it is his doom! He shall be ground between the upper and the nether stones in the towers of anguish, and all that is left of him shall be cast on the accursed stream of the bitter waters, to stink under the blood-grimed sun! And for her—for Marjorie Lindon!—for his dear love!—it shall come to pass that she shall wish that she was never born,—nor he!—and the gods of the shadows shall smell the sweet incense of her suffering!—It shall be! it shall be! It is I that say it,—even I!'

In the madness of his rhapsodical frenzy I believe that he had actually forgotten I was there. But, on a sudden, glancing aside, he saw me, and remembered,—and was prompt to take advantage of an opportunity to wreak his rage upon a tangible object.

'It is you!—you thief!—you still live!—to make a mock of one of the children of the gods!'

He leaped, shrieking, off the bed, and sprang at me, clasping my throat with his horrid hands, bearing me backwards on to the floor; I felt his breath mingle with mine * * * and then God, in His mercy, sent oblivion.

BOOK II.

The Haunted Man

The Story according to Sydney Atherton, Esquire

CHAPTER X.

REJECTED

It was after our second waltz I did it. In the usual quiet corner, —which, that time, was in the shadow of a palm in the hall. Before I had got into my stride she checked me,—touching my sleeve with her fan, turning towards me with startled eyes.

'Stop, please!'

But I was not to be stopped. Cliff Challoner passed, with Gerty Cazell. I fancy that, as he passed, he nodded. I did not care. I was wound up to go, and I went it. No man knows how he can talk till he does talk,—to the girl he wants to marry. It is my impression that I gave her recollections of the Restoration poets. She seemed surprised,—not having previously detected in me the poetic strain, and insisted on cutting in.

'Mr Atherton, I am so sorry.'

Then I did let fly.

'Sorry that I love you!—why? Why should you be sorry that you have become the one thing needful in any man's eyes,—even in mine? The one thing precious,—the one thing to be altogether esteemed! Is it so common for a woman to come across a man who would be willing to lay down his life for her that she should be sorry when she finds him?'

'I did not know that you felt like this, though I confess that I have had my—my doubts.'

'Doubts!—I thank you.'

'You are quite aware, Mr Atherton, that I like you very much.'

'Like me!—Bah!'

'I cannot help liking you,—though it may be "bah."'

'I don't want you to like me,—I want you to love me.'

'Precisely,—that is your mistake.'

'My mistake!—in wanting you to love me!—when I love you—'

'Then you shouldn't,—though I can't help thinking that you are mistaken even there.'

'Mistaken!—in supposing that I love you!—when I assert and reassert it with the whole force of my being! What do you want me to do to prove I love you,—take you in my arms and crush you to my bosom, and make a spectacle of you before every creature in the place?'

'I'd rather you wouldn't, and perhaps you wouldn't mind not talking quite so loud. Mr Challoner seems to be wondering what you're shouting about.'

'You shouldn't torture me.'

She opened and shut her fan,—as she looked down at it I am disposed to suspect that she smiled.

'I am glad we have had this little explanation, because, of course, you are my friend.'

'I am not your friend.'

'Pardon me, you are.'

'I say I'm not,—if I can't be something else, I'll be no friend.'

She went on,—calmly ignoring me,—playing with her fan.

'As it happens, I am, just now, in rather a delicate position, in which a friend is welcome.'

'What's the matter? Who's been worrying you,—your father?'

'Well,—he has not,—as yet; but he may be soon.'

'What's in the wind?'

'Mr Lessingham.'

She dropped her voice,—and her eyes. For the moment I did not catch her meaning.

'What?'

'Your friend, Mr Lessingham.'

'Excuse me, Miss Lindon, but I am by no means sure that anyone is entitled to call Mr Lessingham a friend of mine.'

'What!—Not when I am going to be his wife?'

That took me aback. I had had my suspicions that Paul Lessingham was more with Marjorie than he had any right to be, but I had never supposed that she could see anything desirable in a stick of a man like that. Not to speak of a hundred and one other considerations,—Lessingham on one side of the House, and her father on the other; and old Lindon girding at him anywhere and everywhere—with his high-dried Tory notions of his family importance,—to say nothing of his fortune.

I don't know if I looked what I felt,—if I did, I looked uncommonly blank.

'You have chosen an appropriate moment, Miss Lindon, to make to me such a communication.'

She chose to disregard my irony.

'I am glad you think so, because now you will understand what a difficult position I am in.'

'I offer you my hearty congratulations.'

'And I thank you for them, Mr Atherton, in the spirit in which they are offered, because from you I know they mean so much.'

I bit my lip,—for the life of me I could not tell how she wished me to read her words.

'Do I understand that this announcement has been made to me as one of the public?'

'You do not. It is made to you, in confidence, as my friend,—as my greatest friend; because a husband is something more than friend.' My pulses tingled. 'You will be on my side?'

She had paused,—and I stayed silent.

'On your side,—or Mr Lessingham's?'

'His side is my side, and my side is his side;—you will be on our side?'

'I am not sure that I altogether follow you.'

'You are the first I have told. When papa hears it is possible that there will be trouble,—as you know. He thinks so much of you and of your opinion; when that trouble comes I want you to be on our side,—on my side.'

'Why should I?—what does it matter? You are stronger than your father,—it is just possible that Lessingham is stronger than you; together, from your father's point of view, you will be invincible.'

'You are my friend,—are you not my friend?'

'In effect, you offer me an Apple of Sodom.'

'Thank you;—I did not think you so unkind.'

'And you,—are you kind? I make you an avowal of my love, and, straightway, you ask me to act as chorus to the love of another.'

'How could I tell you loved me,—as you say! I had no notion. You have known me all your life, yet you have not breathed a word of it till now.'

'If I had spoken before?'

I imagine that there was a slight movement of her shoulders, —almost amounting to a shrug.

'I do not know that it would have made any difference.—I do not pretend that it would. But I do know this, I believe that you yourself have only discovered the state of your own mind within the last half-hour.'

If she had slapped my face she could not have startled me more. I had no notion if her words were uttered at random, but they came so near the truth they held me breathless. It was a fact that only during the last few minutes had I really realised how things were with me,—only since the end of that first waltz that the flame had burst out in my soul which was now consuming me. She had read me by what seemed so like a flash of inspiration that I hardly knew what to say to her. I tried to be stinging.

'You flatter me, Miss Lindon, you flatter me at every point. Had you only discovered to me the state of your mind a little sooner I should not have discovered to you the state of mine at all.'

'We will consider it terra incognita.'

'Since you wish it.' Her provoking calmness stung me,—and the suspicion that she was laughing at me in her sleeve. I gave her a glimpse of the cloven hoof. 'But, at the same time, since you assert that you have so long been innocent, I beg that you will continue so no more. At least, your innocence shall be without excuse. For I wish you to understand that I love you, that I have loved you, that I shall love you. Any understanding you may have with Mr Lessingham will not make the slightest difference. I warn you, Miss Lindon, that, until death, you will have to write me down your lover.'

She looked at me, with wide open eyes,—as if I almost frightened her. To be frank, that was what I wished to do.

'Mr Atherton!'

'Miss Lindon?'

'That is not like you at all.'

'We seem to be making each other's acquaintance for the first time.'

She continued to gaze at me with her big eyes,—which, to be candid, I found it difficult to meet. On a sudden her face was lighted by a smile,—which I resented.

'Not after all these years,—not after all these years! I know you, and though I daresay you're not flawless, I fancy you'll be found to ring pretty true.'

Her manner was almost sisterly,—elder-sisterly. I could have shaken her. Hartridge coming to claim his dance gave me an opportunity to escape with such remnants of dignity as I could gather about me. He dawdled up,—his thumbs, as usual, in his waistcoat pockets.

'I believe, Miss Lindon, this is our dance.'

She acknowledged it with a bow, and rose to take his arm. I got up, and left her, without a word.

As I crossed the hall I chanced on Percy Woodville. He was in his familiar state of fluster, and was gaping about him as if he had mislaid the Koh-i-noor, and wondered where in thunder it had got to. When he saw it was I he caught me by the arm.

'I say, Atherton, have you seen Miss Lindon?'

'I have.'

'No!—Have you?—By Jove!—Where? I've been looking for her all over the place, except in the cellars and the attics,—and I was just going to commence on them. This is our dance.'

'In that case, she's shunted you.'

'No!—Impossible!' His mouth went like an O,—and his eyes ditto, his eyeglass clattering down on to his shirt front. 'I expect the mistake's mine. Fact is, I've made a mess of my programme. It's either the last dance, or this dance, or the next, that I've booked with her, but I'm hanged if I know which. Just take a squint at it, there's a good chap, and tell me which one you think it is.'

I 'took a squint'—since he held the thing within an inch of my nose I could hardly help it; one 'squint,' and that was enough—and more. Some men's ball programmes are studies in impressionism, Percy's seemed to me to be a study in madness. It was covered with hieroglyphics, but what they meant, or what they did there anyhow, it was absurd to suppose that I could tell,—I never put them there!—Proverbially, the man's a champion hasher.

'I regret, my dear Percy, that I am not an expert in cuneiform writing. If you have any doubt as to which dance is yours, you'd better ask the lady,—she'll feel flattered.'

Leaving him to do his own addling I went to find my coat,—I panted to get into the open air; as for dancing I felt that I loathed it. Just as I neared the cloak-room someone stopped me. It was Dora Grayling.

'Have you forgotten that this is our dance?'

I had forgotten,—clean. And I was not obliged by her remembering. Though as I looked at her sweet, grey eyes, and at the soft contours of her gentle face, I felt that I deserved well kicking. She is an angel,—one of the best!—but I was in no mood for angels. Not for a very great deal would I have gone through that dance just then, nor, with Dora Grayling, of all women in the world, would I have sat it out.—So I was a brute and blundered.

'You must forgive me, Miss Grayling, but—I am not feeling very well, and—I don't think I'm up to any more dancing.—Good-night.'

CHAPTER XI.

A MIDNIGHT EPISODE

The weather out of doors was in tune with my frame of mind, —I was in a deuce of a temper, and it was a deuce of a night. A keen north-east wind, warranted to take the skin right off you, was playing catch-who-catch-can with intermittent gusts of blinding rain. Since it was not fit for a dog to walk, none of your cabs for me,—nothing would serve but pedestrian exercise.

So I had it.

I went down Park Lane,—and the wind and rain went with me,—also, thoughts of Dora Grayling. What a bounder I had been,—and was! If there is anything in worse taste than to book a lady for a dance, and then to leave her in the lurch, I should like to know what that thing is,—when found it ought to be made a note of. If any man of my acquaintance allowed himself to be guilty of such a felony in the first degree, I should cut him. I wished someone would try to cut me,—I should like to see him at it.

It was all Marjorie's fault,—everything! past, present, and to come! I had known that girl when she was in long frocks—I had, at that period of our acquaintance, pretty recently got out of them; when she was advanced to short ones; and when, once more, she returned to long. And all that time,—well, I was nearly persuaded that the whole of the time I had loved her. If I had not mentioned it, it was because I had suffered my affection, 'like the worm, to lie hidden in the bud,'—or whatever it is the fellow says.

At any rate, I was perfectly positive that if I had had the faintest notion that she would ever seriously consider such a man as Lessingham I should have loved her long ago. Lessingham! Why, he was old enough to be her father,—at least he was a good many years older than I was. And a wretched Radical! It is true that on certain points I, also, am what some people would call a Radical,—but not a Radical of the kind he is. Thank Heaven, no! No doubt I have admired traits in his character, until I learnt this thing of him. I am even prepared to admit that he is a man of ability,—in his way! which is, emphatically, not mine. But to think of him in connection with such a girl as Marjorie Lindon,—preposterous! Why, the man's as dry as a stick,—drier! And cold as an iceberg. Nothing but a politician, absolutely. He a lover!—how I could fancy such a stroke of humour setting all the benches in a roar. Both by education, and by nature, he was incapable of even playing such a part; as for being the thing,—absurd! If you were to sink a shaft from the crown of his head to the soles of his feet, you would find inside him nothing but the dry bones of parties and of politics.

What my Marjorie—if everyone had his own, she is mine, and, in that sense, she always will be mine—what my Marjorie could see in such a dry-as-dust out of which even to construct the rudiments of a husband was beyond my fathoming.

Suchlike agreeable reflections were fit company for the wind and the wet, so they bore me company all down the lane. I crossed at the corner, going round the hospital towards the square. This brought me to the abiding-place of Paul the Apostle. Like the idiot I was, I went out into the middle of the street, and stood awhile in the mud to curse him and his house,—on the whole, when one considers that that is the kind of man I can be, it is, perhaps, not surprising that Marjorie disdained me.

'May your following,' I cried,—it is an absolute fact that the words were shouted!—'both in the House and out of it, no longer regard you as a leader! May your party follow after other gods! May your political aspirations wither, and your speeches be listened to by empty benches! May the Speaker persistently and strenuously refuse to allow you to catch his eye, and, at the next election, may your constituency reject you!—Jehoram!—what's that?'

I might well ask. Until that moment I had appeared to be the only lunatic at large, either outside the house or in it, but, on a sudden, a second lunatic came on the scene, and that with a vengeance. A window was crashed open from within,—the one over the front door, and someone came plunging through it on to the top of the portico. That it was a case of intended suicide I made sure,—and I began to be in hopes that I was about to witness the suicide of Paul. But I was not so assured of the intention when the individual in question began to scramble down the pillar of the porch in the most extraordinary fashion I ever witnessed,—I was not even convinced of a suicidal purpose when he came tumbling down, and lay sprawling in the mud at my feet.

I fancy, if I had performed that portion of the act I should have lain quiet for a second or two, to consider whereabouts I was, and which end of me was uppermost. But there was no nonsense of that sort about that singularly agile stranger,—if he was not made of indiarubber he ought to have been. So to speak, before he was down he was up,—it was all I could do to grab at him before he was off like a rocket.

Such a figure as he presented is seldom seen,—at least, in the streets of London. What he had done with the rest of his apparel I am not in a position to say,—all that was left of it was a long, dark cloak which he strove to wrap round him. Save for that,—and mud!—he was bare as the palm of my hand. Yet it was his face that held me. In my time I have seen strange expressions on men's faces, but never before one such as I saw on his. He looked like a man might look who, after living a life of undiluted crime, at last finds himself face to face with the devil. It was not the look of a madman,—far from it; it was something worse.

It was the expression on the man's countenance, as much as anything else, which made me behave as I did. I said something to him,—some nonsense, I know not what. He regarded me with a silence which was supernatural. I spoke to him again;—not a word issued from those rigid lips; there was not a tremor of those awful eyes,—eyes which I was tolerably convinced saw something which I had never seen, or ever should. Then I took my hand from off his shoulder, and let him go. I know not why,—I did.

He had remained as motionless as a statue while I held him,—indeed, for any evidence of life he gave, he might have been a statue; but, when my grasp was loosed, how he ran! He had turned the corner and was out of sight before I could say, 'How do!'

It was only then,—when he had gone, and I had realised the extra-double-express-flash-of-lightning rate at which he had taken his departure—that it occurred to me of what an extremely sensible act I had been guilty in letting him go at all. Here was an individual who had been committing burglary, or something very like it, in the house of a budding cabinet minister, and who had tumbled plump into my arms, so that all I had to do was to call a policeman and get him quodded,—and all that I had done was something of a totally different kind.

'You're a nice type of an ideal citizen!' I was addressing myself. 'A first chop specimen of a low-down idiot,—to connive at the escape of the robber who's been robbing Paul. Since you've let the villain go, the least you can do is to leave a card on the Apostle, and inquire how he's feeling.'

I went to Lessingham's front door and knocked,—I knocked once, I knocked twice, I knocked thrice, and the third time, I give you my word, I made the echoes ring,—but still there was not a soul that answered.

'If this is a case of a seven or seventy-fold murder, and the gentleman in the cloak has made a fair clearance of every living creature the house contains, perhaps it's just as well I've chanced upon the scene,—still I do think that one of the corpses might get up to answer the door. If it is possible to make noise enough to waken the dead, you bet I'm on to it.'

And I was,—I punished that knocker! until I warrant the pounding I gave it was audible on the other side of Green Park. And, at last, I woke the dead,—or, rather, I roused Matthews to a consciousness that something was going on. Opening the door about six inches, through the interstice he protruded his ancient nose.

'Who's there?'

'Nothing, my dear sir, nothing and no one. It must have been your vigorous imagination which induced you to suppose that there was,—you let it run away with you.'

Then he knew me,—and opened the door about two feet.

'Oh, it's you, Mr Atherton. I beg your pardon, sir,—I thought it might have been the police.'

'What then? Do you stand in terror of the minions of the law,—at last?'

A most discreet servant, Matthews,—just the fellow for a budding cabinet minister. He glanced over his shoulder,—I had suspected the presence of a colleague at his back, now I was assured. He put his hand up to his mouth,—and I thought how exceedingly discreet he looked, in his trousers and his stockinged feet, and with his hair all rumpled, and his braces dangling behind, and his nightshirt creased.

'Well, sir, I have received instructions not to admit the police.'

'The deuce you have!—From whom?'

Coughing behind his hand, leaning forward, he addressed me with an air which was flatteringly confidential.

'From Mr Lessingham, sir.'

'Possibly Mr Lessingham is not aware that a robbery has been committed on his premises, that the burglar has just come out of his drawing-room window with a hop, skip, and a jump, bounded out of the window like a tennis-ball, flashed round the corner like a rocket.'

Again Matthews glanced over his shoulder, as if not clear which way discretion lay, whether fore or aft.

'Thank you, sir. I believe that Mr Lessingham is aware of something of the kind.' He seemed to come to a sudden resolution, dropping his voice to a whisper. 'The fact is, sir, that I fancy Mr Lessingham's a good deal upset.'

'Upset?' I stared at him. There was something in his manner I did not understand. 'What do you mean by upset? Has the scoundrel attempted violence?'

'Who's there?'

The voice was Lessingham's, calling to Matthews from the staircase, though, for an instant, I hardly recognised it, it was so curiously petulant. Pushing past Matthews, I stepped into the hall. A young man, I suppose a footman, in the same undress as Matthews, was holding a candle,—it seemed the only light about the place. By its glimmer I perceived Lessingham standing half-way up the stairs. He was in full war paint,—as he is not the sort of man who dresses for the House, I took it that he had been mixing pleasure with business.

'It's I, Lessingham,—Atherton. Do you know that a fellow has jumped out of your drawing-room window?'

It was a second or two before he answered. When he did, his voice had lost its petulance.

'Has he escaped?'

'Clean,—he's a mile away by now.'

It seemed to me that in his tone, when he spoke again, there was a note of relief.

'I wondered if he had. Poor fellow! more sinned against than sinning! Take my advice, Atherton, and keep out of politics. They bring you into contact with all the lunatics at large. Good night! I am much obliged to you for knocking us up. Matthews, shut the door.'

Tolerably cool, on my honour,—a man who brings news big with the fate of Rome does not expect to receive such treatment. He expects to be listened to with deference, and to hear all that there is to hear, and not to be sent to the right-about before he has had a chance of really opening his lips. Before I knew it—almost!—the door was shut, and I was on the doorstep. Confound the Apostle's impudence! next time he might have his house burnt down—and him in it!—before I took the trouble to touch his dirty knocker.

What did he mean by his allusion to lunatics in politics,—did he think to fool me? There was more in the business than met the eye,—and a good deal more than he wished to meet mine,—hence his insolence. The creature.

What Marjorie Lindon could see in such an opusculum surpassed my comprehension; especially when there was a man of my sort walking about, who adored the very ground she trod upon.

CHAPTER XII.

A MORNING VISITOR

All through the night, waking and sleeping, and in my dreams, I wondered what Marjorie could see in him! In those same dreams I satisfied myself that she could, and did, see nothing in him, but everything in me,—oh the comfort! The misfortune was that when I awoke I knew it was the other way round,—so that it was a sad awakening. An awakening to thoughts of murder.

So, swallowing a mouthful and a peg, I went into my laboratory to plan murder—legalised murder—on the biggest scale it ever has been planned. I was on the track of a weapon which would make war not only an affair of a single campaign, but of a single half-hour. It would not want an army to work it either. Once let an individual, or two or three at most, in possession of my weapon-that-was-to-be, get within a mile or so of even the largest body of disciplined troops that ever yet a nation put into the field, and—pouf!—in about the time it takes you to say that they would be all dead men. If weapons of precision, which may be relied upon to slay, are preservers of the peace—and the man is a fool who says that they are not!—then I was within reach of the finest preserver of the peace imagination ever yet conceived.

What a sublime thought to think that in the hollow of your own hand lies the life and death of nations,—and it was almost in mine.

I had in front of me some of the finest destructive agents you could wish to light upon—carbon-monoxide, chlorine-trioxide, mercuric-oxide, conine, potassamide, potassium-carboxide, cyanogen—when Edwards entered. I was wearing a mask of my own invention, a thing that covered ears and head and everything, something like a diver's helmet—I was dealing with gases a sniff of which meant death; only a few days before, unmasked, I had been doing some fool's trick with a couple of acids—sulphuric and cyanide of potassium—when, somehow, my hand slipped, and, before I knew it, minute portions of them combined. By the mercy of Providence I fell backwards instead of forwards;—sequel, about an hour afterwards Edwards found me on the floor, and it took the remainder of that day, and most of the doctors in town, to bring me back to life again.

Edwards announced his presence by touching me on the shoulder,—when I am wearing that mask it isn't always easy to make me hear.

'Someone wishes to see you, sir.'

'Then tell someone that I don't wish to see him.'

Well-trained servant, Edwards,—he walked off with the message as decorously as you please. And then I thought there was an end,—but there wasn't.

I was regulating the valve of a cylinder in which I was fusing some oxides when, once more, someone touched me on the shoulder. Without turning I took it for granted it was Edwards back again.

'I have only to give a tiny twist to this tap, my good fellow, and you will be in the land where the bogies bloom. Why will you come where you're not wanted?' Then I looked round. 'Who the devil are you?'

For it was not Edwards at all, but quite a different class of character.

I found myself confronting an individual who might almost have sat for one of the bogies I had just alluded to. His costume was reminiscent of the 'Algerians' whom one finds all over France, and who are the most persistent, insolent and amusing of pedlars. I remember one who used to haunt the répétitions at the Alcazar at Tours,—but there! This individual was like the originals, yet unlike,—he was less gaudy, and a good deal dingier, than his Gallic prototypes are apt to be. Then he wore a burnoose,—the yellow, grimy-looking article of the Arab of the Soudan, not the spick and span Arab of the boulevard. Chief difference of all, his face was clean shaven,—and whoever saw an Algerian of Paris whose chiefest glory was not his well-trimmed moustache and beard?

I expected that he would address me in the lingo which these gentlemen call French,—but he didn't.

'You are Mr Atherton?'

'And you are Mr—Who?—how did you come here? Where's my servant?'

The fellow held up his hand. As he did so, as if in accordance with a pre-arranged signal, Edwards came into the room looking excessively startled. I turned to him.

'Is this the person who wished to see me?'

'Yes, sir.'

'Didn't I tell you to say that I didn't wish to see him?'

'Yes, sir.'

'Then why didn't you do as I told you?'

'I did, sir.'

'Then how comes he here?'

'Really, sir,'—Edwards put his hand up to his head as if he was half asleep—'I don't quite know.'

'What do you mean by you don't know? Why didn't you stop him?'

'I think, sir, that I must have had a touch of sudden faintness, because I tried to put out my hand to stop him, and—I couldn't.'

'You're an idiot.—Go!' And he went. I turned to the stranger. 'Pray, sir, are you a magician?'

He replied to my question with another.

'You, Mr Atherton,—are you also a magician?'

He was staring at my mask with an evident lack of comprehension.

'I wear this because, in this place, death lurks in so many subtle forms, that, without it, I dare not breathe.' He inclined his head,—though I doubt if he understood. 'Be so good as to tell me, briefly, what it is you wish with me.'

He slipped his hand into the folds of his burnoose, and, taking out a slip of paper, laid it on the shelf by which we were standing. I glanced at it, expecting to find on it a petition, or a testimonial, or a true statement of his sad case; instead it contained two words only,—'Marjorie Lindon.' The unlooked-for sight of that well-loved name brought the blood into my cheeks.

'You come from Miss Lindon?'

He narrowed his shoulders, brought his finger-tips together, inclined his head, in a fashion which was peculiarly Oriental, but not particularly explanatory, — so I repeated my question.

'Do you wish me to understand that you do come from Miss Lindon?'

Again he slipped his hand into his burnoose, again he produced a slip of paper, again he laid it on the shelf, again I glanced at it, again nothing was written on it but a name, — 'Paul Lessingham.'

'Well? — I see, — Paul Lessingham. — What then?'

'She is good, — he is bad, — is it not so?'

He touched first one scrap of paper, then the other. I stared.

'Pray how do you happen to know?'

'He shall never have her, — eh?'

'What on earth do you mean?'

'Ah! — what do I mean!'

'Precisely, what do you mean? And also, and at the same time, who the devil are you?'

'It is as a friend I come to you.'

'Then in that case you may go; I happen to be overstocked in that line just now.'

'Not with the kind of friend I am!'

'The saints forefend!'

'You love her, — you love Miss Lindon! Can you bear to think of him in her arms?'

I took off my mask, — feeling that the occasion required it. As I did so he brushed aside the hanging folds of the hood of his burnoose, so that I saw more of his face. I was immediately conscious that in his eyes there was, in an especial degree, what, for want of a better term, one may call the mesmeric quality. That his was one of those morbid organisations which are oftener found, thank goodness, in the east than in the west, and which are apt to exercise an uncanny influence over the weak and the foolish folk with whom they come in contact,—the kind of creature for whom it is always just as well to keep a seasoned rope close handy. I was, also, conscious that he was taking advantage of the removal of my mask to try his strength on me,—than which he could not have found a tougher job. The sensitive something which is found in the hypnotic subject happens, in me, to be wholly absent.

'I see you are a mesmerist.'

He started.

'I am nothing,—a shadow!'

'And I'm a scientist. I should like, with your permission—or without it!—to try an experiment or two on you.'

He moved further back. There came a gleam into his eyes which suggested that he possessed his hideous power to an unusual degree,—that, in the estimation of his own people, he was qualified to take his standing as a regular devil-doctor.

'We will try experiments together, you and I,—on Paul Lessingham.'

'Why on him?'

'You do not know?'

'I do not.'

'Why do you lie to me?'

'I don't lie to you,—I haven't the faintest notion what is the nature of your interest in Mr Lessingham.'

'My interest?—that is another thing; it is your interest of which we are speaking.'

'Pardon me,—it is yours.'

'Listen! you love her,—and he! But at a word from you he shall not have her,—never! It is I who say it,—I!'

'And, once more, sir, who are you?'

'I am of the children of Isis!'

'Is that so?—It occurs to me that you have made a slight mistake,—this is London, not a dog-hole in the desert.'

'Do I not know?—what does it matter?—you shall see! There will come a time when you will want me,—you will find that you cannot bear to think of him in her arms,—her whom you love! You will call to me, and I shall come, and of Paul Lessingham there shall be an end.'

While I was wondering whether he was really as mad as he sounded, or whether he was some impudent charlatan who had an axe of his own to grind, and thought that he had found in me a grindstone, he had vanished from the room. I moved after him.

'Hang it all!—stop!' I cried.

He must have made pretty good travelling, because, before I had a foot in the hall, I heard the front door slam, and, when I reached the street, intent on calling him back, neither to the right nor to the left was there a sign of him to be seen.

CHAPTER XIII.

THE PICTURE

'I wonder what that nice-looking beggar really means, and who he happens to be?' That was what I said to myself when I returned to the laboratory. 'If it is true that, now and again, Providence does write a man's character on his face, then there can't be the slightest shred of a doubt that a curious one's been written on his. I wonder what his connection has been with the Apostle,—or if it's only part of his game of bluff.'

I strode up and down,—for the moment my interest in the experiments I was conducting had waned.

'If it was all bluff I never saw a better piece of acting,—and yet what sort of finger can such a precisian as St Paul have in such a pie? The fellow seemed to squirm at the mere mention of the rising-hope-of-the-Radicals' name. Can the objection be political? Let me consider,—what has Lessingham done which could offend the religious or patriotic susceptibilities of the most fanatical of Orientals? Politically, I can recall nothing. Foreign affairs, as a rule, he has carefully eschewed. If he has offended—and if he hasn't the seeming was uncommonly good! —the cause will have to be sought upon some other track. But, then, what track?'

The more I strove to puzzle it out, the greater the puzzlement grew.

'Absurd!—The rascal has had no more connection with St Paul than St Peter. The probability is that he's a crackpot; and if he isn't, he has some little game on foot—in close association with the hunt of the oof-bird!—which he tried to work off on me, but couldn't. As for—for Marjorie—my Marjorie!—only she isn't mine, confound it!—if I had had my senses about me, I should have broken his head in several places for daring to allow her name to pass his lips,—the unbaptised Mohammedan!—Now to return to the chase of splendid murder!'

I snatched up my mask—one of the most ingenious inventions, by the way, of recent years; if the armies of the future wear my mask they will defy my weapon!—and was about to re-adjust it in its place, when someone knocked at the door.

'Who's there?—Come in!'

It was Edwards. He looked round him as if surprised.

'I beg your pardon, sir,—I thought you were engaged. I didn't know that—that gentleman had gone.'

'He went up the chimney, as all that kind of gentlemen do.—Why the deuce did you let him in when I told you not to?'

'Really, sir, I don't know. I gave him your message, and—he looked at me, and—that is all I remember till I found myself standing in this room.'

Had it not been Edwards I might have suspected him of having had his palm well greased,—but, in his case, I knew better. It was as I thought,—my visitor was a mesmerist of the first class; he had actually played some of his tricks, in broad daylight, on my servant, at my own front door,—a man worth studying. Edwards continued.

'There is someone else, sir, who wishes to see you,—Mr Lessingham.'

'Mr Lessingham!' At that moment the juxtaposition seemed odd, though I daresay it was so rather in appearance than in reality. 'Show him in.'

Presently in came Paul.

I am free to confess,—I have owned it before!—that, in a sense, I admire that man,—so long as he does not presume to thrust himself into a certain position. He possesses physical qualities which please my eye—speaking as a mere biologist. I like the suggestion conveyed by his every pose, his every movement, of a tenacious hold on life,—of reserve force, of a repository of bone and gristle on which he can fall back at pleasure. The fellow's lithe and active; not hasty, yet agile; clean built, well hung,—the sort of man who might be relied upon to make a good recovery. You might beat him in a sprint,—mental or physical—though to do that you would have to be spry!—but in a staying race he would see you out. I do not know that he is exactly the kind of man whom I would trust,—unless I knew that he was on the job,—which knowledge, in his case, would be uncommonly hard to attain. He is too calm; too self-contained; with the knack of looking all round him even in moments of extremest peril,—and for whatever he does he has a good excuse. He has the reputation, both in the House and out of it, of being a man of iron nerve,—and with some reason; yet I am not so sure. Unless I read him wrongly his is one of those individualities which, confronted by certain eventualities, collapse,—to rise, the moment of trial having passed, like Phoenix from her ashes. However it might be with his adherents, he would show no trace of his disaster.

And this was the man whom Marjorie loved. Well, she could show some cause. He was a man of position,—destined, probably, to rise much higher; a man of parts,—with capacity to make the most of them; not ill-looking; with agreeable manners,—when he chose; and he came within the lady's definition of a gentleman, 'he always did the right thing, at the right time, in the right way.' And yet—! Well, I take it that we are all cads, and that we most of us are prigs; for mercy's sake do not let us all give ourselves away.

He was dressed as a gentleman should be dressed,—black frock coat, black vest, dark grey trousers, stand-up collar, smartly-tied bow, gloves of the proper shade, neatly brushed hair, and a smile, which if was not childlike, at any rate was bland.

'I am not disturbing you?'

'Not at all.'

'Sure?—I never enter a place like this, where a man is matching himself with nature, to wrest from her her secrets, without feeling that I am crossing the threshold of the unknown. The last time I was in this room was just after you had taken out the final patents for your System of Telegraphy at Sea, which the Admiralty purchased,—wisely—What is it, now?'

'Death.'

'No?—really?—what do you mean?'

'If you are a member of the next government, you will possibly learn; I may offer them the refusal of a new wrinkle in the art of murder.'

'I see,—a new projectile.—How long is this race to continue between attack and defence?'

'Until the sun grows cold.'

'And then?'

'There'll be no defence,—nothing to defend.'

He looked at me with his calm, grave eyes.

'The theory of the Age of Ice towards which we are advancing is not a cheerful one.' He began to finger a glass retort which lay upon a table. 'By the way, it was very good of you to give me a look in last night. I am afraid you thought me peremptory,—I have come to apologise.'

'I don't know that I thought you peremptory; I thought you—queer.'

'Yes.' He glanced at me with that expressionless look upon his face which he could summon at will, and which is at the bottom of the superstition about his iron nerve. 'I was worried, and not well. Besides, one doesn't care to be burgled, even by a maniac.'

'Was he a maniac?'

'Did you see him?'

'Very clearly.'

'Where?'

'In the street.'

'How close were you to him?'

'Closer than I am to you.'

'Indeed. I didn't know you were so close to him as that. Did you try to stop him?'

'Easier said than done,—he was off at such a rate.'

'Did you see how he was dressed,—or, rather, undressed?'

'I did.'

'In nothing but a cloak on such a night. Who but a lunatic would have attempted burglary in such a costume?'

'Did he take anything?'

'Absolutely nothing.'

'It seems to have been a curious episode.'

He moved his eyebrows,—according to members of the House the only gesture in which he has been known to indulge.

'We become accustomed to curious episodes. Oblige me by not mentioning it to anyone,—to anyone.' He repeated the last two words, as if to give them emphasis. I wondered if he was thinking of Marjorie. 'I am communicating with the police. Until they move I don't want it to get into the papers,—or to be talked about. It's a worry,—you understand?'

I nodded. He changed the theme.

'This that you're engaged upon,—is it a projectile or a weapon?'

'If you are a member of the next government you will possibly know; if you aren't you possibly won't.'

'I suppose you have to keep this sort of thing secret?'

'I do. It seems that matters of much less moment you wish to keep secret.'

'You mean that business of last night? If a trifle of that sort gets into the papers, or gets talked about,—which is the same thing!—you have no notion how we are pestered. It becomes an almost unbearable nuisance. Jones the Unknown can commit murder with less inconvenience to himself than Jones the Notorious can have his pocket picked,—there is not so much exaggeration in that as there sounds.—Good-bye,—thanks for your promise.' I had given him no promise, but that was by the way. He turned as to go,—then stopped. 'There's another thing,—I believe you're a specialist on questions of ancient superstitions and extinct religions.'

'I am interested in such subjects, but I am not a specialist.'

'Can you tell me what were the exact tenets of the worshippers of Isis?'

'Neither I nor any man,—with scientific certainty. As you know, she had a brother; the cult of Osiris and Isis was one and the same. What, precisely, were its dogmas, or its practices, or anything about it, none, now, can tell. The Papyri, hieroglyphics, and so on, which remain are very far from being exhaustive, and our knowledge of those which do remain, is still less so.'

'I suppose that the marvels which are told of it are purely legendary?'

'To what marvels do you particularly refer?'

'Weren't supernatural powers attributed to the priests of Isis?'

'Broadly speaking, at that time, supernatural powers were attributed to all the priests of all the creeds.'

'I see.' Presently he continued. 'I presume that her cult is long since extinct,—that none of the worshippers of Isis exist to-day.'

I hesitated,—I was wondering why he had hit on such a subject; if he really had a reason, or if he was merely asking questions as a cover for something else,—you see, I knew my Paul.

'That is not so sure.'

He looked at me with that passionless, yet searching glance of his.

'You think that she still is worshipped?'

'I think it possible, even probable, that, here and there, in Africa—Africa is a large order!—homage is paid to Isis, quite in the good old way.'

'Do you know that as a fact?'

'Excuse me, but do you know it as a fact?—Are you aware that you are treating me as if I was on the witness stand?—Have you any special purpose in making these inquiries?'

He smiled.

'In a kind of a way I have. I have recently come across rather a curious story; I am trying to get to the bottom of it.'

'What is the story?'

'I am afraid that at present I am not at liberty to tell it you; when I am I will. You will find it interesting,—as an instance of a singular survival.—Didn't the followers of Isis believe in transmigration?'

'Some of them,—no doubt.'

'What did they understand by transmigration?'

'Transmigration.'

'Yes,—but of the soul or of the body?'

'How do you mean?—transmigration is transmigration. Are you driving at something in particular? If you'll tell me fairly and squarely what it is I'll do my best to give you the information you require; as it is, your questions are a bit perplexing.'

'Oh, it doesn't matter,—as you say, "transmigration is transmigration."' I was eyeing him keenly; I seemed to detect in his manner an odd reluctance to enlarge on the subject he himself had started. He continued to trifle with the retort upon the table. 'Hadn't the followers of Isis a—what shall I say?—a sacred emblem?'

'How?'

'Hadn't they an especial regard for some sort of a—wasn't it some sort of a—beetle?'

'You mean Scarabaeus sacer,—according to Latreille, Scarabaeus Egyptiorum? Undoubtedly,—the scarab was venerated throughout Egypt,—indeed, speaking generally, most things that had life, for instance, cats; as you know, Orisis continued among men in the figure of Apis, the bull.'

'Weren't the priests of Isis—or some of them—supposed to assume, after death, the form of a—scarabaeus?'

'I never heard of it.'

'Are you sure?—think!'

'I shouldn't like to answer such a question positively, offhand, but I don't, on the spur of the moment, recall any supposition of the kind.'

'Don't laugh at me—I'm not a lunatic!—but I understand that recent researches have shown that even in some of the most astounding of the ancient legends there was a substratum of fact. Is it absolutely certain that there could be no shred of truth in such a belief?'

'In what belief?'

'In the belief that a priest of Isis—or anyone—assumed after death the form of a scarabaeus?'

'It seems to me, Lessingham, that you have lately come across some uncommonly interesting data, of a kind, too, which it is your bounden duty to give to the world,—or, at any rate, to that portion of the world which is represented by me. Come,—tell us all about it!—what are you afraid of?'

'I am afraid of nothing,—and some day you shall be told,—but not now. At present, answer my question.'

'Then repeat your question,—clearly.'

'Is it absolutely certain that there could be no foundation of truth in the belief that a priest of Isis—or anyone—assumed after death the form of a beetle?'

'I know no more than the man in the moon,—how the dickens should I? Such a belief may have been symbolical. Christians believe that after death the body takes the shape of worms—and so, in a sense, it does,—and, sometimes, eels.'

'That is not what I mean.'

'Then what do you mean?'

'Listen. If a person, of whose veracity there could not be a vestige of a doubt, assured you that he had seen such a transformation actually take place, could it conceivably be explained on natural grounds?'

'Seen a priest of Isis assume the form of a beetle?'

'Or a follower of Isis?'

'Before, or after death?'

He hesitated. I had seldom seen him wear such an appearance of interest,—to be frank, I was keenly interested too!—but, on a sudden there came into his eyes a glint of something that was almost terror. When he spoke, it was with the most unwonted awkwardness.

'In—in the very act of dying.'

'In the very act of dying?'

'If—he had seen a follower of Isis in—the very act of dying, assume—the form of a—a beetle, on any conceivable grounds would such a transformation be susceptible of a natural explanation?'

I stared,—as who would not? Such an extraordinary question was rendered more extraordinary by coming from such a man, —yet I was almost beginning to suspect that there was something behind it more extraordinary still.

'Look here, Lessingham, I can see you've a capital tale to tell, —so tell it, man! Unless I'm mistaken, it's not the kind of tale in which ordinary scruples can have any part or parcel,—anyhow, it's hardly fair of you to set my curiosity all agog, and then to leave it unappeased.'

He eyed me steadily, the appearance of interest fading more and more, until, presently, his face assumed its wonted expressionless mask,—somehow I was conscious that what he had seen in my face was not altogether to his liking. His voice was once more bland and self-contained.

'I perceive you are of opinion that I have been told a taradiddle. I suppose I have.'

'But what is the tarradiddle?—don't you see I'm burning?'

'Unfortunately, Atherton, I am on my honour. Until I have permission to unloose it, my tongue is tied.' He picked up his hat and umbrella from where he had placed them on the table. Holding them in his left hand, he advanced to me with his right outstretched. 'It is very good of you to suffer my continued interruption; I know, to my sorrow, what such interruptions mean,—believe me, I am not ungrateful. What is this?'

On the shelf, within a foot or so of where I stood, was a sheet of paper,—the size and shape of half a sheet of post note. At this he stooped to glance. As he did so, something surprising occurred. On the instant a look came on to his face which, literally, transfigured him. His hat and umbrella fell from his grasp on to the floor. He retreated, gibbering, his hands held out as if to ward something off from him, until he reached the wall on the other side of the room. A more amazing spectacle than he presented I never saw.

'Lessingham!' I exclaimed. 'What's wrong with you?'

My first impression was that he was struck by a fit of epilepsy, —though anyone less like an epileptic subject it would be hard to find. In my bewilderment I looked round to see what could be the immediate cause. My eye fell upon the sheet of paper. I stared at it with considerable surprise. I had not noticed it there previously, I had not put it there,—where had it come from? The curious thing was that, on it, produced apparently by some process of photogravure, was an illustration of a species of beetle with which I felt that I ought to be acquainted, and yet was not. It was of a dull golden green; the colour was so well brought out,—even to the extent of seeming to scintillate, and the whole thing was so dexterously done that the creature seemed alive. The semblance of reality was, indeed, so vivid that it needed a second glance to be assured that it was a mere trick of the reproducer. Its presence there was odd,—after what we had been talking about it might seem to need explanation; but it was absurd to suppose that that alone could have had such an effect on a man like Lessingham.

With the thing in my hand, I crossed to where he was,—pressing his back against the wall, he had shrunk lower inch by inch till he was actually crouching on his haunches.

'Lessingham!—come, man, what's wrong with you?'

Taking him by the shoulder, I shook him with some vigour. My touch had on him the effect of seeming to wake him out of a dream, of restoring him to consciousness as against the nightmare horrors with which he was struggling. He gazed up at me with that look of cunning on his face which one associates with abject terror.

'Atherton?—Is it you?—It's all right,—quite right.—I'm well, —very well.'

As he spoke, he slowly drew himself up, till he was standing erect.

'Then, in that case, all I can say is that you have a queer way of being very well.'

He put his hand up to his mouth, as if to hide the trembling of his lips.

'It's the pressure of overwork,—I've had one or two attacks like this,—but it's nothing, only—a local lesion.'

I observed him keenly; to my thinking there was something

about him which was very odd indeed.

'Only a local lesion!—If you take my strongly-urged advice you'll get a medical opinion without delay,—if you haven't been wise enough to have done so already.'

'I'll go to-day;—at once; but I know it's only mental overstrain.'

'You're sure it's nothing to do with this?'

I held out in front of him the photogravure of the beetle. As I did so he backed away from me, shrieking, trembling as with palsy.

'Take it away! take it away!' he screamed.

I stared at him, for some seconds, astonished into speechlessness. Then I found my tongue.

'Lessingham!—It's only a picture!—Are you stark mad?'

He persisted in his ejaculations.

'Take it away! take it away!—Tear it up!—Burn it!'

His agitation was so unnatural,—from whatever cause it arose!—that, fearing the recurrence of the attack from which he had just recovered, I did as he bade me. I tore the sheet of paper into quarters, and, striking a match, set fire to each separate piece. He watched the process of incineration as if fascinated. When it was concluded, and nothing but ashes remained, he gave a gasp of relief.

'Lessingham,' I said, 'you're either mad already, or you're going mad,—which is it?'

'I think it's neither. I believe I am as sane as you. It's—it's that story of which I was speaking; it—it seems curious, but I'll tell you all about it—some day. As I observed, I think you will find it an interesting instance of a singular survival.' He made an obvious effort to become more like his usual self. 'It is extremely unfortunate, Atherton, that I should have troubled you with such a display of weakness,—especially as I am able to offer you so scant an explanation. One thing I would ask of you,—to observe strict confidence. What has taken place has been between ourselves. I am in your hands, but you are my friend, I know I can rely on you not to speak of it to anyone,—and, in particular, not to breathe a hint of it to Miss Lindon.'

'Why, in particular, not to Miss Lindon?'

'Can you not guess?'

I hunched my shoulder.

'If what I guess is what you mean is not that a cause the more why silence would be unfair to her?'

'It is for me to speak, if for anyone. I shall not fail to do what should be done.—Give me your promise that you will not hint a word to her of what you have so unfortunately seen?'

I gave him the promise he required.

****

There was no more work for me that day. The Apostle, his divagations, his example of the coleoptera, his Arabian friend,—these things were as microbes which, acting on a system already predisposed for their reception, produced high fever; I was in a fever,—of unrest. Brain in a whirl!—Marjorie, Paul, Isis, beetle, mesmerism, in delirious jumble. Love's upsetting!—in itself a sufficiently severe disease; but when complications intervene, suggestive of mystery and novelties, so that you do not know if you are moving in an atmosphere of dreams or of frozen facts,—if, then, your temperature does not rise, like that rocket of M. Verne's,—which reached the moon, then you are a freak of an entirely genuine kind, and if the surgeons do not preserve you, and place you on view, in pickle, they ought to, for the sake of historical doubters, for no one will believe that there ever was a man like you, unless you yourself are somewhere around to prove them Thomases.

Myself,—I am not that kind of man. When I get warm I grow heated, and when I am heated there is likely to be a variety show of a gaudy kind. When Paul had gone I tried to think things out, and if I had kept on trying something would have happened—so I went on the river instead.

CHAPTER XIV.

THE DUCHESS' BALL

That night was the Duchess of Datchet's ball—the first person I saw as I entered the dancing-room was Dora Grayling.

I went straight up to her.

'Miss Grayling, I behaved very badly to you last night. I have come to make to you my apologies,—to sue for your forgiveness!'

'My forgiveness?' Her head went back,—she has a pretty bird-like trick of cocking it a little on one side. 'You were not well. Are you better?'

'Quite.—You forgive me? Then grant me plenary absolution by giving me a dance for the one I lost last night.'

She rose. A man came up,—a stranger to me; she's one of the best hunted women in England,—there's a million with her.

'This is my dance, Miss Grayling.'

She looked at him.

'You must excuse me. I am afraid I have made a mistake. I had forgotten that I was already engaged.'

I had not thought her capable of it. She took my arm, and away we went, and left him staring.

'It's he who's the sufferer now,' I whispered, as we went round,—she can waltz!

'You think so? It was I last night,—I did not mean, if I could help it, to suffer again. To me a dance with you means something.' She went all red,—adding, as an afterthought, 'Nowadays so few men really dance. I expect it's because you dance so well.'

'Thank you.'

We danced the waltz right through, then we went to an impromptu shelter which had been rigged up on a balcony. And we talked. There's something sympathetic about Miss Grayling which leads one to talk about one's self,—before I was half aware of it I was telling her of all my plans and projects,—actually telling her of my latest notion which, ultimately, was to result in the destruction of whole armies as by a flash of lightning. She took an amount of interest in it which was surprising.

'What really stands in the way of things of this sort is not theory but practice,—one can prove one's facts on paper, or on a small scale in a room; what is wanted is proof on a large scale, by actual experiment. If, for instance, I could take my plant to one of the forests of South America, where there is plenty of animal life but no human, I could demonstrate the soundness of my position then and there.'

'Why don't you?'

'Think of the money it would cost.'

'I thought I was a friend of yours.'

'I had hoped you were.'

'Then why don't you let me help you?'

'Help me?—How?'

'By letting you have the money for your South American experiment;—it would be an investment on which I should expect to receive good interest.'

I fidgeted.

'It is very good of you, Miss Grayling, to talk like that.'

She became quite frigid.

'Please don't be absurd!—I perceive quite clearly that you are snubbing me, and that you are trying to do it as delicately as you know how.'

'Miss Grayling!'

'I understand that it was an impertinence on my part to volunteer assistance which was unasked; you have made that sufficiently plain.'

'I assure you—'

'Pray don't. Of course, if it had been Miss Lindon it would have been different; she would at least have received a civil answer. But we are not all Miss Lindon.'

I was aghast. The outburst was so uncalled for,—I had not the faintest notion what I had said or done to cause it; she was in such a surprising passion—and it suited her!—I thought I had never seen her look prettier,—I could do nothing else but stare. So she went on,—with just as little reason.

'Here is someone coming to claim this dance,—I can't throw all my partners over. Have I offended you so irremediably that it will be impossible for you to dance with me again?'

'Miss Grayling!—I shall be only too delighted.' She handed me her card. 'Which may I have?'

'For your own sake you had better place it as far off as you possibly can.'

'They all seem taken.'

'That doesn't matter; strike off any name you please, anywhere and put your own instead.'

It was giving me an almost embarrassingly free hand. I booked myself for the next waltz but two,—who it was who would have to give way to me I did not trouble to inquire.

'Mr Atherton!—Is that you?'

It was,—it was also she. It was Marjorie! And so soon as I saw her I knew that there was only one woman in the world for me,—the mere sight of her sent the blood tingling through my veins. Turning to her attendant cavalier, she dismissed him with a bow.

'Is there an empty chair?'

She seated herself in the one Miss Grayling had just vacated. I sat down beside her. She glanced at me, laughter in her eyes. I was all in a stupid tremblement.

'You remember that last night I told you that I might require your friendly services in diplomatic intervention?' I nodded,—I felt that the allusion was unfair. 'Well, the occasion's come,—or, at least, it's very near.' She was still,—and I said nothing to help her. 'You know how unreasonable papa can be.'

I did,—never a more pig-headed man in England than Geoffrey Lindon,—or, in a sense, a duller. But, just then, I was not prepared to admit it to his child.

'You know what an absurd objection he has to—Paul.'

There was an appreciative hesitation before she uttered the fellow's Christian name,—when it came it was with an accent of tenderness which stung me like a gadfly. To speak to me—of all men,—of the fellow in such a tone was—like a woman.

'Has Mr Lindon no notion of how things stand between you?'

'Except what he suspects. That is just where you are to come in, papa thinks so much of you—I want you to sound Paul's praises in his ear—to prepare him for what must come.' Was ever rejected lover burdened with such a task? Its enormity kept me still. 'Sydney, you have always been my friend,—my truest, dearest friend. When I was a little girl you used to come between papa and me, to shield me from his wrath. Now that I am a big girl I want you to be on my side once more, and to shield me still.'

Her voice softened. She laid her hand upon my arm. How, under her touch, I burned.

'But I don't understand what cause there has been for secrecy,—why should there have been any secrecy from the first?'

'It was Paul's wish that papa should not be told.'

'Is Mr Lessingham ashamed of you?'

'Sydney!'

'Or does he fear your father?'

'You are unkind. You know perfectly well that papa has been prejudiced against him all along, you know that his political position is just now one of the greatest difficulty, that every nerve and muscle is kept on the continual strain, that it is in the highest degree essential that further complications of every and any sort should be avoided. He is quite aware that his suit will not be approved of by papa, and he simply wishes that nothing shall be said about it till the end of the session,—that is all.'

'I see! Mr Lessingham is cautious even in love-making,—politician first, and lover afterwards.'

'Well! – why not? – would you have him injure the cause he has at heart for want of a little patience?'

'It depends what cause it is he has at heart.'

'What is the matter with you? – why do you speak to me like that? – it is not like you at all.' She looked at me shrewdly, with flashing eyes. 'Is it possible that you are – jealous? – that you were in earnest in what you said last night? – I thought that was the sort of thing you said to every girl.'

I would have given a great deal to take her in my arms, and press her to my bosom then and there, – to think that she should taunt me with having said to her the sort of thing I said to every girl.

'What do you know of Mr Lessingham?'

'What all the world knows, – that history will be made by him.'

'There are kinds of history in the making of which one would not desire to be associated. What do you know of his private life, – it was to that that I was referring.'

'Really, – you go too far. I know that he is one of the best, just as he is one of the greatest, of men; for me, that is sufficient.'

'If you do know that, it is sufficient.'

'I do know it, – all the world knows it. Everyone with whom he comes in contact is aware – must be aware, that he is incapable of a dishonourable thought or action.'

'Take my advice, don't appreciate any man too highly. In the book of every man's life there is a page which he would wish to keep turned down.'

'There is no such page in Paul's, – there may be in yours; I think that probable.'

'Thank you. I fear it is more than probable. I fear that, in my case, the page may extend to several. There is nothing Apostolic about me, – not even the name.'

'Sydney! – you are unendurable! – It is the more strange to hear you talk like this since Paul regards you as his friend.'

'He flatters me.'

'Are you not his friend?'

'Is it not sufficient to be yours?'

'No,—who is against Paul is against me.'

'That is hard.'

'How is it hard? Who is against the husband can hardly be for the wife,—when the husband and the wife are one.'

'But as yet you are not one.—Is my cause so hopeless?'

'What do you call your cause?—are you thinking of that nonsense you were talking about last night?'

She laughed!

'You call it nonsense.—You ask for sympathy, and give—so much!'

'I will give you all the sympathy you stand in need of,—I promise it! My poor, dear Sydney!—don't be so absurd! Do you think that I don't know you? You're the best of friends, and the worst of lovers,—as the one, so true; so fickle as the other. To my certain knowledge, with how many girls have you been in love,—and out again. It is true that, to the best of my knowledge and belief, you have never been in love with me before,—but that's the merest accident. Believe me, my dear, dear Sydney, you'll be in love with someone else to-morrow,—if you're not half-way there to-night. I confess, quite frankly, that, in that direction, all the experience I have had of you has in nowise strengthened my prophetic instinct. Cheer up!—one never knows!—Who is this that's coming?'

It was Dora Grayling who was coming,—I went off with her without a word,—we were half-way through the dance before she spoke to me.

'I am sorry that I was cross to you just now, and—disagreeable. Somehow I always seem destined to show to you my most unpleasant side.'

'The blame was mine,—what sort of side do I show you? You are far kinder to me than I deserve,—now, and always.'

'That is what you say.'

'Pardon me, it's true,—else how comes it that, at this time of day, I'm without a friend in all the world?'

'You!—without a friend!—I never knew a man who had so many!—I never knew a person of whom so many men and women join in speaking well!'

'Miss Grayling!'

'As for never having done anything worth doing, think of what you have done. Think of your discoveries, think of your inventions, think of—but never mind! The world knows you have done great things, and it confidently looks to you to do still greater. You talk of being friendless, and yet when I ask, as a favour—as a great favour!—to be allowed to do something to show my friendship, you—well, you snub me.'

'I snub you!'

'You know you snubbed me.'

'Do you really mean that you take an interest in—in my work?'

'You know I mean it.'

She turned to me, her face all glowing,—and I did know it.

'Will you come to my laboratory to-morrow morning?'

'Will I!—won't I!'

'With your aunt?'

'Yes, with my aunt.'

'I'll show you round, and tell you all there is to be told, and then if you still think there's anything in it, I'll accept your offer about that South American experiment,—that is, if it still holds good.'

'Of course it still holds good.'

'And we'll be partners.'

'Partners?—Yes,—we will be partners.'

'It will cost a terrific sum.'

'There are some things which never can cost too much.'

'That's not my experience.'

'I hope it will be mine.'

'It's a bargain?'

'On my side, I promise you that it's a bargain.'

When I got outside the room I found that Percy Woodville was at my side. His round face was, in a manner of speaking, as long as my arm. He took his glass out of his eye, and rubbed it with his handkerchief,—and directly he put it back he took it out and rubbed it again. I believe that I never saw him in such a state of fluster,—and, when one speaks of Woodville, that means something.

'Atherton, I am in a devil of a stew.' He looked it. 'All of a heap!—I've had a blow which I shall never get over!'

'Then get under.'

Woodville is one of those fellows who will insist on telling me their most private matters,—even to what they owe their washerwomen for the ruination of their shirts. Why, goodness alone can tell,—heaven knows I am not sympathetic.

'Don't be an idiot!—you don't know what I'm suffering!—I'm as nearly as possible stark mad.'

'That's all right, old chap,—I've seen you that way more than once before.'

'Don't talk like that,—you're not a perfect brute!'

'I bet you a shilling that I am.'

'Don't torture me,—you're not. Atherton!' He seized me by the lapels of my coat, seeming half beside himself,—fortunately he had drawn me into a recess, so that we were noticed by few observers. 'What do you think has happened?'

'My dear chap, how on earth am I to know?'

'She's refused me!'

'Has she!—Well I never!—Buck up,—try some other address,—there are quite as good fish in the sea as ever came out of it.'

'Atherton, you're a blackguard.'

He had crumpled his handkerchief into a ball, and was actually bobbing at his eyes with it,—the idea of Percy Woodville being dissolved in tears was excruciatingly funny,—but, just then, I could hardly tell him so.

'There's not a doubt of it,—it's my way of being sympathetic. Don't be so down, man,—try her again!'

'It's not the slightest use—I know it isn't—from the way she treated me.'

'Don't be so sure—women often say what they mean least. Who's the lady?'

'Who?—Is there more women in the world than one for me, or has there ever been? You ask me who! What does the word mean to me but Marjorie Lindon!'

'Marjorie Lindon?'

I fancy that my jaw dropped open,—that, to use his own vernacular, I was 'all of a heap.' I felt like it.

I strode away—leaving him mazed—and all but ran into Marjorie's arms.

'I'm just leaving. Will you see me to the carriage, Mr Atherton?' I saw her to the carriage. 'Are you off?—can I give you a lift?'

'Thank you,—I am not thinking of being off.'

'I'm going to the House of Commons,—won't you come?'

'What are you going there for?'

Directly she spoke of it I knew why she was going,—and she knew that I knew, as her words showed.

'You are quite well aware of what the magnet is. You are not so ignorant as not to know that the Agricultural Amendment Act is on to-night, and that Paul is to speak. I always try to be there when Paul is to speak, and I mean to always keep on trying.'

'He is a fortunate man.'

'Indeed,—and again indeed. A man with such gifts as his is inadequately described as fortunate.—But I must be off. He expected to be up before, but I heard from him a few minutes ago that there has been a delay, but that he will be up within half-an-hour.—Till our next meeting.'

As I returned into the house, in the hall I met Percy Woodville. He had his hat on.

'Where are you off to?'

'I'm off to the House.'

'To hear Paul Lessingham?'

'Damn Paul Lessingham!'

'With all my heart!'

'There's a division expected,—I've got to go.'

'Someone else has gone to hear Paul Lessingham,—Marjorie Lindon.'

'No!—you don't say so!—by Jove!—I say, Atherton, I wish I could make a speech,—I never can. When I'm electioneering I have to have my speeches written for me, and then I have to read 'em. But, by Jove, if I knew Miss Lindon was in the gallery, and if I knew anything about the thing, or could get someone to tell me something, hang me if I wouldn't speak,—I'd show her I'm not the fool she thinks I am!'

'Speak, Percy, speak!—you'd knock 'em silly, sir!—I tell you what I'll do,—I'll come with you! I'll to the House as well!—Paul Lessingham shall have an audience of three.'

CHAPTER XV.

MR LESSINGHAM SPEAKS

The House was full. Percy and I went upstairs,—to the gallery which is theoretically supposed to be reserved for what are called 'distinguished strangers,'—those curious animals. Trumperton was up, hammering out those sentences which smell, not so much of the lamp as of the dunderhead. Nobody was listening,—except the men in the Press Gallery; where is the brain of the House, and ninety per cent. of its wisdom.

It was not till Trumperton had finished that I discovered Lessingham. The tedious ancient resumed his seat amidst a murmur of sounds which, I have no doubt, some of the pressmen interpreted next day as 'loud and continued applause.' There was movement in the House, possibly expressive of relief; a hum of voices; men came flocking in. Then, from the Opposition benches, there rose a sound which was applause,—and I perceived that, on a cross bench close to the gangway, Paul Lessingham was standing up bareheaded.

I eyed him critically,—as a collector might eye a valuable specimen, or a pathologist a curious subject. During the last four and twenty hours my interest in him had grown apace. Just then, to me, he was the most interesting man the world contained.

When I remembered how I had seen him that same morning, a nerveless, terror-stricken wretch, grovelling, like some craven cur, upon the floor, frightened, to the verge of imbecility, by a shadow, and less than a shadow, I was confronted by two hypotheses. Either I had exaggerated his condition then, or I exaggerated his condition now. So far as appearance went, it was incredible that this man could be that one.

I confess that my feeling rapidly became one of admiration. I love the fighter. I quickly recognised that here we had him in perfection. There was no seeming about him then,—the man was to the manner born. To his finger-tips a fighting man. I had never realised it so clearly before. He was coolness itself. He had all his faculties under complete command. While never, for a moment, really exposing himself, he would be swift in perceiving the slightest weakness in his opponents' defence, and, so soon as he saw it, like lightning, he would slip in a telling blow. Though defeated, he would hardly be disgraced; and one might easily believe that their very victories would be so expensive to his assailants, that, in the end, they would actually conduce to his own triumph.

'Hang me!' I told myself, 'if, after all, I am surprised if Marjorie does see something in him.' For I perceived how a clever and imaginative young woman, seeing him at his best, holding his own, like a gallant knight, against overwhelming odds, in the lists in which he was so much at home, might come to think of him as if he were always and only there, ignoring altogether the kind of man he was when the joust was finished.

It did me good to hear him, I do know that,—and I could easily imagine the effect he had on one particular auditor who was in the Ladies' Cage. It was very far from being an 'oration' in the American sense; it had little or nothing of the fire and fury of the French Tribune; it was marked neither by the ponderosity nor the sentiment of the eloquent German; yet it was as satisfying as are the efforts of either of the three, producing, without doubt, precisely the effect which the speaker intended. His voice was clear and calm, not exactly musical, yet distinctly pleasant, and it was so managed that each word he uttered was as audible to every person present as if it had been addressed particularly to him. His sentences were short and crisp; the words which he used were not big ones, but they came from him with an agreeable ease; and he spoke just fast enough to keep one's interest alert without involving a strain on the attention.

He commenced by making, in the quietest and most courteous manner, sarcastic comments on the speeches and methods of Trumperton and his friends which tickled the House amazingly. But he did not make the mistake of pushing his personalities too far. To a speaker of a certain sort nothing is easier than to sting to madness. If he likes, his every word is barbed. Wounds so given fester; they are not easily forgiven;—it is essential to a politician that he should have his firmest friends among the fools; or his climbing days will soon be over. Soon his sarcasms were at an end. He began to exchange them for sweet-sounding phrases. He actually began to say pleasant things to his opponents; apparently to mean them. To put them in a good conceit with themselves. He pointed out how much truth there was in what they said; and then, as if by accident, with what ease and at how little cost, amendments might be made. He found their arguments, and took them for his own, and flattered them, whether they would or would not, by showing how firmly they were founded upon fact; and grafted other arguments upon them, which seemed their natural sequelae; and transformed them, and drove them hither and thither; and brought them—their own arguments!—to a round, irrefragable conclusion, which was diametrically the reverse of that to which they themselves had brought them. And he did it all with an aptness, a readiness, a grace, which was incontestable. So that, when he sat down, he had performed that most difficult of all feats, he had delivered what, in a House of Commons' sense, was a practical, statesmanlike speech, and yet one which left his hearers in an excellent humour.

It was a great success,—an immense success. A parliamentary triumph of almost the highest order. Paul Lessingham had been coming on by leaps and bounds. When he resumed his seat, amidst applause which, this time, really was applause, there were, probably, few who doubted that he was destined to go still farther. How much farther it is true that time alone could tell; but, so far as appearances went, all the prizes, which are as the crown and climax of a statesman's career, were well within his reach.

For my part, I was delighted. I had enjoyed an intellectual exercise,—a species of enjoyment not so common as it might be. The Apostle had almost persuaded me that the political game was one worth playing, and that its triumphs were things to be desired. It is something, after all, to be able to appeal successfully to the passions and aspirations of your peers; to gain their plaudits; to prove your skill at the game you yourself have chosen; to be looked up to and admired. And when a woman's eyes look down on you, and her ears drink in your every word, and her heart beats time with yours,—each man to his own temperament, but when that woman is the woman whom you love, to know that your triumph means her glory, and her gladness, to me that would be the best part of it all.

In that hour,—the Apostle's hour!—I almost wished that I were a politician too!

The division was over. The business of the night was practically done. I was back again in the lobby! The theme of conversation was the Apostle's speech,—on every side they talked of it.

Suddenly Marjorie was at my side. Her face was glowing. I never saw her look more beautiful,—or happier. She seemed to be alone.

'So you have come, after all!—Wasn't it splendid?—wasn't it magnificent? Isn't it grand to have such great gifts, and to use them to such good purpose?—Speak, Sydney! Don't feign a coolness which is foreign to your nature!'

I saw that she was hungry for me to praise the man whom she delighted to honour. But, somehow, her enthusiasm cooled mine.

'It was not a bad speech, of a kind.'

'Of a kind!' How her eyes flashed fire! With what disdain she treated me! 'What do you mean by "of a kind?" My dear Sydney, are you not aware that it is an attribute of small minds to attempt to belittle those which are greater? Even if you are conscious of inferiority, it's unwise to show it. Mr Lessingham's was a great speech, of any kind; your incapacity to recognise the fact simply reveals your lack of the critical faculty.'

'It is fortunate for Mr Lessingham that there is at least one person in whom the critical faculty is so bountifully developed. Apparently, in your judgment, he who discriminates is lost.'

I thought she was going to burst into passion. But, instead, laughing, she placed her hand upon my shoulder.

'Poor Sydney!—I understand!—It is so sad!—Do you know you are like a little boy who, when he is beaten, declares that the victor has cheated him. Never mind! as you grow older, you will learn better.'

She stung me almost beyond bearing,—I cared not what I said.

'You, unless I am mistaken, will learn better before you are older.'

'What do you mean?'

Before I could have told her—if I had meant to tell; which I did not—Lessingham came up.

'I hope I have not kept you waiting; I have been delayed longer than I expected.'

'Not at all,—though I am quite ready to get away; it's a little tiresome waiting here.'

This with a mischievous glance towards me,—a glance which compelled Lessingham to notice me.

'You do not often favour us.'

'I don't. I find better employment for my time.'

'You are wrong. It's the cant of the day to underrate the House of Commons, and the work which it performs; don't you suffer yourself to join in the chorus of the simpletons. Your time cannot be better employed than in endeavouring to improve the body politic.'

'I am obliged to you.—I hope you are feeling better than when I saw you last.'

A gleam came into his eyes, fading as quickly as it came. He showed no other sign of comprehension, surprise, or resentment.

'Thank you.—I am very well.'

But Marjorie perceived that I meant more than met the eye, and that what I meant was meant unpleasantly.

'Come,—let us be off. It is Mr Atherton to-night who is not well.'

She had just slipped her arm through Lessingham's when her father approached. Old Lindon stared at her on the Apostle's arm, as if he could hardly believe that it was she.

'I thought that you were at the Duchess'?'

'So I have been, papa; and now I'm here.'

'Here!' Old Lindon began to stutter and stammer, and to grow red in the face, as is his wont when at all excited. 'W—what do you mean by here?—wh—where's the carriage?'

'Where should it be, except waiting for me outside,—unless the horses have run away.'

'I—I—I'll take you down to it. I—I don't approve of y—your w—w—waiting in a place like this.'

'Thank you, papa, but Mr Lessingham is going to take me down.—I shall see you afterwards.—Good-bye.'

Anything cooler than the way in which she walked off I do not think I ever saw. This is the age of feminine advancement. Young women think nothing of twisting their mothers round their fingers, let alone their fathers; but the fashion in which that young woman walked off, on the Apostle's arm, and left her father standing there, was, in its way, a study.

Lindon seemed scarcely able to realise that the pair of them had gone. Even after they had disappeared in the crowd he stood staring after them, growing redder and redder, till the veins stood out upon his face, and I thought that an apoplectic seizure threatened. Then, with a gasp, he turned to me.

'Damned scoundrel!' I took it for granted that he alluded to the gentleman,—even though his following words hardly suggested it. 'Only this morning I forbade her to have anything to do with him, and n—now he's w—walked off with her! C—confounded adventurer! That's what he is, an adventurer, and before many hours have passed I'll take the liberty to tell him so!'

Jamming his fists into his pockets, and puffing like a grampus in distress, he took himself away,—and it was time he did, for his words were as audible as they were pointed, and already people were wondering what the matter was. Woodville came up as Lindon was going,—just as sorely distressed as ever.

'She went away with Lessingham,—did you see her?'

'Of course I saw her. When a man makes a speech like Lessingham's any girl would go away with him,—and be proud to. When you are endowed with such great powers as he is, and use them for such lofty purposes, she'll walk away with you,—but, till then, never.'

He was at his old trick of polishing his eyeglass.

'It's bitter hard. When I knew that she was there, I'd half a mind to make a speech myself, upon my word I had, only I didn't know what to speak about, and I can't speak anyhow,—how can a fellow speak when he's shoved into the gallery?'

'As you say, how can he?—he can't stand on the railing and shout,—even with a friend holding him behind.'

'I know I shall speak one day,—bound to; and then she won't be there.'

'It'll be better for you if she isn't.'

'Think so?—Perhaps you're right. I'd be safe to make a mess of it, and then, if she were to see me at it, it'd be the devil! 'Pon my word, I've been wishing, lately, I was clever.'

He rubbed his nose with the rim of his eyeglass, looking the most comically disconsolate figure.

'Put black care behind you, Percy!—buck up, my boy! The division's over—you are free—now we'll go "on the fly."'

And we did 'go on the fly.'

CHAPTER XVI.

ATHERTON'S MAGIC VAPOUR

I bore him off to supper at the Helicon. All the way in the cab he was trying to tell me the story of how he proposed to Marjorie,—and he was very far from being through with it when we reached the club. There was the usual crowd of supperites, but we got a little table to ourselves, in a corner of the room, and before anything was brought for us to eat he was at it again. A good many of the people were pretty near to shouting, and as they seemed to be all speaking at once, and the band was playing, and as the Helicon supper band is not piano, Percy did not have it quite all to himself, but, considering the delicacy of his subject, he talked as loudly as was decent,—getting more so as he went on. But Percy is peculiar.

'I don't know how many times I've tried to tell her,—over and over again.'

'Have you now?'

'Yes, pretty near every time I met her,—but I never seemed to get quite to it, don't you know.'

'How was that?'

'Why, just as I was going to say, "Miss Lindon, may I offer you the gift of my affection—"'

'Was that how you invariably intended to begin?'

'Well, not always—one time like that, another time another way. Fact is, I got off a little speech by heart, but I never got a chance to reel it off, so I made up my mind to just say anything.'

'And what did you say?'

'Well, nothing,—you see, I never got there. Just as I was feeling my way, she'd ask me if I preferred big sleeves to little ones, or top hats to billycocks, or some nonsense of the kind.'

'Would she now?'

'Yes,—of course I had to answer, and by the time I'd answered the chance was lost.' Percy was polishing his eyeglass. 'I tried to get there so many times, and she choked me off so often, that I can't help thinking that she suspected what it was that I was after.'

'You think she did?'

'She must have done. Once I followed her down Piccadilly, and chivied her into a glove shop in the Burlington Arcade. I meant to propose to her in there,—I hadn't had a wink of sleep all night through dreaming of her, and I was just about desperate.'

'And did you propose?'

'The girl behind the counter made me buy a dozen pairs of gloves instead. They turned out to be three sizes too large for me when they came home. I believe she thought I'd gone to spoon the glove girl,—she went out and left me there. That girl loaded me with all sorts of things when she was gone,—I couldn't get away. She held me with her blessed eye. I believe it was a glass one.'

'Miss Lindon's?—or the glove girl's?'

'The glove girl's. She sent me home a whole cartload of green ties, and declared I'd ordered them. I shall never forget that day. I've never been up the Arcade since, and never mean to.'

'You gave Miss Lindon a wrong impression.'

'I don't know. I was always giving her wrong impressions. Once she said that she knew I was not a marrying man, that I was the sort of chap who never would marry, because she saw it in my face.'

'Under the circumstances, that was trying.'

'Bitter hard.' Percy sighed again. 'I shouldn't mind if I wasn't so gone. I'm not a fellow who does get gone, but when I do get gone, I get so beastly gone.'

'I tell you what, Percy,—have a drink!'

'I'm a teetotaler,—you know I am.'

'You talk of your heart being broken, and of your being a teetotaler in the same breath,—if your heart were really broken you'd throw teetotalism to the winds.'

'Do you think so,—why?'

'Because you would, — men whose hearts are broken always do, — you'd swallow a magnum at the least.'

Percy groaned.

'When I drink I'm always ill, — but I'll have a try.'

He had a try, — making a good beginning by emptying at a draught the glass which the waiter had just now filled. Then he relapsed into melancholy.

'Tell me, Percy, — honest Indian! — do you really love her?'

'Love her?' His eyes grew round as saucers. 'Don't I tell you that I love her?'

'I know you tell me, but that sort of thing is easy telling. What does it make you feel like, this love you talk so much about?'

'Feel like? — Just anyhow, — and nohow. You should look inside me, and then you'd know.'

'I see. — It's like that, is it? — Suppose she loved another man, what sort of feeling would you feel towards him?'

'Does she love another man?'

'I say, suppose.'

'I dare say she does. I expect that's it. — What an idiot I am not to have thought of that before.' He sighed, — and refilled his glass. 'He's a lucky chap, whoever he is. I'd — I'd like to tell him so.'

'You'd like to tell him so?'

'He's such a jolly lucky chap, you know.'

'Possibly, — but his jolly good luck is your jolly bad luck. Would you be willing to resign her to him without a word?'

'If she loves him.'

'But you say you love her.'

'Of course I do.'

'Well then?'

'You don't suppose that, because I love her, I shouldn't like to see her happy?—I'm not such a beast!—I'd sooner see her happy than anything else in all the world.'

'I see.—Even happy with another?—I'm afraid that my philosophy is not like yours. If I loved Miss Lindon, and she loved, say, Jones, I'm afraid I shouldn't feel like that towards Jones at all.'

'What would you feel like?'

'Murder.—Percy, you come home with me,—we've begun the night together, let's end it together,—and I'll show you one of the finest notions for committing murder on a scale of real magnificence you ever dreamed of. I should like to make use of it to show my feelings towards the supposititious Jones,—he'd know what I felt for him when once he had been introduced to it.'

Percy went with me without a word. He had not had much to drink, but it had been too much for him, and he was in a condition of maundering sentimentality. I got him into a cab. We dashed along Piccadilly.

He was silent, and sat looking in front of him with an air of vacuous sullenness which ill-became his cast of countenance. I bade the cabman pass though Lowndes Square. As we passed the Apostle's I pulled him up. I pointed out the place to Woodville.

'You see, Percy, that's Lessingham's house!—that's the house of the man who went away with Marjorie!'

'Yes.' Words came from him slowly, with a quite unnecessary stress on each. 'Because he made a speech.—I'd like to make a speech.—One day I'll make a speech.'

'Because he made a speech,—only that, and nothing more! When a man speaks with an Apostle's tongue, he can witch any woman in the land.—Hallo, who's that?—Lessingham, is that you?'

I saw, or thought I saw, someone, or something, glide up the steps, and withdraw into the shadow of the doorway, as if unwilling to be seen. When I hailed no one answered. I called again.

'Don't be shy, my friend!'

I sprang out of the cab, ran across the pavement, and up the steps. To my surprise, there was no one in the doorway. It seemed incredible, but the place was empty. I felt about me with my hands, as if I had been playing at blind man's buff, and grasped at vacancy. I came down a step or two.

'Ostensibly, there's a vacuum,—which nature abhors.—I say, driver, didn't you see someone come up the steps?'

'I thought I did, sir,—I could have sworn I did.'

'So could I.—It's very odd.'

'Perhaps whoever it was has gone into the 'ouse, sir.'

'I don't see how. We should have heard the door open, if we hadn't seen it,—and we should have seen it, it's not so dark as that.—I've half a mind to ring the bell and inquire.'

'I shouldn't do that if I was you, sir,—you jump in, and I'll get along. This is Mr Lessingham's,—the great Mr Lessingham's.'

I believe the cabman thought that I was drunk,—and not respectable enough to claim acquaintance with the great Mr Lessingham.

'Wake up, Woodville! Do you know I believe there's some mystery about this place,—I feel assured of it. I feel as if I were in the presence of something uncanny,—something which I can neither see, nor touch, nor hear.'

The cabman bent down from his seat, wheedling me.

'Jump in, sir, and we'll be getting along.'

I jumped in, and we got along,—but not far. Before we had gone a dozen yards, I was out again, without troubling the driver to stop. He pulled up, aggrieved.

'Well, sir, what's the matter now? You'll be damaging yourself before you've done, and then you'll be blaming me.'

I had caught sight of a cat crouching in the shadow of the railings,—a black one. That cat was my quarry. Either the creature was unusually sleepy, or slow, or stupid, or it had lost its wits—which a cat seldom does lose!—anyhow, without making an attempt to escape it allowed me to grab it by the nape of the neck.

So soon as we were inside my laboratory, I put the cat into my glass box. Percy stared.

'What have you put it there for?'

'That, my dear Percy, is what you are shortly about to see. You are about to be the witness of an experiment which, to a legislator—such as you are!—ought to be of the greatest possible interest. I am going to demonstrate, on a small scale, the action of the force which, on a large scale, I propose to employ on behalf of my native land.'

He showed no signs of being interested. Sinking into a chair, he recommenced his wearisome reiteration.

'I hate cats!—Do let it go!—I'm always miserable when there's a cat in the room.'

'Nonsense,—that's your fancy! What you want's a taste of whisky—you'll be as chirpy as a cricket.'

'I don't want anything more to drink!—I've had too much already!'

I paid no heed to what he said. I poured two stiff doses into a couple of tumblers. Without seeming to be aware of what it was that he was doing he disposed of the better half of the one I gave him at a draught. Putting his glass upon the table, he dropped his head upon his hands, and groaned.

'What would Marjorie think of me if she saw me now?'

'Think?—nothing. Why should she think of a man like you, when she has so much better fish to fry?'

'I'm feeling frightfully ill!—I'll be drunk before I've done!'

'Then be drunk!—only, for gracious sake, be lively drunk, not deadly doleful.—Cheer up, Percy!' I clapped him on the shoulder,—almost knocking him off his seat on to the floor. 'I am now going to show you that little experiment of which I was speaking!—You see that cat?'

'Of course I see it!—the beast!—I wish you'd let it go!'

'Why should I let it go?—Do you know whose cat that is? That cat's Paul Lessingham's.'

'Paul Lessingham's?'

'Yes, Paul Lessingham's,—the man who made the speech,—the man whom Marjorie went away with.'

'How do you know it's his?'

'I don't know it is, but I believe it is,—I choose to believe it is!—I intend to believe it is!—It was outside his house, therefore it's his cat,—that's how I argue. I can't get Lessingham inside that box, so I get his cat instead.'

'Whatever for?'

'You shall see.—You observe how happy it is?'

'It don't seem happy.'

'We've all our ways of seeming happy,—that's its way.'

The creature was behaving like a cat gone mad, dashing itself against the sides of its glass prison, leaping to and fro, and from side to side, squealing with rage, or with terror, or with both. Perhaps it foresaw what was coming,—there is no fathoming the intelligence of what we call the lower animals.

'It's a funny way.'

'We some of us have funny ways, beside cats. Now, attention! Observe this little toy,—you've seen something of its kind before. It's a spring gun; you pull the spring—drop the charge into the barrel—release the spring—and the charge is fired. I'll unlock this safe, which is built into the wall. It's a letter lock, the combination just now, is "whisky,"—you see, that's a hint to you. You'll notice the safe is strongly made,—it's air-tight, fire-proof, the outer casing is of triple-plated drill-proof steel,—the contents are valuable—to me!—and devilish dangerous,—I'd pity the thief who, in his innocent ignorance, broke in to steal. Look inside,—you see it's full of balls,—glass balls, each in its own little separate nest; light as feathers; transparent,—you can see right through them. Here are a couple, like tiny pills. They contain neither dynamite, nor cordite, nor anything of the kind, yet, given a fair field and no favour, they'll work more mischief than all the explosives man has fashioned. Take hold of one—you say your heart is broken!—squeeze this under your nose—it wants but a gentle pressure—and in less time than no time you'll be in the land where they say there are no broken hearts.'

He shrunk back.

'I don't know what you're talking about.—I don't want the thing.—Take it away.'

'Think twice,—the chance may not recur.'

'I tell you I don't want it.'

'Sure?—Consider!'

'Of course I'm sure!'

'Then the cat shall have it.'

'Let the poor brute go!'

'The poor brute's going,—to the land which is so near, and yet so far. Once more, if you please, attention. Notice what I do with this toy gun. I pull back the spring; I insert this small glass pellet; I thrust the muzzle of the gun through the opening in the glass box which contains the Apostle's cat,—you'll observe it fits quite close, which, on the whole, is perhaps as well for us.—I am about to release the spring.—Close attention, please.—Notice the effect.'

'Atherton, let the brute go!'

'The brute's gone! I've released the spring—the pellet has been discharged—it has struck against the roof of the glass box—it has been broken by the contact,—and, hey presto! the cat lies dead,—and that in face of its nine lives. You perceive how still it is,—how still! Let's hope that, now, it's really happy. The cat which I choose to believe is Paul Lessingham's has received its quietus; in the morning I'll send it back to him, with my respectful compliments. He'll miss it if I don't.—Reflect! think of a huge bomb, filled with what we'll call Atherton's Magic Vapour, fired, say, from a hundred and twenty ton gun, bursting at a given elevation over the heads of an opposing force. Properly managed, in less than an instant of time, a hundred thousand men,—quite possibly more!—would drop down dead, as if smitten by the lightning of the skies. Isn't that something like a weapon, sir?'

'I'm not well!—I want to get away!—I wish I'd never come!'

That was all Woodville had to say.

'Rubbish!—You're adding to your stock of information every second, and, in these days, when a member of Parliament is supposed to know all about everything, information's the one thing wanted. Empty your glass, man,—that's the time of day for you!'

I handed him his tumbler. He drained what was left of its contents, then, in a fit of tipsy, childish temper he flung the tumbler from him. I had placed—carelessly enough—the second pellet within a foot of the edge of the table. The shock of the heavy beaker striking the board close to it, set it rolling. I was at the other side. I started forward to stop its motion, but I was too late. Before I could reach the crystal globule, it had fallen off the edge of the table on to the floor at Woodville's feet, and smashed in falling. As it smashed, he was looking down, wondering, no doubt, in his stupidity, what the pother was about,—for I was shouting, and making something of a clatter in my efforts to prevent the catastrophe which I saw was coming. On the instant, as the vapour secreted in the broken pellet gained access to the air, he fell forward on to his face. Rushing to him, I snatched his senseless body from the ground, and dragged it, staggeringly, towards the door which opened on to the yard. Flinging the door open, I got him into the open air.

As I did so, I found myself confronted by someone who stood outside. It was Lessingham's mysterious Egypto-Arabian friend, —my morning's visitor.

CHAPTER XVII.

MAGIC?—OR MIRACLE?

The passage into the yard from the electrically lit laboratory was a passage from brilliancy to gloom. The shrouded figure standing in the shadow, was like some object in a dream. My own senses reeled. It was only because I had resolutely held my breath, and kept my face averted that I had not succumbed to the fate which had overtaken Woodville. Had I been a moment longer in gaining the open air, it would have been too late. As it was, in placing Woodville on the ground, I stumbled over him. My senses left me. Even as they went I was conscious of exclaiming,—remembering the saying about the engineer being hoist by his own petard,

'Atherton's Magic Vapour!'

My sensations on returning to consciousness were curious. I found myself being supported in someone's arms, a stranger's face was bending over me, and the most extraordinary pair of eyes I had ever seen were looking into mine.

'Who the deuce are you?' I asked.

Then, understanding that it was my uninvited visitor, with scant ceremony I drew myself away from him. By the light which was streaming through the laboratory door I saw that Woodville was lying close beside me,—stark and still.

'Is he dead?' I cried. 'Percy!—speak, man!—it's not so bad with you as that!'

But it was pretty bad,—so bad that, as I bent down and looked at him, my heart beat uncomfortably fast lest it was as bad as it could be. His heart seemed still,—the vapour took effect directly on the cardiac centres. To revive their action, and that instantly, was indispensable. Yet my brain was in such a whirl that I could not even think of how to set about beginning. Had I been alone, it is more than probable Woodville would have died. As I stared at him, senselessly, aimlessly, the stranger, passing his arms beneath his body, extended himself at full length upon his motionless form. Putting his lips to Percy's, he seemed to be pumping life from his own body into the unconscious man's. As I gazed bewildered, surprised, presently there came a movement of Percy's body. His limbs twitched, as if he was in pain. By degrees, the motions became convulsive,—till on a sudden he bestirred himself to such effect that the stranger was rolled right off him. I bent down,—to find that the young gentleman's condition still seemed very far from satisfactory. There was a rigidity about the muscles of his face, a clamminess about his skin, a disagreeable suggestiveness about the way in which his teeth and the whites of his eyes were exposed, which was uncomfortable to contemplate.

The stranger must have seen what was passing through my mind,—not a very difficult thing to see. Pointing to the recumbent Percy, he said, with that queer foreign twang of his, which, whatever it had seemed like in the morning, sounded musical enough just then.

'All will be well with him.'

'I am not so sure.'

The stranger did not deign to answer. He was kneeling on one side of the victim of modern science, I on the other. Passing his hand to and fro in front of the unconscious countenance, as if by magic all semblance of discomfort vanished from Percy's features, and, to all appearances, he was placidly asleep.

'Have you hypnotised him?'

'What does it matter?'

If it was a case of hypnotism, it was very neatly done. The conditions were both unusual and trying, the effect produced seemed all that could be desired,—the change brought about in half a dozen seconds was quite remarkable. I began to be aware of a feeling of quasi-respect for Paul Lessingham's friend. His morals might be peculiar, and manners he might have none, but in this case, at any rate, the end seemed to have justified the means. He went on.

'He sleeps. When he awakes he will remember nothing that has been. Leave him,—the night is warm,—all will be well.'

As he said, the night was warm,—and it was dry. Percy would come to little harm by being allowed to enjoy, for a while, the pleasant breezes. So I acted on the stranger's advice, and left him lying in the yard, while I had a little interview with the impromptu physician.

CHAPTER XVIII.

THE APOTHEOSIS OF THE BEETLE

The laboratory door was closed. The stranger was standing a foot or two away from it. I was further within the room, and was subjecting him to as keen a scrutiny as circumstances permitted. Beyond doubt he was conscious of my observation, yet he bore himself with an air of indifference, which was suggestive of perfect unconcern. The fellow was oriental to the finger-tips,—that much was certain; yet in spite of a pretty wide personal knowledge of oriental people I could not make up my mind as to the exact part of the east from which he came. He was hardly an Arab, he was not a fellah,—he was not, unless I erred, a Mohammedan at all. There was something about him which was distinctly not Mussulmanic. So far as looks were concerned, he was not a flattering example of his race, whatever his race might be. The portentous size of his beak-like nose would have been, in itself, sufficient to damn him in any court of beauty. His lips were thick and shapeless,—and this, joined to another peculiarity in his appearance, seemed to suggest that, in his veins there ran more than a streak of negro blood. The peculiarity alluded to was his semblance of great age. As one eyed him one was reminded of the legends told of people who have been supposed to have retained something of their pristine vigour after having lived for centuries. As, however, one continued to gaze, one began to wonder if he really was so old as he seemed,—if, indeed, he was exceptionally old at all. Negroes, and especially negresses, are apt to age with extreme rapidity. Among coloured folk one sometimes encounters women whose faces seem to have been lined by the passage of centuries, yet whose actual tale of years would entitle them to regard themselves, here in England, as in the prime of life. The senility of the fellow's countenance, besides, was contradicted by the juvenescence of his eyes. No really old man could have had eyes like that. They were curiously shaped, reminding me of the elongated, faceted eyes of some queer creature, with whose appearance I was familiar, although I could not, at the instant, recall its name. They glowed not only with the force and fire, but, also, with the frenzy of youth. More uncanny-looking eyes I had never encountered,—their possessor could not be, in any sense of the word, a clubable person. Owing, probably, to some peculiar formation of the optic-nerve one felt, as one met his gaze, that he was looking right through you. More obvious danger signals never yet were placed in a creature's head. The individual who, having once caught sight of him, still sought to cultivate their owner's acquaintance, had only himself to thank if the very worst results of frequenting evil company promptly ensued.

It happens that I am myself endowed with an unusual tenacity of vision. I could, for instance, easily outstare any man I ever met. Yet, as I continued to stare at this man, I was conscious that it was only by an effort of will that I was able to resist a baleful something which seemed to be passing from his eyes to mine. It might have been imagination, but, in that sense, I am not an imaginative man; and, if it was, it was imagination of an unpleasantly vivid kind. I could understand how, in the case of a nervous, or a sensitive temperament, the fellow might exercise, by means of the peculiar quality of his glance alone, an influence of a most disastrous sort, which given an appropriate subject in the manifestation of its power might approach almost to the supernatural. If ever man was endowed with the traditional evil eye, in which Italians, among modern nations, are such profound believers, it was he.

When we had stared at each other for, I daresay, quite five minutes, I began to think I had had about enough of it. So, by way of breaking the ice, I put to him a question.

'May I ask how you found your way into my back yard?'

He did not reply in words, but, raising his hands he lowered them, palms downward, with a gesture which was peculiarly oriental.

'Indeed?—Is that so?—Your meaning may be lucidity itself to you, but, for my benefit, perhaps you would not mind translating it into words. Once more I ask, how did you find your way into my back yard?'

Again nothing but the gesture.

'Possibly you are not sufficiently acquainted with English manners and customs to be aware that you have placed yourself within reach of the pains and penalties of the law. Were I to call in the police you would find yourself in an awkward situation, —and, unless you are presently more explanatory, called in they will be.'

By way of answer he indulged in a distortion of the countenance which might have been meant for a smile,—and which seemed to suggest that he regarded the police with a contempt which was too great for words.

'Why do you laugh—do you think that being threatened with

the police is a joke? You are not likely to find it so.—Have you suddenly been bereft of the use of your tongue?'

He proved that he had not by using it.

'I have still the use of my tongue.'

'That, at least, is something. Perhaps, since the subject of how you got into my back yard seems to be a delicate one, you will tell me why you got there.'

'You know why I have come.'

'Pardon me if I appear to flatly contradict you, but that is precisely what I do not know.'

'You do know.'

'Do I?—Then, in that case, I presume that you are here for the reason which appears upon the surface,—to commit a felony.'

'You call me thief?'

'What else are you?'

'I am no thief.—You know why I have come.'

He raised his head a little. A look came into his eyes which I felt that I ought to understand, yet to the meaning of which I seemed, for the instant, to have mislaid the key. I shrugged my shoulders.

'I have come because you wanted me.'

'Because I wanted you!—On my word!—That's sublime!'

'All night you have wanted me,—do I not know? When she talked to you of him, and the blood boiled in your veins; when he spoke, and all the people listened, and you hated him, because he had honour in her eyes.'

I was startled. Either he meant what it appeared incredible that he could mean, or—there was confusion somewhere.

'Take my advice, my friend, and don't try to come the bunco-steerer over me,—I'm a bit in that line myself, you know.'

This time the score was mine,—he was puzzled.

'I know not what you talk of.'

'In that case, we're equal,—I know not what you talk of either.'

His manner, for him, was childlike and bland.

'What is it you do not know? This morning did I not say,—if you want me, then I come?'

'I fancy I have some faint recollection of your being so good as to say something of the kind, but—where's the application?'

'Do you not feel for him the same as I?'

'Who's the him?'

'Paul Lessingham.'

It was spoken quietly, but with a degree of—to put it gently—spitefulness which showed that at least the will to do the Apostle harm would not be lacking.

'And, pray, what is the common feeling which we have for him?'

'Hate.'

Plainly, with this gentleman, hate meant hate,—in the solid oriental sense. I should hardly have been surprised if the mere utterance of the words had seared his lips.

'I am by no means prepared to admit that I have this feeling which you attribute to me, but, even granting that I have, what then?'

'Those who hate are kin.'

'That, also, I should be slow to admit; but—to go a step farther—what has all this to do with your presence on my premises at this hour of the night?'

'You love her.' This time I did not ask him to supply the name,—being unwilling that it should be soiled by the traffic of his lips. 'She loves him,—that is not well. If you choose, she shall love you,—that will be well.'

'Indeed.—And pray how is this consummation which is so

devoutly to be desired to be brought about?'

'Put your hand into mine. Say that you wish it. It shall be done.'

Moving a step forward, he stretched out his hand towards me. I hesitated. There was that in the fellow's manner which, for the moment, had for me an unwholesome fascination. Memories flashed through my mind of stupid stories which have been told of compacts made with the devil. I almost felt as if I was standing in the actual presence of one of the powers of evil. I thought of my love for Marjorie,—which had revealed itself after all these years; of the delight of holding her in my arms, of feeling the pressure of her lips to mine. As my gaze met his, the lower side of what the conquest of this fair lady would mean, burned in my brain; fierce imaginings blazed before my eyes. To win her,—only to win her!

What nonsense he was talking! What empty brag it was! Suppose, just for the sake of the joke, I did put my hand in his, and did wish, right out, what it was plain he knew. If I wished, what harm would it do! It would be the purest jest. Out of his own mouth he would be confounded, for it was certain that nothing would come of it. Why should I not do it then?

I would act on his suggestion,—I would carry the thing right through. Already I was advancing towards him, when—I stopped. I don't know why. On the instant, my thoughts went off at a tangent.

What sort of a blackguard did I call myself that I should take a woman's name in vain for the sake of playing fool's tricks with such scum of the earth as the hideous vagabond in front of me,—and that the name of the woman whom I loved? Rage took hold of me.

'You hound!' I cried.

In my sudden passage from one mood to another, I was filled with the desire to shake the life half out of him. But so soon as I moved a step in his direction, intending war instead of peace, he altered the position of his hand, holding it out towards me as if forbidding my approach. Directly he did so, quite involuntarily, I pulled up dead,—as if my progress had been stayed by bars of iron and walls of steel.

For the moment, I was astonished to the verge of stupefaction. The sensation was peculiar. I was as incapable of advancing another inch in his direction as if I had lost the use of my limbs,—I was even incapable of attempting to attempt to advance. At first I could only stare and gape. Presently I began to have an inkling of what had happened.

The scoundrel had almost succeeded in hypnotising me.

That was a nice thing to happen to a man of my sort at my time of life. A shiver went down my back,—what might have occurred if I had not pulled up in time! What pranks might a creature of that character not have been disposed to play. It was the old story of the peril of playing with edged tools; I had made the dangerous mistake of underrating the enemy's strength. Evidently, in his own line, the fellow was altogether something out of the usual way.

I believe that even as it was he thought he had me. As I turned away, and leaned against the table at my back, I fancy that he shivered,—as if this proof of my being still my own master was unexpected. I was silent,—it took some seconds to enable me to recover from the shock of the discovery of the peril in which I had been standing. Then I resolved that I would endeavour to do something which should make me equal to this gentleman of many talents.

'Take my advice, my friend, and don't attempt to play that hankey pankey off on to me again.'

'I don't know what you talk of.'

'Don't lie to me,—or I'll burn you into ashes.'

Behind me was an electrical machine, giving an eighteen inch spark. It was set in motion by a lever fitted into the table, which I could easily reach from where I sat. As I spoke the visitor was treated to a little exhibition of electricity. The change in his bearing was amusing. He shook with terror. He salaamed down to the ground.

'My lord!—my lord!—have mercy, oh my lord!'

'Then you be careful, that's all. You may suppose yourself to be something of a magician, but it happens, unfortunately for you, that I can do a bit in that line myself,—perhaps I'm a trifle better at the game than you are. Especially as you have ventured into my stronghold, which contains magic enough to make a show of a hundred thousand such as you.'

Taking down a bottle from a shelf, I sprinkled a drop or two of its contents on the floor. Immediately flames arose, accompanied by a blinding vapour. It was a sufficiently simple illustration of one of the qualities of phosphorous-bromide, but its effect upon my visitor was as startling as it was unexpected. If I could believe the evidence of my own eyesight, in the very act of giving utterance to a scream of terror he disappeared, how, or why, or whither, there was nothing to show,—in his place, where he had been standing, there seemed to be a dim object of some sort in a state of frenzied agitation on the floor. The phosphorescent vapour was confusing; the lights appeared to be suddenly burning low; before I had sense enough to go and see if there was anything there, and, if so, what, the flames had vanished, the man himself had reappeared, and, prostrated on his knees, was salaaming in a condition of abject terror.

'My lord! my lord!' he whined. 'I entreat you, my lord, to use me as your slave!'

'I'll use you as my slave!' Whether he or I was the more agitated it would have been difficult to say,—but, at least, it would not have done to betray my feelings as he did his. 'Stand up!'

He stood up. I eyed him as he did with an interest which, so far as I was concerned, was of a distinctly new and original sort. Whether or not I had been the victim of an ocular delusion I could not be sure. It was incredible to suppose that he could have disappeared as he had seemed to disappear,—it was also incredible that I could have imagined his disappearance. If the thing had been a trick, I had not the faintest notion how it had been worked; and, if it was not a trick, then what was it? Was it something new in scientific marvels? Could he give me as much instruction in the qualities of unknown forces as I could him?

In the meanwhile he stood in an attitude of complete submission, with downcast eyes, and hands crossed upon his breast. I started to cross-examine him.

'I am going to ask you some questions. So long as you answer them promptly, truthfully, you will be safe. Otherwise you had best beware.'

'Ask, oh my lord.'

'What is the nature of your objection to Mr Lessingham?'

'Revenge.'

'What has he done to you that you should wish to be revenged on him?'

'It is the feud of the innocent blood.'

'What do you mean by that?'

'On his hands is the blood of my kin. It cries aloud for vengeance.'

'Who has he killed?'

'That, my lord, is for me,—and for him.'

'I see.—Am I to understand that you do not choose to answer me, and that I am again to use my—magic?'

I saw that he quivered.

'My lord, he has spilled the blood of her who has lain upon his breast.'

I hesitated. What he meant appeared clear enough. Perhaps it would be as well not to press for further details. The words pointed to what it might be courteous to call an Eastern Romance,—though it was hard to conceive of the Apostle figuring as the hero of such a theme. It was the old tale retold, that to the life of every man there is a background,—that it is precisely in the unlikeliest cases that the background's darkest. What would that penny-plain-and-twopence-coloured bogey, the Nonconformist Conscience, make of such a story if it were blazoned through the land. Would Paul not come down with a run?

'"Spilling blood" is a figure of speech; pretty, perhaps, but vague. If you mean that Mr Lessingham has been killing someone, your surest and most effectual revenge would be gained by an appeal to the law.'

'What has the Englishman's law to do with me?'

'If you can prove that he has been guilty of murder it would have a great deal to do with you. I assure you that at any rate, in that sense, the Englishman's law is no respecter of persons. Show him to be guilty, and it would hang Paul Lessingham as indifferently, and as cheerfully, as it would hang Bill Brown.'

'Is that so?'

'It is so, as, if you choose, you will be easily able to prove to your own entire satisfaction.'

He had raised his head, and was looking at something which he seemed to see in front of him with a maleficent glare in his sensitive eyes which it was not nice to see.

'He would be shamed?'

'Indeed he would be shamed.'

'Before all men?'

'Before all men,—and, I take it, before all women too.'

'And he would hang?'

'If shown to have been guilty of wilful murder,—yes.'

His hideous face was lighted up by a sort of diabolical exultation which made it, if that were possible, more hideous still. I had apparently given him a wrinkle which pleased him most consummately.

'Perhaps I will do that in the end,—in the end!' He opened his eyes to their widest limits, then shut them tight,—as if to gloat on the picture which his fancy painted. Then reopened them. 'In the meantime I will have vengeance in my own fashion. He knows already that the avenger is upon him,—he has good reason to know it. And through the days and the nights the knowledge shall be with him still, and it shall be to him as the bitterness of death,—aye, of many deaths. For he will know that escape there is none, and that for him there shall be no more sun in the sky, and that the terror shall be with him by night and by day, at his rising up and at his lying down, wherever his eyes shall turn it shall be there,—yet, behold, the sap and the juice of my vengeance is in this, in that though he shall be very sure that the days that are, are as the days of his death, yet shall he know that THE DEATH, THE GREAT DEATH, is coming—coming—and shall be on him—when I will!'

The fellow spoke like an inspired maniac. If he meant half what he said,—and if he did not then his looks and his tones belied him!—then a promising future bade fair to be in store for Mr Lessingham,—and, also, circumstances being as they were, for Marjorie. It was this latter reflection which gave me pause. Either this imprecatory fanatic would have to be disposed of, by Lessingham himself, or by someone acting on his behalf, and, so far as their power of doing mischief went, his big words proved empty windbags, or Marjorie would have to be warned that there was at least one passage in her suitor's life, into which, ere it was too late, it was advisable that inquiry should be made. To allow Marjorie to irrevocably link her fate with the Apostle's, without being first of all made aware that he was, to all intents and purposes, a haunted man—that was not to be thought of.

'You employ large phrases.'

My words cooled the other's heated blood. Once more his eyes were cast down, his hands crossed upon his breast.

'I crave my lord's pardon. My wound is ever new.'

'By the way, what was the secret history, this morning, of that little incident of the cockroach?'

He glanced up quickly.

'Cockroach?—I know not what you say.'

'Well,—was it beetle, then?'

'Beetle!'

He seemed, all at once, to have lost his voice,—the word was gasped.

'After you went we found, upon a sheet of paper, a capitally executed drawing of a beetle, which, I fancy, you must have left behind you,—Scarabaeus sacer, wasn't it?'

'I know not what you talk of.'

'Its discovery seemed to have quite a singular effect on Mr Lessingham. Now, why was that?'

'I know nothing.'

'Oh yes you do,—and, before you go, I mean to know something too.'

The man was trembling, looking this way and that, showing signs of marked discomfiture. That there was something about that ancient scarab, which figures so largely in the still unravelled tangles of the Egyptian mythologies, and the effect which the mere sight of its cartouch—for the drawing had resembled something of the kind—had had on such a seasoned vessel as Paul Lessingham, which might be well worth my finding out, I felt convinced,—the man's demeanour, on my recurring to the matter, told its own plain tale. I made up my mind, if possible, to probe the business to the bottom, then and there.

'Listen to me, my friend. I am a plain man, and I use plain speech,—it's a kind of hobby I have. You will give me the information I require, and that at once, or I will pit my magic against yours,—in which case I think it extremely probable that you will come off worst from the encounter.'

I reached out for the lever, and the exhibition of electricity recommenced. Immediately his tremors were redoubled.

'My lord, I know not of what you talk.'

'None of your lies for me.—Tell me why, at the sight of the thing on that sheet of paper, Paul Lessingham went green and yellow.'

'Ask him, my lord.'

'Probably, later on, that is what I shall do. In the meantime, I am asking you. Answer,—or look out for squalls.'

The electrical exhibition was going on. He was glaring at it as if he wished that it would stop. As if ashamed of his cowardice, plainly, on a sudden, he made a desperate effort to get the better of his fears,—and succeeded better than I had expected or desired. He drew himself up with what, in him, amounted to an air of dignity.

'I am a child of Isis!'

It struck me that he made this remark, not so much to impress me, as with a view of elevating his own low spirits.

'Are you?—Then, in that case, I regret that I am unable to congratulate the lady on her offspring.'

When I said that, a ring came into his voice which I had not heard before.

'Silence!—You know not of what you speak!—I warn you, as I warned Paul Lessingham, be careful not to go too far. Be not like him,—heed my warning.'

'What is it I am being warned against,—the beetle?'

'Yes,—the beetle!'

Were I upon oath, and this statement being made, in the presence of witnesses, say, in a solicitor's office, I standing in fear of pains and penalties, I think that, at this point, I should leave the paper blank. No man likes to own himself a fool, or that he ever was a fool,—and ever since I have been wondering whether, on that occasion, that 'child of Isis' did, or did not, play the fool with me. His performance was realistic enough at the time, heaven knows. But, as it gets farther and farther away, I ask myself, more and more confidently, as time effluxes, whether, after all, it was not clever juggling,—superhumanly clever juggling, if you will; that, and nothing more. If it was something more, then, with a vengeance! there is more in heaven and earth than is dreamed of in our philosophy. The mere possibility opens vistas which the sane mind fears to contemplate.

Since, then, I am not on oath, and, should I fall short of verbal accuracy, I do not need to fear the engines of the law, what seemed to happen was this.

He was standing within about ten feet of where I leaned against the edge of the table. The light was full on, so that it was difficult to suppose that I could make a mistake as to what took place in front of me. As he replied to my mocking allusion to the beetle by echoing my own words, he vanished,—or, rather, I saw him taking a different shape before my eyes. His loose draperies all fell off him, and, as they were in the very act of falling, there issued, or there seemed to issue out of them, a monstrous creature of the beetle tribe,—the man himself was gone. On the point of size I wish to make myself clear. My impression, when I saw it first, was that it was as large as the man had been, and that it was, in some way, standing up on end, the legs towards me. But, the moment it came in view, it began to dwindle, and that so rapidly that, in a couple of seconds at most, a little heap of drapery was lying on the floor, on which was a truly astonishing example of the coleoptera. It appeared to be a beetle. It was, perhaps, six or seven inches high, and about a foot in length. Its scales were of a vivid golden green. I could distinctly see where the wings were sheathed along the back, and, as they seemed to be slightly agitated, I looked, every moment, to see them opened, and the thing take wing.

I was so astonished,—as who would not have been?—that for

an appreciable space of time I was practically in a state of stupefaction. I could do nothing but stare. I was acquainted with the legendary transmigrations of Isis, and with the story of the beetle which issues from the woman's womb through all eternity, and with the other pretty tales, but this, of which I was an actual spectator, was something new, even in legends. If the man, with whom I had just been speaking, was gone, where had he gone to? If this glittering creature was there, in his stead, whence had it come?

I do protest this much, that, after the first shock of surprise had passed, I retained my presence of mind. I felt as an investigator might feel, who has stumbled, haphazard, on some astounding, some epoch-making, discovery. I was conscious that I should have to make the best use of my mental faculties if I was to take full advantage of so astonishing an accident. I kept my glance riveted on the creature, with the idea of photographing it on my brain. I believe that if it were possible to take a retinal print—which it some day will be—you would have a perfect picture of what it was I saw. Beyond doubt it was a lamellicorn, one of the copridae. With the one exception of its monstrous size, there were the characteristics in plain view;—the convex body, the large head, the projecting clypeus. More, its smooth head and throat seemed to suggest that it was a female. Equally beyond a doubt, apart from its size, there were unusual features present too. The eyes were not only unwontedly conspicuous, they gleamed as if they were lighted by internal flames,—in some indescribable fashion they reminded me of my vanished visitor. The colouring was superb, and the creature appeared to have the chameleonlike faculty of lightening and darkening the shades at will. Its not least curious feature was its restlessness. It was in a state of continual agitation; and, as if it resented my inspection, the more I looked at it the more its agitation grew. As I have said, I expected every moment to see it take wing and circle through the air.

All the while I was casting about in my mind as to what means I could use to effect its capture. I did think of killing it, and, on the whole, I rather wish that I had at any rate attempted slaughter,—there were dozens of things, lying ready to my hand, any one of which would have severely tried its constitution;—but, on the spur of the moment, the only method of taking it alive which occurred to me, was to pop over it a big tin canister which had contained soda-lime. This canister was on the floor to my left. I moved towards it, as nonchalantly as I could, keeping an eye on that shining wonder all the time. Directly I moved, its agitation perceptibly increased,—it was, so to speak, all one whirr of tremblement; it scintillated, as if its coloured scales had been so many prisms; it began to unsheath its wings, as if it had finally decided that it would make use of them. Picking up the tin, disembarrassing it of its lid, I sprang towards my intended victim. Its wings opened wide; obviously it was about to rise; but it was too late. Before it had cleared the ground, the tin was over it.

It remained over it, however, for an instant only. I had stumbled, in my haste, and, in my effort to save myself from falling face foremost on to the floor, I was compelled to remove my hands from the tin. Before I was able to replace them, the tin was sent flying, and, while I was still partially recumbent, within eighteen inches of me, that beetle swelled and swelled, until it had assumed its former portentous dimensions, when, as it seemed, it was enveloped by a human shape, and in less time than no time, there stood in front of me, naked from top to toe, my truly versatile oriental friend. One startling fact nudity revealed,—that I had been egregiously mistaken on the question of sex. My visitor was not a man, but a woman, and, judging from the brief glimpse which I had of her body, by no means old or ill-shaped either.

If that transformation was not a bewildering one, then two and two make five. The most level-headed scientist would temporarily have lost his mental equipoise on witnessing such a quick change as that within a span or two of his own nose I was not only witless, I was breathless too,—I could only gape. And, while I gaped, the woman, stooping down, picking up her draperies, began to huddle them on her anyhow,—and, also, to skedaddle towards the door which led into the yard. When I observed this last manoeuvre, to some extent I did rise to the requirements of the situation. Leaping up, I rushed to stay her flight.

'Stop!' I shouted.

But she was too quick for me. Ere I could reach her, she had opened the door, and was through it,—and, what was more, she had slammed it in my face. In my excitement, I did some fumbling with the handle. When, in my turn, I was in the yard, she was out of sight. I did fancy I saw a dim form disappearing over the wall at the further side, and I made for it as fast as I knew how. I clambered on to the wall, looking this way and that, but there was nothing and no one to be seen. I listened for the sound of retreating footsteps, but all was still. Apparently I had the entire neighbourhood to my own sweet self. My visitor had vanished. Time devoted to pursuit I felt would be time ill-spent.

As I returned across the yard, Woodville, who still was taking his rest under the open canopy of heaven, sat up. Seemingly my approach had roused him out of slumber. At sight of me he rubbed his eyes, and yawned, and blinked.

'I say,' he remarked, not at all unreasonably, 'where am I?'

'You're on holy—or on haunted ground,—hang me if I quite know which!—but that's where you are, my boy.'

'By Jove!—I am feeling queer!—I have got a headache, don't you know.'

'I shouldn't be in the least surprised at anything you have, or haven't,—I'm beyond surprise. It's a drop of whisky you are wanting,—and what I'm wanting too,—only, for goodness sake, drop me none of your drops! Mine is a case for a bottle at the least.'

I put my arm through his, and went with him into the laboratory. And, when we were in, I shut, and locked, and barred the door.

CHAPTER XIX.

THE LADY RAGES

Dora Grayling stood in the doorway.

'I told your servant he need not trouble to show me in,—and I've come without my aunt. I hope I'm not intruding.'

She was—confoundedly; and it was on the tip of my tongue to tell her so. She came into the room, with twinkling eyes, looking radiantly happy,—that sort of look which makes even a plain young woman prepossessing.

'Am I intruding?—I believe I am.'

She held out her hand, while she was still a dozen feet away, and when I did not at once dash forward to make a clutch at it, she shook her head and made a little mouth at me.

'What's the matter with you?—Aren't you well?'

I was not well,—I was very far from well. I was as unwell as I could be without being positively ill, and any person of common discernment would have perceived it at a glance. At the same time I was not going to admit anything of the kind to her.

'Thank you,—I am perfectly well.'

'Then, if I were you, I would endeavour to become imperfectly well; a little imperfection in that direction might make you appear to more advantage.'

'I am afraid that that I am not one of those persons who ever do appear to much advantage,—did I not tell you so last night?'

'I believe you did say something of the kind,—it's very good of you to remember. Have you forgotten something else which you said to me last night?'

'You can hardly expect me to keep fresh in my memory all the follies of which my tongue is guilty.'

'Thank you.—That is quite enough.—Good-day.'

She turned as if to go.

'Miss Grayling!'

'Mr Atherton?'

'What's the matter?—What have I been saying now?'

'Last night you invited me to come and see you this morning,—is that one of the follies of which your tongue was guilty?'

The engagement had escaped my recollection—it is a fact!—and my face betrayed me.

'You had forgotten?' Her cheeks flamed; her eyes sparkled. 'You must pardon my stupidity for not having understood that the invitation was of that general kind which is never meant to be acted on.'

She was half way to the door before I stopped her,—I had to take her by the shoulder to do it.

'Miss Grayling!—You are hard on me.'

'I suppose I am.—Is anything harder than to be intruded on by an undesired, and unexpected, guest?'

'Now you are harder still.—If you knew what I have gone through since our conversation of last night, in your strength you would be merciful.'

'Indeed?—What have you gone through?'

I hesitated. What I actually had gone through I certainly did not propose to tell her. Other reasons apart I did not desire to seem madder than I admittedly am,—and I lacked sufficient plausibility to enable me to concoct, on the spur of the moment, a plain tale of the doings of my midnight visitor which would have suggested that the narrator was perfectly sane. So I fenced,—or tried to.

'For one thing,—I have had no sleep.'

I had not,—not one single wink. When I did get between the sheets, 'all night I lay in agony,' I suffered from that worst form of nightmare,—the nightmare of the man who is wide awake. There was continually before my fevered eyes the strange figure of that Nameless Thing. I had often smiled at tales of haunted folk,—here was I one of them. My feelings were not rendered more agreeable by a strengthening conviction that if I had only retained the normal attitude of a scientific observer I should, in all probability, have solved the mystery of my oriental friend, and that his example of the genus of copridae might have been pinned,—by a very large pin!—on a piece—a monstrous piece!—of cork. It was galling to reflect that he and I had played together a game of bluff,—a game at which civilisation was once more proved to be a failure.

She could not have seen all this in my face; but she saw something—because her own look softened.

'You do look tired.' She seemed to be casting about in her own mind for a cause. 'You have been worrying.' She glanced round the big laboratory. 'Have you been spending the night in this—wizard's cave?'

'Pretty well.'

'Oh!'

The monosyllable, as she uttered it, was big with meaning. Uninvited, she seated herself in an arm-chair, a huge old thing, of shagreen leather, which would have held half a dozen of her. Demure in it she looked, like an agreeable reminiscence, alive, and a little up-to-date, of the women of long ago. Her dove grey eyes seemed to perceive so much more than they cared to show.

'How is it that you have forgotten that you asked me to come?—didn't you mean it?'

'Of course I meant it.'

'Then how is it you've forgotten?'

'I didn't forget.'

'Don't tell fibs.—Something is the matter,—tell me what it is.—Is it that I am too early?'

'Nothing of the sort,—you couldn't be too early.'

'Thank you.—When you pay a compliment, even so neat an one as that, sometimes, you should look as if you meant it.—It is early,—I know it's early, but afterwards I want you to come to lunch. I told aunt that I would bring you back with me.'

'You are much better to me than I deserve.'

'Perhaps.' A tone came into her voice which was almost pathetic. 'I think that to some men women are almost better than they deserve. I don't know why. I suppose it pleases them. It is odd.' There was a different intonation,—a dryness. 'Have you forgotten what I came for?'

'Not a bit of it,—I am not quite the brute I seem. You came to see an illustration of that pleasant little fancy of mine for slaughtering my fellows. The fact is, I'm hardly in a mood for that just now,—I've been illustrating it too much already.'

'What do you mean?'

'Well, for one thing it's been murdering Lessingham's cat.'

'Mr Lessingham's cat?'

'Then it almost murdered Percy Woodville.'

'Mr Atherton!—I wish you wouldn't talk like that.'

'It's a fact. It was a question of a little matter in a wrong place, and, if it hadn't been for something very like a miracle, he'd be dead.'

'I wish you wouldn't have anything to do with such things—I hate them.'

I stared.

'Hate them?—I thought you'd come to see an illustration.'

'And pray what was your notion of an illustration?'

'Well, another cat would have had to be killed, at least.'

'And do you suppose that I would have sat still while a cat was being killed for my—edification?'

'It needn't necessarily have been a cat, but something would have had to be killed,—how are you going to illustrate the death-dealing propensities of a weapon of that sort without it?'

'Is it possible that you imagine that I came here to see something killed?'

'Then for what did you come?'

I do not know what there was about the question which was startling, but as soon as it was out, she went a fiery red.

'Because I was a fool.'

I was bewildered. Either she had got out of the wrong side of bed, or I had,—or we both had. Here she was, assailing me, hammer and tongs, so far as I could see, for absolutely nothing.

'You are pleased to be satirical at my expense.'

'I should not dare. Your detection of me would be so painfully rapid.'

I was in no mood for jangling. I turned a little away from her. Immediately she was at my elbow.

'Mr Atherton?'

'Miss Grayling.'

'Are you cross with me?'

'Why should I be? If it pleases you to laugh at my stupidity you are completely justified.'

'But you are not stupid.'

'No?—Nor you satirical.'

'You are not stupid,—you know you are not stupid; it was only stupidity on my part to pretend that you were.'

'It is very good of you to say so.—But I fear that I am an indifferent host. Although you would not care for an illustration, there may be other things which you might find amusing.'

'Why do you keep on snubbing me?'

'I keep on snubbing you!'

'You are always snubbing me,—you know you are. Some times I feel as if I hated you.'

'Miss Grayling!'

'I do! I do! I do!'

'After all, it is only natural.'

'That is how you talk,—as if I were a child, and you were,—oh I don't know what.—Well, Mr Atherton, I am sorry to be obliged to leave you. I have enjoyed my visit very much. I only hope I have not seemed too intrusive.'

She flounced—'flounce' was the only appropriate word!—out of the room before I could stop her. I caught her in the passage.

'Miss Grayling, I entreat you—'

'Pray do not entreat me, Mr Atherton.' Standing still she turned to me. 'I would rather show myself to the door as I showed myself in, but, if that is impossible, might I ask you not to speak to me between this and the street?'

The hint was broad enough, even for me. I escorted her through the hall without a word,—in perfect silence she shook the dust of my abode from off her feet.

I had made a pretty mess of things. I felt it as I stood on the top of the steps and watched her going,—she was walking off at four miles an hour; I had not even ventured to ask to be allowed to call a hansom.

It was beginning to occur to me that this was a case in which another blow upon the river might be, to say the least of it, advisable—and I was just returning into the house with the intention of putting myself into my flannels, when a cab drew up, and old Lindon got out of it.

CHAPTER XX.

A HEAVY FATHER

Mr Lindon was excited,—there is no mistaking it when he is, because with him excitement means perspiration, and as soon as he was out of the cab he took off his hat and began to wipe the lining.

'Atherton, I want to speak to you—most particularly—somewhere in private.'

I took him into my laboratory. It is my rule to take no one there; it is a workshop, not a playroom,—the place is private; but, recently, my rules had become dead letters. Directly he was inside, Lindon began puffing and stewing, wiping his forehead, throwing out his chest, as if he were oppressed by a sense of his own importance. Then he started off talking at the top of his voice,—and it is not a low one either.

'Atherton, I—I've always looked on you as a—a kind of a son.'

'That's very kind of you.'

'I've always regarded you as a—a level-headed fellow; a man from whom sound advice can be obtained when sound advice—is—is most to be desired.'

'That also is very kind of you.'

'And therefore I make no apology for coming to you at—at what may be regarded as a—a strictly domestic crisis; at a moment in the history of the Lindons when delicacy and common sense are—are essentially required.'

This time I contented myself with nodding. Already I perceived what was coming; somehow, when I am with a man I feel so much more clear-headed than I do when I am with a woman,—realise so much better the nature of the ground on which I am standing.

'What do you know of this man Lessingham?'

I knew it was coming.

'What all the world knows.'

'And what does all the world know of him?—I ask you that! A

flashy, plausible, shallow-pated, carpet-bagger,—that is what all the world knows of him. The man's a political adventurer,—he snatches a precarious, and criminal, notoriety, by trading on the follies of his fellow-countrymen. He is devoid of decency, destitute of principle, and impervious to all the feelings of a gentleman. What do you know of him besides this?'

'I am not prepared to admit that I do know that.'

'Oh yes you do!—don't talk nonsense!—you choose to screen the fellow! I say what I mean,—I always have said, and I always shall say.—What do you know of him outside politics,—of his family—of his private life?'

'Well,—not very much.'

'Of course you don't!—nor does anybody else! The man's a mushroom,—or a toadstool, rather!—sprung up in the course of a single night, apparently out of some dirty ditch.—Why, sir, not only is he without ordinary intelligence, he is even without a Brummagen substitute for manners.'

He had worked himself into a state of heat in which his countenance presented a not too agreeable assortment of scarlets and purples. He flung himself into a chair, threw his coat wide open, and his arms too, and started off again.

'The family of the Lindons is, at this moment, represented by a—a young woman,—by my daughter, sir. She represents me, and it's her duty to represent me adequately—adequately, sir! And what's more, between ourselves, sir, it's her duty to marry. My property's my own, and I wouldn't have it pass to either of my confounded brothers on any account. They're next door to fools, and—and they don't represent me in any possible sense of the word. My daughter, sir, can marry whom she pleases,—whom she pleases! There's no one in England, peer or commoner, who would not esteem it an honour to have her for his wife—I've told her so,—yes, sir, I've told her, though you—you'd think that she, of all people in the world, wouldn't require telling. Yet what do you think she does? She—she actually carries on what I—I can't help calling a—a compromising acquaintance with this man Lessingham!'

'No!'

'But I say yes!—and I wish to heaven I didn't. I—I've warned her against the scoundrel more than once; I—I've told her to cut him dead. And yet, as—as you saw yourself, last night, in—in the face of the assembled House of Commons, after that twaddling clap-trap speech of his, in which there was not one sound sentiment, nor an idea which—which would hold water, she positively went away with him, in—in the most ostentatious and—and disgraceful fashion, on—on his arm, and—and actually snubbed her father.—It is monstrous that a parent—a father!—should be subjected to such treatment by his child.'

The poor old boy polished his brow with his pocket-handkerchief.

'When I got home I—I told her what I thought of her, I promise you that,—and I told her what I thought of him,—I didn't mince my words with her. There are occasions when plain speaking is demanded,—and that was one. I positively forbade her to speak to the fellow again, or to recognise him if she met him in the street. I pointed out to her, with perfect candour, that the fellow was an infernal scoundrel,—that and nothing else!—and that he would bring disgrace on whoever came into contact with him, even with the end of a barge pole.—And what do you think she said?'

'She promised to obey you, I make no doubt.'

'Did she, sir!—By gad, did she!—That shows how much you know her!—She said, and, by gad, by her manner, and—and the way she went on, you'd—you'd have thought that she was the parent and I was the child—she said that I—I grieved her, that she was disappointed in me, that times have changed,—yes, sir, she said that times have changed!—that, nowadays, parents weren't Russian autocrats—no, sir, not Russian autocrats!—that—that she was sorry she couldn't oblige me,—yes, sir, that was how she put it,—she was sorry she couldn't oblige me, but it was altogether out of the question to suppose that she could put a period to a friendship which she valued, simply on account of—of my unreasonable prejudices,—and—and—and, in short, she—she told me to go the devil, sir!'

'And did you—'

I was on the point of asking him if he went,—but I checked myself in time.

'Let us look at the matter as men of the world. What do you know against Lessingham, apart from his politics?'

'That's just it,—I know nothing.'

'In a sense, isn't that in his favour?'

'I don't see how you make that out. I—I don't mind telling you that I—I've had inquiries made. He's not been in the House six years—this is his second Parliament—he's jumped up like a Jack-in-the-box. His first constituency was Harwich—they've got him still, and much good may he do 'em!—but how he came to stand for the place,—or who, or what, or where he was before he stood for the place, no one seems to have the faintest notion.'

'Hasn't he been a great traveller?'

'I never heard of it.'

'Not in the East?'

'Has he told you so?'

'No,—I was only wondering. Well, it seems to me that to find out that nothing is known against him is something in his favour!'

'My dear Sydney, don't talk nonsense. What it proves is simply,—that he's a nothing and a nobody. Had he been anything or anyone, something would have been known about him, either for or against. I don't want my daughter to marry a man who—who—who's shot up through a trap, simply because nothing is known against him. Ha-hang me, if I wouldn't ten times sooner she should marry you.'

When he said that, my heart leaped in my bosom. I had to turn away.

'I am afraid that is out of the question.'

He stopped in his tramping, and looked at me askance.

'Why?'

I felt that, if I was not careful, I should be done for,—and, probably, in his present mood, Marjorie too.

'My dear Lindon, I cannot tell you how grateful I am to you for your suggestion, but I can only repeat that—unfortunately, anything of the kind is out of the question.'

'I don't see why.'

'Perhaps not.'

'You—you're a pretty lot, upon my word!'

'I'm afraid we are.'

'I—I want you to tell her that Lessingham is a damned scoundrel.'

'I see.—But I would suggest that if I am to use the influence with which you credit me to the best advantage, or to preserve a shred of it, I had hardly better state the fact quite so bluntly as that.'

'I don't care how you state it,—state it as you like. Only—only I want you to soak her mind with a loathing of the fellow; I—I—I want you to paint him in his true colours; in—in—in fact, I—I want you to choke him off.'

While he still struggled with his words, and with the perspiration on his brow, Edwards entered. I turned to him.

'What is it?'

'Miss Lindon, sir, wishes to see you particularly, and at once.'

At that moment I found the announcement a trifle perplexing,—it delighted Lindon. He began to stutter and to stammer.

'T-the very thing!—c-couldn't have been better!—show her in here! H-hide me somewhere,—I don't care where,—behind that screen! Y-you use your influence with her;—g-give her a good talking to;—t-tell her what I've told you; and at—at the critical moment I'll come in, and then—then if we can't manage her between us, it'll be a wonder.'

The proposition staggered me.

'But, my dear Mr Lindon, I fear that I cannot—'

He cut me short.

'Here she comes!'

Ere I could stop him he was behind the screen,—I had not seen him move with such agility before!—and before I could expostulate Marjorie was in the room. Something which was in her bearing, in her face, in her eyes, quickened the beating of my pulses,—she looked as if something had come into her life, and taken the joy clean out of it.

CHAPTER XXI.

THE TERROR IN THE NIGHT

'Sydney!' she cried, 'I'm so glad that I can see you!'

She might be,—but, at that moment, I could scarcely assert that I was a sharer of her joy.

'I told you that if trouble overtook me I should come to you, and—I'm in trouble now. Such strange trouble.'

So was I,—and in perplexity as well. An idea occurred to me,—I would outwit her eavesdropping father.

'Come with me into the house,—tell me all about it there.'

She refused to budge.

'No,—I will tell you all about it here.' She looked about her,—as it struck me queerly. 'This is just the sort of place in which to unfold a tale like mine. It looks uncanny.'

'But—'

'"But me no buts!" Sydney, don't torture me,—let me stop here where I am,—don't you see I'm haunted?'

She had seated herself. Now she stood up, holding her hands out in front of her in a state of extraordinary agitation, her manner as wild as her words.

'Why are you staring at me like that? Do you think I'm mad? —I wonder if I'm going mad.—Sydney, do people suddenly go mad? You're a bit of everything, you're a bit of a doctor too, feel my pulse,—there it is!—tell me if I'm ill!'

I felt her pulse,—it did not need its swift beating to inform me that fever of some sort was in her veins. I gave her something in a glass. She held it up to the level of her eyes.

'What's this?'

'It's a decoction of my own. You might not think it, but my brain sometimes gets into a whirl. I use it as a sedative. It will do you good.'

She drained the glass.

'It's done me good already,—I believe it has; that's being something like a doctor.—Well, Sydney, the storm has almost burst. Last night papa forbade me to speak to Paul Lessingham—by way of a prelude.'

'Exactly. Mr Lindon—'

'Yes, Mr Lindon,—that's papa. I fancy we almost quarrelled. I know papa said some surprising things,—but it's a way he has,—he's apt to say surprising things. He's the best father in the world, but—it's not in his nature to like a really clever person; your good high dried old Tory never can;—I've always thought that that's why he's so fond of you.'

'Thank you. I presume that is the reason, though it had not occurred to me before.'

Since her entry, I had, to the best of my ability, been turning the position over in my mind. I came to the conclusion that, all things considered, her father had probably as much right to be a sharer of his daughter's confidence as I had, even from the vantage of the screen,—and that for him to hear a few home truths proceeding from her lips might serve to clear the air. From such a clearance the lady would not be likely to come off worst. I had not the faintest inkling of what was the actual purport of her visit.

She started off, as it seemed to me, at a tangent.

'Did I tell you last night about what took place yesterday morning,—about the adventure of my finding the man?'

'Not a word.'

'I believe I meant to,—I'm half disposed to think he's brought me trouble. Isn't there some superstition about evil befalling whoever shelters a homeless stranger?'

'We'll hope not, for humanity's sake.'

'I fancy there is,—I feel sure there is.—Anyhow, listen to my story. Yesterday morning, before breakfast,—to be accurate, between eight and nine, I looked out of the window, and I saw a crowd in the street. I sent Peter out to see what was the matter. He came back and said there was a man in a fit. I went out to look at the man in the fit. I found, lying on the ground, in the centre of the crowd, a man who, but for the tattered remnants of what had apparently once been a cloak, would have been stark naked. He was covered with dust, and dirt, and blood,—a dreadful sight. As you know, I have had my smattering of instruction in First Aid to the Injured, and that kind of thing, so, as no one else seemed to have any sense, and the man seemed as good as dead, I thought I would try my hand. Directly I knelt down beside him, what do you think he said?'

'Thank you.'

'Nonsense.—He said, in such a queer, hollow, croaking voice, "Paul Lessingham." I was dreadfully startled. To hear a perfect stranger, a man in his condition, utter that name in such a fashion—to me, of all people in the world!—took me aback. The policeman who was holding his head remarked, "That's the first time he's opened his mouth. I thought he was dead." He opened his mouth a second time. A convulsive movement went all over him, and he exclaimed, with the strangest earnestness, and so loudly that you might have heard him at the other end of the street, "Be warned, Paul Lessingham, be warned!" It was very silly of me, perhaps, but I cannot tell you how his words, and his manner—the two together—affected me.—Well, the long and the short of it was, that I had him taken into the house, and washed, and put to bed,—and I had the doctor sent for. The doctor could make nothing of it at all. He reported that the man seemed to be suffering from some sort of cataleptic seizure,—I could see that he thought it likely to turn out almost as interesting a case as I did.'

'Did you acquaint your father with the addition to his household?'

She looked at me, quizzically.

'You see, when one has such a father as mine one cannot tell him everything, at once. There are occasions on which one requires time.'

I felt that this would be wholesome hearing for old Lindon.

'Last night, after papa and I had exchanged our little courtesies,—which, it is to be hoped, were to papa's satisfaction, since they were not to be mine—I went to see the patient. I was told that he had neither eaten nor drunk, moved nor spoken. But, so soon as I approached his bed, he showed signs of agitation. He half raised himself upon his pillow, and he called out, as if he had been addressing some large assembly—I can't describe to you the dreadful something which was in his voice, and on his face,—"Paul Lessingham!—Beware!—The Beetle!"'

When she said that, I was startled.

'Are you sure those were the words he used?'

'Quite sure. Do you think I could mistake them,—especially after what has happened since? I hear them singing in my ears,—they haunt me all the time.'

She put her hands up to her face, as if to veil something from her eyes. I was becoming more and more convinced that there was something about the Apostle's connection with his Oriental friend which needed probing to the bottom.

'What sort of a man is he to look at, this patient of yours?'

I had my doubts as to the gentleman's identity,—which her words dissolved; only, however, to increase my mystification in another direction.

'He seems to be between thirty and forty. He has light hair, and straggling sandy whiskers. He is so thin as to be nothing but skin and bone,—the doctor says it's a case of starvation.'

'You say he has light hair, and sandy whiskers. Are you sure the whiskers are real?'

She opened her eyes.

'Of course they're real. Why shouldn't they be real?'

'Does he strike you as being a—foreigner?'

'Certainly not. He looks like an Englishman, and he speaks like one, and not, I should say, of the lowest class. It is true that there is a very curious, a weird, quality in his voice, what I have heard of it, but it is not un-English. If it is catalepsy he is suffering from, then it is a kind of catalepsy I never heard of. Have you ever seen a clairvoyant?' I nodded. 'He seems to me to be in a state of clairvoyance. Of course the doctor laughed when I told him so, but we know what doctors are, and I still believe that he is in some condition of the kind. When he said that last night he struck me as being under what those sort of people call "influence," and that whoever had him under influence was forcing him to speak against his will, for the words came from his lips as if they had been wrung from him in agony.'

Knowing what I did know, that struck me as being rather a

remarkable conclusion for her to have reached, by the exercise of her own unaided powers of intuition,—but I did not choose to let her know I thought so.

'My dear Marjorie!—you who pride yourself on having your imagination so strictly under control!—on suffering it to take no errant flights!'

'Is not the fact that I do so pride myself proof that I am not likely to make assertions wildly,—proof, at any rate, to you? Listen to me. When I left that unfortunate creature's room,—I had had a nurse sent for, I left him in her charge—and reached my own bedroom, I was possessed by a profound conviction that some appalling, intangible, but very real danger, was at that moment threatening Paul.'

'Remember,—you had had an exciting evening; and a discussion with your father. Your patient's words came as a climax.'

'That is what I told myself,—or, rather, that was what I tried to tell myself; because, in some extraordinary fashion, I had lost the command of my powers of reflection.'

'Precisely.'

'It was not precisely,—or, at least, it was not precisely in the sense you mean. You may laugh at me, Sydney, but I had an altogether indescribable feeling, a feeling which amounted to knowledge, that I was in the presence of the supernatural.'

'Nonsense!'

'It was not nonsense,—I wish it had been nonsense. As I have said, I was conscious, completely conscious, that some frightful peril was assailing Paul. I did not know what it was, but I did know that it was something altogether awful, of which merely to think was to shudder. I wanted to go to his assistance, I tried to, more than once; but I couldn't, and I knew that I couldn't,—I knew that I couldn't move as much as a finger to help him.—Stop,—let me finish!—I told myself that it was absurd, but it wouldn't do; absurd or not, there was the terror with me in the room. I knelt down, and I prayed, but the words wouldn't come. I tried to ask God to remove this burden from my brain, but my longings wouldn't shape themselves into words, and my tongue was palsied. I don't know how long I struggled, but, at last, I came to understand that, for some cause, God had chosen to leave me to fight the fight alone. So I got up, and undressed, and went to bed,—and that was the worst of all. I had sent my maid away in the first rush of my terror, afraid, and, I think, ashamed, to let her see my fear. Now I would have given anything to summon her back again, but I couldn't do it, I couldn't even ring the bell. So, as I say, I got into bed.'

She paused, as if to collect her thoughts. To listen to her words, and to think of the suffering which they meant to her, was almost more than I could endure. I would have thrown away the world to have been able to take her in my arms, and soothe her fears. I knew her to be, in general, the least hysterical of young women; little wont to become the prey of mere delusions; and, incredible though it sounded, I had an innate conviction that, even in its wildest periods, her story had some sort of basis in solid fact. What that basis amounted to, it would be my business, at any and every cost, quickly to determine.

'You know how you have always laughed at me because of my objection to—cockroaches, and how, in spring, the neighbourhood of May-bugs has always made me uneasy. As soon as I got into bed I felt that something of the kind was in the room.'

'Something of what kind?'

'Some kind of—beetle. I could hear the whirring of its wings; I could hear its droning in the air; I knew that it was hovering above my head; that it was coming lower and lower, nearer and nearer. I hid myself; I covered myself all over with the clothes,—then I felt it bumping against the coverlet. And, Sydney!' She drew closer. Her blanched cheeks and frightened eyes made my heart bleed. Her voice became but an echo of itself. 'It followed me.'

'Marjorie!'

'It got into the bed.'

'You imagined it.'

'I didn't imagine it. I heard it crawl along the sheets, till it found a way between them, and then it crawled towards me. And I felt it—against my face.—And it's there now.'

'Where?'

She raised the forefinger of her left hand.

'There!—Can't you hear it droning?'

She listened, intently. I listened too. Oddly enough, at that instant the droning of an insect did become audible.

'It's only a bee, child, which has found its way through the open window.'

'I wish it were only a bee, I wish it were.—Sydney, don't you feel as if you were in the presence of evil? Don't you want to get away from it, back into the presence of God?'

'Marjorie!'

'Pray, Sydney, pray!—I can't!—I don't know why, but I can't!'

She flung her arms about my neck, and pressed herself against me in paroxysmal agitation. The violence of her emotion bade fair to unman me too. It was so unlike Marjorie,—and I would have given my life to save her from a toothache. She kept repeating her own words,—as if she could not help it.

'Pray, Sydney, pray!'

At last I did as she wished me. At least, there is no harm in praying,—I never heard of its bringing hurt to anyone. I repeated aloud the Lord's Prayer,—the first time for I know not how long. As the divine sentences came from my lips, hesitatingly enough, I make no doubt, her tremors ceased. She became calmer. Until, as I reached the last great petition, 'Deliver us from evil,' she loosed her arms from about my neck, and dropped upon her knees, close to my feet. And she joined me in the closing words, as a sort of chorus.

'For Thine is the Kingdom, the Power, and the Glory, for ever and ever. Amen.'

When the prayer was ended, we both of us were still. She with her head bowed, and her hands clasped; and I with something tugging at my heart-strings which I had not felt there for many and many a year, almost as if it had been my mother's hand;—I daresay that sometimes she does stretch out her hand, from her place among the angels, to touch my heart-strings, and I know nothing of it all the while.

As the silence still continued, I chanced to glance up, and there was old Lindon peeping at us from his hiding-place behind the screen. The look of amazed perplexity which was on his big red face struck me with such a keen sense of the incongruous that it was all I could do to keep from laughter. Apparently the sight of us did nothing to lighten the fog which was in his brain, for he stammered out, in what was possibly intended for a whisper,

'Is—is she m-mad?'

The whisper,—if it was meant for a whisper—was more than sufficiently audible to catch his daughter's ears. She started—raised her head—sprang to her feet—turned—and saw her father.

'Papa!'

Immediately her sire was seized with an access of stuttering.

'W-w-what the d-devil's the—the m-m-meaning of this?'

Her utterance was clear enough,—I fancy her parent found it almost painfully clear.

'Rather it is for me to ask, what is the meaning of this! Is it possible, that, all the time, you have actually been concealed behind that—screen?'

Unless I am mistaken the old gentleman cowered before the directness of his daughter's gaze,—and endeavoured to conceal the fact by an explosion of passion.

'Do-don't you s-speak to me li-like that, you un-undutiful girl! I—I'm your father!'

'You certainly are my father; though I was unaware until now that my father was capable of playing the part of eavesdropper.'

Rage rendered him speechless,—or, at any rate, he chose to let us believe that that was the determining cause of his continuing silent. So Marjorie turned to me,—and, on the whole, I had rather she had not. Her manner was very different from what it had been just now,—it was more than civil, it was freezing.

'Am I to understand, Mr Atherton, that this has been done with your cognisance? That while you suffered me to pour out my heart to you unchecked, you were aware, all the time, that there was a listener behind the screen?'

I became keenly aware, on a sudden, that I had borne my

share in playing her a very shabby trick,—I should have liked to throw old Lindon through the window.

'The thing was not of my contriving. Had I had the opportunity I would have compelled Mr Lindon to face you when you came in. But your distress caused me to lose my balance. And you will do me the justice to remember that I endeavoured to induce you to come with me into another room.'

'But I do not seem to remember your hinting at there being any particular reason why I should have gone.'

'You never gave me a chance.'

'Sydney!—I had not thought you would have played me such a trick!'

When she said that—in such a tone!—the woman whom I loved!—I could have hammered my head against the wall. The hound I was to have treated her so scurvily!

Perceiving I was crushed she turned again to face her father, cool, calm, stately;—she was, on a sudden, once more, the Marjorie with whom I was familiar. The demeanour of parent and child was in striking contrast. If appearances went for aught, the odds were heavy that in any encounter which might be coming the senior would suffer.

'I hope, papa, that you are going to tell me that there has been some curious mistake, and that nothing was farther from your intention than to listen at a keyhole. What would you have thought—and said—if I had attempted to play the spy on you? And I have always understood that men were so particular on points of honour.'

Old Lindon was still hardly fit to do much else than splutter, —certainly not qualified to chop phrases with this sharp-tongued maiden.

'D-don't talk to me li-like that, girl!—I—I believe you're s-stark mad!' He turned to me. 'W-what was that tomfoolery she was talking to you about?'

'To what do you allude?'

'About a rub-rubbishing b-beetle, and g-goodness alone knows what,—d-diseased and m-morbid imagination,—rreared on the literature of the gutter!—I never thought that a child of mine could have s-sunk to such a depth!—Now, Atherton, I ask you to t-tell me frankly,—what do you think of a child who behaves as she has done? who t-takes a nameless vagabond into the house and con-conceals his presence from her father? And m-mark the sequel! even the vagabond warns her against the r-rascal Lessingham!—Now, Atherton, tell me what you think of a girl who behaves like that?' I shrugged my shoulders. 'I—I know very well what you d-do think of her,—don't be afraid to say it out because she's present.'

'No; Sydney, don't be afraid.'

I saw that her eyes were dancing,—in a manner of speaking, her looks brightened under the sunshine of her father's displeasure.

'Let's hear what you think of her as a—as a m-man of the world!'

'Pray, Sydney, do!'

'What you feel for her in your—your heart of hearts!'

'Yes, Sydney, what do you feel for me in your heart of hearts?'

The baggage beamed with heartless sweetness,—she was making a mock of me. Her father turned as if he would have rent her.

'D-don't you speak until you're spoken to! Atherton, I—I hope I'm not deceived in you; I—I hope you're the man I—I took you for; that you're willing and—and ready to play the part of a-a-an honest friend to this mis-misguided simpleton. T-this is not the time for mincing words, it—it's the time for candid speech. Tell this—this weak-minded young woman, right out, whether this man Lessingham is, or is not, a damned scoundrel.'

'Papa!—Do you really think that Sydney's opinion, or your opinion, is likely to alter facts?'

'Do you hear, Atherton, tell this wretched girl the truth!'

'My dear Mr Lindon, I have already told you that I know nothing either for or against Mr Lessingham except what is known to all the world.'

'Exactly,—and all the world knows him to be a miserable

adventurer who is scheming to entrap my daughter.'

'I am bound to say, since you press me, that your language appears to me to be unnecessarily strong.'

'Atherton, I—I'm ashamed of you!'

'You see, Sydney, even papa is ashamed of you; now you are outside the pale.—My dear papa, if you will allow me to speak, I will tell you what I know to be the truth, the whole truth, and nothing but the truth.—That Mr Lessingham is a man with great gifts goes without saying,—permit me, papa! He is a man of genius. He is a man of honour. He is a man of the loftiest ambitions, of the highest aims. He has dedicated his whole life to the improvement of the conditions amidst which the less fortunate of his fellow countrymen are at present compelled to exist. That seems to me to be an object well worth having. He has asked me to share his life-work, and I have told him that I will; when, and where, and how, he wants me to. And I will. I do not suppose his life has been free from peccadilloes. I have no delusion on the point. What man's life has? Who among men can claim to be without sin? Even the members of our highest families sometimes hide behind screens. But I know that he is, at least, as good a man as I ever met, I am persuaded that I shall never meet a better; and I thank God that I have found favour in his eyes.—Good-bye, Sydney.—I suppose I shall see you again, papa.'

With the merest inclination of her head to both of us she straightway left the room. Lindon would have stopped her.

'S-stay, y-y-y-you—' he stuttered.

But I caught him by the arm.

'If you will be advised by me, you will let her go. No good purpose will be served by a multiplication of words.'

'Atherton, I—I'm disappointed in you. You—you haven't behaved as I expected. I—I haven't received from you the assistance which I looked for.'

'My dear Lindon, it seems to me that your method of diverting the young lady from the path which she has set herself to tread is calculated to send her furiously along it.'

'C-confound the women! c-confound the women! I don't mind telling you, in c-confidence, that at—at times, her mother was the devil, and I'll be—I'll be hanged if her daughter isn't worse.—What was the tomfoolery she was talking to you about? Is she mad?'

'No,—I don't think she's mad.'

'I never heard such stuff, it made my blood run cold to hear her. What's the matter with the girl?'

'Well,—you must excuse my saying that I don't fancy you quite understand women.'

'I—I don't,—and I—I—I don't want to either.'

I hesitated; then resolved on a taradiddle,—in Marjorie's interest.

'Marjorie is high-strung,—extremely sensitive. Her imagination is quickly aflame. Perhaps, last night, you drove her as far as was safe. You heard for yourself how, in consequence, she suffered. You don't want people to say you have driven her into a lunatic asylum.'

'I—good heavens, no! I—I'll send for the doctor directly I get home,—I—I'll have the best opinion in town.'

'You'll do nothing of the kind,—you'll only make her worse. What you have to do is to be patient with her, and let her have peace.—As for this affair of Lessingham's, I have a suspicion that it may not be all such plain sailing as she supposes.'

'What do you mean?'

'I mean nothing. I only wish you to understand that until you hear from me again you had better let matters slide. Give the girl her head.'

'Give the girl her head! H-haven't I—I g-given the g-girl her h-head all her l-life!' He looked at his watch. 'Why, the day's half gone!' He began scurrying towards the front door, I following at his heels. 'I've got a committee meeting on at the club,—m-most important! For weeks they've been giving us the worst food you ever tasted in your life,—p-played havoc with my digestion, and I—I'm going to tell them if—things aren't changed, they—they'll have to pay my doctor's bills.—As for that man, Lessingham—'

As he spoke, he himself opened the hall door, and there,

standing on the step was 'that man Lessingham' himself. Lindon was a picture. The Apostle was as cool as a cucumber. He held out his hand.

'Good morning, Mr Lindon. What delightful weather we are having.'

Lindon put his hand behind his back,—and behaved as stupidly as he very well could have done.

'You will understand, Mr Lessingham, that, in future, I don't know you, and that I shall decline to recognise you anywhere; and that what I say applies equally to any member of my family.'

With his hat very much on the back of his head he went down the steps like an inflated turkeycock.

CHAPTER XXII.

THE HAUNTED MAN

To have received the cut discourteous from his future father-in-law might have been the most commonplace of incidents,—Lessingham evinced not a trace of discomposure. So far as I could judge, he took no notice of the episode whatever, behaving exactly as if nothing had happened. He merely waited till Mr Lindon was well off the steps; then, turning to me, he placidly observed,

'Interrupting you again, you see.—May I?'

The sight of him had set up such a turmoil in my veins, that, for the moment, I could not trust myself to speak. I felt, acutely, that an explanation with him was, of all things, the thing most to be desired,—and that quickly. Providence could not have thrown him more opportunely in the way. If, before he went away, we did not understand each other a good deal more clearly, upon certain points, the fault should not be mine. Without a responsive word, turning on my heels, I led the way into the laboratory.

Whether he noticed anything peculiar in my demeanour, I could not tell. Within he looked about him with that purely facial smile, the sight of which had always engendered in me a certain distrust of him.

'Do you always receive visitors in here?'

'By no means.'

'What is this?'

Stooping down, he picked up something from the floor. It was a lady's purse,—a gorgeous affair, of crimson leather and gleaming gold. Whether it was Marjorie's or Miss Grayling's I could not tell. He watched me as I examined it.

'Is it yours?'

'No. It is not mine.'

Placing his hat and umbrella on one chair, he placed himself upon another,—very leisurely. Crossing his legs, laying his folded hands upon his knees, he sat and looked at me. I was quite conscious of his observation; but endured it in silence, being a little wishful that he should begin.

Presently he had, as I suppose, enough of looking at me, and spoke.

'Atherton, what is the matter with you?—Have I done something to offend you too?'

'Why do you ask?'

'Your manner seems a little singular.'

'You think so?'

'I do.'

'What have you come to see me about?'

'Just now, nothing.—I like to know where I stand.'

His manner was courteous, easy, even graceful. I was outmanoeuvred. I understood the man sufficiently well to be aware that when once he was on the defensive, the first blow would have to come from me. So I struck it.

'I, also, like to know where I stand.—Lessingham, I am aware, and you know that I am aware, that you have made certain overtures to Miss Lindon. That is a fact in which I am keenly interested.'

'As—how?'

'The Lindons and the Athertons are not the acquaintances of one generation only. Marjorie Lindon and I have been friends since childhood. She looks upon me as a brother—'

'As a brother?'

'As a brother.'

'Yes.'

'Mr Lindon regards me as a son. He has given me his confidence; as I believe you are aware, Marjorie has given me hers; and now I want you to give me yours.'

'What do you want to know?'

'I wish to explain my position before I say what I have to say, because I want you to understand me clearly.—I believe, honestly, that the thing I most desire in this world is to see Marjorie Lindon happy. If I thought she would be happy with you, I should say, God speed you both! and I should congratulate you with all my heart, because I think that you would have won the best girl in the whole world to be your wife.'

'I think so too.'

'But, before I did that, I should have to see, at least, some reasonable probability that she would be happy with you.'

'Why should she not?'

'Will you answer a question?'

'What is the question?'

'What is the story in your life of which you stand in such hideous terror?'

There was a perceptible pause before he answered.

'Explain yourself.'

'No explanation is needed,—you know perfectly well what I mean.'

'You credit me with miraculous acumen.'

'Don't juggle, Lessingham,—be frank!'

'The frankness should not be all on one side.—There is that in your frankness, although you may be unconscious of it, which some men might not unreasonably resent.'

'Do you resent it?'

'That depends. If you are arrogating to yourself the right to place yourself between Miss Lindon and me, I do resent it, strongly.'

'Answer my question!'

'I answer no question which is addressed to me in such a tone.'

He was as calm as you please. I recognised that already I was in peril of losing my temper,—which was not at all what I desired. I eyed him intently, he returning me look for look. His countenance betrayed no sign of a guilty conscience; I had not seen him more completely at his ease. He smiled,—facially, and also, as it seemed to me, a little derisively. I am bound to admit that his bearing showed not the faintest shadow of resentment, and that in his eyes there was a gentleness, a softness, which I had not observed in them before,—I could almost have suspected him of being sympathetic.

'In this matter, you must know, I stand in the place of Mr Lindon.'

'Well?'

'Surely you must understand that before anyone is allowed to think of marriage with Marjorie Lindon he will have to show that his past, as the advertisements have it, will bear the fullest investigation.'

'Is that so?—Will your past bear the fullest investigation?'

I winced.

'At any rate, it is known to all the world.'

'Is it?—Forgive me if I say, I doubt it. I doubt if, of any wise man, that can be said with truth. In all our lives there are episodes which we keep to ourselves.'

I felt that that was so true that, for the instant, I hardly knew what to say.

'But there are episodes and episodes, and when it comes to a man being haunted one draws the line.'

'Haunted?'

'As you are.'

He got up.

'Atherton, I think that I understand you, but I fear that you do not understand me.' He went to where a self-acting mercurial air-pump was standing on a shelf. 'What is this curious arrangement of glass tubes and bulbs?'

'I do not think that you do understand me, or you would know that I am in no mood to be trifled with.'

'Is it some kind of an exhauster?'

'My dear Lessingham, I am entirely at your service. I intend to have an answer to my question before you leave this room, but, in the meanwhile, your convenience is mine. There are some very interesting things here which you might care to see.'

'Marvellous, is it not, how the human intellect progresses,—from conquest unto conquest.'

'Among the ancients the progression had proceeded farther than with us.'

'In what respect?'

'For instance, in the affair of the Apotheosis of the Beetle;—I saw it take place last night.'

'Where?'

'Here,—within a few feet of where you are standing.'

'Are you serious?'

'Perfectly.'

'What did you see?'

'I saw the legendary Apotheosis of the Beetle performed, last night, before my eyes, with a gaudy magnificence at which the legends never hinted.'

'That is odd. I once thought that I saw something of the kind myself.'

'So I understand.'

'From whom?'

'From a friend of yours.'

'From a friend of mine?—Are you sure it was from a friend of mine?'

The man's attempt at coolness did him credit,—but it did not deceive me. That he thought I was endeavouring to bluff him out of his secret I perceived quite clearly; that it was a secret which he would only render with his life I was beginning to suspect. Had it not been for Marjorie, I should have cared nothing,—his affairs were his affairs; though I realised perfectly well that there was something about the man which, from the scientific explorer's point of view, might be well worth finding out. Still, as I say, if it had not been for Marjorie, I should have let it go; but, since she was so intimately concerned in it, I wondered more and more what it could be.

My attitude towards what is called the supernatural is an open one. That all things are possible I unhesitatingly believe,—I have, even in my short time, seen so many so-called impossibilities proved possible. That we know everything, I doubt;—that our great-great-great-great-grandsires, our forebears of thousands of years ago, of the extinct civilisations, knew more on some subjects than we do, I think is, at least, probable. All the legends can hardly be false.

Because men claimed to be able to do things in those days which we cannot do, and which we do not know how they did, we profess to think that their claims are finally dismissed by exclaiming—lies! But it is not so sure.

For my part, what I had seen I had seen. I had seen some devil's trick played before my very eyes. Some trick of the same sort seemed to have been played upon my Marjorie,—I repeat that I write 'my Marjorie' because, to me, she will always be 'my' Marjorie! It had driven her half out of her senses. As I looked at Lessingham, I seemed to see her at his side, as I had seen her not long ago, with her white, drawn face, and staring eyes, dumb with an agony of fear. Her life was bidding fair to be knit with his,—what Upas tree of horror was rooted in his very bones? The thought that her sweet purity was likely to be engulfed in a devil's slough in which he was wallowing was not to be endured. As I realised that the man was more than my match at the game which I was playing—in which such vital interests were at stake!—my hands itched to clutch him by the throat, and try another way.

Doubtless my face revealed my feelings, because, presently, he said,

'Are you aware how strangely you are looking at me, Atherton? Were my countenance a mirror I think you would be surprised to see in it your own.'

I drew back from him, — I daresay, sullenly.

'Not so surprised as, yesterday morning, you would have been to have seen yours, — at the mere sight of a pictured scarab.'

'How easily you quarrel.'

'I do not quarrel.'

'Then perhaps it's I. If that is so, then, at once, the quarrel's ended, — pouf! it's done. Mr Lindon, I fear, because, politically, we differ, regards me as anathema. Has he put some of his spirit into you? — You are a wiser man.'

'I am aware that you are an adept with words. But this is a case in which words only will not serve.'

'Then what will serve?'

'I am myself beginning to wonder.'

'And I.'

'As you so courteously suggest, I believe I am wiser than Lindon. I do not care for your politics, or for what you call your politics, one fig. I do not care if you are as other men are, as I am, — not unspotted from the world! But I do care if you are leprous. And I believe you are.'

'Atherton!'

'Ever since I have known you I have been conscious of there being something about you which I found it difficult to diagnose; — in an unwholesome sense, something out of the common, non-natural; an atmosphere of your own. Events, so far as you are concerned, have, during the last few days moved quickly. They have thrown an uncomfortably lurid light on that peculiarity of yours which I have noticed. Unless you can explain them to my satisfaction, you will withdraw your pretensions to Miss Lindon's hand, or I shall place certain facts before that lady, and, if necessary, publish them to the world.'

He grew visibly paler but he smiled — facially.

'You have your own way of conducting a conversation, Mr Atherton. — What are the events to whose rapid transit you are alluding?'

'Who was the individual, practically stark naked, who came out of your house, in such singular fashion, at dead of night?'

'Is that one of the facts with which you propose to tickle the public ear?'

'Is that the only explanation which you have to offer?'

'Proceed, for the present, with your indictment.'

'I am not so unobservant as you appear to imagine. There were features about the episode which struck me forcibly at the time, and which have struck me more forcibly since. To suggest, as you did yesterday morning, that it was an ordinary case of burglary, or that the man was a lunatic, is an absurdity.'

'Pardon me,—I did nothing of the kind.'

'Then what do you suggest?'

'I suggested, and do suggest, nothing. All the suggestions come from you.'

'You went very much out of your way to beg me to keep the matter quiet. There is an appearance of suggestion about that.'

'You take a jaundiced view of all my actions, Mr Atherton. Nothing, to me, could seem more natural.—However,—proceed.'

He had his hands behind his back, and rested them on the edge of the table against which he was leaning. He was undoubtedly ill at ease; but so far I had not made the impression on him, either mentally or morally, which I desired.

'Who is your Oriental friend?'

'I do not follow you.'

'Are you sure?'

'I am certain. Repeat your question.'

'Who is your Oriental friend?'

'I was not aware that I had one.'

'Do you swear that?'

He laughed, a strange laugh.

'Do you seek to catch me tripping? You conduct your case with too much animus. You must allow me to grasp the exact purport of your inquiry before I can undertake to reply to it on oath.'

'Are you not aware that at present there is in London an individual who claims to have had a very close, and a very curious, acquaintance with you in the East?'

'I am not.'

'That you swear?'

'That I do swear.'

'That is singular.'

'Why is it singular?'

'Because I fancy that that individual haunts you.'

'Haunts me?'

'Haunts you.'

'You jest.'

'You think so?—You remember that picture of the scarabaeus which, yesterday morning, frightened you into a state of semi-idiocy.'

'You use strong language.—I know what you allude to.'

'Do you mean to say that you don't know that you were indebted for that to your Oriental friend?'

'I don't understand you.'

'Are you sure?'

'Certainly I am sure.—It occurs to me, Mr Atherton, that an explanation is demanded from you rather than from me. Are you aware that the purport of my presence here is to ask you how that picture found its way into your room?'

'It was projected by the Lord of the Beetle.'

The words were chance ones,—but they struck a mark.

'The Lord—' He faltered,—and stopped. He showed signs of discomposure. 'I will be frank with you,—since frankness is what you ask.' His smile, that time, was obviously forced. 'Recently I have been the victim of delusions;' there was a pause before the word, 'of a singular kind. I have feared that they were the result of mental overstrain. Is it possible that you can enlighten me as to their source?'

I was silent. He was putting a great strain upon himself, but the twitching of his lips betrayed him. A little more, and I should reach the other side of Mr Lessingham,—the side which he kept hidden from the world.

'Who is this—individual whom you speak of as my—Oriental friend?'

'Being your friend, you should know better than I do.'

'What sort of man is he to look at?'

'I did not say it was a man.'

'But I presume it is a man.'

'I did not say so.'

He seemed, for a moment, to hold his breath,—and he looked at me with eyes which were not friendly. Then, with a display of self-command which did him credit, he drew himself upright, with an air of dignity which well became him.

'Atherton, consciously, or unconsciously, you are doing me a serious injustice. I do not know what conception it is which you have formed of me, or on what the conception is founded, but I protest that, to the best of my knowledge and belief, I am as reputable, as honest, and as clean a man as you are.'

'But you're haunted.'

'Haunted?' He held himself erect, looking me straight in the face. Then a shiver went all over him; the muscles of his mouth twitched; and, in an instant, he was livid. He staggered against the table. 'Yes, God knows it's true,—I'm haunted.'

'So either you're mad, and therefore unfit to marry; or else you've done something which places you outside the tolerably generous boundaries of civilised society, and are therefore still more unfit to marry. You're on the horns of a dilemma.'

'I—I'm the victim of a delusion.'

'What is the nature of the delusion? Does it take the shape of a—beetle?'

'Atherton!'

Without the slightest warning, he collapsed,—was transformed; I can describe the change which took place in him in no other way. He sank in a heap on the floor; he held up his hands above his head; and he gibbered,—like some frenzied animal. A more uncomfortable spectacle than he presented it would be difficult to find. I have seen it matched in the padded rooms of lunatic asylums, but nowhere else. The sight of him set every nerve of my body on edge.

'In Heaven's name, what is the matter with you, man? Are you stark, staring mad? Here,—drink this!'

Filling a tumbler with brandy, I forced it between his quivering fingers. Then it was some moments before I could get him to understand what it was I wanted him to do. When he did get the glass to his lips, he swallowed its contents as if they were so much water. By degrees his senses returned to him. He stood up. He looked about him, with a smile which was positively ghastly.

'It's—it's a delusion.'

'It's a very queer kind of a delusion, if it is.'

I eyed him, curiously. He was evidently making the most strenuous efforts to regain his self-control,—all the while with that horrible smile about his lips.

'Atherton, you—you take me at an advantage.' I was still. 'Who—who's your Oriental friend?'

'My Oriental friend?—you mean yours. I supposed, at first, that the individual in question was a man; but it appears that she's a woman.'

'A woman?—Oh.—How do you mean?'

'Well, the face is a man's—of an uncommonly disagreeable

type, of which the powers forbid that there are many!—and the voice is a man's,—also of a kind!—but the body, as, last night, I chanced to discover, is a woman's.'

'That sounds very odd.' He closed his eyes. I could see that his cheeks were clammy. 'Do you—do you believe in witchcraft?'

'That depends.'

'Have you heard of Obi?'

'I have.'

'I have been told that an Obeah man can put a spell upon a person which compels a person to see whatever he—the Obeah man—may please. Do you think that's possible?'

'It is not a question to which I should be disposed to answer either yes or no.'

He looked at me out of his half-closed eyes. It struck me that he was making conversation,—saying anything for the sake of gaining time.

'I remember reading a book entitled "Obscure Diseases of the Brain." It contained some interesting data on the subject of hallucinations.'

'Possibly.'

'Now, candidly, would you recommend me to place myself in the hands of a mental pathologist?'

'I don't think that you're insane, if that's what you mean.'

'No?—That is good hearing. Of all diseases insanity is the most to be dreaded.—Well, Atherton, I'm keeping you. The truth is that, insane or not, I am very far from well. I think I must give myself a holiday.'

He moved towards his hat and umbrella.

'There is something else which you must do.'

'What is that?'

'You must resign your pretensions to Miss Lindon's hand.'

'My dear Atherton, if my health is really failing me, I shall resign everything,—everything!'

He repeated his own word with a little movement of his hands which was pathetic.

'Understand me, Lessingham. What else you do is no affair of mine. I am concerned only with Miss Lindon. You must give me your definite promise, before you leave this room, to terminate your engagement with her before to-night.'

His back was towards me.

'There will come a time when your conscience will prick you because of your treatment of me; when you will realise that I am the most unfortunate of men.'

'I realise that now. It is because I realise it that I am so desirous that the shadow of your evil fortune shall not fall upon an innocent girl.'

He turned.

'Atherton, what is your actual position with reference to Marjorie Lindon?'

'She regards me as a brother.'

'And do you regard her as a sister? Are your sentiments towards her purely fraternal?'

'You know that I love her.'

'And do you suppose that my removal will clear the path for you?'

'I suppose nothing of the kind. You may believe me or not, but my one desire is for her happiness, and surely, if you love her, that is your desire too.'

'That is so.' He paused. An expression of sadness stole over his face of which I had not thought it capable. 'That is so to an extent of which you do not dream. No man likes to have his hand forced, especially by one whom he regards—may I say it?—as a possible rival. But I will tell you this much. If the blight which has fallen on my life is likely to continue, I would not wish,—God forbid that I should wish to join her fate with mine,—not for all that the world could offer me.'

He stopped. And I was still. Presently he continued.

'When I was younger I was subject to a—similar delusion. But it vanished,—I saw no trace of it for years,—I thought that I had done with it for good. Recently, however, it has returned,—as you have witnessed. I shall institute inquiries into the cause of its reappearance; if it seems likely to be irremovable, or even if it bids fair to be prolonged, I shall not only, as you phrase it, withdraw my pretensions to Miss Lindon's hand, but to all my other ambitions. In the interim, as regards Miss Lindon I shall be careful to hold myself on the footing of a mere acquaintance.'

'You promise me?'

'I do.—And on your side, Atherton, in the meantime, deal with me more gently. Judgment in my case has still to be given. You will find that I am not the guilty wretch you apparently imagine. And there are few things more disagreeable to one's self-esteem than to learn, too late, that one has persisted in judging another man too harshly. Think of all that the world has, at this moment, to offer me, and what it will mean if I have to turn my back on it,—owing to a mischievous twist of fortune's wheel.'

He turned, as if to go. Then stopped, and looked round, in an attitude of listening.

'What's that?'

There was a sound of droning,—I recalled what Marjorie had said of her experiences of the night before, it was like the droning of a beetle. The instant the Apostle heard it, the fashion of his countenance began to change,—it was pitiable to witness. I rushed to him.

'Lessingham!—don't be a fool!—play the man!'

He gripped my left arm with his right hand till it felt as if it were being compressed in a vice.

'Then—I shall have to have some more brandy.'

Fortunately the bottle was within reach from where I stood, otherwise I doubt if he would have released my arm to let me get at it. I gave him the decanter and the glass. He helped himself to a copious libation. By the time that he had swallowed it the droning sound had gone. He put down the empty tumbler.

'When a man has to resort to alcohol to keep his nerves up to concert pitch, things are in a bad way with him, you may be sure of that,—but then you have never known what it is to stand in momentary expectation of a tête-à-tête with the devil.'

Again he turned to leave the room,—and this time he actually went. I let him go alone. I heard his footsteps passing along the passage, and the hall-door close. Then I sat in an arm-chair, stretched my legs out in front of me, thrust my hands in my trouser pockets, and—I wondered.

I had been there, perhaps, four or five minutes, when there was a slight noise at my side. Glancing round, I saw a sheet of paper come fluttering through the open window. It fell almost at my feet. I picked it up. It was a picture of a beetle,—a facsimile of the one which had had such an extraordinary effect on Mr Lessingham the day before.

'If this was intended for St Paul, it's a trifle late;—unless—'

I could hear that someone was approaching along the corridor. I looked up, expecting to see the Apostle reappear;—in which expectation I was agreeably disappointed. The newcomer was feminine. It was Miss Grayling. As she stood in the open doorway, I saw that her cheeks were red as roses.

'I hope I am not interrupting you again, but—I left my purse here.' She stopped; then added, as if it were an afterthought, 'And—I want you to come and lunch with me.'

I locked the picture of the beetle in the drawer,—and I lunched with Dora Grayling.

BOOK III.

The Terror by Night and the Terror by Day

Miss Marjorie Lindon tells the Tale

CHAPTER XXIII.

THE WAY HE TOLD HER

I am the happiest woman in the world! I wonder how many women have said that of themselves in their time,—but I am. Paul has told me that he loves me. How long I have made inward confession of my love for him, I should be ashamed to say. It sounds prosaic, but I believe it is a fact that the first stirring of my pulses was caused by the report of a speech of his which I read in the Times. It was on the Eight Hours' Bill. Papa was most unflattering. He said that he was an oily spouter, an ignorant agitator, an irresponsible firebrand, and a good deal more to the same effect. I remember very well how papa fidgeted with the paper, declaring that it read even worse than it had sounded, and goodness knew that it had sounded bad enough. He was so very emphatic that when he had gone I thought I would see what all the pother was about, and read the speech for myself. So I read it. It affected me quite differently. The speaker's words showed such knowledge, charity, and sympathy that they went straight to my heart.

After that I read everything of Paul Lessingham's which I came across. And the more I read the more I was impressed. But it was some time before we met. Considering what papa's opinions were, it was not likely that he would go out of his way to facilitate a meeting. To him, the mere mention of the name was like a red rag to a bull. But at last we did meet. And then I knew that he was stronger, greater, better even than his words. It is so often the other way; one finds that men, and women too, are so apt to put their best, as it were, into their shop windows, that the discovery was as novel as it was delightful.

When the ice was once broken, we often met. I do not know how it was. We did not plan our meetings,—at first, at any rate. Yet we seemed always meeting. Seldom a day passed on which we did not meet,—sometimes twice or thrice. It was odd how we were always coming across each other in the most unlikely places. I believe we did not notice it at the time, but looking back I can see that we must have managed our engagements so that somewhere, somehow, we should be certain to have an opportunity of exchanging half a dozen words. Those constant encounters could not have all been chance ones.

But I never supposed he loved me,—never. I am not even sure that, for some time, I was aware that I loved him. We were great on friendship, both of us.—I was quite aware that I was his friend,—that he regarded me as his friend; he told me so more than once.

'I tell you this,' he would say, referring to this, that, or the other, 'because I know that, in speaking to you, I am speaking to a friend.'

With him those were not empty words. All kinds of people talk to one like that,—especially men; it is a kind of formula which they use with every woman who shows herself disposed to listen. But Paul is not like that. He is chary of speech; not by any means a woman's man. I tell him that is his weakest point. If legend does not lie more even than is common, few politicians have achieved prosperity without the aid of women. He replies that he is not a politician; that he never means to be a politician. He simply wishes to work for his country; if his country does not need his services—well, let it be. Papa's political friends have always so many axes of their own to grind, that, at first, to hear a member of Parliament talk like that was almost disquieting. I had dreamed of men like that; but I never encountered one till I met Paul Lessingham.

Our friendship was a pleasant one. It became pleasanter and pleasanter. Until there came a time when he told me everything; the dreams he dreamed; the plans which he had planned; the great purposes which, if health and strength were given him, he intended to carry to a great fulfilment. And, at last, he told me something else.

It was after a meeting at a Working Women's Club in Westminster. He had spoken, and I had spoken too. I don't know what papa would have said, if he had known, but I had. A formal resolution had been proposed, and I had seconded it,—in perhaps a couple of hundred words; but that would have been quite enough for papa to have regarded me as an Abandoned Wretch,—papa always puts those sort of words into capitals. Papa regards a speechifying woman as a thing of horror,—I have known him look askance at a Primrose Dame.

The night was fine. Paul proposed that I should walk with him down the Westminster Bridge Road, until we reached the House, and then he would see me into a cab. I did as he suggested. It was still early, not yet ten, and the streets were alive with people. Our conversation, as we went, was entirely political. The Agricultural Amendment Act was then before the Commons, and Paul felt very strongly that it was one of those measures which give with one hand, while taking with the other. The committee stage was at hand, and already several amendments were threatened, the effect of which would be to strengthen the landlord at the expense of the tenant. More than one of these, and they not the most moderate, were to be proposed by papa. Paul was pointing out how it would be his duty to oppose these tooth and nail, when, all at once, he stopped.

'I sometimes wonder how you really feel upon this matter.'

'What matter?'

'On the difference of opinion, in political matters, which exists between your father and myself. I am conscious that Mr Lindon regards my action as a personal question, and resents it so keenly, that I am sometimes moved to wonder if at least a portion of his resentment is not shared by you.'

'I have explained; I consider papa the politician as one person, and papa the father as quite another.'

'You are his daughter.'

'Certainly I am;—but would you, on that account, wish me to share his political opinions, even though I believe them to be wrong?'

'You love him.'

'Of course I do,—he is the best of fathers.'

'Your defection will be a grievous disappointment.'

I looked at him out of the corner of my eye. I wondered what was passing through his mind. The subject of my relations with papa was one which, without saying anything at all about it, we had consented to taboo.

'I am not so sure. I am permeated with a suspicion that papa has no politics.'

'Miss Lindon!—I fancy that I can adduce proof to the contrary.'

'I believe that if papa were to marry again, say, a Home Ruler, within three weeks his wife's politics would be his own.'

Paul thought before he spoke; then he smiled.

'I suppose that men sometimes do change their coats to please their wives,—even their political ones.'

'Papa's opinions are the opinions of those with whom he mixes. The reason why he consorts with Tories of the crusted school is because he fears that if he associated with anybody else—with Radicals, say,—before he knew it, he would be a Radical too. With him, association is synonymous with logic.'

Paul laughed outright. By this time we had reached Westminster Bridge. Standing, we looked down upon the river. A long line of lanterns was gliding mysteriously over the waters; it was a tug towing a string of barges. For some moments neither spoke. Then Paul recurred to what I had just been saying.

'And you,—do you think marriage would colour your convictions?'

'Would it yours?'

'That depends.' He was silent. Then he said, in that tone which I had learned to look for when he was most in earnest, 'It depends on whether you would marry me.'

I was still. His words were so unexpected that they took my breath away. I knew not what to make of them. My head was in a whirl. Then he addressed to me a monosyllabic interrogation.

'Well?'

I found my voice,—or a part of it.

'Well?—to what?'

He came a little closer.

'Will you be my wife?'

The part of my voice which I had found, was lost again. Tears came into my eyes. I shivered. I had not thought that I could be so absurd. Just then the moon came from behind a cloud; the rippling waters were tipped with silver. He spoke again, so gently that his words just reached my ears.

'You know that I love you.'

Then I knew that I loved him too. That what I had fancied was a feeling of friendship was something very different. It was as if somebody, in tearing a veil from before my eyes, had revealed a spectacle which dazzled me. I was speechless. He misconstrued my silence.

'Have I offended you?'

'No.'

I fancy that he noted the tremor which was in my voice, and read it rightly. For he too was still. Presently his hand stole along the parapet, and fastened upon mine, and held it tight.

And that was how it came about. Other things were said; but they were hardly of the first importance. Though I believe we took some time in saying them. Of myself I can say with truth, that my heart was too full for copious speech; I was dumb with a great happiness. And, I believe, I can say the same of Paul. He told me as much when we were parting.

It seemed that we had only just come there when Paul started. Turning, he stared up at Big Ben.

'Midnight!—The House up!—Impossible!'

But it was more than possible, it was fact. We had actually been on the Bridge two hours, and it had not seemed ten minutes. Never had I supposed that the flight of time could have been so entirely unnoticed. Paul was considerably taken aback. His legislative conscience pricked him. He excused himself—in his own fashion.

'Fortunately, for once in a way, my business in the House was not so important as my business out of it.'

He had his arm through mine. We were standing face to face.

'So you call this business!'

He laughed.

He not only saw me into a cab, but he saw me home in it. And in the cab he kissed me. I fancy I was a little out of sorts that night. My nervous system was, perhaps, demoralised. Because, when he kissed me, I did a thing which I never do,—I have my own standard of behaviour, and that sort of thing is quite outside of it; I behaved like a sentimental chit. I cried. And it took him all the way to my father's door to comfort me.

I can only hope that, perceiving the singularity of the occasion, he consented to excuse me.

CHAPTER XXIV.

A WOMAN'S VIEW

Sydney Atherton has asked me to be his wife. It is not only annoying; worse, it is absurd.

This is the result of Paul's wish that our engagement should not be announced. He is afraid of papa;—not really, but for the moment. The atmosphere of the House is charged with electricity. Party feeling runs high. They are at each other, hammer and tongs, about this Agricultural Amendment Act. The strain on Paul is tremendous. I am beginning to feel positively concerned. Little things which I have noticed about him lately convince me that he is being overwrought. I suspect him of having sleepless nights. The amount of work which he has been getting through lately has been too much for any single human being, I care not who he is. He himself admits that he shall be glad when the session is at an end. So shall I.

In the meantime, it is his desire that nothing shall be said about our engagement until the House rises. It is reasonable enough. Papa is sure to be violent,—lately, the barest allusion to Paul's name has been enough to make him explode. When the discovery does come, he will be unmanageable,—I foresee it clearly. From little incidents which have happened recently I predict the worst. He will be capable of making a scene within the precincts of the House. And, as Paul says, there is some truth in the saying that the last straw breaks the camel's back. He will be better able to face papa's wild wrath when the House has risen.

So the news is to bide a wee. Of course Paul is right. And what he wishes I wish too. Still, it is not all such plain sailing for me as he perhaps thinks. The domestic atmosphere is almost as electrical as that in the House. Papa is like the terrier who scents a rat,—he is always sniffing the air. He has not actually forbidden me to speak to Paul,—his courage is not quite at the sticking point; but he is constantly making uncomfortable allusions to persons who number among their acquaintance 'political adventurers,' 'grasping carpet-baggers,' 'Radical riff-raff,' and that kind of thing. Sometimes I venture to call my soul my own; but such a tempest invariably follows that I become discreet again as soon as I possibly can. So, as a rule, I suffer in silence.

Still, I would with all my heart that the concealment were at an end. No one need imagine that I am ashamed of being about to marry Paul,—papa least of all. On the contrary, I am as proud of it as a woman can be. Sometimes, when he has said or done something unusually wonderful, I fear that my pride will out,—I do feel it so strong within me. I should be delighted to have a trial of strength with papa; anywhere, at any time,—I should not be so rude to him as he would be to me. At the bottom of his heart papa knows that I am the more sensible of the two; after a pitched battle or so he would understand it better still. I know papa! I have not been his daughter for all these years in vain. I feel like hot-blooded soldiers must feel, who, burning to attack the enemy in the open field, are ordered to skulk behind hedges, and be shot at.

One result is that Sydney has actually made a proposal of marriage,—he of all people! It is too comical. The best of it was that he took himself quite seriously. I do not know how many times he has confided to me the sufferings which he has endured for love of other women—some of them, I am sorry to say, decent married women too; but this is the first occasion on which the theme has been a personal one. He was so frantic, as he is wont to be, that, to calm him, I told him about Paul,—which, under the circumstances, to him I felt myself at liberty to do. In return, he was melodramatic; hinting darkly at I know not what. I was almost cross with him.

He is a curious person, Sydney Atherton. I suppose it is because I have known him all my life, and have always looked upon him, in cases of necessity, as a capital substitute for a brother, that I criticise him with so much frankness. In some respects, he is a genius; in others—I will not write fool, for that he never is, though he has often done some extremely foolish things. The fame of his inventions is in the mouths of all men; though the half of them has never been told. He is the most extraordinary mixture. The things which most people would like to have proclaimed in the street, he keeps tightly locked in his own bosom; while those which the same persons would be only too glad to conceal, he shouts from the roofs. A very famous man once told me that if Mr Atherton chose to become a specialist, to take up one branch of inquiry, and devote his life to it, his fame, before he died, would bridge the spheres. But sticking to one thing is not in Sydney's line at all. He prefers, like the bee, to roam from flower to flower.

As for his being in love with me; it is ridiculous. He is as much in love with the moon. I cannot think what has put the idea into his head. Some girl must have been ill-using him, or he imagines that she has. The girl whom he ought to marry, and whom he ultimately will marry, is Dora Grayling. She is young, charming, immensely rich, and over head and ears in love with him;—if she were not, then he would be over head and ears in love with her. I believe he is very near it as it is,—sometimes he is so very rude to her. It is a characteristic of Sydney's, that he is apt to be rude to a girl whom he really likes. As for Dora, I suspect she dreams of him. He is tall, straight, very handsome, with a big moustache, and the most extraordinary eyes;—I fancy that those eyes of his have as much to do with Dora's state as anything. I have heard it said that he possesses the hypnotic power to an unusual degree, and that, if he chose to exercise it, he might become a danger to society. I believe he has hypnotised Dora.

He makes an excellent brother. I have gone to him, many and many a time, for help,—and some excellent advice I have received. I daresay I shall consult him still. There are matters of which one would hardly dare to talk to Paul. In all things he is the great man. He could hardly condescend to chiffons. Now Sydney can and does. When he is in the mood, on the vital subject of trimmings a woman could not appeal to a sounder authority. I tell him, if he had been a dressmaker, he would have been magnificent. I am sure he would.

CHAPTER XXV.

THE MAN IN THE STREET

This morning I had an adventure.

I was in the breakfast-room. Papa, as usual, was late for breakfast, and I was wondering whether I should begin without him, when, chancing to look round, something caught my eye in the street. I went to the window to see what it was. A small crowd of people was in the middle of the road, and they were all staring at something which, apparently, was lying on the ground. What it was I could not see.

The butler happened to be in the room. I spoke to him.

'Peter, what is the matter in the street? Go and see.'

He went and saw; and, presently, he returned. Peter is an excellent servant; but the fashion of his speech, even when conveying the most trivial information, is slightly sesquipedalian. He would have made a capital cabinet minister at question time,—he wraps up the smallest portions of meaning in the largest possible words.

'An unfortunate individual appears to have been the victim of a catastrophe. I am informed that he is dead. The constable asserts that he is drunk.'

'Drunk?—dead? Do you mean that he is dead drunk?—at this hour!'

'He is either one or the other. I did not behold the individual myself. I derived my information from a bystander.'

That was not sufficiently explicit for me. I gave way to a, seemingly, quite causeless impulse of curiosity, I went out into the street, just as I was, to see for myself. It was, perhaps, not the most sensible thing I could have done, and papa would have been shocked; but I am always shocking papa. It had been raining in the night, and the shoes which I had on were not so well suited as they might have been for an encounter with the mud.

I made my way to the point of interest.

'What's the matter?' I asked.

A workman, with a bag of tools over his shoulder, answered me.

'There's something wrong with someone. Policeman says he's drunk, but he looks to me as if he was something worse.'

'Will you let me pass, please?'

When they saw I was a woman, they permitted me to reach the centre of the crowd.

A man was lying on his back, in the grease and dirt of the road. He was so plastered with mud, that it was difficult, at first, to be sure that he really was a man. His head and feet were bare. His body was partially covered by a long ragged cloak. It was obvious that that one wretched, dirt-stained, sopping wet rag was all the clothing he had on. A huge constable was holding his shoulders in his hands, and was regarding him as if he could not make him out at all. He seemed uncertain as to whether it was or was not a case of shamming.

He spoke to him as if he had been some refractory child.

'Come, my lad, this won't do! — Wake up! — What's the matter?'

But he neither woke up, nor explained what was the matter. I took hold of his hand. It was icy cold. Apparently the wrist was pulseless. Clearly this was no ordinary case of drunkenness.

'There is something seriously wrong, officer. Medical assistance ought to be had at once.'

'Do you think he's in a fit, miss?'

'That a doctor should be able to tell you better than I can. There seems to be no pulse. I should not be surprised to find that he was — '

The word 'dead' was actually on my lips, when the stranger saved me from making a glaring exposure of my ignorance by snatching his wrist away from me, and sitting up in the mud. He held out his hands in front of him, opened his eyes, and exclaimed, in a loud, but painfully raucous tone of voice, as if he was suffering from a very bad cold,

'Paul Lessingham!'

I was so surprised that I all but sat down in the mud. To hear Paul—my Paul!—apostrophised by an individual of his appearance, in that fashion, was something which I had not expected. Directly the words were uttered, he closed his eyes again, sank backward, and seemingly relapsed into unconsciousness,—the constable gripping him by the shoulder just in time to prevent him banging the back of his head against the road.

The officer shook him,—scarcely gently.

'Now, my lad, it's plain that you're not dead!—What's the meaning of this?—Move yourself!'

Looking round I found that Peter was close behind. Apparently he had been struck by the singularity of his mistress' behaviour, and had followed to see that it did not meet with the reward which it deserved. I spoke to him.

'Peter, let someone go at once for Dr Cotes!'

Dr Cotes lives just round the corner, and since it was evident that the man's lapse into consciousness had made the policeman sceptical as to his case being so serious as it seemed, I thought it might be advisable that a competent opinion should be obtained without delay.

Peter was starting, when again the stranger returned to consciousness,—that is, if it really was consciousness, as to which I was more than a little in doubt. He repeated his previous pantomime; sat up in the mud, stretched out his arms, opened his eyes unnaturally wide,—and yet they appeared unseeing!—a sort of convulsion went all over him, and he shrieked—it really amounted to shrieking—as a man might shriek who was in mortal terror.

'Be warned, Paul Lessingham—be warned!'

For my part, that settled it. There was a mystery here which needed to be unravelled. Twice had he called upon Paul's name,—and in the strangest fashion! It was for me to learn the why and the wherefore; to ascertain what connection there was between this lifeless creature and Paul Lessingham. Providence might have cast him there before my door. I might be entertaining an angel unawares. My mind was made up on the instant.

'Peter, hasten for Dr Cotes.' Peter passed the word, and

immediately a footman started running as fast as his legs would carry him. 'Officer, I will have this man taken into my father's house.—Will some of you men help to carry him?'

There were volunteers enough, and to spare. I spoke to Peter in the hall.

'Is papa down yet?'

'Mr Lindon has sent down to say that you will please not wait for him for breakfast. He has issued instructions to have his breakfast conveyed to him upstairs.'

'That's all right.' I nodded towards the poor wretch who was being carried through the hall. 'You will say nothing to him about this unless he particularly asks. You understand?'

Peter bowed. He is discretion itself. He knows I have my vagaries, and it is not his fault if the savour of them travels to papa.

The doctor was in the house almost as soon as the stranger.

'Wants washing,' he remarked, directly he saw him.

And that certainly was true,—I never saw a man who stood more obviously in need of the good offices of soap and water. Then he went through the usual medical formula, I watching all the while. So far as I could see the man showed not the slightest sign of life.

'Is he dead?'

'He will be soon, if he doesn't have something to eat. The fellow's starving.'

The doctor asked the policeman what he knew of him.

That sagacious officer's reply was vague. A boy had run up to him crying that a man was lying dead in the street. He had straightway followed the boy, and discovered the stranger. That was all he knew.

'What is the matter with the man?' I inquired of the doctor, when the constable had gone.

'Don't know.—It may be catalepsy, and it mayn't.—When I do know, you may ask again.'

Dr Cotes' manner was a trifle brusque,—particularly, I believe, to me. I remember that once he threatened to box my ears. When I was a small child I used to think nothing of boxing his.

Realising that no satisfaction was to be got out of a speechless man—particularly as regards his mysterious references to Paul—I went upstairs. I found that papa was under the impression that he was suffering from a severe attack of gout. But as he was eating a capital breakfast, and apparently enjoying it,—while I was still fasting—I ventured to hope that the matter was not so serious as he feared.

I mentioned nothing to him about the person whom I had found in the street,—lest it should aggravate his gout. When he is like that, the slightest thing does.

CHAPTER XXVI.

A FATHER'S NO

Paul has stormed the House of Commons with one of the greatest speeches which even he has delivered, and I have quarrelled with papa. And, also, I have very nearly quarrelled with Sydney.

Sydney's little affair is nothing. He actually still persists in thinking himself in love with me,—as if, since last night, when he what he calls 'proposed' to me, he has not time to fall out of love, and in again, half a dozen times; and, on the strength of it, he seems to consider himself entitled to make himself as disagreeable as he can. That I should not mind,—for Sydney disagreeable is about as nice as Sydney any other way; but when it comes to his shooting poisoned shafts at Paul, I object. If he imagines that anything he can say, or hint, will lessen my estimation of Paul Lessingham by one hair's breadth, he has less wisdom even than I gave him credit for. By the way, Percy Woodville asked me to be his wife to-night,—which, also, is nothing; he has been trying to do it for the last three years,—though, under the circumstances, it is a little trying; but he would not spit venom merely because I preferred another man,—and he, I believe, does care for me.

Papa's affair is serious. It is the first clashing of the foils,—and this time, I imagine, the buttons are really off. This morning he said a few words, not so much to, as at me. He informed me that Paul was expected to speak to-night,—as if I did not know it!—and availed himself of the opening to load him with the abuse which, in his case, he thinks is not unbecoming to a gentleman. I don't know—or, rather, I do know what he would think, if he heard another man use, in the presence of a woman, the kind of language which he habitually employs. However, I said nothing. I had a motive for allowing the chaff to fly before the wind.

But, to-night, issue was joined.

I, of course, went to hear Paul speak,—as I have done over and over again before. Afterwards, Paul came and fetched me from the cage. He had to leave me for a moment, while he gave somebody a message; and in the lobby, there was Sydney,—all sneers! I could have pinched him. Just as I was coming to the conclusion that I should have to stick a pin into his arm, Paul returned,—and, positively, Sydney was rude to him. I was ashamed, if Mr Atherton was not. As if it was not enough that he should be insulted by a mere popinjay, at the very moment when he had been adding another stone to the fabric of his country's glory,—papa came up. He actually wanted to take me away from Paul. I should have liked to see him do it. Of course I went down with Paul to the carriage, leaving papa to follow if he chose. He did not choose,—but, none the less, he managed to be home within three minutes after I had myself returned.

Then the battle began.

It is impossible for me to give an idea of papa in a rage. There may be men who look well when they lose their temper, but, if there are, papa is certainly not one. He is always talking about the magnificence, and the high breeding of the Lindons, but anything less high-bred than the head of the Lindons, in his moments of wrath, it would be hard to conceive. His language I will not attempt to portray,—but his observations consisted, mainly, of abuse of Paul, glorification of the Lindons, and orders to me.

'I forbid you—I forbid you—' when papa wishes to be impressive he repeats his own words three or four times over; I don't know if he imagines that they are improved by repetition; if he does, he is wrong—'I forbid you ever again to speak to that—that—that—'

Here followed language.

I was silent.

My cue was to keep cool. I believe that, with the exception, perhaps, of being a little white, and exceedingly sorry that papa should so forget himself, I was about the same as I generally am.

'Do you hear me?—do you hear what I say?—do you hear me, miss?'

'Yes, papa; I hear you.'

'Then—then—then promise me!—promise that you will do as I tell you!—mark my words, my girl, you shall promise before you leave this room!'

'My dear papa!—do you intend me to spend the remainder of my life in the drawing-room?'

'Don't you be impertinent!—do-do-don't you speak to me like

that!—I—I—I won't have it!'

'I tell you what it is, papa, if you don't take care you'll have another attack of gout.'

'Damn gout.'

That was the most sensible thing he said; if such a tormentor as gout can be consigned to the nether regions by the mere utterance of a word, by all means let the word be uttered. Off he went again.

'The man's a ruffianly, rascally,—' and so on. 'There's not such a villainous vagabond—' and all the rest of it. 'And I order you, —I'm a Lindon, and I order you! I'm your father, and I order you!—I order you never to speak to such a—such a'—various vain repetitions—'again, and—and—and I order you never to look at him!'

'Listen to me, papa. I will promise you never to speak to Paul Lessingham again, if you will promise me never to speak to Lord Cantilever again,—or to recognise him if you meet him in the street.'

You should have seen how papa glared. Lord Cantilever is the head of his party. Its august, and, I presume, reverenced leader. He is papa's particular fetish. I am not sure that he does regard him as being any lower than the angels, but if he does it is certainly something in decimals. My suggestion seemed as outrageous to him as his suggestion seemed to me. But it is papa's misfortune that he can only see one side of a question,—and that's his own.

'You—you dare to compare Lord Cantilever to—to that—that—that—!'

'I am not comparing them. I am not aware of there being anything in particular against Lord Cantilever,—that is against his character. But, of course, I should not dream of comparing a man of his calibre, with one of real ability, like Paul Lessingham. It would be to treat his lordship with too much severity.'

I could not help it,—but that did it. The rest of papa's conversation was a jumble of explosions. It was all so sad.

Papa poured all the vials of his wrath upon Paul,—to his own sore disfigurement. He threatened me with all the pains and penalties of the inquisition if I did not immediately promise to hold no further communication with Mr Lessingham,—of course I did nothing of the kind. He cursed me, in default, by bell, book, and candle,—and by ever so many other things beside. He called me the most dreadful names,—me! his only child. He warned me that I should find myself in prison before I had done,—I am not sure that he did not hint darkly at the gallows. Finally, he drove me from the room in a whirlwind of anathemas.

CHAPTER XXVII.

THE TERROR BY NIGHT

When I left papa,—or, rather, when papa had driven me from him—I went straight to the man whom I had found in the street. It was late, and I was feeling both tired and worried, so that I only thought of seeing for myself how he was. In some way, he seemed to be a link between Paul and myself, and as, at that moment, links of that kind were precious, I could not have gone to bed without learning something of his condition.

The nurse received me at the door.

'Well, nurse, how's the patient?'

Nurse was a plump, motherly woman, who had attended more than one odd protégé of mine, and whom I kept pretty constantly at my beck and call. She held out her hands.

'It's hard to tell. He hasn't moved since I came.'

'Not moved?—Is he still insensible?'

'He seems to me to be in some sort of trance. He does not appear to breathe, and I can detect no pulsation, but the doctor says he's still alive,—it's the queerest case I ever saw.'

I went farther into the room. Directly I did so the man in the bed gave signs of life which were sufficiently unmistakable. Nurse hastened to him.

'Why,' she exclaimed, 'he's moving!—he might have heard you enter!'

He not only might have done, but it seemed possible that that was what he actually had done. As I approached the bed, he raised himself to a sitting posture, as, in the morning, he had done in the street, and he exclaimed, as if he addressed himself to someone whom he saw in front of him,—I cannot describe the almost more than human agony which was in his voice,

'Paul Lessingham!—Beware!—The Beetle!'

What he meant I had not the slightest notion. Probably that was why what seemed more like a pronouncement of delirium than anything else had such an extraordinary effect upon my nerves. No sooner had he spoken than a sort of blank horror seemed to settle down upon my mind. I actually found myself trembling at the knees. I felt, all at once, as if I was standing in the immediate presence of something awful yet unseen.

As for the speaker, no sooner were the words out of his lips, than, as was the case in the morning, he relapsed into a condition of trance. Nurse, bending over him, announced the fact.

'He's gone off again!—What an extraordinary thing!—I suppose it is real.' It was clear, from the tone of her voice, that she shared the doubt which had troubled the policeman. 'There's not a trace of a pulse. From the look of things he might be dead. Of one thing I'm sure, that there's something unnatural about the man. No natural illness I ever heard of, takes hold of a man like this.'

Glancing up, she saw that there was something unusual in my face; an appearance which startled her.

'Why, Miss Marjorie, what's the matter!—You look quite ill!'

I felt ill, and worse than ill; but, at the same time, I was quite incapable of describing what I felt to nurse. For some inscrutable reason I had even lost the control of my tongue,—I stammered.

'I—I—I'm not feeling very well, nurse; I—I—I think I'll be better in bed.'

As I spoke, I staggered towards the door, conscious, all the while, that nurse was staring at me with eyes wide open. When I got out of the room, it seemed, in some incomprehensible fashion, as if something had left it with me, and that It and I were alone together in the corridor. So overcome was I by the consciousness of its immediate propinquity, that, all at once, I found myself cowering against the wall,—as if I expected something or someone to strike me.

How I reached my bedroom I do not know. I found Fanchette awaiting me. For the moment her presence was a positive comfort,—until I realised the amazement with which she was regarding me.

'Mademoiselle is not well?'

'Thank you, Fanchette, I—I am rather tired. I will undress myself to-night—you can go to bed.'

'But if mademoiselle is so tired, will she not permit me to assist her?'

The suggestion was reasonable enough,—and kindly too; for, to say the least of it, she had as much cause for fatigue as I had. I hesitated. I should have liked to throw my arms about her neck, and beg her not to leave me; but, the plain truth is, I was ashamed. In my inner consciousness I was persuaded that the sense of terror which had suddenly come over me was so absolutely causeless, that I could not bear the notion of playing the craven in my maid's eyes. While I hesitated, something seemed to sweep past me through the air, and to brush against my cheek in passing. I caught at Fanchette's arm.

'Fanchette!—Is there something with us in the room?'

'Something with us in the room?—Mademoiselle?—What does mademoiselle mean?'

She looked disturbed,—which was, on the whole, excusable. Fanchette is not exactly a strong-minded person, and not likely to be much of a support when a support was most required. If I was going to play the fool, I would be my own audience. So I sent her off.

'Did you not hear me tell you that I will undress myself?—you are to go to bed.'

She went to bed,—with quite sufficient willingness.

The instant that she was out of the room I wished that she was back again. Such a paroxysm of fear came over me, that I was incapable of stirring from the spot on which I stood, and it was all I could do to prevent myself from collapsing in a heap on the floor. I had never, till then, had reason to suppose that I was a coward. Nor to suspect myself of being the possessor of 'nerves.' I was as little likely as anyone to be frightened by shadows. I told myself that the whole thing was sheer absurdity, and that I should be thoroughly ashamed of my own conduct when the morning came.

'If you don't want to be self-branded as a contemptible idiot, Marjorie Lindon, you will call up your courage, and these foolish fears will fly.'

But it would not do. Instead of flying, they grew worse. I became convinced,—and the process of conviction was terrible beyond words!—that there actually was something with me in the room, some invisible horror,—which, at any moment, might become visible. I seemed to understand—with a sense of agony which nothing can describe!—that this thing which was with me was with Paul. That we were linked together by the bond of a common, and a dreadful terror. That, at that moment, that same awful peril which was threatening me, was threatening him, and that I was powerless to move a finger in his aid. As with a sort of second sight, I saw out of the room in which I was, into another, in which Paul was crouching on the floor, covering his face with his hands, and shrieking. The vision came again and again with a degree of vividness of which I cannot give the least conception. At last the horror, and the reality of it, goaded me to frenzy.

'Paul! Paul!' I screamed.

As soon as I found my voice, the vision faded. Once more I understood that, as a matter of simple fact, I was standing in my own bedroom; that the lights were burning brightly; that I had not yet commenced to remove a particle of dress.

'Am I going mad?' I wondered.

I had heard of insanity taking extraordinary forms, but what could have caused softening of the brain in me I had not the faintest notion. Surely that sort of thing does not come on one—in such a wholly unmitigated form!—without the slightest notice,—and that my mental faculties were sound enough a few minutes back I was certain. The first premonition of anything of the kind had come upon me with the melodramatic utterance of the man I had found in the street.

'Paul Lessingham!—Beware!—The Beetle!'

The words were ringing in my ears.—What was that?—There was a buzzing sound behind me. I turned to see what it was. It moved as I moved, so that it was still at my back. I swung, swiftly, right round on my heels. It still eluded me,—it was still behind.

I stood and listened,—what was it that hovered so persistently at my back?

The buzzing was distinctly audible. It was like the humming of a bee. Or—could it be a beetle?

My whole life long I have had an antipathy to beetles,—of any sort or kind. I have objected neither to rats nor mice, nor cows, nor bulls, nor snakes, nor spiders, nor toads, nor lizards, nor any of the thousand and one other creatures, animate or otherwise, to which so many people have a rooted, and, apparently, illogical dislike. My pet—and only—horror has been beetles. The mere suspicion of a harmless, and, I am told, necessary cockroach, being within several feet has always made me seriously uneasy. The thought that a great, winged beetle—to me, a flying beetle is the horror of horrors!—was with me in my bedroom,—goodness alone knew how it had got there!—was unendurable. Anyone who had beheld me during the next few moments would certainly have supposed I was deranged. I turned and twisted, sprang from side to side, screwed myself into impossible positions, in order to obtain a glimpse of the detested visitant,—but in vain. I could hear it all the time; but see it—never! The buzzing sound was continually behind.

The terror returned,—I began to think that my brain must be softening. I dashed to the bed. Flinging myself on my knees, I tried to pray. But I was speechless,—words would not come; my thoughts would not take shape. I all at once became conscious, as I struggled to ask help of God, that I was wrestling with something evil,—that if I only could ask help of Him, evil would flee. But I could not. I was helpless,—overmastered. I hid my face in the bedclothes, cramming my fingers into my ears. But the buzzing was behind me all the time.

I sprang up, striking out, blindly, wildly, right and left, hitting nothing,—the buzzing always came from a point at which, at the moment, I was not aiming.

I tore off my clothes. I had on a lovely frock which I had worn for the first time that night; I had had it specially made for the occasion of the Duchess' ball, and—more especially—in honour of Paul's great speech. I had said to myself, when I saw my image in a mirror, that it was the most exquisite gown I had ever had, that it suited me to perfection, and that it should continue in my wardrobe for many a day, if only as a souvenir of a memorable night. Now, in the madness of my terror, all reflections of that sort were forgotten. My only desire was to away with it. I tore it off anyhow, letting it fall in rags on the floor at my feet. All else that I had on I flung in the same way after it; it was a veritable holocaust of dainty garments,—I acting as relentless executioner who am, as a rule, so tender with my things. I leaped upon the bed, switched off the electric light, hurried into bed, burying myself, over head and all, deep down between the sheets.

I had hoped that by shutting out the light, I might regain my senses. That in the darkness I might have opportunity for sane reflection. But I had made a grievous error. I had exchanged bad for worse. The darkness lent added terrors. The light had not been out five seconds before I would have given all that I was worth to be able to switch it on again.

As I cowered beneath the bedclothes I heard the buzzing sound above my head,—the sudden silence of the darkness had rendered it more audible than it had been before. The thing, whatever it was, was hovering above the bed. It came nearer and nearer; it grew clearer and clearer. I felt it alight upon the coverlet;—shall I ever forget the sensations with which I did feel it? It weighed upon me like a ton of lead. How much of the seeming weight was real, and how much imaginary, I cannot pretend to say; but that it was much heavier than any beetle I have ever seen or heard of, I am sure.

For a time it was still,—and during that time I doubt if I even drew my breath. Then I felt it begin to move, in wobbling fashion, with awkward, ungainly gait, stopping every now and then, as if for rest. I was conscious that it was progressing, slowly, yet surely, towards the head of the bed. The emotion of horror with which I realised what this progression might mean, will be, I fear, with me to the end of my life,—not only in dreams, but too often, also, in my waking hours. My heart, as the Psalmist has it, melted like wax within me. I was incapable of movement,—dominated by something as hideous as, and infinitely more powerful than, the fascination of the serpent.

When it reached the head of the bed, what I feared—with what a fear!—would happen, did happen. It began to find its way inside,—to creep between the sheets; the wonder is I did not die! I felt it coming nearer and nearer, inch by inch; I knew that it was upon me, that escape there was none; I felt something touch my hair.

And then oblivion did come to my aid. For the first time in my life I swooned.

CHAPTER XXVIII.

THE STRANGE STORY OF THE MAN IN THE STREET

I have been anticipating for some weeks past, that things would become exciting,—and they have. But hardly in the way which I foresaw. It is the old story of the unexpected happening. Suddenly events of the most extraordinary nature have come crowding on me from the most unlooked-for quarters.

Let me try to take them in something like their proper order.

To begin with, Sydney has behaved very badly. So badly that it seems likely that I shall have to re-cast my whole conception of his character. It was nearly nine o'clock this morning when I,—I cannot say woke up, because I do not believe that I had really been asleep—but when I returned to consciousness. I found myself sitting up in bed, trembling like some frightened child. What had actually happened to me I did not know,—could not guess. I was conscious of an overwhelming sense of nausea, and, generally, I was feeling very far from well. I endeavoured to arrange my thoughts, and to decide upon some plan of action. Finally, I decided to go for advice and help where I had so often gone before,—to Sydney Atherton.

I went to him. I told him the whole gruesome story. He saw, he could not help but see what a deep impress the events of the night had made on me. He heard me to the end with every appearance of sympathy,—and then all at once I discovered that all the time papa had been concealed behind a large screen which was in the room, listening to every word I had been uttering. That I was dumfoundered, goes without saying. It was bad enough in papa, but in Sydney it seemed, and it was, such treachery. He and I have told each other secrets all our lives; it has never entered my imagination, as he very well knows, to play him false, in one jot or tittle; and I have always understood that, in this sort of matter, men pride themselves on their sense of honour being so much keener than women's. I told them some plain truths; and I fancy that I left them both feeling heartily ashamed of themselves.

One result the experience had on me,—it wound me up. It had on me the revivifying effect of a cold douche. I realised that mine was a situation in which I should have to help myself.

When I returned home I learned that the man whom I had

found in the street was himself again, and was as conscious as he was ever likely to be. Burning with curiosity to learn the nature of the connection which existed between Paul and him, and what was the meaning of his oracular apostrophes, I merely paused to remove my hat before hastening into his apartment.

When he saw me, and heard who I was, the expressions of his gratitude were painful in their intensity. The tears streamed down his cheeks. He looked to me like a man who had very little life left in him. He looked weak, and white, and worn to a shadow. Probably he never had been robust, and it was only too plain that privation had robbed him of what little strength he had ever had. He was nothing else but skin and bone. Physical and mental debility was written large all over him.

He was not bad-looking,—in a milk and watery sort of way. He had pale blue eyes and very fair hair, and, I daresay, at one time, had been a spruce enough clerk. It was difficult to guess his age, one ages so rapidly under the stress of misfortune, but I should have set him down as being about forty. His voice, though faint enough at first, was that of an educated man, and as he went on, and gathered courage, and became more and more in earnest, he spoke with a simple directness which was close akin to eloquence. It was a curious story which he had to tell.

So curious, so astounding indeed, that, by the time it was finished, I was in such a state of mind, that I could perceive no alternative but to forgive Sydney, and, in spite of his recent, and scandalous misbehaviour, again appeal to him for assistance. It seemed, if the story told by the man whom I had found in the street was true,—and incredible though it sounded, he spoke like a truthful man!—that Paul was threatened by some dreadful, and, to me, wholly incomprehensible danger; that it was a case in which even moments were precious; and I felt that, with the best will in the world, it was a position in which I could not move alone. The shadow of the terror of the night was with me still, and with that fresh in my recollection how could I hope, single-handed, to act effectually against the mysterious being of whom this amazing tale was told? No! I believed that Sydney did care for me, in his own peculiar way; I knew that he was quick, and cool, and fertile in resource, and that he showed to most advantage in a difficult situation; it was possible that he had a conscience, of a sort, and that, this time, I might not appeal to it in vain.

So I sent a servant off to fetch him, helter skelter.

As luck would have it, the servant returned with him within five minutes. It appeared that he had been lunching with Dora Grayling, who lives just at the end of the street, and the footman had met him coming down the steps. I had him shown into my own room.

'I want you to go to the man whom I found in the street, and listen to what he has to say.'

'With pleasure.'

'Can I trust you?'

'To listen to what he has to say?—I believe so.'

'Can I trust you to respect my confidence?'

He was not at all abashed,—I never saw Sydney Atherton when he was abashed. Whatever the offence of which he has been guilty, he always seems completely at his ease. His eyes twinkled.

'You can,—I will not breathe a syllable even to papa.'

'In that case, come! But, you understand, I am going to put to the test the affirmations which you have made during all these years, and to prove if you have any of the feeling for me which you pretend.'

Directly we were in the stranger's room, Sydney marched straight up to the bed, stared at the man who was lying in it, crammed his hands into his trouser pockets, and whistled. I was amazed.

'So!' he exclaimed. 'It's you!'

'Do you know this man?' I asked.

'I am hardly prepared to go so far as to say that I know him, but, I chance to have a memory for faces, and it happens that I have met this gentleman on at least one previous occasion. Perhaps he remembers me.—Do you?'

The stranger seemed uneasy,—as if he found Sydney's tone and manner disconcerting.

'I do. You are the man in the street.'

'Precisely. I am that—individual. And you are the man who came through the window. And in a much more comfortable condition you appear to be than when first I saw you.' Sydney turned to me. 'It is just possible, Miss Lindon, that I may have a few remarks to make to this gentleman which would be better made in private,—if you don't mind.'

'But I do mind,—I mind very much. What do you suppose I sent for you here for?'

Sydney smiled that absurd, provoking smile of his,—as if the occasion were not sufficiently serious.

'To show that you still repose in me a vestige of your confidence.'

'Don't talk nonsense. This man has told me a most extraordinary story, and I have sent for you—as you may believe, not too willingly'—Sydney bowed—'in order that he may repeat it in your presence, and in mine.'

'Is that so?—Well!—Permit me to offer you a chair,—this tale may turn out to be a trifle long.'

To humour him I accepted the chair he offered, though I should have preferred to stand;—he seated himself on the side of the bed, fixing on the stranger those keen, quizzical, not too merciful, eyes of his.

'Well, sir, we are at your service,—if you will be so good as to favour us with a second edition of that pleasant yarn you have been spinning. But—let us begin at the right end!—what's your name?'

'My name is Robert Holt.'

'That so?—Then, Mr Robert Holt,—let her go!'

Thus encouraged, Mr Holt repeated the tale which he had told me, only in more connected fashion than before. I fancy that Sydney's glances exercised on him a sort of hypnotic effect, and this kept him to the point,—he scarcely needed a word of prompting from the first syllable to the last.

He told how, tired, wet, hungry, desperate, despairing, he had been refused admittance to the casual ward,—that unfailing resource, as one would have supposed, of those who had abandoned even hope. How he had come upon an open window in an apparently empty house, and, thinking of nothing but shelter from the inclement night, he had clambered through it. How he had found himself in the presence of an extraordinary being, who, in his debilitated and nervous state, had seemed to him to be only half human. How this dreadful creature had given utterance to wild sentiments of hatred towards Paul Lessingham,—my Paul! How he had taken advantage of Holt's enfeebled state to gain over him the most complete, horrible, and, indeed, almost incredible ascendency. How he actually had sent Holt, practically naked, into the storm-driven streets, to commit burglary at Paul's house,—and how he,—Holt,—had actually gone without being able to offer even a shadow of opposition. How Paul, suddenly returning home, had come upon Holt engaged in the very act of committing burglary, and how, on his hearing Holt make a cabalistic reference to some mysterious beetle, the manhood had gone out of him, and he had suffered the intruder to make good his escape without an effort to detain him.

The story had seemed sufficiently astonishing the first time, it seemed still more astonishing the second,—but, as I watched Sydney listening, what struck me chiefly was the conviction that he had heard it all before. I charged him with it directly Holt had finished.

'This is not the first time you have been told this tale.'

'Pardon me,—but it is. Do you suppose I live in an atmosphere of fairy tales?'

Something in his manner made me feel sure he was deceiving me.

'Sydney!—Don't tell me a story!—Paul has told you!'

'I am not telling you a story,—at least, on this occasion; and Mr Lessingham has not told me. Suppose we postpone these details to a little later. And perhaps, in the interim, you will permit me to put a question or two to Mr Holt.'

I let him have his way,—though I knew he was concealing something from me; that he had a more intimate acquaintance with Mr Holt's strange tale than he chose to confess. And, for some cause, his reticence annoyed me.

He looked at Mr Holt in silence for a second or two. Then he said, with the quizzical little air of bland impertinence which is peculiarly his own,

'I presume, Mr Holt, you have been entertaining us with a novelty in fables, and that we are not expected to believe this pleasant little yarn of yours.'

'I expect nothing. But I have told you the truth. And you know it.'

This seemed to take Sydney aback.

'I protest that, like Miss Lindon, you credit me with a more extensive knowledge than I possess. However, we will let that pass.—I take it that you paid particular attention to this mysterious habitant of this mysterious dwelling.'

I saw that Mr Holt shuddered.

'I am not likely ever to forget him.'

'Then, in that case, you will be able to describe him to us.'

'To do so adequately would be beyond my powers. But I will do my best.'

If the original was more remarkable than the description which he gave of him, then he must have been remarkable indeed. The impression conveyed to my mind was rather of a monster than a human being. I watched Sydney attentively as he followed Mr Holt's somewhat lurid language, and there was something in his demeanour which made me more and more persuaded that he was more behind the scenes in this strange business than he pretended, or than the speaker suspected. He put a question which seemed uncalled for by anything which Mr Holt had said.

'You are sure this thing of beauty was a man?'

'No, sir, that is exactly what I am not sure.'

There was a note in Sydney's voice which suggested that he had received precisely the answer which he had expected.

'Did you think it was a woman?'

'I did think so, more than once. Though I can hardly explain what made me think so. There was certainly nothing womanly about the face.' He paused, as if to reflect. Then added, 'I suppose it was a question of instinct.'

'I see.—Just so.—It occurs to me, Mr Holt, that you are rather strong on questions of instinct.' Sydney got off the bed. He stretched himself, as if fatigued,—which is a way he has. 'I will not do you the injustice to hint that I do not believe a word of your charming, and simple, narrative. On the contrary, I will demonstrate my perfect credence by remarking that I have not the slightest doubt that you will be able to point out to me, for my particular satisfaction, the delightful residence on which the whole is founded.'

Mr Holt coloured,—Sydney's tone could scarcely have been more significant.

'You must remember, sir, that it was a dark night, that I had never been in that neighbourhood before, and that I was not in a condition to pay much attention to locality.'

'All of which is granted, but—how far was it from Hammersmith Workhouse?'

'Possibly under half a mile.'

'Then, in that case, surely you can remember which turning you took on leaving Hammersmith Workhouse,—I suppose there are not many turnings you could have taken.'

'I think I could remember.'

'Then you shall have an opportunity to try. It isn't a very far cry to Hammersmith,—don't you think you are well enough to drive there now, just you and I together in a cab?'

'I should say so. I wished to get up this morning. It is by the doctor's orders I have stayed in bed.'

'Then, for once in a while, the doctor's orders shall be ignored,—I prescribe fresh air.' Sydney turned to me. 'Since Mr Holt's wardrobe seems rather to seek, don't you think a suit of one of the men might fit him,—if Mr Holt wouldn't mind making shift for the moment?—Then, by the time you've finished dressing, Mr Holt, I shall be ready.'

While they were ascertaining which suit of clothes would be best adapted to his figure, I went with Sydney to my room. So soon as we were in, I let him know that this was not a matter in which I intended to be trifled with.

'Of course you understand, Sydney, that I am coming with

you.'

He pretended not to know what I meant.

'Coming with me?—I am delighted to hear it,—but where?'

'To the house of which Mr Holt has been speaking.'

'Nothing could give me greater pleasure, but—might I point out?—Mr Holt has to find it yet?'

'I will come to help you to help him find it.'

Sydney laughed,—but I could see he did not altogether relish the suggestion.

'Three in a hansom?'

'There is such a thing as a four-wheeled cab,—or I could order a carriage if you'd like one.'

Sydney looked at me out of the corners of his eyes; then began to walk up and down the room, with his hands in his trouser pockets. Presently he began to talk nonsense.

'I need not say with what a sensation of joy I should anticipate the delights of a drive with you,—even in a four-wheeled cab; but, were I in your place, I fancy that I should allow Holt and your humble servant to go hunting out this house of his alone. It may prove a more tedious business than you imagine. I promise that, after the hunt is over, I will describe the proceedings to you with the most literal accuracy.'

'I daresay.—Do you think I don't know you've been deceiving me all the time?'

'Deceiving you?—I!'

'Yes,—you! Do you think I'm quite an idiot?'

'My dear Marjorie!'

'Do you think I can't see that you know all about what Mr Holt has been telling us,—perhaps more about it than he knows himself?'

'On my word!—With what an amount of knowledge you do credit me.'

'Yes, I do,—or discredit you, rather. If I were to trust you, you would tell me just as much as you chose,—which would be nothing. I'm coming with you,—so there's an end.'

'Very well.—Do you happen to know if there are any revolvers in the house?'

'Revolvers?—whatever for?'

'Because I should like to borrow one. I will not conceal from you—since you press me—that this is a case in which a revolver is quite likely to be required.'

'You are trying to frighten me.'

'I am doing nothing of the kind, only, under the circumstances, I am bound to point out to you what it is you may expect.'

'Oh, you think that you're bound to point that out, do you,—then now your bounden duty's done. As for there being any revolvers in the house, papa has a perfect arsenal,—would you like to take them all?'

'Thanks, but I daresay I shall be able to manage with one,—unless you would like one too. You may find yourself in need of it.'

'I am obliged to you, but, on this occasion, I don't think I'll trouble. I'll run the risk.—Oh, Sydney, what a hypocrite you are!'

'It's for your sake, if I seem to be. I tell you most seriously, that I earnestly advise you to allow Mr Holt and I to manage this affair alone. I don't mind going so far as to say that this is a matter with which, in days to come, you will wish that you had not allowed yourself to be associated.'

'What do you mean by that? Do you dare to insinuate anything against—Paul?'

'I insinuate nothing. What I mean, I say right out; and, my dear Marjorie, what I actually do mean is this,—that if, in spite of my urgent solicitations, you will persist in accompanying us, the expedition, so far as I am concerned, will be postponed.'

'That is what you do mean, is it? Then that's settled.' I rang the bell. The servant came. 'Order a four-wheeled cab at once.

And let me know the moment Mr Holt is ready.' The servant went. I turned to Sydney. 'If you will excuse me, I will go and put my hat on. You are, of course, at liberty to please yourself as to whether you will or will not go, but, if you don't, then I shall go with Mr Holt alone.'

I moved to the door. He stopped me.

'My dear Marjorie, why will you persist in treating me with such injustice? Believe me, you have no idea what sort of adventure this is which you are setting out upon, – or you would hear reason. I assure you that you are gratuitously proposing to thrust yourself into imminent peril.'

'What sort of peril? Why do you beat about the bush, – why don't you speak right out?'

'I can't speak right out, there are circumstances which render it practically impossible – and that's the plain truth, – but the danger is none the less real on that account. I am not jesting, – I am in earnest; won't you take my word for it?'

'It is not a question of taking your word only, – it is a question of something else beside. I have not forgotten my adventures of last night, – and Mr Holt's story is mysterious enough in itself; but there is something more mysterious still at the back of it, – something which you appear to suggest points unpleasantly at Paul. My duty is clear, and nothing you can say will turn me from it. Paul, as you are very well aware, is already overweighted with affairs of state, pretty nearly borne down by them, – or I would take the tale to him, and he would talk to you after a fashion of his own. Things being as they are, I propose to show you that, although I am not yet Paul's wife, I can make his interests my own as completely as though I were. I can, therefore, only repeat that it is for you to decide what you intend to do; but, if you prefer to stay, I shall go with Mr Holt, – alone.'

'Understand that, when the time for regret comes – as it will come! – you are not to blame me for having done what I advised you not to do.'

'My dear Mr Atherton, I will undertake to do my utmost to guard your spotless reputation; I should be sorry that anyone should hold you responsible for anything I either said or did.'

'Very well! – Your blood be on your own head!'

'My blood?'

'Yes,—your blood. I shouldn't be surprised if it comes to blood before we're through.—Perhaps you'll oblige me with the loan of one of that arsenal of revolvers of which you spoke.'

I let him have his old revolver,—or, rather, I let him have one of papa's new ones. He put it in the hip pocket in his trousers. And the expedition started,—in a four-wheeled cab.

CHAPTER XXIX.
THE HOUSE ON THE ROAD FROM THE WORKHOUSE

Mr Holt looked as if he was in somebody else's garments. He was so thin, and worn, and wasted, that the suit of clothes which one of the men had lent him hung upon him as on a scarecrow. I was almost ashamed of myself for having incurred a share of the responsibility of taking him out of bed. He seemed so weak and bloodless that I should not have been surprised if he had fainted on the road. I had taken care that he should eat as much as he could eat before we started—the suggestion of starvation which he had conveyed to one's mind was dreadful!—and I had brought a flask of brandy in case of accidents, but, in spite of everything, I could not conceal from myself that he would be more at home in a sick-bed than in a jolting cab.

It was not a cheerful drive. There was in Sydney's manner towards me an air of protection which I instinctively resented,—he appeared to be regarding me as a careful, and anxious, nurse might regard a wrong-headed and disobedient child. Conversation distinctly languished. Since Sydney seemed disposed to patronise me, I was bent on snubbing him. The result was, that the majority of the remarks which were uttered were addressed to Mr Holt.

The cab stopped,—after what had appeared to me to be an interminable journey. I was rejoiced at the prospect of its being at an end. Sydney put his head out of the window. A short parley with the driver ensued.

'This is 'Ammersmith Workhouse, it's a large place, sir,—which part of it might you be wanting?'

Sydney appealed to Mr Holt. He put his head out of the window in his turn,—he did not seem to recognise our surroundings at all.

'We have come a different way,—this is not the way I went; I went through Hammersmith,—and to the casual ward; I don't see that here.'

Sydney spoke to the cabman.

'Driver, where's the casual ward?'

'That's the other end, sir.'

'Then take us there.'

He took us there. Then Sydney appealed again to Mr Holt.

'Shall I dismiss the cabman,—or don't you feel equal to walking?'

'Thank you, I feel quite equal to walking,—I think the exercise will do me good.'

So the cabman was dismissed,—a step which we—and I, in particular—had subsequent cause to regret. Mr Holt took his bearings. He pointed to a door which was just in front of us.

'That's the entrance to the casual ward, and that, over it, is the window through which the other man threw a stone. I went to the right,—back the way I had come.' We went to the right. 'I reached this corner.' We had reached a corner. Mr Holt looked about him, endeavouring to recall the way he had gone. A good many roads appeared to converge at that point, so that he might have wandered in either of several directions.

Presently he arrived at something like a decision.

'I think this is the way I went,—I am nearly sure it is.'

He led the way, with something of an air of dubitation, and we followed. The road he had chosen seemed to lead to nothing and nowhere. We had not gone many yards from the workhouse gates before we were confronted by something like chaos. In front and on either side of us were large spaces of waste land. At some more or less remote period attempts appeared to have been made at brickmaking,—there were untidy stacks of bilious-looking bricks in evidence. Here and there enormous weather-stained boards announced that 'This Desirable Land was to be Let for Building Purposes.' The road itself was unfinished. There was no pavement, and we had the bare uneven ground for sidewalk. It seemed, so far as I could judge, to lose itself in space, and to be swallowed up by the wilderness of 'Desirable Land' which lay beyond. In the near distance there were houses enough, and to spare—of a kind. But they were in other roads. In the one in which we actually were, on the right, at the end, there was a row of unfurnished carcases, but only two buildings which were in anything like a fit state for occupation. One stood on either side, not facing each other,—there was a distance between them of perhaps fifty yards. The sight of them had a more exciting effect on Mr Holt than it had on me. He moved rapidly forward,—coming to a standstill in front of the one upon our left, which was the nearer of the pair.

'This is the house!' he exclaimed.

He seemed almost exhilarated,—I confess that I was depressed. A more dismal-looking habitation one could hardly imagine. It was one of those dreadful jerry-built houses which, while they are still new, look old. It had quite possibly only been built a year or two, and yet, owing to neglect, or to poverty of construction, or to a combination of the two, it was already threatening to tumble down. It was a small place, a couple of storeys high, and would have been dear—I should think!—at thirty pounds a year. The windows had surely never been washed since the house was built,—those on the upper floor seemed all either cracked or broken. The only sign of occupancy consisted in the fact that a blind was down behind the window of the room on the ground floor. Curtains there were none. A low wall ran in front, which had apparently at one time been surmounted by something in the shape of an iron railing,—a rusty piece of metal still remained on one end; but, since there was only about a foot between it and the building, which was practically built upon the road,—whether the wall was intended to ensure privacy, or was merely for ornament, was not clear.

'This is the house!' repeated Mr Holt, showing more signs of life than I had hitherto seen in him.

Sydney looked it up and down,—it apparently appealed to his aesthetic sense as little as it did to mine.

'Are you sure?'

'I am certain.'

'It seems empty.'

'It seemed empty to me that night,—that is why I got into it in search of shelter.'

'Which is the window which served you as a door?'

'This one.' Mr Holt pointed to the window on the ground floor,—the one which was screened by a blind. 'There was no sign of a blind when I first saw it, and the sash was up,—it was that which caught my eye.'

Once more Sydney surveyed the place, in comprehensive fashion, from roof to basement,—then he scrutinisingly regarded Mr Holt.

'You are quite sure this is the house? It might be awkward if you proved mistaken. I am going to knock at the door, and if it turns out that that mysterious acquaintance of yours does not, and never has lived here, we might find an explanation difficult.'

'I am sure it is the house,—certain! I know it,—I feel it here,—and here.'

Mr Holt touched his breast, and his forehead. His manner was distinctly odd. He was trembling, and a fevered expression had come into his eyes. Sydney glanced at him, for a moment, in silence. Then he bestowed his attention upon me.

'May I ask if I may rely upon your preserving your presence of mind?'

The mere question ruffled my plumes.

'What do you mean?'

'What I say. I am going to knock at that door, and I am going to get through it, somehow. It is quite within the range of possibility that, when I am through, there will be some strange happenings,—as you have heard from Mr Holt. The house is commonplace enough without; you may not find it so commonplace within. You may find yourself in a position in which it will be in the highest degree essential that you should keep your wits about you.'

'I am not likely to let them stray.'

'Then that's all right.—Do I understand that you propose to come in with me?'

'Of course I do,—what do you suppose I've come for? What nonsense you are talking.'

'I hope that you will still continue to consider it nonsense by the time this little adventure's done.'

That I resented his impertinence goes without saying—to be talked to in such a strain by Sydney Atherton, whom I had kept in subjection ever since he was in knickerbockers, was a little trying,—but I am forced to admit that I was more impressed by his manner, or his words, or by Mr Holt's manner, or something, than I should have cared to own. I had not the least notion what was going to happen, or what horrors that woebegone-looking dwelling contained. But Mr Holt's story had been of the most astonishing sort, my experiences of the previous night were still fresh, and, altogether, now that I was in such close neighbourhood with the Unknown—with a capital U!—although it was broad daylight, it loomed before me in a shape for which,—candidly!—I was not prepared.

A more disreputable-looking front door I have not seen,—it was in perfect harmony with the remainder of the establishment. The paint was off; the woodwork was scratched and dented; the knocker was red with rust. When Sydney took it in his hand I was conscious of quite a little thrill. As he brought it down with a sharp rat-tat, I half expected to see the door fly open, and disclose some gruesome object glaring out at us. Nothing of the kind took place; the door did not budge,—nothing happened. Sydney waited a second or two, then knocked again; another second or two, then another knock. There was still no sign of any notice being taken of our presence. Sydney turned to Mr Holt.

'Seems as if the place was empty.'

Mr Holt was in the most singular condition of agitation,—it made me uncomfortable to look at him.

'You do not know,—you cannot tell; there may be someone there who hears and pays no heed.'

'I'll give them another chance.'

Sydney brought down the knocker with thundering reverberations. The din must have been audible half a mile away. But from within the house there was still no sign that any heard. Sydney came down the step.

'I'll try another way,—I may have better fortune at the back.'

He led the way round to the rear, Mr Holt and I following in single file. There the place seemed in worse case even than in the front. There were two empty rooms on the ground floor at the back,—there was no mistake about their being empty, without the slightest difficulty we could see right into them. One was apparently intended for a kitchen and wash-house combined, the other for a sitting-room. There was not a stick of furniture in either, nor the slightest sign of human habitation. Sydney commented on the fact.

'Not only is it plain that no one lives in these charming apartments, but it looks to me uncommonly as if no one ever had lived in them.'

To my thinking Mr Holt's agitation was increasing every moment. For some reason of his own, Sydney took no notice of it whatever,—possibly because he judged that to do so would only tend to make it worse. An odd change had even taken place in Mr Holt's voice,—he spoke in a sort of tremulous falsetto.

'It was only the front room which I saw.'

'Very good; then, before very long, you shall see that front room again.'

Sydney rapped with his knuckles on the glass panels of the back door. He tried the handle; when it refused to yield he gave it a vigorous shaking. He saluted the dirty windows,—so far as succeeding in attracting attention was concerned, entirely in vain. Then he turned again to Mr Holt,—half mockingly.

'I call you to witness that I have used every lawful means to gain the favourable notice of your mysterious friend. I must therefore beg to stand excused if I try something slightly unlawful for a change. It is true that you found the window already open; but, in my case, it soon will be.'

He took a knife out of his pocket, and, with the open blade, forced back the catch,—as I am told that burglars do. Then he lifted the sash.

'Behold!' he exclaimed. 'What did I tell you?—Now, my dear Marjorie, if I get in first and Mr Holt gets in after me, we shall be in a position to open the door for you.'

I immediately saw through his design.

'No, Mr Atherton; you will get in first, and I will get in after you, through the window,—before Mr Holt. I don't intend to wait for you to open the door.'

Sydney raised his hands and opened his eyes, as if grieved at my want of confidence. But I did not mean to be left in the lurch, to wait their pleasure, while on pretence of opening the door, they searched the house. So Sydney climbed in first, and I second,—it was not a difficult operation, since the window-sill was under three feet from the ground—and Mr Holt last. Directly we were in, Sydney put his hand up to his mouth, and shouted.

'Is there anybody in this house? If so, will he kindly step this way, as there is someone wishes to see him.'

His words went echoing through the empty rooms in a way which was almost uncanny. I suddenly realised that if, after all, there did happen to be somebody in the house, and he was at all disagreeable, our presence on his premises might prove rather difficult to explain. However, no one answered. While I was waiting for Sydney to make the next move, he diverted my attention to Mr Holt.

'Hollo, Holt, what's the matter with you? Man, don't play the fool like that!'

Something was the matter with Mr Holt. He was trembling all over as if attacked by a shaking palsy. Every muscle in his body seemed twitching at once. A strained look had come on his face, which was not nice to see. He spoke as with an effort.

'I'm all right.—It's nothing.'

'Oh, is it nothing? Then perhaps you'll drop it. Where's that brandy?' I handed Sydney the flask. 'Here, swallow this.'

Mr Holt swallowed the cupful of neat spirit which Sydney offered without an attempt at parley. Beyond bringing some remnants of colour to his ashen cheeks it seemed to have no effect on him whatever. Sydney eyed him with a meaning in his glance which I was at a loss to understand.

'Listen to me, my lad. Don't think you can deceive me by playing any of your fool tricks, and don't delude yourself into supposing that I shall treat you as anything but dangerous if you do. I've got this.' He showed the revolver of papa's which I had lent him. 'Don't imagine that Miss Lindon's presence will deter me from using it.'

Why he addressed Mr Holt in such a strain surpassed my comprehension. Mr Holt, however, evinced not the faintest symptoms of resentment,—he had become, on a sudden, more like an automaton than a man. Sydney continued to gaze at him as if he would have liked his glance to penetrate to his inmost soul.

'Keep in front of me, if you please, Mr Holt, and lead the way to this mysterious apartment in which you claim to have had such a remarkable experience.'

Of me he asked in a whisper,

'Did you bring a revolver?'

I was startled.

'A revolver?—The idea!—How absurd you are!'

Sydney said something which was so rude—and so uncalled for!—that it was worthy of papa in his most violent moments.

'I'd sooner be absurd than a fool in petticoats.' I was so angry that I did not know what to say,—and before I could say it he went on. 'Keep your eyes and ears well open; be surprised at nothing you see or hear. Stick close to me. And for goodness sake remain mistress of as many of your senses as you conveniently can.'

I had not the least idea what was the meaning of it all. To me there seemed nothing to make such a pother about. And yet I was conscious of a fluttering of the heart as if there soon might be something. I knew Sydney sufficiently well to be aware that he was one of the last men in the world to make a fuss without reason,—and that he was as little likely to suppose that there was a reason when as a matter of fact there was none.

Mr Holt led the way, as Sydney desired—or, rather, commanded, to the door of the room which was in front of the house. The door was closed. Sydney tapped on a panel. All was silence. He tapped again.

'Anyone in there?' he demanded.

As there was still no answer, he tried the handle. The door was locked.

'The first sign of the presence of a human being we have had,—doors don't lock themselves. It's just possible that there may have been someone or something about the place, at some time or other, after all.'

Grasping the handle firmly, he shook it with all his might,—as he had done with the door at the back. So flimsily was the place constructed that he made even the walls to tremble.

'Within there!—if anyone is in there!—if you don't open this door, I shall.'

There was no response.

'So be it!—I'm going to pursue my wild career of defiance of established law and order, and gain admission in one way, if I can't in another.'

Putting his right shoulder against the door, he pushed with his whole force. Sydney is a big man, and very strong, and the door was weak. Shortly, the lock yielded before the continuous pressure, and the door flew open. Sydney whistled.

'So!—It begins to occur to me, Mr Holt, that that story of yours may not have been such pure romance as it seemed.'

It was plain enough that, at any rate, this room had been occupied, and that recently,—and, if his taste in furniture could be taken as a test, by an eccentric occupant to boot. My own first impression was that there was someone, or something, living in it still,—an uncomfortable odour greeted our nostrils, which was suggestive of some evil-smelling animal. Sydney seemed to share my thought.

'A pretty perfume, on my word! Let's shed a little more light on the subject, and see what causes it. Marjorie, stop where you are until I tell you.'

I had noticed nothing, from without, peculiar about the appearance of the blind which screened the window, but it must have been made of some unusually thick material, for, within, the room was strangely dark. Sydney entered, with the intention of drawing up the blind, but he had scarcely taken a couple of steps when he stopped.

'What's that?'

'It's it,' said Mr Holt, in a voice which was so unlike his own that it was scarcely recognisable.

'It?—What do you mean by it?'

'The Beetle!'

Judging from the sound of his voice Sydney was all at once in a state of odd excitement.

'Oh, is it!—Then, if this time I don't find out the how and the why and the wherefore of that charming conjuring trick, I'll give you leave to write me down an ass,—with a great, big A.'

He rushed farther into the room,—apparently his efforts to lighten it did not meet with the immediate success which he desired.

'What's the matter with this confounded blind? There's no cord! How do you pull it up?—What the—'

In the middle of his sentence Sydney ceased speaking. Suddenly Mr Holt, who was standing by my side on the threshold of the door, was seized with such a fit of trembling, that, fearing he was going to fall, I caught him by the arm. A most extraordinary look was on his face. His eyes were distended to their fullest width, as if with horror at what they saw in front of them. Great beads of perspiration were on his forehead.

'It's coming!' he screamed.

Exactly what happened I do not know. But, as he spoke, I heard, proceeding from the room, the sound of the buzzing of wings. Instantly it recalled my experiences of the night before,—as it did so I was conscious of a most unpleasant qualm. Sydney swore a great oath, as if he were beside himself with rage.

'If you won't go up, you shall come down.'

I suppose, failing to find a cord, he seized the blind from below, and dragged it down,—it came, roller and all, clattering to the floor. The room was all in light. I hurried in. Sydney was standing by the window, with a look of perplexity upon his face which, under any other circumstances, would have been comical. He was holding papa's revolver in his hand, and was glaring round and round the room, as if wholly at a loss to understand how it was he did not see what he was looking for.

'Marjorie!' he exclaimed. 'Did you hear anything?'

'Of course I did. It was that which I heard last night,—which so frightened me.'

'Oh, was it? Then, by—' in his excitement he must have been

completely oblivious of my presence, for he used the most terrible language, 'when I find it there'll be a small discussion. It can't have got out of the room,—I know the creature's here; I not only heard it, I felt it brush against my face.—Holt, come inside and shut that door.'

Mr Holt raised his arms, as if he were exerting himself to make a forward movement,—but he remained rooted to the spot on which he stood.

'I can't!' he cried.

'You can't!—Why?'

'It won't let me.'

'What won't let you?'

'The Beetle!'

Sydney moved till he was close in front of him. He surveyed him with eager eyes. I was just at his back. I heard him murmur,—possibly to me.

'By George!—It's just as I thought!—The beggar's hypnotised!'

Then he said aloud,

'Can you see it now?'

'Yes.'

'Where?'

'Behind you.'

As Mr Holt spoke, I again heard, quite close to me, that buzzing sound. Sydney seemed to hear it too,—it caused him to swing round so quickly that he all but whirled me off my feet.

'I beg your pardon, Marjorie, but this is of the nature of an unparalleled experience,—didn't you hear something then?'

'I did,—distinctly; it was close to me,—within an inch or two of my face.'

We stared about us, then back at each other,—there was nothing else to be seen. Sydney laughed, doubtfully.

'It's uncommonly queer. I don't want to suggest that there are visions about, or I might suspect myself of softening of the brain. But—it's queer. There's a trick about it somewhere, I am convinced; and no doubt it's simple enough when you know how it's done,—but the difficulty is to find that out.—Do you think our friend over there is acting?'

'He looks to me as if he were ill.'

'He does look ill. He also looks as if he were hypnotised. If he is, it must be by suggestion,—and that's what makes me doubtful, because it will be the first plainly established case of hypnotism by suggestion I've encountered.—Holt!'

'Yes.'

'That,' said Sydney in my ear, 'is the voice and that is the manner of a hypnotised man, but, on the other hand, a person under influence generally responds only to the hypnotist,—which is another feature about our peculiar friend which arouses my suspicions.' Then, aloud, 'Don't stand there like an idiot,—come inside.'

Again Mr Holt made an apparently futile effort to do as he was bid. It was painful to look at him,—he was like a feeble, frightened, tottering child, who would come on, but cannot.

'I can't.'

'No nonsense, my man! Do you think that this is a performance in a booth, and that I am to be taken in by all the humbug of the professional mesmerist? Do as I tell you,—come into the room.'

There was a repetition, on Mr Holt's part, of his previous pitiful struggle; this time it was longer sustained than before,—but the result was the same.

'I can't!' he wailed.

'Then I say you can,—and shall! If I pick you up, and carry you, perhaps you will not find yourself so helpless as you wish me to suppose.'

Sydney moved forward to put his threat into execution. As he did so, a strange alteration took place in Mr Holt's demeanour.

CHAPTER XXX.

THE SINGULAR BEHAVIOUR OF MR HOLT

I was standing in the middle of the room, Sydney was between the door and me; Mr Holt was in the hall, just outside the doorway, in which he, so to speak, was framed. As Sydney advanced towards him he was seized with a kind of convulsion, —he had to lean against the side of the door to save himself from falling. Sydney paused, and watched. The spasm went as suddenly as it came, —Mr Holt became as motionless as he had just now been the other way. He stood in an attitude of febrile expectancy, —his chin raised, his head thrown back, his eyes glancing upwards, —with the dreadful fixed glare which had come into them ever since we had entered the house. He looked to me as if his every faculty was strained in the act of listening, —not a muscle in his body seemed to move; he was as rigid as a figure carved in stone. Presently the rigidity gave place to what, to an onlooker, seemed causeless agitation.

'I hear!' he exclaimed, in the most curious voice I had ever heard. 'I come!'

It was as though he was speaking to someone who was far away. Turning, he walked down the passage to the front door.

'Hollo!' cried Sydney. 'Where are you off to?'

We both of us hastened to see. He was fumbling with the latch; before we could reach him, the door was open, and he was through it. Sydney, rushing after him, caught him on the step and held him by the arm.

'What's the meaning of this little caper?—Where do you think you're going now?'

Mr Holt did not condescend to turn and look at him. He said, in the same dreamy, faraway, unnatural tone of voice, —and he kept his unwavering gaze fixed on what was apparently some distant object which was visible only to himself.

'I am going to him. He calls me.'

'Who calls you?'

'The Lord of the Beetle.'

Whether Sydney released his arm or not I cannot say. As he

spoke, he seemed to me to slip away from Sydney's grasp. Passing through the gateway, turning to the right, he commenced to retrace his steps in the direction we had come. Sydney stared after him in unequivocal amazement. Then he looked at me.

'Well!—this is a pretty fix!—now what's to be done?'

'What's the matter with him?' I inquired. 'Is he mad?'

'There's method in his madness if he is. He's in the same condition in which he was that night I saw him come out of the Apostle's window.' Sydney has a horrible habit of calling Paul 'the Apostle'; I have spoken to him about it over and over again,—but my words have not made much impression. 'He ought to be followed,—he may be sailing off to that mysterious friend of his this instant.—But, on the other hand, he mayn't, and it may be nothing but a trick of our friend the conjurer's to get us away from this elegant abode of his. He's done me twice already, I don't want to be done again,—and I distinctly do not want him to return and find me missing. He's quite capable of taking the hint, and removing himself into the Ewigkeit,—when the clue to as pretty a mystery as ever I came across will have vanished.'

'I can stay,' I said.

'You?—Alone?'

He eyed me doubtingly,—evidently not altogether relishing the proposition.

'Why not? You might send the first person you meet,—policeman, cabman, or whoever it is—to keep me company. It seems a pity now that we dismissed that cab.'

'Yes, it does seem a pity.' Sydney was biting his lip. 'Confound that fellow! how fast he moves.'

Mr Holt was already nearing the end of the road.

'If you think it necessary, by all means follow to see where he goes,—you are sure to meet somebody whom you will be able to send before you have gone very far.'

'I suppose I shall.—You won't mind being left alone?'

'Why should I?—I'm not a child.'

Mr Holt, reaching the corner, turned it, and vanished out of sight. Sydney gave an exclamation of impatience.

'If I don't make haste I shall lose him. I'll do as you suggest—dispatch the first individual I come across to hold watch and ward with you.'

'That'll be all right.'

He started off at a run,—shouting to me as he went.

'It won't be five minutes before somebody comes!'

I waved my hand to him. I watched him till he reached the end of the road. Turning, he waved his hand to me. Then he vanished, as Mr Holt had done.

And I was alone.

CHAPTER XXXI.

THE TERROR BY DAY

My first impulse, after Sydney's disappearance, was to laugh. Why should he display anxiety on my behalf merely because I was to be the sole occupant of an otherwise empty house for a few minutes more or less,—and in broad daylight too! To say the least, the anxiety seemed unwarranted.

I lingered at the gate, for a moment or two, wondering what was at the bottom of Mr Holt's singular proceedings, and what Sydney really proposed to gain by acting as a spy upon his wanderings. Then I turned to re-enter the house. As I did so, another problem suggested itself to my mind,—what connection, of the slightest importance, could a man in Paul Lessingham's position have with the eccentric being who had established himself in such an unsatisfactory dwelling-place? Mr Holt's story I had only dimly understood,—it struck me that it would require a deal of understanding. It was more like a farrago of nonsense, an outcome of delirium, than a plain statement of solid facts. To tell the truth, Sydney had taken it more seriously than I expected. He seemed to see something in it which I emphatically did not. What was double Dutch to me, seemed clear as print to him. So far as I could judge, he actually had the presumption to imagine that Paul—my Paul!—Paul Lessingham!—the great Paul Lessingham!—was mixed up in the very mysterious adventures of poor, weak-minded, hysterical Mr Holt, in a manner which was hardly to his credit.

Of course, any idea of the kind was purely and simply balderdash. Exactly what bee Sydney had got in his bonnet, I could not guess. But I did know Paul. Only let me find myself face to face with the fantastic author of Mr Holt's weird tribulations, and I, a woman, single-handed, would do my best to show him that whoever played pranks with Paul Lessingham trifled with edged tools.

I had returned to that historical front room which, according to Mr Holt, had been the scene of his most disastrous burglarious entry. Whoever had furnished it had had original notions of the resources of modern upholstery. There was not a table in the place,—no chair or couch, nothing to sit down upon except the bed. On the floor there was a marvellous carpet which was apparently of eastern manufacture. It was so thick, and so pliant to the tread, that moving over it was like walking on thousand-year-old turf. It was woven in gorgeous colours, and covered with—

When I discovered what it actually was covered with, I was conscious of a disagreeable sense of surprise.

It was covered with beetles!

All over it, with only a few inches of space between each, were representations of some peculiar kind of beetle,—it was the same beetle, over, and over, and over. The artist had woven his undesirable subject into the warp and woof of the material with such cunning skill that, as one continued to gaze, one began to wonder if by any possibility the creatures could be alive.

In spite of the softness of the texture, and the art—of a kind!—which had been displayed in the workmanship, I rapidly arrived at the conclusion that it was the most uncomfortable carpet I had ever seen. I wagged my finger at the repeated portrayals of the—to me!—unspeakable insect.

'If I had discovered that you were there before Sydney went, I think it just possible that I should have hesitated before I let him go.'

Then there came a revulsion of feeling. I shook myself.

'You ought to be ashamed of yourself, Marjorie Lindon, to even think such nonsense. Are you all nerves and morbid imaginings,—you who have prided yourself on being so strong-minded! A pretty sort you are to do battle for anyone.—Why, they're only make-believes!'

Half involuntarily, I drew my foot over one of the creatures. Of course, it was nothing but imagination; but I seemed to feel it squelch beneath my shoe. It was disgusting.

'Come!' I cried. 'This won't do! As Sydney would phrase it,—am I going to make an idiot of myself?'

I turned to the window,—looking at my watch.

'It's more than five minutes ago since Sydney went. That companion of mine ought to be already on the way. I'll go and see if he is coming.'

I went to the gate. There was not a soul in sight. It was with such a distinct sense of disappointment that I perceived this was so, that I was in two minds what to do. To remain where I was, looking, with gaping eyes, for the policeman, or the cabman, or whoever it was Sydney was dispatching to act as my temporary associate, was tantamount to acknowledging myself a simpleton,—while I was conscious of a most unmistakable reluctance to return within the house.

Common sense, or what I took for common sense, however, triumphed, and, after loitering for another five minutes, I did go in again.

This time, ignoring, to the best of my ability, the beetles on the floor, I proceeded to expend my curiosity—and occupy my thoughts—in an examination of the bed. It only needed a very cursory examination, however, to show that the seeming bed was, in reality, none at all,—or if it was a bed after the manner of the Easterns it certainly was not after the fashion of the Britons. There was no framework,—nothing to represent the bedstead. It was simply a heap of rugs piled apparently indiscriminately upon the floor. A huge mass of them there seemed to be; of all sorts, and shapes, and sizes,—and materials too.

The top one was of white silk,—in quality, exquisite. It was of huge size, yet, with a little compression, one might almost have passed it through the proverbial wedding ring. So far as space admitted I spread it out in front of me. In the middle was a picture,—whether it was embroidered on the substance or woven in it, I could not quite make out. Nor, at first, could I gather what it was the artist had intended to depict,—there was a brilliancy about it which was rather dazzling. By degrees, I realised that the lurid hues were meant for flames,—and, when one had got so far, one perceived that they were by no means badly imitated either. Then the meaning of the thing dawned on me,—it was a representation of a human sacrifice. In its way, as ghastly a piece of realism as one could see.

On the right was the majestic seated figure of a goddess. Her hands were crossed upon her knees, and she was naked from her waist upwards. I fancied it was meant for Isis. On her brow was perched a gaily-apparelled beetle—that ubiquitous beetle!—forming a bright spot of colour against her coppery skin,—it was an exact reproduction of the creatures which were imaged on the carpet. In front of the idol was an enormous fiery furnace. In the very heart of the flames was an altar. On the altar was a naked white woman being burned alive. There could be no doubt as to her being alive, for she was secured by chains in such a fashion that she was permitted a certain amount of freedom, of which she was availing herself to contort and twist her body into shapes which were horribly suggestive of the agony which she was enduring,—the artist, indeed, seemed to have exhausted his powers in his efforts to convey a vivid impression of the pains which were tormenting her.

'A pretty picture, on my word! A pleasant taste in art the garnitures of this establishment suggest! The person who likes to live with this kind of thing, especially as a covering to his bed, must have his own notions as to what constitute agreeable surroundings.'

As I continued staring at the thing, all at once it seemed as if the woman on the altar moved. It was preposterous, but she appeared to gather her limbs together, and turn half over.

'What can be the matter with me? Am I going mad? She can't be moving!'

If she wasn't, then certainly something was,—she was lifted right into the air. An idea occurred to me. I snatched the rug aside.

The mystery was explained!

A thin, yellow, wrinkled hand was protruding from amidst the heap of rugs,—it was its action which had caused the seeming movement of the figure on the altar. I stared, confounded. The hand was followed by an arm; the arm by a shoulder; the shoulder by a head,—and the most awful, hideous, wicked-looking face I had ever pictured even in my most dreadful dreams. A pair of baleful eyes were glaring up at mine.

I understood the position in a flash of startled amazement.

Sydney, in following Mr Holt, had started on a wild goose chase after all. I was alone with the occupant of that mysterious house,—the chief actor in Mr Holt's astounding tale. He had been hidden in the heap of rugs all the while.

BOOK IV.

In Pursuit

The Conclusion of the Matter is extracted from the Case-Book of the Hon. Augustus Champnell, Confidential Agent

CHAPTER XXXII.

A NEW CLIENT

On the afternoon of Friday, June 2, 18—, I was entering in my case-book some memoranda having reference to the very curious matter of the Duchess of Datchet's Deed-box. It was about two o'clock. Andrews came in and laid a card upon my desk. On it was inscribed 'Mr Paul Lessingham.'

'Show Mr Lessingham in.'

Andrews showed him in. I was, of course, familiar with Mr Lessingham's appearance, but it was the first time I had had with him any personal communication. He held out his hand to me.

'You are Mr Champnell?'

'I am.'

'I believe that I have not had the honour of meeting you before, Mr Champnell, but with your father, the Earl of Glenlivet, I have the pleasure of some acquaintance.'

I bowed. He looked at me, fixedly, as if he were trying to make out what sort of man I was.

'You are very young, Mr Champnell.'

'I have been told that an eminent offender in that respect once asserted that youth is not of necessity a crime.'

'And you have chosen a singular profession,—one in which one hardly looks for juvenility.'

'You yourself, Mr Lessingham, are not old. In a statesman one expects grey hairs.—I trust that I am sufficiently ancient to be able to do you service.'

He smiled.

'I think it possible. I have heard of you more than once, Mr Champnell, always to your advantage. My friend, Sir John Seymour, was telling me, only the other day, that you have recently conducted for him some business, of a very delicate nature, with much skill and tact; and he warmly advised me, if ever I found myself in a predicament, to come to you. I find myself in a predicament now.'

Again I bowed.

'A predicament, I fancy, of an altogether unparalleled sort. I take it that anything I may say to you will be as though it were said to a father confessor.'

'You may rest assured of that.'

'Good.—Then, to make the matter clear to you I must begin by telling you a story,—if I may trespass on your patience to that extent. I will endeavour not to be more verbose than the occasion requires.'

I offered him a chair, placing it in such a position that the light from the window would have shone full upon his face. With the calmest possible air, as if unconscious of my design, he carried the chair to the other side of my desk, twisting it right round before he sat on it,—so that now the light was at his back and on my face. Crossing his legs, clasping his hands about his knee, he sat in silence for some moments, as if turning something over in his mind. He glanced round the room.

'I suppose, Mr Champnell, that some singular tales have been told in here.'

'Some very singular tales indeed. I am never appalled by singularity. It is my normal atmosphere.'

'And yet I should be disposed to wager that you have never listened to so strange a story as that which I am about to tell you now. So astonishing, indeed, is the chapter in my life which I am about to open out to you, that I have more than once had to take myself to task, and fit the incidents together with mathematical accuracy in order to assure myself of its perfect truth.'

He paused. There was about his demeanour that suggestion of reluctance which I not uncommonly discover in individuals who are about to take the skeletons from their cupboards and parade them before my eyes. His next remark seemed to point to the fact that he perceived what was passing through my thoughts.

'My position is not rendered easier by the circumstance that I am not of a communicative nature. I am not in sympathy with the spirit of the age which craves for personal advertisement. I hold that the private life even of a public man should be held inviolate. I resent, with peculiar bitterness, the attempts of prying eyes to peer into matters which, as it seems to me, concern myself alone. You must, therefore, bear with me, Mr Champnell, if I seem awkward in disclosing to you certain incidents in my career which I had hoped would continue locked in the secret depository of my own bosom, at any rate till I was carried to the grave. I am sure you will suffer me to stand excused if I frankly admit that it is only an irresistible chain of incidents which has constrained me to make of you a confidant.'

'My experience tells me, Mr Lessingham, that no one ever does come to me until they are compelled. In that respect I am regarded as something worse even than a medical man.'

A wintry smile flitted across his features,—it was clear that he regarded me as a good deal worse than a medical man. Presently he began to tell me one of the most remarkable tales which even I had heard. As he proceeded I understood how strong, and how natural, had been his desire for reticence. On the mere score of credibility he must have greatly preferred to have kept his own counsel. For my part I own, unreservedly, that I should have deemed the tale incredible had it been told me by Tom, Dick, or Harry, instead of by Paul Lessingham.

CHAPTER XXXIII.
WHAT CAME OF LOOKING THROUGH A LATTICE

He began in accents which halted not a little. By degrees his voice grew firmer. Words came from him with greater fluency.

'I am not yet forty. So when I tell you that twenty years ago I was a mere youth I am stating what is a sufficiently obvious truth. It is twenty years ago since the events of which I am going to speak transpired.

'I lost both my parents when I was quite a lad, and by their death I was left in a position in which I was, to an unusual extent in one so young, my own master. I was ever of a rambling turn of mind, and when, at the mature age of eighteen, I left school, I decided that I should learn more from travel than from sojourn at a university. So, since there was no one to say me nay, instead of going either to Oxford or Cambridge, I went abroad. After a few months I found myself in Egypt,—I was down with fever at Shepheard's Hotel in Cairo. I had caught it by drinking polluted water during an excursion with some Bedouins to Palmyra.

'When the fever had left me I went out one night into the town in search of amusement. I went, unaccompanied, into the native quarter, not a wise thing to do, especially at night, but at eighteen one is not always wise, and I was weary of the monotony of the sick-room, and eager for something which had in it a spice of adventure. I found myself in a street which I have reason to believe is no longer existing. It had a French name, and was called the Rue de Rabagas,—I saw the name on the corner as I turned into it, and it has left an impress on the tablets of my memory which is never likely to be obliterated.

'It was a narrow street, and, of course, a dirty one, ill-lit, and, apparently, at the moment of my appearance, deserted. I had gone, perhaps, half-way down its tortuous length, blundering more than once into the kennel, wondering what fantastic whim had brought me into such unsavoury quarters, and what would happen to me if, as seemed extremely possible, I lost my way. On a sudden my ears were saluted by sounds which proceeded from a house which I was passing,—sounds of music and of singing.

'I paused. I stood awhile to listen.

'There was an open window on my right, which was screened by latticed blinds. From the room which was behind these blinds the sounds were coming. Someone was singing, accompanied by an instrument resembling a guitar,—singing uncommonly well.'

Mr Lessingham stopped. A stream of recollection seemed to come flooding over him. A dreamy look came into his eyes.

'I remember it all as clearly as if it were yesterday. How it all comes back,—the dirty street, the evil smells, the imperfect light, the girl's voice filling all at once the air. It was a girl's voice,—full, and round, and sweet; an organ seldom met with, especially in such a place as that. She sang a little chansonnette, which, just then, half Europe was humming,—it occurred in an opera which they were acting at one of the Boulevard theatres, —"La P'tite Voyageuse." The effect, coming so unexpectedly, was startling. I stood and heard her to an end.

'Inspired by I know not what impulse of curiosity, when the song was finished, I moved one of the lattice blinds a little aside, so as to enable me to get a glimpse of the singer. I found myself looking into what seemed to be a sort of café,—one of those places which are found all over the Continent, in which women sing in order to attract custom. There was a low platform at one end of the room, and on it were seated three women. One of them had evidently just been accompanying her own song,—she still had an instrument of music in her hands, and was striking a few idle notes. The other two had been acting as audience. They were attired in the fantastic apparel which the women who are found in such places generally wear. An old woman was sitting knitting in a corner, whom I took to be the inevitable patronne. With the exception of these four the place was empty.

'They must have heard me touch the lattice, or seen it moving, for no sooner did I glance within than the three pairs of eyes on the platform were raised and fixed on mine. The old woman in the corner alone showed no consciousness of my neighbourhood. We eyed one another in silence for a second or two. Then the girl with the harp,—the instrument she was manipulating proved to be fashioned more like a harp than a guitar—called out to me,

'"Entrez, monsieur!—Soyez le bienvenu!"

'I was a little tired. Rather curious as to whereabouts I was,—the place struck me, even at that first momentary glimpse, as hardly in the ordinary line of that kind of thing. And not unwilling to listen to a repetition of the former song, or to another sung by the same singer.

'"On condition," I replied, "that you sing me another song."

'"Ah, monsieur, with the greatest pleasure in the world I will sing you twenty."

'She was almost, if not quite, as good as her word. She entertained me with song after song. I may safely say that I have seldom if ever heard melody more enchanting. All languages seemed to be the same to her. She sang in French and Italian, German and English,—in tongues with which I was unfamiliar. It was in these Eastern harmonies that she was most successful. They were indescribably weird and thrilling, and she delivered them with a verve and sweetness which was amazing. I sat at one of the little tables with which the room was dotted, listening entranced.

'Time passed more rapidly than I supposed. While she sang I sipped the liquor with which the old woman had supplied me. So enthralled was I by the display of the girl's astonishing gifts that I did not notice what it was I was drinking. Looking back I can only surmise that it was some poisonous concoction of the creature's own. That one small glass had on me the strangest effect. I was still weak from the fever which I had only just succeeded in shaking off, and that, no doubt, had something to do with the result. But, as I continued to sit, I was conscious that I was sinking into a lethargic condition, against which I was incapable of struggling.

'After a while the original performer ceased her efforts, and, her companions taking her place, she came and joined me at the little table. Looking at my watch I was surprised to perceive the lateness of the hour. I rose to leave. She caught me by the wrist.

'"Do not go," she said;—she spoke English of a sort, and with the queerest accent. "All is well with you. Rest awhile."

'You will smile,—I should smile, perhaps, were I the listener instead of you, but it is the simple truth that her touch had on me what I can only describe as a magnetic influence. As her fingers closed upon my wrist, I felt as powerless in her grasp as if she held me with bands of steel. What seemed an invitation was virtually a command. I had to stay whether I would or wouldn't. She called for more liquor, and at what again was really her command I drank of it. I do not think that after she touched my wrist I uttered a word. She did all the talking. And, while she talked, she kept her eyes fixed on my face. Those eyes of hers! They were a devil's. I can positively affirm that they had on me a diabolical effect. They robbed me of my consciousness, of my power of volition, of my capacity to think,—they made me as wax in her hands. My last recollection of that fatal night is of her sitting in front of me, bending over the table, stroking my wrist with her extended fingers, staring at me with her awful eyes. After that, a curtain seems to descend. There comes a period of oblivion.'

Mr Lessingham ceased. His manner was calm and self-contained enough; but, in spite of that I could see that the mere recollection of the things which he told me moved his nature to its foundations. There was eloquence in the drawn lines about his mouth, and in the strained expression of his eyes.

So far his tale was sufficiently commonplace. Places such as the one which he described abound in the Cairo of to-day; and many are the Englishmen who have entered them to their exceeding bitter cost. With that keen intuition which has done him yeoman's service in the political arena, Mr Lessingham at once perceived the direction my thoughts were taking.

'You have heard this tale before?—No doubt. And often. The traps are many, and the fools and the unwary are not a few. The singularity of my experience is still to come. You must forgive me if I seem to stumble in the telling. I am anxious to present my case as baldly, and with as little appearance of exaggeration as possible. I say with as little appearance, for some appearance of exaggeration I fear is unavoidable. My case is so unique, and so out of the common run of our every-day experience, that the plainest possible statement must smack of the sensational.

'As, I fancy, you have guessed, when understanding returned to me, I found myself in an apartment with which I was unfamiliar. I was lying, undressed, on a heap of rugs in a corner of a low-pitched room which was furnished in a fashion which, when I grasped the details, filled me with amazement. By my side knelt the Woman of the Songs. Leaning over, she wooed my mouth with kisses. I cannot describe to you the sense of horror and of loathing with which the contact of her lips oppressed me. There was about her something so unnatural, so inhuman, that I believe even then I could have destroyed her with as little sense of moral turpitude as if she had been some noxious insect.

'"Where am I?" I exclaimed.

'"You are with the children of Isis," she replied. What she meant I did not know, and do not to this hour. "You are in the hands of the great goddess,—of the mother of men."

'"How did I come here?"

'"By the loving kindness of the great mother."

'I do not, of course, pretend to give you the exact text of her words, but they were to that effect.

'Half raising myself on the heap of rugs, I gazed about me,—and was astounded at what I saw.

'The place in which I was, though the reverse of lofty, was of considerable size,—I could not conceive whereabouts it could be. The walls and roof were of bare stone,—as though the whole had been hewed out of the solid rock. It seemed to be some sort of temple, and was redolent with the most extraordinary odour. An altar stood about the centre, fashioned out of a single block of stone. On it a fire burned with a faint blue flame,—the fumes which rose from it were no doubt chiefly responsible for the prevailing perfumes. Behind it was a huge bronze figure, more than life size. It was in a sitting posture, and represented a woman. Although it resembled no portrayal of her I have seen either before or since, I came afterwards to understand that it was meant for Isis. On the idol's brow was poised a beetle. That the creature was alive seemed clear, for, as I looked at it, it opened and shut its wings.

'If the one on the forehead of the goddess was the only live beetle which the place contained, it was not the only representation. It was modelled in the solid stone of the roof, and depicted in flaming colours on hangings which here and there were hung against the walls. Wherever the eye turned it rested on a scarab. The effect was bewildering. It was as though one saw things through the distorted glamour of a nightmare. I asked myself if I were not still dreaming; if my appearance of consciousness were not after all a mere delusion; if I had really regained my senses.

'And, here, Mr Champnell, I wish to point out, and to emphasise the fact, that I am not prepared to positively affirm what portion of my adventures in that extraordinary, and horrible place, was actuality, and what the product of a feverish imagination. Had I been persuaded that all I thought I saw, I really did see, I should have opened my lips long ago, let the consequences to myself have been what they might. But there is the crux. The happenings were of such an incredible character, and my condition was such an abnormal one,—I was never really myself from the first moment to the last—that I have hesitated, and still do hesitate, to assert where, precisely, fiction ended and fact began.

'With some misty notion of testing my actual condition I endeavoured to get off the heap of rugs on which I reclined. As I did so the woman at my side laid her hand against my chest, lightly. But, had her gentle pressure been the equivalent of a ton of iron, it could not have been more effectual. I collapsed, sank back upon the rugs, and lay there, panting for breath, wondering if I had crossed the border line which divides madness from sanity.

'"Let me get up!—let me go!" I gasped.

'"Nay," she murmured, "stay with me yet awhile, O my beloved."

'And again she kissed me.'

Once more Mr Lessingham paused. An involuntary shudder went all over him. In spite of the evidently great effort which he was making to retain his self-control his features were contorted by an anguished spasm. For some seconds he seemed at a loss to find words to enable him to continue.

When he did go on, his voice was harsh and strained.

'I am altogether incapable of even hinting to you the nauseous nature of that woman's kisses. They filled me with an indescribable repulsion. I look back at them with a feeling of physical, mental, and moral horror, across an interval of twenty years. The most dreadful part of it was that I was wholly incapable of offering even the faintest resistance to her caresses. I lay there like a log. She did with me as she would, and in dumb agony I endured.'

He took his handkerchief from his pocket, and, although the day was cool, with it he wiped the perspiration from his brow.

'To dwell in detail on what occurred during my involuntary sojourn in that fearful place is beyond my power. I cannot even venture to attempt it. The attempt, were it made, would be futile, and, to me, painful beyond measure. I seem to have seen all that happened as in a glass darkly,—with about it all an element of unreality. As I have already remarked, the things which revealed themselves, dimly, to my perception, seemed too bizarre, too hideous, to be true.

'It was only afterwards, when I was in a position to compare dates, that I was enabled to determine what had been the length of my imprisonment. It appears that I was in that horrible den more than two months,—two unspeakable months. And the whole time there were comings and goings, a phantasmagoric array of eerie figures continually passed to and fro before my hazy eyes. What I judge to have been religious services took place; in which the altar, the bronze image, and the beetle on its brow, figure largely. Not only were they conducted with a bewildering confusion of mysterious rites, but, if my memory is in the least degree trustworthy, they were orgies of nameless horrors. I seem to have seen things take place at them at the mere thought of which the brain reels and trembles.

'Indeed it is in connection with the cult of the obscene deity to whom these wretched creatures paid their scandalous vows that my most awful memories seem to have been associated. It may have been—I hope it was, a mirage born of my half delirious state, but it seemed to me that they offered human sacrifices.'

When Mr Lessingham said this, I pricked up my ears. For reasons of my own, which will immediately transpire, I had been wondering if he would make any reference to a human sacrifice. He noted my display of interest,—but misapprehended the cause.

'I see you start, I do not wonder. But I repeat that unless I was the victim of some extraordinary species of double sight—in which case the whole business would resolve itself into the fabric of a dream, and I should indeed thank God!—I saw, on more than one occasion, a human sacrifice offered on that stone altar, presumably to the grim image which looked down on it. And, unless I err, in each case the sacrificial object was a woman, stripped to the skin, as white as you or I,—and before they burned her they subjected her to every variety of outrage of which even the minds of demons could conceive. More than once since then I have seemed to hear the shrieks of the victims ringing through the air, mingled with the triumphant cries of her frenzied murderers, and the music of their harps.

'It was the cumulative horrors of such a scene which gave me the strength, or the courage, or the madness, I know not which it was, to burst the bonds which bound me, and which, even in the bursting, made of me, even to this hour, a haunted man.

'There had been a sacrifice,—unless, as I have repeatedly observed, the whole was nothing but a dream. A woman—a young and lovely Englishwoman, if I could believe the evidence of my own eyes, had been outraged, and burnt alive, while I lay there helpless, looking on. The business was concluded. The ashes of the victim had been consumed by the participants. The worshippers had departed. I was left alone with the woman of the songs, who apparently acted as the guardian of that worse than slaughterhouse. She was, as usual after such an orgie, rather a devil than a human being, drunk with an insensate frenzy, delirious with inhuman longings. As she approached to offer to me her loathed caresses, I was on a sudden conscious of something which I had not felt before when in her company. It was as though something had slipped away from me,—some weight which had oppressed me, some bond by which I had been bound. I was aroused, all at once, to a sense of freedom; to a knowledge that the blood which coursed through my veins was after all my own, that I was master of my own honour.

'I can only suppose that through all those weeks she had kept me there in a state of mesmeric stupor. That, taking advantage of the weakness which the fever had left behind, by the exercise of her diabolical arts, she had not allowed me to pass out of a condition of hypnotic trance. Now, for some reason, the cord was loosed. Possibly her absorption in her religious duties had caused her to forget to tighten it. Anyhow, as she approached me, she approached a man, and one who, for the first time for many a day, was his own man. She herself seemed wholly unconscious of anything of the kind. As she drew nearer to me, and nearer, she appeared to be entirely oblivious of the fact that I was anything but the fibreless, emasculated creature which, up to that moment, she had made of me.

'But she knew it when she touched me,—when she stooped to press her lips to mine. At that instant the accumulating rage which had been smouldering in my breast through all those leaden torturing hours, sprang into flame. Leaping off my couch of rugs, I flung my hands about her throat,—and then she knew I was awake. Then she strove to tighten the cord which she had suffered to become unduly loose. Her baleful eyes were fixed on mine. I knew that she was putting out her utmost force to trick me of my manhood. But I fought with her like one possessed, and I conquered—in a fashion. I compressed her throat with my two hands as with an iron vice. I knew that I was struggling for more than life, that the odds were all against me, that I was staking my all upon the casting of a die,—I stuck at nothing which could make me victor.

'Tighter and tighter my pressure grew,—I did not stay to think if I was killing her—till on a sudden—'

Mr Lessingham stopped. He stared with fixed, glassy eyes, as if the whole was being re-enacted in front of him. His voice faltered. I thought he would break down. But, with an effort, he continued.

'On a sudden, I felt her slipping from between my fingers. Without the slightest warning, in an instant she had vanished, and where, not a moment before, she herself had been, I found myself confronting a monstrous beetle,—a huge, writhing creation of some wild nightmare.

'At first the creature stood as high as I did. But, as I stared at it, in stupefied amazement,—as you may easily imagine,—the thing dwindled while I gazed. I did not stop to see how far the process of dwindling continued,—a stark raving madman for the nonce, I fled as if all the fiends in hell were at my heels.'

CHAPTER XXXIV.

AFTER TWENTY YEARS

'How I reached the open air I cannot tell you,—I do not know. I have a confused recollection of rushing through vaulted passages, through endless corridors, of trampling over people who tried to arrest my passage,—and the rest is blank.

'When I again came to myself I was lying in the house of an American missionary named Clements. I had been found, at early dawn, stark naked, in a Cairo street, and picked up for dead. Judging from appearances I must have wandered for miles, all through the night. Whence I had come, or whither I was going, none could tell,—I could not tell myself. For weeks I hovered between life and death. The kindness of Mr and Mrs Clements was not to be measured by words. I was brought to their house a penniless, helpless, battered stranger, and they gave me all they had to offer, without money and without price,—with no expectation of an earthly reward. Let no one pretend that there is no Christian charity under the sun. The debt I owed that man and woman I was never able to repay. Before I was properly myself again, and in a position to offer some adequate testimony of the gratitude I felt, Mrs Clements was dead, drowned during an excursion on the Nile, and her husband had departed on a missionary expedition into Central Africa, from which he never returned.

'Although, in a measure, my physical health returned, for months after I had left the roof of my hospitable hosts, I was in a state of semi-imbecility. I suffered from a species of aphasia. For days together I was speechless, and could remember nothing,—not even my own name. And, when that stage had passed, and I began to move more freely among my fellows, for years I was but a wreck of my former self. I was visited, at all hours of the day and night, by frightful—I know not whether to call them visions, they were real enough to me, but since they were visible to no one but myself, perhaps that is the word which best describes them. Their presence invariably plunged me into a state of abject terror, against which I was unable to even make a show of fighting. To such an extent did they embitter my existence, that I voluntarily placed myself under the treatment of an expert in mental pathology. For a considerable period of time I was under his constant supervision, but the visitations were as inexplicable to him as they were to me.

'By degrees, however, they became rarer and rarer, until at last I flattered myself that I had once more become as other men. After an interval, to make sure, I devoted myself to politics. Thenceforward I have lived, as they phrase it, in the public eye. Private life, in any peculiar sense of the term, I have had none.'

Mr Lessingham ceased. His tale was not uninteresting, and, to say the least of it, was curious. But I still was at a loss to understand what it had to do with me, or what was the purport of his presence in my room. Since he remained silent, as if the matter, so far as he was concerned, was at an end, I told him so.

'I presume, Mr Lessingham, that all this is but a prelude to the play. At present I do not see where it is that I come in.'

Still for some seconds he was silent. When he spoke his voice was grave and sombre, as if he were burdened by a weight of woe.

'Unfortunately, as you put it, all this has been but a prelude to the play. Were it not so I should not now stand in such pressing want of the services of a confidential agent,—that is, of an experienced man of the world, who has been endowed by nature with phenomenal perceptive faculties, and in whose capacity and honour I can place the completest confidence.'

I smiled,—the compliment was a pointed one.

'I hope your estimate of me is not too high.'

'I hope not,—for my sake, as well as for your own. I have heard great things of you. If ever man stood in need of all that human skill and acumen can do for him, I certainly am he.'

His words aroused my curiosity. I was conscious of feeling more interested than heretofore.

'I will do my best for you. Man can do no more. Only give my best a trial.'

'I will. At once.'

He looked at me long and earnestly. Then, leaning forward, he said, lowering his voice perhaps unconsciously,

'The fact is, Mr Champnell, that quite recently events have happened which threaten to bridge the chasm of twenty years, and to place me face to face with that plague spot of the past. At this moment I stand in imminent peril of becoming again the wretched thing I was when I fled from that den of all the devils. It is to guard me against this that I have come to you. I want you to unravel the tangled thread which threatens to drag me to my doom,—and, when unravelled to sunder it—for ever, if God wills!—in twain.'

'Explain.'

To be frank, for the moment I thought him mad. He went on.

'Three weeks ago, when I returned late one night from a sitting in the House of Commons, I found, on my study table, a sheet of paper on which there was a representation—marvellously like!—of the creature into which, as it seemed to me, the woman of the songs was transformed as I clutched her throat between my hands. The mere sight of it brought back one of those visitations of which I have told you, and which I thought I had done with for ever,—I was convulsed by an agony of fear, thrown into a state approximating to a paralysis both of mind and body.'

'But why?'

'I cannot tell you. I only know that I have never dared to allow my thoughts to recur to that last dread scene, lest the mere recurrence should drive me mad.'

'What was this you found upon your study table,—merely a drawing?'

'It was a representation, produced by what process I cannot say, which was so wonderfully, so diabolically, like the original, that for a moment I thought the thing itself was on my table.'

'Who put it there?'

'That is precisely what I wish you to find out,—what I wish you to make it your instant business to ascertain. I have found the thing, under similar circumstances, on three separate occasions, on my study table,—and each time it has had on me the same hideous effect.'

'Each time after you have returned from a late sitting in the House of Commons?'

'Exactly.'

'Where are these—what shall I call them—delineations?'

'That, again, I cannot tell you.'

'What do you mean?'

'What I say. Each time, when I recovered, the thing had vanished.'

'Sheet of paper and all?'

'Apparently,—though on that point I could not be positive. You will understand that my study table is apt to be littered with sheets of paper, and I could not absolutely determine that the thing had not stared at me from one of those. The delineation itself, to use your word, certainly had vanished.'

I began to suspect that this was a case rather for a doctor than for a man of my profession. And hinted as much.

'Don't you think it is possible, Mr Lessingham, that you have been overworking yourself—that you have been driving your brain too hard, and that you have been the victim of an optical delusion?'

'I thought so myself; I may say that I almost hoped so. But wait till I have finished. You will find that there is no loophole in that direction.'

He appeared to be recalling events in their due order. His manner was studiously cold,—as if he were endeavouring, despite the strangeness of his story, to impress me with the literal accuracy of each syllable he uttered.

'The night before last, on returning home, I found in my study a stranger.'

'A stranger?'

'Yes.—In other words, a burglar.'

'A burglar?—I see.—Go on.'

He had paused. His demeanour was becoming odder and odder.

'On my entry he was engaged in forcing an entry into my bureau. I need hardly say that I advanced to seize him. But—I could not.'

'You could not?—How do you mean you could not?'

'I mean simply what I say. You must understand that this was no ordinary felon. Of what nationality he was I cannot tell you. He only uttered two words, and they were certainly in English, but apart from that he was dumb. He wore no covering on his head or feet. Indeed, his only garment was a long dark flowing cloak which, as it fluttered about him, revealed that his limbs were bare.'

'An unique costume for a burglar.'

'The instant I saw him I realised that he was in some way connected with that adventure in the Rue de Rabagas. What he said and did, proved it to the hilt.'

'What did he say and do?'

'As I approached to effect his capture, he pronounced aloud two words which recalled that awful scene the recollection of which always lingers in my brain, and of which I never dare to permit myself to think. Their very utterance threw me into a sort of convulsion.'

'What were the words?'

Mr Lessingham opened his mouth,—and shut it. A marked change took place in the expression of his countenance. His eyes became fixed and staring,—resembling the glassy orbs of the somnambulist. For a moment I feared that he was going to give me an object lesson in the 'visitations' of which I had heard so much. I rose, with a view of offering him assistance. He motioned me back.

'Thank you.—It will pass away.'

His voice was dry and husky,—unlike his usual silvern tones. After an uncomfortable interval he managed to continue.

'You see for yourself, Mr Champnell, what a miserable weakling, when this subject is broached, I still remain. I cannot utter the words the stranger uttered, I cannot even write them down. For some inscrutable reason they have on me an effect similar to that which spells and incantations had on people in tales of witchcraft.'

'I suppose, Mr Lessingham, that there is no doubt that this mysterious stranger was not himself an optical delusion?'

'Scarcely. There is the evidence of my servants to prove the contrary.'

'Did your servants see him?'

'Some of them,—yes. Then there is the evidence of the bureau. The fellow had smashed the top right in two. When I came to examine the contents I learned that a packet of letters was missing. They were letters which I had received from Miss Lindon, a lady whom I hope to make my wife. This, also, I state to you in confidence.'

'What use would he be likely to make of them?'

'If matters stand as I fear they do, he might make a very serious misuse of them. If the object of these wretches, after all these years, is a wild revenge, they would be capable, having discovered what she is to me, of working Miss Lindon a fatal mischief,—or, at the very least, of poisoning her mind.'

'I see.—How did the thief escape,—did he, like the delineation, vanish into air?'

'He escaped by the much more prosaic method of dashing through the drawing-room window, and clambering down from the verandah into the street, where he ran right into someone's arms.'

'Into whose arms,—a constable's?'

'No; into Mr Atherton's,—Sydney Atherton's.'

'The inventor?'

'The same.—Do you know him?'

'I do. Sydney Atherton and I are friends of a good many years' standing.—But Atherton must have seen where he came from;—and, anyhow, if he was in the state of undress which you have described, why didn't he stop him?'

'Mr Atherton's reasons were his own. He did not stop him, and, so far as I can learn, he did not attempt to stop him. Instead, he knocked at my hall door to inform me that he had seen a man climb out of my window.'

'I happen to know that, at certain seasons, Atherton is a queer fish,—but that sounds very queer indeed.'

'The truth is, Mr Champnell, that, if it were not for Mr Atherton, I doubt if I should have troubled you even now. The accident of his being an acquaintance of yours makes my task easier.'

He drew his chair closer to me with an air of briskness which had been foreign to him before. For some reason, which I was unable to fathom, the introduction of Atherton's name seemed to have enlivened him. However, I was not long to remain in darkness. In half a dozen sentences he threw more light on the real cause of his visit to me than he had done in all that had gone before. His bearing, too, was more businesslike and to the point. For the first time I had some glimmerings of the politician,—alert, keen, eager,—as he is known to all the world.

'Mr Atherton, like myself, has been a postulant for Miss Lindon's hand. Because I have succeeded where he has failed, he has chosen to be angry. It seems that he has had dealings, either with my visitor of Tuesday night, or with some other his acquaintance, and he proposes to use what he has gleaned from him to the disadvantage of my character. I have just come from Mr Atherton. From hints he dropped I conclude that, probably during the last few hours, he has had an interview with someone who was connected in some way with that lurid patch in my career; that this person made so-called revelations, which were nothing but a series of monstrous lies; and these so-called revelations Mr Atherton has threatened, in so many words, to place before Miss Lindon. That is an eventuality which I wish to avoid. My own conviction is that there is at this moment in London an emissary from that den in the whilom Rue de Rabagas—for all I know it may be the Woman of the Songs herself. Whether the sole purport of this individual's presence is to do me injury, I am, as yet, in no position to say, but that it is proposed to work me mischief, at any rate, by the way, is plain. I believe that Mr Atherton knows more about this person's individuality and whereabouts than he has been willing, so far, to admit. I want you, therefore, to ascertain these things on my behalf; to find out what, and where, this person is, to drag her! —or him;—out into the light of day. In short, I want you to effectually protect me from the terrorism which threatens once more to overwhelm my mental and my physical powers,—which bids fair to destroy my intellect, my career, my life, my all.'

'What reason have you for suspecting that Mr Atherton has seen this individual of whom you speak,—has he told you so?'

'Practically,—yes.'

'I know Atherton well. In his not infrequent moments of excitement he is apt to use strong language, but it goes no further. I believe him to be the last person in the world to do anyone an intentional injustice, under any circumstances whatever. If I go to him, armed with credentials from you, when he understands the real gravity of the situation,—which it will be my business to make him do, I believe that, spontaneously, of his own accord, he will tell me as much about this mysterious individual as he knows himself.'

'Then go to him at once.'

'Good. I will. The result I will communicate to you.'

I rose from my seat. As I did so, someone rushed into the outer office with a din and a clatter. Andrews' voice, and another, became distinctly audible,—Andrews' apparently raised in vigorous expostulation. Raised, seemingly, in vain, for presently the door of my own particular sanctum was thrown open with a crash, and Mr Sydney Atherton himself came dashing in,—evidently conspicuously under the influence of one of those not infrequent 'moments of excitement' of which I had just been speaking.

CHAPTER XXXV.

A BRINGER OF TIDINGS

Atherton did not wait to see who might or might not be present, but, without even pausing to take breath, he broke into full cry on the instant,—as is occasionally his wont.

'Champnell!—Thank goodness I've found you in!—I want you!—At once!—Don't stop to talk, but stick your hat on, and put your best foot forward,—I'll tell you all about it in the cab.'

I endeavoured to call his attention to Mr Lessingham's presence,—but without success.

'My dear fellow—'

When I had got as far as that he cut me short.

'Don't "dear fellow" me!—None of your jabber! And none of your excuses either! I don't care if you've got an engagement with the Queen, you'll have to chuck it. Where's that dashed hat of yours,—or are you going without it? Don't I tell you that every second cut to waste may mean the difference between life and death?—Do you want me to drag you down to the cab by the hair of your head?'

'I will try not to constrain you to quite so drastic a resource,—and I was coming to you at once in any case. I only want to call your attention to the fact that I am not alone.—Here is Mr Lessingham.'

In his harum-scarum haste Mr Lessingham had gone unnoticed. Now that his observation was particularly directed to him, Atherton started, turned, and glared at my latest client in a fashion which was scarcely flattering.

'Oh!—It's you, is it?—What the deuce are you doing here?'

Before Lessingham could reply to this most unceremonious query, Atherton, rushing forward, gripped him by the arm.

'Have you seen her?'

Lessingham, not unnaturally nonplussed by the other's curious conduct, stared at him in unmistakable amazement.

'Have I seen whom?'

'Marjorie Lindon!'

'Marjorie Lindon?'

Lessingham paused. He was evidently asking himself what the inquiry meant.

'I have not seen Miss Lindon since last night. Why do you ask?'

'Then Heaven help us!—As I'm a living man I believe he, she, or it has got her!'

His words were incomprehensible enough to stand in copious need of explanation,—as Mr Lessingham plainly thought.

'What is it that you mean, sir?'

'What I say,—I believe that that Oriental friend of yours has got her in her clutches,—if it is a "her;" goodness alone knows what the infernal conjurer's real sex may be.'

'Atherton!—Explain yourself!'

On a sudden Lessingham's tones rang out like a trumpet call.

'If damage comes to her I shall be fit to cut my throat,—and yours!'

Mr Lessingham's next proceeding surprised me,—I imagine it surprised Atherton still more. Springing at Sydney like a tiger, he caught him by the throat.

'You——you hound! Of what wretched folly have you been guilty? If so much as a hair of her head is injured you shall repay it me ten thousandfold!—You mischief-making, intermeddling, jealous fool!'

He shook Sydney as if he had been a rat,—then flung him from him headlong on to the floor. It reminded me of nothing so much as Othello's treatment of Iago. Never had I seen a man so transformed by rage. Lessingham seemed to have positively increased in stature. As he stood glowering down at the prostrate Sydney, he might have stood for a materialistic conception of human retribution.

Sydney, I take it, was rather surprised than hurt. For a moment or two he lay quite still. Then, lifting his head, he looked up his assailant. Then, raising himself to his feet, he shook himself,—as if with a view of learning if all his bones were whole. Putting his hands up to his neck, he rubbed it, gently. And he grinned.

'By God, Lessingham, there's more in you than I thought. After all, you are a man. There's some holding power in those wrists of yours,—they've nearly broken my neck. When this business is finished, I should like to put on the gloves with you, and fight it out. You're clean wasted upon politics.—Damn it, man, give me your hand!'

Mr Lessingham did not give him his hand. Atherton took it,—and gave it a hearty shake with both of his.

If the first paroxysm of his passion had passed, Lessingham was still sufficiently stern.

'Be so good as not to trifle, Mr Atherton. If what you say is correct, and the wretch to whom you allude really has Miss Lindon at her mercy, then the woman I love—and whom you also pretend to love!—stands in imminent peril not only of a ghastly death, but of what is infinitely worse than death.'

'The deuce she does!' Atherton wheeled round towards me. 'Champnell, haven't you got that dashed hat of yours yet? Don't stand there like a tailor's dummy, keeping me on tenter-hooks, —move yourself! I'll tell you all about it in the cab.—And, Lessingham, if you'll come with us I'll tell you too.'

CHAPTER XXXVI.

WHAT THE TIDINGS WERE

Three in a hansom cab is not, under all circumstances, the most comfortable method of conveyance,—when one of the trio happens to be Sydney Atherton in one of his 'moments of excitement' it is distinctly the opposite; as, on that occasion, Mr Lessingham and I both quickly found. Sometimes he sat on my knees, sometimes on Lessingham's, and frequently, when he unexpectedly stood up, and all but precipitated himself on to the horse's back, on nobody's. In the eagerness of his gesticulations, first he knocked off my hat, then he knocked off Lessingham's, then his own, then all three together,—once, his own hat rolling into the mud, he sprang into the road, without previously going through the empty form of advising the driver of his intention, to pick it up. When he turned to speak to Lessingham, he thrust his elbow into my eye; and when he turned to speak to me, he thrust it into Lessingham's. Never, for one solitary instant, was he at rest, or either of us at ease. The wonder is that the gymnastics in which he incessantly indulged did not sufficiently attract public notice to induce a policeman to put at least a momentary period to our progress. Had speed not been of primary importance I should have insisted on the transference of the expedition to the somewhat wider limits of a four-wheeler.

His elucidation of the causes of his agitation was apparently more comprehensible to Lessingham than it was to me. I had to piece this and that together under considerable difficulties. By degrees I did arrive at something like a clear notion of what had actually taken place.

He commenced by addressing Lessingham,—and thrusting his elbow into my eye.

'Did Marjorie tell you about the fellow she found in the street?' Up went his arm to force the trap-door open overhead,—and off went my hat. 'Now then, William Henry!—let her go!—if you kill the horse I'll buy you another!'

We were already going much faster than, legally, we ought to have done,—but that, seemingly to him was not a matter of the slightest consequence. Lessingham replied to his inquiry.

'She did not.'

'You know the fellow I saw coming out of your drawing-room

window?'

'Yes.'

'Well, Marjorie found him the morning after in front of her breakfast-room window—in the middle of the street. Seems he had been wandering about all night, unclothed,—in the rain and the mud, and all the rest of it,—in a condition of hypnotic trance.'

'Who is the— —gentleman you are alluding to?'

'Says his name's Holt, Robert Holt.'

'Holt?—Is he an Englishman?'

'Very much so,—City quilldriver out of a shop,—stony broke absolutely! Got the chuck from the casual ward,—wouldn't let him in,—house full, and that sort of thing,—poor devil! Pretty passes you politicians bring men to!'

'Are you sure?'

'Of what?'

'Are you sure that this man, Robert Holt, is the same person whom, as you put it, you saw coming out of my drawing-room window?'

'Sure!—Of course I'm sure!—Think I didn't recognise him?—Besides, there was the man's own tale,—owned to it himself,—besides all the rest, which sent one rushing Fulham way.'

'You must remember, Mr Atherton, that I am wholly in the dark as to what has happened. What has the man, Holt, to do with the errand on which we are bound?'

'Am I not coming to it? If you would let me tell the tale in my own way I should get there in less than no time, but you will keep on cutting in,—how the deuce do you suppose Champnell is to make head or tail of the business if you will persist in interrupting?—Marjorie took the beggar in,—he told his tale to her,—she sent for me—that was just now; caught me on the steps after I had been lunching with Dora Grayling. Holt re-dished his yarn—I smelt a rat—saw that a connection possibly existed between the thief who'd been playing confounded conjuring tricks off on to me and this interesting party down Fulham way—'

'What party down Fulham way?'

'This friend of Holt's—am I not telling you? There you are, you see,—won't let me finish! When Holt slipped through the window—which is the most sensible thing he seems to have done; if I'd been in his shoes I'd have slipped through forty windows!—dusky coloured charmer caught him on the hop,—doctored him—sent him out to commit burglary by deputy. I said to Holt, "Show us this agreeable little crib, young man." Holt was game—then Marjorie chipped in—she wanted to go and see it too. I said, "You'll be sorry if you do,"—that settled it! After that she'd have gone if she'd died,—I never did have a persuasive way with women. So off we toddled, Marjorie, Holt, and I, in a growler,—spotted the crib in less than no time,—invited ourselves in by the kitchen window—house seemed empty. Presently Holt became hypnotised before my eyes,—the best established case of hypnotism by suggestion I ever yet encountered—started off on a pilgrimage of one. Like an idiot I followed, leaving Marjorie to wait for me—'

'Alone?'

'Alone!—Am I not telling you?—Great Scott, Lessingham, in the House of Commons they must be hazy to think you smart! I said, "I'll send the first sane soul I meet to keep you company." As luck would have it, I never met one,—only kids, and a baker, who wouldn't leave his cart, or take it with him either. I'd covered pretty nearly two miles before I came across a peeler,—and when I did the man was cracked—and he thought me mad, or drunk, or both. By the time I'd got myself within nodding distance of being run in for obstructing the police in the execution of their duty, without inducing him to move a single one of his twenty-four-inch feet, Holt was out of sight. So, since all my pains in his direction were clean thrown away, there was nothing left for me but to scurry back to Marjorie,—so I scurried, and I found the house empty, no one there, and Marjorie gone.'

'But, I don't quite follow—'

Atherton impetuously declined to allow Mr Lessingham to conclude.

'Of course you don't quite follow, and you'll follow still less if you will keep getting in front. I went upstairs and downstairs, inside and out—shouted myself hoarse as a crow—nothing was to be seen of Marjorie,—or heard; until, as I was coming down the stairs for about the five-and-fiftieth time, I stepped on something hard which was lying in the passage. I picked it up,—it was a ring; this ring. Its shape is not just what it was,—I'm not as light as gossamer, especially when I come jumping downstairs six at a time,—but what's left of it is here.'

Sydney held something in front of him. Mr Lessingham wriggled to one side to enable him to see. Then he made a snatch at it.

'It's mine!'

Sydney dodged it out of his reach.

'What do you mean, it's yours?'

'It's the ring I gave Marjorie for an engagement ring. Give it me, you hound!—unless you wish me to do you violence in the cab.'

With complete disregard of the limitations of space,—or of my comfort,—Lessingham thrust him vigorously aside. Then gripping Sydney by the wrist, he seized the gaud,—Sydney yielding it just in time to save himself from being precipitated into the street. Ravished of his treasure, Sydney turned and surveyed the ravisher with something like a glance of admiration.

'Hang me, Lessingham, if I don't believe there is some warm blood in those fishlike veins of yours. Please the piper, I'll live to fight you after all,—with the bare ones, sir, as a gentleman should do.'

Lessingham seemed to pay no attention to him whatever. He was surveying the ring, which Sydney had trampled out of shape, with looks of the deepest concern.

'Marjorie's ring!—The one I gave her! Something serious must have happened to her before she would have dropped my ring, and left it lying where it fell.'

Atherton went on.

'That's it!—What has happened to her!—I'll be dashed if I know!—When it was clear that there she wasn't, I tore off to find out where she was. Came across old Lindon,—he knew nothing;—I rather fancy I startled him in the middle of Pall Mall, when I left he stared after me like one possessed, and his hat was lying in the gutter. Went home,—she wasn't there.

Asked Dora Grayling,—she'd seen nothing of her. No one had seen anything of her,—she had vanished into air. Then I said to myself, "You're a first-class idiot, on my honour! While you're looking for her, like a lost sheep, the betting is that the girl's in Holt's friend's house the whole jolly time. When you were there, the chances are that she'd just stepped out for a stroll, and that now she's back again, and wondering where on earth you've gone!" So I made up my mind that I'd fly back and see,—because the idea of her standing on the front doorstep looking for me, while I was going off my nut looking for her, commended itself to what I call my sense of humour; and on my way it struck me that it would be the part of wisdom to pick up Champnell, because if there is a man who can be backed to find a needle in any amount of haystacks it is the great Augustus.—That horse has moved itself after all, because here we are. Now, cabman, don't go driving further on,—you'll have to put a girdle round the earth if you do; because you'll have to reach this point again before you get your fare.—This is the magician's house!'

CHAPTER XXXVII.

WHAT WAS HIDDEN UNDER THE FLOOR

The cab pulled up in front of a tumbledown cheap 'villa' in an unfinished cheap neighbourhood,—the whole place a living monument of the defeat of the speculative builder.

Atherton leaped out on to the grass-grown rubble which was meant for a footpath.

'I don't see Marjorie looking for me on the doorstep.'

Nor did I,—I saw nothing but what appeared to be an unoccupied ramshackle brick abomination. Suddenly Sydney gave an exclamation.

'Hullo!—The front door's closed!'

I was hard at his heels.

'What do you mean?'

'Why, when I went I left the front door open. It looks as if I've made an idiot of myself after all, and Marjorie's returned,—let's hope to goodness that I have.'

He knocked. While we waited for a response I questioned him.

'Why did you leave the door open when you went?'

'I hardly know,—I imagine that it was with some dim idea of Marjorie's being able to get in if she returned while I was absent,—but the truth is I was in such a condition of helter skelter that I am not prepared to swear that I had any reasonable reason.'

'I suppose there is no doubt that you did leave it open?'

'Absolutely none,—on that I'll stake my life.'

'Was it open when you returned from your pursuit of Holt?'

'Wide open,—I walked straight in expecting to find her waiting for me in the front room,—I was struck all of a heap when I found she wasn't there.'

'Were there any signs of a struggle?'

'None,—there were no signs of anything. Everything was just as I had left it, with the exception of the ring which I trod on in the passage, and which Lessingham has.'

'If Miss Lindon has returned, it does not look as if she were in the house at present.'

It did not,—unless silence had such meaning. Atherton had knocked loudly three times without succeeding in attracting the slightest notice from within.

'It strikes me that this is another case of seeking admission through that hospitable window at the back.'

Atherton led the way to the rear. Lessingham and I followed. There was not even an apology for a yard, still less a garden,—there was not even a fence of any sort, to serve as an enclosure, and to shut off the house from the wilderness of waste land. The kitchen window was open. I asked Sydney if he had left it so.

'I don't know,—I dare say we did; I don't fancy that either of us stood on the order of his coming.'

While he spoke, he scrambled over the sill. We followed. When he was in, he shouted at the top of his voice,

'Marjorie! Marjorie! Speak to me, Marjorie,—it is I,—Sydney!'

The words echoed through the house. Only silence answered. He led the way to the front room. Suddenly he stopped.

'Hollo!' he cried. 'The blind's down!' I had noticed, when we were outside, that the blind was down at the front room window. 'It was up when I went, that I'll swear. That someone has been here is pretty plain,—let's hope it's Marjorie.'

He had only taken a step forward into the room when he again stopped short to exclaim.

'My stars!—here's a sudden clearance!—Why, the place is empty,—everything's clean gone!'

'What do you mean?—was it furnished when you left?'

The room was empty enough then.

'Furnished?—I don't know that it was exactly what you'd call furnished,—the party who ran this establishment had a taste in upholstery which was all his own,—but there was a carpet, and a bed, and—and lots of things,—for the most part, I should have said, distinctly Eastern curiosities. They seem to have evaporated into smoke,—which may be a way which is common enough among Eastern curiosities, though it's queer to me.'

Atherton was staring about him as if he found it difficult to credit the evidence of his own eyes.

'How long ago is it since you left?'

He referred to his watch.

'Something over an hour,—possibly an hour and a half; I couldn't swear to the exact moment, but it certainly isn't more.'

'Did you notice any signs of packing up?'

'Not a sign.' Going to the window he drew up the blind,—speaking as he did so. 'The queer thing about this business is that when we first got in this blind wouldn't draw up a little bit, so, since it wouldn't go up I pulled it down, roller and all, now it draws up as easily and smoothly as if it had always been the best blind that ever lived.'

Standing at Sydney's back I saw that the cabman on his box was signalling to us with his outstretched hand. Sydney perceived him too. He threw up the sash.

'What's the matter with you?'

'Excuse me, sir, but who's the old gent?'

'What old gent?'

'Why the old gent peeping through the window of the room upstairs?'

The words were hardly out of the driver's mouth when Sydney was through the door and flying up the staircase. I followed rather more soberly,—his methods were a little too flighty for me. When I reached the landing, dashing out of the front room he rushed into the one at the back,—then through a door at the side. He came out shouting.

'What's the idiot mean! – with his old gent! I'd old gent him if I got him! – There's not a creature about the place!'

He returned into the front room, – I at his heels. That certainly was empty, – and not only empty, but it showed no traces of recent occupation. The dust lay thick upon the floor, – there was that mouldy, earthy smell which is so frequently found in apartments which have been long untenanted.

'Are you sure, Atherton, that there is no one at the back?'

'Of course I'm sure, – you can go and see for yourself if you like; do you think I'm blind? Jehu's drunk.' Throwing up the sash he addressed the driver. 'What do you mean with your old gent at the window? – what window?'

'That window, sir.'

'Go to! – you're dreaming, man! – there's no one here.'

'Begging your pardon, sir, but there was someone there not a minute ago.'

'Imagination, cabman, – the slant of the light on the glass, – or your eyesight's defective.'

'Excuse me, sir, but it's not my imagination, and my eyesight's as good as any man's in England, – and as for the slant of the light on the glass, there ain't much glass for the light to slant on. I saw him peeping through that bottom broken pane on your left hand as plainly as I see you. He must be somewhere about, – he can't have got away, – he's at the back. Ain't there a cupboard nor nothing where he could hide?'

The cabman's manner was so extremely earnest that I went myself to see. There was a cupboard on the landing, but the door of that stood wide open, and that obviously was bare. The room behind was small, and, despite the splintered glass in the window frame, stuffy. Fragments of glass kept company with the dust on the floor, together with a choice collection of stones, brickbats, and other missiles, – which not improbably were the cause of their being there. In the corner stood a cupboard, – but a momentary examination showed that that was as bare as the other. The door at the side, which Sydney had left wide open, opened on to a closet, and that was empty. I glanced up, – there was no trap door which led to the roof. No practicable nook or cranny, in which a living being could lie concealed, was anywhere at hand.

I returned to Sydney's shoulder to tell the cabman so.

'There is no place in which anyone could hide, and there is no one in either of the rooms,—you must have been mistaken, driver.'

The man waxed wroth.

'Don't tell me! How could I come to think I saw something when I didn't?'

'One's eyes are apt to play us tricks;—how could you see what wasn't there?'

'That's what I want to know. As I drove up, before you told me to stop, I saw him looking through the window,—the one at which you are. He'd got his nose glued to the broken pane, and was staring as hard as he could stare. When I pulled up, off he started,—I saw him get up off his knees, and go to the back of the room. When the gentleman took to knocking, back he came,—to the same old spot, and flopped down on his knees. I didn't know what caper you was up to,—you might be bum bailiffs for all I knew!—and I supposed that he wasn't so anxious to let you in as you might be to get inside, and that was why he didn't take no notice of your knocking, while all the while he kept a eye on what was going on. When you goes round to the back, up he gets again, and I reckoned that he was going to meet yer, and perhaps give yer a bit of his mind, and that presently I should hear a shindy, or that something would happen. But when you pulls up the blind downstairs, to my surprise back he come once more. He shoves his old nose right through the smash in the pane, and wags his old head at me like a chattering magpie. That didn't seem to me quite the civil thing to do,—I hadn't done no harm to him; so I gives you the office, and lets you know that he was there. But for you to say that he wasn't there, and never had been,—blimey! that cops the biscuit. If he wasn't there, all I can say is I ain't here, and my 'orse ain't here, and my cab ain't neither,—damn it!—the house ain't here, and nothing ain't!'

He settled himself on his perch with an air of the most extreme ill usage,—he had been standing up to tell his tale. That the man was serious was unmistakable. As he himself suggested, what inducement could he have had to tell a lie like that? That he believed himself to have seen what he declared he saw was plain. But, on the other hand, what could have become—in the space of fifty seconds!—of his 'old gent'?

Atherton put a question.

'What did he look like,—this old gent of yours?'

'Well, that I shouldn't hardly like to say. It wasn't much of his face I could see, only his face and his eyes,—and they wasn't pretty. He kept a thing over his head all the time, as if he didn't want too much to be seen.'

'What sort of a thing?'

'Why,—one of them cloak sort of things, like them Arab blokes used to wear what used to be at Earl's Court Exhibition,—you know!'

This piece of information seemed to interest my companions more than anything he had said before.

'A burnoose do you mean?'

'How am I to know what the thing's called? I ain't up in foreign languages,—'tain't likely! All I know that them Arab blokes what was at Earl's Court used to walk about in them all over the place,—sometimes they wore them over their heads, and sometimes they didn't. In fact if you'd asked me, instead of trying to make out as I sees double, or things what was only inside my own noddle, or something or other, I should have said this here old gent what I've been telling you about was a Arab bloke,—when he gets off his knees to sneak away from the window, I could see that he had his cloak thing, what was over his head, wrapped all round him.'

Mr Lessingham turned to me, all quivering with excitement.

'I believe that what he says is true!'

'Then where can this mysterious old gentleman have got to,—can you suggest an explanation? It is strange, to say the least of it, that the cabman should be the only person to see or hear anything of him.'

'Some devil's trick has been played,—I know it, I feel it!—my instinct tells me so!'

I stared. In such a matter one hardly expects a man of Paul Lessingham's stamp to talk of 'instinct.' Atherton stared too. Then, on a sudden, he burst out,

'By the Lord, I believe the Apostle's right,—the whole place reeks to me of hankey-pankey,—it did as soon as I put my nose inside. In matters of prestidigitation, Champnell, we Westerns are among the rudiments,—we've everything to learn,—Orientals leave us at the post. If their civilisation's what we're pleased to call extinct, their conjuring—when you get to know it!—is all alive oh!'

He moved towards the door. As he went he slipped, or seemed to, all but stumbling on to his knees.

'Something tripped me up,—what's this?' He was stamping on the floor with his foot. 'Here's a board loose. Come and lend me a hand, one of you fellows, to get it up. Who knows what mystery's beneath?'

I went to his aid. As he said, a board in the floor was loose. His stepping on it unawares had caused his stumble. Together we prised it out of its place,—Lessingham standing by and watching us the while. Having removed it, we peered into the cavity it disclosed.

There was something there.

'Why,' cried Atherton, 'it's a woman's clothing!'

CHAPTER XXXVIII.

THE REST OF THE FIND

It was a woman's clothing, beyond a doubt, all thrown in anyhow,—as if the person who had placed it there had been in a desperate hurry. An entire outfit was there, shoes, stockings, body linen, corsets, and all,—even to hat, gloves, and hairpins; —these latter were mixed up with the rest of the garments in strange confusion. It seemed plain that whoever had worn those clothes had been stripped to the skin.

Lessingham and Sydney stared at me in silence as I dragged them out and laid them on the floor. The dress was at the bottom,—it was an alpaca, of a pretty shade in blue, bedecked with lace and ribbons, as is the fashion of the hour, and lined with sea-green silk. It had perhaps been a 'charming confection' once—and that a very recent one!—but now it was all soiled and creased and torn and tumbled. The two spectators made a simultaneous pounce at it as I brought it to the light.

'My God!' cried Sydney, 'it's Marjorie's!—she was wearing it when I saw her last!'

'It's Marjorie's!' gasped Lessingham,—he was clutching at the ruined costume, staring at it like a man who has just received sentence of death. 'She wore it when she was with me yesterday,—I told her how it suited her, and how pretty it was!'

There was silence,—it was an eloquent find; it spoke for itself. The two men gazed at the heap of feminine glories,—it might have been the most wonderful sight they ever had seen. Lessingham was the first to speak,—his face had all at once grown grey and haggard.

'What has happened to her?'

I replied to his question with another.

'Are you sure this is Miss Lindon's dress?'

'I am sure,—and were proof needed, here it is.'

He had found the pocket, and was turning out the contents. There was a purse, which contained money and some visiting cards on which were her name and address; a small bunch of keys, with her nameplate attached; a handkerchief, with her initials in a corner. The question of ownership was placed beyond a doubt.

'You see,' said Lessingham, exhibiting the money which was in the purse, 'it is not robbery which has been attempted. Here are two ten-pound notes, and one for five, besides gold and silver,—over thirty pounds in all.'

Atherton, who had been turning over the accumulation of rubbish between the joists, proclaimed another find.

'Here are her rings, and watch, and a bracelet,—no, it certainly does not look as if theft had been an object.'

Lessingham was glowering at him with knitted brows.

'I have to thank you for this.'

Sydney was unwontedly meek.

'You are hard on me, Lessingham, harder than I deserve,—I had rather have thrown away my own life than have suffered misadventure to have come to her.'

'Yours are idle words. Had you not meddled this would not have happened. A fool works more mischief with his folly than of malice prepense. If hurt has befallen Marjorie Lindon you shall account for it to me with your life's blood.'

'Let it be so,' said Sydney. 'I am content. If hurt has come to Marjorie, God knows that I am willing enough that death should come to me.'

While they wrangled, I continued to search. A little to one side, under the flooring which was still intact, I saw something gleam. By stretching out my hand, I could just manage to reach it,—it was a long plait of woman's hair. It had been cut off at the roots,—so close to the head in one place that the scalp itself had been cut, so that the hair was clotted with blood.

They were so occupied with each other that they took no notice of me. I had to call their attention to my discovery.

'Gentlemen, I fear that I have here something which will distress you,—is not this Miss Lindon's hair?'

They recognised it on the instant. Lessingham, snatching it from my hands, pressed it to his lips.

'This is mine,—I shall at least have something.' He spoke with a grimness which was a little startling. He held the silken tresses at arm's length. 'This points to murder,—foul, cruel, causeless murder. As I live, I will devote my all,—money, time, reputation!—to gaining vengeance on the wretch who did this deed.'

Atherton chimed in.

'To that I say, Amen!' He lifted his hand. 'God is my witness!'

'It seems to me, gentlemen, that we move too fast,—to my mind it does not by any means of necessity point to murder. On the contrary, I doubt if murder has been done. Indeed, I don't mind owning that I have a theory of my own which points all the other way.'

Lessingham caught me by the sleeve.

'Mr Champnell, tell me your theory.'

'I will, a little later. Of course it may be altogether wrong;—though I fancy it is not; I will explain my reasons when we come to talk of it. But, at present, there are things which must be done.'

'I vote for tearing up every board in the house!' cried Sydney. 'And for pulling the whole infernal place to pieces. It's a conjurer's den.—I shouldn't be surprised if cabby's old gent is staring at us all the while from some peephole of his own.'

We examined the entire house, methodically, so far as we were able, inch by inch. Not another board proved loose,—to lift those which were nailed down required tools, and those we were without. We sounded all the walls,—with the exception of the party walls they were the usual lath and plaster constructions, and showed no signs of having been tampered with. The ceilings were intact; if anything was concealed in them it must have been there some time,—the cement was old and dirty. We took the closet to pieces; examined the chimneys; peered into the kitchen oven and the copper;—in short, we pried into everything which, with the limited means at our disposal, could be pried into,—without result. At the end we found ourselves dusty, dirty, and discomfited. The cabman's 'old gent' remained as much a mystery as ever, and no further trace had been discovered of Miss Lindon.

Atherton made no effort to disguise his chagrin.

'Now what's to be done? There seems to be just nothing in the place at all, and yet that there is, and that it's the key to the whole confounded business I should be disposed to swear.'

'In that case I would suggest that you should stay and look for it. The cabman can go and look for the requisite tools, or a workman to assist you, if you like. For my part it appears to me that evidence of another sort is, for the moment, of paramount importance; and I propose to commence my search for it by making a call at the house which is over the way.'

I had observed, on our arrival, that the road only contained two houses which were in anything like a finished state,—that which we were in, and another, some fifty or sixty yards further down, on the opposite side. It was to this I referred. The twain immediately proffered their companionship.

'I will come with you,' said Mr Lessingham.

'And I,' echoed Sydney. 'We'll leave this sweet homestead in charge of the cabman,—I'll pull it to pieces afterwards.' He went out and spoke to the driver. 'Cabby, we're going to pay a visit to the little crib over there,—you keep an eye on this one. And if you see a sign of anyone being about the place,—living, or dead, or anyhow—you give me a yell. I shall be on the lookout, and I'll be with you before you can say Jack Robinson.'

'You bet I'll yell,—I'll raise the hair right off you.' The fellow grinned. 'But I don't know if you gents are hiring me by the day,—I want to change my horse; he ought to have been in his stable a couple of hours ago.'

'Never mind your horse,—let him rest a couple of hours extra to-morrow to make up for those he has lost to-day. I'll take care you don't lose anything by this little job,—or your horse either. —By the way, look here,—this will be better than yelling.'

Taking a revolver out of his trousers' pocket he handed it up to the grinning driver.

'If that old gent of yours does appear, you have a pop at him, —I shall hear that easier than a yell. You can put a bullet through him if you like,—I give you my word it won't be murder.'

'I don't care if it is,' declared the cabman, handling the weapon like one who was familiar with arms of precision. 'I used to fancy my revolver shooting when I was with the colours, and if I do get a chance I'll put a shot through the old hunks, if only to prove to you that I'm no liar.'

Whether the man was in earnest or not I could not tell, — nor whether Atherton meant what he said in answer.

'If you shoot him I'll give you fifty pounds.'

'All right!' The driver laughed. 'I'll do my best to earn that fifty!'

CHAPTER XXXIX.

MISS LOUISA COLEMAN

That the house over the way was tenanted was plain to all the world,—at least one occupant sat gazing through the window of the first floor front room. An old woman in a cap,—one of those large old-fashioned caps which our grandmothers used to wear, tied with strings under the chin. It was a bow window, and as she was seated in the bay looking right in our direction she could hardly have failed to see us as we advanced,—indeed she continued to stare at us all the while with placid calmness. Yet I knocked once, twice, and yet again without the slightest notice being taken of my summons.

Sydney gave expression to his impatience in his own peculiar vein.

'Knockers in this part of the world seem intended for ornament only,—nobody seems to pay any attention to them when they're used. The old lady upstairs must be either deaf or dotty.' He went out into the road to see if she still was there. 'She's looking at me as calmly as you please,—what does she think we're doing here, I wonder; playing a tune on her front door by way of a little amusement?—Madam!' He took off his hat and waved it to her. 'Madam! might I observe that if you won't condescend to notice that we're here your front door will run the risk of being severely injured!—She don't care for me any more than if I was nothing at all,—sound another tattoo upon that knocker. Perhaps she's so deaf that nothing short of a cataclysmal uproar will reach her auditory nerves.'

She immediately proved, however, that she was nothing of the sort. Hardly had the sounds of my further knocking died away than, throwing up the window, she thrust out her head and addressed me in a fashion which, under the circumstances, was as unexpected as it was uncalled for.

'Now, young man, you needn't be in such a hurry!'

Sydney explained.

'Pardon me, madam, it's not so much a hurry we're in as pressed for time,—this is a matter of life and death.'

She turned her attention to Sydney,—speaking with a frankness for which, I imagine, he was unprepared.

'I don't want none of your imperence, young man. I've seen you before,—you've been hanging about here the whole day long!—and I don't like the looks of you, and so I'll let you know. That's my front door, and that's my knocker,—I'll come down and open when I like, but I'm not going to be hurried, and if the knocker's so much as touched again, I won't come down at all.'

She closed the window with a bang. Sydney seemed divided between mirth and indignation.

'That's a nice old lady, on my honour,—one of the good old crusty sort. Agreeable characters this neighbourhood seems to grow,—a sojourn hereabouts should do one good. Unfortunately I don't feel disposed just now to stand and kick my heels in the road.' Again saluting the old dame by raising his hat he shouted to her at the top of his voice. 'Madam, I beg ten thousand pardons for troubling you, but this is a matter in which every second is of vital importance,—would you allow me to ask you one or two questions?'

Up went the window; out came the old lady's head.

'Now, young man, you needn't put yourself out to holler at me,—I won't be hollered at! I'll come down and open that door in five minutes by the clock on my mantelpiece, and not a moment before.'

The fiat delivered, down came the window. Sydney looked rueful,—he consulted his watch.

'I don't know what you think, Champnell, but I really doubt if this comfortable creature can tell us anything worth waiting another five minutes to hear. We mustn't let the grass grow under our feet, and time is getting on.'

I was of a different opinion,—and said so.

'I'm afraid, Atherton, that I can't agree with you. She seems to have noticed you hanging about all day; and it is at least possible that she has noticed a good deal which would be well worth our hearing. What more promising witness are we likely to find?—her house is the only one which overlooks the one we have just quitted. I am of opinion that it may not only prove well worth our while to wait five minutes, but also that it would be as well, if possible, not to offend her by the way. She's not likely to afford us the information we require if you do.'

'Good. If that's what you think I'm sure I'm willing to wait,—only it's to be hoped that that clock upon her mantelpiece moves quicker than its mistress.'

Presently, when about a minute had gone, he called to the cabman.

'Seen a sign of anything?'

The cabman shouted back.

'Ne'er a sign,—you'll hear a sound of popguns when I do.'

Those five minutes did seem long ones. But at last Sydney, from his post of vantage in the road, informed us that the old lady was moving.

'She's getting up;—she's leaving the window;—let's hope to goodness she's coming down to open the door. That's been the longest five minutes I've known.'

I could hear uncertain footsteps descending the stairs. They came along the passage. The door was opened—'on the chain.' The old lady peered at us through an aperture of about six inches.

'I don't know what you young men think you're after, but have all three of you in my house I won't. I'll have him and you'—a skinny finger was pointed to Lessingham and me; then it was directed towards Atherton—'but have him I won't. So if it's anything particular you want to say to me, you'll just tell him to go away.'

On hearing this Sydney's humility was abject. His hat was in his hand,—he bent himself double.

'Suffer me to make you a million apologies, madam, if I have in any way offended you; nothing, I assure you, could have been farther from my intention, or from my thoughts.'

'I don't want none of your apologies, and I don't want none of you neither; I don't like the looks of you, and so I tell you. Before I let anybody into my house you'll have to sling your hook.'

The door was banged in our faces. I turned to Sydney.

'The sooner you go the better it will be for us. You can wait for us over the way.'

He shrugged his shoulders, and groaned,—half in jest, half in earnest.

'If I must I suppose I must,—it's the first time I've been refused admittance to a lady's house in all my life! What have I done to deserve this thing?—If you keep me waiting long I'll tear that infernal den to pieces!'

He sauntered across the road, viciously kicking the stones as he went. The door reopened.

'Has that other young man gone?'

'He has.'

'Then now I'll let you in. Have him inside my house I won't.'

The chain was removed. Lessingham and I entered. Then the door was refastened and the chain replaced. Our hostess showed us into the front room on the ground floor; it was sparsely furnished and not too clean,—but there were chairs enough for us to sit upon; which she insisted on our occupying.

'Sit down, do,—I can't abide to see folks standing; it gives me the fidgets.'

So soon as we were seated, without any overture on our parts she plunged in medias res.

'I know what it is you've come about,—I know! You want me to tell you who it is as lives in the house over the road. Well, I can tell you,—and I dare bet a shilling that I'm about the only one who can.'

I inclined my head.

'Indeed. Is that so, madam?'

She was huffed at once.

'Don't madam me,—I can't bear none of your lip service. I'm a plain-spoken woman, that's what I am, and I like other people's tongues to be as plain as mine. My name's Miss Louisa Coleman; but I'm generally called Miss Coleman,—I'm only called Louisa by my relatives.'

Since she was apparently between seventy and eighty—and looked every year of her apparent age—I deemed that possible. Miss Coleman was evidently a character. If one was desirous of getting information out of her it would be necessary to allow her to impart it in her own manner,—to endeavour to induce her to impart it in anybody else's would be time clean wasted. We had Sydney's fate before our eyes.

She started with a sort of roundabout preamble.

'This property is mine; it was left me by my uncle, the late George Henry Jobson,—he's buried in Hammersmith Cemetery just over the way,—he left me the whole of it. It's one of the finest building sites near London, and it increases in value every year, and I'm not going to let it for another twenty, by which time the value will have more than trebled,—so if that is what you've come about, as heaps of people do, you might have saved yourselves the trouble. I keep the boards standing, just to let people know that the ground is to let,—though, as I say, it won't be for another twenty years, when it'll be for the erection of high-class mansions only, same as there is in Grosvenor Square,—no shops or public houses, and none of your shanties. I live in this place just to keep an eye upon the property,—and as for the house over the way, I've never tried to let it, and it never has been let, not until a month ago, when, one morning, I had this letter. You can see it if you like.'

She handed me a greasy envelope which she ferreted out of a capacious pocket which was suspended from her waist, and which she had to lift up her skirt to reach. The envelope was addressed, in unformed characters, 'Miss Louisa Coleman, The Rhododendrons, Convolvulus Avenue, High Oaks Park, West Kensington.'—I felt, if the writer had not been of a humorous turn of mind, and drawn on his imagination, and this really was the lady's correct address, then there must be something in a name.

The letter within was written in the same straggling, characterless caligraphy,—I should have said, had I been asked offhand, that the whole thing was the composition of a servant girl. The composition was about on a par with the writing.

'The undersigned would be oblidged if Miss Coleman would let her empty house. I do not know the rent but send fifty pounds. If more will send. Please address, Mohamed el Kheir, Post Office, Sligo Street, London.'

It struck me as being as singular an application for a tenancy as I remembered to have encountered. When I passed it on to Lessingham, he seemed to think so too.

'This is a curious letter, Miss Coleman.'

'So I thought,—and still more so when I found the fifty pounds inside. There were five ten-pound notes, all loose, and the letter not even registered. If I had been asked what was the rent of the house, I should have said, at the most, not more than twenty pounds,—because, between you and me, it wants a good bit of doing up, and is hardly fit to live in as it stands.'

I had had sufficient evidence of the truth of this altogether apart from the landlady's frank admission.

'Why, for all he could have done to help himself I might have kept the money, and only sent him a receipt for a quarter. And some folks would have done,—but I'm not one of that sort myself, and shouldn't care to be. So I sent this here party,—I never could pronounce his name, and never shall—a receipt for a year.'

Miss Coleman paused to smooth her apron, and consider.

'Well, the receipt should have reached this here party on the Thursday morning, as it were,—I posted it on the Wednesday night, and on the Thursday, after breakfast, I thought I'd go over the way to see if there was any little thing I could do,—because there wasn't hardly a whole pane of glass in the place,—when I all but went all of a heap. When I looked across the road, blessed if the party wasn't in already,—at least as much as he ever was in, which, so far as I can make out, never has been anything particular,—though how he had got in, unless it was through a window in the middle of the night, is more than I should care to say,—there was nobody in the house when I went to bed, that I could pretty nearly take my Bible oath,—yet there was the blind up at the parlour, and, what's more, it was down, and it's been down pretty nearly ever since.

'"Well," I says to myself, "for right down imperence this beats anything,—why he's in the place before he knows if I'll let him have it. Perhaps he thinks I haven't got a word to say in the matter,—fifty pounds or no fifty pounds, I'll soon show him." So I slips on my bonnet, and I walks over the road, and I hammers at the door.

'Well, I have seen people hammering since then, many a one, and how they've kept it up has puzzled me,—for an hour, some of them,—but I was the first one as begun it. I hammers, and I hammers, and I kept on hammering, but it wasn't no more use than if I'd been hammering at a tombstone. So I starts rapping at the window, but that wasn't no use neither. So I goes round behind, and I hammers at the back door,—but there, I couldn't make anyone hear nohow. So I says to myself, "Perhaps the party as is in, ain't in, in a manner of speaking; but I'll keep an eye on the house, and when he is in I'll take care that he ain't out again before I've had a word to say."

'So I come back home, and as I said I would, I kept an eye on the house the whole of that livelong day, but never a soul went either out or in. But the next day, which it was a Friday, I got out of bed about five o'clock, to see if it was raining, through my having an idea of taking a little excursion if the weather was fine, when I see a party coming down the road. He had on one of them dirty-coloured bed-cover sort of things, and it was wrapped all over his head and round his body, like, as I have been told, them there Arabs wear,—and, indeed, I've seen them in them myself at West Brompton, when they was in the exhibition there. It was quite fine, and broad day, and I see him as plainly as I see you,—he comes skimming along at a tear of a pace, pulls up at the house over the way, opens the front door, and lets himself in.

'"So," I says to myself, "there you are. Well, Mr Arab, or whatever, or whoever, you may be, I'll take good care that you don't go out again before you've had a word from me. I'll show you that landladies have their rights, like other Christians, in this country, however it may be in yours." So I kept an eye on the house, to see that he didn't go out again, and nobody never didn't, and between seven and eight I goes and I knocks at the door,—because I thought to myself that the earlier I was the better it might be.

'If you'll believe me, no more notice was taken of me than if I was one of the dead. I hammers, and I hammers, till my wrist was aching, I daresay I hammered twenty times,—and then I went round to the back door, and I hammers at that,—but it wasn't the least good in the world. I was that provoked to think I should be treated as if I was nothing and nobody, by a dirty foreigner, who went about in a bed-gown through the public streets, that it was all I could do to hold myself.

'I comes round to the front again, and I starts hammering at the window, with every knuckle on my hands, and I calls out, "I'm Miss Louisa Coleman, and I'm the owner of this house, and you can't deceive me,—I saw you come in, and you're in now, and if you don't come and speak to me this moment I'll have the police."

'All of a sudden, when I was least expecting it, and was hammering my very hardest at the pane, up goes the blind, and up goes the window too, and the most awful-looking creature ever I heard of, not to mention seeing, puts his head right into my face,—he was more like a hideous baboon than anything else, let alone a man. I was struck all of a heap, and plumps down on the little wall, and all but tumbles head over heels backwards. And he starts shrieking, in a sort of a kind of English, and in such a voice as I'd never heard the like,—it was like a rusty steam engine.

'"Go away! go away! I don't want you! I will not have you,—never! You have your fifty pounds,—you have your money,—that is the whole of you,—that is all you want! You come to me no more!—never!—never no more!—or you be sorry!—Go away!"

'I did go away, and that as fast as ever my legs would carry me,—what with his looks, and what with his voice, and what with the way that he went on, I was nothing but a mass of trembling. As for answering him back, or giving him a piece of my mind, as I had meant to, I wouldn't have done it not for a thousand pounds. I don't mind confessing, between you and me, that I had to swallow four cups of tea, right straight away, before my nerves was steady.

'"Well," I says to myself, when I did feel, as it might be, a little more easy, "you never have let that house before, and now you've let it with a vengeance,—so you have. If that there new tenant of yours isn't the greatest villain that ever went unhung it must be because he's got near relations what's as bad as himself,—because two families like his I'm sure there can't be. A nice sort of Arab party to have sleeping over the road he is!"

'But after a time I cools down, as it were,—because I'm one of them sort as likes to see on both sides of a question. "After all," I says to myself, "he has paid his rent, and fifty pounds is fifty pounds,—I doubt if the whole house is worth much more, and he can't do much damage to it whatever he does."

'I shouldn't have minded, so far as that went, if he'd set fire to the place, for, between ourselves, it's insured for a good bit over its value. So I decided that I'd let things be as they were, and see how they went on. But from that hour to this I've never spoken to the man, and never wanted to, and wouldn't, not of my own free will, not for a shilling a time,—that face of his will haunt me if I live till Noah, as the saying is. I've seen him going in and out at all hours of the day and night,—that Arab party's a mystery if ever there was one,—he always goes tearing along as if he's flying for his life. Lots of people have come to the house, all sorts and kinds, men and women—they've been mostly women, and even little children. I've seen them hammer and hammer at that front door, but never a one have I seen let in,—or yet seen taken any notice of, and I think I may say, and yet tell no lie, that I've scarcely took my eye off the house since he's been inside it, over and over again in the middle of the night have I got up to have a look, so that I've not missed much that has took place.

'What's puzzled me is the noises that's come from the house. Sometimes for days together there's not been a sound, it might have been a house of the dead; and then, all through the night, there've been yells and screeches, squawks and screams,—I never heard nothing like it. I have thought, and more than once, that the devil himself must be in that front room, let alone all the rest of his demons. And as for cats!—where they've come from I can't think. I didn't use to notice hardly a cat in the neighbourhood till that there Arab party came,—there isn't much to attract them; but since he came there's been regiments. Sometimes at night there's been troops about the place, screeching like mad,—I've wished them farther, I can tell you. That Arab party must be fond of 'em. I've seen them inside the house, at the windows, upstairs and downstairs, as it seemed to me, a dozen at a time.'

CHAPTER XL.

WHAT MISS COLEMAN SAW THROUGH THE WINDOW

As Miss Coleman had paused, as if her narrative was approaching a conclusion, I judged it expedient to make an attempt to bring the record as quickly as possible up to date.

'I take it, Miss Coleman, that you have observed what has occurred in the house to-day.'

She tightened her nut-cracker jaws and glared at me disdainfully,—her dignity was ruffled.

'I'm coming to it, aren't I?—if you'll let me. If you've got no manners I'll learn you some. One doesn't like to be hurried at my time of life, young man.'

I was meekly silent;—plainly, if she was to talk, every one else must listen.

'During the last few days there have been some queer goings on over the road,—out of the common queer, I mean, for goodness knows that they always have been queer enough. That Arab party has been flitting about like a creature possessed,—I've seen him going in and out twenty times a day. This morning—'

She paused,—to fix her eyes on Lessingham. She apparently observed his growing interest as she approached the subject which had brought us there,—and resented it.

'Don't look at me like that, young man, because I won't have it. And as for questions, I may answer questions when I'm done, but don't you dare to ask me one before, because I won't be interrupted.'

Up to then Lessingham had not spoken a word,—but it seemed as if she was endowed with the faculty of perceiving the huge volume of the words which he had left unuttered.

'This morning—as I've said already,—' she glanced at Lessingham as if she defied his contradiction—'when that Arab party came home it was just on the stroke of seven. I know what was the exact time because, when I went to the door to the milkman, my clock was striking the half hour, and I always keep it thirty minutes fast. As I was taking the milk, the man said to me, "Hollo, Miss Coleman, here's your friend coming along." "What friend?" I says,—for I ain't got no friends, as I know, round here, nor yet, I hope no enemies neither.

'And I looks round, and there was the Arab party coming tearing down the road, his bedcover thing all flying in the wind, and his arms straight out in front of him,—I never did see anyone go at such a pace. "My goodness," I says, "I wonder he don't do himself an injury." "I wonder someone else don't do him an injury," says the milkman. "The very sight of him is enough to make my milk go sour." And he picked up his pail and went away quite grumpy,—though what that Arab party's done to him is more than I can say.—I have always noticed that milkman's temper's short like his measure. I wasn't best pleased with him for speaking of that Arab party as my friend, which he never has been, and never won't be, and never could be neither.

'Five persons went to the house after the milkman was gone, and that there Arab party was safe inside,—three of them was commercials, that I know, because afterwards they came to me. But of course they none of them got no chance with that there Arab party except of hammering at his front door, which ain't what you might call a paying game, nor nice for the temper, but for that I don't blame him, for if once those commercials do begin talking they'll talk for ever.

'Now I'm coming to this afternoon.'

I thought it was about time,—though for the life of me, I did not dare to hint as much.

'Well, it might have been three, or it might have been half past, anyhow it was thereabouts, when up there comes two men and a woman, which one of the men was that young man what's a friend of yours. "Oh," I says to myself, "here's something new in callers, I wonder what it is they're wanting." That young man what was a friend of yours, he starts hammering, and hammering, as the custom was with every one who came, and, as usual, no more notice was taken of him than nothing,—though I knew that all the time the Arab party was indoors.'

At this point I felt that at all hazards I must interpose a question.

'You are sure he was indoors?'

She took it better than I feared she might.

'Of course I'm sure,—hadn't I seen him come in at seven, and he never hadn't gone out since, for I don't believe that I'd taken my eyes off the place not for two minutes together, and I'd never had a sight of him. If he wasn't indoors, where was he then?'

For the moment, so far as I was concerned, the query was unanswerable. She triumphantly continued:

'Instead of doing what most did, when they'd had enough of hammering, and going away, these three they went round to the back, and I'm blessed if they mustn't have got through the kitchen window, woman and all, for all of a sudden the blind in the front room was pulled not up, but down—dragged down it was, and there was that young man what's a friend of yours standing with it in his hand.

'"Well," I says to myself, "if that ain't cool I should like to know what is. If, when you ain't let in, you can let yourself in, and that without so much as saying by your leave, or with your leave, things is coming to a pretty pass. Wherever can that Arab party be, and whatever can he be thinking of, to let them go on like that because that he's the sort to allow a liberty to be took with him, and say nothing, I don't believe."

'Every moment I expects to hear a noise and see a row begin, but, so far as I could make out, all was quiet and there wasn't nothing of the kind. So I says to myself, "There's more in this than meets the eye, and them three parties must have right upon their side, or they wouldn't be doing what they are doing in the way they are, there'd be a shindy."

'Presently, in about five minutes, the front door opens, and a young man—not the one what's your friend, but the other—comes sailing out, and through the gate, and down the road, as stiff and upright as a grenadier,—I never see anyone walk more upright, and few as fast. At his heels comes the young man what is your friend, and it seems to me that he couldn't make out what this other was a-doing of. I says to myself, "There's been a quarrel between them two, and him as has gone has hooked it." This young man what is your friend he stood at the gate, all of a fidget, staring after the other with all his eyes, as if he couldn't think what to make of him, and the young woman, she stood on the doorstep, staring after him too.

'As the young man what had hooked it turned the corner, and

was out of sight, all at once your friend he seemed to make up his mind, and he started off running as hard as he could pelt,—and the young woman was left alone. I expected, every minute, to see him come back with the other young man, and the young woman, by the way she hung about the gate, she seemed to expect it too. But no, nothing of the kind. So when, as I expect, she'd had enough of waiting, she went into the house again, and I see her pass the front room window. After a while, back she comes to the gate, and stands looking and looking, but nothing was to be seen of either of them young men. When she'd been at the gate, I daresay five minutes, back she goes into the house,—and I never saw nothing of her again.'

'You never saw anything of her again?—Are you sure she went back into the house?'

'As sure as I am that I see you.'

'I suppose that you didn't keep a constant watch upon the premises?'

'But that's just what I did do. I felt something queer was going on, and I made up my mind to see it through. And when I make up my mind to a thing like that I'm not easy to turn aside. I never moved off the chair at my bedroom window, and I never took my eyes off the house, not till you come knocking at my front door.'

'But, since the young lady is certainly not in the house at present, she must have eluded your observation, and, in some manner, have left it without your seeing her.'

'I don't believe she did, I don't see how she could have done,—there's something queer about that house, since that Arab party's been inside it. But though I didn't see her, I did see someone else.'

'Who was that?'

'A young man.'

'A young man?'

'Yes, a young man, and that's what puzzled me, and what's been puzzling me ever since, for see him go in I never did do.'

'Can you describe him?'

'Not as to the face, for he wore a dirty cloth cap pulled down right over it, and he walked so quickly that I never had a proper look. But I should know him anywhere if I saw him, if only because of his clothes and his walk.'

'What was there peculiar about his clothes and his walk?'

'Why, his clothes were that old, and torn, and dirty, that a ragman wouldn't have given a thank you for them,—and as for fit,—there wasn't none, they hung upon him like a scarecrow—he was a regular figure of fun; I should think the boys would call after him if they saw him in the street. As for his walk, he walked off just like the first young man had done, he strutted along with his shoulders back, and his head in the air, and that stiff and straight that my kitchen poker would have looked crooked beside of him.'

'Did nothing happen to attract your attention between the young lady's going back into the house and the coming out of this young man?'

Miss Coleman cogitated.

'Now you mention it there did,—though I should have forgotten all about it if you hadn't asked me,—that comes of your not letting me tell the tale in my own way. About twenty minutes after the young woman had gone in someone put up the blind in the front room, which that young man had dragged right down, I couldn't see who it was for the blind was between us, and it was about ten minutes after that that young man came marching out.'

'And then what followed?'

'Why, in about another ten minutes that Arab party himself comes scooting through the door.'

'The Arab party?'

'Yes, the Arab party! The sight of him took me clean aback. Where he'd been, and what he'd been doing with himself while them there people played hi-spy-hi about his premises I'd have given a shilling out of my pocket to have known, but there he was, as large as life, and carrying a bundle.'

'A bundle?'

'A bundle, on his head, like a muffin-man carries his tray. It was a great thing, you never would have thought he could have carried it, and it was easy to see that it was as much as he could manage; it bent him nearly double, and he went crawling along like a snail,—it took him quite a time to get to the end of the road.'

Mr Lessingham leaped up from his seat, crying,

'Marjorie was in that bundle!'

'I doubt it,' I said.

He moved about the room distractedly, wringing his hands.

'She was! she must have been! God help us all!'

'I repeat that I doubt it. If you will be advised by me you will wait awhile before you arrive at any such conclusion.'

All at once there was a tapping at the window pane. Atherton was staring at us from without.

He shouted through the glass,

'Come out of that, you fossils!—I've news for you!'

CHAPTER XLI.

THE CONSTABLE,—HIS CLUE, —AND THE CAB

Miss Coleman, getting up in a fluster, went hurrying to the door.

'I won't have that young man in my house. I won't have him! Don't let him dare to put his nose across my doorstep.'

I endeavoured to appease her perturbation.

'I promise you that he shall not come in, Miss Coleman. My friend here, and I, will go and speak to him outside.'

She held the front door open just wide enough to enable Lessingham and me to slip through, then she shut it after us with a bang. She evidently had a strong objection to any intrusion on Sydney's part.

Standing just without the gate he saluted us with a characteristic vigour which was scarcely flattering to our late hostess. Behind him was a constable.

'I hope you two have been mewed in with that old pussy long enough. While you've been tittle-tattling I've been doing,—listen to what this bobby's got to say.'

The constable, his thumbs thrust inside his belt, wore an indulgent smile upon his countenance. He seemed to find Sydney amusing. He spoke in a deep bass voice,—as if it issued from his boots.

'I don't know that I've got anything to say.'

It was plain that Sydney thought otherwise.

'You wait till I've given this pretty pair of gossips a lead, officer, then I'll trot you out.' He turned to us.

'After I'd poked my nose into every dashed hole in that infernal den, and been rewarded with nothing but a pain in the back for my trouble, I stood cooling my heels on the doorstep, wondering if I should fight the cabman, or get him to fight me, just to pass the time away,—for he says he can box, and he looks it,—when who should come strolling along but this magnificent example of the metropolitan constabulary.' He waved his hand towards the policeman, whose grin grew wider. 'I looked at him, and he looked at me, and then when we'd had enough of admiring each other's fine features and striking proportions, he said to me, "Has he gone?" I said, "Who?—Baxter?—or Bob Brown?" He said, "No, the Arab." I said, "What do you know about any Arab?" He said, "Well, I saw him in the Broadway about three-quarters of an hour ago, and then, seeing you here, and the house all open, I wondered if he had gone for good." With that I almost jumped out of my skin, though you can bet your life I never showed it. I said, "How do you know it was he?" He said, "It was him right enough, there's no doubt about that. If you've seen him once, you're not likely to forget him." "Where was he going?" "He was talking to a cabman,—four-wheeler. He'd got a great bundle on his head,—wanted to take it inside with him. Cabman didn't seem to see it." That was enough for me,—I picked this most deserving officer up in my arms, and carried him across the road to you two fellows like a flash of lightning.'

Since the policeman was six feet three or four, and more than sufficiently broad in proportion, his scarcely seemed the kind of figure to be picked up in anybody's arms and carried like a 'flash of lightning,' which,—as his smile grew more indulgent, he himself appeared to think.

Still, even allowing for Atherton's exaggeration, the news which he had brought was sufficiently important. I questioned the constable upon my own account.

'There is my card, officer, probably, before the day is over, a charge of a very serious character will be preferred against the person who has been residing in the house over the way. In the meantime it is of the utmost importance that a watch should be kept upon his movements. I suppose you have no sort of doubt that the person you saw in the Broadway was the one in question?'

'Not a morsel. I know him as well as I do my own brother,—we all do upon this beat. He's known amongst us as the Arab. I've had my eye on him ever since he came to the place. A queer fish he is. I always have said that he's up to some game or other. I never came across one like him for flying about in all sorts of weather, at all hours of the night, always tearing along as if for his life. As I was telling this gentleman I saw him in the Broadway,—well, now it's about an hour since, perhaps a little more. I was coming on duty when I saw a crowd in front of the District Railway Station,—and there was the Arab, having a sort of argument with the cabman. He had a great bundle on his head, five or six feet long, perhaps longer. He wanted to take this great bundle with him into the cab, and the cabman, he didn't see it.'

'You didn't wait to see him drive off.'

'No,—I hadn't time. I was due at the station,—I was cutting it pretty fine as it was.'

'You didn't speak to him,—or to the cabman?'

'No, it wasn't any business of mine you understand. The whole thing just caught my eye as I was passing.'

'And you didn't take the cabman's number?'

'No, well, as far as that goes it wasn't needful. I know the cabman, his name and all about him, his stable's in Bradmore.'

I whipped out my note-book.

'Give me his address.'

'I don't know what his Christian name is, Tom, I believe, but I'm not sure. Anyhow his surname's Ellis and his address is Church Mews, St John's Road, Bradmore,—I don't know his number, but any one will tell you which is his place, if you ask for Four-Wheel Ellis,—that's the name he's known by among his pals because of his driving a four-wheeler.'

'Thank you, officer. I am obliged to you.' Two half-crowns changed hands. 'If you will keep an eye on the house and advise me at the address which you will find on my card, of any thing which takes place there during the next few days, you will do me a service.'

We had clambered back into the hansom, the driver was just about to start, when the constable was struck by a sudden thought.

'One moment, sir,—blessed if I wasn't going to forget the most important bit of all. I did hear him tell Ellis where to drive him to,—he kept saying it over and over again, in that queer lingo of his. "Waterloo Railway Station, Waterloo Railway Station." "All right," said Ellis, "I'll drive you to Waterloo Railway Station right enough, only I'm not going to have that bundle of yours inside my cab. There isn't room for it, so you put it on the roof."

"To Waterloo Railway Station," said the Arab, "I take my bundle with me to Waterloo Railway Station,—I take it with me." "Who says you don't take it with you?" said Ellis. "You can take it, and twenty more besides, for all I care, only you don't take it inside my cab,—put it on the roof." "I take it with me to Waterloo Railway Station," said the Arab, and there they were, wrangling and jangling, and neither seeming to be able to make out what the other was after, and the people all laughing.'

'Waterloo Railway Station,—you are sure that was what he said?'

'I'll take my oath to it, because I said to myself, when I heard it, "I wonder what you'll have to pay for that little lot, for the District Railway Station's outside the four-mile radius."'

As we drove off I was inclined to ask myself, a little bitterly—and perhaps unjustly—if it were not characteristic of the average London policeman to almost forget the most important part of his information,—at any rate to leave it to the last and only to bring it to the front on having his palm crossed with silver.

As the hansom bowled along we three had what occasionally approached a warm discussion.

'Marjorie was in that bundle,' began Lessingham, in the most lugubrious of tones, and with the most woebegone of faces.

'I doubt it,' I observed.

'She was,—I feel it,—I know it. She was either dead and mutilated, or gagged and drugged and helpless. All that remains is vengeance.'

'I repeat that I doubt it.'

Atherton struck in.

'I am bound to say, with the best will in the world to think otherwise, that I agree with Lessingham.'

'You are wrong.'

'It's all very well for you to talk in that cocksure way, but it's easier for you to say I'm wrong than to prove it. If I am wrong, and if Lessingham's wrong, how do you explain his extraordinary insistence on taking it inside the cab with him, which the bobby describes? If there wasn't something horrible, awful in that bundle of his, of which he feared the discovery, why was he so reluctant to have it placed upon the roof?'

'There probably was something in it which he was particularly anxious should not be discovered, but I doubt if it was anything of the kind which you suggest.'

'Here is Marjorie in a house alone—nothing has been seen of her since,—her clothing, her hair, is found hidden away under the floor. This scoundrel sallies forth with a huge bundle on his head,—the bobby speaks of it being five or six feet long, or longer,—a bundle which he regards with so much solicitude that he insists on never allowing it to go, for a single instant, out of his sight and reach. What is in the thing? don't all the facts most unfortunately point in one direction?'

Mr Lessingham covered his face with his hands, and groaned.

'I fear that Mr Atherton is right.'

'I differ from you both.'

Sydney at once became heated.

'Then perhaps you can tell us what was in the bundle?'

'I fancy I could make a guess at the contents.'

'Oh you could, could you, then, perhaps, for our sakes, you'll make it,—and not play the oracular owl!—Lessingham and I are interested in this business, after all.'

'It contained the bearer's personal property: that, and nothing more. Stay! before you jeer at me, suffer me to finish. If I am not mistaken as to the identity of the person whom the constable describes as the Arab, I apprehend that the contents of that bundle were of much more importance to him than if they had consisted of Miss Lindon, either dead or living. More. I am inclined to suspect that if the bundle was placed on the roof of the cab, and if the driver did meddle with it, and did find out the contents, and understand them, he would have been driven, out of hand, stark staring mad.'

Sydney was silent, as if he reflected. I imagine he perceived there was something in what I said.

'But what has become of Miss Lindon?'

'I fancy that Miss Lindon, at this moment, is—somewhere; I don't, just now, know exactly where, but I hope very shortly to be able to give you a clearer notion,—attired in a rotten, dirty pair of boots; a filthy, tattered pair of trousers; a ragged, unwashed apology for a shirt; a greasy, ancient, shapeless coat; and a frowsy peaked cloth cap.'

They stared at me, opened-eyed. Atherton was the first to speak.

'What on earth do you mean?'

'I mean that it seems to me that the facts point in the direction of my conclusions rather than yours—and that very strongly too. Miss Coleman asserts that she saw Miss Lindon return into the house; that within a few minutes the blind was replaced at the front window; and that shortly after a young man, attired in the costume I have described, came walking out of the front door. I believe that young man was Miss Marjorie Lindon.'

Lessingham and Atherton both broke out into interrogations, with Sydney, as usual, loudest.

'But—man alive! what on earth should make her do a thing like that? Marjorie, the most retiring, modest girl on all God's earth, walk about in broad daylight, in such a costume, and for no reason at all! my dear Champnell, you are suggesting that she first of all went mad.'

'She was in a state of trance.'

'Good God!—Champnell!'

'Well?'

'Then you think that—juggling villain did get hold of her?'

'Undoubtedly. Here is my view of the case, mind it is only a hypothesis and you must take it for what it is worth. It seems to me quite clear that the Arab, as we will call the person for the sake of identification, was somewhere about the premises when you thought he wasn't.'

'But—where? We looked upstairs, and downstairs, and everywhere—where could he have been?'

'That, as at present advised, I am not prepared to say, but I think you may take it for granted that he was there. He hypnotised the man Holt, and sent him away, intending you to go after him, and so being rid of you both—'

'The deuce he did, Champnell! You write me down an ass!'

'As soon as the coast was clear he discovered himself to Miss Lindon, who, I expect, was disagreeably surprised, and hypnotised her.'

'The hound!'

'The devil!'

The first exclamation was Lessingham's, the second Sydney's.

'He then constrained her to strip herself to the skin—'

'The wretch!'

'The fiend!'

'He cut off her hair; he hid it and her clothes under the floor where we found them—where I think it probable that he had already some ancient masculine garments concealed—'

'By Jove! I shouldn't be surprised if they were Holt's. I remember the man saying that that nice joker stripped him of his duds,—and certainly when I saw him,—and when Marjorie found him!—he had absolutely nothing on but a queer sort of cloak. Can it be possible that that humorous professor of hankey-pankey—may all the maledictions of the accursed alight upon his head!—can have sent Marjorie Lindon, the daintiest damsel in the land!—into the streets of London rigged out in Holt's old togs!'

'As to that, I am not able to give an authoritative opinion, but, if I understand you aright, it at least is possible. Anyhow I am disposed to think that he sent Miss Lindon after the man Holt, taking it for granted that he had eluded you.—'

'That's it. Write me down an ass again!'

'That he did elude you, you have yourself admitted.'

'That's because I stopped talking with that mutton-headed bobby,—I'd have followed the man to the ends of the earth if it hadn't been for that.'

'Precisely; the reason is immaterial, it is the fact with which we are immediately concerned. He did elude you. And I think you will find that Miss Lindon and Mr Holt are together at this moment.'

'In men's clothing?'

'Both in men's clothing, or, rather, Miss Lindon is in a man's rags.'

'Great Potiphar! To think of Marjorie like that!'

'And where they are, the Arab is not very far off either.'

Lessingham caught me by the arm.

'And what diabolical mischief do you imagine that he proposes to do to her?'

I shirked the question.

'Whatever it is, it is our business to prevent his doing it.'

'And where do you think they have been taken?'

'That it will be our immediate business to endeavour to discover,—and here, at any rate, we are at Waterloo.'

CHAPTER XLII.

THE QUARRY DOUBLES

I turned towards the booking-office on the main departure platform. As I went, the chief platform inspector, George Bellingham, with whom I had some acquaintance, came out of his office. I stopped him.

'Mr Bellingham, will you be so good as to step with me to the booking-office, and instruct the clerk in charge to answer one or two questions which I wish to put to him. I will explain to you afterwards what is their exact import, but you know me sufficiently to be able to believe me when I say that they refer to a matter in which every moment is of the first importance.'

He turned and accompanied us into the interior of the booking-case.

'To which of the clerks, Mr Champnell, do you wish to put your questions?'

'To the one who issues third-class tickets to Southampton.'

Bellingham beckoned to a man who was counting a heap of money, and apparently seeking to make it tally with the entries in a huge ledger which lay open before him,—he was a short, slightly-built young fellow, with a pleasant face and smiling eyes.

'Mr Stone, this gentleman wishes to ask you one or two questions.'

'I am at his service.'

I put my questions.

'I want to know, Mr Stone, if, in the course of the day, you have issued any tickets to a person dressed in Arab costume?'

His reply was prompt.

'I have—by the last train, the 7.25,—three singles.'

Three singles! Then my instinct had told me rightly.

'Can you describe the person?'

Mr Stone's eyes twinkled.

'I don't know that I can, except in a general way,—he was uncommonly old and uncommonly ugly, and he had a pair of the most extraordinary eyes I ever saw,—they gave me a sort of all-overish feeling when I saw them glaring at me through the pigeon hole. But I can tell you one thing about him, he had a great bundle on his head, which he steadied with one hand, and as it bulged out in all directions its presence didn't make him popular with other people who wanted tickets too.'

Undoubtedly this was our man.

'You are sure he asked for three tickets?'

'Certain. He said three tickets to Southampton; laid down the exact fare,—nineteen and six—and held up three fingers—like that. Three nasty looking fingers they were, with nails as long as talons.'

'You didn't see who were his companions?'

'I didn't,—I didn't try to look. I gave him his tickets and off he went,—with the people grumbling at him because that bundle of his kept getting in their way.'

Bellingham touched me on the arm.

'I can tell you about the Arab of whom Mr Stone speaks. My attention was called to him by his insisting on taking his bundle with him into the carriage,—it was an enormous thing, he could hardly squeeze it through the door; it occupied the entire seat. But as there weren't as many passengers as usual, and he wouldn't or couldn't be made to understand that his precious bundle would be safe in the luggage van along with the rest of the luggage, and as he wasn't the sort of person you could argue with to any advantage, I had him put into an empty compartment, bundle and all.'

'Was he alone then?'

'I thought so at the time, he said nothing about having more than one ticket, or any companions, but just before the train started two other men—English men—got into his compartment; and as I came down the platform, the ticket inspector at the barrier informed me that these two men were with him, because he held tickets for the three, which, as he was a foreigner, and they seemed English, struck the inspector as odd.'

'Could you describe the two men?'

'I couldn't, not particularly, but the man who had charge of the barrier might. I was at the other end of the train when they got in. All I noticed was that one seemed to be a commonplace looking individual and that the other was dressed like a tramp, all rags and tatters, a disreputable looking object he appeared to be.'

'That,' I said to myself, 'was Miss Marjorie Lindon, the lovely daughter of a famous house; the wife-elect of a coming statesman.'

To Bellingham I remarked aloud:

'I want you to strain a point, Mr Bellingham, and to do me a service which I assure you you shall never have any cause to regret. I want you to wire instructions down the line to detain this Arab and his companions and to keep them in custody until the receipt of further instructions. They are not wanted by the police as yet, but they will be as soon as I am able to give certain information to the authorities at Scotland Yard,—and wanted very badly. But, as you will perceive for yourself, until I am able to give that information every moment is important.—Where's the Station Superintendent?'

'He's gone. At present I'm in charge.'

'Then will you do this for me? I repeat that you shall never have any reason to regret it.'

'I will if you'll accept all responsibility.'

'I'll do that with the greatest pleasure.'

Bellingham looked at his watch.

'It's about twenty minutes to nine. The train's scheduled for Basingstoke at 9.6. If we wire to Basingstoke at once they ought to be ready for them when they come.'

'Good!'

The wire was sent.

We were shown into Bellingham's office to await results.

Lessingham paced agitatedly to and fro; he seemed to have reached the limits of his self-control, and to be in a condition in which movement of some sort was an absolute necessity. The mercurial Sydney, on the contrary, leaned back in a chair, his legs stretched out in front of him, his hands thrust deep into his trouser pockets, and stared at Lessingham, as if he found relief to his feelings in watching his companion's restlessness. I, for my part, drew up as full a précis of the case as I deemed advisable, and as time permitted, which I despatched by one of the company's police to Scotland Yard.

Then I turned to my associates.

'Now, gentlemen, it's past dinner time. We may have a journey in front of us. If you take my advice you'll have something to eat.'

Lessingham shook his head.

'I want nothing.'

'Nor I,' echoed Sydney.

I started up.

'You must pardon my saying nonsense, but surely you of all men, Mr Lessingham, should be aware that you will not improve the situation by rendering yourself incapable of seeing it through. Come and dine.'

I haled them off with me, willy nilly, to the refreshment room. I dined,—after a fashion; Mr Lessingham swallowed with difficulty, a plate of soup; Sydney nibbled at a plate of the most unpromising looking 'chicken and ham,'—he proved, indeed, more intractable than Lessingham, and was not to be persuaded to tackle anything easier of digestion.

I was just about to take cheese after chop when Bellingham came hastening in, in his hand an open telegram.

'The birds have flown,' he cried.

'Flown!—How?'

In reply he gave me the telegram. I glanced at it. It ran:

'Persons described not in the train. Guard says they got out at Vauxhall. Have wired Vauxhall to advise you.'

'That's a level-headed chap,' said Bellingham. 'The man who sent that telegram. His wiring to Vauxhall should save us a lot of time,—we ought to hear from there directly. Hollo! what's this? I shouldn't be surprised if this is it.'

As he spoke a porter entered,—he handed an envelope to Bellingham. We all three kept our eyes fixed on the inspector's face as he opened it. When he perceived the contents he gave an exclamation of surprise.

'This Arab of yours, and his two friends, seem rather a curious lot, Mr Champnell.'

He passed the paper on to me. It took the form of a report. Lessingham and Sydney, regardless of forms and ceremonies, leaned over my shoulder as I read it.

'Passengers by 7.30 Southampton, on arrival of train, complained of noises coming from a compartment in coach 8964. Stated that there had been shrieks and yells ever since the train left Waterloo, as if someone was being murdered. An Arab and two Englishmen got out of the compartment in question, apparently the party referred to in wire just to hand from Basingstoke. All three declared that there was nothing the matter. That they had been shouting for fun. Arab gave up three third singles for Southampton, saying, in reply to questions, that they had changed their minds, and did not want to go any farther. As there were no signs of a struggle or of violence, nor, apparently, any definite cause for detention, they were allowed to pass. They took a four-wheeler, No. 09435. The Arab and one man went inside, and the other man on the box. They asked to be driven to Commercial Road, Limehouse. The cab has since returned. Driver says he put the three men down, at their request, in Commercial Road, at the corner of Sutcliffe Street, near the East India Docks. They walked up Sutcliffe Street, the Englishmen in front, and the Arab behind, took the first turning to the right, and after that he saw nothing of them. The driver further states that all the way the Englishman inside, who was so ragged and dirty that he was reluctant to carry him, kept up a sort of wailing noise which so attracted his attention that he twice got off his box to see what was the matter, and each time he said it was nothing. The cabman is of opinion that both the Englishmen were of weak intellect. We were of the same impression here. They said nothing, except at the seeming instigation of the Arab, but when spoken to stared and gaped like lunatics.

'It may be mentioned that the Arab had with him an

enormous bundle, which he persisted, in spite of all remonstrances, on taking with him inside the cab.'

As soon as I had mastered the contents of the report, and perceived what I believed to be—unknown to the writer himself—its hideous inner meaning, I turned to Bellingham.

'With your permission, Mr Bellingham, I will keep this communication,—it will be safe in my hands, you will be able to get a copy, and it may be necessary that I should have the original to show to the police. If any inquiries are made for me from Scotland Yard, tell them that I have gone to the Commercial Road, and that I will report my movements from Limehouse Police Station.'

In another minute we were once more traversing the streets of London,—three in a hansom cab.

CHAPTER XLIII.

THE MURDER AT MRS 'ENDERSON'S

It is something of a drive from Waterloo to Limehouse,—it seems longer when all your nerves are tingling with anxiety to reach your journey's end; and the cab I had hit upon proved to be not the fastest I might have chosen. For some time after our start, we were silent. Each was occupied with his own thoughts.

Then Lessingham, who was sitting at my side, said to me,

'Mr Champnell, you have that report.'

'I have.'

'Will you let me see it once more?'

I gave it to him. He read it once, twice,—and I fancy yet again. I purposely avoided looking at him as he did so. Yet all the while I was conscious of his pallid cheeks, the twitched muscles of his mouth, the feverish glitter of his eyes,—this Leader of Men, whose predominate characteristic in the House of Commons was immobility, was rapidly approximating to the condition of a hysterical woman. The mental strain which he had been recently undergoing was proving too much for his physical strength. This disappearance of the woman he loved bade fair to be the final straw. I felt convinced that unless something was done quickly to relieve the strain upon his mind he was nearer to a state of complete mental and moral collapse than he himself imagined. Had he been under my orders I should have commanded him to at once return home, and not to think; but conscious that, as things were, such a direction would be simply futile, I decided to do something else instead. Feeling that suspense was for him the worst possible form of suffering I resolved to explain, so far as I was able, precisely what it was I feared, and how I proposed to prevent it.

Presently there came the question for which I had been waiting, in a harsh, broken voice which no one who had heard him speak on a public platform, or in the House of Commons, would have recognised as his.

'Mr Champnell,—who do you think this person is of whom the report from Vauxhall Station speaks as being all in rags and tatters?'

He knew perfectly well,—but I understood the mental attitude which induced him to prefer that the information should seem to come from me.

'I hope that it will prove to be Miss Lindon.'

'Hope!' He gave a sort of gasp.

'Yes, hope,—because if it is I think it possible, nay probable, that within a few hours you will have her again enfolded in your arms.'

'Pray God that it may be so! pray God!—pray the good God!'

I did not dare to look round for, from the tremor which was in his tone, I was persuaded that in the speaker's eyes were tears. Atherton continued silent. He was leaning half out of the cab, staring straight ahead, as if he saw in front a young girl's face, from which he could not remove his glance, and which beckoned him on.

After a while Lessingham spoke again, as if half to himself and half to me.

'This mention of the shrieks on the railway, and of the wailing noise in the cab,—what must this wretch have done to her? How my darling must have suffered!'

That was a theme on which I myself scarcely ventured to allow my thoughts to rest. The notion of a gently-nurtured girl being at the mercy of that fiend incarnate, possessed—as I believed that so-called Arab to be possessed—of all the paraphernalia of horror and of dread, was one which caused me tangible shrinkings of the body. Whence had come those shrieks and yells, of which the writer of the report spoke, which had caused the Arab's fellow-passengers to think that murder was being done? What unimaginable agony had caused them? what speechless torture? And the 'wailing noise,' which had induced the prosaic, indurated London cabman to get twice off his box to see what was the matter, what anguish had been provocative of that? The helpless girl who had already endured so much, endured, perhaps, that to which death would have been preferred!—shut up in that rattling, jolting box on wheels, alone with that diabolical Asiatic, with the enormous bundle, which was but the lurking place of nameless terrors,—what might she not, while being borne through the heart of civilised London, have been made to suffer? What had she not been made to suffer to have kept up that continued 'wailing noise'?

It was not a theme on which it was wise to permit one's thoughts to linger,—and particularly was it clear that it was one from which Lessingham's thoughts should have been kept as far as possible away.

'Come, Mr Lessingham, neither you nor I will do himself any good by permitting his reflections to flow in a morbid channel. Let us talk of something else. By the way, weren't you due to speak in the House to-night?'

'Due!—Yes, I was due,—but what does it matter?'

'But have you acquainted no one with the cause of your non-attendance?'

'Acquaint!—whom should I acquaint?'

'My good sir! Listen to me, Mr Lessingham. Let me entreat you very earnestly, to follow my advice. Call another cab,—or take this! and go at once to the House. It is not too late. Play the man, deliver the speech you have undertaken to deliver, perform your political duties. By coming with me you will be a hindrance rather than a help, and you may do your reputation an injury from which it never may recover. Do as I counsel you, and I will undertake to do my very utmost to let you have good news by the time your speech is finished.'

He turned on me with a bitterness for which I was unprepared.

'If I were to go down to the House, and try to speak in the state in which I am now, they would laugh at me, I should be ruined.'

'Do you not run an equally great risk of being ruined by staying away?'

He gripped me by the arm.

'Mr Champnell, do you know that I am on the verge of madness? Do you know that as I am sitting here by your side I am living in a dual world? I am going on and on to catch that—that fiend, and I am back again in that Egyptian den, upon that couch of rugs, with the Woman of the Songs beside me, and Marjorie is being torn and tortured, and burnt before my eyes! God help me! Her shrieks are ringing in my ears!'

He did not speak loudly, but his voice was none the less

impressive on that account. I endeavoured my hardest to be stern.

'I confess that you disappoint me, Mr Lessingham. I have always understood that you were a man of unusual strength; you appear instead, to be a man of extraordinary weakness; with an imagination so ill-governed that its ebullitions remind me of nothing so much as feminine hysterics. Your wild language is not warranted by circumstances. I repeat that I think it quite possible that by to-morrow morning she will be returned to you.'

'Yes, — but how? as the Marjorie I have known, as I saw her last, — or how?'

That was the question which I had already asked myself, in what condition would she be when we had succeeded in snatching her from her captor's grip? It was a question to which I had refused to supply an answer. To him I lied by implication.

'Let us hope that, with the exception of being a trifle scared, she will be as sound and hale and hearty as ever in her life.'

'Do you yourself believe that she'll be like that, — untouched, unchanged, unstained?'

Then I lied right out, — it seemed to me necessary to calm his growing excitement.

'I do.'

'You don't!'

'Mr Lessingham!'

'Do you think that I can't see your face and read in it the same thoughts which trouble me? As a man of honour do you care to deny that when Marjorie Lindon is restored to me, — if she ever is! — you fear she will be but the mere soiled husk of the Marjorie whom I knew and loved?'

'Even supposing that there may be a modicum of truth in what you say, — which I am far from being disposed to admit — what good purpose do you propose to serve by talking in such a strain?'

'None, — no good purpose, — unless it be the desire of looking the truth in the face. For, Mr Champnell, you must not seek to play with me the hypocrite, nor try to hide things from me as if I were a child. If my life is ruined—it is ruined,—let me know it, and look the knowledge in the face. That, to me, is to play the man.'

I was silent.

The wild tale he had told me of that Cairene inferno, oddly enough—yet why oddly, for the world is all coincidence!—had thrown a flood of light on certain events which had happened some three years previously and which ever since had remained shrouded in mystery. The conduct of the business afterwards came into my hands,—and briefly, what had occurred was this:

Three persons,—two sisters and their brother, who was younger than themselves, members of a decent English family, were going on a trip round the world. They were young, adventurous, and—not to put too fine a point on it—foolhardy. The evening after their arrival in Cairo, by way of what is called 'a lark,' in spite of the protestations of people who were better informed than themselves, they insisted on going, alone, for a ramble through the native quarter.

They went,—but they never returned. Or, rather the two girls never returned. After an interval the young man was found again,—what was left of him. A fuss was made when there were no signs of their re-appearance, but as there were no relations, nor even friends of theirs, but only casual acquaintances on board the ship by which they had travelled, perhaps not so great a fuss as might have been was made. Anyhow, nothing was discovered. Their widowed mother, alone in England, wondering how it was that beyond the receipt of a brief wire, acquainting her with their arrival at Cairo, she had heard nothing further of their wanderings, placed herself in communication with the diplomatic people over there,—to learn that, to all appearances, her three children had vanished from off the face of the earth.

Then a fuss was made,—with a vengeance. So far as one can judge the whole town and neighbourhood was turned pretty well upside down. But nothing came of it,—so far as any results were concerned, the authorities might just as well have left the mystery of their vanishment alone. It continued where it was in spite of them.

However, some three months afterwards a youth was brought to the British Embassy by a party of friendly Arabs who asserted that they had found him naked and nearly dying in some remote spot in the Wady Halfa desert. It was the brother of the two lost girls. He was as nearly dying as he very well could be without being actually dead when they brought him to the Embassy,—and in a state of indescribable mutilation. He seemed to rally for a time under careful treatment, but he never again uttered a coherent word. It was only from his delirious ravings that any idea was formed of what had really occurred.

Shorthand notes were taken of some of the utterances of his delirium. Afterwards they were submitted to me. I remembered the substance of them quite well, and when Mr Lessingham began to tell me of his own hideous experiences they came back to me more clearly still. Had I laid those notes before him I have little doubt but that he would have immediately perceived that seventeen years after the adventure which had left such an indelible scar upon his own life, this youth—he was little more than a boy—had seen the things which he had seen, and suffered the nameless agonies and degradations which he had suffered. The young man was perpetually raving about some indescribable den of horror which was own brother to Lessingham's temple and about some female monster, whom he regarded with such fear and horror that every allusion he made to her was followed by a convulsive paroxysm which taxed all the ingenuity of his medical attendants to bring him out of. He frequently called upon his sisters by name, speaking of them in a manner which inevitably suggested that he had been an unwilling and helpless witness of hideous tortures which they had undergone; and then he would rise in bed, screaming, 'They're burning them! they're burning them! Devils! devils!' And at those times it required all the strength of those who were in attendance to restrain his maddened frenzy.

The youth died in one of these fits of great preternatural excitement, without, as I have previously written, having given utterance to one single coherent word, and by some of those who were best able to judge it was held to have been a mercy that he did die without having been restored to consciousness. And, presently, tales began to be whispered, about some idolatrous sect, which was stated to have its headquarters somewhere in the interior of the country—some located it in this neighbourhood, and some in that—which was stated to still practise, and to always have practised, in unbroken historical continuity, the debased, unclean, mystic, and bloody rites, of a form of idolatry which had had its birth in a period of the world's story which was so remote, that to all intents and purposes it might be described as pre-historic.

While the ferment was still at its height, a man came to the

British Embassy who said that he was a member of a tribe which had its habitat on the banks of the White Nile. He asserted that he was in association with this very idolatrous sect,—though he denied that he was one of the actual sectaries. He did admit, however, that he had assisted more than once at their orgies, and declared that it was their constant practice to offer young women as sacrifices—preferably white Christian women, with a special preference, if they could get them, to young English women. He vowed that he himself had seen with his own eyes, English girls burnt alive. The description which he gave of what preceded and followed these foul murders appalled those who listened. He finally wound up by offering, on payment of a stipulated sum of money, to guide a troop of soldiers to this den of demons, so that they should arrive there at a moment when it was filled with worshippers, who were preparing to participate in an orgie which was to take place during the next few days.

His offer was conditionally accepted. He was confined in an apartment with one man on guard inside and another on guard outside the room. That night the sentinel without was startled by hearing a great noise and frightful screams issuing from the chamber in which the native was interned. He summoned assistance. The door was opened. The soldier on guard within was stark, staring mad,—he died within a few months, a gibbering maniac to the end. The native was dead. The window, which was a very small one, was securely fastened inside and strongly barred without. There was nothing to show by what means entry had been gained. Yet it was the general opinion of those who saw the corpse that the man had been destroyed by some wild beast. A photograph was taken of the body after death, a copy of which is still in my possession. In it are distinctly shown lacerations about the neck and the lower portion of the abdomen, as if they had been produced by the claws of some huge and ferocious animal. The skull is splintered in half-a-dozen places, and the face is torn to rags.

That was more than three years ago. The whole business has remained as great a mystery as ever. But my attention has once or twice been caught by trifling incidents, which have caused me to more than suspect that the wild tale told by that murdered native had in it at least the elements of truth; and which have even led me to wonder if the trade in kidnapping was not being carried on to this very hour, and if women of my own flesh and blood were not still being offered up on that infernal altar. And now, here was Paul Lessingham, a man of world-wide reputation, of great intellect, of undoubted honour, who had come to me with a wholly unconscious verification of all my worst suspicions!

That the creature spoken of as an Arab,—and who was probably no more an Arab than I was, and whose name was certainly not Mohamed el Kheir!—was an emissary from that den of demons, I had no doubt. What was the exact purport of the creature's presence in England was another question. Possibly part of the intention was the destruction of Paul Lessingham, body, soul and spirit; possibly another part was the procuration of fresh victims for that long-drawn-out holocaust. That this latter object explained the disappearance of Miss Lindon I felt persuaded. That she was designed by the personification of evil who was her captor, to suffer all the horrors at which the stories pointed, and then to be burned alive, amidst the triumphant yells of the attendant demons, I was certain. That the wretch, aware that the pursuit was in full cry, was tearing, twisting, doubling, and would stick at nothing which would facilitate the smuggling of the victim out of England, was clear.

My interest in the quest was already far other than a merely professional one. The blood in my veins tingled at the thought of such a woman as Miss Lindon being in the power of such a monster. I may assuredly claim that throughout the whole business I was urged forward by no thought of fee or of reward. To have had a share in rescuing that unfortunate girl, and in the destruction of her noxious persecutor, would have been reward enough for me.

One is not always, even in strictly professional matters, influenced by strictly professional instincts.

The cab slowed. A voice descended through the trap door.

'This is Commercial Road, sir,—what part of it do you want?'

'Drive me to Limehouse Police Station.'

We were driven there. I made my way to the usual inspector behind the usual pigeon-hole.

'My name is Champnell. Have you received any communication from Scotland Yard to-night having reference to a matter in which I am interested?'

'Do you mean about the Arab? We received a telephonic message about half an hour ago.'

'Since communicating with Scotland Yard this has come to hand from the authorities at Vauxhall Station. Can you tell me if anything has been seen of the person in question by the men of your division?'

I handed the Inspector the 'report.' His reply was laconic.

'I will inquire.'

He passed through a door into an inner room and the 'report' went with him.

'Beg pardon, sir, but was that a Harab you was a-talking about to the Hinspector?'

The speaker was a gentleman unmistakably of the guttersnipe class. He was seated on a form. Close at hand hovered a policeman whose special duty it seemed to be to keep an eye upon his movements.

'Why do you ask?'

'I beg your pardon, sir, but I saw a Harab myself about a hour ago,—leastways he looked like as if he was a Harab.'

'What sort of a looking person was he?'

'I can't 'ardly tell you that, sir, because I didn't never have a proper look at him,—but I know he had a bloomin' great bundle on 'is 'ead.... It was like this, 'ere. I was comin' round the corner, as he was passin', I never see 'im till I was right atop of 'im, so that I haccidentally run agin 'im,—my heye! didn't 'e give me a downer! I was down on the back of my 'ead in the middle of the road before I knew where I was and 'e was at the other end of the street. If 'e 'adn't knocked me more'n 'arf silly I'd been after 'im, sharp,—I tell you! and hasked 'im what 'e thought 'e was a-doin' of, but afore my senses was back agin 'e was out o' sight,—clean!'

'You are sure he had a bundle on his head?'

'I noticed it most particular.'

'How long ago do you say this was? and where?'

'About a hour ago,—perhaps more, perhaps less.'

'Was he alone?'

'It seemed to me as if a cove was a follerin' 'im, leastways there was a bloke as was a-keepin' close at 'is 'eels,—though I don't know what 'is little game was, I'm sure. Ask the pleesman—he knows, he knows everythink, the pleesman do.'

I turned to the 'pleesman.'

'Who is this man?'

The 'pleesman' put his hands behind his back, and threw out his chest. His manner was distinctly affable.

'Well,—he's being detained upon suspicion. He's given us an address at which to make inquiries, and inquiries are being made. I shouldn't pay too much attention to what he says if I were you. I don't suppose he'd be particular about a lie or two.'

This frank expression of opinion re-aroused the indignation of the gentleman on the form.

'There you hare! at it again! That's just like you peelers,—you're all the same! What do you know about me?—Nuffink! This gen'leman ain't got no call to believe me, not as I knows on,—it's all the same to me if 'e do or don't, but it's trewth what I'm sayin', all the same.'

At this point the Inspector re-appeared at the pigeon-hole. He cut short the flow of eloquence.

'Now then, not so much noise outside there!' He addressed me. 'None of our men have seen anything of the person you're inquiring for, so far as we're aware. But, if you like, I will place a man at your disposal, and he will go round with you, and you will be able to make your own inquiries.'

A capless, wildly excited young ragamuffin came dashing in at the street door. He gasped out, as clearly as he could for the speed which he had made:

'There's been murder done, Mr Pleesman,—a Harab's killed a bloke.'

'Mr Pleesman' gripped him by the shoulder.

'What's that?'

The youngster put up his arm, and ducked his head, instinctively, as if to ward off a blow.

'Leave me alone! I don't want none of your 'andling! – I ain't done nuffink to you! I tell you 'e 'as!'

The Inspector spoke through the pigeon-hole.

'He has what, my lad? What do you say has happened?'

'There's been murder done – it's right enough! – there 'as! – up at Mrs 'Enderson's, in Paradise Place, – a Harab's been and killed a bloke!'

CHAPTER XLIV.

THE MAN WHO WAS MURDERED

The Inspector spoke to me.

'If what the boy says is correct it sounds as if the person whom you are seeking may have had a finger in the pie.'

I was of the same opinion, as, apparently, were Lessingham and Sydney. Atherton collared the youth by the shoulder which Mr Pleesman had left disengaged.

'What sort of looking bloke is it who's been murdered?'

'I dunno! I 'aven't seen 'im! Mrs 'Enderson, she says to me! "'Gustus Barley," she says, "a bloke's been murdered. That there Harab what I chucked out 'alf a hour ago been and murdered 'im, and left 'im behind up in my back room. You run as 'ard as you can tear and tell them there dratted pleese what's so fond of shovin' their dirty noses into respectable people's 'ouses." So I comes and tells yer. That's all I knows about it.'

We went four in the hansom which had been waiting in the street to Mrs Henderson's in Paradise Place,—the Inspector and we three. 'Mr Pleesman' and ''Gustus Barley' followed on foot. The Inspector was explanatory.

'Mrs Henderson keeps a sort of lodging-house,—a "Sailors' Home" she calls it, but no one could call it sweet. It doesn't bear the best of characters, and if you asked me what I thought of it, I should say in plain English that it was a disorderly house.'

Paradise Place proved to be within three or four hundred yards of the Station House. So far as could be seen in the dark it consisted of a row of houses of considerable dimensions,—and also of considerable antiquity. They opened on to two or three stone steps which led directly into the street. At one of the doors stood an old lady with a shawl drawn over her head. This was Mrs Henderson. She greeted us with garrulous volubility.

'So you 'ave come, 'ave you? I thought you never was a-comin' that I did.' She recognised the Inspector. 'It's you, Mr Phillips, is it?' Perceiving us, she drew a little back. 'Who's them 'ere parties? They ain't coppers?'

Mr Phillips dismissed her inquiry, curtly.

'Never you mind who they are. What's this about someone being murdered.'

'Ssh!' The old lady glanced round. 'Don't you speak so loud, Mr Phillips. No one don't know nothing about it as yet. The parties what's in my 'ouse is most respectable,—most! and they couldn't abide the notion of there being police about the place.'

'We quite believe that, Mrs Henderson.'

The Inspector's tone was grim.

Mrs Henderson led the way up a staircase which would have been distinctly the better for repairs. It was necessary to pick one's way as one went, and as the light was defective stumbles were not infrequent.

Our guide paused outside a door on the topmost landing. From some mysterious recess in her apparel she produced a key.

'It's in 'ere. I locked the door so that nothing mightn't be disturbed. I knows 'ow particular you pleesmen is.'

She turned the key. We all went in—we, this time, in front, and she behind.

A candle was guttering on a broken and dilapidated single washhand stand. A small iron bedstead stood by its side, the clothes on which were all tumbled and tossed. There was a rush-seated chair with a hole in the seat,—and that, with the exception of one or two chipped pieces of stoneware, and a small round mirror which was hung on a nail against the wall, seemed to be all that the room contained. I could see nothing in the shape of a murdered man. Nor, it appeared, could the Inspector either.

'What's the meaning of this, Mrs Henderson? I don't see anything here.'

'It's be'ind the bed, Mr Phillips. I left 'im just where I found 'im, I wouldn't 'ave touched 'im not for nothing, nor yet 'ave let nobody else 'ave touched 'im neither, because, as I say, I know 'ow particular you pleesmen is.'

We all four went hastily forward. Atherton and I went to the head of the bed, Lessingham and the Inspector, leaning right across the bed, peeped over the side. There, on the floor in the space which was between the bed and the wall, lay the murdered man.

At sight of him an exclamation burst from Sydney's lips.

'It's Holt!'

'Thank God!' cried Lessingham. 'It isn't Marjorie!'

The relief in his tone was unmistakable. That the one was gone was plainly nothing to him in comparison with the fact that the other was left.

Thrusting the bed more into the centre of the room I knelt down beside the man on the floor. A more deplorable spectacle than he presented I have seldom witnessed. He was decently clad in a grey tweed suit, white hat, collar and necktie, and it was perhaps that fact which made his extreme attenuation the more conspicuous. I doubt if there was an ounce of flesh on the whole of his body. His cheeks and the sockets of his eyes were hollow. The skin was drawn tightly over his cheek bones,—the bones themselves were staring through. Even his nose was wasted, so that nothing but a ridge of cartilage remained. I put my arm beneath his shoulder and raised him from the floor; no resistance was offered by the body's gravity,—he was as light as a little child.

'I doubt,' I said, 'if this man has been murdered. It looks to me like a case of starvation, or exhaustion,—possibly a combination of both.'

'What's that on his neck?' asked the Inspector,—he was kneeling at my side.

He referred to two abrasions of the skin,—one on either side of the man's neck.

'They look to me like scratches. They seem pretty deep, but I don't think they're sufficient in themselves to cause death.'

'They might be, joined to an already weakened constitution. Is there anything in his pockets?—let's lift him on to the bed.'

We lifted him on to the bed,—a featherweight he was to lift. While the Inspector was examining his pockets—to find them empty—a tall man with a big black beard came bustling in. He proved to be Dr Glossop, the local police surgeon, who had been sent for before our quitting the Station House.

His first pronouncement, made as soon as he commenced his examination, was, under the circumstances, sufficiently startling.

'I don't believe the man's dead. Why didn't you send for me directly you found him?'

The question was put to Mrs Henderson.

'Well, Dr Glossop, I wouldn't touch 'im myself, and I wouldn't 'ave 'im touched by no one else, because, as I've said afore, I know 'ow particular them pleesmen is.'

'Then in that case, if he does die you'll have had a hand in murdering him,—that's all.'

The lady sniggered. 'Of course Dr Glossop, we all knows that you'll always 'ave your joke.'

'You'll find it a joke if you have to hang, as you ought to, you——' The doctor said what he did say to himself, under his breath. I doubt if it was flattering to Mrs Henderson. 'Have you got any brandy in the house?'

'We've got everythink in the 'ouse for them as likes to pay for it,—everythink.' Then, suddenly remembering that the police were present, and that hers were not exactly licensed premises, 'Leastways we can send out for it for them parties as gives us the money, being, as is well known, always willing to oblige.'

'Then send for some,—to the tap downstairs, if that's the nearest! If this man dies before you've brought it I'll have you locked up as sure as you're a living woman.'

The arrival of the brandy was not long delayed,—but the man on the bed had regained consciousness before it came. Opening his eyes he looked up at the doctor bending over him.

'Hollo, my man! that's more like the time of day! How are you feeling?'

The patient stared hazily up at the doctor, as if his sense of perception was not yet completely restored,—as if this big bearded man was something altogether strange. Atherton bent down beside the doctor.

'I'm glad to see you looking better, Mr Holt. You know me don't you? I've been running about after you all day long.'

'You are—you are—' The man's eyes closed, as if the effort at recollection exhausted him. He kept them closed as he continued to speak.

'I know who you are. You are—the gentleman.'

'Yes, that's it, I'm the gentleman,—name of Atherton.—Miss Lindon's friend. And I daresay you're feeling pretty well done up, and in want of something to eat and drink,—here's some brandy for you.'

The doctor had some in a tumbler. He raised the patient's head, allowing it to trickle down his throat. The man swallowed it mechanically, motionless, as if unconscious what it was that he was doing. His cheeks flushed, the passing glow of colour caused their condition of extraordinary, and, indeed, extravagant attenuation, to be more prominent than ever. The doctor laid him back upon the bed, feeling his pulse with one hand, while he stood and regarded him in silence.

Then, turning to the Inspector, he said to him in an undertone:

'If you want him to make a statement he'll have to make it now, he's going fast. You won't be able to get much out of him,—he's too far gone, and I shouldn't bustle him, but get what you can.'

The Inspector came to the front, a notebook in his hand.

'I understand from this gentleman—' signifying Atherton—'that your name's Robert Holt. I'm an Inspector of police, and I want you to tell me what has brought you into this condition. Has anyone been assaulting you?'

Holt, opening his eyes, glanced up at the speaker mistily, as if he could not see him clearly,—still less understand what it was that he was saying. Sydney, stooping over him, endeavoured to explain.

'The Inspector wants to know how you got here, has anyone been doing anything to you? Has anyone been hurting you?'

The man's eyelids were partially closed. Then they opened wider and wider. His mouth opened too. On his skeleton features there came a look of panic fear. He was evidently struggling to speak. At last words came.

'The beetle!' He stopped. Then, after an effort, spoke again.

'The beetle!'

'What's he mean?' asked the Inspector.

'I think I understand,' Sydney answered; then turning again to the man in the bed. 'Yes, I hear what you say,—the beetle. Well, has the beetle done anything to you?'

'It took me by the throat!'

'Is that the meaning of the marks upon your neck?'

'The beetle killed me.'

The lids closed. The man relapsed into a state of lethargy. The Inspector was puzzled;—and said so.

'What's he mean about a beetle?'

Atherton replied.

'I think I understand what he means,—and my friends do too. We'll explain afterwards. In the meantime I think I'd better get as much out of him as I can,—while there's time.'

'Yes,' said the doctor, his hand upon the patient's pulse, 'while there's time. There isn't much—only seconds.'

Sydney endeavoured to rouse the man from his stupor.

'You've been with Miss Lindon all the afternoon and evening, haven't you, Mr Holt?'

Atherton had reached a chord in the man's consciousness. His lips moved,—in painful articulation.

'Yes—all the afternoon—and evening—God help me!'

'I hope God will help you my poor fellow; you've been in need of His help if ever man was. Miss Lindon is disguised in your old clothes, isn't she?'

'Yes,—in my old clothes. My God!'

'And where is Miss Lindon now?'

The man had been speaking with his eyes closed. Now he opened them, wide; there came into them the former staring horror. He became possessed by uncontrollable agitation,—half raising himself in bed. Words came from his quivering lips as if they were only drawn from him by the force of his anguish.

'The beetle's going to kill Miss Lindon.'

A momentary paroxysm seemed to shake the very foundations of his being. His whole frame quivered. He fell back on to the bed,—ominously. The doctor examined him in silence—while we too were still.

'This time he's gone for good, there'll be no conjuring him back again.'

I felt a sudden pressure on my arm, and found that Lessingham was clutching me with probably unconscious violence. The muscles of his face were twitching. He trembled. I turned to the doctor.

'Doctor, if there is any of that brandy left will you let me have it for my friend?'

Lessingham disposed of the remainder of the 'shillings worth.' I rather fancy it saved us from a scene.

The Inspector was speaking to the woman of the house.

'Now, Mrs Henderson, perhaps you'll tell us what all this means. Who is this man, and how did he come in here, and who came in with him, and what do you know about it altogether? If you've got anything to say, say it, only you'd better be careful, because it's my duty to warn you that anything you do say may be used against you.'

CHAPTER XLV.

ALL THAT MRS 'ENDERSON KNEW

Mrs Henderson put her hands under her apron and smirked.

'Well, Mr Phillips, it do sound strange to 'ear you talkin' to me like that. Anybody'd think I'd done something as I didn't ought to 'a' done to 'ear you going on. As for what's 'appened, I'll tell you all I know with the greatest willingness on earth. And as for bein' careful, there ain't no call for you to tell me to be that, for that I always am, as by now you ought to know.'

'Yes,—I do know. Is that all you have to say?'

'Rilly, Mr Phillips, what a man you are for catching people up, you rilly are. O' course that ain't all I've got to say,—ain't I just a-comin' to it?'

'Then come.'

'If you presses me so you'll muddle of me up, and then if I do 'appen to make a herror, you'll say I'm a liar, when goodness knows there ain't no more truthful woman not in Limehouse.'

Words plainly trembled on the Inspector's lips,—which he refrained from uttering. Mrs Henderson cast her eyes upwards, as if she sought for inspiration from the filthy ceiling.

'So far as I can swear it might 'ave been a hour ago, or it might 'ave been a hour and a quarter, or it might 'ave been a hour and twenty minutes—'

'We're not particular as to the seconds.'

'When I 'ears a knockin' at my front door, and when I comes to open it, there was a Harab party, with a great bundle on 'is 'ead, bigger nor 'isself, and two other parties along with him. This Harab party says, in that queer foreign way them Harab parties 'as of talkin', "A room for the night, a room." Now I don't much care for foreigners, and never did, especially them Harabs, which their 'abits ain't my own,—so I as much 'ints the same. But this 'ere Harab party, he didn't seem to quite foller of my meaning, for all he done was to say as he said afore, "A room for the night, a room." And he shoves a couple of 'arf crowns into my 'and. Now it's always been a motter o' mine, that money is money, and one man's money is as good as another man's. So, not wishing to be disagreeable—which other people would have taken 'em if I 'adn't, I shows 'em up 'ere. I'd been downstairs it might 'ave been 'arf a hour, when I 'ears a shindy a-coming from this room—'

'What sort of a shindy?'

'Yelling and shrieking—oh my gracious, it was enough to set your blood all curdled,—for ear-piercingness I never did 'ear nothing like it. We do 'ave troublesome parties in 'ere, like they do elsewhere, but I never did 'ear nothing like that before. I stood it for about a minute, but it kep' on, and kep' on, and every moment I expected as the other parties as was in the 'ouse would be complainin', so up I comes and I thumps at the door, and it seemed that thump I might for all the notice that was took of me.'

'Did the noise keep on?'

'Keep on! I should think it did keep on! Lord love you! shriek after shriek, I expected to see the roof took off.'

'Were there any other noises? For instance, were there any sounds of struggling, or of blows?'

'There weren't no sounds except of the party hollering.'

'One party only?'

'One party only. As I says afore, shriek after shriek,—when you put your ear to the panel there was a noise like some other party blubbering, but that weren't nothing, as for the hollering you wouldn't have thought that nothing what you might call 'umin could 'ave kep' up such a screechin'. I thumps and thumps and at last when I did think that I should 'ave to 'ave the door broke down, the Harab says to me from inside, "Go away! I pay for the room! go away!" I did think that pretty good, I tell you that. So I says, "Pay for the room or not pay for the room, you didn't pay to make that shindy!" And what's more I says, "If I 'ear it again," I says, "out you goes! And if you don't go quiet I'll 'ave somebody in as'll pretty quickly make you!"'

'Then was there silence?'

'So to speak there was,—only there was this sound as if some party was a-blubbering, and another sound as if a party was a-panting for his breath.'

'Then what happened?'

'Seeing that, so to speak, all was quiet, down I went again. And in another quarter of a hour, or it might 'ave been twenty minutes, I went to the front door to get a mouthful of hair. And Mrs Barker, what lives over the road, at No. 24, she comes to me and says, "That there Arab party of yours didn't stop long." I looks at 'er, "I don't quite foller you," I says,—which I didn't. "I saw him come in," she says, "and then, a few minutes back, I see 'im go again, with a great bundle on 'is 'ead he couldn't 'ardly stagger under!" "Oh," I says, "that's news to me, I didn't know 'e'd gone, nor see him neither—" which I didn't. So, up I comes again, and, sure enough, the door was open, and it seems to me that the room was empty, till I come upon this poor young man what was lying be'ind the bed.'

There was a growl from the doctor.

'If you'd had any sense, and sent for me at once, he might have been alive at this moment.'

''Ow was I to know that, Dr Glossop? I couldn't tell. My finding 'im there murdered was quite enough for me. So I runs downstairs, and I nips 'old of 'Gustus Barley, what was leaning against the wall, and I says to him, "'Gustus Barley, run to the station as fast as you can and tell 'em that a man's been murdered,—that Harab's been and killed a bloke." And that's all I know about it, and I couldn't tell you no more, Mr Phillips, not if you was to keep on asking me questions not for hours and hours.'

'Then you think it was this man'—with a motion towards the bed—'who was shrieking?'

'To tell you the truth, Mr Phillips, about that I don't 'ardly know what to think. If you 'ad asked me I should 'ave said it was a woman. I ought to know a woman's holler when I 'ear it, if any one does, I've 'eard enough of 'em in my time, goodness knows. And I should 'ave said that only a woman could 'ave hollered like that and only 'er when she was raving mad. But there weren't no woman with him. There was only this man what's murdered, and the other man,—and as for the other man I will say this, that 'e 'adn't got twopennyworth of clothes to cover 'im. But, Mr Phillips, howsomever that may be, that's the last Harab I'll 'ave under my roof, no matter what they pays, and you may mark my words I'll 'ave no more.'

Mrs Henderson, once more glancing upward, as if she

imagined herself to have made some declaration of a religious nature, shook her head with much solemnity.

CHAPTER XLVI.

THE SUDDEN STOPPING

As we were leaving the house a constable gave the Inspector a note. Having read it he passed it to me. It was from the local office.

'Message received that an Arab with a big bundle on his head has been noticed loitering about the neighbourhood of St Pancras Station. He seemed to be accompanied by a young man who had the appearance of a tramp. Young man seemed ill. They appeared to be waiting for a train, probably to the North. Shall I advise detention?'

I scribbled on the flyleaf of the note.

'Have them detained. If they have gone by train have a special in readiness.'

In a minute we were again in the cab. I endeavoured to persuade Lessingham and Atherton to allow me to conduct the pursuit alone,—in vain. I had no fear of Atherton's succumbing, but I was afraid for Lessingham. What was more almost than the expectation of his collapse was the fact that his looks and manner, his whole bearing, so eloquent of the agony and agitation of his mind, was beginning to tell upon my nerves. A catastrophe of some sort I foresaw. Of the curtain's fall upon one tragedy we had just been witnesses. That there was worse—much worse, to follow I did not doubt. Optimistic anticipations were out of the question,—that the creature we were chasing would relinquish the prey uninjured, no one, after what we had seen and heard, could by any possibility suppose. Should a necessity suddenly arise for prompt and immediate action, that Lessingham would prove a hindrance rather than a help I felt persuaded.

But since moments were precious, and Lessingham was not to be persuaded to allow the matter to proceed without him, all that remained was to make the best of his presence.

The great arch of St Pancras was in darkness. An occasional light seemed to make the darkness still more visible. The station seemed deserted. I thought, at first, that there was not a soul about the place, that our errand was in vain, that the only thing for us to do was to drive to the police station and to pursue our inquiries there. But as we turned towards the booking-office, our footsteps ringing out clearly through the silence and the night, a door opened, a light shone out from the room within, and a voice inquired:

'Who's that?'

'My name's Champnell. Has a message been received from me from the Limehouse Police Station?'

'Step this way.'

We stepped that way,—into a snug enough office, of which one of the railway inspectors was apparently in charge. He was a big man, with a fair beard. He looked me up and down, as if doubtfully. Lessingham he recognised at once. He took off his cap to him.

'Mr Lessingham, I believe?'

'I am Mr Lessingham. Have you any news for me?'

I fancy, by his looks,—that the official was struck by the pallor of the speaker's face,—and by his tremulous voice.

'I am instructed to give certain information to a Mr Augustus Champnell.'

'I am Mr Champnell. What's your information?'

'With reference to the Arab about whom you have been making inquiries. A foreigner, dressed like an Arab, with a great bundle on his head, took two single thirds for Hull by the midnight express.'

'Was he alone?'

'It is believed that he was accompanied by a young man of very disreputable appearance. They were not together at the booking-office, but they had been seen together previously. A minute or so after the Arab had entered the train this young man got into the same compartment—they were in the front waggon.'

'Why were they not detained?'

'We had no authority to detain them, nor any reason. Until your message was received a few minutes ago we at this station were not aware that inquiries were being made for them.'

'You say he booked to Hull,—does the train run through to Hull?'

'No—it doesn't go to Hull at all. Part of it's the Liverpool and Manchester Express, and part of it's for Carlisle. It divides at Derby. The man you're looking for will change either at Sheffield or at Cudworth Junction and go on to Hull by the first train in the morning. There's a local service.'

I looked at my watch.

'You say the train left at midnight. It's now nearly five-and-twenty past. Where's it now?'

'Nearing St Albans, it's due there 12.35.'

'Would there be time for a wire to reach St Albans?'

'Hardly,—and anyhow there'll only be enough railway officials about the place to receive and despatch the train. They'll be fully occupied with their ordinary duties. There won't be time to get the police there.'

'You could wire to St Albans to inquire if they were still in the train?'

'That could be done,—certainly. I'll have it done at once if you like.'

'Then where's the next stoppage?'

'Well, they're at Luton at 12.51. But that's another case of St Albans. You see there won't be much more than twenty minutes by the time you've got your wire off, and I don't expect there'll be many people awake at Luton. At these country places sometimes there's a policeman hanging about the station to see the express go through, but, on the other hand, very often there isn't, and if there isn't, probably at this time of night it'll take a good bit of time to get the police on the premises. I tell you what I should advise.'

'What's that?'

'The train is due at Bedford at 1.29—send your wire there. There ought to be plenty of people about at Bedford, and anyhow there'll be time to get the police to the station.'

'Very good. I instructed them to tell you to have a special

ready, – have you got one?'

'There's an engine with steam up in the shed, – we'll have all ready for you in less than ten minutes. And I tell you what, – you'll have about fifty minutes before the train is due at Bedford. It's a fifty mile run. With luck you ought to get there pretty nearly as soon as the express does. – Shall I tell them to get ready?'

'At once.'

While he issued directions through a telephone to what, I presume, was the engine shed, I drew up a couple of telegrams. Having completed his orders he turned to me.

'They're coming out of the siding now – they'll be ready in less than ten minutes. I'll see that the line's kept clear. Have you got those wires?'

'Here is one, – this is for Bedford.'

It ran:

'Arrest the Arab who is in train due at 1.29. When leaving St Pancras he was in a third-class compartment in front waggon. He has a large bundle, which detain. He took two third singles for Hull. Also detain his companion, who is dressed like a tramp. This is a young lady whom the Arab has disguised and kidnapped while in a condition of hypnotic trance. Let her have medical assistance and be taken to a hotel. All expenses will be paid on the arrival of the undersigned who is following by special train. As the Arab will probably be very violent a sufficient force of police should be in waiting.

'Augustus Champnell.'

'And this is the other. It is probably too late to be of any use at St Albans, – but send it there, and also to Luton.'

'Is Arab with companion in train which left St Pancras at 12.0? If so, do not let them get out till train reaches Bedford, where instructions are being wired for arrest.'

The Inspector rapidly scanned them both.

'They ought to do your business, I should think. Come along with me – I'll have them sent at once, and we'll see if your train's ready.'

The train was not ready,—nor was it ready within the prescribed ten minutes. There was some hitch, I fancy, about a saloon. Finally we had to be content with an ordinary old-fashioned first-class carriage. The delay, however, was not altogether time lost. Just as the engine with its solitary coach was approaching the platform someone came running up with an envelope in his hand.

'Telegram from St Albans.'

I tore it open. It was brief and to the point.

'Arab with companion was in train when it left here. Am wiring Luton.'

'That's all right. Now unless something wholly unforeseen takes place, we ought to have them.'

That unforeseen!

I went forward with the Inspector and the guard of our train to exchange a few final words with the driver. The Inspector explained what instructions he had given.

'I've told the driver not to spare his coal but to take you into Bedford within five minutes after the arrival of the express. He says he thinks that he can do it.'

The driver leaned over his engine, rubbing his hands with the usual oily rag. He was a short, wiry man with grey hair and a grizzled moustache, with about him that bearing of semi-humorous, frank-faced resolution which one notes about engine-drivers as a class.

'We ought to do it, the gradients are against us, but it's a clear night and there's no wind. The only thing that will stop us will be if there's any shunting on the road, or any luggage trains; of course, if we are blocked, we are blocked, but the Inspector says he'll clear the way for us.'

'Yes,' said the Inspector, 'I'll clear the way. I've wired down the road already.'

Atherton broke in.

'Driver, if you get us into Bedford within five minutes of the arrival of the mail there'll be a five-pound note to divide between your mate and you.'

The driver grinned.

'We'll get you there in time, sir, if we have to go clear through the shunters. It isn't often we get a chance of a five-pound note for a run to Bedford, and we'll do our best to earn it.'

The fireman waved his hand in the rear.

'That's right, sir!' he cried. 'We'll have to trouble you for that five-pound note.'

So soon as we were clear of the station it began to seem probable that, as the fireman put it, Atherton would be 'troubled.' Journeying in a train which consists of a single carriage attached to an engine which is flying at topmost speed is a very different business from being an occupant of an ordinary train which is travelling at ordinary express rates. I had discovered that for myself before. That night it was impressed on me more than ever. A tyro—or even a nervous 'season'—might have been excused for expecting at every moment we were going to be derailed. It was hard to believe that the carriage had any springs,—it rocked and swung, and jogged and jolted. Of smooth travelling had we none. Talking was out of the question;—and for that, I, personally, was grateful. Quite apart from the difficulty we experienced in keeping our seats—and when every moment our position was being altered and we were jerked backwards and forwards up and down, this way and that, that was a business which required care,—the noise was deafening. It was as though we were being pursued by a legion of shrieking, bellowing, raging demons.

'George!' shrieked Atherton, 'he does mean to earn that fiver. I hope I'll be alive to pay it him!'

He was only at the other end of the carriage, but though I could see by the distortion of his visage that he was shouting at the top of his voice,—and he has a voice,—I only caught here and there a word or two of what he was saying. I had to make sense of the whole.

Lessingham's contortions were a study. Few of that large multitude of persons who are acquainted with him only by means of the portraits which have appeared in the illustrated papers, would then have recognised the rising statesman. Yet I believe that few things could have better fallen in with his mood than that wild travelling. He might have been almost shaken to pieces,—but the very severity of the shaking served to divert his thoughts from the one dread topic which threatened to absorb them to the exclusion of all else beside. Then there was the tonic influence of the element of risk. The pick-me-up effect of a spice of peril. Actual danger there quite probably was none; but there very really seemed to be. And one thing was absolutely certain, that if we did come to smash while going at that speed we should come to as everlasting smash as the heart of man could by any possibility desire. It is probable that the knowledge that this was so warmed the blood in Lessingham's veins. At any rate as—to use what in this case, was simply a form of speech—I sat and watched him, it seemed to me that he was getting a firmer hold of the strength which had all but escaped him, and that with every jog and jolt he was becoming more and more of a man.

On and on we went dashing, crashing, smashing, roaring, rumbling. Atherton, who had been endeavouring to peer through the window, strained his lungs again in the effort to make himself audible.

'Where the devil are we?'

Looking at my watch I screamed back at him.

'It's nearly one, so I suppose we're somewhere in the neighbourhood of Luton.—Hollo! What's the matter?'

That something was the matter seemed certain. There was a shrill whistle from the engine. In a second we were conscious—almost too conscious—of the application of the Westinghouse brake. Of all the jolting that was ever jolted! the mere reverberation of the carriage threatened to resolve our bodies into their component parts. Feeling what we felt then helped us to realise the retardatory force which that vacuum brake must be exerting,—it did not seem at all surprising that the train should have been brought to an almost instant standstill.

Simultaneously all three of us were on our feet. I let down my window and Atherton let down his,—he shouting out,

'I should think that Inspector's wire hasn't had it's proper effect, looks as if we're blocked—or else we've stopped at Luton. It can't be Bedford.'

It wasn't Bedford—so much seemed clear. Though at first from my window I could make out nothing. I was feeling more than a trifle dazed,—there was a singing in my ears,—the sudden darkness was impenetrable. Then I became conscious that the guard was opening the door of his compartment. He stood on the step for a moment, seeming to hesitate. Then, with a lamp in his hand, he descended on to the line.

'What's the matter?' I asked.

'Don't know, sir. Seems as if there was something on the road. What's up there?'

This was to the man on the engine. The fireman replied:

'Someone in front there's waving a red light like mad,—lucky I caught sight of him, we should have been clean on top of him in another moment. Looks as if there was something wrong. Here he comes.'

As my eyes grew more accustomed to the darkness I became aware that someone was making what haste he could along the six-foot way, swinging a red light as he came. Our guard advanced to meet him, shouting as he went:

'What's the matter! Who's that?'

A voice replied,

'My God! Is that George Hewett. I thought you were coming right on top of us!'

Our guard again.

'What! Jim Branson! What the devil are you doing here, what's wrong? I thought you were on the twelve out, we're chasing you.'

'Are you? Then you've caught us. Thank God for it!—We're a wreck.'

I had already opened the carriage door. With that we all three clambered out on to the line.

CHAPTER XLVII.
THE CONTENTS OF THE THIRD-CLASS CARRIAGE

I moved to the stranger who was holding the lamp. He was in official uniform.

'Are you the guard of the 12.0 out from St Pancras?'

'I am.'

'Where's your train? What's happened?'

'As for where it is, there it is, right in front of you, what's left of it. As to what's happened, why, we're wrecked.'

'What do you mean by you're wrecked?'

'Some heavy loaded trucks broke loose from a goods in front and came running down the hill on top of us.'

'How long ago was it?'

'Not ten minutes. I was just starting off down the road to the signal box, it's a good two miles away, when I saw you coming. My God! I thought there was going to be another smash.'

'Much damage done?'

'Seems to me as if we're all smashed up. As far as I can make out they're matchboxed up in front. I feel as if I was all broken up inside of me. I've been in the service going on for thirty years, and this is the first accident I've been in.'

It was too dark to see the man's face, but judging from his tone he was either crying or very near to it.

Our guard turned and shouted back to our engine,

'You'd better go back to the box and let 'em know!'

'All right!' came echoing back.

The special immediately commenced retreating, whistling continually as it went. All the country side must have heard the engine shrieking, and all who did hear must have understood that on the line something was seriously wrong.

The smashed train was all in darkness, the force of the collision had put out all the carriage lamps. Here was a flickering candle, there the glimmer of a match, these were all the lights which shone upon the scene. People were piling up débris by the side of the line, for the purpose of making a fire,—more for illumination than for warmth.

Many of the passengers had succeeded in freeing themselves, and were moving hither and thither about the line. But the majority appeared to be still imprisoned. The carriage doors were jammed. Without the necessary tools it was impossible to open them. Every step we took our ears were saluted by piteous cries. Men, women, children, appealed to us for help.

'Open the door, sir!' 'In the name of God, sir, open the door!'

Over and over again, in all sorts of tones, with all degrees of violence, the supplication was repeated.

The guards vainly endeavoured to appease the, in many cases, half-frenzied creatures.

'All right, sir! If you'll only wait a minute or two, madam! We can't get the doors open without tools, a special train's just started off to get them. If you'll only have patience there'll be plenty of help for everyone of you directly. You'll be quite safe in there, if you'll only keep still.'

But that was just what they found it most difficult to do—keep still!

In the front of the train all was chaos. The trucks which had done the mischief—there were afterwards shown to be six of them, together with two guards' vans—appeared to have been laden with bags of Portland cement. The bags had burst, and everything was covered with what seemed gritty dust. The air was full of the stuff, it got into our eyes, half blinding us. The engine of the express had turned a complete somersault. It vomited forth smoke, and steam, and flames,—every moment it seemed as if the woodwork of the carriages immediately behind and beneath would catch fire.

The front coaches were, as the guard had put it, 'matchboxed.' They were nothing but a heap of débris,—telescoped into one another in a state of apparently inextricable confusion. It was broad daylight before access was gained to what had once been the interiors. The condition of the first third-class compartment revealed an extraordinary state of things.

Scattered all over it were pieces of what looked like partially burnt rags, and fragments of silk and linen. I have those fragments now. Experts have assured me that they are actually neither of silk nor linen! but of some material—animal rather than vegetable—with which they are wholly unacquainted. On the cushions and woodwork—especially on the woodwork of the floor—were huge blotches,—stains of some sort. When first noticed they were damp, and gave out a most unpleasant smell. One of the pieces of woodwork is yet in my possession,—with the stain still on it. Experts have pronounced upon it too,—with the result that opinions are divided. Some maintain that the stain was produced by human blood, which had been subjected to a great heat, and, so to speak, parboiled. Others declare that it is the blood of some wild animal,—possibly of some creature of the cat species. Yet others affirm that it is not blood at all, but merely paint. While a fourth describes it as—I quote the written opinion which lies in front of me—'caused apparently by a deposit of some sort of viscid matter, probably the excretion of some variety of lizard.'

In a corner of the carriage was the body of what seemed a young man costumed like a tramp. It was Marjorie Lindon.

So far as a most careful search revealed, that was all the compartment contained.

CHAPTER XLVIII.

THE CONCLUSION OF THE MATTER

It is several years since I bore my part in the events which I have rapidly sketched,—or I should not have felt justified in giving them publicity. Exactly how many years, for reasons which should be sufficiently obvious, I must decline to say.

Marjorie Lindon still lives. The spark of life which was left in her, when she was extricated from among the débris of the wrecked express, was fanned again into flame. Her restoration was, however, not merely an affair of weeks or months, it was a matter of years. I believe that, even after her physical powers were completely restored—in itself a tedious task—she was for something like three years under medical supervision as a lunatic. But all that skill and money could do was done, and in course of time—the great healer—the results were entirely satisfactory.

Her father is dead,—and has left her in possession of the family estates. She is married to the individual who, in these pages, has been known as Paul Lessingham. Were his real name divulged she would be recognised as the popular and universally reverenced wife of one of the greatest statesmen the age has seen.

Nothing has been said to her about the fateful day on which she was—consciously or unconsciously—paraded through London in the tattered masculine habiliments of a vagabond. She herself has never once alluded to it. With the return of reason the affair seems to have passed from her memory as wholly as if it had never been, which, although she may not know it, is not the least cause she has for thankfulness. Therefore what actually transpired will never, in all human probability, be certainly known and particularly what precisely occurred in the railway carriage during that dreadful moment of sudden passing from life unto death. What became of the creature who all but did her to death; who he was—if it was a 'he,' which is extremely doubtful; whence he came; whither he went; what was the purport of his presence here,—to this hour these things are puzzles.

Paul Lessingham has not since been troubled by his old tormentor. He has ceased to be a haunted man. None the less he continues to have what seems to be a constitutional disrelish for the subject of beetles, nor can he himself be induced to speak of them. Should they be mentioned in a general conversation, should he be unable to immediately bring about a change of theme, he will, if possible, get up and leave the room. More, on this point he and his wife are one.

The fact may not be generally known, but it is so. Also I have reason to believe that there still are moments in which he harks back, with something like physical shrinking, to that awful nightmare of the past, and in which he prays God, that as it is distant from him now so may it be kept far off from him for ever.

Before closing, one matter may be casually mentioned. The tale has never been told, but I have unimpeachable authority for its authenticity.

During the recent expeditionary advance towards Dongola, a body of native troops which was encamped at a remote spot in the desert was aroused one night by what seemed to be the sound of a loud explosion. The next morning, at a distance of about a couple of miles from the camp, a huge hole was discovered in the ground,—as if blasting operations, on an enormous scale, had recently been carried on. In the hole itself, and round about it, were found fragments of what seemed bodies; credible witnesses have assured me that they were bodies neither of men nor women, but of creatures of some monstrous growth. I prefer to believe, since no scientific examination of the remains took place, that these witnesses ignorantly, though innocently, erred.

One thing is sure. Numerous pieces, both of stone and of metal, were seen, which went far to suggest that some curious subterranean building had been blown up by the force of the explosion. Especially were there portions of moulded metal which seemed to belong to what must have been an immense bronze statue. There were picked up also, more than a dozen replicas in bronze of the whilom sacred scarabaeus.

That the den of demons described by Paul Lessingham, had, that night, at last come to an end, and that these things which lay scattered, here and there, on that treeless plain, were the evidences of its final destruction, is not a hypothesis which I should care to advance with any degree of certainty. But, putting this and that together, the facts seem to point that way, —and it is a consummation devoutly to be desired.

By-the-bye, Sydney Atherton has married Miss Dora Grayling. Her wealth has made him one of the richest men in England. She began, the story goes, by loving him immensely; I can answer for the fact that he has ended by loving her as much. Their devotion to each other contradicts the pessimistic nonsense which supposes that every marriage must be of necessity a failure. He continues his career of an inventor. His investigations into the subject of aërial flight, which have brought the flying machine within the range of practical politics, are on everybody's tongue.

The best man at Atherton's wedding was Percy Woodville, now the Earl of Barnes. Within six months afterwards he married one of Mrs Atherton's bridesmaids.

It was never certainly shown how Robert Holt came to his end. At the inquest the coroner's jury was content to return a verdict of 'Died of exhaustion.' He lies buried in Kensal Green Cemetery, under a handsome tombstone, the cost of which, had he had it in his pockets, might have indefinitely prolonged his days.

It should be mentioned that that portion of this strange history which purports to be The Surprising Narration of Robert Holt was compiled from the statements which Holt made to Atherton, and to Miss Lindon, as she then was, when, a mud-stained, shattered derelict he lay at the lady's father's house.

Miss Lindon's contribution towards the elucidation of the mystery was written with her own hand. After her physical strength had come back to her, and, while mentally, she still hovered between the darkness and the light, her one relaxation was writing. Although she would never speak of what she had written, it was found that her theme was always the same. She confided to pen and paper what she would not speak of with her lips. She told, and re-told, and re-told again, the story of her love, and of her tribulation so far as it is contained in the present volume. Her MSS. invariably began and ended at the same point. They have all of them been destroyed, with one exception. That exception is herein placed before the reader.

On the subject of the Mystery of the Beetle I do not propose to pronounce a confident opinion. Atherton and I have talked it over many and many a time, and at the end we have got no 'forrarder.' So far as I am personally concerned, experience has taught me that there are indeed more things in heaven and earth than are dreamed of in our philosophy, and I am quite prepared to believe that the so-called Beetle, which others saw, but I never, was—or is, for it cannot be certainly shown that the Thing is not still existing—a creature born neither of God nor man.

THE END

The Hound of the Baskervilles

By Arthur Conan Doyle

Chapter 1.

Mr. Sherlock Holmes

Mr. Sherlock Holmes, who was usually very late in the mornings, save upon those not infrequent occasions when he was up all night, was seated at the breakfast table. I stood upon the hearth-rug and picked up the stick which our visitor had left behind him the night before. It was a fine, thick piece of wood, bulbous-headed, of the sort which is known as a "Penang lawyer." Just under the head was a broad silver band nearly an inch across. "To James Mortimer, M.R.C.S., from his friends of the C.C.H.," was engraved upon it, with the date "1884." It was just such a stick as the old-fashioned family practitioner used to carry—dignified, solid, and reassuring.

"Well, Watson, what do you make of it?"

Holmes was sitting with his back to me, and I had given him no sign of my occupation.

"How did you know what I was doing? I believe you have eyes in the back of your head."

"I have, at least, a well-polished, silver-plated coffee-pot in front of me," said he. "But, tell me, Watson, what do you make of our visitor's stick? Since we have been so unfortunate as to miss him and have no notion of his errand, this accidental souvenir becomes of importance. Let me hear you reconstruct the man by an examination of it."

"I think," said I, following as far as I could the methods of my companion, "that Dr. Mortimer is a successful, elderly medical man, well-esteemed since those who know him give him this mark of their appreciation."

"Good!" said Holmes. "Excellent!"

"I think also that the probability is in favour of his being a country practitioner who does a great deal of his visiting on foot."

"Why so?"

"Because this stick, though originally a very handsome one has been so knocked about that I can hardly imagine a town practitioner carrying it. The thick-iron ferrule is worn down, so it is evident that he has done a great amount of walking with it."

"Perfectly sound!" said Holmes.

"And then again, there is the 'friends of the C.C.H.' I should guess that to be the Something Hunt, the local hunt to whose members he has possibly given some surgical assistance, and which has made him a small presentation in return."

"Really, Watson, you excel yourself," said Holmes, pushing back his chair and lighting a cigarette. "I am bound to say that in all the accounts which you have been so good as to give of my own small achievements you have habitually underrated your own abilities. It may be that you are not yourself luminous, but you are a conductor of light. Some people without possessing genius have a remarkable power of stimulating it. I confess, my dear fellow, that I am very much in your debt."

He had never said as much before, and I must admit that his words gave me keen pleasure, for I had often been piqued by his indifference to my admiration and to the attempts which I had made to give publicity to his methods. I was proud, too, to think that I had so far mastered his system as to apply it in a way which earned his approval. He now took the stick from my hands and examined it for a few minutes with his naked eyes. Then with an expression of interest he laid down his cigarette, and carrying the cane to the window, he looked over it again with a convex lens.

"Interesting, though elementary," said he as he returned to his favourite corner of the settee. "There are certainly one or two indications upon the stick. It gives us the basis for several deductions."

"Has anything escaped me?" I asked with some self-importance. "I trust that there is nothing of consequence which I have overlooked?"

"I am afraid, my dear Watson, that most of your conclusions were erroneous. When I said that you stimulated me I meant, to be frank, that in noting your fallacies I was occasionally guided towards the truth. Not that you are entirely wrong in this instance. The man is certainly a country practitioner. And he walks a good deal."

"Then I was right."

"To that extent."

"But that was all."

"No, no, my dear Watson, not all—by no means all. I would suggest, for example, that a presentation to a doctor is more likely to come from a hospital than from a hunt, and that when the initials 'C.C.' are placed before that hospital the words 'Charing Cross' very naturally suggest themselves."

"You may be right."

"The probability lies in that direction. And if we take this as a working hypothesis we have a fresh basis from which to start our construction of this unknown visitor."

"Well, then, supposing that 'C.C.H.' does stand for 'Charing Cross Hospital,' what further inferences may we draw?"

"Do none suggest themselves? You know my methods. Apply them!"

"I can only think of the obvious conclusion that the man has practised in town before going to the country."

"I think that we might venture a little farther than this. Look at it in this light. On what occasion would it be most probable that such a presentation would be made? When would his friends unite to give him a pledge of their good will? Obviously at the moment when Dr. Mortimer withdrew from the service of the hospital in order to start a practice for himself. We know there has been a presentation. We believe there has been a change from a town hospital to a country practice. Is it, then, stretching our inference too far to say that the presentation was on the occasion of the change?"

"It certainly seems probable."

"Now, you will observe that he could not have been on the

staff of the hospital, since only a man well-established in a London practice could hold such a position, and such a one would not drift into the country. What was he, then? If he was in the hospital and yet not on the staff he could only have been a house-surgeon or a house-physician—little more than a senior student. And he left five years ago—the date is on the stick. So your grave, middle-aged family practitioner vanishes into thin air, my dear Watson, and there emerges a young fellow under thirty, amiable, unambitious, absent-minded, and the possessor of a favourite dog, which I should describe roughly as being larger than a terrier and smaller than a mastiff."

I laughed incredulously as Sherlock Holmes leaned back in his settee and blew little wavering rings of smoke up to the ceiling.

"As to the latter part, I have no means of checking you," said I, "but at least it is not difficult to find out a few particulars about the man's age and professional career." From my small medical shelf I took down the Medical Directory and turned up the name. There were several Mortimers, but only one who could be our visitor. I read his record aloud.

"Mortimer, James, M.R.C.S., 1882, Grimpen, Dartmoor, Devon. House-surgeon, from 1882 to 1884, at Charing Cross Hospital. Winner of the Jackson prize for Comparative Pathology, with essay entitled 'Is Disease a Reversion?' Corresponding member of the Swedish Pathological Society. Author of 'Some Freaks of Atavism' (Lancet 1882). 'Do We Progress?' (Journal of Psychology, March, 1883). Medical Officer for the parishes of Grimpen, Thorsley, and High Barrow."

"No mention of that local hunt, Watson," said Holmes with a mischievous smile, "but a country doctor, as you very astutely observed. I think that I am fairly justified in my inferences. As to the adjectives, I said, if I remember right, amiable, unambitious, and absent-minded. It is my experience that it is only an amiable man in this world who receives testimonials, only an unambitious one who abandons a London career for the country, and only an absent-minded one who leaves his stick and not his visiting-card after waiting an hour in your room."

"And the dog?"

"Has been in the habit of carrying this stick behind his master. Being a heavy stick the dog has held it tightly by the middle, and the marks of his teeth are very plainly visible. The dog's jaw, as shown in the space between these marks, is too broad in my opinion for a terrier and not broad enough for a mastiff. It may have been—yes, by Jove, it is a curly-haired spaniel."

He had risen and paced the room as he spoke. Now he halted in the recess of the window. There was such a ring of conviction in his voice that I glanced up in surprise.

"My dear fellow, how can you possibly be so sure of that?"

"For the very simple reason that I see the dog himself on our very door-step, and there is the ring of its owner. Don't move, I beg you, Watson. He is a professional brother of yours, and your presence may be of assistance to me. Now is the dramatic moment of fate, Watson, when you hear a step upon the stair which is walking into your life, and you know not whether for good or ill. What does Dr. James Mortimer, the man of science, ask of Sherlock Holmes, the specialist in crime? Come in!"

The appearance of our visitor was a surprise to me, since I had expected a typical country practitioner. He was a very tall, thin man, with a long nose like a beak, which jutted out between two keen, grey eyes, set closely together and sparkling brightly from behind a pair of gold-rimmed glasses. He was clad in a professional but rather slovenly fashion, for his frock-coat was dingy and his trousers frayed. Though young, his long back was already bowed, and he walked with a forward thrust of his head and a general air of peering benevolence. As he entered his eyes fell upon the stick in Holmes's hand, and he ran towards it with an exclamation of joy. "I am so very glad," said he. "I was not sure whether I had left it here or in the Shipping Office. I would not lose that stick for the world."

"A presentation, I see," said Holmes.

"Yes, sir."

"From Charing Cross Hospital?"

"From one or two friends there on the occasion of my marriage."

"Dear, dear, that's bad!" said Holmes, shaking his head.

Dr. Mortimer blinked through his glasses in mild astonishment. "Why was it bad?"

"Only that you have disarranged our little deductions. Your

marriage, you say?"

"Yes, sir. I married, and so left the hospital, and with it all hopes of a consulting practice. It was necessary to make a home of my own."

"Come, come, we are not so far wrong, after all," said Holmes. "And now, Dr. James Mortimer—"

"Mister, sir, Mister—a humble M.R.C.S."

"And a man of precise mind, evidently."

"A dabbler in science, Mr. Holmes, a picker up of shells on the shores of the great unknown ocean. I presume that it is Mr. Sherlock Holmes whom I am addressing and not—"

"No, this is my friend Dr. Watson."

"Glad to meet you, sir. I have heard your name mentioned in connection with that of your friend. You interest me very much, Mr. Holmes. I had hardly expected so dolichocephalic a skull or such well-marked supra-orbital development. Would you have any objection to my running my finger along your parietal fissure? A cast of your skull, sir, until the original is available, would be an ornament to any anthropological museum. It is not my intention to be fulsome, but I confess that I covet your skull."

Sherlock Holmes waved our strange visitor into a chair. "You are an enthusiast in your line of thought, I perceive, sir, as I am in mine," said he. "I observe from your forefinger that you make your own cigarettes. Have no hesitation in lighting one."

The man drew out paper and tobacco and twirled the one up in the other with surprising dexterity. He had long, quivering fingers as agile and restless as the antennæ of an insect.

Holmes was silent, but his little darting glances showed me the interest which he took in our curious companion. "I presume, sir," said he at last, "that it was not merely for the purpose of examining my skull that you have done me the honour to call here last night and again today?"

"No, sir, no; though I am happy to have had the opportunity of doing that as well. I came to you, Mr. Holmes, because I recognized that I am myself an unpractical man and because I am suddenly confronted with a most serious and extraordinary problem. Recognizing, as I do, that you are the second highest expert in Europe—"

"Indeed, sir! May I inquire who has the honour to be the first?" asked Holmes with some asperity.

"To the man of precisely scientific mind the work of Monsieur Bertillon must always appeal strongly."

"Then had you not better consult him?"

"I said, sir, to the precisely scientific mind. But as a practical man of affairs it is acknowledged that you stand alone. I trust, sir, that I have not inadvertently—"

"Just a little," said Holmes. "I think, Dr. Mortimer, you would do wisely if without more ado you would kindly tell me plainly what the exact nature of the problem is in which you demand my assistance."

Chapter 2.

The Curse of the Baskervilles

"I have in my pocket a manuscript," said Dr. James Mortimer.

"I observed it as you entered the room," said Holmes.

"It is an old manuscript."

"Early eighteenth century, unless it is a forgery."

"How can you say that, sir?"

"You have presented an inch or two of it to my examination all the time that you have been talking. It would be a poor expert who could not give the date of a document within a decade or so. You may possibly have read my little monograph upon the subject. I put that at 1730."

"The exact date is 1742." Dr. Mortimer drew it from his breast-pocket. "This family paper was committed to my care by Sir Charles Baskerville, whose sudden and tragic death some three months ago created so much excitement in Devonshire. I may say that I was his personal friend as well as his medical attendant. He was a strong-minded man, sir, shrewd, practical, and as unimaginative as I am myself. Yet he took this document very seriously, and his mind was prepared for just such an end as did eventually overtake him."

Holmes stretched out his hand for the manuscript and flattened it upon his knee. "You will observe, Watson, the alternative use of the long s and the short. It is one of several indications which enabled me to fix the date."

I looked over his shoulder at the yellow paper and the faded script. At the head was written: "Baskerville Hall," and below in large, scrawling figures: "1742."

"It appears to be a statement of some sort."

"Yes, it is a statement of a certain legend which runs in the Baskerville family."

"But I understand that it is something more modern and practical upon which you wish to consult me?"

"Most modern. A most practical, pressing matter, which must be decided within twenty-four hours. But the manuscript is short and is intimately connected with the affair. With your permission I will read it to you."

Holmes leaned back in his chair, placed his finger-tips together, and closed his eyes, with an air of resignation. Dr. Mortimer turned the manuscript to the light and read in a high, cracking voice the following curious, old-world narrative:

"Of the origin of the Hound of the Baskervilles there have been many statements, yet as I come in a direct line from Hugo Baskerville, and as I had the story from my father, who also had it from his, I have set it down with all belief that it occurred even as is here set forth. And I would have you believe, my sons, that the same Justice which punishes sin may also most graciously forgive it, and that no ban is so heavy but that by prayer and repentance it may be removed. Learn then from this story not to fear the fruits of the past, but rather to be circumspect in the future, that those foul passions whereby our family has suffered so grievously may not again be loosed to our undoing.

"Know then that in the time of the Great Rebellion (the history of which by the learned Lord Clarendon I most earnestly commend to your attention) this Manor of Baskerville was held by Hugo of that name, nor can it be gainsaid that he was a most wild, profane, and godless man. This, in truth, his neighbours might have pardoned, seeing that saints have never flourished in those parts, but there was in him a certain wanton and cruel humour which made his name a by-word through the West. It chanced that this Hugo came to love (if, indeed, so dark a passion may be known under so bright a name) the daughter of a yeoman who held lands near the Baskerville estate. But the young maiden, being discreet and of good repute, would ever avoid him, for she feared his evil name. So it came to pass that one Michaelmas this Hugo, with five or six of his idle and wicked companions, stole down upon the farm and carried off the maiden, her father and brothers being from home, as he well knew. When they had brought her to the Hall the maiden was placed in an upper chamber, while Hugo and his friends sat down to a long carouse, as was their nightly custom. Now, the poor lass upstairs was like to have her wits turned at the singing and shouting and terrible oaths which came up to her from below, for they say that the words used by Hugo Baskerville, when he was in wine, were such as might blast the man who said them. At last in the stress of her fear she did that which might have daunted the bravest or most active man, for by the aid of the growth of ivy which covered (and still covers) the south wall she came down from under the eaves, and so homeward across the moor, there being three leagues betwixt the Hall and her father's farm.

"It chanced that some little time later Hugo left his guests to carry food and drink—with other worse things, perchance—to his captive, and so found the cage empty and the bird escaped. Then, as it would seem, he became as one that hath a devil, for, rushing down the stairs into the dining-hall, he sprang upon the great table, flagons and trenchers flying before him, and he cried aloud before all the company that he would that very night render his body and soul to the Powers of Evil if he might but overtake the wench. And while the revellers stood aghast at the fury of the man, one more wicked or, it may be, more drunken than the rest, cried out that they should put the hounds upon her. Whereat Hugo ran from the house, crying to his grooms that they should saddle his mare and unkennel the pack, and giving the hounds a kerchief of the maid's, he swung them to the line, and so off full cry in the moonlight over the moor.

"Now, for some space the revellers stood agape, unable to understand all that had been done in such haste. But anon their bemused wits awoke to the nature of the deed which was like to be done upon the moorlands. Everything was now in an uproar, some calling for their pistols, some for their horses, and some for another flask of wine. But at length some sense came back to their crazed minds, and the whole of them, thirteen in number, took horse and started in pursuit. The moon shone clear above them, and they rode swiftly abreast, taking that course which the maid must needs have taken if she were to reach her own home.

"They had gone a mile or two when they passed one of the night shepherds upon the moorlands, and they cried to him to know if he had seen the hunt. And the man, as the story goes, was so crazed with fear that he could scarce speak, but at last he said that he had indeed seen the unhappy maiden, with the hounds upon her track. 'But I have seen more than that,' said he, 'for Hugo Baskerville passed me upon his black mare, and there ran mute behind him such a hound of hell as God forbid should ever be at my heels.' So the drunken squires cursed the shepherd and rode onward. But soon their skins turned cold, for there came a galloping across the moor, and the black mare, dabbled with white froth, went past with trailing bridle and empty saddle. Then the revellers rode close together, for a great fear was on them, but they still followed over the moor, though each, had he been alone, would have been right glad to have turned his horse's head. Riding slowly in this fashion they came at last upon the hounds. These, though known for their valour and their breed, were whimpering in a cluster at the head of a deep dip or goyal, as we call it, upon the moor, some slinking away and some, with starting hackles and staring eyes, gazing down the narrow valley before them.

"The company had come to a halt, more sober men, as you may guess, than when they started. The most of them would by no means advance, but three of them, the boldest, or it may be the most drunken, rode forward down the goyal. Now, it opened into a broad space in which stood two of those great stones, still to be seen there, which were set by certain forgotten peoples in the days of old. The moon was shining bright upon the clearing, and there in the centre lay the unhappy maid where she had fallen, dead of fear and of fatigue. But it was not the sight of her body, nor yet was it that of the body of Hugo Baskerville lying near her, which raised the hair upon the heads of these three dare-devil roysterers, but it was that, standing over Hugo, and plucking at his throat, there stood a foul thing, a great, black beast, shaped like a hound, yet larger than any hound that ever mortal eye has rested upon. And even as they looked the thing tore the throat out of Hugo Baskerville, on which, as it turned its blazing eyes and dripping jaws upon them, the three shrieked with fear and rode for dear life, still screaming, across the moor. One, it is said, died that very night of what he had seen, and the other twain were but broken men for the rest of their days.

"Such is the tale, my sons, of the coming of the hound which is said to have plagued the family so sorely ever since. If I have set it down it is because that which is clearly known hath less terror than that which is but hinted at and guessed. Nor can it be denied that many of the family have been unhappy in their deaths, which have been sudden, bloody, and mysterious. Yet may we shelter ourselves in the infinite goodness of Providence, which would not forever punish the innocent beyond that third or fourth generation which is threatened in Holy Writ. To that Providence, my sons, I hereby commend you, and I counsel you by way of caution to forbear from crossing the moor in those dark hours when the powers of evil are exalted.

"[This from Hugo Baskerville to his sons Rodger and John, with instructions that they say nothing thereof to their sister Elizabeth.]"

When Dr. Mortimer had finished reading this singular

narrative he pushed his spectacles up on his forehead and stared across at Mr. Sherlock Holmes. The latter yawned and tossed the end of his cigarette into the fire.

"Well?" said he.

"Do you not find it interesting?"

"To a collector of fairy tales."

Dr. Mortimer drew a folded newspaper out of his pocket.

"Now, Mr. Holmes, we will give you something a little more recent. This is the Devon County Chronicle of May 14th of this year. It is a short account of the facts elicited at the death of Sir Charles Baskerville which occurred a few days before that date."

My friend leaned a little forward and his expression became intent. Our visitor readjusted his glasses and began:

"The recent sudden death of Sir Charles Baskerville, whose name has been mentioned as the probable Liberal candidate for Mid-Devon at the next election, has cast a gloom over the county. Though Sir Charles had resided at Baskerville Hall for a comparatively short period his amiability of character and extreme generosity had won the affection and respect of all who had been brought into contact with him. In these days of nouveaux riches it is refreshing to find a case where the scion of an old county family which has fallen upon evil days is able to make his own fortune and to bring it back with him to restore the fallen grandeur of his line. Sir Charles, as is well known, made large sums of money in South African speculation. More wise than those who go on until the wheel turns against them, he realised his gains and returned to England with them. It is only two years since he took up his residence at Baskerville Hall, and it is common talk how large were those schemes of reconstruction and improvement which have been interrupted by his death. Being himself childless, it was his openly expressed desire that the whole countryside should, within his own lifetime, profit by his good fortune, and many will have personal reasons for bewailing his untimely end. His generous donations to local and county charities have been frequently chronicled in these columns.

"The circumstances connected with the death of Sir Charles cannot be said to have been entirely cleared up by the inquest, but at least enough has been done to dispose of those rumours to which local superstition has given rise. There is no reason whatever to suspect foul play, or to imagine that death could be from any but natural causes. Sir Charles was a widower, and a man who may be said to have been in some ways of an eccentric habit of mind. In spite of his considerable wealth he was simple in his personal tastes, and his indoor servants at Baskerville Hall consisted of a married couple named Barrymore, the husband acting as butler and the wife as housekeeper. Their evidence, corroborated by that of several friends, tends to show that Sir Charles's health has for some time been impaired, and points especially to some affection of the heart, manifesting itself in changes of colour, breathlessness, and acute attacks of nervous depression. Dr. James Mortimer, the friend and medical attendant of the deceased, has given evidence to the same effect.

"The facts of the case are simple. Sir Charles Baskerville was in the habit every night before going to bed of walking down the famous yew alley of Baskerville Hall. The evidence of the Barrymores shows that this had been his custom. On the fourth of May Sir Charles had declared his intention of starting next day for London, and had ordered Barrymore to prepare his luggage. That night he went out as usual for his nocturnal walk, in the course of which he was in the habit of smoking a cigar. He never returned. At twelve o'clock Barrymore, finding the hall door still open, became alarmed, and, lighting a lantern, went in search of his master. The day had been wet, and Sir Charles's footmarks were easily traced down the alley. Halfway down this walk there is a gate which leads out on to the moor. There were indications that Sir Charles had stood for some little time here. He then proceeded down the alley, and it was at the far end of it that his body was discovered. One fact which has not been explained is the statement of Barrymore that his master's footprints altered their character from the time that he passed the moor-gate, and that he appeared from thence onward to have been walking upon his toes. One Murphy, a gipsy horse-dealer, was on the moor at no great distance at the time, but he appears by his own confession to have been the worse for drink. He declares that he heard cries but is unable to state from what direction they came. No signs of violence were to be discovered upon Sir Charles's person, and though the doctor's evidence pointed to an almost incredible facial distortion—so great that Dr. Mortimer refused at first to believe that it was indeed his friend and patient who lay before him—it was explained that that is a symptom which is not unusual in cases of dyspnœa and death from cardiac exhaustion. This explanation was borne out by the post-mortem examination, which showed long-standing organic disease, and the coroner's jury returned a verdict in accordance with the medical evidence. It is well that this is so, for it is obviously of the utmost importance that Sir Charles's heir should settle at the Hall and continue the good work which has been so sadly interrupted. Had the prosaic finding of the coroner not finally put an end to the romantic stories which have been whispered in connection with the affair, it might have been difficult to find a tenant for Baskerville Hall. It is understood that the next of kin is Mr. Henry Baskerville, if he be still alive, the son of Sir Charles Baskerville's younger brother. The young man when last heard of was in America, and inquiries are being instituted with a view to informing him of his good fortune."

Dr. Mortimer refolded his paper and replaced it in his pocket. "Those are the public facts, Mr. Holmes, in connection with the death of Sir Charles Baskerville."

"I must thank you," said Sherlock Holmes, "for calling my attention to a case which certainly presents some features of interest. I had observed some newspaper comment at the time, but I was exceedingly preoccupied by that little affair of the Vatican cameos, and in my anxiety to oblige the Pope I lost touch with several interesting English cases. This article, you say, contains all the public facts?"

"It does."

"Then let me have the private ones." He leaned back, put his finger-tips together, and assumed his most impassive and judicial expression.

"In doing so," said Dr. Mortimer, who had begun to show signs of some strong emotion, "I am telling that which I have not confided to anyone. My motive for withholding it from the coroner's inquiry is that a man of science shrinks from placing himself in the public position of seeming to indorse a popular superstition. I had the further motive that Baskerville Hall, as the paper says, would certainly remain untenanted if anything were done to increase its already rather grim reputation. For both these reasons I thought that I was justified in telling rather less than I knew, since no practical good could result from it, but with you there is no reason why I should not be perfectly frank.

"The moor is very sparsely inhabited, and those who live near each other are thrown very much together. For this reason I saw a good deal of Sir Charles Baskerville. With the exception of Mr. Frankland, of Lafter Hall, and Mr. Stapleton, the naturalist, there are no other men of education within many miles. Sir Charles was a retiring man, but the chance of his illness brought us together, and a community of interests in science kept us so. He had brought back much scientific information from South Africa, and many a charming evening we have spent together discussing the comparative anatomy of the Bushman and the Hottentot.

"Within the last few months it became increasingly plain to me that Sir Charles's nervous system was strained to the breaking point. He had taken this legend which I have read you exceedingly to heart—so much so that, although he would walk in his own grounds, nothing would induce him to go out upon the moor at night. Incredible as it may appear to you, Mr. Holmes, he was honestly convinced that a dreadful fate overhung his family, and certainly the records which he was able to give of his ancestors were not encouraging. The idea of some ghastly presence constantly haunted him, and on more than one occasion he has asked me whether I had on my medical journeys at night ever seen any strange creature or heard the baying of a hound. The latter question he put to me several times, and always with a voice which vibrated with excitement.

"I can well remember driving up to his house in the evening some three weeks before the fatal event. He chanced to be at his hall door. I had descended from my gig and was standing in front of him, when I saw his eyes fix themselves over my shoulder and stare past me with an expression of the most dreadful horror. I whisked round and had just time to catch a glimpse of something which I took to be a large black calf passing at the head of the drive. So excited and alarmed was he that I was compelled to go down to the spot where the animal had been and look around for it. It was gone, however, and the incident appeared to make the worst impression upon his mind. I stayed with him all the evening, and it was on that occasion, to explain the emotion which he had shown, that he confided to my keeping that narrative which I read to you when first I came. I mention this small episode because it assumes some importance in view of the tragedy which followed, but I was convinced at the time that the matter was entirely trivial and that his excitement had no justification.

"It was at my advice that Sir Charles was about to go to London. His heart was, I knew, affected, and the constant anxiety in which he lived, however chimerical the cause of it might be, was evidently having a serious effect upon his health. I thought that a few months among the distractions of town would send him back a new man. Mr. Stapleton, a mutual friend who was much concerned at his state of health, was of the same opinion. At the last instant came this terrible catastrophe.

"On the night of Sir Charles's death Barrymore the butler, who made the discovery, sent Perkins the groom on horseback to me, and as I was sitting up late I was able to reach Baskerville Hall within an hour of the event. I checked and corroborated all the facts which were mentioned at the inquest. I followed the footsteps down the yew alley, I saw the spot at the moor-gate where he seemed to have waited, I remarked the change in the shape of the prints after that point, I noted that there were no other footsteps save those of Barrymore on the soft gravel, and finally I carefully examined the body, which had not been touched until my arrival. Sir Charles lay on his face, his arms out, his fingers dug into the ground, and his features convulsed with some strong emotion to such an extent that I could hardly have sworn to his identity. There was certainly no physical injury of any kind. But one false statement was made by Barrymore at the inquest. He said that there were no traces upon the ground round the body. He did not observe any. But I did—some little distance off, but fresh and clear."

"Footprints?"

"Footprints."

"A man's or a woman's?"

Dr. Mortimer looked strangely at us for an instant, and his voice sank almost to a whisper as he answered.

"Mr. Holmes, they were the footprints of a gigantic hound!"

Chapter 3.
The Problem

I confess at these words a shudder passed through me. There was a thrill in the doctor's voice which showed that he was himself deeply moved by that which he told us. Holmes leaned forward in his excitement and his eyes had the hard, dry glitter which shot from them when he was keenly interested.

"You saw this?"

"As clearly as I see you."

"And you said nothing?"

"What was the use?"

"How was it that no one else saw it?"

"The marks were some twenty yards from the body and no one gave them a thought. I don't suppose I should have done so had I not known this legend."

"There are many sheep-dogs on the moor?"

"No doubt, but this was no sheep-dog."

"You say it was large?"

"Enormous."

"But it had not approached the body?"

"No."

"What sort of night was it?'

"Damp and raw."

"But not actually raining?"

"No."

"What is the alley like?"

"There are two lines of old yew hedge, twelve feet high and impenetrable. The walk in the centre is about eight feet across."

"Is there anything between the hedges and the walk?"

"Yes, there is a strip of grass about six feet broad on either side."

"I understand that the yew hedge is penetrated at one point by a gate?"

"Yes, the wicket-gate which leads on to the moor."

"Is there any other opening?"

"None."

"So that to reach the yew alley one either has to come down it from the house or else to enter it by the moor-gate?"

"There is an exit through a summer-house at the far end."

"Had Sir Charles reached this?"

"No; he lay about fifty yards from it."

"Now, tell me, Dr. Mortimer—and this is important—the marks which you saw were on the path and not on the grass?"

"No marks could show on the grass."

"Were they on the same side of the path as the moor-gate?"

"Yes; they were on the edge of the path on the same side as the moor-gate."

"You interest me exceedingly. Another point. Was the wicket-gate closed?"

"Closed and padlocked."

"How high was it?"

"About four feet high."

"Then anyone could have got over it?"

"Yes."

"And what marks did you see by the wicket-gate?"

"None in particular."

"Good heaven! Did no one examine?"

"Yes, I examined, myself."

"And found nothing?"

"It was all very confused. Sir Charles had evidently stood there for five or ten minutes."

"How do you know that?"

"Because the ash had twice dropped from his cigar."

"Excellent! This is a colleague, Watson, after our own heart. But the marks?"

"He had left his own marks all over that small patch of gravel. I could discern no others."

Sherlock Holmes struck his hand against his knee with an impatient gesture.

"If I had only been there!" he cried. "It is evidently a case of extraordinary interest, and one which presented immense opportunities to the scientific expert. That gravel page upon which I might have read so much has been long ere this smudged by the rain and defaced by the clogs of curious peasants. Oh, Dr. Mortimer, Dr. Mortimer, to think that you should not have called me in! You have indeed much to answer for."

"I could not call you in, Mr. Holmes, without disclosing these facts to the world, and I have already given my reasons for not wishing to do so. Besides, besides—"

"Why do you hesitate?"

"There is a realm in which the most acute and most experienced of detectives is helpless."

"You mean that the thing is supernatural?"

"I did not positively say so."

"No, but you evidently think it."

"Since the tragedy, Mr. Holmes, there have come to my ears several incidents which are hard to reconcile with the settled order of Nature."

"For example?"

"I find that before the terrible event occurred several people had seen a creature upon the moor which corresponds with this Baskerville demon, and which could not possibly be any animal known to science. They all agreed that it was a huge creature, luminous, ghastly, and spectral. I have cross-examined these men, one of them a hard-headed countryman, one a farrier, and one a moorland farmer, who all tell the same story of this dreadful apparition, exactly corresponding to the hell-hound of the legend. I assure you that there is a reign of terror in the district, and that it is a hardy man who will cross the moor at night."

"And you, a trained man of science, believe it to be supernatural?"

"I do not know what to believe."

Holmes shrugged his shoulders. "I have hitherto confined my investigations to this world," said he. "In a modest way I have combated evil, but to take on the Father of Evil himself would, perhaps, be too ambitious a task. Yet you must admit that the footmark is material."

"The original hound was material enough to tug a man's throat out, and yet he was diabolical as well."

"I see that you have quite gone over to the supernaturalists. But now, Dr. Mortimer, tell me this. If you hold these views, why have you come to consult me at all? You tell me in the same breath that it is useless to investigate Sir Charles's death, and that you desire me to do it."

"I did not say that I desired you to do it."

"Then, how can I assist you?"

"By advising me as to what I should do with Sir Henry Baskerville, who arrives at Waterloo Station"—Dr. Mortimer looked at his watch—"in exactly one hour and a quarter."

"He being the heir?"

"Yes. On the death of Sir Charles we inquired for this young gentleman and found that he had been farming in Canada. From the accounts which have reached us he is an excellent fellow in every way. I speak now not as a medical man but as a trustee and executor of Sir Charles's will."

"There is no other claimant, I presume?"

"None. The only other kinsman whom we have been able to trace was Rodger Baskerville, the youngest of three brothers of whom poor Sir Charles was the elder. The second brother, who died young, is the father of this lad Henry. The third, Rodger, was the black sheep of the family. He came of the old masterful Baskerville strain and was the very image, they tell me, of the family picture of old Hugo. He made England too hot to hold him, fled to Central America, and died there in 1876 of yellow fever. Henry is the last of the Baskervilles. In one hour and five minutes I meet him at Waterloo Station. I have had a wire that he arrived at Southampton this morning. Now, Mr. Holmes, what would you advise me to do with him?"

"Why should he not go to the home of his fathers?"

"It seems natural, does it not? And yet, consider that every Baskerville who goes there meets with an evil fate. I feel sure that if Sir Charles could have spoken with me before his death he would have warned me against bringing this, the last of the old race, and the heir to great wealth, to that deadly place. And yet it cannot be denied that the prosperity of the whole poor, bleak countryside depends upon his presence. All the good work which has been done by Sir Charles will crash to the ground if there is no tenant of the Hall. I fear lest I should be swayed too much by my own obvious interest in the matter, and that is why I bring the case before you and ask for your advice."

Holmes considered for a little time.

"Put into plain words, the matter is this," said he. "In your opinion there is a diabolical agency which makes Dartmoor an unsafe abode for a Baskerville—that is your opinion?"

"At least I might go the length of saying that there is some evidence that this may be so."

"Exactly. But surely, if your supernatural theory be correct, it could work the young man evil in London as easily as in Devonshire. A devil with merely local powers like a parish vestry would be too inconceivable a thing."

"You put the matter more flippantly, Mr. Holmes, than you would probably do if you were brought into personal contact with these things. Your advice, then, as I understand it, is that the young man will be as safe in Devonshire as in London. He comes in fifty minutes. What would you recommend?"

"I recommend, sir, that you take a cab, call off your spaniel who is scratching at my front door, and proceed to Waterloo to meet Sir Henry Baskerville."

"And then?"

"And then you will say nothing to him at all until I have made up my mind about the matter."

"How long will it take you to make up your mind?"

"Twenty-four hours. At ten o'clock tomorrow, Dr. Mortimer, I will be much obliged to you if you will call upon me here, and it will be of help to me in my plans for the future if you will bring Sir Henry Baskerville with you."

"I will do so, Mr. Holmes." He scribbled the appointment on his shirt-cuff and hurried off in his strange, peering, absent-minded fashion. Holmes stopped him at the head of the stair.

"Only one more question, Dr. Mortimer. You say that before Sir Charles Baskerville's death several people saw this apparition upon the moor?"

"Three people did."

"Did any see it after?"

"I have not heard of any."

"Thank you. Good-morning."

Holmes returned to his seat with that quiet look of inward satisfaction which meant that he had a congenial task before him.

"Going out, Watson?"

"Unless I can help you."

"No, my dear fellow, it is at the hour of action that I turn to you for aid. But this is splendid, really unique from some points of view. When you pass Bradley's, would you ask him to send up a pound of the strongest shag tobacco? Thank you. It would be as well if you could make it convenient not to return before evening. Then I should be very glad to compare impressions as to this most interesting problem which has been submitted to us this morning."

I knew that seclusion and solitude were very necessary for my friend in those hours of intense mental concentration during which he weighed every particle of evidence, constructed alternative theories, balanced one against the other, and made up his mind as to which points were essential and which immaterial. I therefore spent the day at my club and did not return to Baker Street until evening. It was nearly nine o'clock when I found myself in the sitting-room once more.

My first impression as I opened the door was that a fire had broken out, for the room was so filled with smoke that the light of the lamp upon the table was blurred by it. As I entered, however, my fears were set at rest, for it was the acrid fumes of strong coarse tobacco which took me by the throat and set me coughing. Through the haze I had a vague vision of Holmes in his dressing-gown coiled up in an armchair with his black clay pipe between his lips. Several rolls of paper lay around him.

"Caught cold, Watson?" said he.

"No, it's this poisonous atmosphere."

"I suppose it is pretty thick, now that you mention it."

"Thick! It is intolerable."

"Open the window, then! You have been at your club all day, I perceive."

"My dear Holmes!"

"Am I right?"

"Certainly, but how?"

He laughed at my bewildered expression. "There is a delightful freshness about you, Watson, which makes it a pleasure to exercise any small powers which I possess at your expense. A gentleman goes forth on a showery and miry day.

He returns immaculate in the evening with the gloss still on his hat and his boots. He has been a fixture therefore all day. He is not a man with intimate friends. Where, then, could he have been? Is it not obvious?"

"Well, it is rather obvious."

"The world is full of obvious things which nobody by any chance ever observes. Where do you think that I have been?"

"A fixture also."

"On the contrary, I have been to Devonshire."

"In spirit?"

"Exactly. My body has remained in this armchair and has, I regret to observe, consumed in my absence two large pots of coffee and an incredible amount of tobacco. After you left I sent down to Stamford's for the Ordnance map of this portion of the moor, and my spirit has hovered over it all day. I flatter myself that I could find my way about."

"A large-scale map, I presume?"

"Very large."

He unrolled one section and held it over his knee. "Here you have the particular district which concerns us. That is Baskerville Hall in the middle."

"With a wood round it?"

"Exactly. I fancy the yew alley, though not marked under that name, must stretch along this line, with the moor, as you perceive, upon the right of it. This small clump of buildings here is the hamlet of Grimpen, where our friend Dr. Mortimer has his headquarters. Within a radius of five miles there are, as you see, only a very few scattered dwellings. Here is Lafter Hall, which was mentioned in the narrative. There is a house indicated here which may be the residence of the naturalist—Stapleton, if I remember right, was his name. Here are two moorland farmhouses, High Tor and Foulmire. Then fourteen miles away the great convict prison of Princetown. Between and around these scattered points extends the desolate, lifeless moor. This, then, is the stage upon which tragedy has been played, and upon which we may help to play it again."

"It must be a wild place."

"Yes, the setting is a worthy one. If the devil did desire to have a hand in the affairs of men—"

"Then you are yourself inclining to the supernatural explanation."

"The devil's agents may be of flesh and blood, may they not? There are two questions waiting for us at the outset. The one is whether any crime has been committed at all; the second is, what is the crime and how was it committed? Of course, if Dr. Mortimer's surmise should be correct, and we are dealing with forces outside the ordinary laws of Nature, there is an end of our investigation. But we are bound to exhaust all other hypotheses before falling back upon this one. I think we'll shut that window again, if you don't mind. It is a singular thing, but I find that a concentrated atmosphere helps a concentration of thought. I have not pushed it to the length of getting into a box to think, but that is the logical outcome of my convictions. Have you turned the case over in your mind?"

"Yes, I have thought a good deal of it in the course of the day."

"What do you make of it?"

"It is very bewildering."

"It has certainly a character of its own. There are points of distinction about it. That change in the footprints, for example. What do you make of that?"

"Mortimer said that the man had walked on tiptoe down that portion of the alley."

"He only repeated what some fool had said at the inquest. Why should a man walk on tiptoe down the alley?"

"What then?"

"He was running, Watson—running desperately, running for his life, running until he burst his heart—and fell dead upon his face."

"Running from what?"

"There lies our problem. There are indications that the man

was crazed with fear before ever he began to run."

"How can you say that?"

"I am presuming that the cause of his fears came to him across the moor. If that were so, and it seems most probable, only a man who had lost his wits would have run from the house instead of towards it. If the gipsy's evidence may be taken as true, he ran with cries for help in the direction where help was least likely to be. Then, again, whom was he waiting for that night, and why was he waiting for him in the yew alley rather than in his own house?"

"You think that he was waiting for someone?"

"The man was elderly and infirm. We can understand his taking an evening stroll, but the ground was damp and the night inclement. Is it natural that he should stand for five or ten minutes, as Dr. Mortimer, with more practical sense than I should have given him credit for, deduced from the cigar ash?"

"But he went out every evening."

"I think it unlikely that he waited at the moor-gate every evening. On the contrary, the evidence is that he avoided the moor. That night he waited there. It was the night before he made his departure for London. The thing takes shape, Watson. It becomes coherent. Might I ask you to hand me my violin, and we will postpone all further thought upon this business until we have had the advantage of meeting Dr. Mortimer and Sir Henry Baskerville in the morning."

Chapter 4.

Sir Henry Baskerville

Our breakfast table was cleared early, and Holmes waited in his dressing-gown for the promised interview. Our clients were punctual to their appointment, for the clock had just struck ten when Dr. Mortimer was shown up, followed by the young baronet. The latter was a small, alert, dark-eyed man about thirty years of age, very sturdily built, with thick black eyebrows and a strong, pugnacious face. He wore a ruddy-tinted tweed suit and had the weather-beaten appearance of one who has spent most of his time in the open air, and yet there was something in his steady eye and the quiet assurance of his bearing which indicated the gentleman.

"This is Sir Henry Baskerville," said Dr. Mortimer.

"Why, yes," said he, "and the strange thing is, Mr. Sherlock Holmes, that if my friend here had not proposed coming round to you this morning I should have come on my own account. I understand that you think out little puzzles, and I've had one this morning which wants more thinking out than I am able to give it."

"Pray take a seat, Sir Henry. Do I understand you to say that you have yourself had some remarkable experience since you arrived in London?"

"Nothing of much importance, Mr. Holmes. Only a joke, as like as not. It was this letter, if you can call it a letter, which reached me this morning."

He laid an envelope upon the table, and we all bent over it. It was of common quality, greyish in colour. The address, "Sir Henry Baskerville, Northumberland Hotel," was printed in rough characters; the post-mark "Charing Cross," and the date of posting the preceding evening.

"Who knew that you were going to the Northumberland Hotel?" asked Holmes, glancing keenly across at our visitor.

"No one could have known. We only decided after I met Dr. Mortimer."

"But Dr. Mortimer was no doubt already stopping there?"

"No, I had been staying with a friend," said the doctor.

"There was no possible indication that we intended to go to this hotel."

"Hum! Someone seems to be very deeply interested in your movements." Out of the envelope he took a half-sheet of foolscap paper folded into four. This he opened and spread flat upon the table. Across the middle of it a single sentence had been formed by the expedient of pasting printed words upon it. It ran:

As you value your life or your reason keep away from the moor.

The word "moor" only was printed in ink.

"Now," said Sir Henry Baskerville, "perhaps you will tell me, Mr. Holmes, what in thunder is the meaning of that, and who it is that takes so much interest in my affairs?"

"What do you make of it, Dr. Mortimer? You must allow that there is nothing supernatural about this, at any rate?"

"No, sir, but it might very well come from someone who was convinced that the business is supernatural."

"What business?" asked Sir Henry sharply. "It seems to me that all you gentlemen know a great deal more than I do about my own affairs."

"You shall share our knowledge before you leave this room, Sir Henry. I promise you that," said Sherlock Holmes. "We will confine ourselves for the present with your permission to this very interesting document, which must have been put together and posted yesterday evening. Have you yesterday's Times, Watson?"

"It is here in the corner."

"Might I trouble you for it—the inside page, please, with the leading articles?" He glanced swiftly over it, running his eyes up and down the columns. "Capital article this on free trade. Permit me to give you an extract from it.

'You may be cajoled into imagining that your own special trade or your own industry will be encouraged by a protective tariff, but it stands to reason that such legislation must in the long run keep away wealth from the country, diminish the value of our imports, and lower the general conditions of life in this island.'

"What do you think of that, Watson?" cried Holmes in high glee, rubbing his hands together with satisfaction. "Don't you think that is an admirable sentiment?"

Dr. Mortimer looked at Holmes with an air of professional interest, and Sir Henry Baskerville turned a pair of puzzled dark eyes upon me.

"I don't know much about the tariff and things of that kind," said he, "but it seems to me we've got a bit off the trail so far as that note is concerned."

"On the contrary, I think we are particularly hot upon the trail, Sir Henry. Watson here knows more about my methods than you do, but I fear that even he has not quite grasped the significance of this sentence."

"No, I confess that I see no connection."

"And yet, my dear Watson, there is so very close a connection that the one is extracted out of the other. 'You,' 'your,' 'your,' 'life,' 'reason,' 'value,' 'keep away,' 'from the.' Don't you see now whence these words have been taken?"

"By thunder, you're right! Well, if that isn't smart!" cried Sir Henry.

"If any possible doubt remained it is settled by the fact that 'keep away' and 'from the' are cut out in one piece."

"Well, now—so it is!"

"Really, Mr. Holmes, this exceeds anything which I could have imagined," said Dr. Mortimer, gazing at my friend in amazement. "I could understand anyone saying that the words were from a newspaper; but that you should name which, and add that it came from the leading article, is really one of the most remarkable things which I have ever known. How did you do it?"

"I presume, Doctor, that you could tell the skull of a negro from that of an Esquimau?"

"Most certainly."

"But how?"

"Because that is my special hobby. The differences are obvious. The supra-orbital crest, the facial angle, the maxillary curve, the—"

"But this is my special hobby, and the differences are equally obvious. There is as much difference to my eyes between the leaded bourgeois type of a Times article and the slovenly print of an evening half-penny paper as there could be between your negro and your Esquimau. The detection of types is one of the most elementary branches of knowledge to the special expert in crime, though I confess that once when I was very young I confused the Leeds Mercury with the Western Morning News. But a Times leader is entirely distinctive, and these words could have been taken from nothing else. As it was done yesterday the strong probability was that we should find the words in yesterday's issue."

"So far as I can follow you, then, Mr. Holmes," said Sir Henry Baskerville, "someone cut out this message with a scissors—"

"Nail-scissors," said Holmes. "You can see that it was a very short-bladed scissors, since the cutter had to take two snips over 'keep away.'"

"That is so. Someone, then, cut out the message with a pair of short-bladed scissors, pasted it with paste—"

"Gum," said Holmes.

"With gum on to the paper. But I want to know why the word 'moor' should have been written?"

"Because he could not find it in print. The other words were all simple and might be found in any issue, but 'moor' would be less common."

"Why, of course, that would explain it. Have you read anything else in this message, Mr. Holmes?"

"There are one or two indications, and yet the utmost pains have been taken to remove all clues. The address, you observe is printed in rough characters. But the Times is a paper which is seldom found in any hands but those of the highly educated. We may take it, therefore, that the letter was composed by an educated man who wished to pose as an uneducated one, and his effort to conceal his own writing suggests that that writing might be known, or come to be known, by you. Again, you will observe that the words are not gummed on in an accurate line, but that some are much higher than others. 'Life,' for example is quite out of its proper place. That may point to carelessness or it may point to agitation and hurry upon the part of the cutter. On the whole I incline to the latter view, since the matter was evidently important, and it is unlikely that the composer of such a letter would be careless. If he were in a hurry it opens up the interesting question why he should be in a hurry, since any letter posted up to early morning would reach Sir Henry before he would leave his hotel. Did the composer fear an interruption—and from whom?"

"We are coming now rather into the region of guesswork," said Dr. Mortimer.

"Say, rather, into the region where we balance probabilities and choose the most likely. It is the scientific use of the imagination, but we have always some material basis on which to start our speculation. Now, you would call it a guess, no doubt, but I am almost certain that this address has been written in a hotel."

"How in the world can you say that?"

"If you examine it carefully you will see that both the pen and the ink have given the writer trouble. The pen has spluttered twice in a single word and has run dry three times in a short address, showing that there was very little ink in the bottle. Now, a private pen or ink-bottle is seldom allowed to be in such a state, and the combination of the two must be quite rare. But you know the hotel ink and the hotel pen, where it is rare to get anything else. Yes, I have very little hesitation in saying that could we examine the waste-paper baskets of the hotels around Charing Cross until we found the remains of the mutilated Times leader we could lay our hands straight upon the person who sent this singular message. Halloa! Halloa! What's this?"

He was carefully examining the foolscap, upon which the words were pasted, holding it only an inch or two from his eyes.

"Well?"

"Nothing," said he, throwing it down. "It is a blank half-sheet of paper, without even a water-mark upon it. I think we have drawn as much as we can from this curious letter; and now, Sir Henry, has anything else of interest happened to you since you have been in London?"

"Why, no, Mr. Holmes. I think not."

"You have not observed anyone follow or watch you?"

"I seem to have walked right into the thick of a dime novel," said our visitor. "Why in thunder should anyone follow or watch me?"

"We are coming to that. You have nothing else to report to us before we go into this matter?"

"Well, it depends upon what you think worth reporting."

"I think anything out of the ordinary routine of life well worth reporting."

Sir Henry smiled. "I don't know much of British life yet, for I have spent nearly all my time in the States and in Canada. But I hope that to lose one of your boots is not part of the ordinary routine of life over here."

"You have lost one of your boots?"

"My dear sir," cried Dr. Mortimer, "it is only mislaid. You will find it when you return to the hotel. What is the use of troubling Mr. Holmes with trifles of this kind?"

"Well, he asked me for anything outside the ordinary routine."

"Exactly," said Holmes, "however foolish the incident may seem. You have lost one of your boots, you say?"

"Well, mislaid it, anyhow. I put them both outside my door last night, and there was only one in the morning. I could get no sense out of the chap who cleans them. The worst of it is that I only bought the pair last night in the Strand, and I have never had them on."

"If you have never worn them, why did you put them out to be cleaned?"

"They were tan boots and had never been varnished. That was why I put them out."

"Then I understand that on your arrival in London

yesterday you went out at once and bought a pair of boots?"

"I did a good deal of shopping. Dr. Mortimer here went round with me. You see, if I am to be squire down there I must dress the part, and it may be that I have got a little careless in my ways out West. Among other things I bought these brown boots—gave six dollars for them—and had one stolen before ever I had them on my feet."

"It seems a singularly useless thing to steal," said Sherlock Holmes. "I confess that I share Dr. Mortimer's belief that it will not be long before the missing boot is found."

"And, now, gentlemen," said the baronet with decision, "it seems to me that I have spoken quite enough about the little that I know. It is time that you kept your promise and gave me a full account of what we are all driving at."

"Your request is a very reasonable one," Holmes answered. "Dr. Mortimer, I think you could not do better than to tell your story as you told it to us."

Thus encouraged, our scientific friend drew his papers from his pocket and presented the whole case as he had done upon the morning before. Sir Henry Baskerville listened with the deepest attention and with an occasional exclamation of surprise.

"Well, I seem to have come into an inheritance with a vengeance," said he when the long narrative was finished. "Of course, I've heard of the hound ever since I was in the nursery. It's the pet story of the family, though I never thought of taking it seriously before. But as to my uncle's death—well, it all seems boiling up in my head, and I can't get it clear yet. You don't seem quite to have made up your mind whether it's a case for a policeman or a clergyman."

"Precisely."

"And now there's this affair of the letter to me at the hotel. I suppose that fits into its place."

"It seems to show that someone knows more than we do about what goes on upon the moor," said Dr. Mortimer.

"And also," said Holmes, "that someone is not ill-disposed towards you, since they warn you of danger."

"Or it may be that they wish, for their own purposes, to scare me away."

"Well, of course, that is possible also. I am very much indebted to you, Dr. Mortimer, for introducing me to a problem which presents several interesting alternatives. But the practical point which we now have to decide, Sir Henry, is whether it is or is not advisable for you to go to Baskerville Hall."

"Why should I not go?"

"There seems to be danger."

"Do you mean danger from this family fiend or do you mean danger from human beings?"

"Well, that is what we have to find out."

"Whichever it is, my answer is fixed. There is no devil in hell, Mr. Holmes, and there is no man upon earth who can prevent me from going to the home of my own people, and you may take that to be my final answer." His dark brows knitted and his face flushed to a dusky red as he spoke. It was evident that the fiery temper of the Baskervilles was not extinct in this their last representative. "Meanwhile," said he, "I have hardly had time to think over all that you have told me. It's a big thing for a man to have to understand and to decide at one sitting. I should like to have a quiet hour by myself to make up my mind. Now, look here, Mr. Holmes, it's half-past eleven now and I am going back right away to my hotel. Suppose you and your friend, Dr. Watson, come round and lunch with us at two. I'll be able to tell you more clearly then how this thing strikes me."

"Is that convenient to you, Watson?"

"Perfectly."

"Then you may expect us. Shall I have a cab called?"

"I'd prefer to walk, for this affair has flurried me rather."

"I'll join you in a walk, with pleasure," said his companion.

"Then we meet again at two o'clock. Au revoir, and good-morning!"

We heard the steps of our visitors descend the stair and the bang of the front door. In an instant Holmes had changed from the languid dreamer to the man of action.

"Your hat and boots, Watson, quick! Not a moment to lose!" He rushed into his room in his dressing-gown and was back again in a few seconds in a frock-coat. We hurried together down the stairs and into the street. Dr. Mortimer and Baskerville were still visible about two hundred yards ahead of us in the direction of Oxford Street.

"Shall I run on and stop them?"

"Not for the world, my dear Watson. I am perfectly satisfied with your company if you will tolerate mine. Our friends are wise, for it is certainly a very fine morning for a walk."

He quickened his pace until we had decreased the distance which divided us by about half. Then, still keeping a hundred yards behind, we followed into Oxford Street and so down Regent Street. Once our friends stopped and stared into a shop window, upon which Holmes did the same. An instant afterwards he gave a little cry of satisfaction, and, following the direction of his eager eyes, I saw that a hansom cab with a man inside which had halted on the other side of the street was now proceeding slowly onward again.

"There's our man, Watson! Come along! We'll have a good look at him, if we can do no more."

At that instant I was aware of a bushy black beard and a pair of piercing eyes turned upon us through the side window of the cab. Instantly the trapdoor at the top flew up, something was screamed to the driver, and the cab flew madly off down Regent Street. Holmes looked eagerly round for another, but no empty one was in sight. Then he dashed in wild pursuit amid the stream of the traffic, but the start was too great, and already the cab was out of sight.

"There now!" said Holmes bitterly as he emerged panting and white with vexation from the tide of vehicles. "Was ever such bad luck and such bad management, too? Watson, Watson, if you are an honest man you will record this also and set it against my successes!"

"Who was the man?"

"I have not an idea."

"A spy?"

"Well, it was evident from what we have heard that Baskerville has been very closely shadowed by someone since he has been in town. How else could it be known so quickly that it was the Northumberland Hotel which he had chosen? If they had followed him the first day I argued that they would follow him also the second. You may have observed that I twice strolled over to the window while Dr. Mortimer was reading his legend."

"Yes, I remember."

"I was looking out for loiterers in the street, but I saw none. We are dealing with a clever man, Watson. This matter cuts very deep, and though I have not finally made up my mind whether it is a benevolent or a malevolent agency which is in touch with us, I am conscious always of power and design. When our friends left I at once followed them in the hopes of marking down their invisible attendant. So wily was he that he had not trusted himself upon foot, but he had availed himself of a cab so that he could loiter behind or dash past them and so escape their notice. His method had the additional advantage that if they were to take a cab he was all ready to follow them. It has, however, one obvious disadvantage."

"It puts him in the power of the cabman."

"Exactly."

"What a pity we did not get the number!"

"My dear Watson, clumsy as I have been, you surely do not seriously imagine that I neglected to get the number? No. 2704 is our man. But that is no use to us for the moment."

"I fail to see how you could have done more."

"On observing the cab I should have instantly turned and walked in the other direction. I should then at my leisure have hired a second cab and followed the first at a respectful distance, or, better still, have driven to the Northumberland Hotel and waited there. When our unknown had followed Baskerville home we should have had the opportunity of playing his own game upon himself and seeing where he made for. As it is, by an indiscreet eagerness, which was taken advantage of with extraordinary quickness and energy by our opponent, we have betrayed ourselves and lost our man."

We had been sauntering slowly down Regent Street during

this conversation, and Dr. Mortimer, with his companion, had long vanished in front of us.

"There is no object in our following them," said Holmes. "The shadow has departed and will not return. We must see what further cards we have in our hands and play them with decision. Could you swear to that man's face within the cab?"

"I could swear only to the beard."

"And so could I—from which I gather that in all probability it was a false one. A clever man upon so delicate an errand has no use for a beard save to conceal his features. Come in here, Watson!"

He turned into one of the district messenger offices, where he was warmly greeted by the manager.

"Ah, Wilson, I see you have not forgotten the little case in which I had the good fortune to help you?"

"No, sir, indeed I have not. You saved my good name, and perhaps my life."

"My dear fellow, you exaggerate. I have some recollection, Wilson, that you had among your boys a lad named Cartwright, who showed some ability during the investigation."

"Yes, sir, he is still with us."

"Could you ring him up?—thank you! And I should be glad to have change of this five-pound note."

A lad of fourteen, with a bright, keen face, had obeyed the summons of the manager. He stood now gazing with great reverence at the famous detective.

"Let me have the Hotel Directory," said Holmes. "Thank you! Now, Cartwright, there are the names of twenty-three hotels here, all in the immediate neighbourhood of Charing Cross. Do you see?"

"Yes, sir."

"You will visit each of these in turn."

"Yes, sir."

"You will begin in each case by giving the outside porter one shilling. Here are twenty-three shillings."

"Yes, sir."

"You will tell him that you want to see the waste-paper of yesterday. You will say that an important telegram has miscarried and that you are looking for it. You understand?"

"Yes, sir."

"But what you are really looking for is the centre page of the Times with some holes cut in it with scissors. Here is a copy of the Times. It is this page. You could easily recognize it, could you not?"

"Yes, sir."

"In each case the outside porter will send for the hall porter, to whom also you will give a shilling. Here are twenty-three shillings. You will then learn in possibly twenty cases out of the twenty-three that the waste of the day before has been burned or removed. In the three other cases you will be shown a heap of paper and you will look for this page of the Times among it. The odds are enormously against your finding it. There are ten shillings over in case of emergencies. Let me have a report by wire at Baker Street before evening. And now, Watson, it only remains for us to find out by wire the identity of the cabman, No. 2704, and then we will drop into one of the Bond Street picture galleries and fill in the time until we are due at the hotel."

Chapter 5.

Three Broken Threads

Sherlock Holmes had, in a very remarkable degree, the power of detaching his mind at will. For two hours the strange business in which we had been involved appeared to be forgotten, and he was entirely absorbed in the pictures of the modern Belgian masters. He would talk of nothing but art, of which he had the crudest ideas, from our leaving the gallery until we found ourselves at the Northumberland Hotel.

"Sir Henry Baskerville is upstairs expecting you," said the clerk. "He asked me to show you up at once when you came."

"Have you any objection to my looking at your register?" said Holmes.

"Not in the least."

The book showed that two names had been added after that of Baskerville. One was Theophilus Johnson and family, of Newcastle; the other Mrs. Oldmore and maid, of High Lodge, Alton.

"Surely that must be the same Johnson whom I used to know," said Holmes to the porter. "A lawyer, is he not, grey-headed, and walks with a limp?"

"No, sir, this is Mr. Johnson, the coal-owner, a very active gentleman, not older than yourself."

"Surely you are mistaken about his trade?"

"No, sir! he has used this hotel for many years, and he is very well known to us."

"Ah, that settles it. Mrs. Oldmore, too; I seem to remember the name. Excuse my curiosity, but often in calling upon one friend one finds another."

"She is an invalid lady, sir. Her husband was once mayor of Gloucester. She always comes to us when she is in town."

"Thank you; I am afraid I cannot claim her acquaintance. We have established a most important fact by these questions, Watson," he continued in a low voice as we went upstairs together. "We know now that the people who are so interested in our friend have not settled down in his own hotel. That means that while they are, as we have seen, very anxious to watch him, they are equally anxious that he should not see them. Now, this is a most suggestive fact."

"What does it suggest?"

"It suggests—halloa, my dear fellow, what on earth is the matter?"

As we came round the top of the stairs we had run up against Sir Henry Baskerville himself. His face was flushed with anger, and he held an old and dusty boot in one of his hands. So furious was he that he was hardly articulate, and when he did speak it was in a much broader and more Western dialect than any which we had heard from him in the morning.

"Seems to me they are playing me for a sucker in this hotel," he cried. "They'll find they've started in to monkey with the wrong man unless they are careful. By thunder, if that chap can't find my missing boot there will be trouble. I can take a joke with the best, Mr. Holmes, but they've got a bit over the mark this time."

"Still looking for your boot?"

"Yes, sir, and mean to find it."

"But, surely, you said that it was a new brown boot?"

"So it was, sir. And now it's an old black one."

"What! you don't mean to say—?"

"That's just what I do mean to say. I only had three pairs in the world—the new brown, the old black, and the patent leathers, which I am wearing. Last night they took one of my brown ones, and today they have sneaked one of the black. Well, have you got it? Speak out, man, and don't stand staring!"

An agitated German waiter had appeared upon the scene.

"No, sir; I have made inquiry all over the hotel, but I can hear no word of it."

"Well, either that boot comes back before sundown or I'll see the manager and tell him that I go right straight out of this hotel."

"It shall be found, sir—I promise you that if you will have a little patience it will be found."

"Mind it is, for it's the last thing of mine that I'll lose in this den of thieves. Well, well, Mr. Holmes, you'll excuse my troubling you about such a trifle—"

"I think it's well worth troubling about."

"Why, you look very serious over it."

"How do you explain it?"

"I just don't attempt to explain it. It seems the very maddest, queerest thing that ever happened to me."

"The queerest perhaps—" said Holmes thoughtfully.

"What do you make of it yourself?"

"Well, I don't profess to understand it yet. This case of yours is very complex, Sir Henry. When taken in conjunction with your uncle's death I am not sure that of all the five hundred cases of capital importance which I have handled there is one which cuts so deep. But we hold several threads in our hands, and the odds are that one or other of them guides us to the truth. We may waste time in following the wrong one, but sooner or later we must come upon the right."

We had a pleasant luncheon in which little was said of the business which had brought us together. It was in the private sitting-room to which we afterwards repaired that Holmes asked Baskerville what were his intentions.

"To go to Baskerville Hall."

"And when?"

"At the end of the week."

"On the whole," said Holmes, "I think that your decision is a wise one. I have ample evidence that you are being dogged in London, and amid the millions of this great city it is difficult to discover who these people are or what their object can be. If their intentions are evil they might do you a mischief, and we should be powerless to prevent it. You did not know, Dr. Mortimer, that you were followed this morning from my house?"

Dr. Mortimer started violently. "Followed! By whom?"

"That, unfortunately, is what I cannot tell you. Have you among your neighbours or acquaintances on Dartmoor any man with a black, full beard?"

"No—or, let me see—why, yes. Barrymore, Sir Charles's butler, is a man with a full, black beard."

"Ha! Where is Barrymore?"

"He is in charge of the Hall."

"We had best ascertain if he is really there, or if by any possibility he might be in London."

"How can you do that?"

"Give me a telegraph form. 'Is all ready for Sir Henry?' That will do. Address to Mr. Barrymore, Baskerville Hall. What is the nearest telegraph-office? Grimpen. Very good, we will send a second wire to the postmaster, Grimpen: 'Telegram to Mr. Barrymore to be delivered into his own hand. If absent, please return wire to Sir Henry Baskerville, Northumberland Hotel.' That should let us know before evening whether Barrymore is at his post in Devonshire or not."

"That's so," said Baskerville. "By the way, Dr. Mortimer, who is this Barrymore, anyhow?"

"He is the son of the old caretaker, who is dead. They have looked after the Hall for four generations now. So far as I know, he and his wife are as respectable a couple as any in the county."

"At the same time," said Baskerville, "it's clear enough that so long as there are none of the family at the Hall these people have a mighty fine home and nothing to do."

"That is true."

"Did Barrymore profit at all by Sir Charles's will?" asked Holmes.

"He and his wife had five hundred pounds each."

"Ha! Did they know that they would receive this?"

"Yes; Sir Charles was very fond of talking about the provisions of his will."

"That is very interesting."

"I hope," said Dr. Mortimer, "that you do not look with suspicious eyes upon everyone who received a legacy from Sir Charles, for I also had a thousand pounds left to me."

"Indeed! And anyone else?"

"There were many insignificant sums to individuals, and a large number of public charities. The residue all went to Sir Henry."

"And how much was the residue?"

"Seven hundred and forty thousand pounds."

Holmes raised his eyebrows in surprise. "I had no idea that so gigantic a sum was involved," said he.

"Sir Charles had the reputation of being rich, but we did not know how very rich he was until we came to examine his securities. The total value of the estate was close on to a million."

"Dear me! It is a stake for which a man might well play a desperate game. And one more question, Dr. Mortimer. Supposing that anything happened to our young friend here—you will forgive the unpleasant hypothesis!—who would inherit the estate?"

"Since Rodger Baskerville, Sir Charles's younger brother died unmarried, the estate would descend to the Desmonds, who are distant cousins. James Desmond is an elderly clergyman in Westmoreland."

"Thank you. These details are all of great interest. Have you met Mr. James Desmond?"

"Yes; he once came down to visit Sir Charles. He is a man of venerable appearance and of saintly life. I remember that he refused to accept any settlement from Sir Charles, though he pressed it upon him."

"And this man of simple tastes would be the heir to Sir Charles's thousands."

"He would be the heir to the estate because that is entailed. He would also be the heir to the money unless it were willed otherwise by the present owner, who can, of course, do what he likes with it."

"And have you made your will, Sir Henry?"

"No, Mr. Holmes, I have not. I've had no time, for it was only yesterday that I learned how matters stood. But in any case I feel that the money should go with the title and estate. That was my poor uncle's idea. How is the owner going to restore the glories of the Baskervilles if he has not money enough to keep up the property? House, land, and dollars must go together."

"Quite so. Well, Sir Henry, I am of one mind with you as to the advisability of your going down to Devonshire without delay. There is only one provision which I must make. You certainly must not go alone."

"Dr. Mortimer returns with me."

"But Dr. Mortimer has his practice to attend to, and his house is miles away from yours. With all the goodwill in the world he may be unable to help you. No, Sir Henry, you must take with you someone, a trusty man, who will be always by your side."

"Is it possible that you could come yourself, Mr. Holmes?"

"If matters came to a crisis I should endeavour to be present in person; but you can understand that, with my extensive consulting practice and with the constant appeals which reach me from many quarters, it is impossible for me to be absent from London for an indefinite time. At the present instant one of the most revered names in England is being besmirched by a blackmailer, and only I can stop a disastrous scandal. You will see how impossible it is for me to go to Dartmoor."

"Whom would you recommend, then?"

Holmes laid his hand upon my arm. "If my friend would undertake it there is no man who is better worth having at your side when you are in a tight place. No one can say so more confidently than I."

The proposition took me completely by surprise, but before I had time to answer, Baskerville seized me by the hand and wrung it heartily.

"Well, now, that is real kind of you, Dr. Watson," said he. "You see how it is with me, and you know just as much about the matter as I do. If you will come down to Baskerville Hall and see me through I'll never forget it."

The promise of adventure had always a fascination for me, and I was complimented by the words of Holmes and by the eagerness with which the baronet hailed me as a companion.

"I will come, with pleasure," said I. "I do not know how I could employ my time better."

"And you will report very carefully to me," said Holmes. "When a crisis comes, as it will do, I will direct how you shall act. I suppose that by Saturday all might be ready?"

"Would that suit Dr. Watson?"

"Perfectly."

"Then on Saturday, unless you hear to the contrary, we shall meet at the ten-thirty train from Paddington."

We had risen to depart when Baskerville gave a cry of triumph, and diving into one of the corners of the room he drew a brown boot from under a cabinet.

"My missing boot!" he cried.

"May all our difficulties vanish as easily!" said Sherlock Holmes.

"But it is a very singular thing," Dr. Mortimer remarked. "I searched this room carefully before lunch."

"And so did I," said Baskerville. "Every inch of it."

"There was certainly no boot in it then."

"In that case the waiter must have placed it there while we were lunching."

The German was sent for but professed to know nothing of the matter, nor could any inquiry clear it up. Another item had been added to that constant and apparently purposeless series of small mysteries which had succeeded each other so rapidly.

Setting aside the whole grim story of Sir Charles's death, we had a line of inexplicable incidents all within the limits of two days, which included the receipt of the printed letter, the black-bearded spy in the hansom, the loss of the new brown boot, the loss of the old black boot, and now the return of the new brown boot. Holmes sat in silence in the cab as we drove back to Baker Street, and I knew from his drawn brows and keen face that his mind, like my own, was busy in endeavouring to frame some scheme into which all these strange and apparently disconnected episodes could be fitted. All afternoon and late into the evening he sat lost in tobacco and thought.

Just before dinner two telegrams were handed in. The first ran:

Have just heard that Barrymore is at the Hall. BASKERVILLE.

The second:

Visited twenty-three hotels as directed, but sorry to report unable to trace cut sheet of Times. CARTWRIGHT.

"There go two of my threads, Watson. There is nothing more stimulating than a case where everything goes against you. We must cast round for another scent."

"We have still the cabman who drove the spy."

"Exactly. I have wired to get his name and address from the Official Registry. I should not be surprised if this were an answer to my question."

The ring at the bell proved to be something even more satisfactory than an answer, however, for the door opened and a rough-looking fellow entered who was evidently the man himself.

"I got a message from the head office that a gent at this address had been inquiring for No. 2704," said he. "I've driven my cab this seven years and never a word of complaint. I came here straight from the Yard to ask you to your face what you had against me."

"I have nothing in the world against you, my good man," said Holmes. "On the contrary, I have half a sovereign for you if you will give me a clear answer to my questions."

"Well, I've had a good day and no mistake," said the cabman with a grin. "What was it you wanted to ask, sir?"

"First of all your name and address, in case I want you again."

"John Clayton, 3 Turpey Street, the Borough. My cab is out of Shipley's Yard, near Waterloo Station."

Sherlock Holmes made a note of it.

"Now, Clayton, tell me all about the fare who came and watched this house at ten o'clock this morning and afterwards followed the two gentlemen down Regent Street."

The man looked surprised and a little embarrassed. "Why, there's no good my telling you things, for you seem to know as much as I do already," said he. "The truth is that the gentleman told me that he was a detective and that I was to say nothing about him to anyone."

"My good fellow; this is a very serious business, and you may find yourself in a pretty bad position if you try to hide anything from me. You say that your fare told you that he was a detective?"

"Yes, he did."

"When did he say this?"

"When he left me."

"Did he say anything more?"

"He mentioned his name."

Holmes cast a swift glance of triumph at me. "Oh, he mentioned his name, did he? That was imprudent. What was the name that he mentioned?"

"His name," said the cabman, "was Mr. Sherlock Holmes."

Never have I seen my friend more completely taken aback than by the cabman's reply. For an instant he sat in silent amazement. Then he burst into a hearty laugh.

"A touch, Watson—an undeniable touch!" said he. "I feel a foil as quick and supple as my own. He got home upon me very prettily that time. So his name was Sherlock Holmes, was it?"

"Yes, sir, that was the gentleman's name."

"Excellent! Tell me where you picked him up and all that occurred."

"He hailed me at half-past nine in Trafalgar Square. He said that he was a detective, and he offered me two guineas if I would do exactly what he wanted all day and ask no questions. I was glad enough to agree. First we drove down to the Northumberland Hotel and waited there until two gentlemen came out and took a cab from the rank. We followed their cab until it pulled up somewhere near here."

"This very door," said Holmes.

"Well, I couldn't be sure of that, but I dare say my fare knew all about it. We pulled up halfway down the street and waited an hour and a half. Then the two gentlemen passed us, walking, and we followed down Baker Street and along—"

"I know," said Holmes.

"Until we got three-quarters down Regent Street. Then my gentleman threw up the trap, and he cried that I should drive right away to Waterloo Station as hard as I could go. I whipped up the mare and we were there under the ten minutes. Then he paid up his two guineas, like a good one, and away he went into the station. Only just as he was leaving he turned round and he said: 'It might interest you to know that you have been driving Mr. Sherlock Holmes.' That's how I come to know the name."

"I see. And you saw no more of him?"

"Not after he went into the station."

"And how would you describe Mr. Sherlock Holmes?"

The cabman scratched his head. "Well, he wasn't altogether such an easy gentleman to describe. I'd put him at forty years of age, and he was of a middle height, two or three inches shorter than you, sir. He was dressed like a toff, and he had a black beard, cut square at the end, and a pale face. I don't know as I could say more than that."

"Colour of his eyes?"

"No, I can't say that."

"Nothing more that you can remember?"

"No, sir; nothing."

"Well, then, here is your half-sovereign. There's another one waiting for you if you can bring any more information. Good-night!"

"Good-night, sir, and thank you!"

John Clayton departed chuckling, and Holmes turned to me with a shrug of his shoulders and a rueful smile.

"Snap goes our third thread, and we end where we began," said he. "The cunning rascal! He knew our number, knew that Sir Henry Baskerville had consulted me, spotted who I was in Regent Street, conjectured that I had got the number of the cab and would lay my hands on the driver, and so sent back this audacious message. I tell you, Watson, this time we have got a foeman who is worthy of our steel. I've been checkmated in London. I can only wish you better luck in Devonshire. But I'm not easy in my mind about it."

"About what?"

"About sending you. It's an ugly business, Watson, an ugly dangerous business, and the more I see of it the less I like it. Yes, my dear fellow, you may laugh, but I give you my word that I shall be very glad to have you back safe and sound in Baker Street once more."

Chapter 6.

Baskerville Hall

Sir Henry Baskerville and Dr. Mortimer were ready upon the appointed day, and we started as arranged for Devonshire. Mr. Sherlock Holmes drove with me to the station and gave me his last parting injunctions and advice.

"I will not bias your mind by suggesting theories or suspicions, Watson," said he; "I wish you simply to report facts in the fullest possible manner to me, and you can leave me to do the theorizing."

"What sort of facts?" I asked.

"Anything which may seem to have a bearing however indirect upon the case, and especially the relations between young Baskerville and his neighbours or any fresh particulars concerning the death of Sir Charles. I have made some inquiries myself in the last few days, but the results have, I fear, been negative. One thing only appears to be certain, and that is that Mr. James Desmond, who is the next heir, is an elderly gentleman of a very amiable disposition, so that this persecution does not arise from him. I really think that we may eliminate him entirely from our calculations. There remain the people who will actually surround Sir Henry Baskerville upon the moor."

"Would it not be well in the first place to get rid of this Barrymore couple?"

"By no means. You could not make a greater mistake. If they are innocent it would be a cruel injustice, and if they are guilty we should be giving up all chance of bringing it home to them. No, no, we will preserve them upon our list of suspects. Then there is a groom at the Hall, if I remember right. There are two moorland farmers. There is our friend Dr. Mortimer, whom I believe to be entirely honest, and there is his wife, of whom we know nothing. There is this naturalist, Stapleton, and there is his sister, who is said to be a young lady of attractions. There is Mr. Frankland, of Lafter Hall, who is also an unknown factor, and there are one or two other neighbours. These are the folk who must be your very special study."

"I will do my best."

"You have arms, I suppose?"

"Yes, I thought it as well to take them."

"Most certainly. Keep your revolver near you night and day, and never relax your precautions."

Our friends had already secured a first-class carriage and were waiting for us upon the platform.

"No, we have no news of any kind," said Dr. Mortimer in answer to my friend's questions. "I can swear to one thing, and that is that we have not been shadowed during the last two days. We have never gone out without keeping a sharp watch, and no one could have escaped our notice."

"You have always kept together, I presume?"

"Except yesterday afternoon. I usually give up one day to pure amusement when I come to town, so I spent it at the Museum of the College of Surgeons."

"And I went to look at the folk in the park," said Baskerville.

"But we had no trouble of any kind."

"It was imprudent, all the same," said Holmes, shaking his head and looking very grave. "I beg, Sir Henry, that you will not go about alone. Some great misfortune will befall you if you do. Did you get your other boot?"

"No, sir, it is gone forever."

"Indeed. That is very interesting. Well, good-bye," he added as the train began to glide down the platform. "Bear in mind, Sir Henry, one of the phrases in that queer old legend which Dr. Mortimer has read to us, and avoid the moor in those hours of darkness when the powers of evil are exalted."

I looked back at the platform when we had left it far behind and saw the tall, austere figure of Holmes standing motionless and gazing after us.

The journey was a swift and pleasant one, and I spent it in making the more intimate acquaintance of my two companions and in playing with Dr. Mortimer's spaniel. In a very few hours the brown earth had become ruddy, the brick had changed to granite, and red cows grazed in well-hedged fields where the lush grasses and more luxuriant vegetation spoke of a richer, if a damper, climate. Young Baskerville stared eagerly out of the window and cried aloud with delight as he recognized the familiar features of the Devon scenery.

"I've been over a good part of the world since I left it, Dr. Watson," said he; "but I have never seen a place to compare with it."

"I never saw a Devonshire man who did not swear by his county," I remarked.

"It depends upon the breed of men quite as much as on the county," said Dr. Mortimer. "A glance at our friend here reveals the rounded head of the Celt, which carries inside it the Celtic enthusiasm and power of attachment. Poor Sir Charles's head was of a very rare type, half Gaelic, half Ivernian in its characteristics. But you were very young when you last saw Baskerville Hall, were you not?"

"I was a boy in my teens at the time of my father's death and had never seen the Hall, for he lived in a little cottage on the South Coast. Thence I went straight to a friend in America. I tell you it is all as new to me as it is to Dr. Watson, and I'm as keen as possible to see the moor."

"Are you? Then your wish is easily granted, for there is your first sight of the moor," said Dr. Mortimer, pointing out of the carriage window.

Over the green squares of the fields and the low curve of a wood there rose in the distance a grey, melancholy hill, with a strange jagged summit, dim and vague in the distance, like some fantastic landscape in a dream. Baskerville sat for a long time, his eyes fixed upon it, and I read upon his eager face how much it meant to him, this first sight of that strange spot where the men of his blood had held sway so long and left their mark so deep. There he sat, with his tweed suit and his American accent, in the corner of a prosaic railway-carriage, and yet as I looked at his dark and expressive face I felt more than ever how true a descendant he was of that long line of high-blooded, fiery, and masterful men. There were pride, valour, and strength in his thick brows, his sensitive nostrils, and his large hazel eyes. If on that forbidding moor a difficult and dangerous quest should lie before us, this was at least a comrade for whom one might venture to take a risk with the certainty that he would bravely share it.

The train pulled up at a small wayside station and we all descended. Outside, beyond the low, white fence, a wagonette with a pair of cobs was waiting. Our coming was evidently a great event, for station-master and porters clustered round us to carry out our luggage. It was a sweet, simple country spot, but I was surprised to observe that by the gate there stood two soldierly men in dark uniforms who leaned upon their short rifles and glanced keenly at us as we passed. The coachman, a hard-faced, gnarled little fellow, saluted Sir Henry Baskerville, and in a few minutes we were flying swiftly down the broad, white road. Rolling pasture lands curved upward on either side of us, and old gabled houses peeped out from amid the thick green foliage, but behind the peaceful and sunlit countryside there rose ever, dark against the evening sky, the long, gloomy curve of the moor, broken by the jagged and sinister hills.

The wagonette swung round into a side road, and we curved upward through deep lanes worn by centuries of wheels, high banks on either side, heavy with dripping moss and fleshy hart's-tongue ferns. Bronzing bracken and mottled bramble gleamed in the light of the sinking sun. Still steadily rising, we passed over a narrow granite bridge and skirted a noisy stream which gushed swiftly down, foaming and roaring amid the grey boulders. Both road and stream wound up through a valley dense with scrub oak and fir. At every turn Baskerville gave an exclamation of delight, looking eagerly about him and asking countless questions. To his eyes all seemed beautiful, but to me a tinge of melancholy lay upon the countryside, which bore so clearly the mark of the waning year. Yellow leaves carpeted the lanes and fluttered down upon us as we passed. The rattle of our wheels died away as we drove through drifts of rotting vegetation—sad gifts, as it seemed to me, for Nature to throw before the carriage of the returning heir of the Baskervilles.

"Halloa!" cried Dr. Mortimer, "what is this?"

A steep curve of heath-clad land, an outlying spur of the moor, lay in front of us. On the summit, hard and clear like an equestrian statue upon its pedestal, was a mounted soldier, dark and stern, his rifle poised ready over his forearm. He was watching the road along which we travelled.

"What is this, Perkins?" asked Dr. Mortimer.

Our driver half turned in his seat. "There's a convict escaped from Princetown, sir. He's been out three days now, and the warders watch every road and every station, but they've had no sight of him yet. The farmers about here don't like it, sir, and that's a fact."

"Well, I understand that they get five pounds if they can give information."

"Yes, sir, but the chance of five pounds is but a poor thing compared to the chance of having your throat cut. You see, it isn't like any ordinary convict. This is a man that would stick at nothing."

"Who is he, then?"

"It is Selden, the Notting Hill murderer."

I remembered the case well, for it was one in which Holmes had taken an interest on account of the peculiar ferocity of the crime and the wanton brutality which had marked all the actions of the assassin. The commutation of his death sentence had been due to some doubts as to his complete sanity, so atrocious was his conduct. Our wagonette had topped a rise and in front of us rose the huge expanse of the moor, mottled with gnarled and craggy cairns and tors. A cold wind swept down from it and set us shivering. Somewhere there, on that desolate plain, was lurking this fiendish man, hiding in a burrow like a wild beast, his heart full of malignancy against the whole race which had cast him out. It needed but this to complete the grim suggestiveness of the barren waste, the chilling wind, and the darkling sky. Even Baskerville fell silent and pulled his overcoat more closely around him.

We had left the fertile country behind and beneath us. We looked back on it now, the slanting rays of a low sun turning the streams to threads of gold and glowing on the red earth new turned by the plough and the broad tangle of the woodlands. The road in front of us grew bleaker and wilder over huge russet and olive slopes, sprinkled with giant boulders. Now and then we passed a moorland cottage, walled and roofed with stone, with no creeper to break its harsh outline. Suddenly we looked down into a cuplike depression, patched with stunted oaks and firs which had been twisted and bent by the fury of years of storm. Two high, narrow towers rose over the trees. The driver pointed with his whip.

"Baskerville Hall," said he.

Its master had risen and was staring with flushed cheeks and shining eyes. A few minutes later we had reached the lodge-gates, a maze of fantastic tracery in wrought iron, with weather-bitten pillars on either side, blotched with lichens, and surmounted by the boars' heads of the Baskervilles. The lodge was a ruin of black granite and bared ribs of rafters, but facing it was a new building, half constructed, the first fruit of Sir Charles's South African gold.

Through the gateway we passed into the avenue, where the wheels were again hushed amid the leaves, and the old trees shot their branches in a sombre tunnel over our heads. Baskerville shuddered as he looked up the long, dark drive to where the house glimmered like a ghost at the farther end.

"Was it here?" he asked in a low voice.

"No, no, the yew alley is on the other side."

The young heir glanced round with a gloomy face.

"It's no wonder my uncle felt as if trouble were coming on him in such a place as this," said he. "It's enough to scare any man. I'll have a row of electric lamps up here inside of six months, and you won't know it again, with a thousand candle-power Swan and Edison right here in front of the hall door."

The avenue opened into a broad expanse of turf, and the house lay before us. In the fading light I could see that the centre was a heavy block of building from which a porch projected. The whole front was draped in ivy, with a patch clipped bare here and there where a window or a coat of arms broke through the dark veil. From this central block rose the twin towers, ancient, crenelated, and pierced with many loopholes. To right and left of the turrets were more modern wings of black granite. A dull light shone through heavy mullioned windows, and from the high chimneys which rose from the steep, high-angled roof there sprang a single black column of smoke.

"Welcome, Sir Henry! Welcome to Baskerville Hall!"

A tall man had stepped from the shadow of the porch to open the door of the wagonette. The figure of a woman was silhouetted against the yellow light of the hall. She came out and helped the man to hand down our bags.

"You don't mind my driving straight home, Sir Henry?" said Dr. Mortimer. "My wife is expecting me."

"Surely you will stay and have some dinner?"

"No, I must go. I shall probably find some work awaiting

me. I would stay to show you over the house, but Barrymore will be a better guide than I. Good-bye, and never hesitate night or day to send for me if I can be of service."

The wheels died away down the drive while Sir Henry and I turned into the hall, and the door clanged heavily behind us. It was a fine apartment in which we found ourselves, large, lofty, and heavily raftered with huge baulks of age-blackened oak. In the great old-fashioned fireplace behind the high iron dogs a log-fire crackled and snapped. Sir Henry and I held out our hands to it, for we were numb from our long drive. Then we gazed round us at the high, thin window of old stained glass, the oak panelling, the stags' heads, the coats of arms upon the walls, all dim and sombre in the subdued light of the central lamp.

"It's just as I imagined it," said Sir Henry. "Is it not the very picture of an old family home? To think that this should be the same hall in which for five hundred years my people have lived. It strikes me solemn to think of it."

I saw his dark face lit up with a boyish enthusiasm as he gazed about him. The light beat upon him where he stood, but long shadows trailed down the walls and hung like a black canopy above him. Barrymore had returned from taking our luggage to our rooms. He stood in front of us now with the subdued manner of a well-trained servant. He was a remarkable-looking man, tall, handsome, with a square black beard and pale, distinguished features.

"Would you wish dinner to be served at once, sir?"

"Is it ready?"

"In a very few minutes, sir. You will find hot water in your rooms. My wife and I will be happy, Sir Henry, to stay with you until you have made your fresh arrangements, but you will understand that under the new conditions this house will require a considerable staff."

"What new conditions?"

"I only meant, sir, that Sir Charles led a very retired life, and we were able to look after his wants. You would, naturally, wish to have more company, and so you will need changes in your household."

"Do you mean that your wife and you wish to leave?"

"Only when it is quite convenient to you, sir."

"But your family have been with us for several generations, have they not? I should be sorry to begin my life here by breaking an old family connection."

I seemed to discern some signs of emotion upon the butler's white face.

"I feel that also, sir, and so does my wife. But to tell the truth, sir, we were both very much attached to Sir Charles, and his death gave us a shock and made these surroundings very painful to us. I fear that we shall never again be easy in our minds at Baskerville Hall."

"But what do you intend to do?"

"I have no doubt, sir, that we shall succeed in establishing ourselves in some business. Sir Charles's generosity has given us the means to do so. And now, sir, perhaps I had best show you to your rooms."

A square balustraded gallery ran round the top of the old hall, approached by a double stair. From this central point two long corridors extended the whole length of the building, from which all the bedrooms opened. My own was in the same wing as Baskerville's and almost next door to it. These rooms appeared to be much more modern than the central part of the house, and the bright paper and numerous candles did something to remove the sombre impression which our arrival had left upon my mind.

But the dining-room which opened out of the hall was a place of shadow and gloom. It was a long chamber with a step separating the dais where the family sat from the lower portion reserved for their dependents. At one end a minstrel's gallery overlooked it. Black beams shot across above our heads, with a smoke-darkened ceiling beyond them. With rows of flaring torches to light it up, and the colour and rude hilarity of an old-time banquet, it might have softened; but now, when two black-clothed gentlemen sat in the little circle of light thrown by a shaded lamp, one's voice became hushed and one's spirit subdued. A dim line of ancestors, in every variety of dress, from the Elizabethan knight to the buck of the Regency, stared down upon us and daunted us by their silent company. We talked little, and I for one was glad when the meal was over and we were able to retire into the modern billiard-room and smoke a cigarette.

"My word, it isn't a very cheerful place," said Sir Henry. "I suppose one can tone down to it, but I feel a bit out of the picture at present. I don't wonder that my uncle got a little jumpy if he lived all alone in such a house as this. However, if it suits you, we will retire early tonight, and perhaps things may seem more cheerful in the morning."

I drew aside my curtains before I went to bed and looked out from my window. It opened upon the grassy space which lay in front of the hall door. Beyond, two copses of trees moaned and swung in a rising wind. A half moon broke through the rifts of racing clouds. In its cold light I saw beyond the trees a broken fringe of rocks, and the long, low curve of the melancholy moor. I closed the curtain, feeling that my last impression was in keeping with the rest.

And yet it was not quite the last. I found myself weary and yet wakeful, tossing restlessly from side to side, seeking for the sleep which would not come. Far away a chiming clock struck out the quarters of the hours, but otherwise a deathly silence lay upon the old house. And then suddenly, in the very dead of the night, there came a sound to my ears, clear, resonant, and unmistakable. It was the sob of a woman, the muffled, strangling gasp of one who is torn by an uncontrollable sorrow. I sat up in bed and listened intently. The noise could not have been far away and was certainly in the house. For half an hour I waited with every nerve on the alert, but there came no other sound save the chiming clock and the rustle of the ivy on the wall.

Chapter 7.

The Stapletons of Merripit House

The fresh beauty of the following morning did something to efface from our minds the grim and grey impression which had been left upon both of us by our first experience of Baskerville Hall. As Sir Henry and I sat at breakfast the sunlight flooded in through the high mullioned windows, throwing watery patches of colour from the coats of arms which covered them. The dark panelling glowed like bronze in the golden rays, and it was hard to realise that this was indeed the chamber which had struck such a gloom into our souls upon the evening before.

"I guess it is ourselves and not the house that we have to blame!" said the baronet. "We were tired with our journey and chilled by our drive, so we took a grey view of the place. Now we are fresh and well, so it is all cheerful once more."

"And yet it was not entirely a question of imagination," I answered. "Did you, for example, happen to hear someone, a woman I think, sobbing in the night?"

"That is curious, for I did when I was half asleep fancy that I heard something of the sort. I waited quite a time, but there was no more of it, so I concluded that it was all a dream."

"I heard it distinctly, and I am sure that it was really the sob of a woman."

"We must ask about this right away." He rang the bell and asked Barrymore whether he could account for our experience. It seemed to me that the pallid features of the butler turned a shade paler still as he listened to his master's question.

"There are only two women in the house, Sir Henry," he answered. "One is the scullery-maid, who sleeps in the other wing. The other is my wife, and I can answer for it that the sound could not have come from her."

And yet he lied as he said it, for it chanced that after breakfast I met Mrs. Barrymore in the long corridor with the sun full upon her face. She was a large, impassive, heavy-featured woman with a stern set expression of mouth. But her telltale eyes were red and glanced at me from between swollen lids. It was she, then, who wept in the night, and if she did so her husband must know it. Yet he had taken the obvious risk of discovery in declaring that it was not so. Why had he done this?

And why did she weep so bitterly? Already round this pale-faced, handsome, black-bearded man there was gathering an atmosphere of mystery and of gloom. It was he who had been the first to discover the body of Sir Charles, and we had only his word for all the circumstances which led up to the old man's death. Was it possible that it was Barrymore, after all, whom we had seen in the cab in Regent Street? The beard might well have been the same. The cabman had described a somewhat shorter man, but such an impression might easily have been erroneous. How could I settle the point forever? Obviously the first thing to do was to see the Grimpen postmaster and find whether the test telegram had really been placed in Barrymore's own hands. Be the answer what it might, I should at least have something to report to Sherlock Holmes.

Sir Henry had numerous papers to examine after breakfast, so that the time was propitious for my excursion. It was a pleasant walk of four miles along the edge of the moor, leading me at last to a small grey hamlet, in which two larger buildings, which proved to be the inn and the house of Dr. Mortimer, stood high above the rest. The postmaster, who was also the village grocer, had a clear recollection of the telegram.

"Certainly, sir," said he, "I had the telegram delivered to Mr. Barrymore exactly as directed."

"Who delivered it?"

"My boy here. James, you delivered that telegram to Mr. Barrymore at the Hall last week, did you not?"

"Yes, father, I delivered it."

"Into his own hands?" I asked.

"Well, he was up in the loft at the time, so that I could not put it into his own hands, but I gave it into Mrs. Barrymore's hands, and she promised to deliver it at once."

"Did you see Mr. Barrymore?"

"No, sir; I tell you he was in the loft."

"If you didn't see him, how do you know he was in the loft?"

"Well, surely his own wife ought to know where he is," said the postmaster testily. "Didn't he get the telegram? If there is any mistake it is for Mr. Barrymore himself to complain."

It seemed hopeless to pursue the inquiry any farther, but it was clear that in spite of Holmes's ruse we had no proof that Barrymore had not been in London all the time. Suppose that it were so—suppose that the same man had been the last who had seen Sir Charles alive, and the first to dog the new heir when he returned to England. What then? Was he the agent of others or had he some sinister design of his own? What interest could he have in persecuting the Baskerville family? I thought of the strange warning clipped out of the leading article of the Times. Was that his work or was it possibly the doing of someone who was bent upon counteracting his schemes? The only conceivable motive was that which had been suggested by Sir Henry, that if the family could be scared away a comfortable and permanent home would be secured for the Barrymores. But surely such an explanation as that would be quite inadequate to account for the deep and subtle scheming which seemed to be weaving an invisible net round the young baronet. Holmes himself had said that no more complex case had come to him in all the long series of his sensational investigations. I prayed, as I walked back along the grey, lonely road, that my friend might soon be freed from his preoccupations and able to come down to take this heavy burden of responsibility from my shoulders.

Suddenly my thoughts were interrupted by the sound of running feet behind me and by a voice which called me by name. I turned, expecting to see Dr. Mortimer, but to my surprise it was a stranger who was pursuing me. He was a small, slim, clean-shaven, prim-faced man, flaxen-haired and lean-jawed, between thirty and forty years of age, dressed in a grey suit and wearing a straw hat. A tin box for botanical specimens hung over his shoulder and he carried a green butterfly-net in one of his hands.

"You will, I am sure, excuse my presumption, Dr. Watson," said he as he came panting up to where I stood. "Here on the moor we are homely folk and do not wait for formal introductions. You may possibly have heard my name from our mutual friend, Mortimer. I am Stapleton, of Merripit House."

"Your net and box would have told me as much," said I, "for I knew that Mr. Stapleton was a naturalist. But how did you know me?"

"I have been calling on Mortimer, and he pointed you out to me from the window of his surgery as you passed. As our road lay the same way I thought that I would overtake you and introduce myself. I trust that Sir Henry is none the worse for his journey?"

"He is very well, thank you."

"We were all rather afraid that after the sad death of Sir Charles the new baronet might refuse to live here. It is asking much of a wealthy man to come down and bury himself in a place of this kind, but I need not tell you that it means a very great deal to the countryside. Sir Henry has, I suppose, no superstitious fears in the matter?"

"I do not think that it is likely."

"Of course you know the legend of the fiend dog which haunts the family?"

"I have heard it."

"It is extraordinary how credulous the peasants are about here! Any number of them are ready to swear that they have seen such a creature upon the moor." He spoke with a smile, but I seemed to read in his eyes that he took the matter more seriously. "The story took a great hold upon the imagination of Sir Charles, and I have no doubt that it led to his tragic end."

"But how?"

"His nerves were so worked up that the appearance of any dog might have had a fatal effect upon his diseased heart. I fancy that he really did see something of the kind upon that last night in the yew alley. I feared that some disaster might occur, for I was very fond of the old man, and I knew that his heart was weak."

"How did you know that?"

"My friend Mortimer told me."

"You think, then, that some dog pursued Sir Charles, and that he died of fright in consequence?"

"Have you any better explanation?"

"I have not come to any conclusion."

"Has Mr. Sherlock Holmes?"

The words took away my breath for an instant but a glance at the placid face and steadfast eyes of my companion showed that no surprise was intended.

"It is useless for us to pretend that we do not know you, Dr. Watson," said he. "The records of your detective have reached us here, and you could not celebrate him without being known yourself. When Mortimer told me your name he could not deny your identity. If you are here, then it follows that Mr. Sherlock Holmes is interesting himself in the matter, and I am naturally curious to know what view he may take."

"I am afraid that I cannot answer that question."

"May I ask if he is going to honour us with a visit himself?"

"He cannot leave town at present. He has other cases which engage his attention."

"What a pity! He might throw some light on that which is so dark to us. But as to your own researches, if there is any possible way in which I can be of service to you I trust that you will command me. If I had any indication of the nature of your suspicions or how you propose to investigate the case, I might perhaps even now give you some aid or advice."

"I assure you that I am simply here upon a visit to my friend, Sir Henry, and that I need no help of any kind."

"Excellent!" said Stapleton. "You are perfectly right to be wary and discreet. I am justly reproved for what I feel was an unjustifiable intrusion, and I promise you that I will not mention the matter again."

We had come to a point where a narrow grassy path struck off from the road and wound away across the moor. A steep, boulder-sprinkled hill lay upon the right which had in bygone days been cut into a granite quarry. The face which was turned towards us formed a dark cliff, with ferns and brambles growing in its niches. From over a distant rise there floated a grey plume of smoke.

"A moderate walk along this moor-path brings us to Merripit House," said he. "Perhaps you will spare an hour that I may have the pleasure of introducing you to my sister."

My first thought was that I should be by Sir Henry's side. But then I remembered the pile of papers and bills with which his study table was littered. It was certain that I could not help with those. And Holmes had expressly said that I should study the neighbours upon the moor. I accepted Stapleton's invitation, and we turned together down the path.

"It is a wonderful place, the moor," said he, looking round over the undulating downs, long green rollers, with crests of jagged granite foaming up into fantastic surges. "You never tire of the moor. You cannot think the wonderful secrets which it contains. It is so vast, and so barren, and so mysterious."

"You know it well, then?"

"I have only been here two years. The residents would call me a newcomer. We came shortly after Sir Charles settled. But my tastes led me to explore every part of the country round, and I should think that there are few men who know it better than I do."

"Is it hard to know?"

"Very hard. You see, for example, this great plain to the north here with the queer hills breaking out of it. Do you observe anything remarkable about that?"

"It would be a rare place for a gallop."

"You would naturally think so and the thought has cost several their lives before now. You notice those bright green spots scattered thickly over it?"

"Yes, they seem more fertile than the rest."

Stapleton laughed. "That is the great Grimpen Mire," said he. "A false step yonder means death to man or beast. Only yesterday I saw one of the moor ponies wander into it. He never came out. I saw his head for quite a long time craning out of the bog-hole, but it sucked him down at last. Even in dry seasons it is a danger to cross it, but after these autumn rains it is an awful place. And yet I can find my way to the very heart of it and return alive. By George, there is another of those miserable ponies!"

Something brown was rolling and tossing among the green sedges. Then a long, agonised, writhing neck shot upward and a dreadful cry echoed over the moor. It turned me cold with horror, but my companion's nerves seemed to be stronger than mine.

"It's gone!" said he. "The mire has him. Two in two days, and many more, perhaps, for they get in the way of going there in the dry weather and never know the difference until the mire has them in its clutches. It's a bad place, the great Grimpen Mire."

"And you say you can penetrate it?"

"Yes, there are one or two paths which a very active man can take. I have found them out."

"But why should you wish to go into so horrible a place?"

"Well, you see the hills beyond? They are really islands cut off on all sides by the impassable mire, which has crawled round them in the course of years. That is where the rare plants and the butterflies are, if you have the wit to reach them."

"I shall try my luck some day."

He looked at me with a surprised face. "For God's sake put such an idea out of your mind," said he. "Your blood would be upon my head. I assure you that there would not be the least chance of your coming back alive. It is only by remembering certain complex landmarks that I am able to do it."

"Halloa!" I cried. "What is that?"

A long, low moan, indescribably sad, swept over the moor. It filled the whole air, and yet it was impossible to say whence it came. From a dull murmur it swelled into a deep roar, and then sank back into a melancholy, throbbing murmur once again. Stapleton looked at me with a curious expression in his face.

"Queer place, the moor!" said he.

"But what is it?"

"The peasants say it is the Hound of the Baskervilles calling for its prey. I've heard it once or twice before, but never quite so loud."

I looked round, with a chill of fear in my heart, at the huge swelling plain, mottled with the green patches of rushes. Nothing stirred over the vast expanse save a pair of ravens, which croaked loudly from a tor behind us.

"You are an educated man. You don't believe such nonsense

as that?" said I. "What do you think is the cause of so strange a sound?"

"Bogs make queer noises sometimes. It's the mud settling, or the water rising, or something."

"No, no, that was a living voice."

"Well, perhaps it was. Did you ever hear a bittern booming?"

"No, I never did."

"It's a very rare bird—practically extinct—in England now, but all things are possible upon the moor. Yes, I should not be surprised to learn that what we have heard is the cry of the last of the bitterns."

"It's the weirdest, strangest thing that ever I heard in my life."

"Yes, it's rather an uncanny place altogether. Look at the hillside yonder. What do you make of those?"

The whole steep slope was covered with grey circular rings of stone, a score of them at least.

"What are they? Sheep-pens?"

"No, they are the homes of our worthy ancestors. Prehistoric man lived thickly on the moor, and as no one in particular has lived there since, we find all his little arrangements exactly as he left them. These are his wigwams with the roofs off. You can even see his hearth and his couch if you have the curiosity to go inside.

"But it is quite a town. When was it inhabited?"

"Neolithic man—no date."

"What did he do?"

"He grazed his cattle on these slopes, and he learned to dig for tin when the bronze sword began to supersede the stone axe. Look at the great trench in the opposite hill. That is his mark. Yes, you will find some very singular points about the moor, Dr. Watson. Oh, excuse me an instant! It is surely Cyclopides."

A small fly or moth had fluttered across our path, and in an instant Stapleton was rushing with extraordinary energy and speed in pursuit of it. To my dismay the creature flew straight for the great mire, and my acquaintance never paused for an instant, bounding from tuft to tuft behind it, his green net waving in the air. His grey clothes and jerky, zigzag, irregular progress made him not unlike some huge moth himself. I was standing watching his pursuit with a mixture of admiration for his extraordinary activity and fear lest he should lose his footing in the treacherous mire, when I heard the sound of steps and, turning round, found a woman near me upon the path. She had come from the direction in which the plume of smoke indicated the position of Merripit House, but the dip of the moor had hid her until she was quite close.

I could not doubt that this was the Miss Stapleton of whom I had been told, since ladies of any sort must be few upon the moor, and I remembered that I had heard someone describe her as being a beauty. The woman who approached me was certainly that, and of a most uncommon type. There could not have been a greater contrast between brother and sister, for Stapleton was neutral tinted, with light hair and grey eyes, while she was darker than any brunette whom I have seen in England—slim, elegant, and tall. She had a proud, finely cut face, so regular that it might have seemed impassive were it not for the sensitive mouth and the beautiful dark, eager eyes. With her perfect figure and elegant dress she was, indeed, a strange apparition upon a lonely moorland path. Her eyes were on her brother as I turned, and then she quickened her pace towards me. I had raised my hat and was about to make some explanatory remark when her own words turned all my thoughts into a new channel.

"Go back!" she said. "Go straight back to London, instantly."

I could only stare at her in stupid surprise. Her eyes blazed at me, and she tapped the ground impatiently with her foot.

"Why should I go back?" I asked.

"I cannot explain." She spoke in a low, eager voice, with a curious lisp in her utterance. "But for God's sake do what I ask you. Go back and never set foot upon the moor again."

"But I have only just come."

"Man, man!" she cried. "Can you not tell when a warning is for your own good? Go back to London! Start tonight! Get away from this place at all costs! Hush, my brother is coming! Not a word of what I have said. Would you mind getting that orchid for me among the mare's-tails yonder? We are very rich in orchids on the moor, though, of course, you are rather late to see the beauties of the place."

Stapleton had abandoned the chase and came back to us breathing hard and flushed with his exertions.

"Halloa, Beryl!" said he, and it seemed to me that the tone of his greeting was not altogether a cordial one.

"Well, Jack, you are very hot."

"Yes, I was chasing a Cyclopides. He is very rare and seldom found in the late autumn. What a pity that I should have missed him!" He spoke unconcernedly, but his small light eyes glanced incessantly from the girl to me.

"You have introduced yourselves, I can see."

"Yes. I was telling Sir Henry that it was rather late for him to see the true beauties of the moor."

"Why, who do you think this is?"

"I imagine that it must be Sir Henry Baskerville."

"No, no," said I. "Only a humble commoner, but his friend. My name is Dr. Watson."

A flush of vexation passed over her expressive face. "We have been talking at cross purposes," said she.

"Why, you had not very much time for talk," her brother remarked with the same questioning eyes.

"I talked as if Dr. Watson were a resident instead of being merely a visitor," said she. "It cannot much matter to him whether it is early or late for the orchids. But you will come on, will you not, and see Merripit House?"

A short walk brought us to it, a bleak moorland house, once the farm of some grazier in the old prosperous days, but now put into repair and turned into a modern dwelling. An orchard surrounded it, but the trees, as is usual upon the moor, were stunted and nipped, and the effect of the whole place was mean and melancholy. We were admitted by a strange, wizened, rusty-coated old manservant, who seemed in keeping with the house. Inside, however, there were large rooms furnished with an elegance in which I seemed to recognize the taste of the lady. As I looked from their windows at the interminable granite-flecked moor rolling unbroken to the farthest horizon I could not but marvel at what could have brought this highly educated man and this beautiful woman to live in such a place.

"Queer spot to choose, is it not?" said he as if in answer to my thought. "And yet we manage to make ourselves fairly happy, do we not, Beryl?"

"Quite happy," said she, but there was no ring of conviction in her words.

"I had a school," said Stapleton. "It was in the north country. The work to a man of my temperament was mechanical and uninteresting, but the privilege of living with youth, of helping to mould those young minds, and of impressing them with one's own character and ideals was very dear to me. However, the fates were against us. A serious epidemic broke out in the school and three of the boys died. It never recovered from the blow, and much of my capital was irretrievably swallowed up. And yet, if it were not for the loss of the charming companionship of the boys, I could rejoice over my own misfortune, for, with my strong tastes for botany and zoology, I find an unlimited field of work here, and my sister is as devoted to Nature as I am. All this, Dr. Watson, has been brought upon your head by your expression as you surveyed the moor out of our window."

"It certainly did cross my mind that it might be a little dull—less for you, perhaps, than for your sister."

"No, no, I am never dull," said she quickly.

"We have books, we have our studies, and we have interesting neighbours. Dr. Mortimer is a most learned man in his own line. Poor Sir Charles was also an admirable companion. We knew him well and miss him more than I can tell. Do you think that I should intrude if I were to call this afternoon and make the acquaintance of Sir Henry?"

"I am sure that he would be delighted."

"Then perhaps you would mention that I propose to do so. We may in our humble way do something to make things more easy for him until he becomes accustomed to his new surroundings. Will you come upstairs, Dr. Watson, and inspect my collection of Lepidoptera? I think it is the most complete one in the south-west of England. By the time that you have looked through them lunch will be almost ready."

But I was eager to get back to my charge. The melancholy of the moor, the death of the unfortunate pony, the weird sound which had been associated with the grim legend of the Baskervilles, all these things tinged my thoughts with sadness. Then on the top of these more or less vague impressions there had come the definite and distinct warning of Miss Stapleton, delivered with such intense earnestness that I could not doubt that some grave and deep reason lay behind it. I resisted all pressure to stay for lunch, and I set off at once upon my return journey, taking the grass-grown path by which we had come.

It seems, however, that there must have been some short cut for those who knew it, for before I had reached the road I was astounded to see Miss Stapleton sitting upon a rock by the side of the track. Her face was beautifully flushed with her exertions and she held her hand to her side.

"I have run all the way in order to cut you off, Dr. Watson," said she. "I had not even time to put on my hat. I must not stop, or my brother may miss me. I wanted to say to you how sorry I am about the stupid mistake I made in thinking that you were Sir Henry. Please forget the words I said, which have no application whatever to you."

"But I can't forget them, Miss Stapleton," said I. "I am Sir Henry's friend, and his welfare is a very close concern of mine. Tell me why it was that you were so eager that Sir Henry should return to London."

"A woman's whim, Dr. Watson. When you know me better you will understand that I cannot always give reasons for what I say or do."

"No, no. I remember the thrill in your voice. I remember the look in your eyes. Please, please, be frank with me, Miss Stapleton, for ever since I have been here I have been conscious of shadows all round me. Life has become like that great Grimpen Mire, with little green patches everywhere into which one may sink and with no guide to point the track. Tell me then what it was that you meant, and I will promise to convey your warning to Sir Henry."

An expression of irresolution passed for an instant over her face, but her eyes had hardened again when she answered me.

"You make too much of it, Dr. Watson," said she. "My brother and I were very much shocked by the death of Sir Charles. We knew him very intimately, for his favourite walk was over the moor to our house. He was deeply impressed with the curse which hung over the family, and when this tragedy came I naturally felt that there must be some grounds for the fears which he had expressed. I was distressed therefore when another member of the family came down to live here, and I felt that he should be warned of the danger which he will run. That was all which I intended to convey.

"But what is the danger?"

"You know the story of the hound?"

"I do not believe in such nonsense."

"But I do. If you have any influence with Sir Henry, take him away from a place which has always been fatal to his family. The world is wide. Why should he wish to live at the place of danger?"

"Because it is the place of danger. That is Sir Henry's nature. I fear that unless you can give me some more definite information than this it would be impossible to get him to move."

"I cannot say anything definite, for I do not know anything definite."

"I would ask you one more question, Miss Stapleton. If you meant no more than this when you first spoke to me, why should you not wish your brother to overhear what you said? There is nothing to which he, or anyone else, could object."

"My brother is very anxious to have the Hall inhabited, for he thinks it is for the good of the poor folk upon the moor. He would be very angry if he knew that I have said anything which might induce Sir Henry to go away. But I have done my duty now and I will say no more. I must go back, or he will miss me and suspect that I have seen you. Good-bye!" She turned and had disappeared in a few minutes among the scattered boulders, while I, with my soul full of vague fears, pursued my way to Baskerville Hall.

Chapter 8.

First Report of Dr. Watson

From this point onward I will follow the course of events by transcribing my own letters to Mr. Sherlock Holmes which lie before me on the table. One page is missing, but otherwise they are exactly as written and show my feelings and suspicions of the moment more accurately than my memory, clear as it is upon these tragic events, can possibly do.

Baskerville Hall, October 13th.

MY DEAR HOLMES,

My previous letters and telegrams have kept you pretty well up to date as to all that has occurred in this most God-forsaken corner of the world. The longer one stays here the more does the spirit of the moor sink into one's soul, its vastness, and also its grim charm. When you are once out upon its bosom you have left all traces of modern England behind you, but, on the other hand, you are conscious everywhere of the homes and the work of the prehistoric people. On all sides of you as you walk are the houses of these forgotten folk, with their graves and the huge monoliths which are supposed to have marked their temples. As you look at their grey stone huts against the scarred hillsides you leave your own age behind you, and if you were to see a skin-clad, hairy man crawl out from the low door fitting a flint-tipped arrow on to the string of his bow, you would feel that his presence there was more natural than your own. The strange thing is that they should have lived so thickly on what must always have been most unfruitful soil. I am no antiquarian, but I could imagine that they were some unwarlike and harried race who were forced to accept that which none other would occupy.

All this, however, is foreign to the mission on which you sent me and will probably be very uninteresting to your severely practical mind. I can still remember your complete indifference as to whether the sun moved round the earth or the earth round the sun. Let me, therefore, return to the facts concerning Sir Henry Baskerville.

If you have not had any report within the last few days it is because up to today there was nothing of importance to relate. Then a very surprising circumstance occurred, which I shall tell you in due course. But, first of all, I must keep you in touch with some of the other factors in the situation.

One of these, concerning which I have said little, is the escaped convict upon the moor. There is strong reason now to believe that he has got right away, which is a considerable relief to the lonely householders of this district. A fortnight has passed since his flight, during which he has not been seen and nothing has been heard of him. It is surely inconceivable that he could have held out upon the moor during all that time. Of course, so far as his concealment goes there is no difficulty at all. Any one of these stone huts would give him a hiding-place. But there is nothing to eat unless he were to catch and slaughter one of the moor sheep. We think, therefore, that he has gone, and the outlying farmers sleep the better in consequence.

We are four able-bodied men in this household, so that we could take good care of ourselves, but I confess that I have had uneasy moments when I have thought of the Stapletons. They live miles from any help. There are one maid, an old manservant, the sister, and the brother, the latter not a very strong man. They would be helpless in the hands of a desperate fellow like this Notting Hill criminal if he could once effect an entrance. Both Sir Henry and I were concerned at their situation, and it was suggested that Perkins the groom should go over to sleep there, but Stapleton would not hear of it.

The fact is that our friend, the baronet, begins to display a considerable interest in our fair neighbour. It is not to be wondered at, for time hangs heavily in this lonely spot to an active man like him, and she is a very fascinating and beautiful woman. There is something tropical and exotic about her which forms a singular contrast to her cool and unemotional brother. Yet he also gives the idea of hidden fires. He has certainly a very marked influence over her, for I have seen her continually glance at him as she talked as if seeking approbation for what she said. I trust that he is kind to her. There is a dry glitter in his eyes and a firm set of his thin lips, which goes with a positive and possibly a harsh nature. You would find him an interesting study.

He came over to call upon Baskerville on that first day, and the very next morning he took us both to show us the spot where the legend of the wicked Hugo is supposed to have had its origin. It was an excursion of some miles across the moor to a place which is so dismal that it might have suggested the story. We found a short valley between rugged tors which led to an open, grassy space flecked over with the white cotton grass. In the middle of it rose two great stones, worn and sharpened at the upper end until they looked like the huge corroding fangs of some monstrous beast. In every way it corresponded with the scene of the old tragedy. Sir Henry was much interested and asked Stapleton more than once whether he did really believe in the possibility of the interference of the supernatural in the affairs of men. He spoke lightly, but it was evident that he was very much in earnest. Stapleton was guarded in his replies, but it was easy to see that he said less than he might, and that he would not express his whole opinion out of consideration for the feelings of the baronet. He told us of similar cases, where families had suffered from some evil influence, and he left us with the impression that he shared the popular view upon the matter.

On our way back we stayed for lunch at Merripit House, and it was there that Sir Henry made the acquaintance of Miss Stapleton. From the first moment that he saw her he appeared to be strongly attracted by her, and I am much mistaken if the feeling was not mutual. He referred to her again and again on our walk home, and since then hardly a day has passed that we have not seen something of the brother and sister. They dine here tonight, and there is some talk of our going to them next week. One would imagine that such a match would be very welcome to Stapleton, and yet I have more than once caught a look of the strongest disapprobation in his face when Sir Henry has been paying some attention to his sister. He is much attached to her, no doubt, and would lead a lonely life without her, but it would seem the height of selfishness if he were to stand in the way of her making so brilliant a marriage. Yet I am certain that he does not wish their intimacy to ripen into love, and I have several times observed that he has taken pains to prevent them from being tête-à-tête. By the way, your instructions to me never to allow Sir Henry to go out alone will become very much more onerous if a love affair were to be added to our other difficulties. My popularity would soon suffer if I were to carry out your orders to the letter.

The other day—Thursday, to be more exact—Dr. Mortimer lunched with us. He has been excavating a barrow at Long Down and has got a prehistoric skull which fills him with great joy. Never was there such a single-minded enthusiast as he! The Stapletons came in afterwards, and the good doctor took us all to the yew alley at Sir Henry's request to show us exactly how everything occurred upon that fatal night. It is a long, dismal walk, the yew alley, between two high walls of clipped hedge, with a narrow band of grass upon either side. At the far end is an old tumble-down summer-house. Halfway down is the moor-gate, where the old gentleman left his cigar-ash. It is a white wooden gate with a latch. Beyond it lies the wide moor. I remembered your theory of the affair and tried to picture all that had occurred. As the old man stood there he saw something coming across the moor, something which terrified him so that he lost his wits and ran and ran until he died of sheer horror and exhaustion. There was the long, gloomy tunnel down which he fled. And from what? A sheep-dog of the moor? Or a spectral hound, black, silent, and monstrous? Was there a human agency in the matter? Did the pale, watchful Barrymore know more than he cared to say? It was all dim and vague, but always there is the dark shadow of crime behind it.

One other neighbour I have met since I wrote last. This is Mr. Frankland, of Lafter Hall, who lives some four miles to the south of us. He is an elderly man, red-faced, white-haired, and choleric. His passion is for the British law, and he has spent a large fortune in litigation. He fights for the mere pleasure of fighting and is equally ready to take up either side of a question, so that it is no wonder that he has found it a costly amusement. Sometimes he will shut up a right of way and defy the parish to make him open it. At others he will with his own hands tear down some other man's gate and declare that a path has existed there from time immemorial, defying the owner to prosecute him for trespass. He is learned in old manorial and communal rights, and he applies his knowledge sometimes in favour of the villagers of Fernworthy and sometimes against them, so that he is periodically either carried in triumph down the village street or else burned in effigy, according to his latest exploit. He is said to have about seven lawsuits upon his hands at present, which will probably swallow up the remainder of his fortune and so draw his sting and leave him harmless for the future. Apart from the law he seems a kindly, good-natured person, and I only mention him because you were particular that I should send some description of the people who surround us. He is curiously employed at present, for, being an amateur astronomer, he has an excellent telescope, with which he lies upon the roof of his own house and sweeps the moor all day in the hope of catching a glimpse of the escaped convict. If he would confine his energies to this all would be well, but there are rumours that he intends to prosecute Dr. Mortimer for opening a grave without the consent of the next of kin because he dug up the Neolithic skull in the barrow on Long Down. He helps to keep our lives from being monotonous and gives a little comic relief where it is badly needed.

And now, having brought you up to date in the escaped convict, the Stapletons, Dr. Mortimer, and Frankland, of Lafter Hall, let me end on that which is most important and tell you more about the Barrymores, and especially about the surprising development of last night.

First of all about the test telegram, which you sent from London in order to make sure that Barrymore was really here. I have already explained that the testimony of the postmaster shows that the test was worthless and that we have no proof one way or the other. I told Sir Henry how the matter stood, and he at once, in his downright fashion, had Barrymore up and asked him whether he had received the telegram himself. Barrymore said that he had.

"Did the boy deliver it into your own hands?" asked Sir Henry.

Barrymore looked surprised, and considered for a little time.

"No," said he, "I was in the box-room at the time, and my wife brought it up to me."

"Did you answer it yourself?"

"No; I told my wife what to answer and she went down to write it."

In the evening he recurred to the subject of his own accord.

"I could not quite understand the object of your questions this morning, Sir Henry," said he. "I trust that they do not mean that I have done anything to forfeit your confidence?"

Sir Henry had to assure him that it was not so and pacify him by giving him a considerable part of his old wardrobe, the London outfit having now all arrived.

Mrs. Barrymore is of interest to me. She is a heavy, solid person, very limited, intensely respectable, and inclined to be puritanical. You could hardly conceive a less emotional subject. Yet I have told you how, on the first night here, I heard her sobbing bitterly, and since then I have more than once observed traces of tears upon her face. Some deep sorrow gnaws ever at her heart. Sometimes I wonder if she has a guilty memory which haunts her, and sometimes I suspect Barrymore of being a domestic tyrant. I have always felt that there was something singular and questionable in this man's character, but the adventure of last night brings all my suspicions to a head.

And yet it may seem a small matter in itself. You are aware that I am not a very sound sleeper, and since I have been on guard in this house my slumbers have been lighter than ever. Last night, about two in the morning, I was aroused by a stealthy step passing my room. I rose, opened my door, and peeped out. A long black shadow was trailing down the corridor. It was thrown by a man who walked softly down the passage with a candle held in his hand. He was in shirt and trousers, with no covering to his feet. I could merely see the outline, but his height told me that it was Barrymore. He walked very slowly and circumspectly, and there was something indescribably guilty and furtive in his whole appearance.

I have told you that the corridor is broken by the balcony which runs round the hall, but that it is resumed upon the farther side. I waited until he had passed out of sight and then I followed him. When I came round the balcony he had reached the end of the farther corridor, and I could see from the glimmer of light through an open door that he had entered one of the rooms. Now, all these rooms are unfurnished and unoccupied so that his expedition became more mysterious than ever. The light shone steadily as if he were standing motionless. I crept down the passage as noiselessly as I could and peeped round the corner of the door.

Barrymore was crouching at the window with the candle held against the glass. His profile was half turned towards me, and his face seemed to be rigid with expectation as he stared out into the blackness of the moor. For some minutes he stood watching intently. Then he gave a deep groan and with an impatient gesture he put out the light. Instantly I made my way back to my room, and very shortly came the stealthy steps passing once more upon their return journey. Long afterwards when I had fallen into a light sleep I heard a key turn somewhere in a lock, but I could not tell whence the sound came. What it all means I cannot guess, but there is some secret business going on in this house of gloom which sooner or later we shall get to the bottom of. I do not trouble you with my theories, for you asked me to furnish you only with facts. I have had a long talk with Sir Henry this morning, and we have made a plan of campaign founded upon my observations of last night. I will not speak about it just now, but it should make my next report interesting reading.

Chapter 9.

The Light upon the Moor

[Second Report of Dr. Watson]

Baskerville Hall, Oct. 15th.

MY DEAR HOLMES,

If I was compelled to leave you without much news during the early days of my mission you must acknowledge that I am making up for lost time, and that events are now crowding thick and fast upon us. In my last report I ended upon my top note with Barrymore at the window, and now I have quite a budget already which will, unless I am much mistaken, considerably surprise you. Things have taken a turn which I could not have anticipated. In some ways they have within the last forty-eight hours become much clearer and in some ways they have become more complicated. But I will tell you all and you shall judge for yourself.

Before breakfast on the morning following my adventure I went down the corridor and examined the room in which Barrymore had been on the night before. The western window through which he had stared so intently has, I noticed, one peculiarity above all other windows in the house—it commands the nearest outlook on to the moor. There is an opening between two trees which enables one from this point of view to look right down upon it, while from all the other windows it is only a distant glimpse which can be obtained. It follows, therefore, that Barrymore, since only this window would serve the purpose, must have been looking out for something or somebody upon the moor. The night was very dark, so that I can hardly imagine how he could have hoped to see anyone. It had struck me that it was possible that some love intrigue was on foot. That would have accounted for his stealthy movements and also for the uneasiness of his wife. The man is a striking-looking fellow, very well equipped to steal the heart of a country girl, so that this theory seemed to have something to support it. That opening of the door which I had heard after I had returned to my room might mean that he had gone out to keep some clandestine appointment. So I reasoned with myself in the morning, and I tell you the direction of my suspicions, however much the result may have shown that they were unfounded.

But whatever the true explanation of Barrymore's

movements might be, I felt that the responsibility of keeping them to myself until I could explain them was more than I could bear. I had an interview with the baronet in his study after breakfast, and I told him all that I had seen. He was less surprised than I had expected.

"I knew that Barrymore walked about nights, and I had a mind to speak to him about it," said he. "Two or three times I have heard his steps in the passage, coming and going, just about the hour you name."

"Perhaps then he pays a visit every night to that particular window," I suggested.

"Perhaps he does. If so, we should be able to shadow him and see what it is that he is after. I wonder what your friend Holmes would do if he were here."

"I believe that he would do exactly what you now suggest," said I. "He would follow Barrymore and see what he did."

"Then we shall do it together."

"But surely he would hear us."

"The man is rather deaf, and in any case we must take our chance of that. We'll sit up in my room tonight and wait until he passes." Sir Henry rubbed his hands with pleasure, and it was evident that he hailed the adventure as a relief to his somewhat quiet life upon the moor.

The baronet has been in communication with the architect who prepared the plans for Sir Charles, and with a contractor from London, so that we may expect great changes to begin here soon. There have been decorators and furnishers up from Plymouth, and it is evident that our friend has large ideas and means to spare no pains or expense to restore the grandeur of his family. When the house is renovated and refurnished, all that he will need will be a wife to make it complete. Between ourselves there are pretty clear signs that this will not be wanting if the lady is willing, for I have seldom seen a man more infatuated with a woman than he is with our beautiful neighbour, Miss Stapleton. And yet the course of true love does not run quite as smoothly as one would under the circumstances expect. Today, for example, its surface was broken by a very unexpected ripple, which has caused our friend considerable perplexity and annoyance.

After the conversation which I have quoted about Barrymore, Sir Henry put on his hat and prepared to go out. As a matter of course I did the same.

"What, are you coming, Watson?" he asked, looking at me in a curious way.

"That depends on whether you are going on the moor," said I.

"Yes, I am."

"Well, you know what my instructions are. I am sorry to intrude, but you heard how earnestly Holmes insisted that I should not leave you, and especially that you should not go alone upon the moor."

Sir Henry put his hand upon my shoulder with a pleasant smile.

"My dear fellow," said he, "Holmes, with all his wisdom, did not foresee some things which have happened since I have been on the moor. You understand me? I am sure that you are the last man in the world who would wish to be a spoil-sport. I must go out alone."

It put me in a most awkward position. I was at a loss what to say or what to do, and before I had made up my mind he picked up his cane and was gone.

But when I came to think the matter over my conscience reproached me bitterly for having on any pretext allowed him to go out of my sight. I imagined what my feelings would be if I had to return to you and to confess that some misfortune had occurred through my disregard for your instructions. I assure you my cheeks flushed at the very thought. It might not even now be too late to overtake him, so I set off at once in the direction of Merripit House.

I hurried along the road at the top of my speed without seeing anything of Sir Henry, until I came to the point where the moor path branches off. There, fearing that perhaps I had come in the wrong direction after all, I mounted a hill from which I could command a view—the same hill which is cut into the dark quarry. Thence I saw him at once. He was on the moor path about a quarter of a mile off, and a lady was by his side who could only be Miss Stapleton. It was clear that there was already an understanding between them and that they had met by appointment. They were walking slowly along in deep conversation, and I saw her making quick little movements of her hands as if she were very earnest in what she was saying, while he listened intently, and once or twice shook his head in strong dissent. I stood among the rocks watching them, very much puzzled as to what I should do next. To follow them and break into their intimate conversation seemed to be an outrage, and yet my clear duty was never for an instant to let him out of my sight. To act the spy upon a friend was a hateful task. Still, I could see no better course than to observe him from the hill, and to clear my conscience by confessing to him afterwards what I had done. It is true that if any sudden danger had threatened him I was too far away to be of use, and yet I am sure that you will agree with me that the position was very difficult, and that there was nothing more which I could do.

Our friend, Sir Henry, and the lady had halted on the path and were standing deeply absorbed in their conversation, when I was suddenly aware that I was not the only witness of their interview. A wisp of green floating in the air caught my eye, and another glance showed me that it was carried on a stick by a man who was moving among the broken ground. It was Stapleton with his butterfly-net. He was very much closer to the pair than I was, and he appeared to be moving in their direction. At this instant Sir Henry suddenly drew Miss Stapleton to his side. His arm was round her, but it seemed to me that she was straining away from him with her face averted. He stooped his head to hers, and she raised one hand as if in protest. Next moment I saw them spring apart and turn hurriedly round. Stapleton was the cause of the interruption. He was running wildly towards them, his absurd net dangling behind him. He gesticulated and almost danced with excitement in front of the lovers. What the scene meant I could not imagine, but it seemed to me that Stapleton was abusing Sir Henry, who offered explanations, which became more angry as the other refused to accept them. The lady stood by in haughty silence. Finally Stapleton turned upon his heel and beckoned in a peremptory way to his sister, who, after an irresolute glance at Sir Henry, walked off by the side of her brother. The naturalist's angry gestures showed that the lady was included in his displeasure. The baronet stood for a minute looking after them, and then he walked slowly back the way that he had come, his head hanging, the very picture of dejection.

What all this meant I could not imagine, but I was deeply ashamed to have witnessed so intimate a scene without my friend's knowledge. I ran down the hill therefore and met the baronet at the bottom. His face was flushed with anger and his brows were wrinkled, like one who is at his wit's ends what to do.

"Halloa, Watson! Where have you dropped from?" said he. "You don't mean to say that you came after me in spite of all?"

I explained everything to him: how I had found it impossible to remain behind, how I had followed him, and how I had witnessed all that had occurred. For an instant his eyes blazed at me, but my frankness disarmed his anger, and he broke at last into a rather rueful laugh.

"You would have thought the middle of that prairie a fairly safe place for a man to be private," said he, "but, by thunder, the whole countryside seems to have been out to see me do my wooing—and a mighty poor wooing at that! Where had you engaged a seat?"

"I was on that hill."

"Quite in the back row, eh? But her brother was well up to the front. Did you see him come out on us?"

"Yes, I did."

"Did he ever strike you as being crazy—this brother of hers?"

"I can't say that he ever did."

"I dare say not. I always thought him sane enough until today, but you can take it from me that either he or I ought to be in a straitjacket. What's the matter with me, anyhow? You've lived near me for some weeks, Watson. Tell me straight, now! Is there anything that would prevent me from making a good husband to a woman that I loved?"

"I should say not."

"He can't object to my worldly position, so it must be myself that he has this down on. What has he against me? I never hurt man or woman in my life that I know of. And yet he would not so much as let me touch the tips of her fingers."

"Did he say so?"

"That, and a deal more. I tell you, Watson, I've only known her these few weeks, but from the first I just felt that she was made for me, and she, too—she was happy when she was with me, and that I'll swear. There's a light in a woman's eyes that speaks louder than words. But he has never let us get together and it was only today for the first time that I saw a chance of having a few words with her alone. She was glad to meet me, but when she did it was not love that she would talk about, and she wouldn't have let me talk about it either if she could have stopped it. She kept coming back to it that this was a place of danger, and that she would never be happy until I had left it. I told her that since I had seen her I was in no hurry to leave it, and that if she really wanted me to go, the only way to work it was for her to arrange to go with me. With that I offered in as many words to marry her, but before she could answer, down came this brother of hers, running at us with a face on him like a madman. He was just white with rage, and those light eyes of his were blazing with fury. What was I doing with the lady? How dared I offer her attentions which were distasteful to her? Did I think that because I was a baronet I could do what I liked? If he had not been her brother I should have known better how to answer him. As it was I told him that my feelings towards his sister were such as I was not ashamed of, and that I hoped that she might honour me by becoming my wife. That seemed to make the matter no better, so then I lost my temper too, and I answered him rather more hotly than I should perhaps, considering that she was standing by. So it ended by his going off with her, as you saw, and here am I as badly puzzled a man as any in this county. Just tell me what it all means, Watson, and I'll owe you more than ever I can hope to pay."

I tried one or two explanations, but, indeed, I was completely puzzled myself. Our friend's title, his fortune, his age, his character, and his appearance are all in his favour, and I know nothing against him unless it be this dark fate which runs in his family. That his advances should be rejected so brusquely without any reference to the lady's own wishes and that the lady should accept the situation without protest is very amazing. However, our conjectures were set at rest by a visit from Stapleton himself that very afternoon. He had come to offer apologies for his rudeness of the morning, and after a long private interview with Sir Henry in his study the upshot of their conversation was that the breach is quite healed, and that we are to dine at Merripit House next Friday as a sign of it.

"I don't say now that he isn't a crazy man," said Sir Henry; "I can't forget the look in his eyes when he ran at me this morning, but I must allow that no man could make a more handsome apology than he has done."

"Did he give any explanation of his conduct?"

"His sister is everything in his life, he says. That is natural enough, and I am glad that he should understand her value. They have always been together, and according to his account he has been a very lonely man with only her as a companion, so that the thought of losing her was really terrible to him. He had not understood, he said, that I was becoming attached to her, but when he saw with his own eyes that it was really so, and that she might be taken away from him, it gave him such a shock that for a time he was not responsible for what he said or did. He was very sorry for all that had passed, and he recognized how foolish and how selfish it was that he should imagine that he could hold a beautiful woman like his sister to himself for her whole life. If she had to leave him he had rather it was to a neighbour like myself than to anyone else. But in any case it was a blow to him and it would take him some time before he could prepare himself to meet it. He would withdraw all opposition upon his part if I would promise for three months to let the matter rest and to be content with cultivating the lady's friendship during that time without claiming her love. This I promised, and so the matter rests."

So there is one of our small mysteries cleared up. It is something to have touched bottom anywhere in this bog in which we are floundering. We know now why Stapleton looked with disfavour upon his sister's suitor—even when that suitor was so eligible a one as Sir Henry. And now I pass on to another thread which I have extricated out of the tangled skein, the mystery of the sobs in the night, of the tear-stained face of Mrs. Barrymore, of the secret journey of the butler to the western lattice window. Congratulate me, my dear Holmes, and tell me that I have not disappointed you as an agent—that you do not regret the confidence which you showed in me when you sent me down. All these things have by one night's work been thoroughly cleared.

I have said "by one night's work," but, in truth, it was by two nights' work, for on the first we drew entirely blank. I sat up with Sir Henry in his rooms until nearly three o'clock in the morning, but no sound of any sort did we hear except the chiming clock upon the stairs. It was a most melancholy vigil and ended by each of us falling asleep in our chairs. Fortunately we were not discouraged, and we determined to try again. The next night we lowered the lamp and sat smoking cigarettes without making the least sound. It was incredible how slowly the hours crawled by, and yet we were helped through it by the same sort of patient interest which the hunter must feel as he watches the trap into which he hopes the game may wander. One struck, and two, and we had almost for the second time given it up in despair when in an instant we both sat bolt upright in our chairs with all our weary senses keenly on the alert once more. We had heard the creak of a step in the passage.

Very stealthily we heard it pass along until it died away in the distance. Then the baronet gently opened his door and we set out in pursuit. Already our man had gone round the gallery and the corridor was all in darkness. Softly we stole along until we had come into the other wing. We were just in time to catch a glimpse of the tall, black-bearded figure, his shoulders rounded as he tiptoed down the passage. Then he passed through the same door as before, and the light of the candle framed it in the darkness and shot one single yellow beam across the gloom of the corridor. We shuffled cautiously towards it, trying every plank before we dared to put our whole weight upon it. We had taken the precaution of leaving our boots behind us, but, even so, the old boards snapped and creaked beneath our tread. Sometimes it seemed impossible that he should fail to hear our approach. However, the man is fortunately rather deaf, and he was entirely preoccupied in that which he was doing. When at last we reached the door and peeped through we found him crouching at the window, candle in hand, his white, intent face pressed against the pane, exactly as I had seen him two nights before.

We had arranged no plan of campaign, but the baronet is a man to whom the most direct way is always the most natural. He walked into the room, and as he did so Barrymore sprang up from the window with a sharp hiss of his breath and stood, livid and trembling, before us. His dark eyes, glaring out of the white mask of his face, were full of horror and astonishment as he gazed from Sir Henry to me.

"What are you doing here, Barrymore?"

"Nothing, sir." His agitation was so great that he could hardly speak, and the shadows sprang up and down from the shaking of his candle. "It was the window, sir. I go round at night to see that they are fastened."

"On the second floor?"

"Yes, sir, all the windows."

"Look here, Barrymore," said Sir Henry sternly, "we have

made up our minds to have the truth out of you, so it will save you trouble to tell it sooner rather than later. Come, now! No lies! What were you doing at that window?"

The fellow looked at us in a helpless way, and he wrung his hands together like one who is in the last extremity of doubt and misery.

"I was doing no harm, sir. I was holding a candle to the window."

"And why were you holding a candle to the window?"

"Don't ask me, Sir Henry—don't ask me! I give you my word, sir, that it is not my secret, and that I cannot tell it. If it concerned no one but myself I would not try to keep it from you."

A sudden idea occurred to me, and I took the candle from the trembling hand of the butler.

"He must have been holding it as a signal," said I. "Let us see if there is any answer." I held it as he had done, and stared out into the darkness of the night. Vaguely I could discern the black bank of the trees and the lighter expanse of the moor, for the moon was behind the clouds. And then I gave a cry of exultation, for a tiny pinpoint of yellow light had suddenly transfixed the dark veil, and glowed steadily in the centre of the black square framed by the window.

"There it is!" I cried.

"No, no, sir, it is nothing—nothing at all!" the butler broke in; "I assure you, sir—"

"Move your light across the window, Watson!" cried the baronet. "See, the other moves also! Now, you rascal, do you deny that it is a signal? Come, speak up! Who is your confederate out yonder, and what is this conspiracy that is going on?"

The man's face became openly defiant. "It is my business, and not yours. I will not tell."

"Then you leave my employment right away."

"Very good, sir. If I must I must."

"And you go in disgrace. By thunder, you may well be ashamed of yourself. Your family has lived with mine for over a hundred years under this roof, and here I find you deep in some dark plot against me."

"No, no, sir; no, not against you!" It was a woman's voice, and Mrs. Barrymore, paler and more horror-struck than her husband, was standing at the door. Her bulky figure in a shawl and skirt might have been comic were it not for the intensity of feeling upon her face.

"We have to go, Eliza. This is the end of it. You can pack our things," said the butler.

"Oh, John, John, have I brought you to this? It is my doing, Sir Henry—all mine. He has done nothing except for my sake and because I asked him."

"Speak out, then! What does it mean?"

"My unhappy brother is starving on the moor. We cannot let him perish at our very gates. The light is a signal to him that food is ready for him, and his light out yonder is to show the spot to which to bring it."

"Then your brother is—"

"The escaped convict, sir—Selden, the criminal."

"That's the truth, sir," said Barrymore. "I said that it was not my secret and that I could not tell it to you. But now you have heard it, and you will see that if there was a plot it was not against you."

This, then, was the explanation of the stealthy expeditions at night and the light at the window. Sir Henry and I both stared at the woman in amazement. Was it possible that this stolidly respectable person was of the same blood as one of the most notorious criminals in the country?

"Yes, sir, my name was Selden, and he is my younger brother. We humoured him too much when he was a lad and gave him his own way in everything until he came to think that the world was made for his pleasure, and that he could do what he liked in it. Then as he grew older he met wicked companions, and the devil entered into him until he broke my mother's heart and dragged our name in the dirt. From crime to crime he sank lower and lower until it is only the mercy of God which has snatched him from the scaffold; but to me, sir, he was always the little curly-headed boy that I had nursed and played with as an elder sister would. That was why he broke prison, sir. He knew that I was here and that we could not refuse to help him. When he dragged himself here one night, weary and starving, with the warders hard at his heels, what could we do? We took him in and fed him and cared for him. Then you returned, sir, and my brother thought he would be safer on the moor than anywhere else until the hue and cry was over, so he lay in hiding there. But every second night we made sure if he was still there by putting a light in the window, and if there was an answer my husband took out some bread and meat to him. Every day we hoped that he was gone, but as long as he was there we could not desert him. That is the whole truth, as I am an honest Christian woman and you will see that if there is blame in the matter it does not lie with my husband but with me, for whose sake he has done all that he has."

The woman's words came with an intense earnestness which carried conviction with them.

"Is this true, Barrymore?"

"Yes, Sir Henry. Every word of it."

"Well, I cannot blame you for standing by your own wife. Forget what I have said. Go to your room, you two, and we shall talk further about this matter in the morning."

When they were gone we looked out of the window again. Sir Henry had flung it open, and the cold night wind beat in upon our faces. Far away in the black distance there still glowed that one tiny point of yellow light.

"I wonder he dares," said Sir Henry.

"It may be so placed as to be only visible from here."

"Very likely. How far do you think it is?"

"Out by the Cleft Tor, I think."

"Not more than a mile or two off."

"Hardly that."

"Well, it cannot be far if Barrymore had to carry out the food to it. And he is waiting, this villain, beside that candle. By thunder, Watson, I am going out to take that man!"

The same thought had crossed my own mind. It was not as if the Barrymores had taken us into their confidence. Their secret had been forced from them. The man was a danger to the community, an unmitigated scoundrel for whom there was neither pity nor excuse. We were only doing our duty in taking this chance of putting him back where he could do no harm. With his brutal and violent nature, others would have to pay the price if we held our hands. Any night, for example, our neighbours the Stapletons might be attacked by him, and it may have been the thought of this which made Sir Henry so keen upon the adventure.

"I will come," said I.

"Then get your revolver and put on your boots. The sooner we start the better, as the fellow may put out his light and be off."

In five minutes we were outside the door, starting upon our expedition. We hurried through the dark shrubbery, amid the dull moaning of the autumn wind and the rustle of the falling leaves. The night air was heavy with the smell of damp and decay. Now and again the moon peeped out for an instant, but clouds were driving over the face of the sky, and just as we came out on the moor a thin rain began to fall. The light still burned steadily in front.

"Are you armed?" I asked.

"I have a hunting-crop."

"We must close in on him rapidly, for he is said to be a desperate fellow. We shall take him by surprise and have him at our mercy before he can resist."

"I say, Watson," said the baronet, "what would Holmes say to this? How about that hour of darkness in which the power of evil is exalted?"

As if in answer to his words there rose suddenly out of the vast gloom of the moor that strange cry which I had already heard upon the borders of the great Grimpen Mire. It came with the wind through the silence of the night, a long, deep mutter, then a rising howl, and then the sad moan in which it died away. Again and again it sounded, the whole air throbbing with it, strident, wild, and menacing. The baronet caught my sleeve and his face glimmered white through the darkness.

"My God, what's that, Watson?"

"I don't know. It's a sound they have on the moor. I heard it once before."

It died away, and an absolute silence closed in upon us. We stood straining our ears, but nothing came.

"Watson," said the baronet, "it was the cry of a hound."

My blood ran cold in my veins, for there was a break in his voice which told of the sudden horror which had seized him.

"What do they call this sound?" he asked.

"Who?"

"The folk on the countryside."

"Oh, they are ignorant people. Why should you mind what they call it?"

"Tell me, Watson. What do they say of it?"

I hesitated but could not escape the question.

"They say it is the cry of the Hound of the Baskervilles."

He groaned and was silent for a few moments.

"A hound it was," he said at last, "but it seemed to come from miles away, over yonder, I think."

"It was hard to say whence it came."

"It rose and fell with the wind. Isn't that the direction of the great Grimpen Mire?"

"Yes, it is."

"Well, it was up there. Come now, Watson, didn't you think yourself that it was the cry of a hound? I am not a child. You need not fear to speak the truth."

"Stapleton was with me when I heard it last. He said that it might be the calling of a strange bird."

"No, no, it was a hound. My God, can there be some truth in all these stories? Is it possible that I am really in danger from so dark a cause? You don't believe it, do you, Watson?"

"No, no."

"And yet it was one thing to laugh about it in London, and it is another to stand out here in the darkness of the moor and to hear such a cry as that. And my uncle! There was the footprint of the hound beside him as he lay. It all fits together. I don't think that I am a coward, Watson, but that sound seemed to freeze my very blood. Feel my hand!"

It was as cold as a block of marble.

"You'll be all right tomorrow."

"I don't think I'll get that cry out of my head. What do you advise that we do now?"

"Shall we turn back?"

"No, by thunder; we have come out to get our man, and we will do it. We after the convict, and a hell-hound, as likely as not, after us. Come on! We'll see it through if all the fiends of the pit were loose upon the moor."

We stumbled slowly along in the darkness, with the black loom of the craggy hills around us, and the yellow speck of light burning steadily in front. There is nothing so deceptive as the distance of a light upon a pitch-dark night, and sometimes the glimmer seemed to be far away upon the horizon and sometimes it might have been within a few yards of us. But at last we could see whence it came, and then we knew that we were indeed very close. A guttering candle was stuck in a crevice of the rocks which flanked it on each side so as to keep the wind from it and also to prevent it from being visible, save in the direction of Baskerville Hall. A boulder of granite concealed our approach, and crouching behind it we gazed over it at the signal light. It was strange to see this single candle burning there in the middle of the moor, with no sign of life near it—just the one straight yellow flame and the gleam of the rock on each side of it.

"What shall we do now?" whispered Sir Henry.

"Wait here. He must be near his light. Let us see if we can get a glimpse of him."

The words were hardly out of my mouth when we both saw him. Over the rocks, in the crevice of which the candle burned, there was thrust out an evil yellow face, a terrible animal face, all seamed and scored with vile passions. Foul with mire, with a bristling beard, and hung with matted hair, it might well have belonged to one of those old savages who dwelt in the burrows on the hillsides. The light beneath him was reflected in his small, cunning eyes which peered fiercely to right and left through the darkness like a crafty and savage animal who has heard the steps of the hunters.

Something had evidently aroused his suspicions. It may have been that Barrymore had some private signal which we had neglected to give, or the fellow may have had some other reason for thinking that all was not well, but I could read his fears upon his wicked face. Any instant he might dash out the light and vanish in the darkness. I sprang forward therefore, and Sir Henry did the same. At the same moment the convict screamed out a curse at us and hurled a rock which splintered up against the boulder which had sheltered us. I caught one glimpse of his short, squat, strongly built figure as he sprang to his feet and turned to run. At the same moment by a lucky chance the moon broke through the clouds. We rushed over the brow of the hill, and there was our man running with great speed down the other side, springing over the stones in his way with the activity of a mountain goat. A lucky long shot of my revolver might have crippled him, but I had brought it only to defend myself if attacked and not to shoot an unarmed man who was running away.

We were both swift runners and in fairly good training, but we soon found that we had no chance of overtaking him. We saw him for a long time in the moonlight until he was only a small speck moving swiftly among the boulders upon the side of a distant hill. We ran and ran until we were completely blown, but the space between us grew ever wider. Finally we stopped and sat panting on two rocks, while we watched him disappearing in the distance.

And it was at this moment that there occurred a most strange and unexpected thing. We had risen from our rocks and were turning to go home, having abandoned the hopeless chase. The moon was low upon the right, and the jagged pinnacle of a granite tor stood up against the lower curve of its silver disc. There, outlined as black as an ebony statue on that shining background, I saw the figure of a man upon the tor. Do not think that it was a delusion, Holmes. I assure you that I have never in my life seen anything more clearly. As far as I could judge, the figure was that of a tall, thin man. He stood with his legs a little separated, his arms folded, his head bowed, as if he were brooding over that enormous wilderness of peat and granite which lay before him. He might have been the very spirit of that terrible place. It was not the convict. This man was far from the place where the latter had disappeared. Besides, he was a much taller man. With a cry of surprise I pointed him out to the baronet, but in the instant during which I had turned to grasp his arm the man was gone. There was the sharp pinnacle of granite still cutting the lower edge of the moon, but its peak bore no trace of that silent and motionless figure.

I wished to go in that direction and to search the tor, but it was some distance away. The baronet's nerves were still quivering from that cry, which recalled the dark story of his family, and he was not in the mood for fresh adventures. He had not seen this lonely man upon the tor and could not feel the thrill which his strange presence and his commanding attitude had given to me. "A warder, no doubt," said he. "The moor has been thick with them since this fellow escaped." Well, perhaps his explanation may be the right one, but I should like to have some further proof of it. Today we mean to communicate to the Princetown people where they should look for their missing man, but it is hard lines that we have not actually had the triumph of bringing him back as our own prisoner. Such are the adventures of last night, and you must acknowledge, my dear Holmes, that I have done you very well in the matter of a report. Much of what I tell you is no doubt quite irrelevant, but still I feel that it is best that I should let you have all the facts and leave you to select for yourself those which will be of most service to you in helping you to your conclusions. We are certainly making some progress. So far as the Barrymores go we have found the motive of their actions, and that has cleared up the situation very much. But the moor with its mysteries and its strange inhabitants remains as inscrutable as ever. Perhaps in my next I may be able to throw some light upon this also. Best of all would it be if you could come down to us. In any case you will hear from me again in the course of the next few days.

Chapter 10.

Extract from the Diary of Dr. Watson

So far I have been able to quote from the reports which I have forwarded during these early days to Sherlock Holmes. Now, however, I have arrived at a point in my narrative where I am compelled to abandon this method and to trust once more to my recollections, aided by the diary which I kept at the time. A few extracts from the latter will carry me on to those scenes which are indelibly fixed in every detail upon my memory. I proceed, then, from the morning which followed our abortive chase of the convict and our other strange experiences upon the moor.

October 16th.—A dull and foggy day with a drizzle of rain. The house is banked in with rolling clouds, which rise now and then to show the dreary curves of the moor, with thin, silver veins upon the sides of the hills, and the distant boulders gleaming where the light strikes upon their wet faces. It is melancholy outside and in. The baronet is in a black reaction after the excitements of the night. I am conscious myself of a weight at my heart and a feeling of impending danger—ever present danger, which is the more terrible because I am unable to define it.

And have I not cause for such a feeling? Consider the long sequence of incidents which have all pointed to some sinister influence which is at work around us. There is the death of the last occupant of the Hall, fulfilling so exactly the conditions of the family legend, and there are the repeated reports from peasants of the appearance of a strange creature upon the moor. Twice I have with my own ears heard the sound which resembled the distant baying of a hound. It is incredible, impossible, that it should really be outside the ordinary laws of nature. A spectral hound which leaves material footmarks and fills the air with its howling is surely not to be thought of. Stapleton may fall in with such a superstition, and Mortimer also, but if I have one quality upon earth it is common sense, and nothing will persuade me to believe in such a thing. To do so would be to descend to the level of these poor peasants, who are not content with a mere fiend dog but must needs describe him with hell-fire shooting from his mouth and eyes. Holmes would not listen to such fancies, and I am his agent. But facts are facts, and I have twice heard this crying upon the moor. Suppose that there were really some huge hound loose upon it; that would go far to explain everything. But where could such a hound lie concealed, where did it get its food, where did it come from, how was it that no one saw it by day? It must be confessed that the natural explanation offers almost as many difficulties as the other. And always, apart from the hound, there is the fact of the human agency in London, the man in the cab, and the letter which warned Sir Henry against the moor. This at least was real, but it might have been the work of a protecting friend as easily as of an enemy. Where is that friend or enemy now? Has he remained in London, or has he followed us down here? Could he—could he be the stranger whom I saw upon the tor?

It is true that I have had only the one glance at him, and yet there are some things to which I am ready to swear. He is no one whom I have seen down here, and I have now met all the neighbours. The figure was far taller than that of Stapleton, far thinner than that of Frankland. Barrymore it might possibly have been, but we had left him behind us, and I am certain that he could not have followed us. A stranger then is still dogging us, just as a stranger dogged us in London. We have never shaken him off. If I could lay my hands upon that man, then at last we might find ourselves at the end of all our difficulties. To this one purpose I must now devote all my energies.

My first impulse was to tell Sir Henry all my plans. My second and wisest one is to play my own game and speak as little as possible to anyone. He is silent and distrait. His nerves have been strangely shaken by that sound upon the moor. I will say nothing to add to his anxieties, but I will take my own steps to attain my own end.

We had a small scene this morning after breakfast. Barrymore asked leave to speak with Sir Henry, and they were closeted in his study some little time. Sitting in the billiard-room I more than once heard the sound of voices raised, and I had a pretty good idea what the point was which was under discussion. After a time the baronet opened his door and called for me. "Barrymore considers that he has a grievance," he said. "He thinks that it was unfair on our part to hunt his brother-in-law down when he, of his own free will, had told us the secret."

The butler was standing very pale but very collected before us.

"I may have spoken too warmly, sir," said he, "and if I have, I am sure that I beg your pardon. At the same time, I was very much surprised when I heard you two gentlemen come back this morning and learned that you had been chasing Selden. The poor fellow has enough to fight against without my putting more upon his track."

"If you had told us of your own free will it would have been a different thing," said the baronet, "you only told us, or rather your wife only told us, when it was forced from you and you could not help yourself."

"I didn't think you would have taken advantage of it, Sir Henry—indeed I didn't."

"The man is a public danger. There are lonely houses scattered over the moor, and he is a fellow who would stick at nothing. You only want to get a glimpse of his face to see that. Look at Mr. Stapleton's house, for example, with no one but himself to defend it. There's no safety for anyone until he is under lock and key."

"He'll break into no house, sir. I give you my solemn word upon that. But he will never trouble anyone in this country again. I assure you, Sir Henry, that in a very few days the necessary arrangements will have been made and he will be on his way to South America. For God's sake, sir, I beg of you not to let the police know that he is still on the moor. They have given up the chase there, and he can lie quiet until the ship is ready for him. You can't tell on him without getting my wife and me into trouble. I beg you, sir, to say nothing to the police."

"What do you say, Watson?"

I shrugged my shoulders. "If he were safely out of the country it would relieve the tax-payer of a burden."

"But how about the chance of his holding someone up before he goes?"

"He would not do anything so mad, sir. We have provided him with all that he can want. To commit a crime would be to show where he was hiding."

"That is true," said Sir Henry. "Well, Barrymore—"

"God bless you, sir, and thank you from my heart! It would have killed my poor wife had he been taken again."

"I guess we are aiding and abetting a felony, Watson? But, after what we have heard I don't feel as if I could give the man up, so there is an end of it. All right, Barrymore, you can go."

With a few broken words of gratitude the man turned, but he hesitated and then came back.

"You've been so kind to us, sir, that I should like to do the best I can for you in return. I know something, Sir Henry, and perhaps I should have said it before, but it was long after the inquest that I found it out. I've never breathed a word about it yet to mortal man. It's about poor Sir Charles's death."

The baronet and I were both upon our feet. "Do you know how he died?"

"No, sir, I don't know that."

"What then?"

"I know why he was at the gate at that hour. It was to meet a woman."

"To meet a woman! He?"

"Yes, sir."

"And the woman's name?"

"I can't give you the name, sir, but I can give you the initials. Her initials were L. L."

"How do you know this, Barrymore?"

"Well, Sir Henry, your uncle had a letter that morning. He had usually a great many letters, for he was a public man and well known for his kind heart, so that everyone who was in trouble was glad to turn to him. But that morning, as it chanced, there was only this one letter, so I took the more notice of it. It was from Coombe Tracey, and it was addressed in a woman's hand."

"Well?"

"Well, sir, I thought no more of the matter, and never would have done had it not been for my wife. Only a few weeks ago she was cleaning out Sir Charles's study—it had never been touched since his death—and she found the ashes of a burned letter in the back of the grate. The greater part of it was charred to pieces, but one little slip, the end of a page, hung together, and the writing could still be read, though it was grey on a black ground. It seemed to us to be a postscript at the end of the letter and it said: 'Please, please, as you are a gentleman, burn this letter, and be at the gate by ten o clock. Beneath it were signed the initials L. L."

"Have you got that slip?"

"No, sir, it crumbled all to bits after we moved it."

"Had Sir Charles received any other letters in the same writing?"

"Well, sir, I took no particular notice of his letters. I should not have noticed this one, only it happened to come alone."

"And you have no idea who L. L. is?"

"No, sir. No more than you have. But I expect if we could lay our hands upon that lady we should know more about Sir Charles's death."

"I cannot understand, Barrymore, how you came to conceal this important information."

"Well, sir, it was immediately after that our own trouble came to us. And then again, sir, we were both of us very fond of Sir Charles, as we well might be considering all that he has done for us. To rake this up couldn't help our poor master, and it's well to go carefully when there's a lady in the case. Even the best of us—"

"You thought it might injure his reputation?"

"Well, sir, I thought no good could come of it. But now you have been kind to us, and I feel as if it would be treating you unfairly not to tell you all that I know about the matter."

"Very good, Barrymore; you can go." When the butler had left us Sir Henry turned to me. "Well, Watson, what do you think of this new light?"

"It seems to leave the darkness rather blacker than before."

"So I think. But if we can only trace L. L. it should clear up the whole business. We have gained that much. We know that there is someone who has the facts if we can only find her. What do you think we should do?"

"Let Holmes know all about it at once. It will give him the

clue for which he has been seeking. I am much mistaken if it does not bring him down."

I went at once to my room and drew up my report of the morning's conversation for Holmes. It was evident to me that he had been very busy of late, for the notes which I had from Baker Street were few and short, with no comments upon the information which I had supplied and hardly any reference to my mission. No doubt his blackmailing case is absorbing all his faculties. And yet this new factor must surely arrest his attention and renew his interest. I wish that he were here.

October 17th.—All day today the rain poured down, rustling on the ivy and dripping from the eaves. I thought of the convict out upon the bleak, cold, shelterless moor. Poor devil! Whatever his crimes, he has suffered something to atone for them. And then I thought of that other one—the face in the cab, the figure against the moon. Was he also out in that deluged—the unseen watcher, the man of darkness? In the evening I put on my waterproof and I walked far upon the sodden moor, full of dark imaginings, the rain beating upon my face and the wind whistling about my ears. God help those who wander into the great mire now, for even the firm uplands are becoming a morass. I found the black tor upon which I had seen the solitary watcher, and from its craggy summit I looked out myself across the melancholy downs. Rain squalls drifted across their russet face, and the heavy, slate-coloured clouds hung low over the landscape, trailing in grey wreaths down the sides of the fantastic hills. In the distant hollow on the left, half hidden by the mist, the two thin towers of Baskerville Hall rose above the trees. They were the only signs of human life which I could see, save only those prehistoric huts which lay thickly upon the slopes of the hills. Nowhere was there any trace of that lonely man whom I had seen on the same spot two nights before.

As I walked back I was overtaken by Dr. Mortimer driving in his dog-cart over a rough moorland track which led from the outlying farmhouse of Foulmire. He has been very attentive to us, and hardly a day has passed that he has not called at the Hall to see how we were getting on. He insisted upon my climbing into his dog-cart, and he gave me a lift homeward. I found him much troubled over the disappearance of his little spaniel. It had wandered on to the moor and had never come back. I gave him such consolation as I might, but I thought of the pony on the Grimpen Mire, and I do not fancy that he will see his little dog again.

"By the way, Mortimer," said I as we jolted along the rough

road, "I suppose there are few people living within driving distance of this whom you do not know?"

"Hardly any, I think."

"Can you, then, tell me the name of any woman whose initials are L. L.?"

He thought for a few minutes.

"No," said he. "There are a few gipsies and labouring folk for whom I can't answer, but among the farmers or gentry there is no one whose initials are those. Wait a bit though," he added after a pause. "There is Laura Lyons—her initials are L. L.—but she lives in Coombe Tracey."

"Who is she?" I asked.

"She is Frankland's daughter."

"What! Old Frankland the crank?"

"Exactly. She married an artist named Lyons, who came sketching on the moor. He proved to be a blackguard and deserted her. The fault from what I hear may not have been entirely on one side. Her father refused to have anything to do with her because she had married without his consent and perhaps for one or two other reasons as well. So, between the old sinner and the young one the girl has had a pretty bad time."

"How does she live?"

"I fancy old Frankland allows her a pittance, but it cannot be more, for his own affairs are considerably involved. Whatever she may have deserved one could not allow her to go hopelessly to the bad. Her story got about, and several of the people here did something to enable her to earn an honest living. Stapleton did for one, and Sir Charles for another. I gave a trifle myself. It was to set her up in a typewriting business."

He wanted to know the object of my inquiries, but I managed to satisfy his curiosity without telling him too much, for there is no reason why we should take anyone into our confidence. Tomorrow morning I shall find my way to Coombe Tracey, and if I can see this Mrs. Laura Lyons, of equivocal reputation, a long step will have been made towards clearing one incident in this chain of mysteries. I am certainly developing the wisdom of the serpent, for when Mortimer pressed his questions to an inconvenient extent I asked him casually to what type Frankland's skull belonged, and so heard nothing but craniology for the rest of our drive. I have not lived for years with Sherlock Holmes for nothing.

I have only one other incident to record upon this tempestuous and melancholy day. This was my conversation with Barrymore just now, which gives me one more strong card which I can play in due time.

Mortimer had stayed to dinner, and he and the baronet played écarté afterwards. The butler brought me my coffee into the library, and I took the chance to ask him a few questions.

"Well," said I, "has this precious relation of yours departed, or is he still lurking out yonder?"

"I don't know, sir. I hope to heaven that he has gone, for he has brought nothing but trouble here! I've not heard of him since I left out food for him last, and that was three days ago."

"Did you see him then?"

"No, sir, but the food was gone when next I went that way."

"Then he was certainly there?"

"So you would think, sir, unless it was the other man who took it."

I sat with my coffee-cup halfway to my lips and stared at Barrymore.

"You know that there is another man then?"

"Yes, sir; there is another man upon the moor."

"Have you seen him?"

"No, sir."

"How do you know of him then?"

"Selden told me of him, sir, a week ago or more. He's in hiding, too, but he's not a convict as far as I can make out. I don't like it, Dr. Watson—I tell you straight, sir, that I don't like it." He spoke with a sudden passion of earnestness.

"Now, listen to me, Barrymore! I have no interest in this matter but that of your master. I have come here with no object except to help him. Tell me, frankly, what it is that you don't like."

Barrymore hesitated for a moment, as if he regretted his outburst or found it difficult to express his own feelings in words.

"It's all these goings-on, sir," he cried at last, waving his hand towards the rain-lashed window which faced the moor. "There's foul play somewhere, and there's black villainy brewing, to that I'll swear! Very glad I should be, sir, to see Sir Henry on his way back to London again!"

"But what is it that alarms you?"

"Look at Sir Charles's death! That was bad enough, for all that the coroner said. Look at the noises on the moor at night. There's not a man would cross it after sundown if he was paid for it. Look at this stranger hiding out yonder, and watching and waiting! What's he waiting for? What does it mean? It means no good to anyone of the name of Baskerville, and very glad I shall be to be quit of it all on the day that Sir Henry's new servants are ready to take over the Hall."

"But about this stranger," said I. "Can you tell me anything about him? What did Selden say? Did he find out where he hid, or what he was doing?"

"He saw him once or twice, but he is a deep one and gives nothing away. At first he thought that he was the police, but soon he found that he had some lay of his own. A kind of gentleman he was, as far as he could see, but what he was doing he could not make out."

"And where did he say that he lived?"

"Among the old houses on the hillside—the stone huts where the old folk used to live."

"But how about his food?"

"Selden found out that he has got a lad who works for him and brings all he needs. I dare say he goes to Coombe Tracey for what he wants."

"Very good, Barrymore. We may talk further of this some

other time." When the butler had gone I walked over to the black window, and I looked through a blurred pane at the driving clouds and at the tossing outline of the wind-swept trees. It is a wild night indoors, and what must it be in a stone hut upon the moor. What passion of hatred can it be which leads a man to lurk in such a place at such a time! And what deep and earnest purpose can he have which calls for such a trial! There, in that hut upon the moor, seems to lie the very centre of that problem which has vexed me so sorely. I swear that another day shall not have passed before I have done all that man can do to reach the heart of the mystery.

Chapter 11.

The Man on the Tor

The extract from my private diary which forms the last chapter has brought my narrative up to the eighteenth of October, a time when these strange events began to move swiftly towards their terrible conclusion. The incidents of the next few days are indelibly graven upon my recollection, and I can tell them without reference to the notes made at the time. I start them from the day which succeeded that upon which I had established two facts of great importance, the one that Mrs. Laura Lyons of Coombe Tracey had written to Sir Charles Baskerville and made an appointment with him at the very place and hour that he met his death, the other that the lurking man upon the moor was to be found among the stone huts upon the hillside. With these two facts in my possession I felt that either my intelligence or my courage must be deficient if I could not throw some further light upon these dark places.

I had no opportunity to tell the baronet what I had learned about Mrs. Lyons upon the evening before, for Dr. Mortimer remained with him at cards until it was very late. At breakfast, however, I informed him about my discovery and asked him whether he would care to accompany me to Coombe Tracey. At first he was very eager to come, but on second thoughts it seemed to both of us that if I went alone the results might be better. The more formal we made the visit the less information we might obtain. I left Sir Henry behind, therefore, not without some prickings of conscience, and drove off upon my new quest.

When I reached Coombe Tracey I told Perkins to put up the horses, and I made inquiries for the lady whom I had come to interrogate. I had no difficulty in finding her rooms, which were central and well appointed. A maid showed me in without ceremony, and as I entered the sitting-room a lady, who was sitting before a Remington typewriter, sprang up with a pleasant smile of welcome. Her face fell, however, when she saw that I was a stranger, and she sat down again and asked me the object of my visit.

The first impression left by Mrs. Lyons was one of extreme beauty. Her eyes and hair were of the same rich hazel colour, and her cheeks, though considerably freckled, were flushed with the exquisite bloom of the brunette, the dainty pink which lurks at the heart of the sulphur rose. Admiration was, I repeat, the first impression. But the second was criticism. There was something subtly wrong with the face, some coarseness of expression, some hardness, perhaps, of eye, some looseness of lip which marred its perfect beauty. But these, of course, are afterthoughts. At the moment I was simply conscious that I was in the presence of a very handsome woman, and that she was asking me the reasons for my visit. I had not quite understood until that instant how delicate my mission was.

"I have the pleasure," said I, "of knowing your father."

It was a clumsy introduction, and the lady made me feel it. "There is nothing in common between my father and me," she said. "I owe him nothing, and his friends are not mine. If it were not for the late Sir Charles Baskerville and some other kind hearts I might have starved for all that my father cared."

"It was about the late Sir Charles Baskerville that I have come here to see you."

The freckles started out on the lady's face.

"What can I tell you about him?" she asked, and her fingers played nervously over the stops of her typewriter.

"You knew him, did you not?"

"I have already said that I owe a great deal to his kindness. If I am able to support myself it is largely due to the interest which he took in my unhappy situation."

"Did you correspond with him?"

The lady looked quickly up with an angry gleam in her hazel eyes.

"What is the object of these questions?" she asked sharply.

"The object is to avoid a public scandal. It is better that I should ask them here than that the matter should pass outside our control."

She was silent and her face was still very pale. At last she looked up with something reckless and defiant in her manner.

"Well, I'll answer," she said. "What are your questions?"

"Did you correspond with Sir Charles?"

"I certainly wrote to him once or twice to acknowledge his delicacy and his generosity."

"Have you the dates of those letters?"

"No."

"Have you ever met him?"

"Yes, once or twice, when he came into Coombe Tracey. He was a very retiring man, and he preferred to do good by stealth."

"But if you saw him so seldom and wrote so seldom, how did he know enough about your affairs to be able to help you, as you say that he has done?"

She met my difficulty with the utmost readiness.

"There were several gentlemen who knew my sad history and united to help me. One was Mr. Stapleton, a neighbour and intimate friend of Sir Charles's. He was exceedingly kind, and it was through him that Sir Charles learned about my affairs."

I knew already that Sir Charles Baskerville had made Stapleton his almoner upon several occasions, so the lady's statement bore the impress of truth upon it.

"Did you ever write to Sir Charles asking him to meet you?" I continued.

Mrs. Lyons flushed with anger again. "Really, sir, this is a very extraordinary question."

"I am sorry, madam, but I must repeat it."

"Then I answer, certainly not."

"Not on the very day of Sir Charles's death?"

The flush had faded in an instant, and a deathly face was before me. Her dry lips could not speak the "No" which I saw rather than heard.

"Surely your memory deceives you," said I. "I could even quote a passage of your letter. It ran 'Please, please, as you are a gentleman, burn this letter, and be at the gate by ten o'clock.'"

I thought that she had fainted, but she recovered herself by a supreme effort.

"Is there no such thing as a gentleman?" she gasped.

"You do Sir Charles an injustice. He did burn the letter. But sometimes a letter may be legible even when burned. You acknowledge now that you wrote it?"

"Yes, I did write it," she cried, pouring out her soul in a torrent of words. "I did write it. Why should I deny it? I have no reason to be ashamed of it. I wished him to help me. I believed that if I had an interview I could gain his help, so I asked him to meet me."

"But why at such an hour?"

"Because I had only just learned that he was going to London next day and might be away for months. There were reasons why I could not get there earlier."

"But why a rendezvous in the garden instead of a visit to the house?"

"Do you think a woman could go alone at that hour to a bachelor's house?"

"Well, what happened when you did get there?"

"I never went."

"Mrs. Lyons!"

"No, I swear it to you on all I hold sacred. I never went. Something intervened to prevent my going."

"What was that?"

"That is a private matter. I cannot tell it."

"You acknowledge then that you made an appointment with Sir Charles at the very hour and place at which he met his death, but you deny that you kept the appointment."

"That is the truth."

Again and again I cross-questioned her, but I could never get past that point.

"Mrs. Lyons," said I as I rose from this long and inconclusive interview, "you are taking a very great responsibility and putting yourself in a very false position by not making an absolutely clean breast of all that you know. If I have to call in the aid of the police you will find how seriously you are compromised. If your position is innocent, why did you in the first instance deny having written to Sir Charles upon that date?"

"Because I feared that some false conclusion might be drawn from it and that I might find myself involved in a scandal."

"And why were you so pressing that Sir Charles should destroy your letter?"

"If you have read the letter you will know."

"I did not say that I had read all the letter."

"You quoted some of it."

"I quoted the postscript. The letter had, as I said, been burned and it was not all legible. I ask you once again why it was that you were so pressing that Sir Charles should destroy this letter which he received on the day of his death."

"The matter is a very private one."

"The more reason why you should avoid a public investigation."

"I will tell you, then. If you have heard anything of my unhappy history you will know that I made a rash marriage and had reason to regret it."

"I have heard so much."

"My life has been one incessant persecution from a husband whom I abhor. The law is upon his side, and every day I am faced by the possibility that he may force me to live with him. At the time that I wrote this letter to Sir Charles I had learned that there was a prospect of my regaining my freedom if certain expenses could be met. It meant everything to me—peace of mind, happiness, self-respect—everything. I knew Sir Charles's generosity, and I thought that if he heard the story from my own lips he would help me."

"Then how is it that you did not go?"

"Because I received help in the interval from another source."

"Why then, did you not write to Sir Charles and explain this?"

"So I should have done had I not seen his death in the paper next morning."

The woman's story hung coherently together, and all my questions were unable to shake it. I could only check it by finding if she had, indeed, instituted divorce proceedings against her husband at or about the time of the tragedy.

It was unlikely that she would dare to say that she had not been to Baskerville Hall if she really had been, for a trap would be necessary to take her there, and could not have returned to Coombe Tracey until the early hours of the morning. Such an excursion could not be kept secret. The probability was, therefore, that she was telling the truth, or, at least, a part of the truth. I came away baffled and disheartened. Once again I had reached that dead wall which seemed to be built across every path by which I tried to get at the object of my mission. And yet the more I thought of the lady's face and of her manner the more I felt that something was being held back from me. Why should she turn so pale? Why should she fight against every admission until it was forced from her? Why should she have been so reticent at the time of the tragedy? Surely the explanation of all this could not be as innocent as she would have me believe. For the moment I could proceed no farther in that direction, but must turn back to that other clue which was to be sought for among the stone huts upon the moor.

And that was a most vague direction. I realised it as I drove back and noted how hill after hill showed traces of the ancient people. Barrymore's only indication had been that the stranger lived in one of these abandoned huts, and many hundreds of them are scattered throughout the length and breadth of the moor. But I had my own experience for a guide since it had shown me the man himself standing upon the summit of the Black Tor. That, then, should be the centre of my search. From there I should explore every hut upon the moor until I lighted upon the right one. If this man were inside it I should find out from his own lips, at the point of my revolver if necessary, who he was and why he had dogged us so long. He might slip away from us in the crowd of Regent Street, but it would puzzle him to do so upon the lonely moor. On the other hand, if I should find the hut and its tenant should not be within it I must remain there, however long the vigil, until he returned. Holmes had missed him in London. It would indeed be a triumph for me if I could run him to earth where my master had failed.

Luck had been against us again and again in this inquiry, but now at last it came to my aid. And the messenger of good fortune was none other than Mr. Frankland, who was standing, grey-whiskered and red-faced, outside the gate of his garden, which opened on to the highroad along which I travelled.

"Good-day, Dr. Watson," cried he with unwonted good humour, "you must really give your horses a rest and come in to have a glass of wine and to congratulate me."

My feelings towards him were very far from being friendly after what I had heard of his treatment of his daughter, but I was anxious to send Perkins and the wagonette home, and the opportunity was a good one. I alighted and sent a message to Sir Henry that I should walk over in time for dinner. Then I followed Frankland into his dining-room.

"It is a great day for me, sir—one of the red-letter days of my life," he cried with many chuckles. "I have brought off a double event. I mean to teach them in these parts that law is law, and that there is a man here who does not fear to invoke it. I have established a right of way through the centre of old Middleton's park, slap across it, sir, within a hundred yards of his own front door. What do you think of that? We'll teach these magnates that they cannot ride roughshod over the rights of the commoners, confound them! And I've closed the wood where the Fernworthy folk used to picnic. These infernal people seem to think that there are no rights of property, and that they can swarm where they like with their papers and their bottles. Both cases decided, Dr. Watson, and both in my favour. I haven't had such a day since I had Sir John Morland for trespass because he shot in his own warren."

"How on earth did you do that?"

"Look it up in the books, sir. It will repay reading—Frankland v. Morland, Court of Queen's Bench. It cost me £200, but I got my verdict."

"Did it do you any good?"

"None, sir, none. I am proud to say that I had no interest in the matter. I act entirely from a sense of public duty. I have no doubt, for example, that the Fernworthy people will burn me in effigy tonight. I told the police last time they did it that they should stop these disgraceful exhibitions. The County Constabulary is in a scandalous state, sir, and it has not afforded me the protection to which I am entitled. The case of Frankland v. Regina will bring the matter before the attention of the public. I told them that they would have occasion to regret their treatment of me, and already my words have come true."

"How so?" I asked.

The old man put on a very knowing expression. "Because I could tell them what they are dying to know; but nothing would induce me to help the rascals in any way."

I had been casting round for some excuse by which I could get away from his gossip, but now I began to wish to hear more of it. I had seen enough of the contrary nature of the old sinner to understand that any strong sign of interest would be the surest way to stop his confidences.

"Some poaching case, no doubt?" said I with an indifferent manner.

"Ha, ha, my boy, a very much more important matter than that! What about the convict on the moor?"

I stared. "You don't mean that you know where he is?" said I.

"I may not know exactly where he is, but I am quite sure that I could help the police to lay their hands on him. Has it never struck you that the way to catch that man was to find out where he got his food and so trace it to him?"

He certainly seemed to be getting uncomfortably near the truth. "No doubt," said I; "but how do you know that he is anywhere upon the moor?"

"I know it because I have seen with my own eyes the messenger who takes him his food."

My heart sank for Barrymore. It was a serious thing to be in the power of this spiteful old busybody. But his next remark took a weight from my mind.

"You'll be surprised to hear that his food is taken to him by a child. I see him every day through my telescope upon the roof. He passes along the same path at the same hour, and to whom should he be going except to the convict?"

Here was luck indeed! And yet I suppressed all appearance of interest. A child! Barrymore had said that our unknown was supplied by a boy. It was on his track, and not upon the convict's, that Frankland had stumbled. If I could get his knowledge it might save me a long and weary hunt. But incredulity and indifference were evidently my strongest cards.

"I should say that it was much more likely that it was the son of one of the moorland shepherds taking out his father's dinner."

The least appearance of opposition struck fire out of the old autocrat. His eyes looked malignantly at me, and his grey whiskers bristled like those of an angry cat.

"Indeed, sir!" said he, pointing out over the wide-stretching moor. "Do you see that Black Tor over yonder? Well, do you see the low hill beyond with the thornbush upon it? It is the stoniest part of the whole moor. Is that a place where a shepherd would be likely to take his station? Your suggestion, sir, is a most absurd one."

I meekly answered that I had spoken without knowing all the facts. My submission pleased him and led him to further confidences.

"You may be sure, sir, that I have very good grounds before I come to an opinion. I have seen the boy again and again with his bundle. Every day, and sometimes twice a day, I have been able—but wait a moment, Dr. Watson. Do my eyes deceive me, or is there at the present moment something moving upon that hillside?"

It was several miles off, but I could distinctly see a small dark dot against the dull green and grey.

"Come, sir, come!" cried Frankland, rushing upstairs. "You will see with your own eyes and judge for yourself."

The telescope, a formidable instrument mounted upon a tripod, stood upon the flat leads of the house. Frankland clapped his eye to it and gave a cry of satisfaction.

"Quick, Dr. Watson, quick, before he passes over the hill!"

There he was, sure enough, a small urchin with a little

bundle upon his shoulder, toiling slowly up the hill. When he reached the crest I saw the ragged uncouth figure outlined for an instant against the cold blue sky. He looked round him with a furtive and stealthy air, as one who dreads pursuit. Then he vanished over the hill.

"Well! Am I right?"

"Certainly, there is a boy who seems to have some secret errand."

"And what the errand is even a county constable could guess. But not one word shall they have from me, and I bind you to secrecy also, Dr. Watson. Not a word! You understand!"

"Just as you wish."

"They have treated me shamefully—shamefully. When the facts come out in Frankland v. Regina I venture to think that a thrill of indignation will run through the country. Nothing would induce me to help the police in any way. For all they cared it might have been me, instead of my effigy, which these rascals burned at the stake. Surely you are not going! You will help me to empty the decanter in honour of this great occasion!"

But I resisted all his solicitations and succeeded in dissuading him from his announced intention of walking home with me. I kept the road as long as his eye was on me, and then I struck off across the moor and made for the stony hill over which the boy had disappeared. Everything was working in my favour, and I swore that it should not be through lack of energy or perseverance that I should miss the chance which fortune had thrown in my way.

The sun was already sinking when I reached the summit of the hill, and the long slopes beneath me were all golden-green on one side and grey shadow on the other. A haze lay low upon the farthest sky-line, out of which jutted the fantastic shapes of Belliver and Vixen Tor. Over the wide expanse there was no sound and no movement. One great grey bird, a gull or curlew, soared aloft in the blue heaven. He and I seemed to be the only living things between the huge arch of the sky and the desert beneath it. The barren scene, the sense of loneliness, and the mystery and urgency of my task all struck a chill into my heart. The boy was nowhere to be seen. But down beneath me in a cleft of the hills there was a circle of the old stone huts, and in the middle of them there was one which retained sufficient roof to act as a screen against the weather. My heart leaped within me as I saw it. This must be the burrow where the stranger lurked. At last my foot was on the threshold of his hiding place—his secret was within my grasp.

As I approached the hut, walking as warily as Stapleton would do when with poised net he drew near the settled butterfly, I satisfied myself that the place had indeed been used as a habitation. A vague pathway among the boulders led to the dilapidated opening which served as a door. All was silent within. The unknown might be lurking there, or he might be prowling on the moor. My nerves tingled with the sense of adventure. Throwing aside my cigarette, I closed my hand upon the butt of my revolver and, walking swiftly up to the door, I looked in. The place was empty.

But there were ample signs that I had not come upon a false scent. This was certainly where the man lived. Some blankets rolled in a waterproof lay upon that very stone slab upon which Neolithic man had once slumbered. The ashes of a fire were heaped in a rude grate. Beside it lay some cooking utensils and a bucket half-full of water. A litter of empty tins showed that the place had been occupied for some time, and I saw, as my eyes became accustomed to the checkered light, a pannikin and a half-full bottle of spirits standing in the corner. In the middle of the hut a flat stone served the purpose of a table, and upon this stood a small cloth bundle—the same, no doubt, which I had seen through the telescope upon the shoulder of the boy. It contained a loaf of bread, a tinned tongue, and two tins of preserved peaches. As I set it down again, after having examined it, my heart leaped to see that beneath it there lay a sheet of paper with writing upon it. I raised it, and this was what I read, roughly scrawled in pencil: "Dr. Watson has gone to Coombe Tracey."

For a minute I stood there with the paper in my hands thinking out the meaning of this curt message. It was I, then, and not Sir Henry, who was being dogged by this secret man. He had not followed me himself, but he had set an agent—the boy, perhaps—upon my track, and this was his report. Possibly I had taken no step since I had been upon the moor which had not been observed and reported. Always there was this feeling of an unseen force, a fine net drawn round us with infinite skill and delicacy, holding us so lightly that it was only at some supreme moment that one realised that one was indeed entangled in its meshes.

If there was one report there might be others, so I looked round the hut in search of them. There was no trace, however, of anything of the kind, nor could I discover any sign which might indicate the character or intentions of the man who lived in this singular place, save that he must be of Spartan habits and cared little for the comforts of life. When I thought of the heavy rains and looked at the gaping roof I understood how strong and immutable must be the purpose which had kept him in that inhospitable abode. Was he our malignant enemy, or was he by chance our guardian angel? I swore that I would not leave the hut until I knew.

Outside the sun was sinking low and the west was blazing with scarlet and gold. Its reflection was shot back in ruddy patches by the distant pools which lay amid the great Grimpen Mire. There were the two towers of Baskerville Hall, and there a distant blur of smoke which marked the village of Grimpen. Between the two, behind the hill, was the house of the Stapletons. All was sweet and mellow and peaceful in the golden evening light, and yet as I looked at them my soul shared none of the peace of Nature but quivered at the vagueness and the terror of that interview which every instant was bringing nearer. With tingling nerves but a fixed purpose, I sat in the dark recess of the hut and waited with sombre patience for the coming of its tenant.

And then at last I heard him. Far away came the sharp clink of a boot striking upon a stone. Then another and yet another, coming nearer and nearer. I shrank back into the darkest corner and cocked the pistol in my pocket, determined not to discover myself until I had an opportunity of seeing something of the stranger. There was a long pause which showed that he had stopped. Then once more the footsteps approached and a shadow fell across the opening of the hut.

"It is a lovely evening, my dear Watson," said a well-known voice. "I really think that you will be more comfortable outside than in."

Chapter 12.

Death on the Moor

For a moment or two I sat breathless, hardly able to believe my ears. Then my senses and my voice came back to me, while a crushing weight of responsibility seemed in an instant to be lifted from my soul. That cold, incisive, ironical voice could belong to but one man in all the world.

"Holmes!" I cried—"Holmes!"

"Come out," said he, "and please be careful with the revolver."

I stooped under the rude lintel, and there he sat upon a stone outside, his grey eyes dancing with amusement as they fell upon my astonished features. He was thin and worn, but clear and alert, his keen face bronzed by the sun and roughened by the wind. In his tweed suit and cloth cap he looked like any other tourist upon the moor, and he had contrived, with that catlike love of personal cleanliness which was one of his characteristics, that his chin should be as smooth and his linen as perfect as if he were in Baker Street.

"I never was more glad to see anyone in my life," said I as I wrung him by the hand.

"Or more astonished, eh?"

"Well, I must confess to it."

"The surprise was not all on one side, I assure you. I had no idea that you had found my occasional retreat, still less that you were inside it, until I was within twenty paces of the door."

"My footprint, I presume?"

"No, Watson, I fear that I could not undertake to recognize your footprint amid all the footprints of the world. If you seriously desire to deceive me you must change your tobacconist; for when I see the stub of a cigarette marked Bradley, Oxford Street, I know that my friend Watson is in the neighbourhood. You will see it there beside the path. You threw it down, no doubt, at that supreme moment when you charged into the empty hut."

"Exactly."

"I thought as much—and knowing your admirable tenacity I was convinced that you were sitting in ambush, a weapon within reach, waiting for the tenant to return. So you actually thought that I was the criminal?"

"I did not know who you were, but I was determined to find out."

"Excellent, Watson! And how did you localise me? You saw me, perhaps, on the night of the convict hunt, when I was so imprudent as to allow the moon to rise behind me?"

"Yes, I saw you then."

"And have no doubt searched all the huts until you came to this one?"

"No, your boy had been observed, and that gave me a guide where to look."

"The old gentleman with the telescope, no doubt. I could not make it out when first I saw the light flashing upon the lens." He rose and peeped into the hut. "Ha, I see that Cartwright has brought up some supplies. What's this paper? So you have been to Coombe Tracey, have you?"

"Yes."

"To see Mrs. Laura Lyons?"

"Exactly."

"Well done! Our researches have evidently been running on parallel lines, and when we unite our results I expect we shall have a fairly full knowledge of the case."

"Well, I am glad from my heart that you are here, for indeed the responsibility and the mystery were both becoming too much for my nerves. But how in the name of wonder did you come here, and what have you been doing? I thought that you were in Baker Street working out that case of blackmailing."

"That was what I wished you to think."

"Then you use me, and yet do not trust me!" I cried with some bitterness. "I think that I have deserved better at your hands, Holmes."

"My dear fellow, you have been invaluable to me in this as in many other cases, and I beg that you will forgive me if I have seemed to play a trick upon you. In truth, it was partly for your own sake that I did it, and it was my appreciation of the danger which you ran which led me to come down and examine the matter for myself. Had I been with Sir Henry and you it is confident that my point of view would have been the same as yours, and my presence would have warned our very formidable opponents to be on their guard. As it is, I have been able to get about as I could not possibly have done had I been living in the Hall, and I remain an unknown factor in the business, ready to throw in all my weight at a critical moment."

"But why keep me in the dark?"

"For you to know could not have helped us and might possibly have led to my discovery. You would have wished to tell me something, or in your kindness you would have brought me out some comfort or other, and so an unnecessary risk would be run. I brought Cartwright down with me—you remember the little chap at the express office—and he has seen after my simple wants: a loaf of bread and a clean collar. What does man want more? He has given me an extra pair of eyes upon a very active pair of feet, and both have been invaluable."

"Then my reports have all been wasted!"—My voice trembled as I recalled the pains and the pride with which I had composed them.

Holmes took a bundle of papers from his pocket.

"Here are your reports, my dear fellow, and very well thumbed, I assure you. I made excellent arrangements, and they are only delayed one day upon their way. I must compliment you exceedingly upon the zeal and the intelligence which you have shown over an extraordinarily difficult case."

I was still rather raw over the deception which had been practised upon me, but the warmth of Holmes's praise drove my anger from my mind. I felt also in my heart that he was right in what he said and that it was really best for our purpose that I should not have known that he was upon the moor.

"That's better," said he, seeing the shadow rise from my face. "And now tell me the result of your visit to Mrs. Laura Lyons—it was not difficult for me to guess that it was to see her that you had gone, for I am already aware that she is the one person in Coombe Tracey who might be of service to us in the matter. In fact, if you had not gone today it is exceedingly probable that I should have gone tomorrow."

The sun had set and dusk was settling over the moor. The air had turned chill and we withdrew into the hut for warmth. There, sitting together in the twilight, I told Holmes of my conversation with the lady. So interested was he that I had to repeat some of it twice before he was satisfied.

"This is most important," said he when I had concluded. "It fills up a gap which I had been unable to bridge in this most complex affair. You are aware, perhaps, that a close intimacy exists between this lady and the man Stapleton?"

"I did not know of a close intimacy."

"There can be no doubt about the matter. They meet, they write, there is a complete understanding between them. Now, this puts a very powerful weapon into our hands. If I could only use it to detach his wife—"

"His wife?"

"I am giving you some information now, in return for all that you have given me. The lady who has passed here as Miss Stapleton is in reality his wife."

"Good heavens, Holmes! Are you sure of what you say? How could he have permitted Sir Henry to fall in love with her?"

"Sir Henry's falling in love could do no harm to anyone except Sir Henry. He took particular care that Sir Henry did not make love to her, as you have yourself observed. I repeat that the lady is his wife and not his sister."

"But why this elaborate deception?"

"Because he foresaw that she would be very much more useful to him in the character of a free woman."

All my unspoken instincts, my vague suspicions, suddenly took shape and centred upon the naturalist. In that impassive colourless man, with his straw hat and his butterfly-net, I seemed to see something terrible—a creature of infinite patience and craft, with a smiling face and a murderous heart.

"It is he, then, who is our enemy—it is he who dogged us in

London?"

"So I read the riddle."

"And the warning—it must have come from her!"

"Exactly."

The shape of some monstrous villainy, half seen, half guessed, loomed through the darkness which had girt me so long.

"But are you sure of this, Holmes? How do you know that the woman is his wife?"

"Because he so far forgot himself as to tell you a true piece of autobiography upon the occasion when he first met you, and I dare say he has many a time regretted it since. He was once a schoolmaster in the north of England. Now, there is no one more easy to trace than a schoolmaster. There are scholastic agencies by which one may identify any man who has been in the profession. A little investigation showed me that a school had come to grief under atrocious circumstances, and that the man who had owned it—the name was different—had disappeared with his wife. The descriptions agreed. When I learned that the missing man was devoted to entomology the identification was complete."

The darkness was rising, but much was still hidden by the shadows.

"If this woman is in truth his wife, where does Mrs. Laura Lyons come in?" I asked.

"That is one of the points upon which your own researches have shed a light. Your interview with the lady has cleared the situation very much. I did not know about a projected divorce between herself and her husband. In that case, regarding Stapleton as an unmarried man, she counted no doubt upon becoming his wife."

"And when she is undeceived?"

"Why, then we may find the lady of service. It must be our first duty to see her—both of us—tomorrow. Don't you think, Watson, that you are away from your charge rather long? Your place should be at Baskerville Hall."

The last red streaks had faded away in the west and night had settled upon the moor. A few faint stars were gleaming in a violet sky.

"One last question, Holmes," I said as I rose. "Surely there is no need of secrecy between you and me. What is the meaning of it all? What is he after?"

Holmes's voice sank as he answered:

"It is murder, Watson—refined, cold-blooded, deliberate murder. Do not ask me for particulars. My nets are closing upon him, even as his are upon Sir Henry, and with your help he is already almost at my mercy. There is but one danger which can threaten us. It is that he should strike before we are ready to do so. Another day—two at the most—and I have my case complete, but until then guard your charge as closely as ever a fond mother watched her ailing child. Your mission today has justified itself, and yet I could almost wish that you had not left his side. Hark!"

A terrible scream—a prolonged yell of horror and anguish—burst out of the silence of the moor. That frightful cry turned the blood to ice in my veins.

"Oh, my God!" I gasped. "What is it? What does it mean?"

Holmes had sprung to his feet, and I saw his dark, athletic outline at the door of the hut, his shoulders stooping, his head thrust forward, his face peering into the darkness.

"Hush!" he whispered. "Hush!"

The cry had been loud on account of its vehemence, but it had pealed out from somewhere far off on the shadowy plain. Now it burst upon our ears, nearer, louder, more urgent than before.

"Where is it?" Holmes whispered; and I knew from the thrill of his voice that he, the man of iron, was shaken to the soul. "Where is it, Watson?"

"There, I think." I pointed into the darkness.

"No, there!"

Again the agonised cry swept through the silent night, louder and much nearer than ever. And a new sound mingled with it, a deep, muttered rumble, musical and yet menacing, rising and falling like the low, constant murmur of the sea.

"The hound!" cried Holmes. "Come, Watson, come! Great heavens, if we are too late!"

He had started running swiftly over the moor, and I had followed at his heels. But now from somewhere among the broken ground immediately in front of us there came one last despairing yell, and then a dull, heavy thud. We halted and listened. Not another sound broke the heavy silence of the windless night.

I saw Holmes put his hand to his forehead like a man distracted. He stamped his feet upon the ground.

"He has beaten us, Watson. We are too late."

"No, no, surely not!"

"Fool that I was to hold my hand. And you, Watson, see what comes of abandoning your charge! But, by Heaven, if the worst has happened we'll avenge him!"

Blindly we ran through the gloom, blundering against boulders, forcing our way through gorse bushes, panting up hills and rushing down slopes, heading always in the direction whence those dreadful sounds had come. At every rise Holmes looked eagerly round him, but the shadows were thick upon the moor, and nothing moved upon its dreary face.

"Can you see anything?"

"Nothing."

"But, hark, what is that?"

A low moan had fallen upon our ears. There it was again upon our left! On that side a ridge of rocks ended in a sheer cliff which overlooked a stone-strewn slope. On its jagged face was spread-eagled some dark, irregular object. As we ran towards it the vague outline hardened into a definite shape. It was a prostrate man face downward upon the ground, the head doubled under him at a horrible angle, the shoulders rounded and the body hunched together as if in the act of throwing a somersault. So grotesque was the attitude that I could not for the instant realise that that moan had been the passing of his soul. Not a whisper, not a rustle, rose now from the dark figure over which we stooped. Holmes laid his hand upon him and held it up again with an exclamation of horror. The gleam of the match which he struck shone upon his clotted fingers and upon the ghastly pool which widened slowly from the crushed skull of the victim. And it shone upon something else which turned our hearts sick and faint within us—the body of Sir Henry Baskerville!

There was no chance of either of us forgetting that peculiar ruddy tweed suit—the very one which he had worn on the first morning that we had seen him in Baker Street. We caught the one clear glimpse of it, and then the match flickered and went out, even as the hope had gone out of our souls. Holmes groaned, and his face glimmered white through the darkness.

"The brute! The brute!" I cried with clenched hands. "Oh Holmes, I shall never forgive myself for having left him to his fate."

"I am more to blame than you, Watson. In order to have my case well rounded and complete, I have thrown away the life of my client. It is the greatest blow which has befallen me in my career. But how could I know—how could I know—that he would risk his life alone upon the moor in the face of all my warnings?"

"That we should have heard his screams—my God, those screams!—and yet have been unable to save him! Where is this brute of a hound which drove him to his death? It may be lurking among these rocks at this instant. And Stapleton, where is he? He shall answer for this deed."

"He shall. I will see to that. Uncle and nephew have been murdered—the one frightened to death by the very sight of a beast which he thought to be supernatural, the other driven to his end in his wild flight to escape from it. But now we have to prove the connection between the man and the beast. Save from what we heard, we cannot even swear to the existence of the latter, since Sir Henry has evidently died from the fall. But, by heavens, cunning as he is, the fellow shall be in my power before another day is past!"

We stood with bitter hearts on either side of the mangled body, overwhelmed by this sudden and irrevocable disaster which had brought all our long and weary labours to so piteous an end. Then as the moon rose we climbed to the top of the rocks over which our poor friend had fallen, and from the summit we gazed out over the shadowy moor, half silver and half gloom. Far away, miles off, in the direction of Grimpen, a single steady yellow light was shining. It could only come from the lonely abode of the Stapletons. With a bitter curse I shook my fist at it as I gazed.

"Why should we not seize him at once?"

"Our case is not complete. The fellow is wary and cunning to the last degree. It is not what we know, but what we can prove. If we make one false move the villain may escape us yet."

"What can we do?"

"There will be plenty for us to do tomorrow. Tonight we can only perform the last offices to our poor friend."

Together we made our way down the precipitous slope and approached the body, black and clear against the silvered stones. The agony of those contorted limbs struck me with a spasm of pain and blurred my eyes with tears.

"We must send for help, Holmes! We cannot carry him all the way to the Hall. Good heavens, are you mad?"

He had uttered a cry and bent over the body. Now he was dancing and laughing and wringing my hand. Could this be my stern, self-contained friend? These were hidden fires, indeed!

"A beard! A beard! The man has a beard!"

"A beard?"

"It is not the baronet—it is—why, it is my neighbour, the convict!"

With feverish haste we had turned the body over, and that dripping beard was pointing up to the cold, clear moon. There could be no doubt about the beetling forehead, the sunken animal eyes. It was indeed the same face which had glared upon me in the light of the candle from over the rock—the face of Selden, the criminal.

Then in an instant it was all clear to me. I remembered how the baronet had told me that he had handed his old wardrobe to Barrymore. Barrymore had passed it on in order to help Selden in his escape. Boots, shirt, cap—it was all Sir Henry's. The tragedy was still black enough, but this man had at least deserved death by the laws of his country. I told Holmes how the matter stood, my heart bubbling over with thankfulness and joy.

"Then the clothes have been the poor devil's death," said he. "It is clear enough that the hound has been laid on from some article of Sir Henry's—the boot which was abstracted in the hotel, in all probability—and so ran this man down. There is one very singular thing, however: How came Selden, in the darkness, to know that the hound was on his trail?"

"He heard him."

"To hear a hound upon the moor would not work a hard man like this convict into such a paroxysm of terror that he would risk recapture by screaming wildly for help. By his cries he must have run a long way after he knew the animal was on his track. How did he know?"

"A greater mystery to me is why this hound, presuming that all our conjectures are correct—"

"I presume nothing."

"Well, then, why this hound should be loose tonight. I suppose that it does not always run loose upon the moor. Stapleton would not let it go unless he had reason to think that Sir Henry would be there."

"My difficulty is the more formidable of the two, for I think that we shall very shortly get an explanation of yours, while mine may remain forever a mystery. The question now is, what shall we do with this poor wretch's body? We cannot leave it here to the foxes and the ravens."

"I suggest that we put it in one of the huts until we can communicate with the police."

"Exactly. I have no doubt that you and I could carry it so far. Halloa, Watson, what's this? It's the man himself, by all that's wonderful and audacious! Not a word to show your suspicions—not a word, or my plans crumble to the ground."

A figure was approaching us over the moor, and I saw the dull red glow of a cigar. The moon shone upon him, and I could distinguish the dapper shape and jaunty walk of the naturalist. He stopped when he saw us, and then came on again.

"Why, Dr. Watson, that's not you, is it? You are the last man that I should have expected to see out on the moor at this time of night. But, dear me, what's this? Somebody hurt? Not—don't tell me that it is our friend Sir Henry!" He hurried past me and stooped over the dead man. I heard a sharp intake of his breath and the cigar fell from his fingers.

"Who—who's this?" he stammered.

"It is Selden, the man who escaped from Princetown."

Stapleton turned a ghastly face upon us, but by a supreme effort he had overcome his amazement and his disappointment. He looked sharply from Holmes to me. "Dear me! What a very shocking affair! How did he die?"

"He appears to have broken his neck by falling over these rocks. My friend and I were strolling on the moor when we heard a cry."

"I heard a cry also. That was what brought me out. I was uneasy about Sir Henry."

"Why about Sir Henry in particular?" I could not help asking.

"Because I had suggested that he should come over. When he did not come I was surprised, and I naturally became alarmed for his safety when I heard cries upon the moor. By the way"—his eyes darted again from my face to Holmes's—"did you hear anything else besides a cry?"

"No," said Holmes; "did you?"

"No."

"What do you mean, then?"

"Oh, you know the stories that the peasants tell about a phantom hound, and so on. It is said to be heard at night upon the moor. I was wondering if there were any evidence of such a sound tonight."

"We heard nothing of the kind," said I.

"And what is your theory of this poor fellow's death?"

"I have no doubt that anxiety and exposure have driven him

off his head. He has rushed about the moor in a crazy state and eventually fallen over here and broken his neck."

"That seems the most reasonable theory," said Stapleton, and he gave a sigh which I took to indicate his relief. "What do you think about it, Mr. Sherlock Holmes?"

My friend bowed his compliments. "You are quick at identification," said he.

"We have been expecting you in these parts since Dr. Watson came down. You are in time to see a tragedy."

"Yes, indeed. I have no doubt that my friend's explanation will cover the facts. I will take an unpleasant remembrance back to London with me tomorrow."

"Oh, you return tomorrow?"

"That is my intention."

"I hope your visit has cast some light upon those occurrences which have puzzled us?"

Holmes shrugged his shoulders.

"One cannot always have the success for which one hopes. An investigator needs facts and not legends or rumours. It has not been a satisfactory case."

My friend spoke in his frankest and most unconcerned manner. Stapleton still looked hard at him. Then he turned to me.

"I would suggest carrying this poor fellow to my house, but it would give my sister such a fright that I do not feel justified in doing it. I think that if we put something over his face he will be safe until morning."

And so it was arranged. Resisting Stapleton's offer of hospitality, Holmes and I set off to Baskerville Hall, leaving the naturalist to return alone. Looking back we saw the figure moving slowly away over the broad moor, and behind him that one black smudge on the silvered slope which showed where the man was lying who had come so horribly to his end.

"We're at close grips at last," said Holmes as we walked together across the moor. "What a nerve the fellow has! How he pulled himself together in the face of what must have been a paralyzing shock when he found that the wrong man had fallen a victim to his plot. I told you in London, Watson, and I tell you now again, that we have never had a foeman more worthy of our steel."

"I am sorry that he has seen you."

"And so was I at first. But there was no getting out of it."

"What effect do you think it will have upon his plans now that he knows you are here?"

"It may cause him to be more cautious, or it may drive him to desperate measures at once. Like most clever criminals, he may be too confident in his own cleverness and imagine that he has completely deceived us."

"Why should we not arrest him at once?"

"My dear Watson, you were born to be a man of action. Your instinct is always to do something energetic. But supposing, for argument's sake, that we had him arrested tonight, what on earth the better off should we be for that? We could prove nothing against him. There's the devilish cunning of it! If he were acting through a human agent we could get some evidence, but if we were to drag this great dog to the light of day it would not help us in putting a rope round the neck of its master."

"Surely we have a case."

"Not a shadow of one—only surmise and conjecture. We should be laughed out of court if we came with such a story and such evidence."

"There is Sir Charles's death."

"Found dead without a mark upon him. You and I know that he died of sheer fright, and we know also what frightened him, but how are we to get twelve stolid jurymen to know it? What signs are there of a hound? Where are the marks of its fangs? Of course we know that a hound does not bite a dead body and that Sir Charles was dead before ever the brute overtook him. But we have to prove all this, and we are not in a position to do it."

"Well, then, tonight?"

"We are not much better off tonight. Again, there was no direct connection between the hound and the man's death. We never saw the hound. We heard it, but we could not prove that it was running upon this man's trail. There is a complete absence of motive. No, my dear fellow; we must reconcile ourselves to the fact that we have no case at present, and that it is worth our while to run any risk in order to establish one."

"And how do you propose to do so?"

"I have great hopes of what Mrs. Laura Lyons may do for us when the position of affairs is made clear to her. And I have my own plan as well. Sufficient for tomorrow is the evil thereof; but I hope before the day is past to have the upper hand at last."

I could draw nothing further from him, and he walked, lost in thought, as far as the Baskerville gates.

"Are you coming up?"

"Yes; I see no reason for further concealment. But one last word, Watson. Say nothing of the hound to Sir Henry. Let him think that Selden's death was as Stapleton would have us believe. He will have a better nerve for the ordeal which he will have to undergo tomorrow, when he is engaged, if I remember your report aright, to dine with these people."

"And so am I."

"Then you must excuse yourself and he must go alone. That will be easily arranged. And now, if we are too late for dinner, I think that we are both ready for our suppers."

Chapter 13.

Fixing the Nets

Sir Henry was more pleased than surprised to see Sherlock Holmes, for he had for some days been expecting that recent events would bring him down from London. He did raise his eyebrows, however, when he found that my friend had neither any luggage nor any explanations for its absence. Between us we soon supplied his wants, and then over a belated supper we explained to the baronet as much of our experience as it seemed desirable that he should know. But first I had the unpleasant duty of breaking the news to Barrymore and his wife. To him it may have been an unmitigated relief, but she wept bitterly in her apron. To all the world he was the man of violence, half animal and half demon; but to her he always remained the little wilful boy of her own girlhood, the child who had clung to her hand. Evil indeed is the man who has not one woman to mourn him.

"I've been moping in the house all day since Watson went off in the morning," said the baronet. "I guess I should have some credit, for I have kept my promise. If I hadn't sworn not to go about alone I might have had a more lively evening, for I had a message from Stapleton asking me over there."

"I have no doubt that you would have had a more lively evening," said Holmes drily. "By the way, I don't suppose you appreciate that we have been mourning over you as having broken your neck?"

Sir Henry opened his eyes. "How was that?"

"This poor wretch was dressed in your clothes. I fear your servant who gave them to him may get into trouble with the police."

"That is unlikely. There was no mark on any of them, as far as I know."

"That's lucky for him—in fact, it's lucky for all of you, since you are all on the wrong side of the law in this matter. I am not sure that as a conscientious detective my first duty is not to arrest the whole household. Watson's reports are most incriminating documents."

"But how about the case?" asked the baronet. "Have you made anything out of the tangle? I don't know that Watson and

I are much the wiser since we came down."

"I think that I shall be in a position to make the situation rather more clear to you before long. It has been an exceedingly difficult and most complicated business. There are several points upon which we still want light—but it is coming all the same."

"We've had one experience, as Watson has no doubt told you. We heard the hound on the moor, so I can swear that it is not all empty superstition. I had something to do with dogs when I was out West, and I know one when I hear one. If you can muzzle that one and put him on a chain I'll be ready to swear you are the greatest detective of all time."

"I think I will muzzle him and chain him all right if you will give me your help."

"Whatever you tell me to do I will do."

"Very good; and I will ask you also to do it blindly, without always asking the reason."

"Just as you like."

"If you will do this I think the chances are that our little problem will soon be solved. I have no doubt—"

He stopped suddenly and stared fixedly up over my head into the air. The lamp beat upon his face, and so intent was it and so still that it might have been that of a clear-cut classical statue, a personification of alertness and expectation.

"What is it?" we both cried.

I could see as he looked down that he was repressing some internal emotion. His features were still composed, but his eyes shone with amused exultation.

"Excuse the admiration of a connoisseur," said he as he waved his hand towards the line of portraits which covered the opposite wall. "Watson won't allow that I know anything of art but that is mere jealousy because our views upon the subject differ. Now, these are a really very fine series of portraits."

"Well, I'm glad to hear you say so," said Sir Henry, glancing with some surprise at my friend. "I don't pretend to know much about these things, and I'd be a better judge of a horse or a steer than of a picture. I didn't know that you found time for such things."

"I know what is good when I see it, and I see it now. That's a Kneller, I'll swear, that lady in the blue silk over yonder, and the stout gentleman with the wig ought to be a Reynolds. They are all family portraits, I presume?"

"Every one."

"Do you know the names?"

"Barrymore has been coaching me in them, and I think I can say my lessons fairly well."

"Who is the gentleman with the telescope?"

"That is Rear-Admiral Baskerville, who served under Rodney in the West Indies. The man with the blue coat and the roll of paper is Sir William Baskerville, who was Chairman of Committees of the House of Commons under Pitt."

"And this Cavalier opposite to me—the one with the black velvet and the lace?"

"Ah, you have a right to know about him. That is the cause of all the mischief, the wicked Hugo, who started the Hound of the Baskervilles. We're not likely to forget him."

I gazed with interest and some surprise upon the portrait.

"Dear me!" said Holmes, "he seems a quiet, meek-mannered man enough, but I dare say that there was a lurking devil in his eyes. I had pictured him as a more robust and ruffianly person."

"There's no doubt about the authenticity, for the name and the date, 1647, are on the back of the canvas."

Holmes said little more, but the picture of the old roysterer seemed to have a fascination for him, and his eyes were continually fixed upon it during supper. It was not until later, when Sir Henry had gone to his room, that I was able to follow the trend of his thoughts. He led me back into the banqueting-hall, his bedroom candle in his hand, and he held it up against the time-stained portrait on the wall.

"Do you see anything there?"

I looked at the broad plumed hat, the curling love-locks, the white lace collar, and the straight, severe face which was framed between them. It was not a brutal countenance, but it was prim, hard, and stern, with a firm-set, thin-lipped mouth, and a coldly intolerant eye.

"Is it like anyone you know?"

"There is something of Sir Henry about the jaw."

"Just a suggestion, perhaps. But wait an instant!" He stood upon a chair, and, holding up the light in his left hand, he curved his right arm over the broad hat and round the long ringlets.

"Good heavens!" I cried in amazement.

The face of Stapleton had sprung out of the canvas.

"Ha, you see it now. My eyes have been trained to examine faces and not their trimmings. It is the first quality of a criminal investigator that he should see through a disguise."

"But this is marvellous. It might be his portrait."

"Yes, it is an interesting instance of a throwback, which appears to be both physical and spiritual. A study of family portraits is enough to convert a man to the doctrine of reincarnation. The fellow is a Baskerville—that is evident."

"With designs upon the succession."

"Exactly. This chance of the picture has supplied us with one of our most obvious missing links. We have him, Watson, we have him, and I dare swear that before tomorrow night he will be fluttering in our net as helpless as one of his own butterflies. A pin, a cork, and a card, and we add him to the Baker Street collection!" He burst into one of his rare fits of laughter as he turned away from the picture. I have not heard him laugh often, and it has always boded ill to somebody.

I was up betimes in the morning, but Holmes was afoot earlier still, for I saw him as I dressed, coming up the drive.

"Yes, we should have a full day today," he remarked, and he rubbed his hands with the joy of action. "The nets are all in place, and the drag is about to begin. We'll know before the day is out whether we have caught our big, lean-jawed pike, or whether he has got through the meshes."

"Have you been on the moor already?"

"I have sent a report from Grimpen to Princetown as to the death of Selden. I think I can promise that none of you will be troubled in the matter. And I have also communicated with my faithful Cartwright, who would certainly have pined away at the door of my hut, as a dog does at his master's grave, if I had not set his mind at rest about my safety."

"What is the next move?"

"To see Sir Henry. Ah, here he is!"

"Good-morning, Holmes," said the baronet. "You look like a general who is planning a battle with his chief of the staff."

"That is the exact situation. Watson was asking for orders."

"And so do I."

"Very good. You are engaged, as I understand, to dine with our friends the Stapletons tonight."

"I hope that you will come also. They are very hospitable people, and I am sure that they would be very glad to see you."

"I fear that Watson and I must go to London."

"To London?"

"Yes, I think that we should be more useful there at the present juncture."

The baronet's face perceptibly lengthened.

"I hoped that you were going to see me through this business. The Hall and the moor are not very pleasant places when one is alone."

"My dear fellow, you must trust me implicitly and do exactly what I tell you. You can tell your friends that we should have been happy to have come with you, but that urgent business required us to be in town. We hope very soon to return to Devonshire. Will you remember to give them that message?"

"If you insist upon it."

"There is no alternative, I assure you."

I saw by the baronet's clouded brow that he was deeply hurt by what he regarded as our desertion.

"When do you desire to go?" he asked coldly.

"Immediately after breakfast. We will drive in to Coombe Tracey, but Watson will leave his things as a pledge that he will come back to you. Watson, you will send a note to Stapleton to tell him that you regret that you cannot come."

"I have a good mind to go to London with you," said the baronet. "Why should I stay here alone?"

"Because it is your post of duty. Because you gave me your word that you would do as you were told, and I tell you to stay."

"All right, then, I'll stay."

"One more direction! I wish you to drive to Merripit House. Send back your trap, however, and let them know that you intend to walk home."

"To walk across the moor?"

"Yes."

"But that is the very thing which you have so often cautioned me not to do."

"This time you may do it with safety. If I had not every confidence in your nerve and courage I would not suggest it, but it is essential that you should do it."

"Then I will do it."

"And as you value your life do not go across the moor in any direction save along the straight path which leads from Merripit House to the Grimpen Road, and is your natural way home."

"I will do just what you say."

"Very good. I should be glad to get away as soon after breakfast as possible, so as to reach London in the afternoon."

I was much astounded by this programme, though I

remembered that Holmes had said to Stapleton on the night before that his visit would terminate next day. It had not crossed my mind however, that he would wish me to go with him, nor could I understand how we could both be absent at a moment which he himself declared to be critical. There was nothing for it, however, but implicit obedience; so we bade good-bye to our rueful friend, and a couple of hours afterwards we were at the station of Coombe Tracey and had dispatched the trap upon its return journey. A small boy was waiting upon the platform.

"Any orders, sir?"

"You will take this train to town, Cartwright. The moment you arrive you will send a wire to Sir Henry Baskerville, in my name, to say that if he finds the pocketbook which I have dropped he is to send it by registered post to Baker Street."

"Yes, sir."

"And ask at the station office if there is a message for me."

The boy returned with a telegram, which Holmes handed to me. It ran:

Wire received. Coming down with unsigned warrant. Arrive five-forty. Lestrade.

"That is in answer to mine of this morning. He is the best of the professionals, I think, and we may need his assistance. Now, Watson, I think that we cannot employ our time better than by calling upon your acquaintance, Mrs. Laura Lyons."

His plan of campaign was beginning to be evident. He would use the baronet in order to convince the Stapletons that we were really gone, while we should actually return at the instant when we were likely to be needed. That telegram from London, if mentioned by Sir Henry to the Stapletons, must remove the last suspicions from their minds. Already I seemed to see our nets drawing closer around that lean-jawed pike.

Mrs. Laura Lyons was in her office, and Sherlock Holmes opened his interview with a frankness and directness which considerably amazed her.

"I am investigating the circumstances which attended the death of the late Sir Charles Baskerville," said he. "My friend here, Dr. Watson, has informed me of what you have communicated, and also of what you have withheld in connection with that matter."

"What have I withheld?" she asked defiantly.

"You have confessed that you asked Sir Charles to be at the gate at ten o'clock. We know that that was the place and hour of his death. You have withheld what the connection is between these events."

"There is no connection."

"In that case the coincidence must indeed be an extraordinary one. But I think that we shall succeed in establishing a connection, after all. I wish to be perfectly frank with you, Mrs. Lyons. We regard this case as one of murder, and the evidence may implicate not only your friend Mr. Stapleton but his wife as well."

The lady sprang from her chair.

"His wife!" she cried.

"The fact is no longer a secret. The person who has passed for his sister is really his wife."

Mrs. Lyons had resumed her seat. Her hands were grasping the arms of her chair, and I saw that the pink nails had turned white with the pressure of her grip.

"His wife!" she said again. "His wife! He is not a married man."

Sherlock Holmes shrugged his shoulders.

"Prove it to me! Prove it to me! And if you can do so—!"

The fierce flash of her eyes said more than any words.

"I have come prepared to do so," said Holmes, drawing several papers from his pocket. "Here is a photograph of the couple taken in York four years ago. It is indorsed 'Mr. and Mrs. Vandeleur,' but you will have no difficulty in recognizing him, and her also, if you know her by sight. Here are three written descriptions by trustworthy witnesses of Mr. and Mrs. Vandeleur, who at that time kept St. Oliver's private school. Read them and see if you can doubt the identity of these people."

She glanced at them, and then looked up at us with the set, rigid face of a desperate woman.

"Mr. Holmes," she said, "this man had offered me marriage on condition that I could get a divorce from my husband. He has lied to me, the villain, in every conceivable way. Not one word of truth has he ever told me. And why—why? I imagined that all was for my own sake. But now I see that I was never anything but a tool in his hands. Why should I preserve faith with him who never kept any with me? Why should I try to shield him from the consequences of his own wicked acts? Ask me what you like, and there is nothing which I shall hold back. One thing I swear to you, and that is that when I wrote the letter I never dreamed of any harm to the old gentleman, who had been my kindest friend."

"I entirely believe you, madam," said Sherlock Holmes. "The recital of these events must be very painful to you, and perhaps it will make it easier if I tell you what occurred, and you can check me if I make any material mistake. The sending of this letter was suggested to you by Stapleton?"

"He dictated it."

"I presume that the reason he gave was that you would receive help from Sir Charles for the legal expenses connected with your divorce?"

"Exactly."

"And then after you had sent the letter he dissuaded you from keeping the appointment?"

"He told me that it would hurt his self-respect that any other man should find the money for such an object, and that though he was a poor man himself he would devote his last penny to removing the obstacles which divided us."

"He appears to be a very consistent character. And then you heard nothing until you read the reports of the death in the paper?"

"No."

"And he made you swear to say nothing about your appointment with Sir Charles?"

"He did. He said that the death was a very mysterious one,

and that I should certainly be suspected if the facts came out. He frightened me into remaining silent."

"Quite so. But you had your suspicions?"

She hesitated and looked down.

"I knew him," she said. "But if he had kept faith with me I should always have done so with him."

"I think that on the whole you have had a fortunate escape," said Sherlock Holmes. "You have had him in your power and he knew it, and yet you are alive. You have been walking for some months very near to the edge of a precipice. We must wish you good-morning now, Mrs. Lyons, and it is probable that you will very shortly hear from us again."

"Our case becomes rounded off, and difficulty after difficulty thins away in front of us," said Holmes as we stood waiting for the arrival of the express from town. "I shall soon be in the position of being able to put into a single connected narrative one of the most singular and sensational crimes of modern times. Students of criminology will remember the analogous incidents in Godno, in Little Russia, in the year '66, and of course there are the Anderson murders in North Carolina, but this case possesses some features which are entirely its own. Even now we have no clear case against this very wily man. But I shall be very much surprised if it is not clear enough before we go to bed this night."

The London express came roaring into the station, and a small, wiry bulldog of a man had sprung from a first-class carriage. We all three shook hands, and I saw at once from the reverential way in which Lestrade gazed at my companion that he had learned a good deal since the days when they had first worked together. I could well remember the scorn which the theories of the reasoner used then to excite in the practical man.

"Anything good?" he asked.

"The biggest thing for years," said Holmes. "We have two hours before we need think of starting. I think we might employ it in getting some dinner and then, Lestrade, we will take the London fog out of your throat by giving you a breath of the pure night air of Dartmoor. Never been there? Ah, well, I don't suppose you will forget your first visit."

Chapter 14.

The Hound of the Baskervilles

One of Sherlock Holmes's defects—if, indeed, one may call it a defect—was that he was exceedingly loath to communicate his full plans to any other person until the instant of their fulfilment. Partly it came no doubt from his own masterful nature, which loved to dominate and surprise those who were around him. Partly also from his professional caution, which urged him never to take any chances. The result, however, was very trying for those who were acting as his agents and assistants. I had often suffered under it, but never more so than during that long drive in the darkness. The great ordeal was in front of us; at last we were about to make our final effort, and yet Holmes had said nothing, and I could only surmise what his course of action would be. My nerves thrilled with anticipation when at last the cold wind upon our faces and the dark, void spaces on either side of the narrow road told me that we were back upon the moor once again. Every stride of the horses and every turn of the wheels was taking us nearer to our supreme adventure.

Our conversation was hampered by the presence of the driver of the hired wagonette, so that we were forced to talk of trivial matters when our nerves were tense with emotion and anticipation. It was a relief to me, after that unnatural restraint, when we at last passed Frankland's house and knew that we were drawing near to the Hall and to the scene of action. We did not drive up to the door but got down near the gate of the avenue. The wagonette was paid off and ordered to return to Coombe Tracey forthwith, while we started to walk to Merripit House.

"Are you armed, Lestrade?"

The little detective smiled. "As long as I have my trousers I have a hip-pocket, and as long as I have my hip-pocket I have something in it."

"Good! My friend and I are also ready for emergencies."

"You're mighty close about this affair, Mr. Holmes. What's the game now?"

"A waiting game."

"My word, it does not seem a very cheerful place," said the

detective with a shiver, glancing round him at the gloomy slopes of the hill and at the huge lake of fog which lay over the Grimpen Mire. "I see the lights of a house ahead of us."

"That is Merripit House and the end of our journey. I must request you to walk on tiptoe and not to talk above a whisper."

We moved cautiously along the track as if we were bound for the house, but Holmes halted us when we were about two hundred yards from it.

"This will do," said he. "These rocks upon the right make an admirable screen."

"We are to wait here?"

"Yes, we shall make our little ambush here. Get into this hollow, Lestrade. You have been inside the house, have you not, Watson? Can you tell the position of the rooms? What are those latticed windows at this end?"

"I think they are the kitchen windows."

"And the one beyond, which shines so brightly?"

"That is certainly the dining-room."

"The blinds are up. You know the lie of the land best. Creep forward quietly and see what they are doing—but for heaven's sake don't let them know that they are watched!"

I tiptoed down the path and stooped behind the low wall which surrounded the stunted orchard. Creeping in its shadow I reached a point whence I could look straight through the uncurtained window.

There were only two men in the room, Sir Henry and Stapleton. They sat with their profiles towards me on either side of the round table. Both of them were smoking cigars, and coffee and wine were in front of them. Stapleton was talking with animation, but the baronet looked pale and distrait. Perhaps the thought of that lonely walk across the ill-omened moor was weighing heavily upon his mind.

As I watched them Stapleton rose and left the room, while Sir Henry filled his glass again and leaned back in his chair, puffing at his cigar. I heard the creak of a door and the crisp sound of boots upon gravel. The steps passed along the path on the other side of the wall under which I crouched. Looking over, I saw the naturalist pause at the door of an out-house in the corner of the orchard. A key turned in a lock, and as he passed in there was a curious scuffling noise from within. He was only a minute or so inside, and then I heard the key turn once more and he passed me and reentered the house. I saw him rejoin his guest, and I crept quietly back to where my companions were waiting to tell them what I had seen.

"You say, Watson, that the lady is not there?" Holmes asked when I had finished my report.

"No."

"Where can she be, then, since there is no light in any other room except the kitchen?"

"I cannot think where she is."

I have said that over the great Grimpen Mire there hung a dense, white fog. It was drifting slowly in our direction and banked itself up like a wall on that side of us, low but thick and well defined. The moon shone on it, and it looked like a great shimmering ice-field, with the heads of the distant tors as rocks borne upon its surface. Holmes's face was turned towards it, and he muttered impatiently as he watched its sluggish drift.

"It's moving towards us, Watson."

"Is that serious?"

"Very serious, indeed—the one thing upon earth which could have disarranged my plans. He can't be very long, now. It is already ten o'clock. Our success and even his life may depend upon his coming out before the fog is over the path."

The night was clear and fine above us. The stars shone cold and bright, while a half-moon bathed the whole scene in a soft, uncertain light. Before us lay the dark bulk of the house, its serrated roof and bristling chimneys hard outlined against the silver-spangled sky. Broad bars of golden light from the lower windows stretched across the orchard and the moor. One of them was suddenly shut off. The servants had left the kitchen. There only remained the lamp in the dining-room where the two men, the murderous host and the unconscious guest, still chatted over their cigars.

Every minute that white woolly plain which covered one-half of the moor was drifting closer and closer to the house. Already the first thin wisps of it were curling across the golden square of the lighted window. The farther wall of the orchard was already invisible, and the trees were standing out of a swirl of white vapour. As we watched it the fog-wreaths came crawling round both corners of the house and rolled slowly into one dense bank on which the upper floor and the roof floated like a strange ship upon a shadowy sea. Holmes struck his hand passionately upon the rock in front of us and stamped his feet in his impatience.

"If he isn't out in a quarter of an hour the path will be covered. In half an hour we won't be able to see our hands in front of us."

"Shall we move farther back upon higher ground?"

"Yes, I think it would be as well."

So as the fog-bank flowed onward we fell back before it until we were half a mile from the house, and still that dense white sea, with the moon silvering its upper edge, swept slowly and inexorably on.

"We are going too far," said Holmes. "We dare not take the chance of his being overtaken before he can reach us. At all costs we must hold our ground where we are." He dropped on his knees and clapped his ear to the ground. "Thank God, I think that I hear him coming."

A sound of quick steps broke the silence of the moor. Crouching among the stones we stared intently at the silver-tipped bank in front of us. The steps grew louder, and through the fog, as through a curtain, there stepped the man whom we were awaiting. He looked round him in surprise as he emerged into the clear, starlit night. Then he came swiftly along the path, passed close to where we lay, and went on up the long slope behind us. As he walked he glanced continually over either shoulder, like a man who is ill at ease.

"Hist!" cried Holmes, and I heard the sharp click of a cocking pistol. "Look out! It's coming!"

There was a thin, crisp, continuous patter from somewhere in the heart of that crawling bank. The cloud was within fifty yards of where we lay, and we glared at it, all three, uncertain what horror was about to break from the heart of it. I was at Holmes's elbow, and I glanced for an instant at his face. It was pale and exultant, his eyes shining brightly in the moonlight. But suddenly they started forward in a rigid, fixed stare, and his lips parted in amazement. At the same instant Lestrade gave a yell of terror and threw himself face downward upon the ground. I sprang to my feet, my inert hand grasping my pistol, my mind paralyzed by the dreadful shape which had sprung out upon us from the shadows of the fog. A hound it was, an enormous coal-black hound, but not such a hound as mortal eyes have ever seen. Fire burst from its open mouth, its eyes glowed with a smouldering glare, its muzzle and hackles and dewlap were outlined in flickering flame. Never in the delirious dream of a disordered brain could anything more savage, more appalling, more hellish be conceived than that dark form and savage face which broke upon us out of the wall of fog.

With long bounds the huge black creature was leaping down the track, following hard upon the footsteps of our friend. So paralyzed were we by the apparition that we allowed him to pass before we had recovered our nerve. Then Holmes and I both fired together, and the creature gave a hideous howl, which showed that one at least had hit him. He did not pause, however, but bounded onward. Far away on the path we saw Sir Henry looking back, his face white in the moonlight, his hands raised in horror, glaring helplessly at the frightful thing which was hunting him down. But that cry of pain from the hound had blown all our fears to the winds. If he was vulnerable he was mortal, and if we could wound him we could kill him. Never have I seen a man run as Holmes ran that night. I am reckoned fleet of foot, but he outpaced me as much as I outpaced the little professional. In front of us as we flew up the track we heard scream after scream from Sir Henry and the deep roar of the hound. I was in time to see the beast spring upon its victim, hurl him to the ground, and worry at his throat. But the next instant Holmes had emptied five barrels of his revolver into the creature's flank. With a last howl of agony and a vicious snap in the air, it rolled upon its back, four feet pawing furiously, and then fell limp upon its side. I stooped, panting, and pressed my pistol to the dreadful, shimmering head, but it was useless to press the trigger. The giant hound was dead.

Sir Henry lay insensible where he had fallen. We tore away his collar, and Holmes breathed a prayer of gratitude when we saw that there was no sign of a wound and that the rescue had been in time. Already our friend's eyelids shivered and he made a feeble effort to move. Lestrade thrust his brandy-flask between the baronet's teeth, and two frightened eyes were looking up at us.

"My God!" he whispered. "What was it? What, in heaven's name, was it?"

"It's dead, whatever it is," said Holmes. "We've laid the family ghost once and forever."

In mere size and strength it was a terrible creature which was lying stretched before us. It was not a pure bloodhound and it was not a pure mastiff; but it appeared to be a combination of the two—gaunt, savage, and as large as a small lioness. Even now in the stillness of death, the huge jaws seemed to be dripping with a bluish flame and the small, deep-set, cruel eyes were ringed with fire. I placed my hand upon the glowing muzzle, and as I held them up my own fingers smouldered and gleamed in the darkness.

"Phosphorus," I said.

"A cunning preparation of it," said Holmes, sniffing at the dead animal. "There is no smell which might have interfered with his power of scent. We owe you a deep apology, Sir Henry, for having exposed you to this fright. I was prepared for a hound, but not for such a creature as this. And the fog gave us little time to receive him."

"You have saved my life."

"Having first endangered it. Are you strong enough to stand?"

"Give me another mouthful of that brandy and I shall be ready for anything. So! Now, if you will help me up. What do you propose to do?"

"To leave you here. You are not fit for further adventures tonight. If you will wait, one or other of us will go back with you to the Hall."

He tried to stagger to his feet; but he was still ghastly pale and trembling in every limb. We helped him to a rock, where he sat shivering with his face buried in his hands.

"We must leave you now," said Holmes. "The rest of our work must be done, and every moment is of importance. We have our case, and now we only want our man.

"It's a thousand to one against our finding him at the house," he continued as we retraced our steps swiftly down the path. "Those shots must have told him that the game was up."

"We were some distance off, and this fog may have deadened them."

"He followed the hound to call him off—of that you may be certain. No, no, he's gone by this time! But we'll search the house and make sure."

The front door was open, so we rushed in and hurried from room to room to the amazement of a doddering old manservant, who met us in the passage. There was no light save in the dining-room, but Holmes caught up the lamp and left no corner of the house unexplored. No sign could we see of the man whom we were chasing. On the upper floor, however, one of the bedroom doors was locked.

"There's someone in here," cried Lestrade. "I can hear a movement. Open this door!"

A faint moaning and rustling came from within. Holmes struck the door just over the lock with the flat of his foot and it flew open. Pistol in hand, we all three rushed into the room.

But there was no sign within it of that desperate and defiant villain whom we expected to see. Instead we were faced by an object so strange and so unexpected that we stood for a moment staring at it in amazement.

The room had been fashioned into a small museum, and the walls were lined by a number of glass-topped cases full of that collection of butterflies and moths the formation of which had been the relaxation of this complex and dangerous man. In the centre of this room there was an upright beam, which had been placed at some period as a support for the old worm-eaten baulk of timber which spanned the roof. To this post a figure was tied, so swathed and muffled in the sheets which had been used to secure it that one could not for the moment tell whether it was that of a man or a woman. One towel passed round the throat and was secured at the back of the pillar. Another covered the lower part of the face, and over it two dark eyes—eyes full of grief and shame and a dreadful questioning—stared back at us. In a minute we had torn off the gag, unswathed the bonds, and Mrs. Stapleton sank upon the floor in front of us. As her beautiful head fell upon her chest I saw the clear red weal of a whiplash across her neck.

"The brute!" cried Holmes. "Here, Lestrade, your brandy-bottle! Put her in the chair! She has fainted from ill-usage and exhaustion."

She opened her eyes again.

"Is he safe?" she asked. "Has he escaped?"

"He cannot escape us, madam."

"No, no, I did not mean my husband. Sir Henry? Is he safe?"

"Yes."

"And the hound?"

"It is dead."

She gave a long sigh of satisfaction.

"Thank God! Thank God! Oh, this villain! See how he has treated me!" She shot her arms out from her sleeves, and we saw with horror that they were all mottled with bruises. "But this is nothing—nothing! It is my mind and soul that he has tortured and defiled. I could endure it all, ill-usage, solitude, a life of deception, everything, as long as I could still cling to the hope that I had his love, but now I know that in this also I have been his dupe and his tool." She broke into passionate sobbing as she spoke.

"You bear him no good will, madam," said Holmes. "Tell us then where we shall find him. If you have ever aided him in evil, help us now and so atone."

"There is but one place where he can have fled," she answered. "There is an old tin mine on an island in the heart of the mire. It was there that he kept his hound and there also he had made preparations so that he might have a refuge. That is where he would fly."

The fog-bank lay like white wool against the window. Holmes held the lamp towards it.

"See," said he. "No one could find his way into the Grimpen Mire tonight."

She laughed and clapped her hands. Her eyes and teeth gleamed with fierce merriment.

"He may find his way in, but never out," she cried. "How can he see the guiding wands tonight? We planted them together, he and I, to mark the pathway through the mire. Oh, if I could only have plucked them out today. Then indeed you would have had him at your mercy!"

It was evident to us that all pursuit was in vain until the fog had lifted. Meanwhile we left Lestrade in possession of the house while Holmes and I went back with the baronet to Baskerville Hall. The story of the Stapletons could no longer be withheld from him, but he took the blow bravely when he learned the truth about the woman whom he had loved. But the shock of the night's adventures had shattered his nerves, and before morning he lay delirious in a high fever under the care of Dr. Mortimer. The two of them were destined to travel together round the world before Sir Henry had become once more the hale, hearty man that he had been before he became master of that ill-omened estate.

And now I come rapidly to the conclusion of this singular narrative, in which I have tried to make the reader share those dark fears and vague surmises which clouded our lives so long and ended in so tragic a manner. On the morning after the death of the hound the fog had lifted and we were guided by Mrs. Stapleton to the point where they had found a pathway through the bog. It helped us to realise the horror of this woman's life when we saw the eagerness and joy with which she laid us on her husband's track. We left her standing upon the thin peninsula of firm, peaty soil which tapered out into the widespread bog. From the end of it a small wand planted here and there showed where the path zigzagged from tuft to tuft of rushes among those green-scummed pits and foul quagmires which barred the way to the stranger. Rank reeds and lush, slimy water-plants sent an odour of decay and a heavy miasmatic vapour onto our faces, while a false step plunged us more than once thigh-deep into the dark, quivering mire, which shook for yards in soft undulations around our feet. Its tenacious grip plucked at our heels as we walked, and when we sank into it it was as if some malignant hand was tugging us down into those obscene depths, so grim and purposeful was the clutch in which it held us. Once only we saw a trace that someone had passed that perilous way before us. From amid a tuft of cotton grass which bore it up out of the slime some dark thing was projecting. Holmes sank to his waist as he stepped from the path to seize it, and had we not been there to drag him out he could never have set his foot upon firm land again. He held an old black boot in the air. "Meyers, Toronto," was printed on the leather inside.

"It is worth a mud bath," said he. "It is our friend Sir Henry's missing boot."

"Thrown there by Stapleton in his flight."

"Exactly. He retained it in his hand after using it to set the hound upon the track. He fled when he knew the game was up, still clutching it. And he hurled it away at this point of his flight. We know at least that he came so far in safety."

But more than that we were never destined to know, though there was much which we might surmise. There was no chance of finding footsteps in the mire, for the rising mud oozed swiftly in upon them, but as we at last reached firmer ground beyond the morass we all looked eagerly for them. But no slightest sign of them ever met our eyes. If the earth told a true story, then Stapleton never reached that island of refuge towards which he struggled through the fog upon that last night. Somewhere in the heart of the great Grimpen Mire, down in the foul slime of the huge morass which had sucked him in, this cold and cruel-hearted man is forever buried.

Many traces we found of him in the bog-girt island where he had hid his savage ally. A huge driving-wheel and a shaft half-filled with rubbish showed the position of an abandoned mine. Beside it were the crumbling remains of the cottages of the miners, driven away no doubt by the foul reek of the surrounding swamp. In one of these a staple and chain with a quantity of gnawed bones showed where the animal had been confined. A skeleton with a tangle of brown hair adhering to it lay among the débris.

"A dog!" said Holmes. "By Jove, a curly-haired spaniel. Poor Mortimer will never see his pet again. Well, I do not know that this place contains any secret which we have not already fathomed. He could hide his hound, but he could not hush its voice, and hence came those cries which even in daylight were not pleasant to hear. On an emergency he could keep the hound in the out-house at Merripit, but it was always a risk, and it was only on the supreme day, which he regarded as the end of all his efforts, that he dared do it. This paste in the tin is no doubt the luminous mixture with which the creature was daubed. It was suggested, of course, by the story of the family hell-hound, and by the desire to frighten old Sir Charles to death. No wonder the poor devil of a convict ran and screamed, even as our friend did, and as we ourselves might have done, when he saw such a creature bounding through the darkness of the moor upon his track. It was a cunning device, for, apart from the chance of driving your victim to his death, what peasant would venture to inquire too closely into such a creature should he get sight of it, as many have done, upon the moor? I said it in London, Watson, and I say it again now, that never yet have we helped to hunt down a more dangerous man than he who is lying yonder" — he swept his long arm towards the huge mottled expanse of green-splotched bog which stretched away until it merged into the russet slopes of the moor.

Chapter 15.

A Retrospection

It was the end of November, and Holmes and I sat, upon a raw and foggy night, on either side of a blazing fire in our sitting-room in Baker Street. Since the tragic upshot of our visit to Devonshire he had been engaged in two affairs of the utmost importance, in the first of which he had exposed the atrocious conduct of Colonel Upwood in connection with the famous card scandal of the Nonpareil Club, while in the second he had defended the unfortunate Mme. Montpensier from the charge of murder which hung over her in connection with the death of her step-daughter, Mlle. Carére, the young lady who, as it will be remembered, was found six months later alive and married in New York. My friend was in excellent spirits over the success which had attended a succession of difficult and important cases, so that I was able to induce him to discuss the details of the Baskerville mystery. I had waited patiently for the opportunity for I was aware that he would never permit cases to overlap, and that his clear and logical mind would not be drawn from its present work to dwell upon memories of the past. Sir Henry and Dr. Mortimer were, however, in London, on their way to that long voyage which had been recommended for the restoration of his shattered nerves. They had called upon us that very afternoon, so that it was natural that the subject should come up for discussion.

"The whole course of events," said Holmes, "from the point of view of the man who called himself Stapleton was simple and direct, although to us, who had no means in the beginning of knowing the motives of his actions and could only learn part of the facts, it all appeared exceedingly complex. I have had the advantage of two conversations with Mrs. Stapleton, and the case has now been so entirely cleared up that I am not aware that there is anything which has remained a secret to us. You will find a few notes upon the matter under the heading B in my indexed list of cases."

"Perhaps you would kindly give me a sketch of the course of events from memory."

"Certainly, though I cannot guarantee that I carry all the facts in my mind. Intense mental concentration has a curious way of blotting out what has passed. The barrister who has his case at his fingers' ends and is able to argue with an expert upon his own subject finds that a week or two of the courts will drive it all out of his head once more. So each of my cases displaces the last, and Mlle. Carére has blurred my recollection of Baskerville Hall. Tomorrow some other little problem may be submitted to my notice which will in turn dispossess the fair French lady and the infamous Upwood. So far as the case of the hound goes, however, I will give you the course of events as nearly as I can, and you will suggest anything which I may have forgotten.

"My inquiries show beyond all question that the family portrait did not lie, and that this fellow was indeed a Baskerville. He was a son of that Rodger Baskerville, the younger brother of Sir Charles, who fled with a sinister reputation to South America, where he was said to have died unmarried. He did, as a matter of fact, marry, and had one child, this fellow, whose real name is the same as his father's. He married Beryl Garcia, one of the beauties of Costa Rica, and, having purloined a considerable sum of public money, he changed his name to Vandeleur and fled to England, where he established a school in the east of Yorkshire. His reason for attempting this special line of business was that he had struck up an acquaintance with a consumptive tutor upon the voyage home, and that he had used this man's ability to make the undertaking a success. Fraser, the tutor, died however, and the school which had begun well sank from disrepute into infamy. The Vandeleurs found it convenient to change their name to Stapleton, and he brought the remains of his fortune, his schemes for the future, and his taste for entomology to the south of England. I learned at the British Museum that he was a recognized authority upon the subject, and that the name of Vandeleur has been permanently attached to a certain moth which he had, in his Yorkshire days, been the first to describe.

"We now come to that portion of his life which has proved to be of such intense interest to us. The fellow had evidently made inquiry and found that only two lives intervened between him and a valuable estate. When he went to Devonshire his plans were, I believe, exceedingly hazy, but that he meant mischief from the first is evident from the way in which he took his wife with him in the character of his sister. The idea of using her as a decoy was clearly already in his mind, though he may not have been certain how the details of his plot were to be arranged. He meant in the end to have the estate, and he was ready to use any tool or run any risk for that end. His first act was to establish himself as near to his ancestral home as he could, and his second was to cultivate a friendship with Sir Charles Baskerville and with the neighbours.

"The baronet himself told him about the family hound, and

so prepared the way for his own death. Stapleton, as I will continue to call him, knew that the old man's heart was weak and that a shock would kill him. So much he had learned from Dr. Mortimer. He had heard also that Sir Charles was superstitious and had taken this grim legend very seriously. His ingenious mind instantly suggested a way by which the baronet could be done to death, and yet it would be hardly possible to bring home the guilt to the real murderer.

"Having conceived the idea he proceeded to carry it out with considerable finesse. An ordinary schemer would have been content to work with a savage hound. The use of artificial means to make the creature diabolical was a flash of genius upon his part. The dog he bought in London from Ross and Mangles, the dealers in Fulham Road. It was the strongest and most savage in their possession. He brought it down by the North Devon line and walked a great distance over the moor so as to get it home without exciting any remarks. He had already on his insect hunts learned to penetrate the Grimpen Mire, and so had found a safe hiding-place for the creature. Here he kennelled it and waited his chance.

"But it was some time coming. The old gentleman could not be decoyed outside of his grounds at night. Several times Stapleton lurked about with his hound, but without avail. It was during these fruitless quests that he, or rather his ally, was seen by peasants, and that the legend of the demon dog received a new confirmation. He had hoped that his wife might lure Sir Charles to his ruin, but here she proved unexpectedly independent. She would not endeavour to entangle the old gentleman in a sentimental attachment which might deliver him over to his enemy. Threats and even, I am sorry to say, blows refused to move her. She would have nothing to do with it, and for a time Stapleton was at a deadlock.

"He found a way out of his difficulties through the chance that Sir Charles, who had conceived a friendship for him, made him the minister of his charity in the case of this unfortunate woman, Mrs. Laura Lyons. By representing himself as a single man he acquired complete influence over her, and he gave her to understand that in the event of her obtaining a divorce from her husband he would marry her. His plans were suddenly brought to a head by his knowledge that Sir Charles was about to leave the Hall on the advice of Dr. Mortimer, with whose opinion he himself pretended to coincide. He must act at once, or his victim might get beyond his power. He therefore put pressure upon Mrs. Lyons to write this letter, imploring the old man to give her an interview on the evening before his departure for London. He then, by a specious argument, prevented her from going, and so had the chance for which he had waited.

"Driving back in the evening from Coombe Tracey he was in time to get his hound, to treat it with his infernal paint, and to bring the beast round to the gate at which he had reason to expect that he would find the old gentleman waiting. The dog, incited by its master, sprang over the wicket-gate and pursued the unfortunate baronet, who fled screaming down the yew alley. In that gloomy tunnel it must indeed have been a dreadful sight to see that huge black creature, with its flaming jaws and blazing eyes, bounding after its victim. He fell dead at the end of the alley from heart disease and terror. The hound had kept upon the grassy border while the baronet had run down the path, so that no track but the man's was visible. On seeing him lying still the creature had probably approached to sniff at him, but finding him dead had turned away again. It was then that it left the print which was actually observed by Dr. Mortimer. The hound was called off and hurried away to its lair in the Grimpen Mire, and a mystery was left which puzzled the authorities, alarmed the countryside, and finally brought the case within the scope of our observation.

"So much for the death of Sir Charles Baskerville. You perceive the devilish cunning of it, for really it would be almost impossible to make a case against the real murderer. His only accomplice was one who could never give him away, and the grotesque, inconceivable nature of the device only served to make it more effective. Both of the women concerned in the case, Mrs. Stapleton and Mrs. Laura Lyons, were left with a strong suspicion against Stapleton. Mrs. Stapleton knew that he had designs upon the old man, and also of the existence of the hound. Mrs. Lyons knew neither of these things, but had been impressed by the death occurring at the time of an uncancelled appointment which was only known to him. However, both of them were under his influence, and he had nothing to fear from them. The first half of his task was successfully accomplished but the more difficult still remained.

"It is possible that Stapleton did not know of the existence of an heir in Canada. In any case he would very soon learn it from his friend Dr. Mortimer, and he was told by the latter all details about the arrival of Henry Baskerville. Stapleton's first idea was that this young stranger from Canada might possibly be done to death in London without coming down to Devonshire at all. He distrusted his wife ever since she had refused to help him in laying a trap for the old man, and he dared not leave her long out of his sight for fear he should lose his influence over her. It was for this reason that he took her to London with him. They lodged, I find, at the Mexborough Private Hotel, in Craven Street, which was actually one of those called upon by my agent in search of evidence. Here he kept his wife imprisoned in her room while he, disguised in a beard, followed Dr. Mortimer to Baker Street and afterwards to the station and to the Northumberland Hotel. His wife had some inkling of his plans; but she had such a fear of her husband—a fear founded upon brutal ill-treatment—that she dare not write to warn the man whom she knew to be in danger. If the letter should fall into Stapleton's hands her own life would not be safe. Eventually, as we know, she adopted the expedient of cutting out the words which would form the message, and addressing the letter in a disguised hand. It reached the baronet, and gave him the first warning of his danger.

"It was very essential for Stapleton to get some article of Sir Henry's attire so that, in case he was driven to use the dog, he might always have the means of setting him upon his track. With characteristic promptness and audacity he set about this at once, and we cannot doubt that the boots or chamber-maid of the hotel was well bribed to help him in his design. By chance, however, the first boot which was procured for him was a new one and, therefore, useless for his purpose. He then had it returned and obtained another—a most instructive incident, since it proved conclusively to my mind that we were dealing with a real hound, as no other supposition could explain this anxiety to obtain an old boot and this indifference to a new one. The more outré and grotesque an incident is the more carefully it deserves to be examined, and the very point which appears to complicate a case is, when duly considered and scientifically handled, the one which is most likely to elucidate it.

"Then we had the visit from our friends next morning, shadowed always by Stapleton in the cab. From his knowledge of our rooms and of my appearance, as well as from his general conduct, I am inclined to think that Stapleton's career of crime has been by no means limited to this single Baskerville affair. It is suggestive that during the last three years there have been four considerable burglaries in the west country, for none of which was any criminal ever arrested. The last of these, at Folkestone Court, in May, was remarkable for the cold-blooded pistolling of the page, who surprised the masked and solitary burglar. I cannot doubt that Stapleton recruited his waning resources in this fashion, and that for years he has been a desperate and dangerous man.

"We had an example of his readiness of resource that morning when he got away from us so successfully, and also of his audacity in sending back my own name to me through the cabman. From that moment he understood that I had taken over the case in London, and that therefore there was no chance for him there. He returned to Dartmoor and awaited the arrival of the baronet."

"One moment!" said I. "You have, no doubt, described the sequence of events correctly, but there is one point which you have left unexplained. What became of the hound when its master was in London?"

"I have given some attention to this matter and it is undoubtedly of importance. There can be no question that Stapleton had a confidant, though it is unlikely that he ever placed himself in his power by sharing all his plans with him. There was an old manservant at Merripit House, whose name was Anthony. His connection with the Stapletons can be traced for several years, as far back as the school-mastering days, so that he must have been aware that his master and mistress were really husband and wife. This man has disappeared and has escaped from the country. It is suggestive that Anthony is not a common name in England, while Antonio is so in all Spanish or Spanish-American countries. The man, like Mrs. Stapleton herself, spoke good English, but with a curious lisping accent. I have myself seen this old man cross the Grimpen Mire by the path which Stapleton had marked out. It is very probable, therefore, that in the absence of his master it was he who cared for the hound, though he may never have known the purpose for which the beast was used.

"The Stapletons then went down to Devonshire, whither they were soon followed by Sir Henry and you. One word now as to how I stood myself at that time. It may possibly recur to your memory that when I examined the paper upon which the printed words were fastened I made a close inspection for the water-mark. In doing so I held it within a few inches of my eyes, and was conscious of a faint smell of the scent known as white jessamine. There are seventy-five perfumes, which it is very necessary that a criminal expert should be able to distinguish from each other, and cases have more than once within my own experience depended upon their prompt recognition. The scent suggested the presence of a lady, and already my thoughts began to turn towards the Stapletons. Thus I had made certain of the hound, and had guessed at the criminal before ever we went to the west country.

"It was my game to watch Stapleton. It was evident, however, that I could not do this if I were with you, since he would be keenly on his guard. I deceived everybody, therefore, yourself included, and I came down secretly when I was supposed to be in London. My hardships were not so great as you imagined, though such trifling details must never interfere with the investigation of a case. I stayed for the most part at Coombe Tracey, and only used the hut upon the moor when it was necessary to be near the scene of action. Cartwright had come down with me, and in his disguise as a country boy he was of great assistance to me. I was dependent upon him for food and clean linen. When I was watching Stapleton, Cartwright was frequently watching you, so that I was able to keep my hand upon all the strings.

"I have already told you that your reports reached me rapidly, being forwarded instantly from Baker Street to Coombe Tracey. They were of great service to me, and especially that one incidentally truthful piece of biography of Stapleton's. I was able to establish the identity of the man and the woman and knew at last exactly how I stood. The case had been considerably complicated through the incident of the escaped convict and the relations between him and the Barrymores. This also you cleared up in a very effective way, though I had already come to the same conclusions from my own observations.

"By the time that you discovered me upon the moor I had a complete knowledge of the whole business, but I had not a case which could go to a jury. Even Stapleton's attempt upon Sir Henry that night which ended in the death of the unfortunate convict did not help us much in proving murder against our man. There seemed to be no alternative but to catch him red-handed, and to do so we had to use Sir Henry, alone and apparently unprotected, as a bait. We did so, and at the cost of a severe shock to our client we succeeded in completing our case and driving Stapleton to his destruction. That Sir Henry should have been exposed to this is, I must confess, a reproach to my management of the case, but we had no means of foreseeing the terrible and paralyzing spectacle which the beast presented, nor could we predict the fog which enabled him to burst upon us at such short notice. We succeeded in our object at a cost which both the specialist and Dr. Mortimer assure me will be a temporary one. A long journey may enable our friend to recover not only from his shattered nerves but also from his wounded feelings. His love for the lady was deep and sincere, and to him the saddest part of all this black business was that he should have been deceived by her.

"It only remains to indicate the part which she had played throughout. There can be no doubt that Stapleton exercised an influence over her which may have been love or may have been fear, or very possibly both, since they are by no means incompatible emotions. It was, at least, absolutely effective. At his command she consented to pass as his sister, though he found the limits of his power over her when he endeavoured to make her the direct accessory to murder. She was ready to warn Sir Henry so far as she could without implicating her husband, and again and again she tried to do so. Stapleton himself seems to have been capable of jealousy, and when he saw the baronet paying court to the lady, even though it was part of his own plan, still he could not help interrupting with a passionate outburst which revealed the fiery soul which his self-contained manner so cleverly concealed. By encouraging the intimacy he made it certain that Sir Henry would frequently come to Merripit House and that he would sooner or later get the opportunity which he desired. On the day of the crisis, however, his wife turned suddenly against him. She had learned something of the death of the convict, and she knew that the hound was being kept in the outhouse on the evening that Sir Henry was coming to dinner. She taxed her husband with his intended crime, and a furious scene followed in which he showed her for the first time that she had a rival in his love. Her fidelity turned in an instant to bitter hatred, and he saw that she would betray him. He tied her up, therefore, that she might have no chance of warning Sir Henry, and he hoped, no doubt, that when the whole countryside put down the baronet's death to the curse of his family, as they certainly would do, he could win his wife back to accept an accomplished fact and to keep silent upon what she knew. In this I fancy that in any case he made a miscalculation, and that, if we had not been there, his doom would none the less have been sealed. A woman of Spanish blood does not condone such an injury so lightly. And now, my dear Watson, without referring to my notes, I cannot give you a more detailed account of this curious case. I do not know that anything essential has been left unexplained."

"He could not hope to frighten Sir Henry to death as he had done the old uncle with his bogie hound."

"The beast was savage and half-starved. If its appearance did not frighten its victim to death, at least it would paralyze the resistance which might be offered."

"No doubt. There only remains one difficulty. If Stapleton came into the succession, how could he explain the fact that he, the heir, had been living unannounced under another name so close to the property? How could he claim it without causing suspicion and inquiry?"

"It is a formidable difficulty, and I fear that you ask too much when you expect me to solve it. The past and the present are within the field of my inquiry, but what a man may do in the future is a hard question to answer. Mrs. Stapleton has heard her husband discuss the problem on several occasions. There were three possible courses. He might claim the property from South America, establish his identity before the British authorities there and so obtain the fortune without ever coming to England at all, or he might adopt an elaborate disguise during the short time that he need be in London; or, again, he might furnish an accomplice with the proofs and papers, putting him in as heir, and retaining a claim upon some proportion of his income. We cannot doubt from what we know of him that he would have found some way out of the difficulty. And now, my dear Watson, we have had some weeks of severe work, and for one evening, I think, we may turn our thoughts into more pleasant channels. I have a box for Les Huguenots. Have you heard the De Reszkes? Might I trouble you then to be ready in half an hour, and we can stop at Marcini's for a little dinner on the way?"

THE END

Milton Keynes UK
Ingram Content Group UK Ltd.
UKHW021939081024
449407UK00008B/162

9 781965 179154